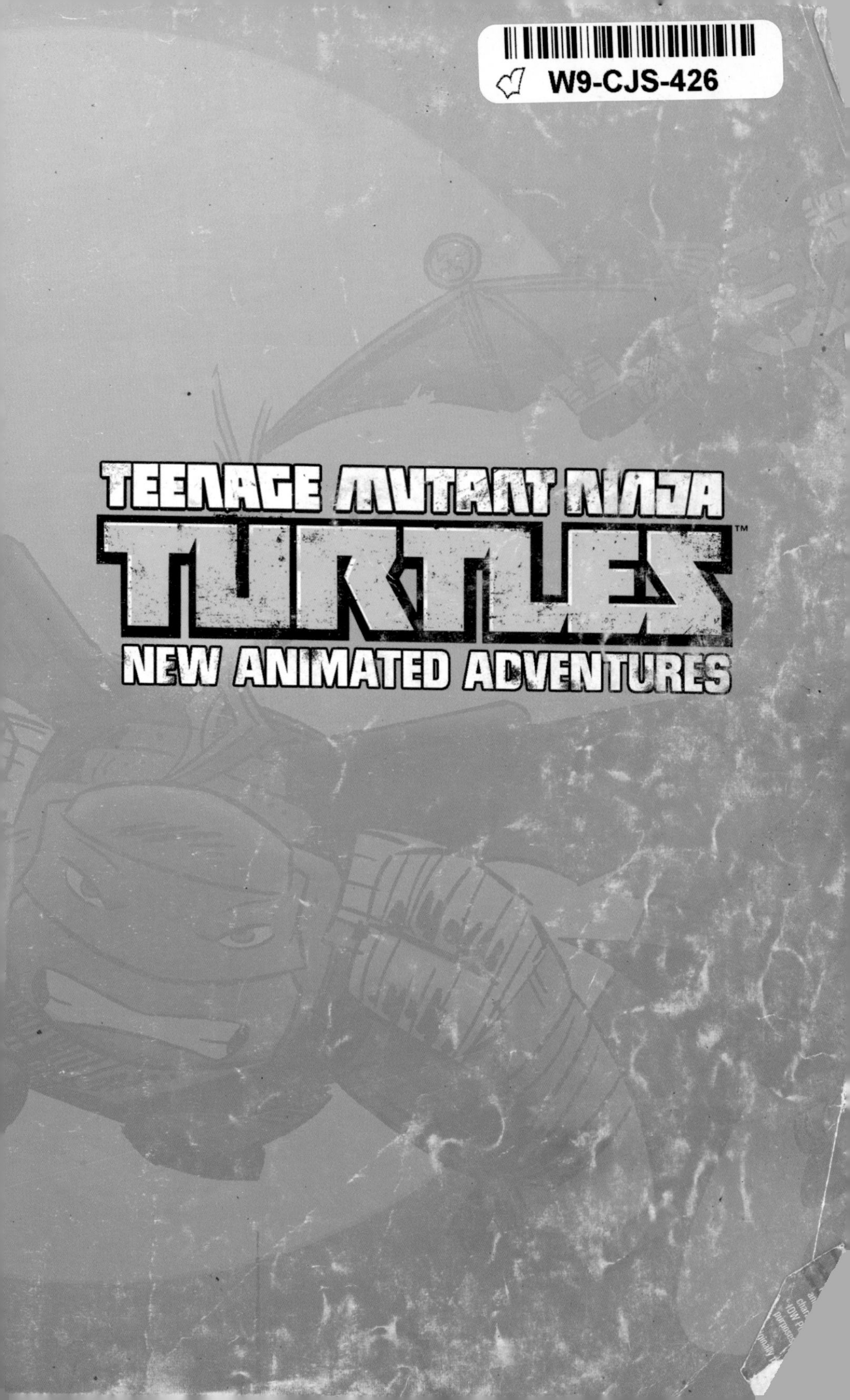

TEENAGE MUTANT NINJA TURTLES™
NEW ANIMATED ADVENTURES

TEENAGE MUTANT NINJA
TURTLES
NEW ANIMATED ADVENTURES

Special thanks to Joan Hilty & Linda Lee for their invaluable assistance.

ISBN: 978-1-63140-806-9

nickelodeon™

For international rights, contact licensing@idwpublishing.com

19 18 17 16   1 2 3

IDW®
www.IDWPUBLISHING.com

Ted Adams, CEO & Publisher • Greg Goldstein, President & COO • Robbie Robbins, EVP/Sr. Graphic Artist • Chris Ryall, Chief Creative Office
David Hedgecock, Editor-in-Chief • Laurie Windrow, Senior Vice President of Sales & Marketing • Matthew Ruzicka, CPA, Chief Financial Offic
Dirk Wood, VP of Marketing • Lorelei Bunjes, VP of Digital Services • Jeff Webber, VP of Licensing, Digital and Subsidiary Rights • Jerry Benning
VP of New Product Development

Facebook: facebook.com/idwpublishing • Twitter: @idwpublishing • YouTube: youtube.com/idwpublishing
Tumblr: tumblr.idwpublishing.com • Instagram: instagram.com/idwpublishing

TEENAGE MUTANT NINJA TURTLES: NEW ANIMATED ADVENTURES OMNIBUS, VOLUME 2. DECEMBER 2016. FIRST PRINTING. © 2016 Viacom International Inc. All Rights Reserved. Nickelodeon, TEENAGE MUTANT NINJA TURT
all related titles, logos and characters are trademarks of Viacom International Inc. © 2016 Viacom Overseas Holdings C.V. All Rights Reserved. Nickelodeon, TEENAGE MUTANT NINJA TURTLES, and all related titles, logos
ters are trademarks of Viacom Overseas Holdings C.V. Based on characters created by Peter Laird and Kevin Eastman. © 2016 Idea and Design Works, LLC. The IDW logo is registered in the U.S. Patent and Trademark O
lishing, a division of Idea and Design Works, LLC. Editorial offices: 2765 Truxtun Road, San Diego, CA 92106. Any similarities to persons living or dead are purely coincidental. With the exception of artwork used for re
none of the contents of this publication may be reprinted without the permission of Idea and Design Works, LLC. Printed in Korea. IDW Publishing does not read or accept unsolicited submissions of ideas, stories, or
ished as TEENAGE MUTANT NINJA TURTLES: NEW ANIMATED ADVENTURES issues #13–24.

COLORS BY
HEATHER BRECKEL

LETTERS BY
SHAWN LEE

SERIES EDITS BY
BOBBY CURNOW

COVER BY
PAULINA GANUCHEAU

COLLECTION EDITS BY
JUSTIN EISINGER AND **ALONZO SIMON**

PRODUCTION ASSISTANCE BY
SHAWN LEE

PUBLISHER
TED ADAMS

Cover by **DARIO BRIZUELA**

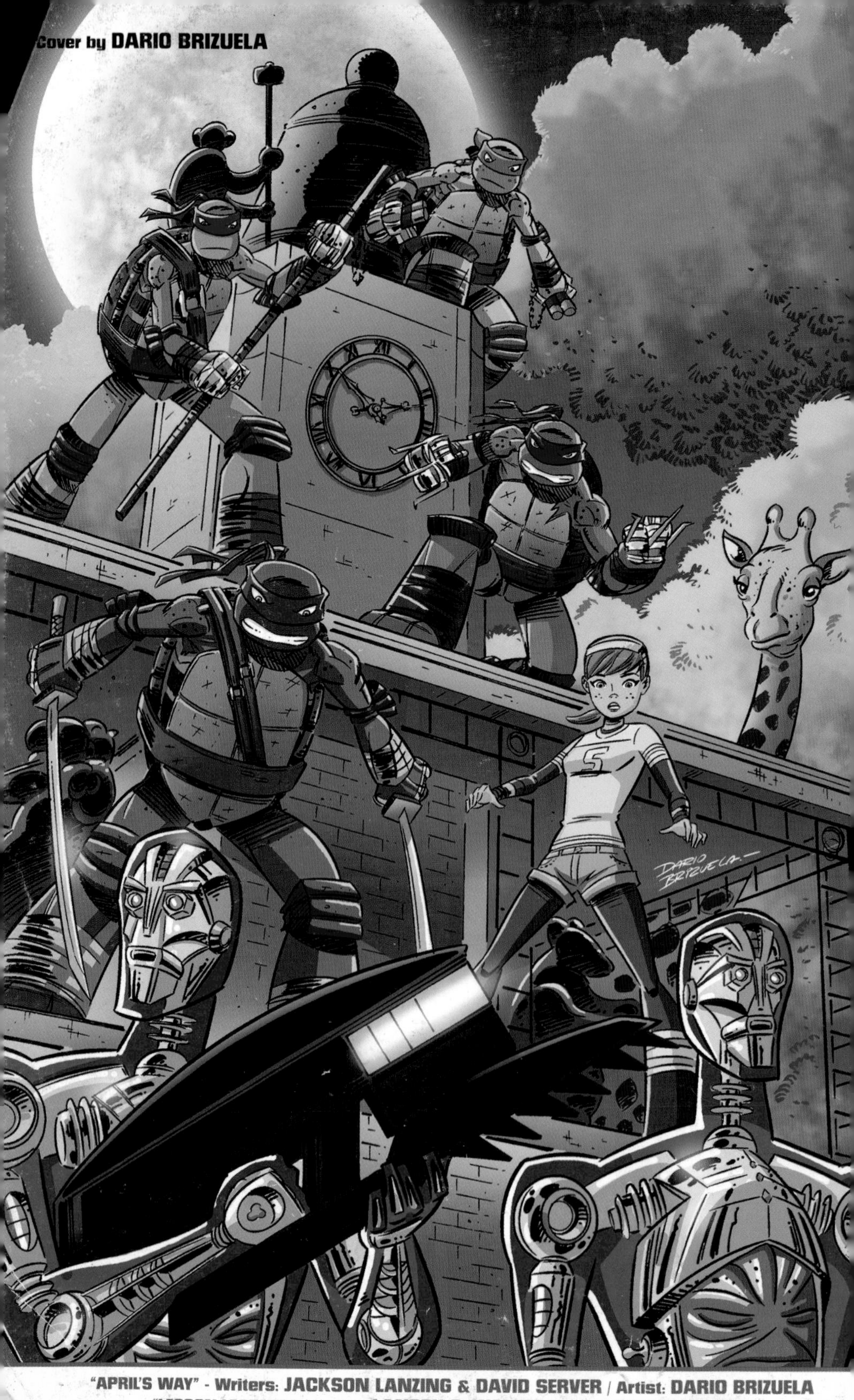

DARIO BRIZUELA

"APRIL'S WAY" - Writers: **JACKSON LANZING & DAVID SERVER** / Artist: **DARIO BRIZUELA**
"LESSON LEARNED" - Writer: **LANDRY Q. WALKER** / Artist: **DAVID ALVAREZ**

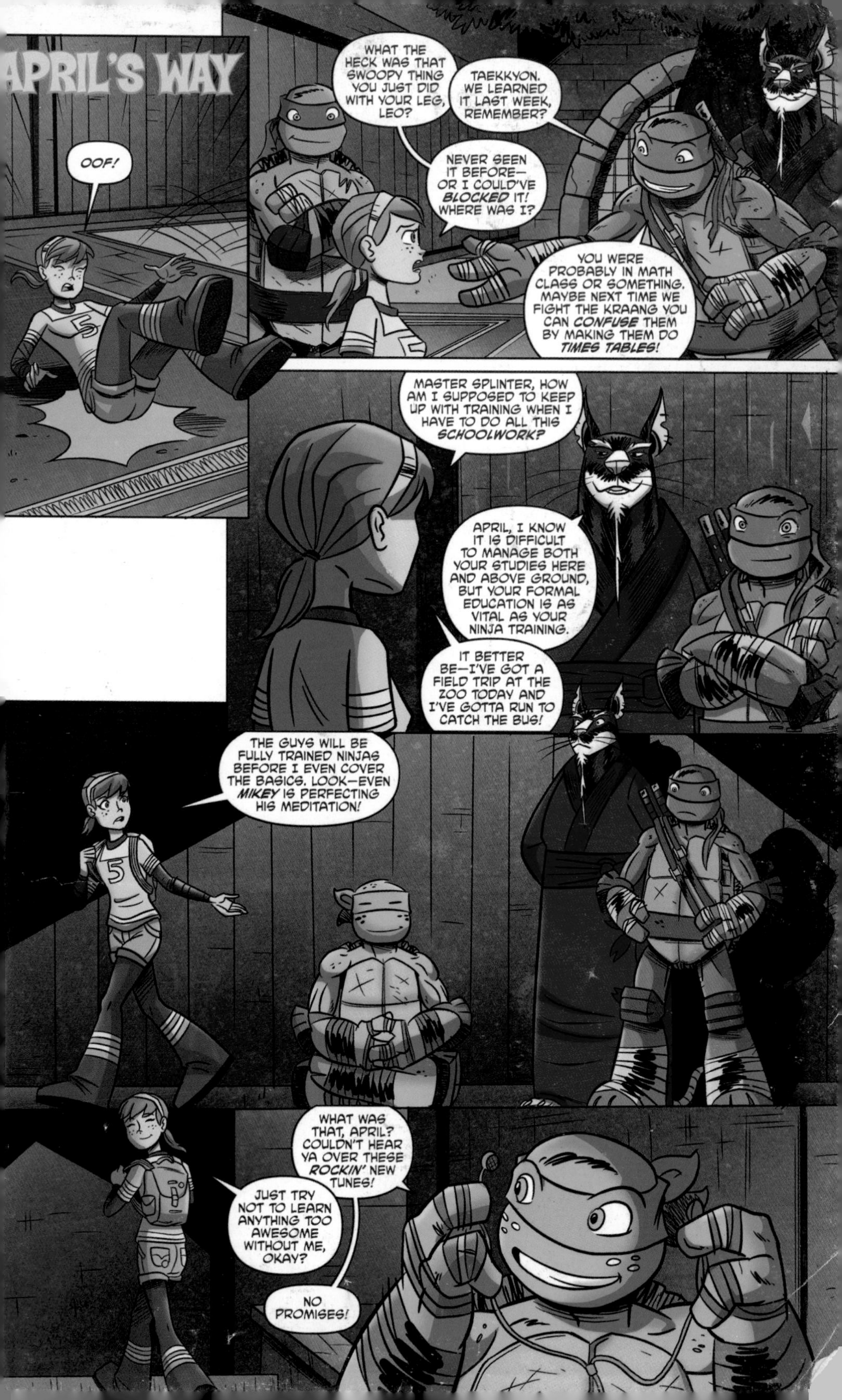

APRIL'S WAY
OOF!
WHAT THE HECK WAS THAT SWOOPY THING YOU JUST DID WITH YOUR LEG, LEO?
TAEKKYON. WE LEARNED IT LAST WEEK, REMEMBER?
NEVER SEEN IT BEFORE— OR I COULD'VE *BLOCKED* IT! WHERE WAS I?
YOU WERE PROBABLY IN MATH CLASS OR SOMETHING. MAYBE NEXT TIME WE FIGHT THE KRAANG YOU CAN *CONFUSE* THEM BY MAKING THEM DO *TIMES TABLES!*
MASTER SPLINTER, HOW AM I SUPPOSED TO KEEP UP WITH TRAINING WHEN I HAVE TO DO ALL THIS *SCHOOLWORK?*
APRIL, I KNOW IT IS DIFFICULT TO MANAGE BOTH YOUR STUDIES HERE AND ABOVE GROUND, BUT YOUR FORMAL EDUCATION IS AS VITAL AS YOUR NINJA TRAINING.
IT BETTER BE—I'VE GOT A FIELD TRIP AT THE ZOO TODAY AND I'VE GOTTA RUN TO CATCH THE BUS!
THE GUYS WILL BE FULLY TRAINED NINJAS BEFORE I EVEN COVER THE BASICS. LOOK—EVEN *MIKEY* IS PERFECTING HIS MEDITATION!
JUST TRY NOT TO LEARN ANYTHING TOO AWESOME WITHOUT ME, OKAY?
WHAT WAS THAT, APRIL? COULDN'T HEAR YA OVER THESE *ROCKIN'* NEW TUNES!
NO PROMISES!

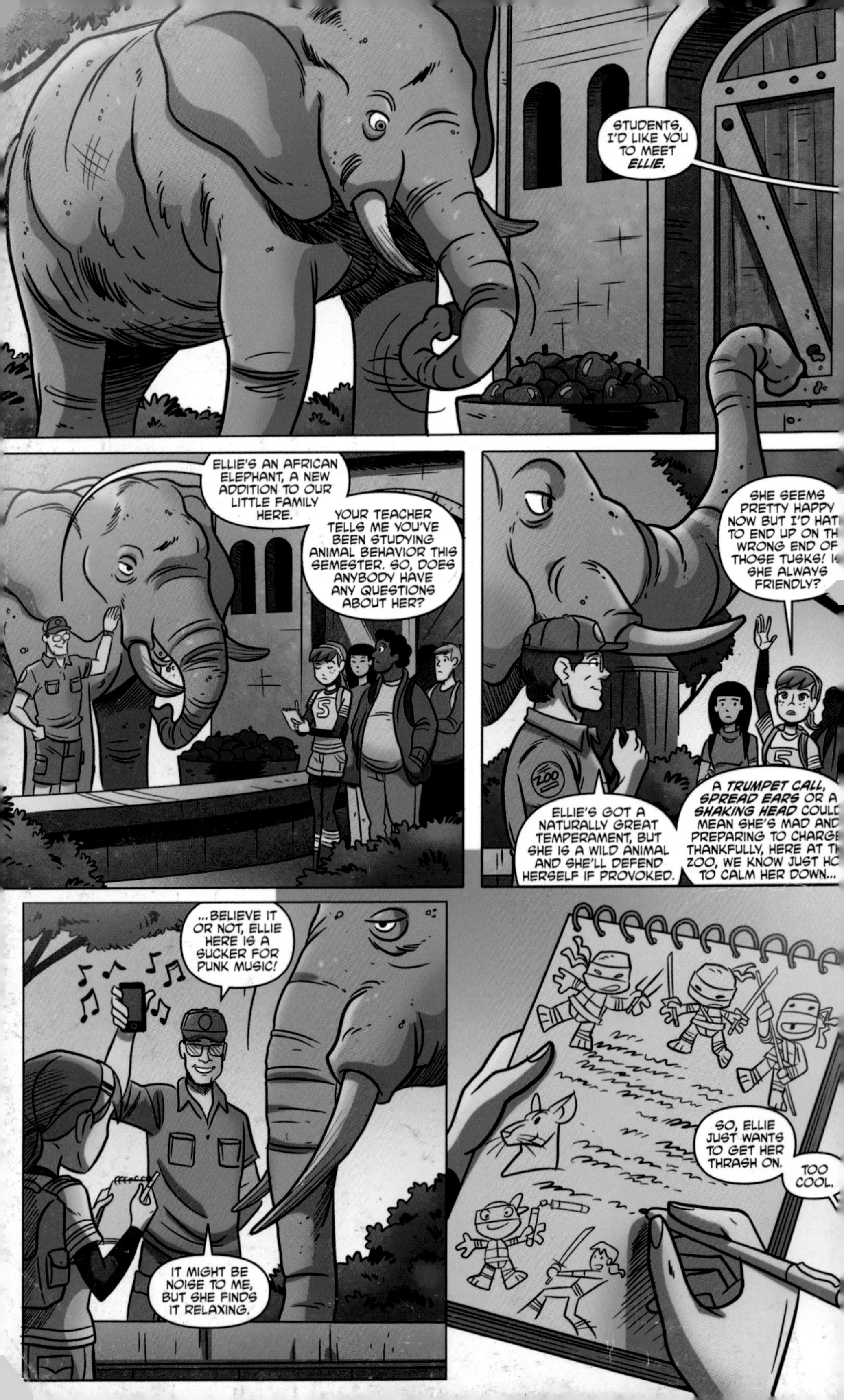
STUDENTS, I'D LIKE YOU TO MEET *ELLIE.*
ELLIE'S AN AFRICAN ELEPHANT, A NEW ADDITION TO OUR LITTLE FAMILY HERE.
YOUR TEACHER TELLS ME YOU'VE BEEN STUDYING ANIMAL BEHAVIOR THIS SEMESTER. SO, DOES ANYBODY HAVE ANY QUESTIONS ABOUT HER?
SHE SEEMS PRETTY HAPPY NOW BUT I'D HAT TO END UP ON TH WRONG END OF THOSE TUSKS! I SHE ALWAYS FRIENDLY?
ZOO
ELLIE'S GOT A NATURALLY GREAT TEMPERAMENT, BUT SHE IS A WILD ANIMAL AND SHE'LL DEFEND HERSELF IF PROVOKED.
A ***TRUMPET CALL, SPREAD EARS*** OR A ***SHAKING HEAD*** COUL MEAN SHE'S MAD AND PREPARING TO CHARG THANKFULLY, HERE AT T ZOO, WE KNOW JUST H TO CALM HER DOWN...
...BELIEVE IT OR NOT, ELLIE HERE IS A SUCKER FOR PUNK MUSIC!
IT MIGHT BE NOISE TO ME, BUT SHE FINDS IT RELAXING.
SO, ELLIE JUST WANTS TO GET HER THRASH ON.
TOO COOL.

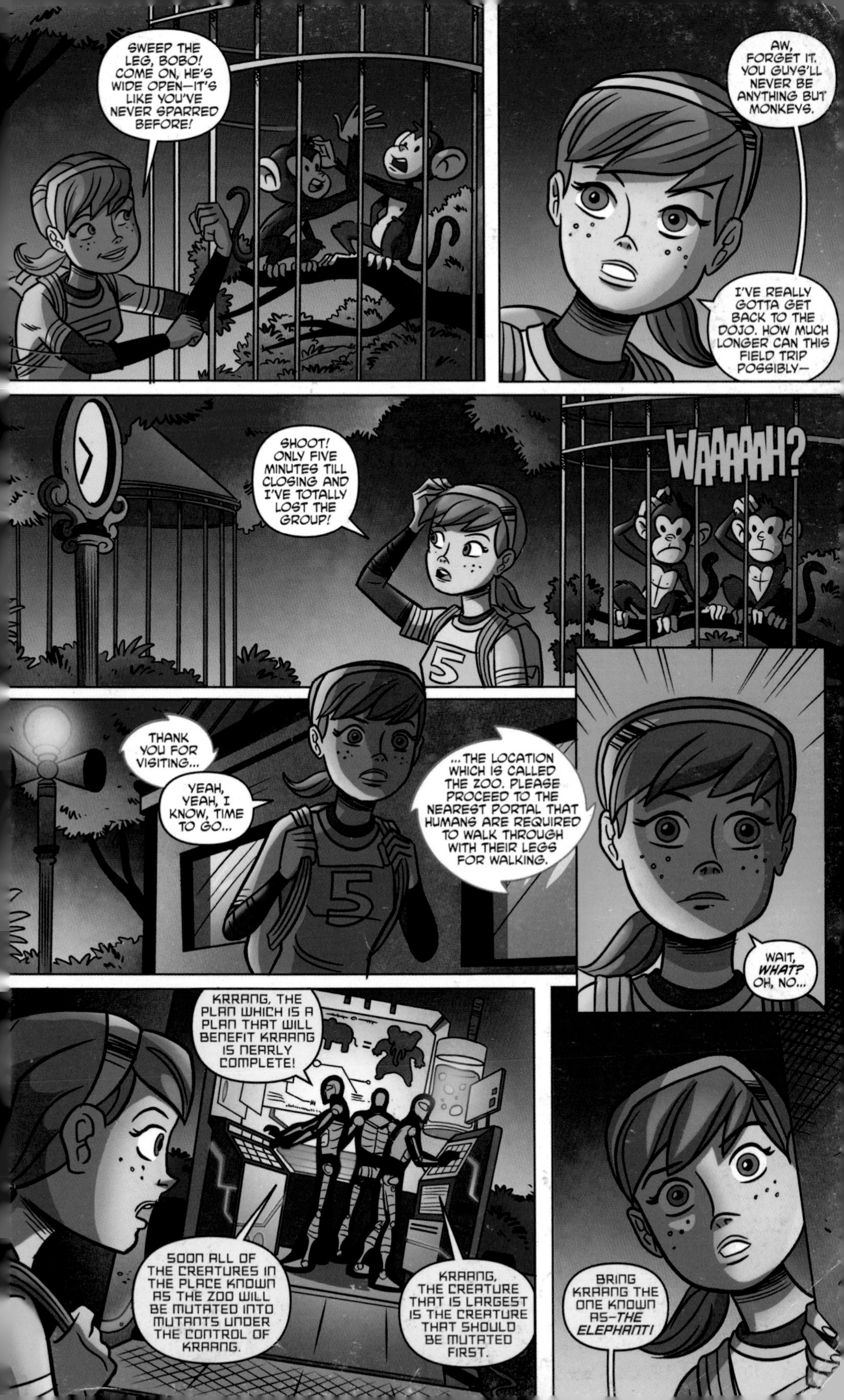
SWEEP THE LEG, BOBO! COME ON, HE'S WIDE OPEN—IT'S LIKE YOU'VE NEVER SPARRED BEFORE!
AW, FORGET IT. YOU GUYS'LL NEVER BE ANYTHING BUT MONKEYS.
I'VE REALLY GOTTA GET BACK TO THE DOJO. HOW MUCH LONGER CAN THIS FIELD TRIP POSSIBLY—
SHOOT! ONLY FIVE MINUTES TILL CLOSING AND I'VE TOTALLY LOST THE GROUP!
WAAAAAH?
THANK YOU FOR VISITING...
YEAH, YEAH, I KNOW, TIME TO GO...
...THE LOCATION WHICH IS CALLED THE ZOO. PLEASE PROCEED TO THE NEAREST PORTAL THAT HUMANS ARE REQUIRED TO WALK THROUGH WITH THEIR LEGS FOR WALKING.
WAIT, *WHAT?* OH, NO...
KRRANG, THE PLAN WHICH IS A PLAN THAT WILL BENEFIT KRAANG IS NEARLY COMPLETE!
SOON ALL OF THE CREATURES IN THE PLACE KNOWN AS THE ZOO WILL BE MUTATED INTO MUTANTS UNDER THE CONTROL OF KRAANG.
KRAANG, THE CREATURE THAT IS LARGEST IS THE CREATURE THAT SHOULD BE MUTATED FIRST.
BRING KRAANG THE ONE KNOWN AS—*THE ELEPHANT!*

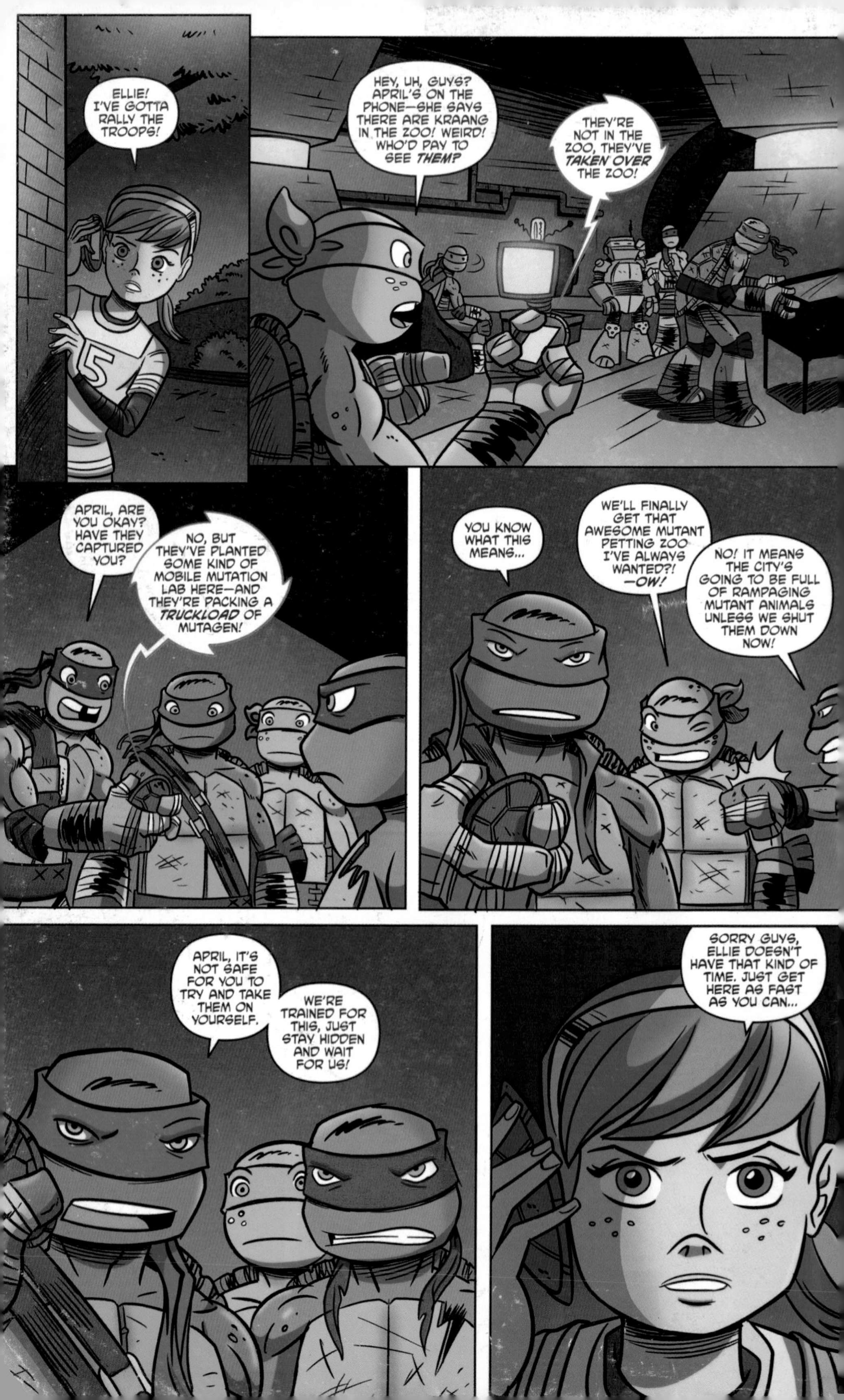
ELLIE! I'VE GOTTA RALLY THE TROOPS!
HEY, UH, GUYS? APRIL'S ON THE PHONE—SHE SAYS THERE ARE KRAANG IN THE ZOO! WEIRD! WHO'D PAY TO SEE *THEM?*
THEY'RE NOT IN THE ZOO, THEY'VE *TAKEN OVER* THE ZOO!
APRIL, ARE YOU OKAY? HAVE THEY CAPTURED YOU?
NO, BUT THEY'VE PLANTED SOME KIND OF MOBILE MUTATION LAB HERE—AND THEY'RE PACKING A *TRUCKLOAD* OF MUTAGEN!
YOU KNOW WHAT THIS MEANS...
WE'LL FINALLY GET THAT AWESOME MUTANT PETTING ZOO I'VE ALWAYS WANTED?! *—OW!*
NO! IT MEANS THE CITY'S GOING TO BE FULL OF RAMPAGING MUTANT ANIMALS UNLESS WE SHUT THEM DOWN NOW!
APRIL, IT'S NOT SAFE FOR YOU TO TRY AND TAKE THEM ON YOURSELF.
WE'RE TRAINED FOR THIS, JUST STAY HIDDEN AND WAIT FOR US!
SORRY GUYS, ELLIE DOESN'T HAVE THAT KIND OF TIME. JUST GET HERE AS FAST AS YOU CAN...

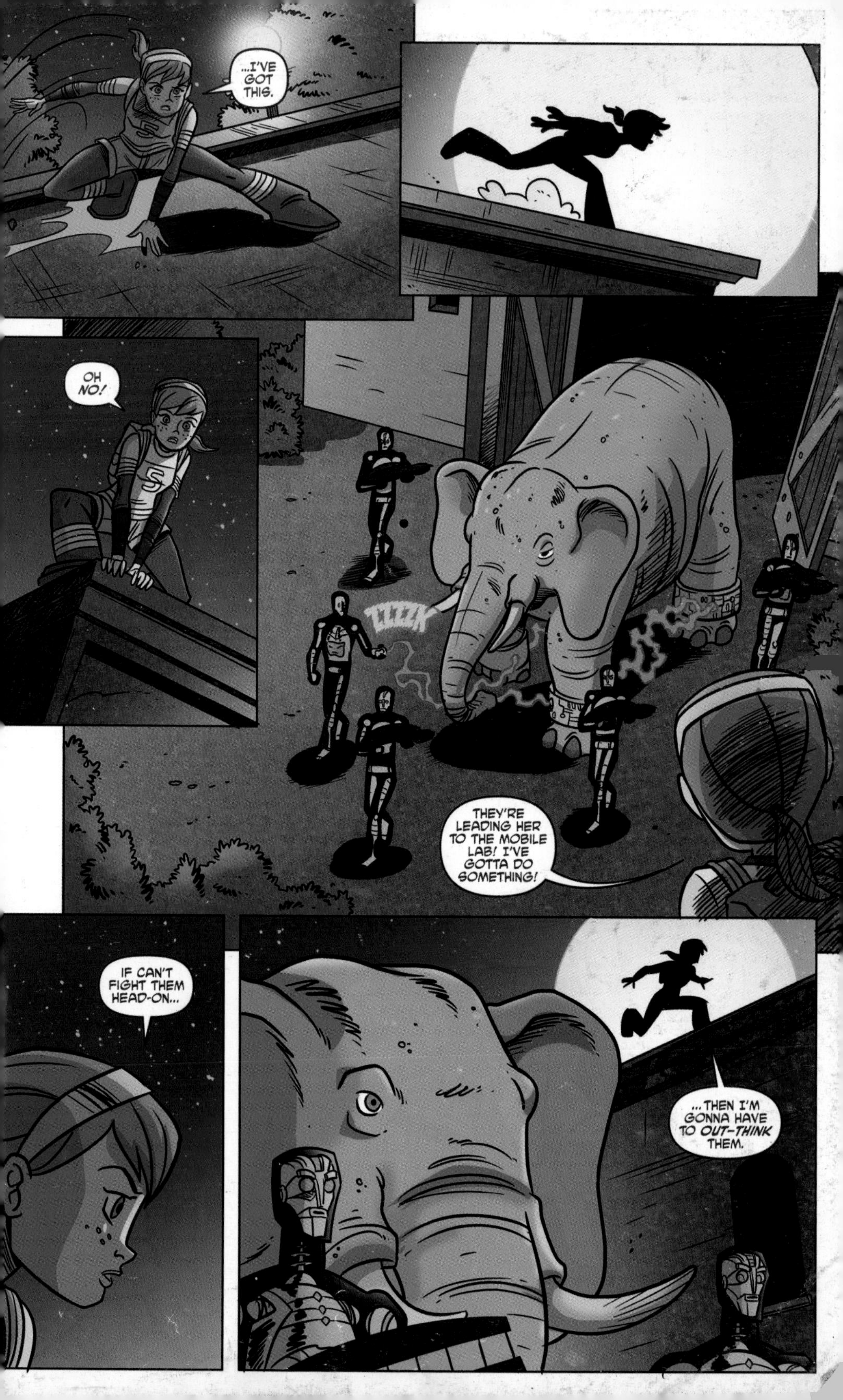
...I'VE GOT THIS.
OH NO!
ZZZZK
THEY'RE LEADING HER TO THE MOBILE LAB! I'VE GOTTA DO SOMETHING!
IF CAN'T FIGHT THEM HEAD-ON...
...THEN I'M GONNA HAVE TO OUT-THINK THEM.

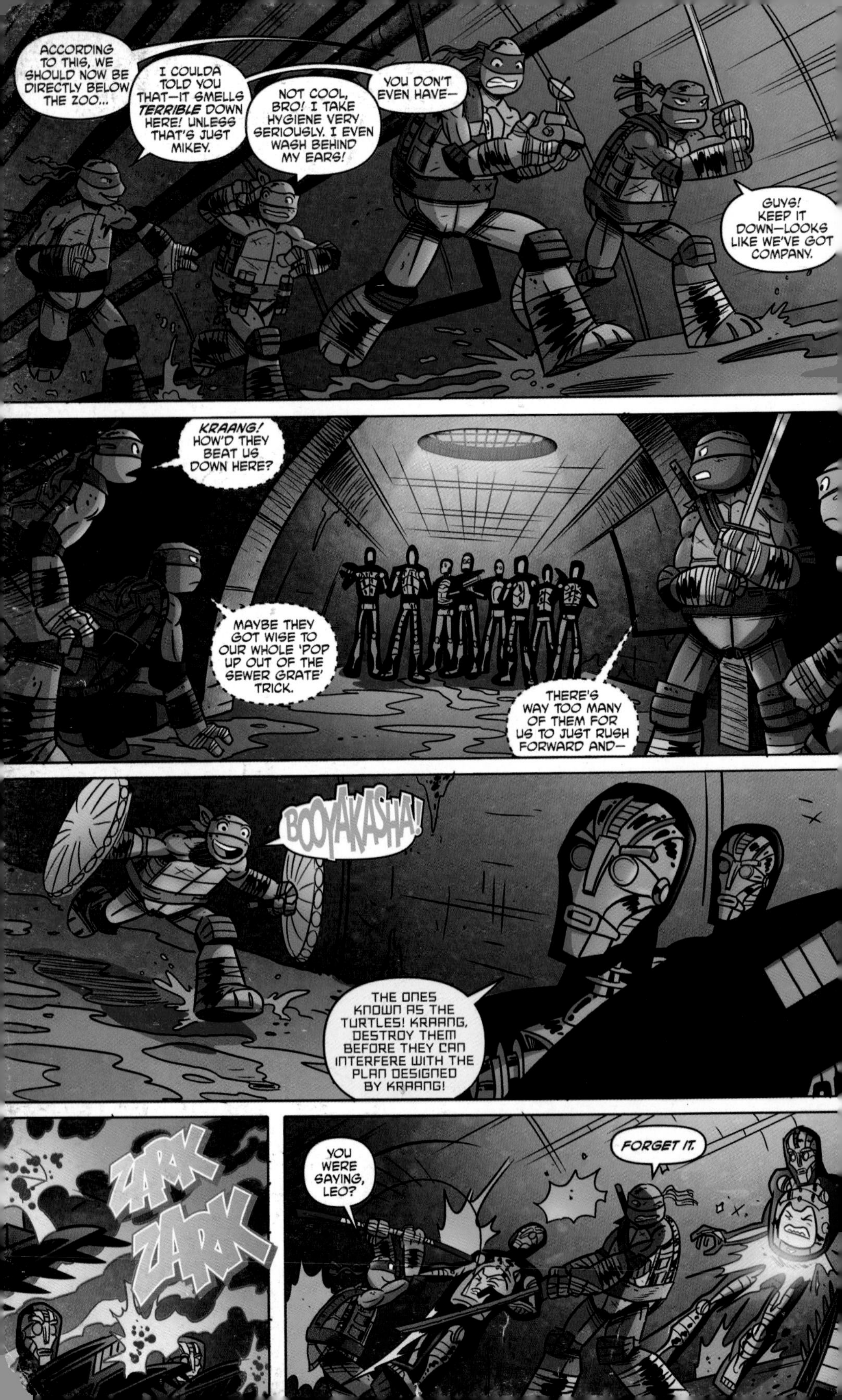
ACCORDING TO THIS, WE SHOULD NOW BE DIRECTLY BELOW THE ZOO...
I COULDA TOLD YOU THAT—IT SMELLS *TERRIBLE* DOWN HERE! UNLESS THAT'S JUST MIKEY.
NOT COOL, BRO! I TAKE HYGIENE VERY SERIOUSLY. I EVEN WASH BEHIND MY EARS!
YOU DON'T EVEN HAVE—
GUYS! KEEP IT DOWN—LOOKS LIKE WE'VE GOT COMPANY.
KRAANG! HOW'D THEY BEAT US DOWN HERE?
MAYBE THEY GOT WISE TO OUR WHOLE 'POP UP OUT OF THE SEWER GRATE' TRICK.
THERE'S WAY TOO MANY OF THEM FOR US TO JUST RUSH FORWARD AND—
BOOYAKASHA!
THE ONES KNOWN AS THE TURTLES! KRAANG, DESTROY THEM BEFORE THEY CAN INTERFERE WITH THE PLAN DESIGNED BY KRAANG!
ZARK ZARK
YOU WERE SAYING, LEO?
FORGET IT.

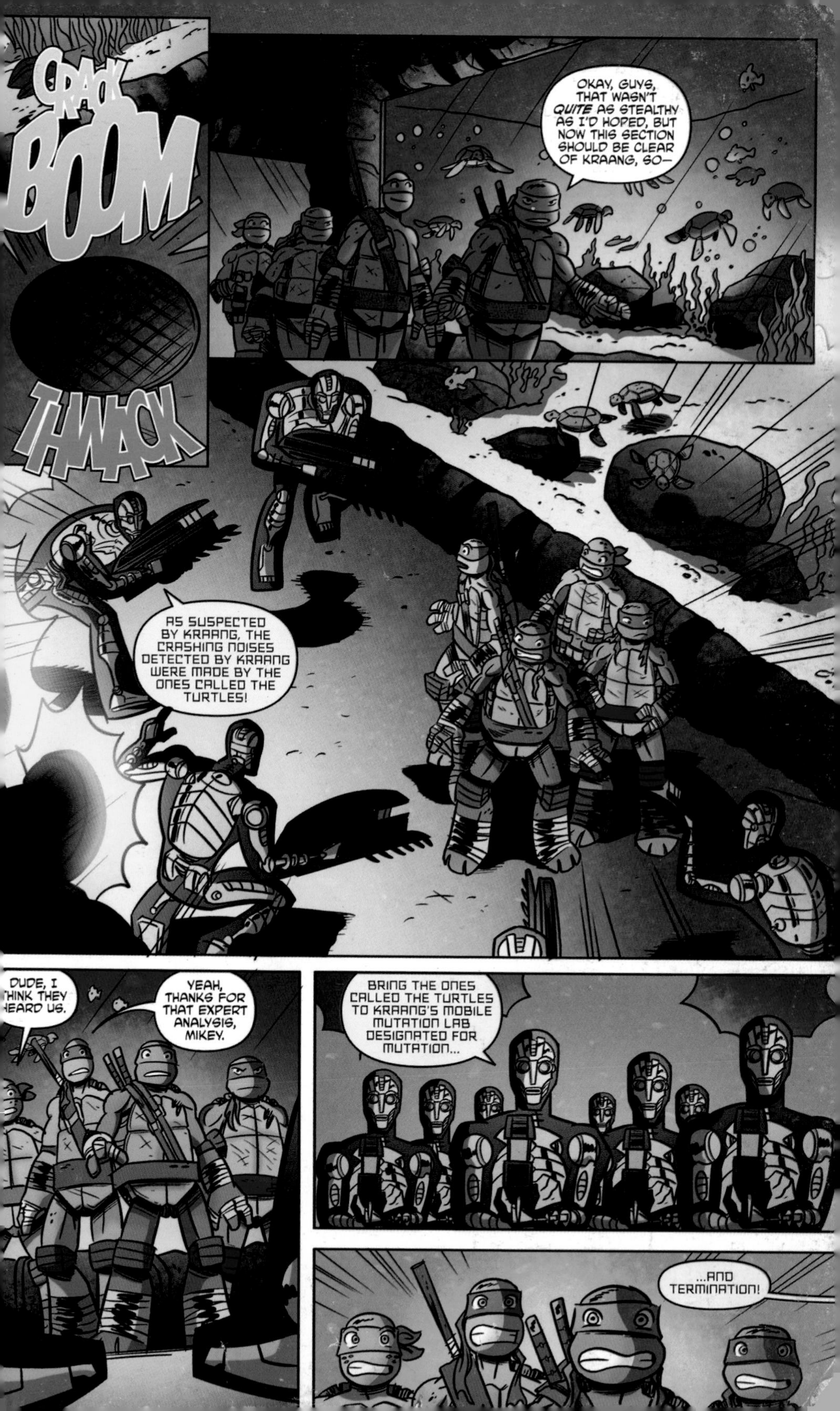
CRACK
BOOM
OKAY, GUYS, THAT WASN'T QUITE AS STEALTHY AS I'D HOPED, BUT NOW THIS SECTION SHOULD BE CLEAR OF KRAANG, SO—
THWACK
AS SUSPECTED BY KRAANG, THE CRASHING NOISES DETECTED BY KRAANG WERE MADE BY THE ONES CALLED THE TURTLES!
DUDE, I THINK THEY HEARD US.
YEAH, THANKS FOR THAT EXPERT ANALYSIS, MIKEY.
BRING THE ONES CALLED THE TURTLES TO KRAANG'S MOBILE MUTATION LAB DESIGNATED FOR MUTATION...
...AND TERMINATION!

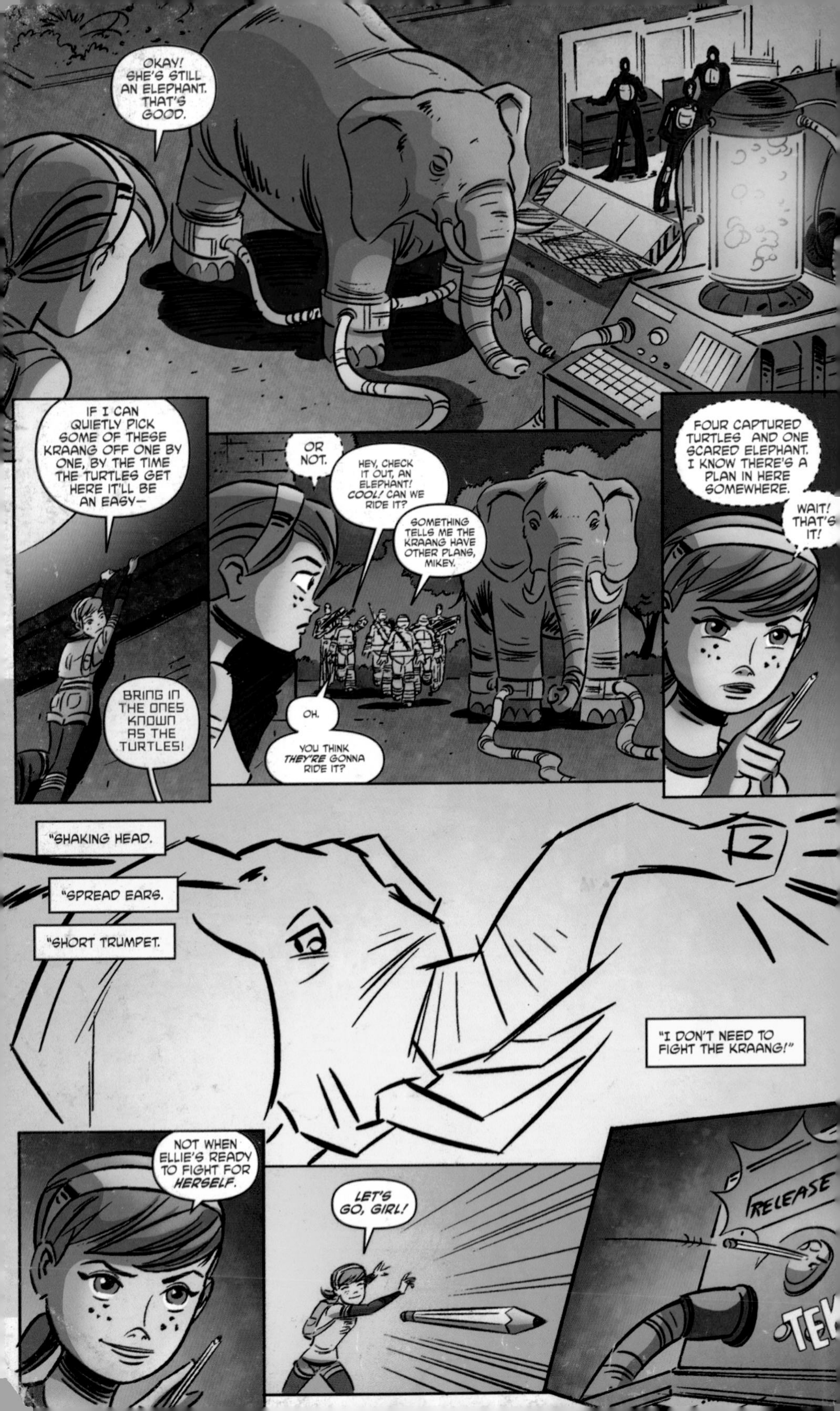

OKAY! SHE'S STILL AN ELEPHANT. THAT'S GOOD.
IF I CAN QUIETLY PICK SOME OF THESE KRAANG OFF ONE BY ONE, BY THE TIME THE TURTLES GET HERE IT'LL BE AN EASY—
BRING IN THE ONES KNOWN AS THE TURTLES!
OR NOT.
HEY, CHECK IT OUT, AN ELEPHANT! COOL! CAN WE RIDE IT?
SOMETHING TELLS ME THE KRAANG HAVE OTHER PLANS, MIKEY.
OH.
YOU THINK THEY'RE GONNA RIDE IT?
FOUR CAPTURED TURTLES AND ONE SCARED ELEPHANT. I KNOW THERE'S A PLAN IN HERE SOMEWHERE.
WAIT! THAT'S IT!
"SHAKING HEAD.
"SPREAD EARS.
"SHORT TRUMPET.
"I DON'T NEED TO FIGHT THE KRAANG!"
NOT WHEN ELLIE'S READY TO FIGHT FOR HERSELF.
LET'S GO, GIRL!
RELEASE

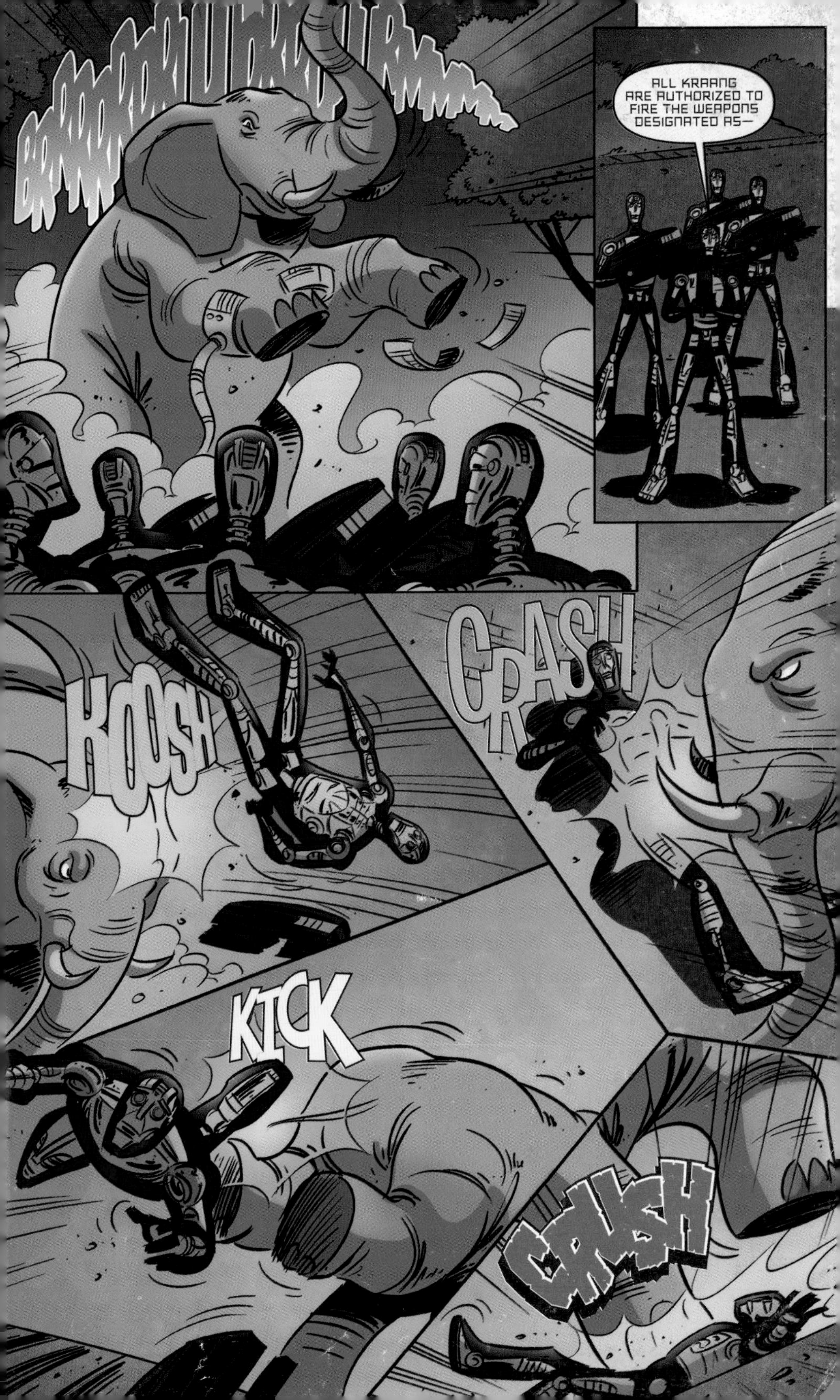
BRRRRRRRUUUURRRRRAAAAAA
ALL KRAANG
ARE AUTHORIZED TO
FIRE THE WEAPONS
DESIGNATED AS—
KOOSH
CRASH
KICK
CRASH

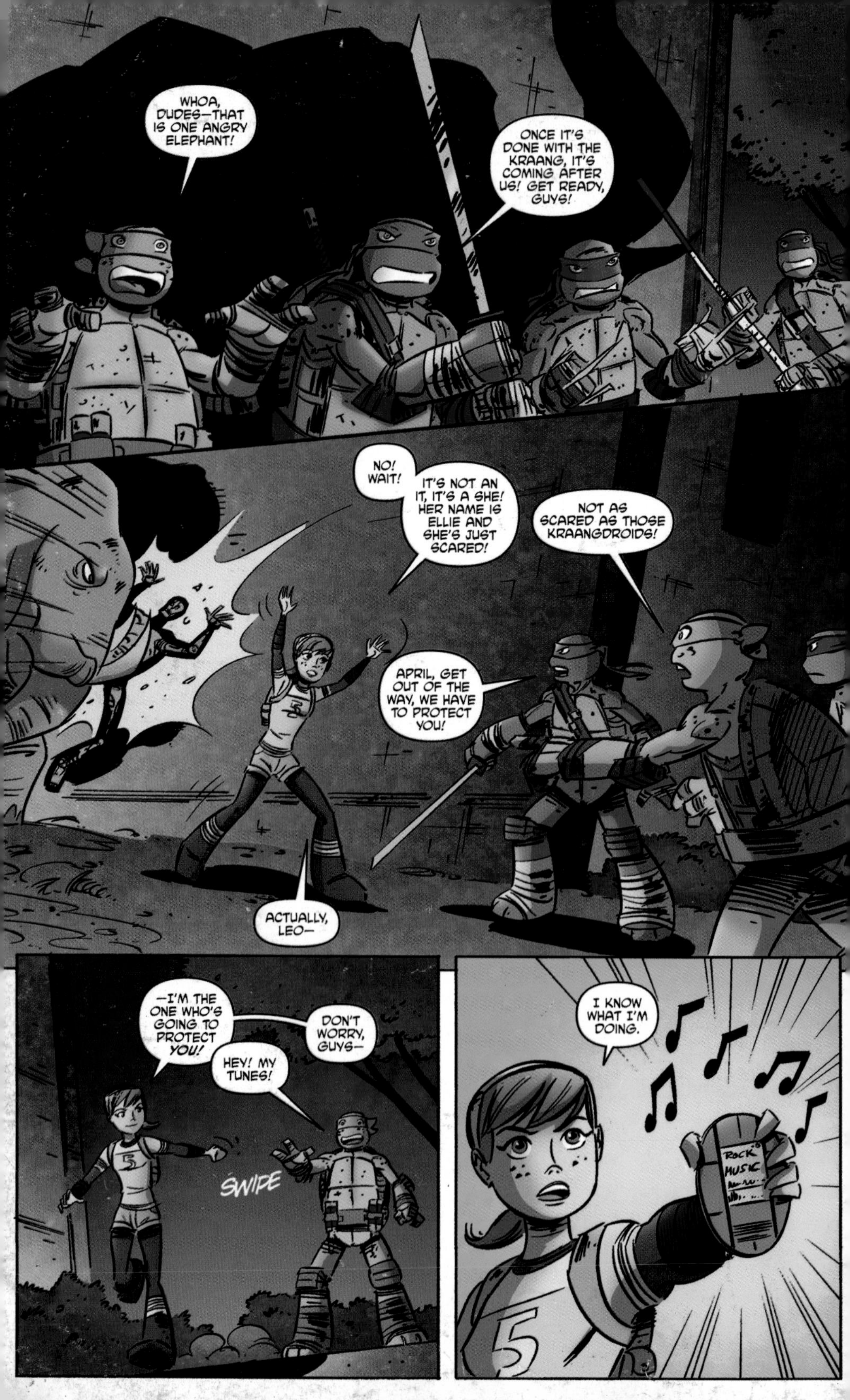
WHOA, DUDES—THAT IS ONE ANGRY ELEPHANT!
ONCE IT'S DONE WITH THE KRAANG, IT'S COMING AFTER US! GET READY, GUYS!
NO! WAIT!
IT'S NOT AN IT, IT'S A SHE! HER NAME IS ELLIE AND SHE'S JUST SCARED!
NOT AS SCARED AS THOSE KRAANGDROIDS!
APRIL, GET OUT OF THE WAY, WE HAVE TO PROTECT YOU!
ACTUALLY, LEO—
—I'M THE ONE WHO'S GOING TO PROTECT YOU!
DON'T WORRY, GUYS—
HEY! MY TUNES!
SWIPE
I KNOW WHAT I'M DOING.
ROCK MUSIC

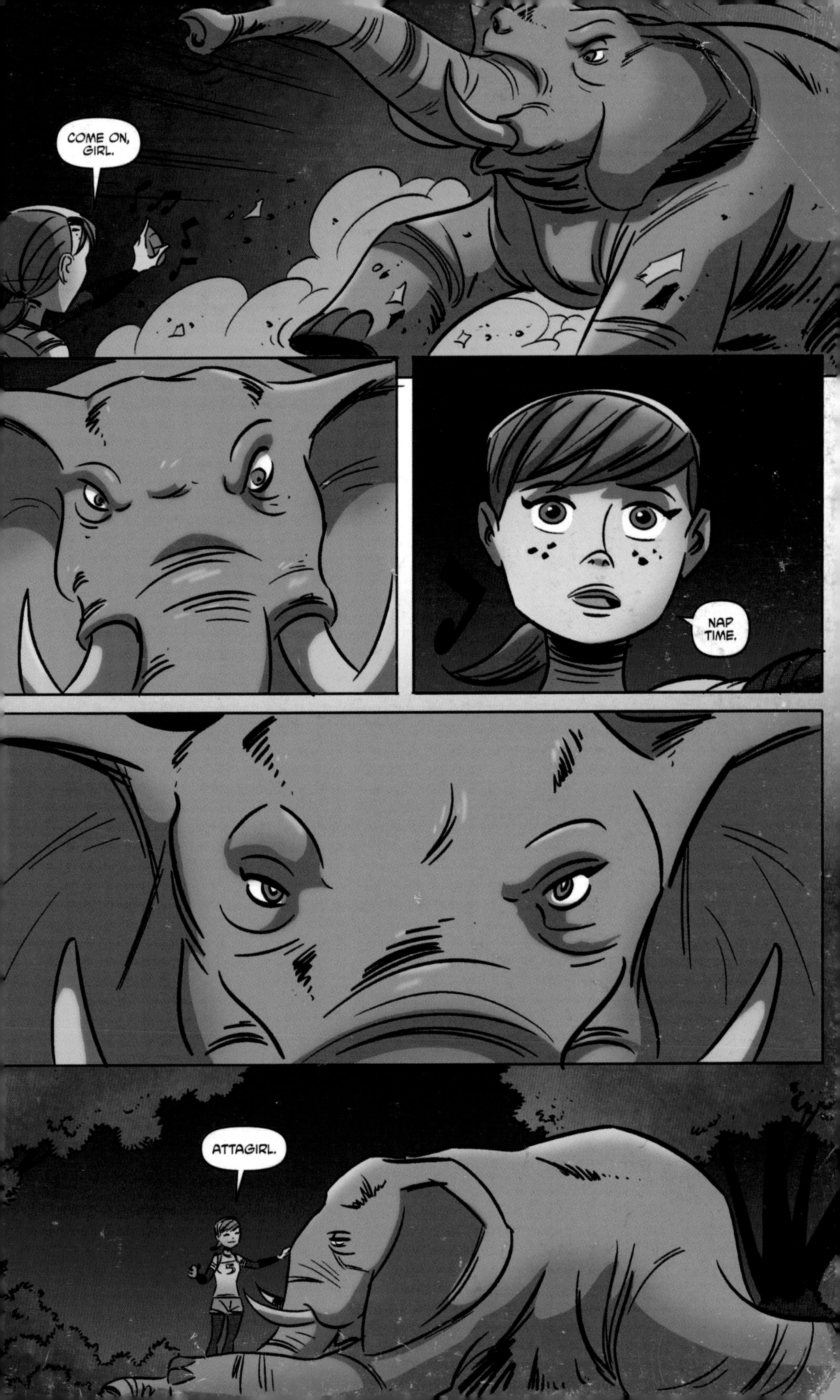
COME ON, GIRL.
NAP TIME.
ATTAGIRL.

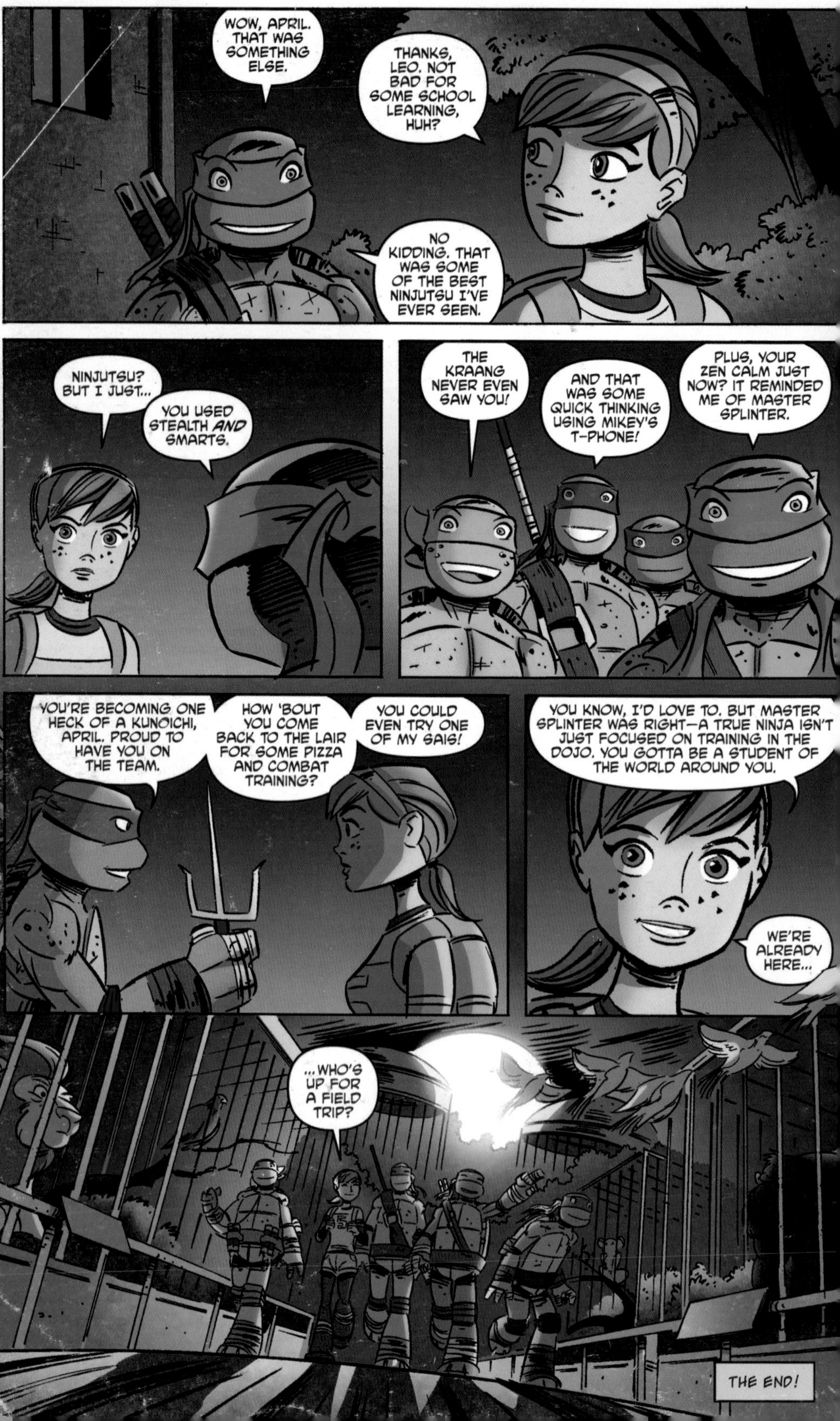
WOW, APRIL. THAT WAS SOMETHING ELSE.
THANKS, LEO. NOT BAD FOR SOME SCHOOL LEARNING, HUH?
NO KIDDING. THAT WAS SOME OF THE BEST NINJUTSU I'VE EVER SEEN.
NINJUTSU? BUT I JUST...
YOU USED STEALTH AND SMARTS.
THE KRAANG NEVER EVEN SAW YOU!
AND THAT WAS SOME QUICK THINKING USING MIKEY'S T-PHONE!
PLUS, YOUR ZEN CALM JUST NOW? IT REMINDED ME OF MASTER SPLINTER.
YOU'RE BECOMING ONE HECK OF A KUNOICHI, APRIL. PROUD TO HAVE YOU ON THE TEAM.
HOW 'BOUT YOU COME BACK TO THE LAIR FOR SOME PIZZA AND COMBAT TRAINING?
YOU COULD EVEN TRY ONE OF MY SAIS!
YOU KNOW, I'D LOVE TO. BUT MASTER SPLINTER WAS RIGHT—A TRUE NINJA ISN'T JUST FOCUSED ON TRAINING IN THE DOJO. YOU GOTTA BE A STUDENT OF THE WORLD AROUND YOU.
WE'RE ALREADY HERE...
...WHO'S UP FOR A FIELD TRIP?
THE END!

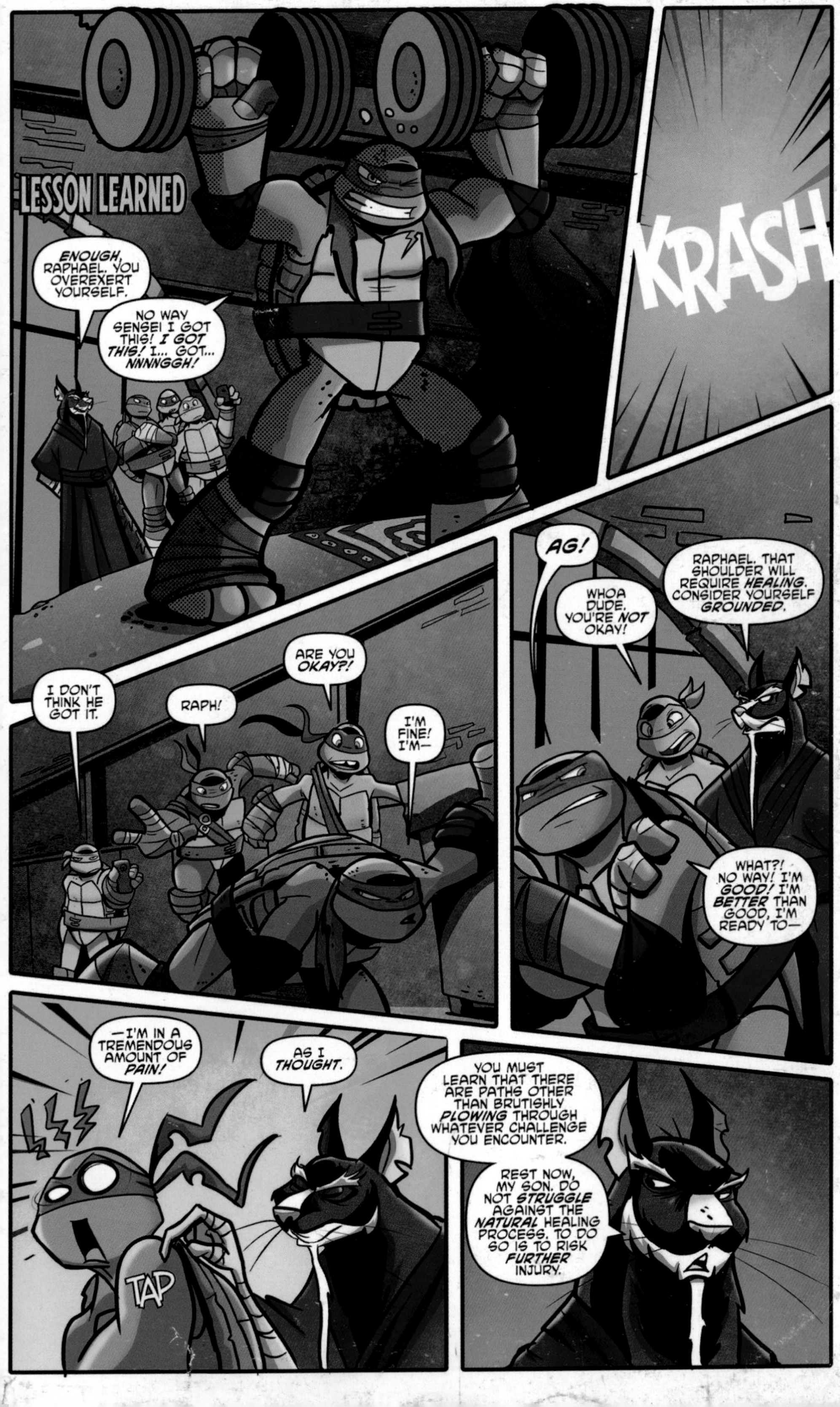
LESSON LEARNED
ENOUGH, RAPHAEL. YOU OVEREXERT YOURSELF.
NO WAY SENSEI I GOT THIS! I GOT THIS! I... GOT... NNNNGGH!
KRASH
I DON'T THINK HE GOT IT.
RAPH!
ARE YOU OKAY?!
I'M FINE! I'M—
AG!
WHOA DUDE. YOU'RE NOT OKAY!
RAPHAEL. THAT SHOULDER WILL REQUIRE HEALING. CONSIDER YOURSELF GROUNDED.
WHAT?! NO WAY! I'M GOOD! I'M BETTER THAN GOOD, I'M READY TO—
—I'M IN A TREMENDOUS AMOUNT OF PAIN!
AS I THOUGHT.
TAP
YOU MUST LEARN THAT THERE ARE PATHS OTHER THAN BRUTISHLY PLOWING THROUGH WHATEVER CHALLENGE YOU ENCOUNTER.
REST NOW, MY SON. DO NOT STRUGGLE AGAINST THE NATURAL HEALING PROCESS. TO DO SO IS TO RISK FURTHER INJURY.

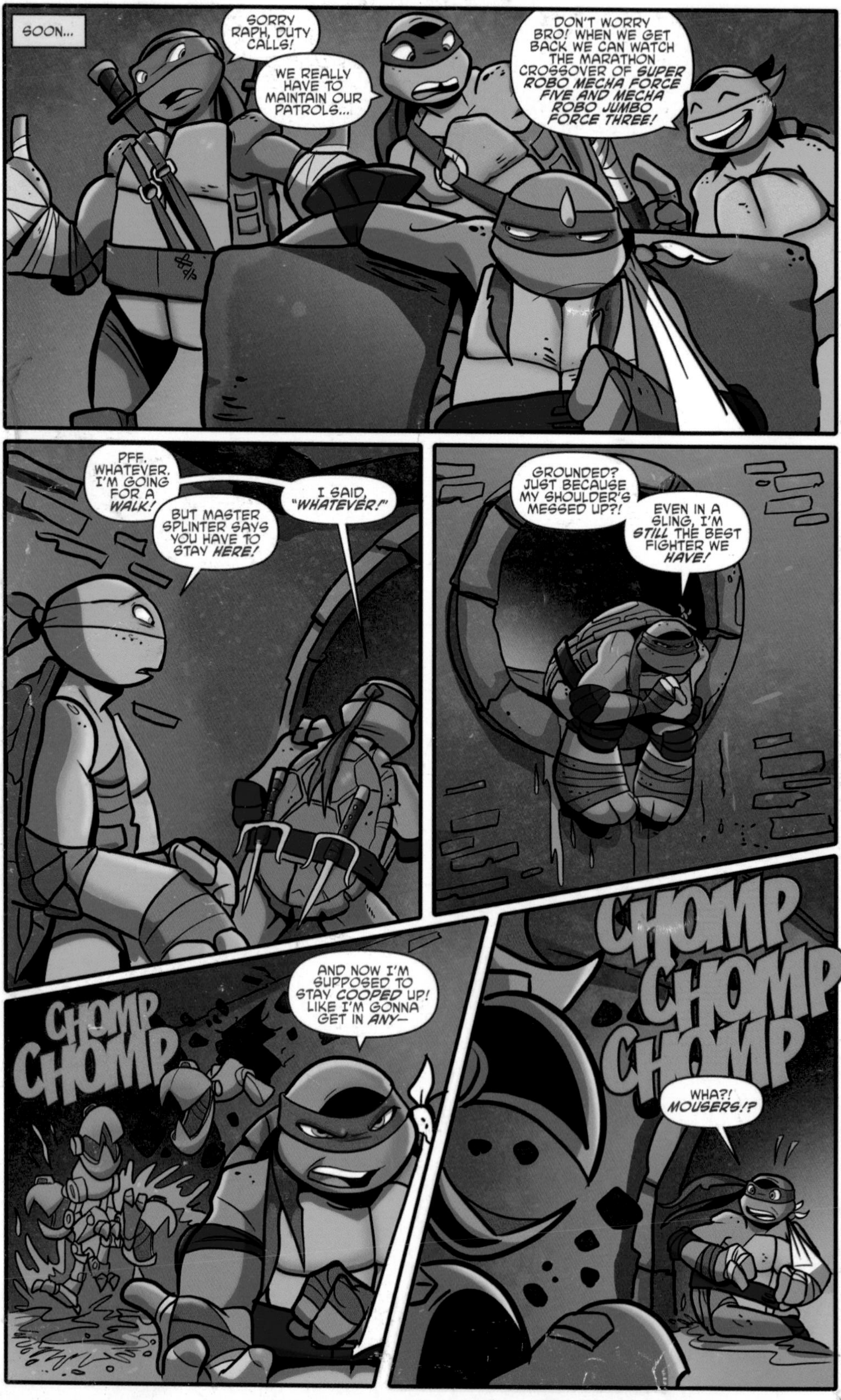
SOON...
SORRY RAPH, DUTY CALLS!
WE REALLY HAVE TO MAINTAIN OUR PATROLS...
DON'T WORRY BRO! WHEN WE GET BACK WE CAN WATCH THE MARATHON CROSSOVER OF SUPER ROBO MECHA FORCE FIVE AND MECHA ROBO JUMBO FORCE THREE!
PFF. WHATEVER. I'M GOING FOR A WALK!
BUT MASTER SPLINTER SAYS YOU HAVE TO STAY HERE!
I SAID, "WHATEVER!"
GROUNDED? JUST BECAUSE MY SHOULDER'S MESSED UP?!
EVEN IN A SLING, I'M STILL THE BEST FIGHTER WE HAVE!
CHOMP CHOMP
AND NOW I'M SUPPOSED TO STAY COOPED UP! LIKE I'M GONNA GET IN ANY—
CHOMP CHOMP CHOMP
WHA?! MOUSERS!?

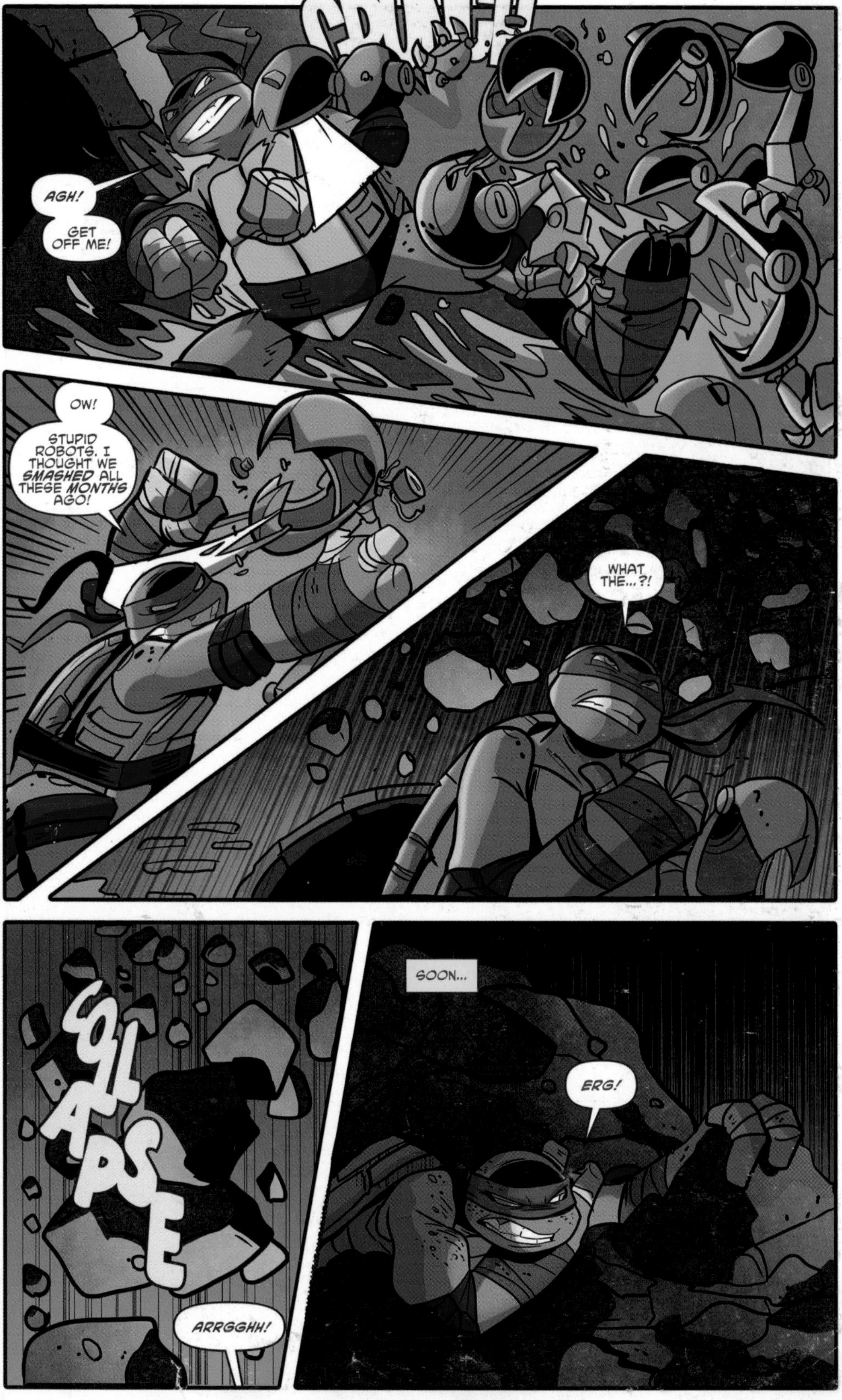
CRUNCH!
AGH!
GET OFF ME!
OW!
STUPID ROBOTS. I THOUGHT WE SMASHED ALL THESE MONTHS AGO!
WHAT THE...?!
COLLAPSE
ARRGGHH!
SOON...
ERG!

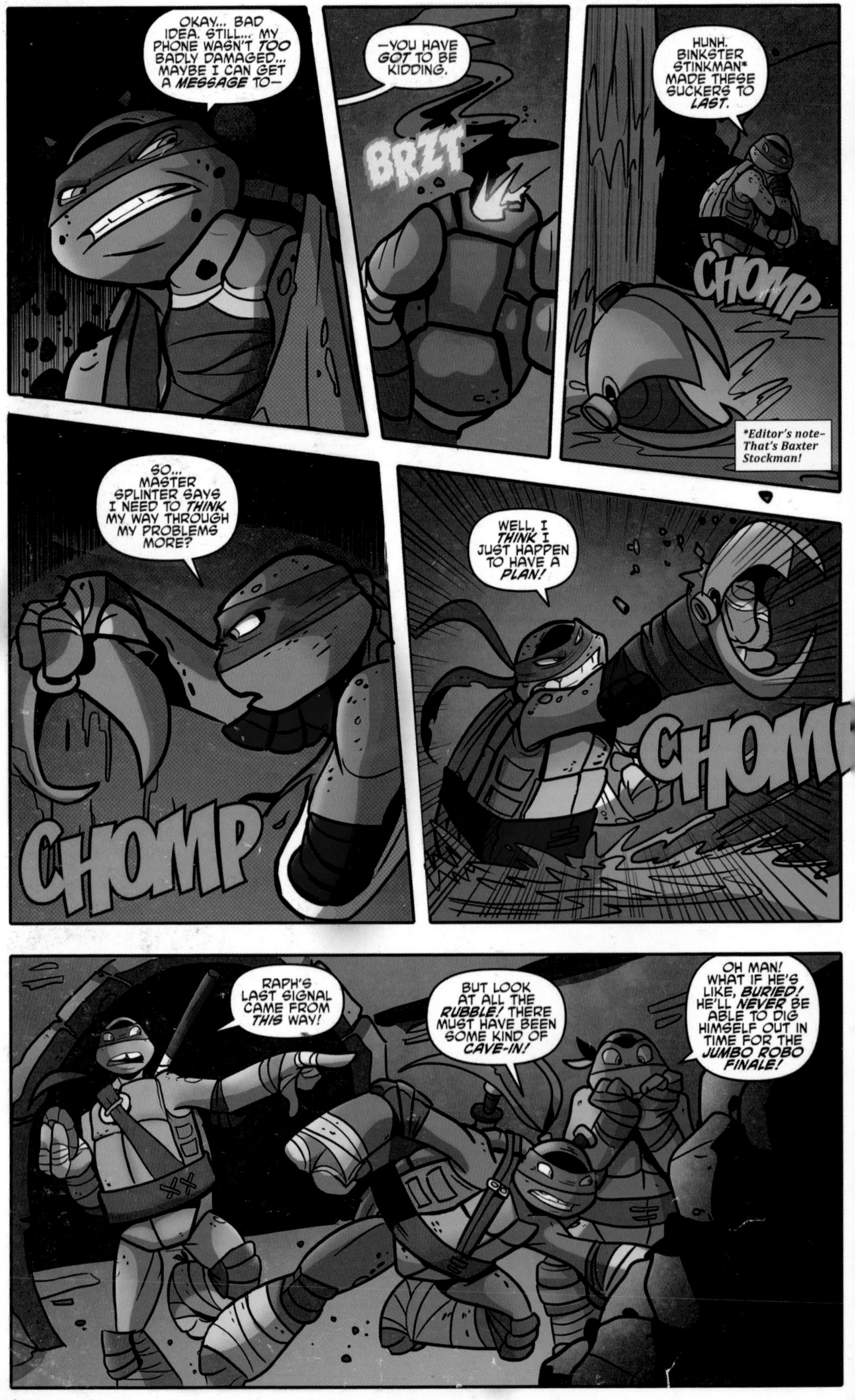
OKAY... BAD IDEA. STILL... MY PHONE WASN'T TOO BADLY DAMAGED... MAYBE I CAN GET A MESSAGE TO—
—YOU HAVE GOT TO BE KIDDING.
BRZT
HUNH. BINKSTER STINKMAN* MADE THESE SUCKERS TO LAST.
CHOMP
*Editor's note– That's Baxter Stockman!
SO... MASTER SPLINTER SAYS I NEED TO THINK MY WAY THROUGH MY PROBLEMS MORE?
CHOMP
WELL, I THINK I JUST HAPPEN TO HAVE A PLAN!
CHOMP
RAPH'S LAST SIGNAL CAME FROM THIS WAY!
BUT LOOK AT ALL THE RUBBLE! THERE MUST HAVE BEEN SOME KIND OF CAVE-IN!
OH MAN! WHAT IF HE'S LIKE, BURIED! HE'LL NEVER BE ABLE TO DIG HIMSELF OUT IN TIME FOR THE JUMBO ROBO FINALE!

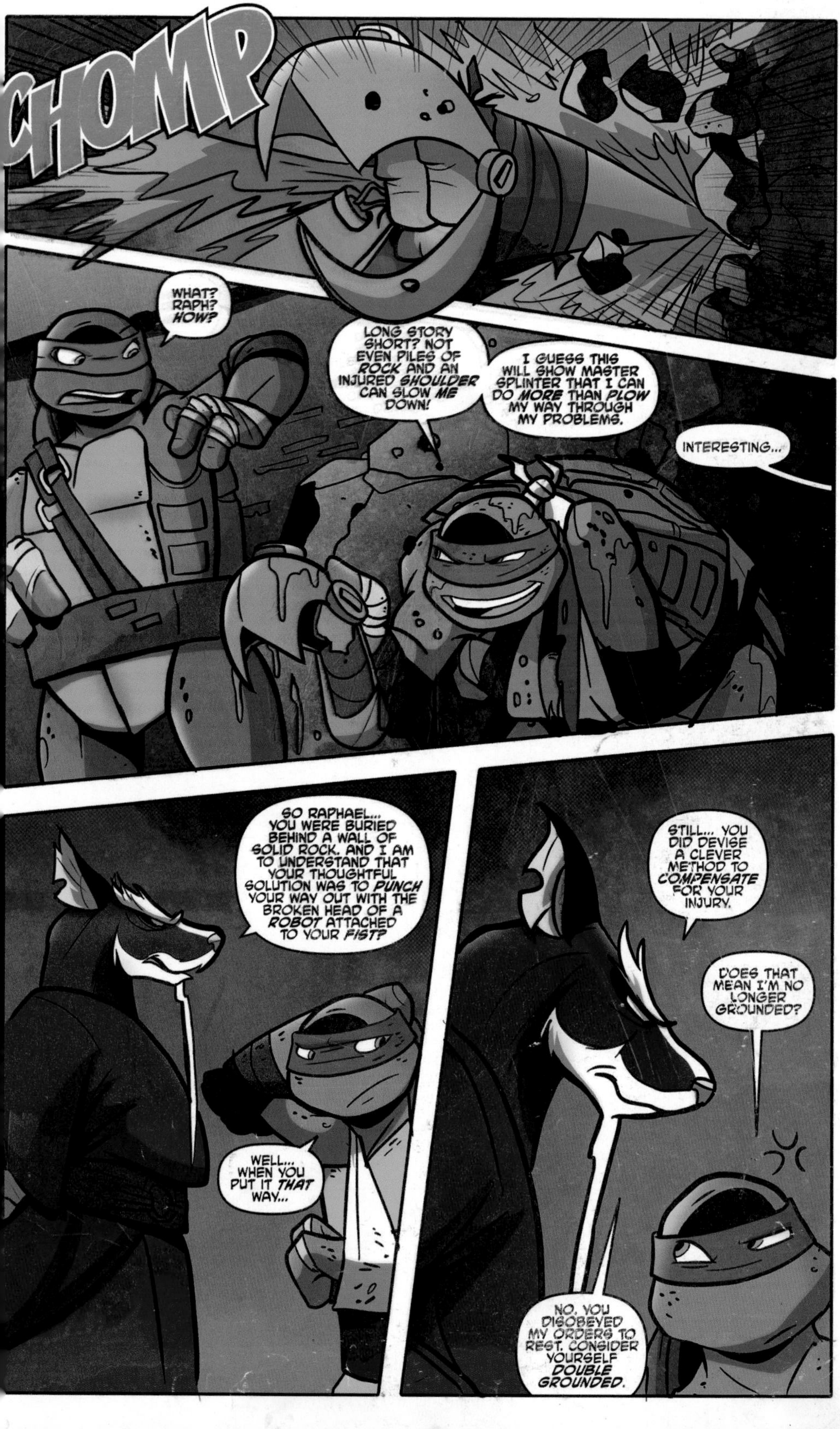
CHOMP
WHAT? RAPH? HOW?
LONG STORY SHORT? NOT EVEN PILES OF ROCK AND AN INJURED SHOULDER CAN SLOW ME DOWN!
I GUESS THIS WILL SHOW MASTER SPLINTER THAT I CAN DO MORE THAN PLOW MY WAY THROUGH MY PROBLEMS.
INTERESTING...
SO RAPHAEL... YOU WERE BURIED BEHIND A WALL OF SOLID ROCK. AND I AM TO UNDERSTAND THAT YOUR THOUGHTFUL SOLUTION WAS TO PUNCH YOUR WAY OUT WITH THE BROKEN HEAD OF A ROBOT ATTACHED TO YOUR FIST?
WELL... WHEN YOU PUT IT THAT WAY...
STILL... YOU DID DEVISE A CLEVER METHOD TO COMPENSATE FOR YOUR INJURY.
DOES THAT MEAN I'M NO LONGER GROUNDED?
NO. YOU DISOBEYED MY ORDERS TO REST. CONSIDER YOURSELF DOUBLE GROUNDED.

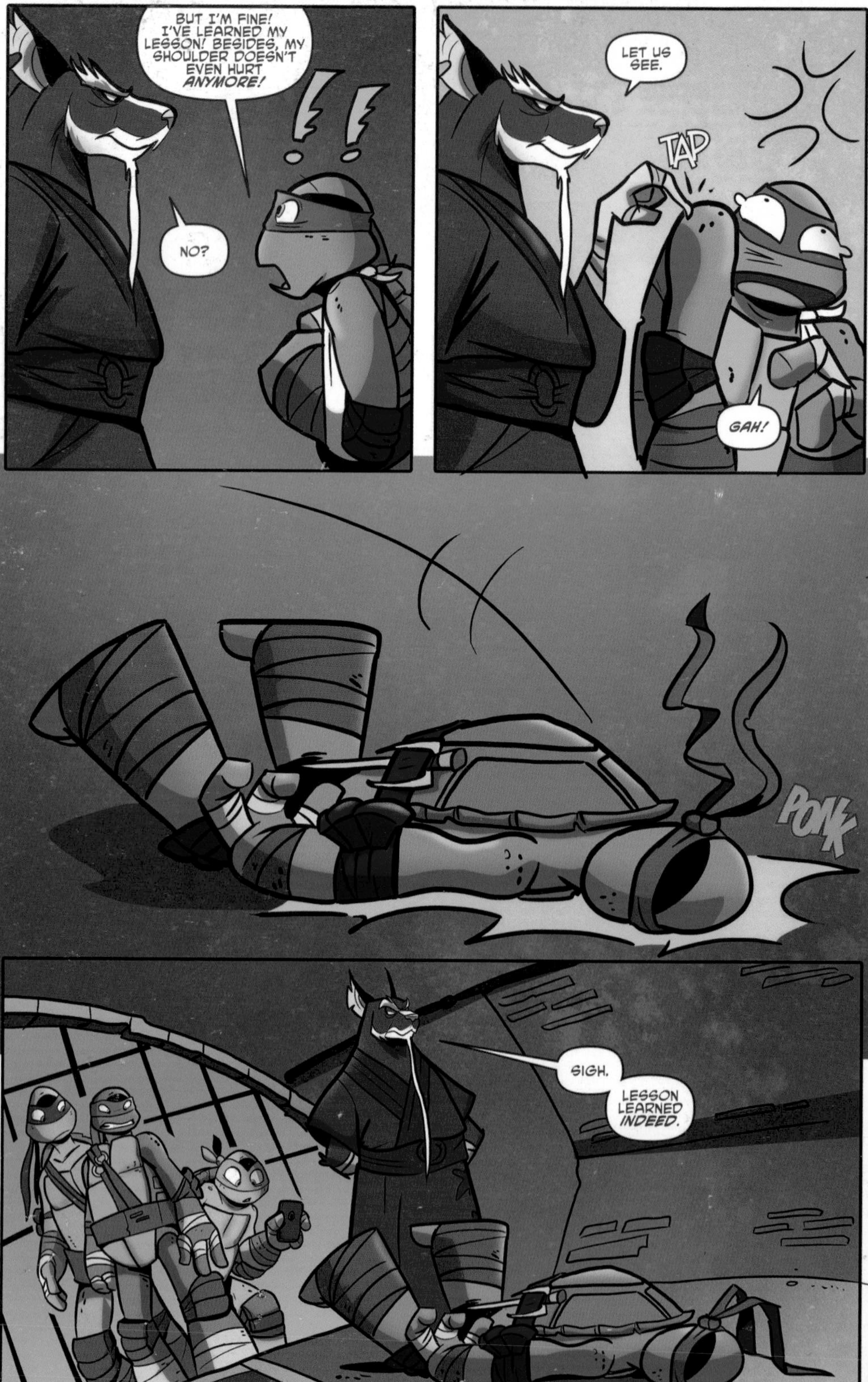
BUT I'M FINE! I'VE LEARNED MY LESSON! BESIDES, MY SHOULDER DOESN'T EVEN HURT ANYMORE!
NO?
LET US SEE.
TAP
GAH!
PONK
SIGH.
LESSON LEARNED INDEED.
THE END!

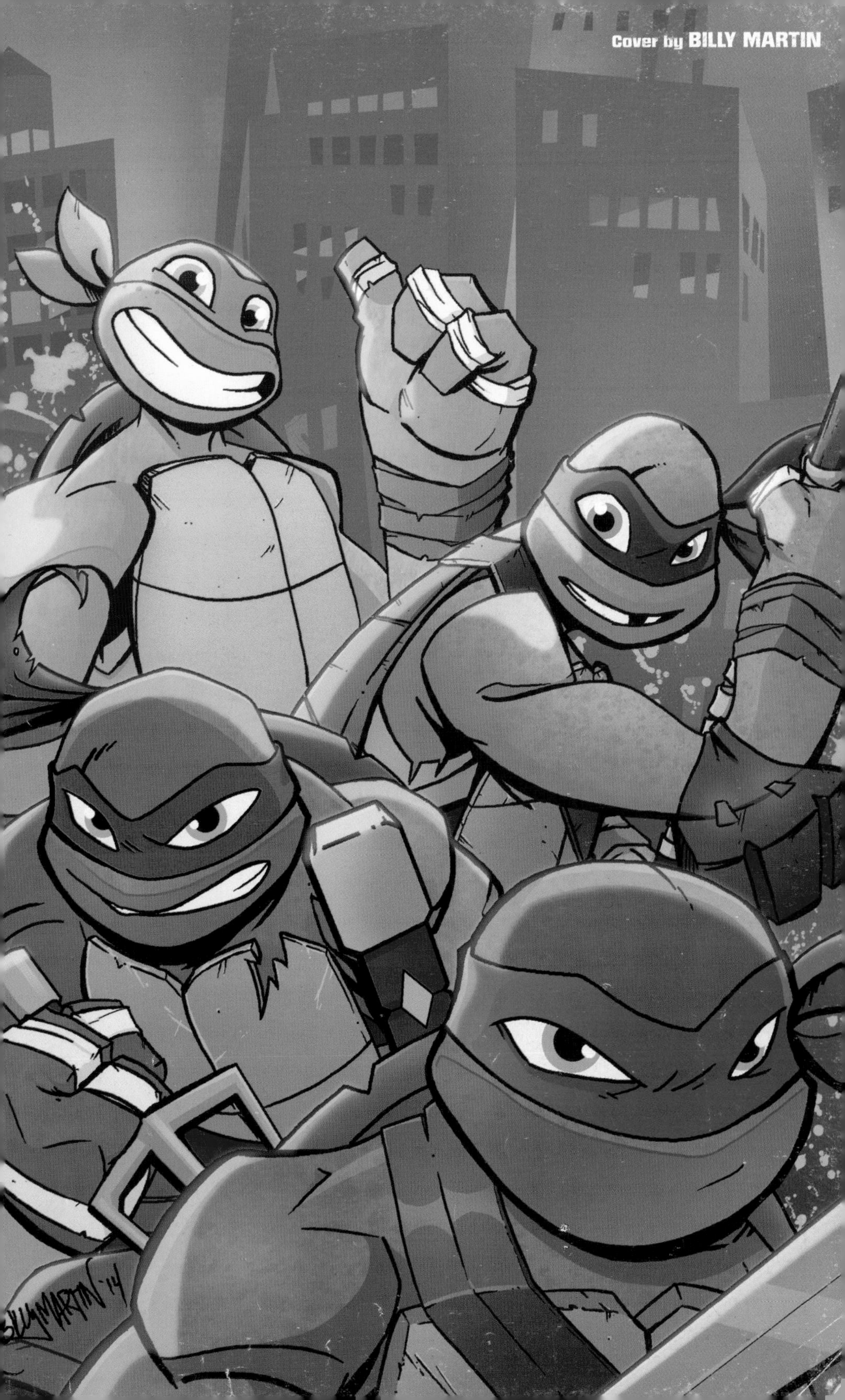

Cover by **BILLY MARTIN**

Cover by DARIO BRIZUELA

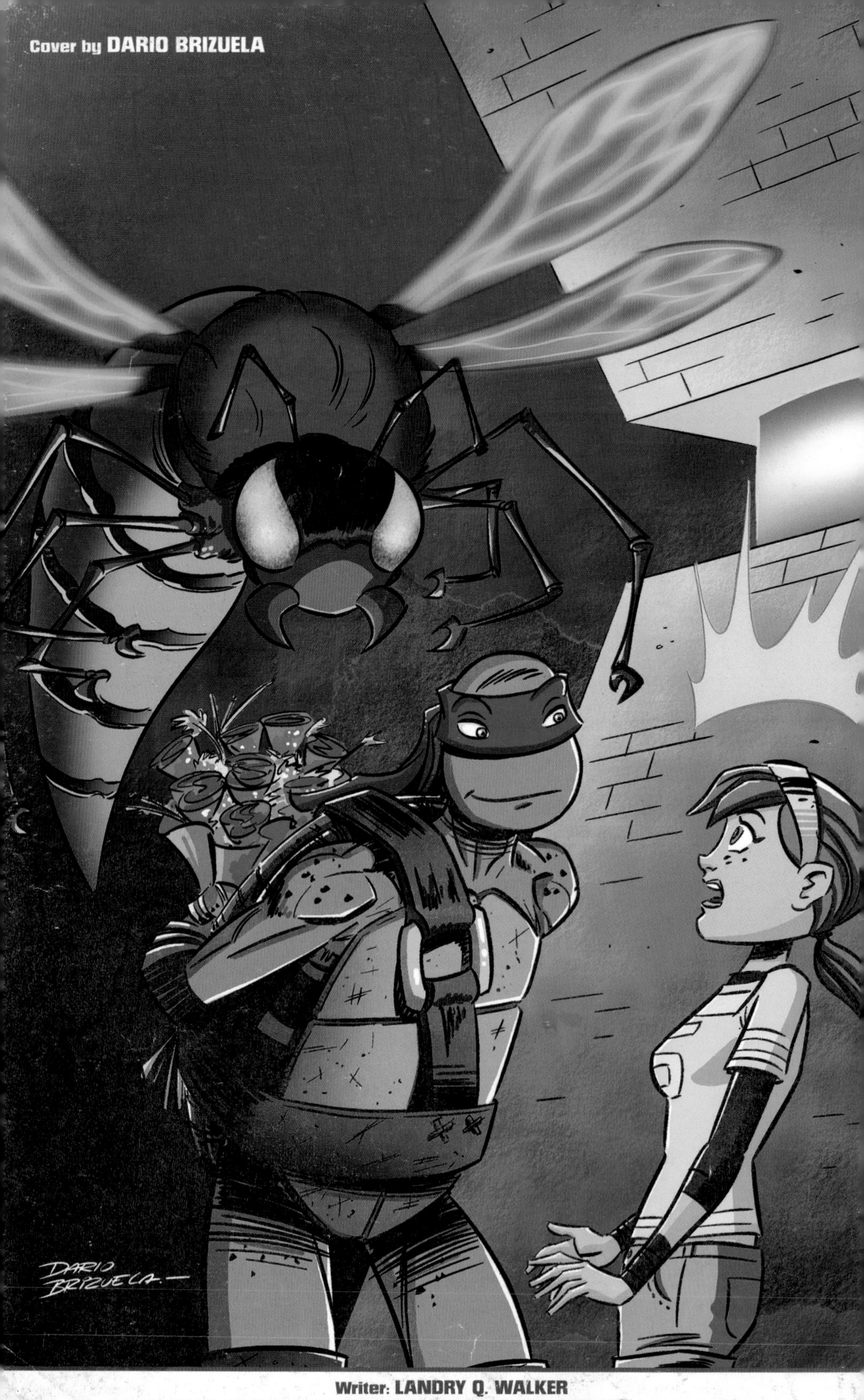
DARIO BRIZUELA

Writer: LANDRY Q. WALKER
Artists: CHAD THOMAS "THE SWARM" / MARCELO FERREIRA "MIKEY & THE MACHINE"

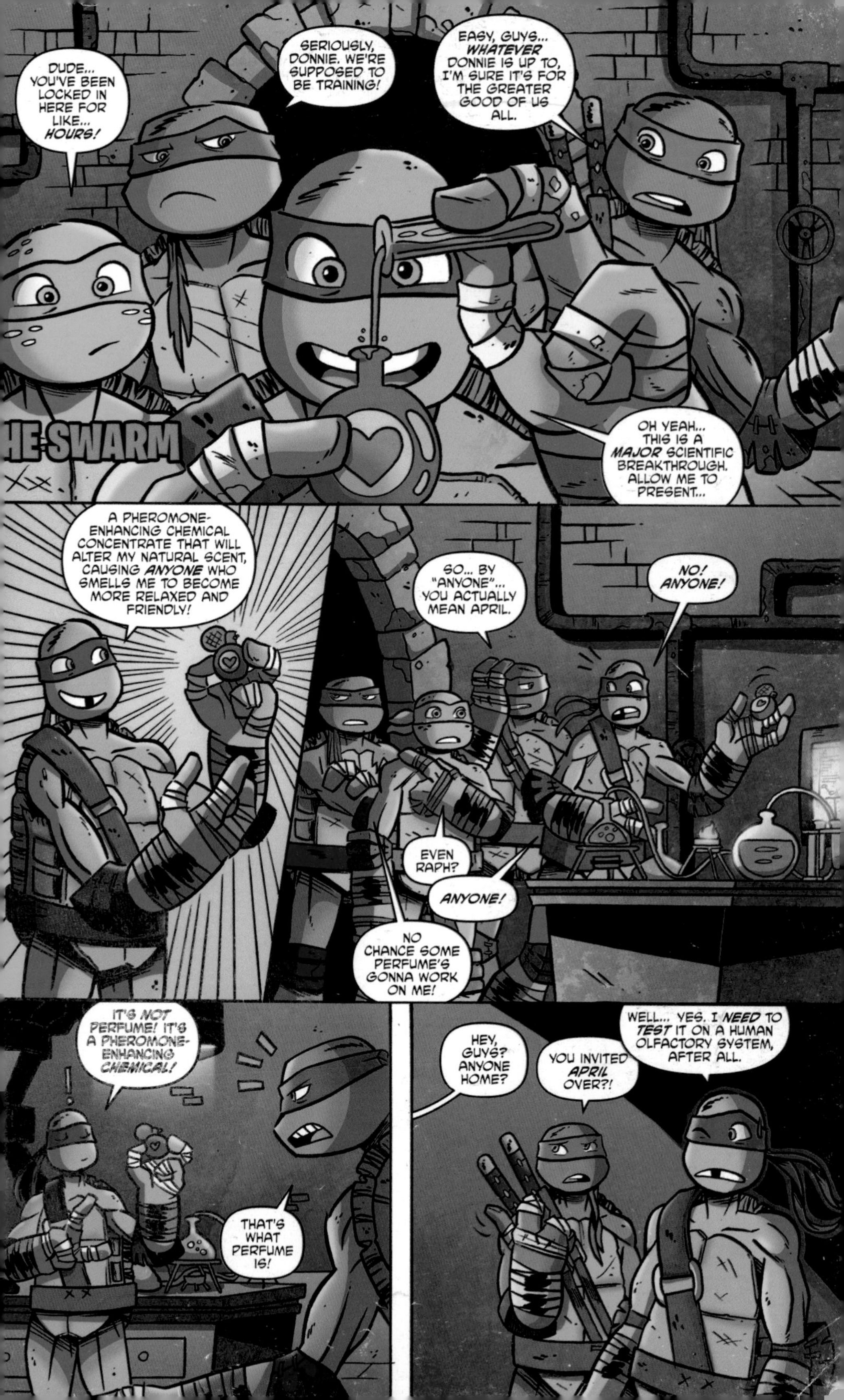
DUDE... YOU'VE BEEN LOCKED IN HERE FOR LIKE... HOURS!
SERIOUSLY, DONNIE. WE'RE SUPPOSED TO BE TRAINING!
EASY, GUYS... WHATEVER DONNIE IS UP TO, I'M SURE IT'S FOR THE GREATER GOOD OF US ALL.
HE SWARM
OH YEAH... THIS IS A MAJOR SCIENTIFIC BREAKTHROUGH. ALLOW ME TO PRESENT...
A PHEROMONE-ENHANCING CHEMICAL CONCENTRATE THAT WILL ALTER MY NATURAL SCENT, CAUSING ANYONE WHO SMELLS ME TO BECOME MORE RELAXED AND FRIENDLY!
SO... BY "ANYONE"... YOU ACTUALLY MEAN APRIL.
NO! ANYONE!
EVEN RAPH?
ANYONE!
NO CHANCE SOME PERFUME'S GONNA WORK ON ME!
IT'S NOT PERFUME! IT'S A PHEROMONE-ENHANCING CHEMICAL!
THAT'S WHAT PERFUME IS!
HEY, GUYS? ANYONE HOME?
YOU INVITED APRIL OVER?!
WELL... YES. I NEED TO TEST IT ON A HUMAN OLFACTORY SYSTEM, AFTER ALL.

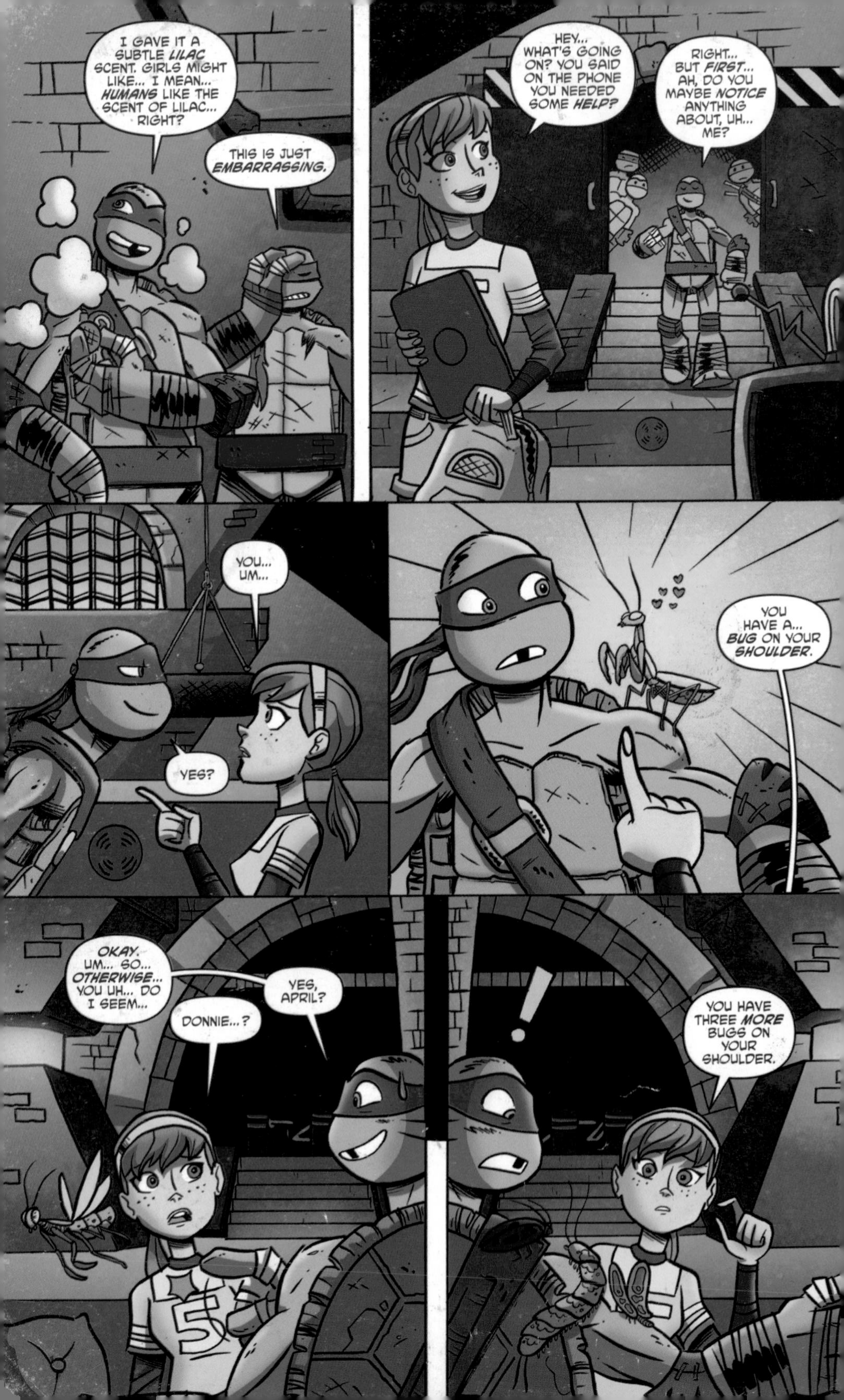
I GAVE IT A SUBTLE LILAC SCENT. GIRLS MIGHT LIKE... I MEAN... HUMANS LIKE THE SCENT OF LILAC... RIGHT?
THIS IS JUST EMBARRASSING.
HEY... WHAT'S GOING ON? YOU SAID ON THE PHONE YOU NEEDED SOME HELP?
RIGHT... BUT FIRST... AH, DO YOU MAYBE NOTICE ANYTHING ABOUT, UH... ME?
YOU... UM...
YES?
YOU HAVE A... BUG ON YOUR SHOULDER.
OKAY. UM... SO... OTHERWISE... YOU UH... DO I SEEM...
YES, APRIL?
DONNIE...?
!
YOU HAVE THREE MORE BUGS ON YOUR SHOULDER.

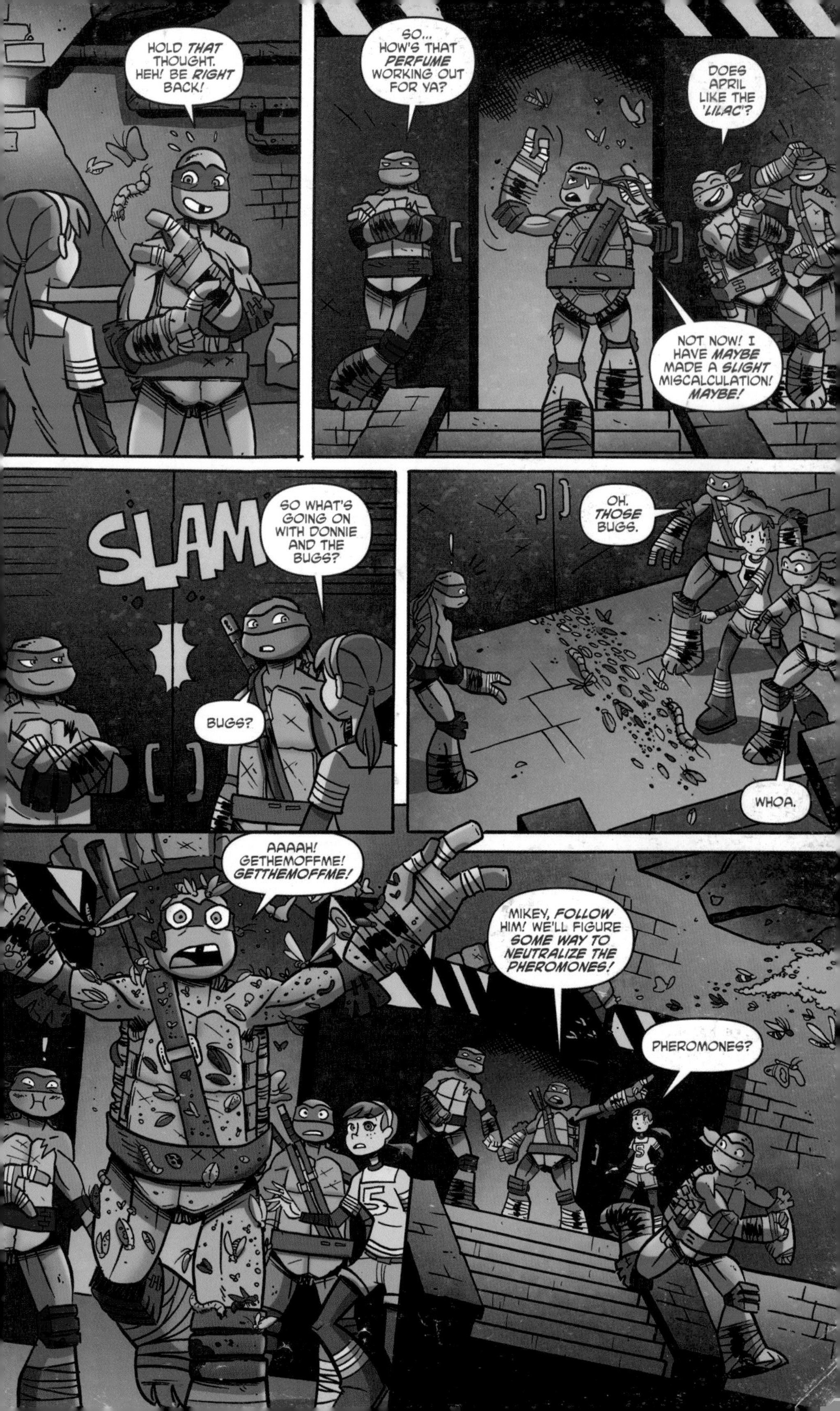
HOLD THAT THOUGHT. HEH! BE RIGHT BACK!
SO... HOW'S THAT PERFUME WORKING OUT FOR YA?
DOES APRIL LIKE THE 'LILAC'?
NOT NOW! I HAVE MAYBE MADE A SLIGHT MISCALCULATION! MAYBE!
SLAM
SO WHAT'S GOING ON WITH DONNIE AND THE BUGS?
BUGS?
!
OH. THOSE BUGS.
WHOA.
AAAAH! GETHEMOFFME! GETTHEMOFFME!
MIKEY, FOLLOW HIM! WE'LL FIGURE SOME WAY TO NEUTRALIZE THE PHEROMONES!
PHEROMONES?
!

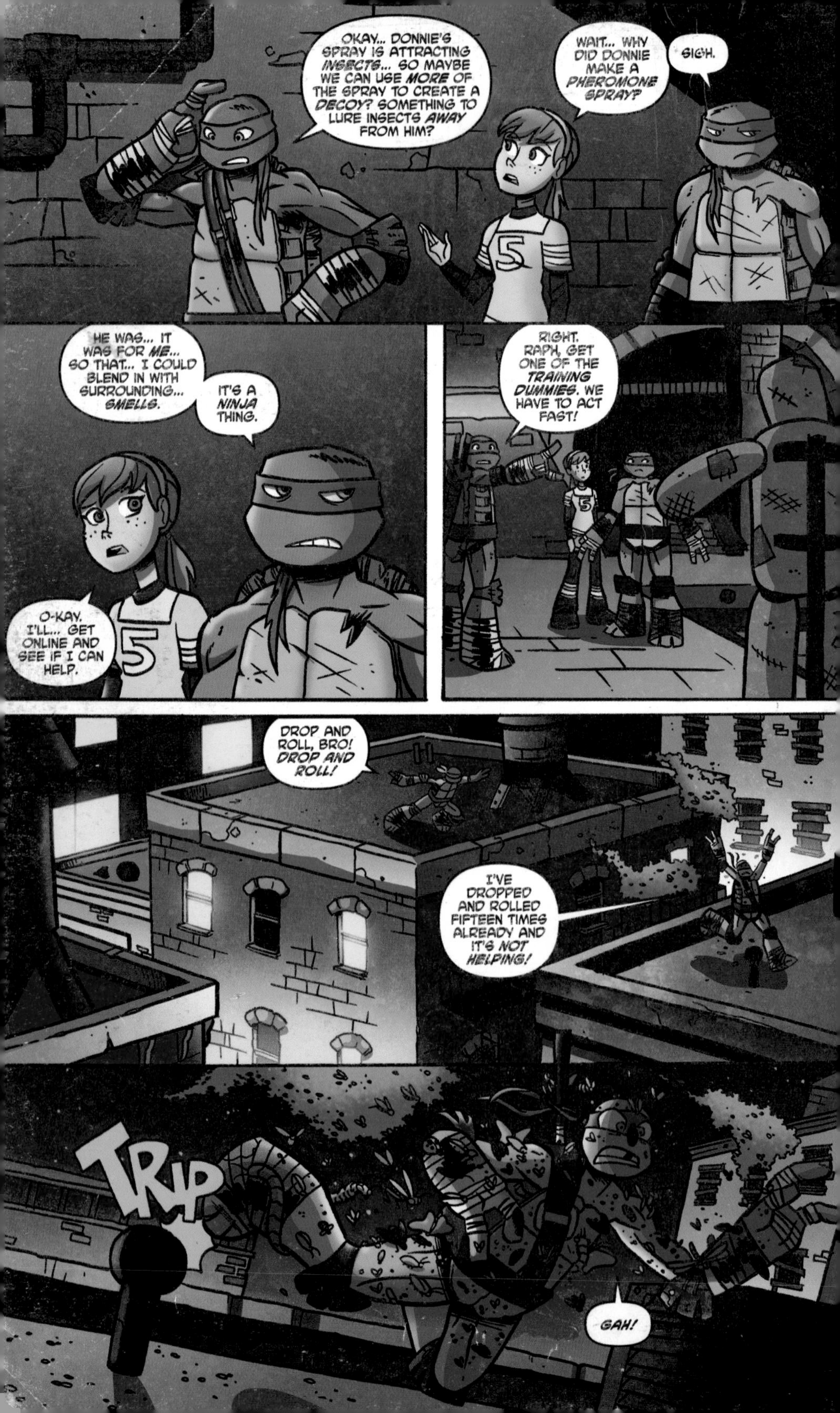
OKAY... DONNIE'S SPRAY IS ATTRACTING *INSECTS*... SO MAYBE WE CAN USE *MORE* OF THE SPRAY TO CREATE A *DECOY?* SOMETHING TO LURE INSECTS *AWAY* FROM HIM?
WAIT... WHY DID DONNIE MAKE A *PHEROMONE SPRAY?*
SIGH.
HE WAS... IT WAS FOR *ME*... SO THAT... I COULD BLEND IN WITH SURROUNDING... *SMELLS*.
IT'S A *NINJA* THING.
O-KAY. I'LL... GET ONLINE AND SEE IF I CAN HELP.
RIGHT. RAPH, GET ONE OF THE *TRAINING DUMMIES*. WE HAVE TO ACT FAST!
DROP AND ROLL, BRO! *DROP AND ROLL!*
I'VE DROPPED AND ROLLED FIFTEEN TIMES ALREADY AND IT'S *NOT HELPING!*
TRIP
GAH!

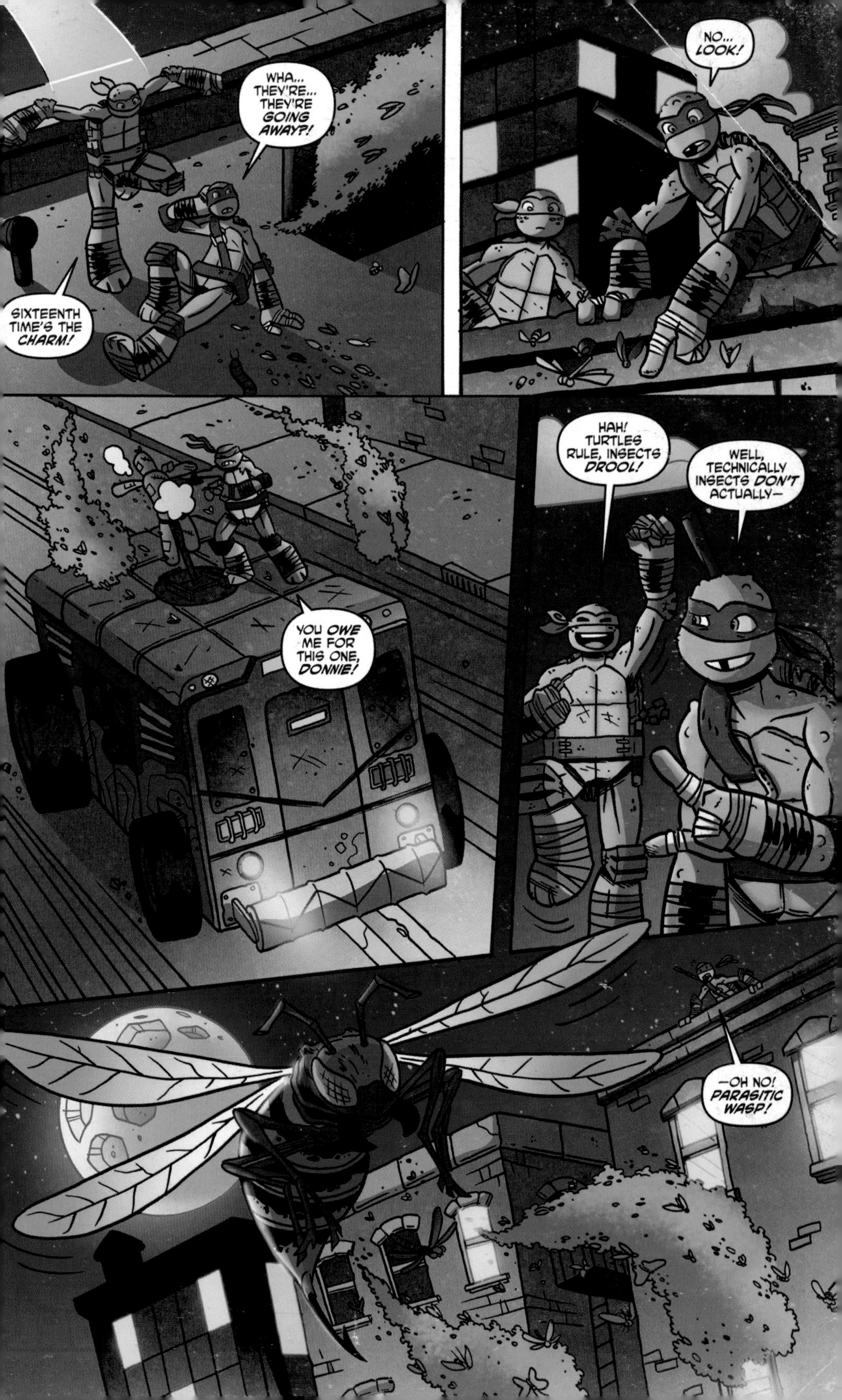
WHA... THEY'RE... THEY'RE GOING AWAY?!
SIXTEENTH TIME'S THE CHARM!
NO... LOOK!
YOU OWE ME FOR THIS ONE, DONNIE!
HAH! TURTLES RULE, INSECTS DROOL!
WELL, TECHNICALLY INSECTS DON'T ACTUALLY—
—OH NO! PARASITIC WASP!

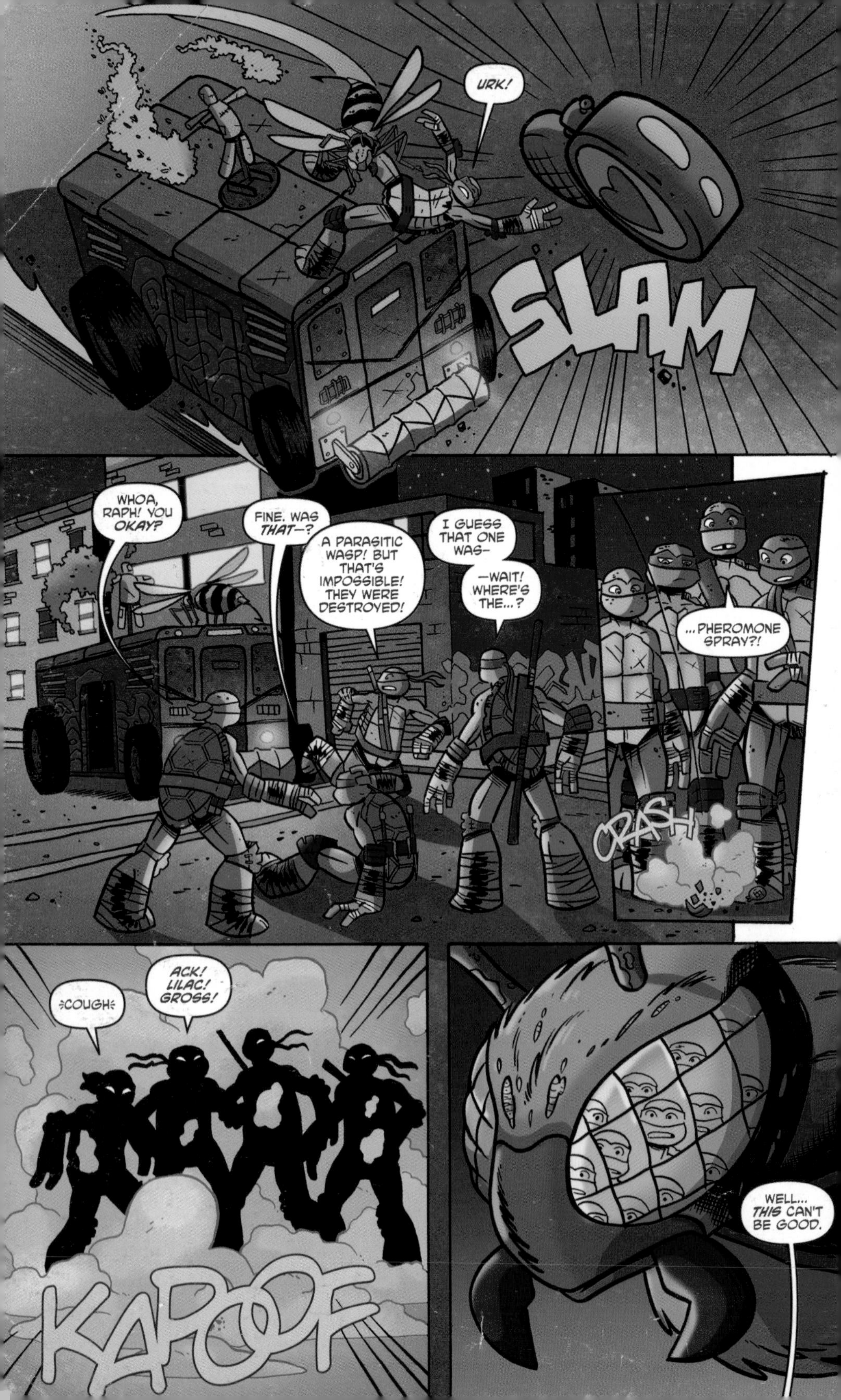
URK!
SLAM
WHOA, RAPH! YOU OKAY?
FINE. WAS THAT—?
A PARASITIC WASP! BUT THAT'S IMPOSSIBLE! THEY WERE DESTROYED!
I GUESS THAT ONE WAS-
—WAIT! WHERE'S THE...?
...PHEROMONE SPRAY?!
CRASH
COUGH
ACK! LILAC! GROSS!
KAPOOF
WELL... THIS CAN'T BE GOOD.

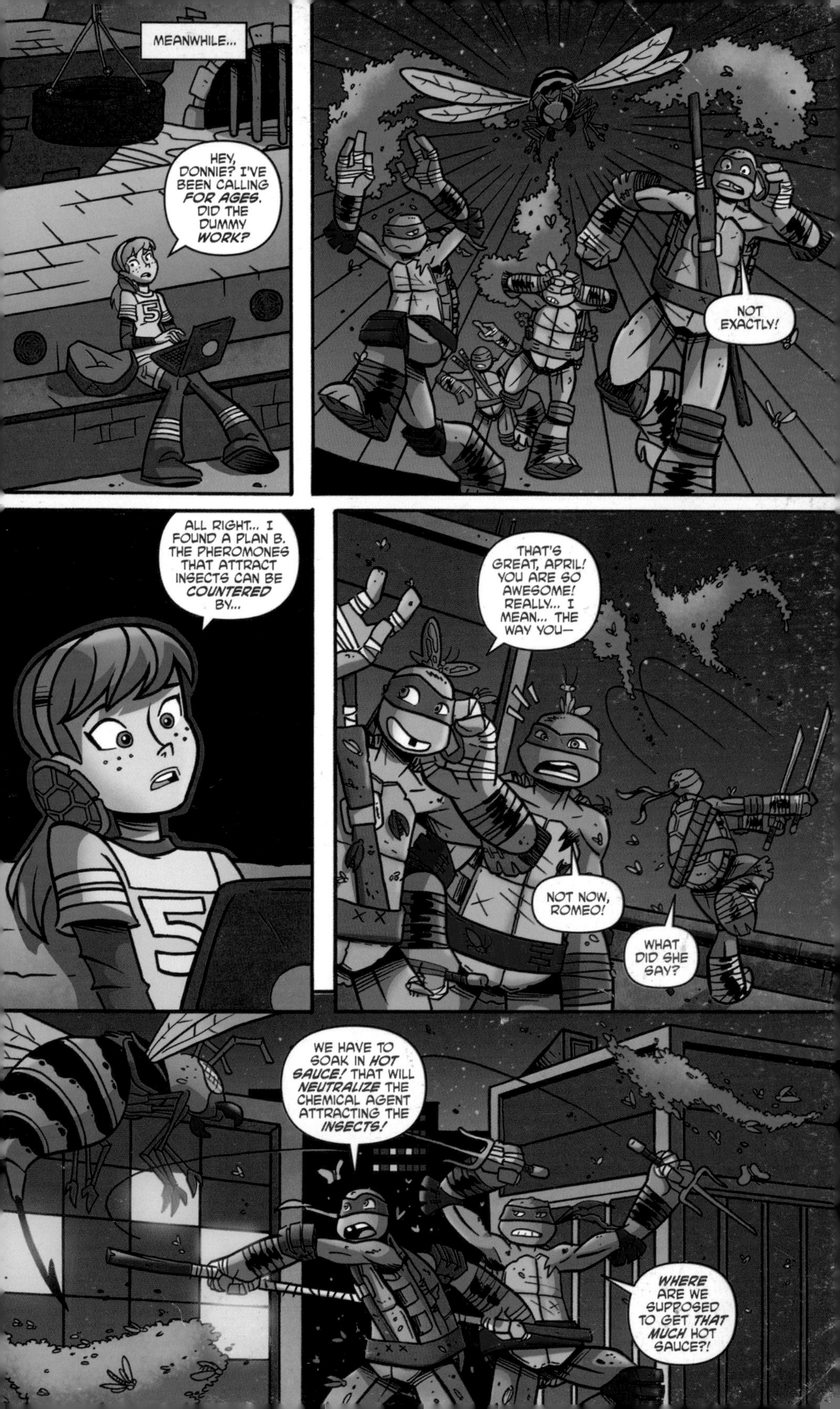
MEANWHILE...
HEY, DONNIE? I'VE BEEN CALLING FOR AGES. DID THE DUMMY WORK?
NOT EXACTLY!
ALL RIGHT... I FOUND A PLAN B. THE PHEROMONES THAT ATTRACT INSECTS CAN BE COUNTERED BY...
THAT'S GREAT, APRIL! YOU ARE SO AWESOME! REALLY... I MEAN... THE WAY YOU—
NOT NOW, ROMEO!
WHAT DID SHE SAY?
WE HAVE TO SOAK IN HOT SAUCE! THAT WILL NEUTRALIZE THE CHEMICAL AGENT ATTRACTING THE INSECTS!
WHERE ARE WE SUPPOSED TO GET THAT MUCH HOT SAUCE?!

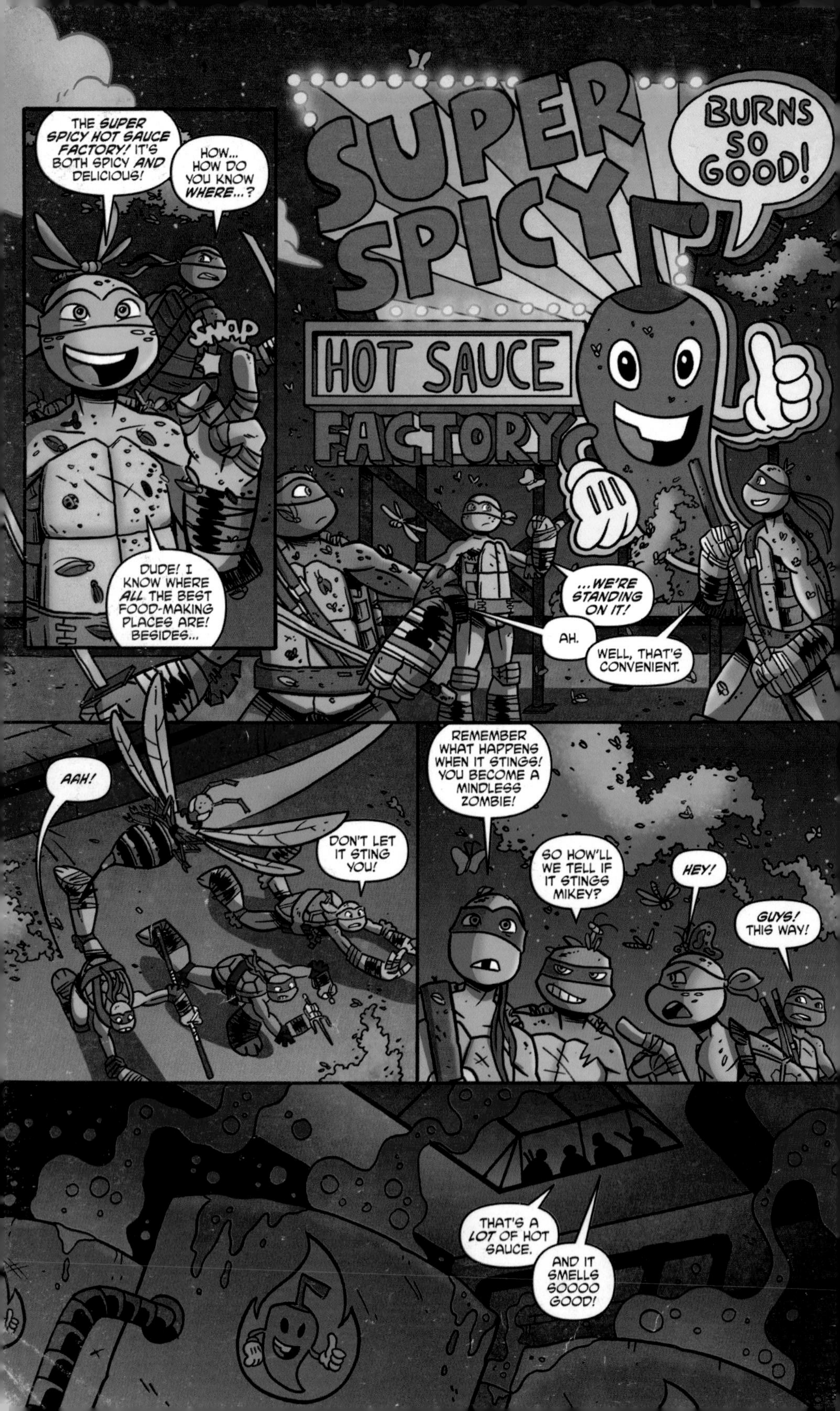

SUPER SPICY
BURNS SO GOOD!
HOT SAUCE
FACTORY
THE SUPER SPICY HOT SAUCE FACTORY! IT'S BOTH SPICY AND DELICIOUS!
HOW... HOW DO YOU KNOW WHERE...?
SNAP
DUDE! I KNOW WHERE ALL THE BEST FOOD-MAKING PLACES ARE! BESIDES...
...WE'RE STANDING ON IT!
AH.
WELL, THAT'S CONVENIENT.
AAH!
DON'T LET IT STING YOU!
REMEMBER WHAT HAPPENS WHEN IT STINGS! YOU BECOME A MINDLESS ZOMBIE!
SO HOW'LL WE TELL IF IT STINGS MIKEY?
HEY!
GUYS! THIS WAY!
THAT'S A LOT OF HOT SAUCE.
AND IT SMELLS SOOOO GOOD!

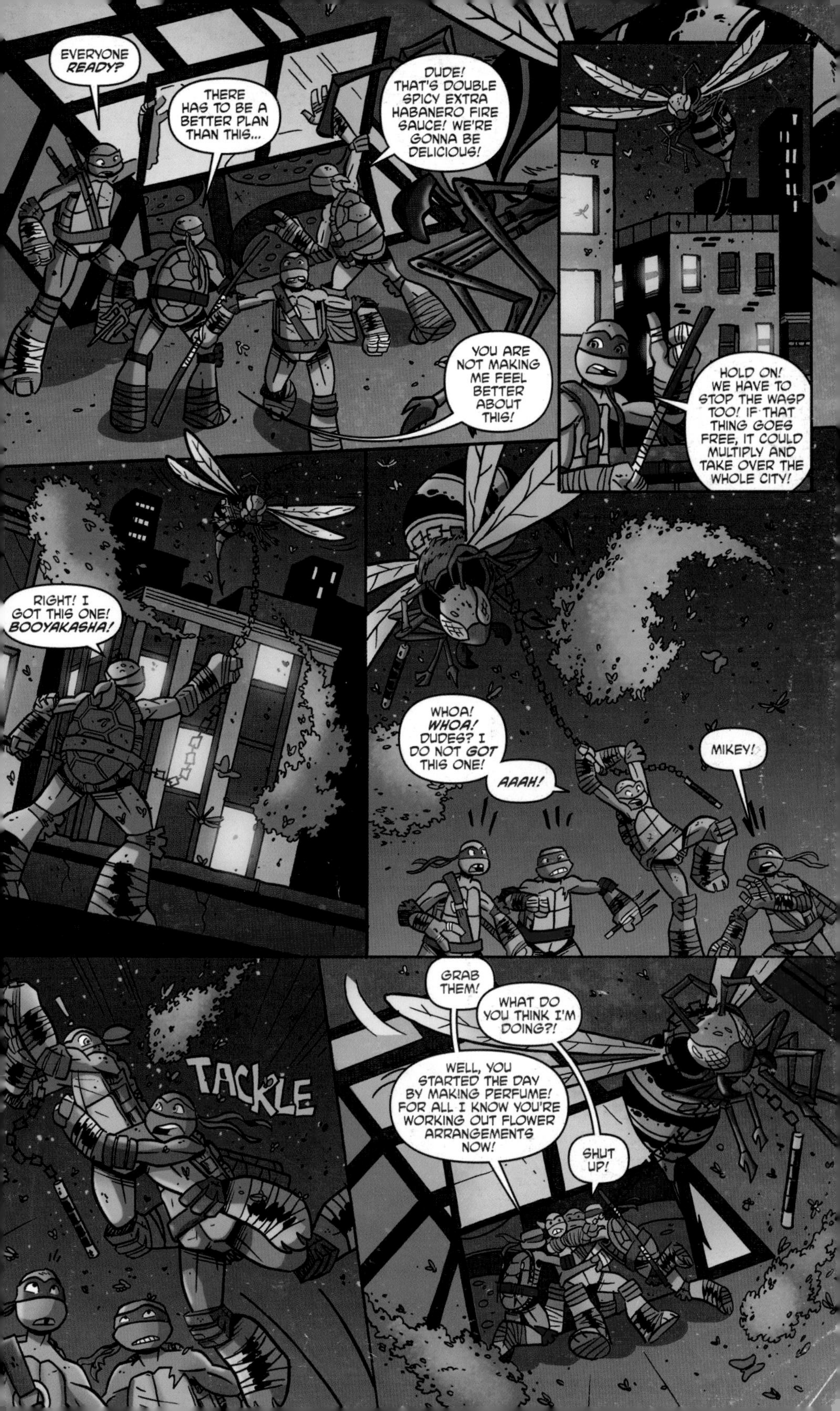
EVERYONE READY?
THERE HAS TO BE A BETTER PLAN THAN THIS...
DUDE! THAT'S DOUBLE SPICY EXTRA HABANERO FIRE SAUCE! WE'RE GONNA BE DELICIOUS!
YOU ARE NOT MAKING ME FEEL BETTER ABOUT THIS!
HOLD ON! WE HAVE TO STOP THE WASP TOO! IF THAT THING GOES FREE, IT COULD MULTIPLY AND TAKE OVER THE WHOLE CITY!
RIGHT! I GOT THIS ONE! BOOYAKASHA!
WHOA! WHOA! DUDES? I DO NOT GOT THIS ONE!
AAAH!
MIKEY!
TACKLE
GRAB THEM!
WHAT DO YOU THINK I'M DOING?!
WELL, YOU STARTED THE DAY BY MAKING PERFUME! FOR ALL I KNOW YOU'RE WORKING OUT FLOWER ARRANGEMENTS NOW!
SHUT UP!

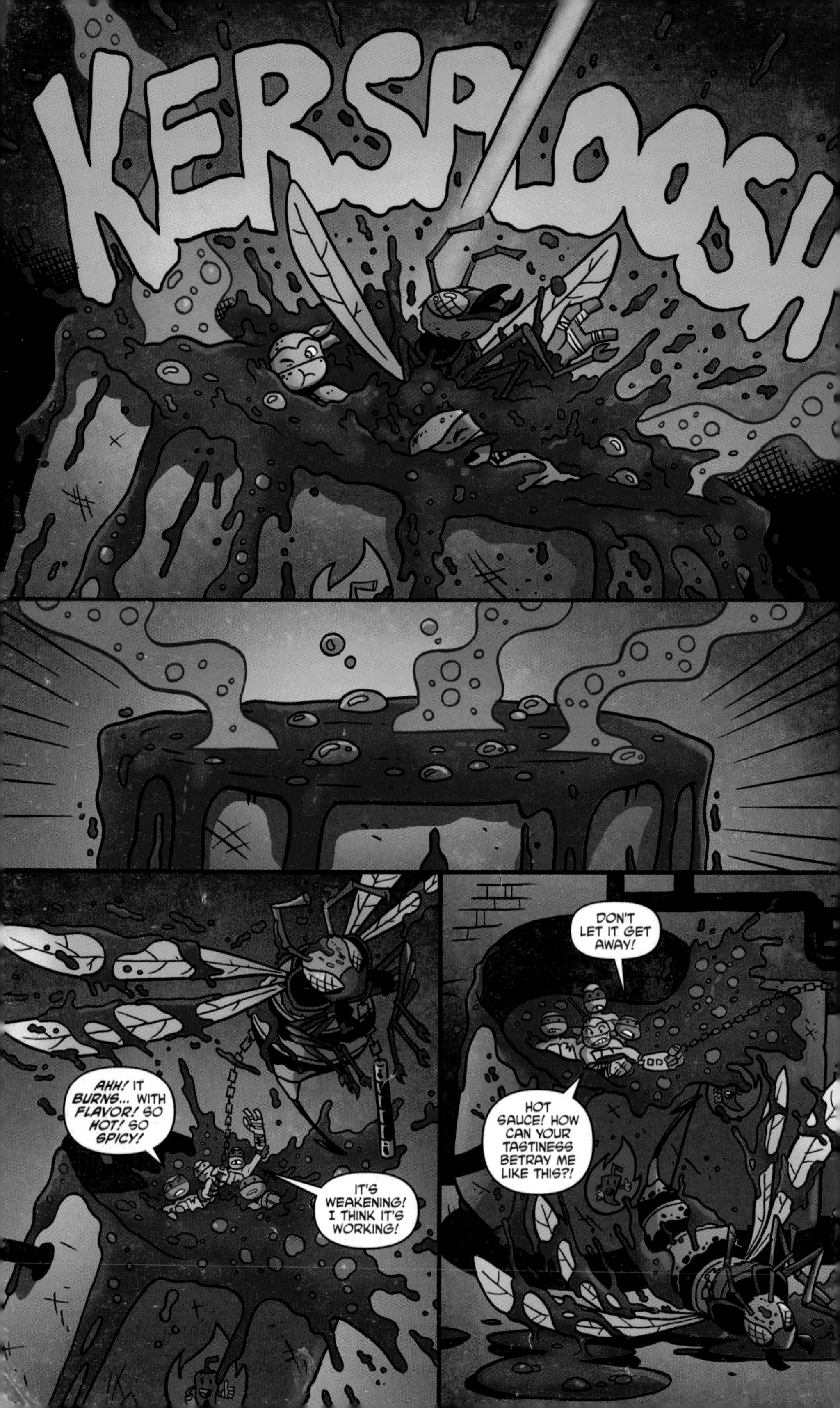
KERSPLOOSH!
AHH! IT BURNS... WITH FLAVOR! SO HOT! SO SPICY!
IT'S WEAKENING! I THINK IT'S WORKING!
DON'T LET IT GET AWAY!
HOT SAUCE! HOW CAN YOUR TASTINESS BETRAY ME LIKE THIS?!

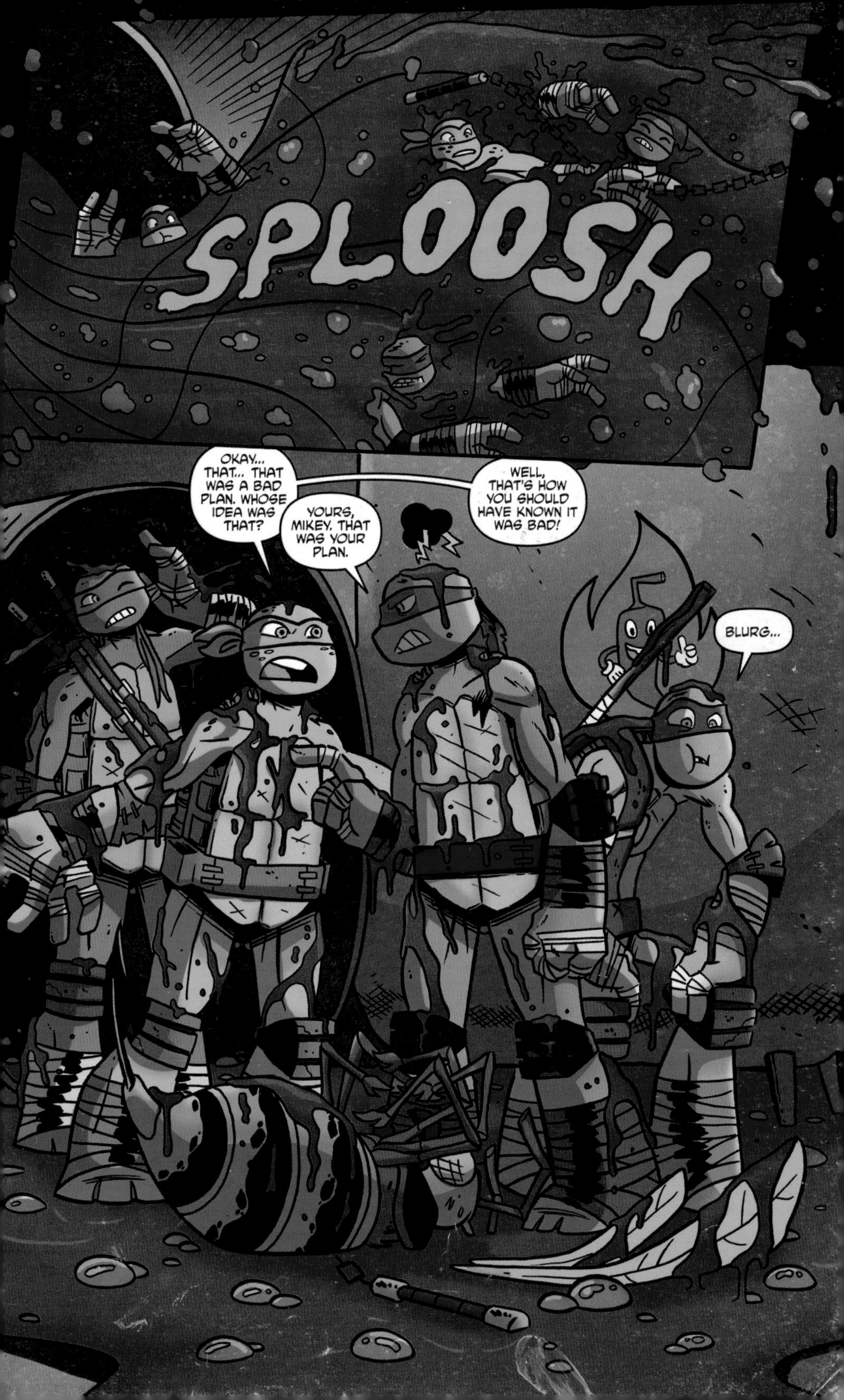
SPLOOSH
OKAY... THAT... THAT WAS A BAD PLAN. WHOSE IDEA WAS THAT?
YOURS, MIKEY. THAT WAS YOUR PLAN.
WELL, THAT'S HOW YOU SHOULD HAVE KNOWN IT WAS BAD!
BLURG...

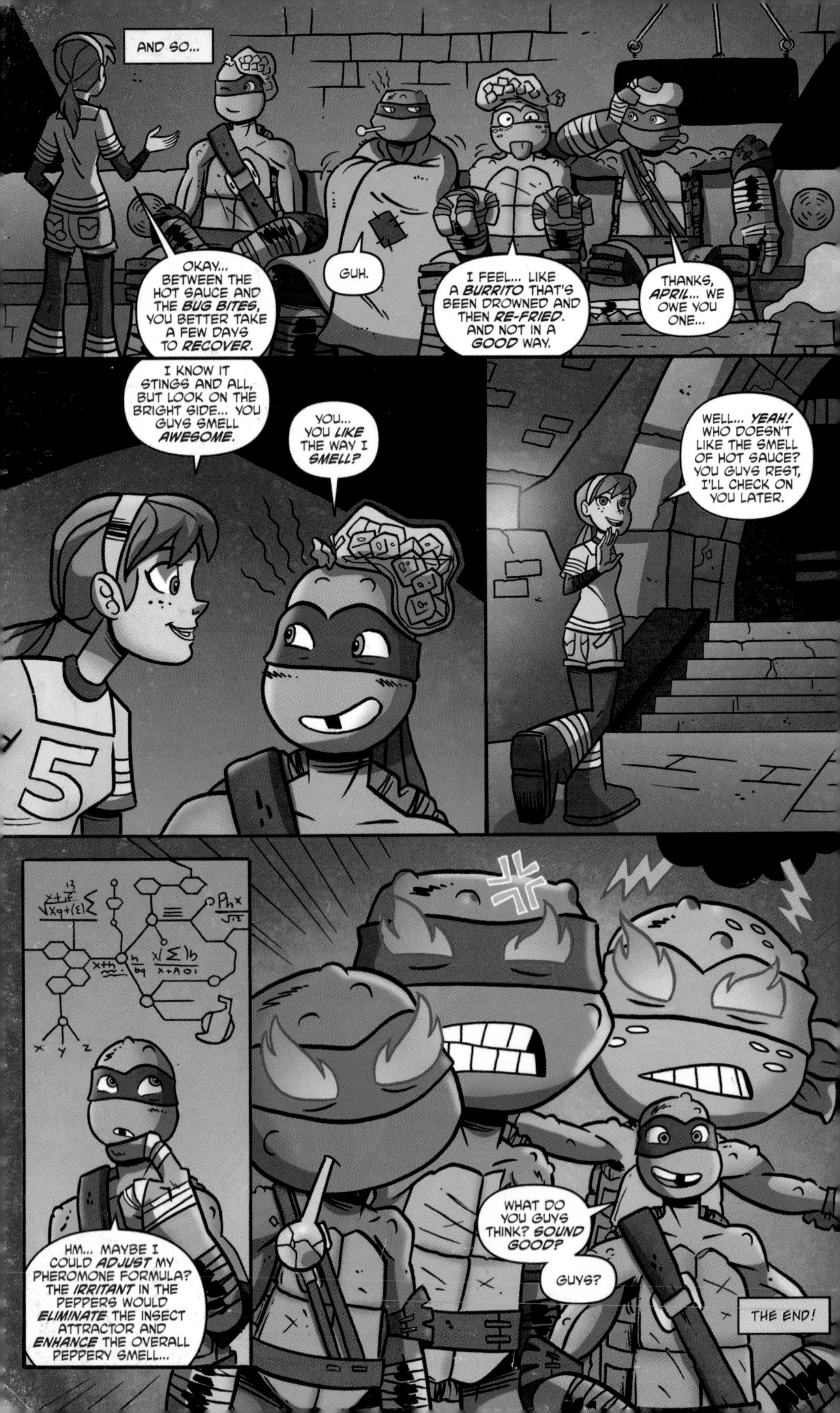
AND SO...
OKAY... BETWEEN THE HOT SAUCE AND THE BUG BITES, YOU BETTER TAKE A FEW DAYS TO RECOVER.
GUH.
I FEEL... LIKE A BURRITO THAT'S BEEN DROWNED AND THEN RE-FRIED. AND NOT IN A GOOD WAY.
THANKS, APRIL... WE OWE YOU ONE...
I KNOW IT STINGS AND ALL, BUT LOOK ON THE BRIGHT SIDE... YOU GUYS SMELL AWESOME.
YOU... YOU LIKE THE WAY I SMELL?
WELL... YEAH! WHO DOESN'T LIKE THE SMELL OF HOT SAUCE? YOU GUYS REST, I'LL CHECK ON YOU LATER.
HM... MAYBE I COULD ADJUST MY PHEROMONE FORMULA? THE IRRITANT IN THE PEPPERS WOULD ELIMINATE THE INSECT ATTRACTOR AND ENHANCE THE OVERALL PEPPERY SMELL...
WHAT DO YOU GUYS THINK? SOUND GOOD?
GUYS?
THE END!

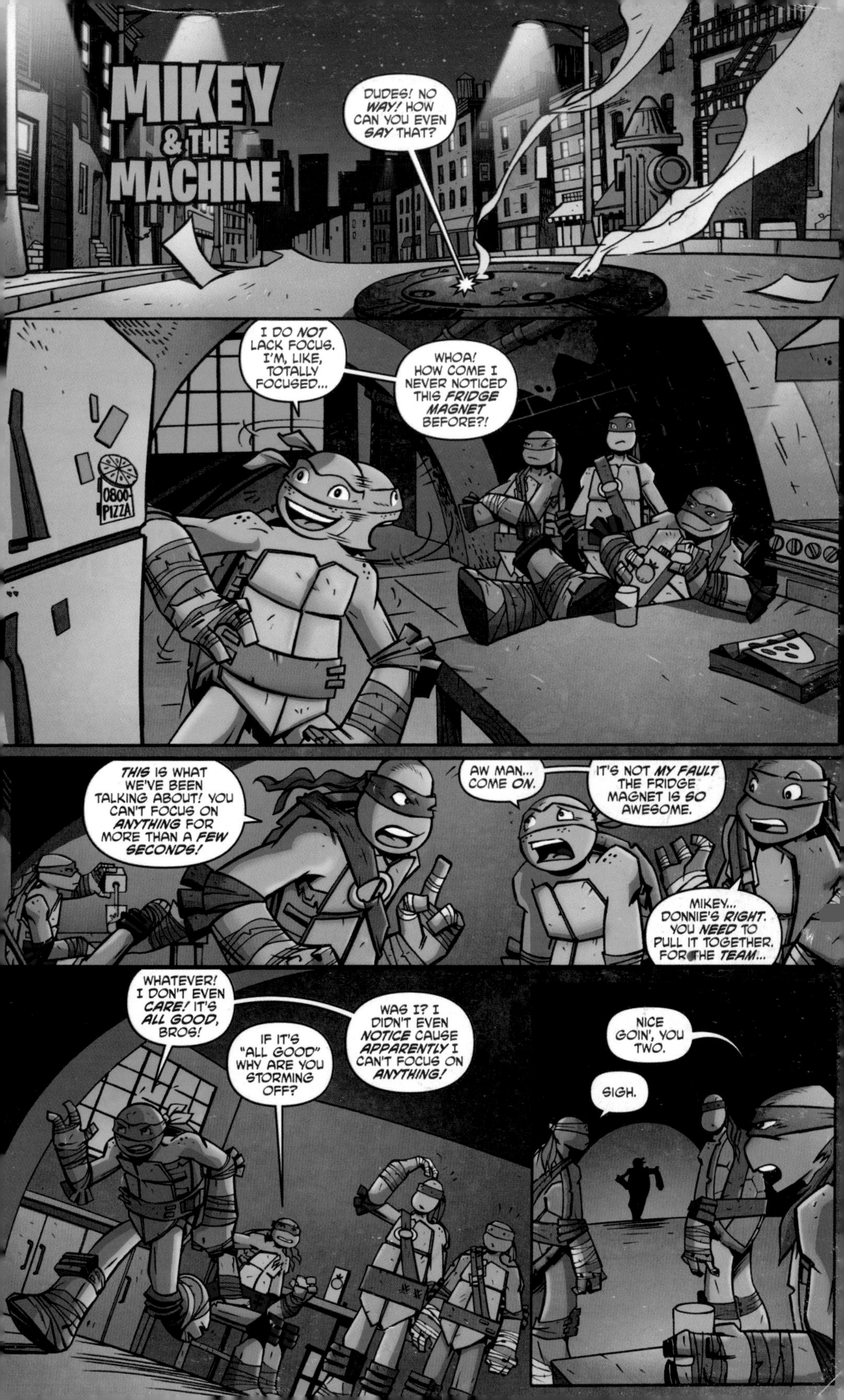

MIKEY & THE MACHINE
DUDES! NO WAY! HOW CAN YOU EVEN SAY THAT?
I DO NOT LACK FOCUS. I'M, LIKE, TOTALLY FOCUSED...
WHOA! HOW COME I NEVER NOTICED THIS FRIDGE MAGNET BEFORE?!
0800-PIZZA
THIS IS WHAT WE'VE BEEN TALKING ABOUT! YOU CAN'T FOCUS ON ANYTHING FOR MORE THAN A FEW SECONDS!
AW MAN... COME ON.
IT'S NOT MY FAULT THE FRIDGE MAGNET IS SO AWESOME.
MIKEY... DONNIE'S RIGHT. YOU NEED TO PULL IT TOGETHER. FOR THE TEAM...
WHATEVER! I DON'T EVEN CARE! IT'S ALL GOOD, BROS!
IF IT'S "ALL GOOD" WHY ARE YOU STORMING OFF?
WAS I? I DIDN'T EVEN NOTICE CAUSE APPARENTLY I CAN'T FOCUS ON ANYTHING!
NICE GOIN', YOU TWO.
SIGH.

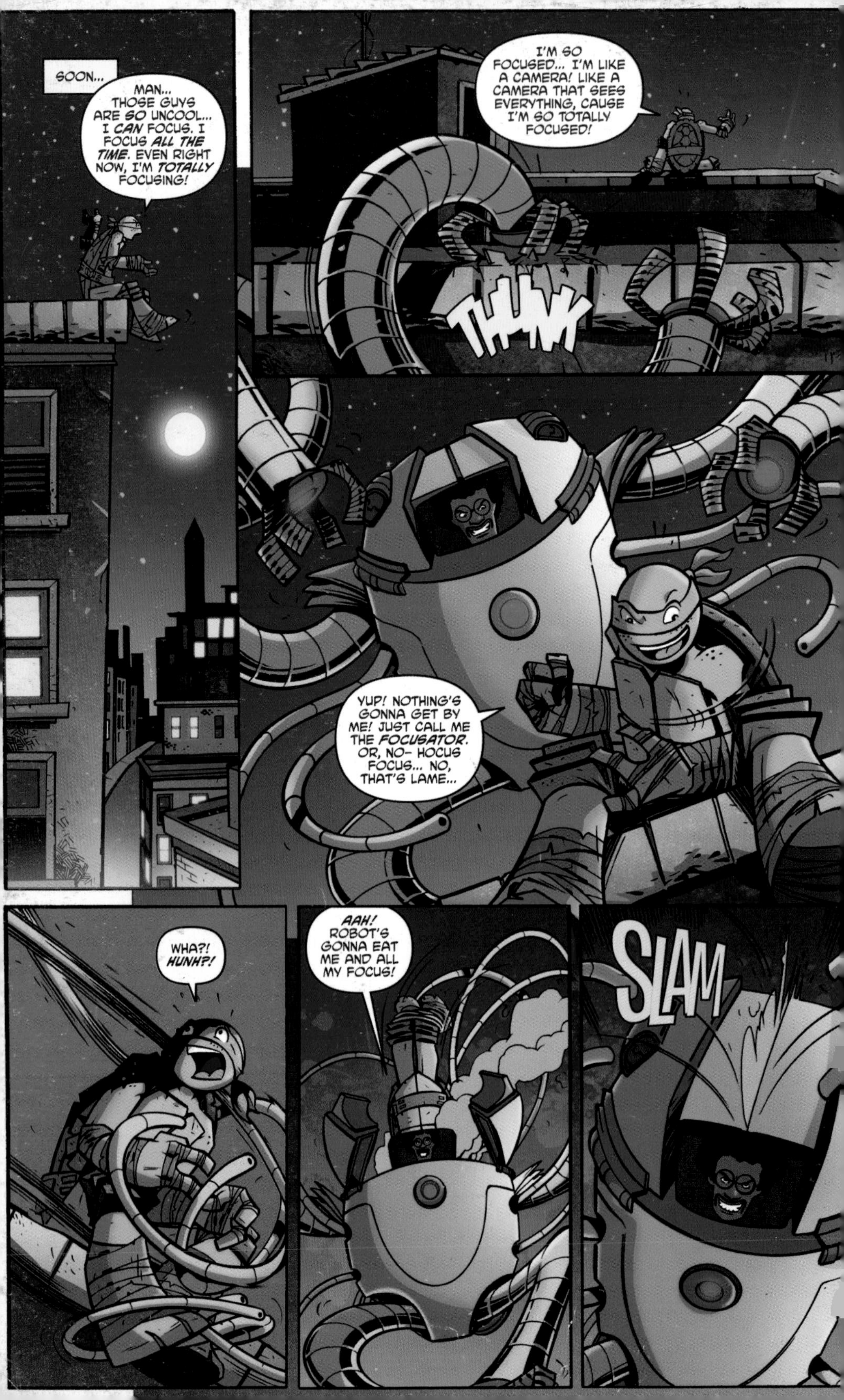

SOON...
MAN... THOSE GUYS ARE SO UNCOOL... I CAN FOCUS. I FOCUS ALL THE TIME. EVEN RIGHT NOW, I'M TOTALLY FOCUSING!
I'M SO FOCUSED... I'M LIKE A CAMERA! LIKE A CAMERA THAT SEES EVERYTHING, CAUSE I'M SO TOTALLY FOCUSED!
THUNK
YUP! NOTHING'S GONNA GET BY ME! JUST CALL ME THE FOCUSATOR. OR, NO- HOCUS FOCUS... NO, THAT'S LAME...
WHA?! HUNH?!
AAH! ROBOT'S GONNA EAT ME AND ALL MY FOCUS!
SLAM

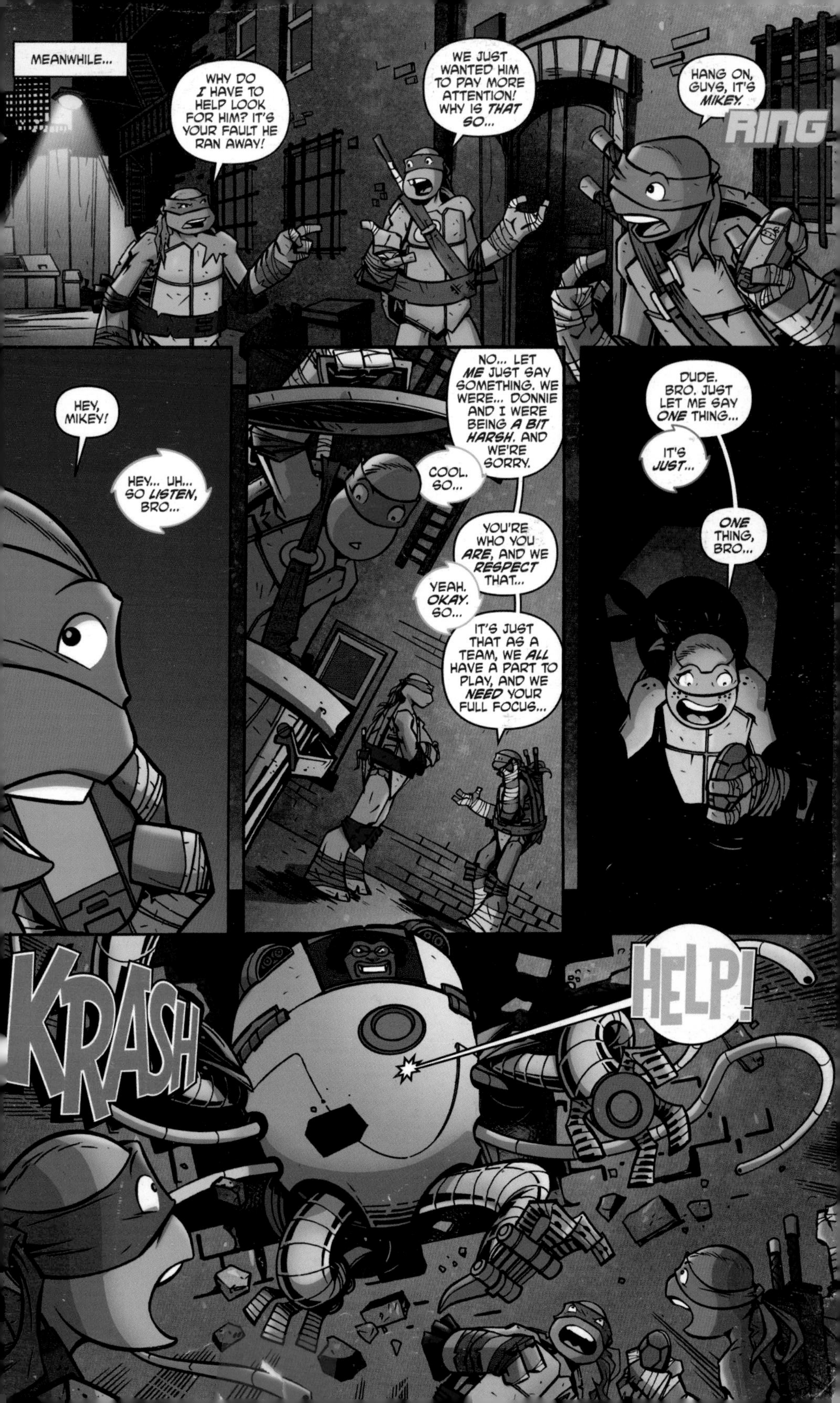
MEANWHILE...
WHY DO I HAVE TO HELP LOOK FOR HIM? IT'S YOUR FAULT HE RAN AWAY!
WE JUST WANTED HIM TO PAY MORE ATTENTION! WHY IS THAT SO...
HANG ON, GUYS, IT'S MIKEY.
RING
HEY, MIKEY!
HEY... UH... SO LISTEN, BRO...
NO... LET ME JUST SAY SOMETHING. WE WERE... DONNIE AND I WERE BEING A BIT HARSH. AND WE'RE SORRY.
COOL. SO...
YOU'RE WHO YOU ARE, AND WE RESPECT THAT...
YEAH. OKAY. SO...
IT'S JUST THAT AS A TEAM, WE ALL HAVE A PART TO PLAY, AND WE NEED YOUR FULL FOCUS...
DUDE. BRO. JUST LET ME SAY ONE THING...
IT'S JUST...
ONE THING, BRO...
KRASH
HELP!

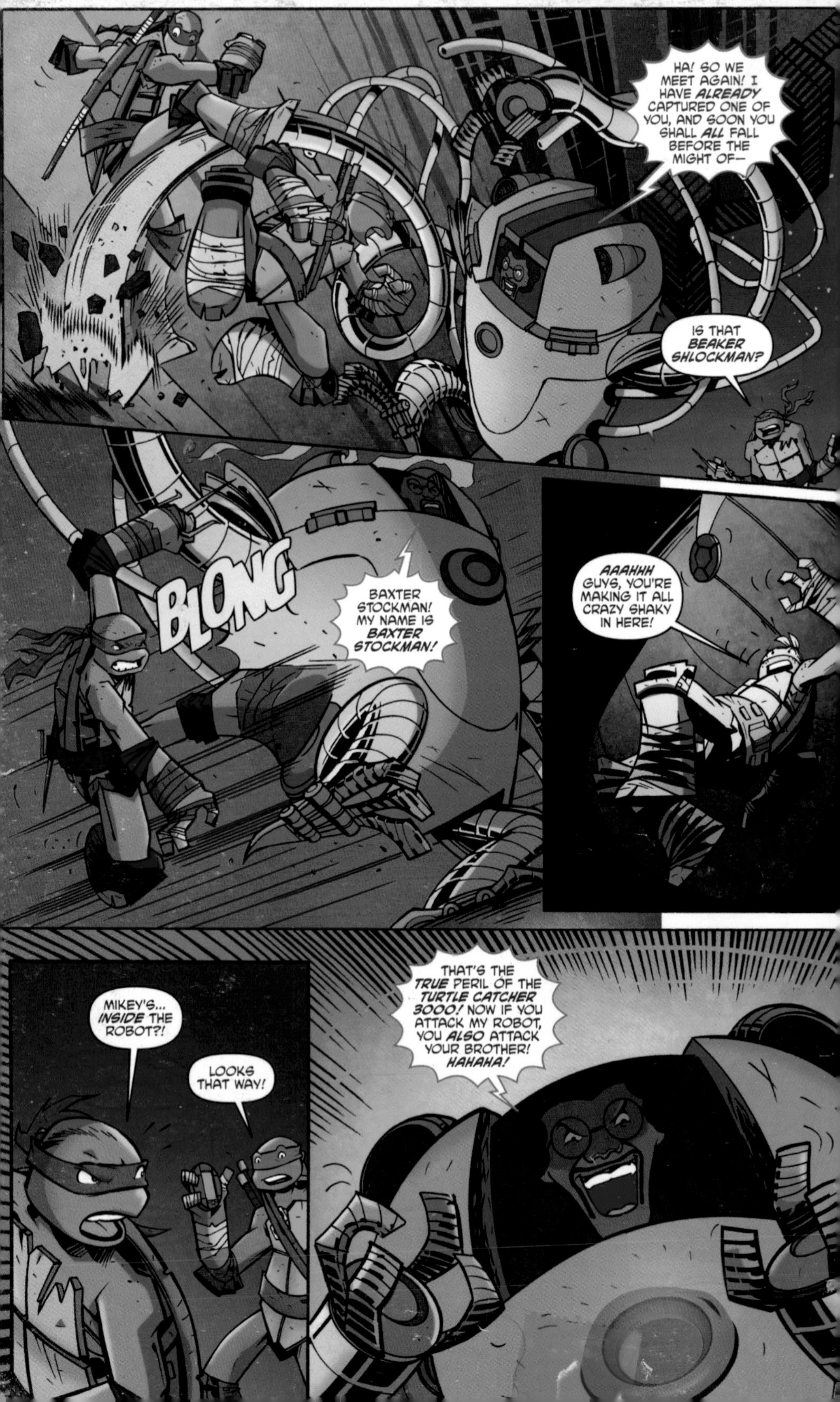
HA! SO WE MEET AGAIN! I HAVE *ALREADY* CAPTURED ONE OF YOU, AND SOON YOU SHALL *ALL* FALL BEFORE THE MIGHT OF—
IS THAT *BEAKER SHLOCKMAN?*
BLONG
BAXTER STOCKMAN! MY NAME IS *BAXTER STOCKMAN!*
AAAHHH GUYS, YOU'RE MAKING IT ALL CRAZY SHAKY IN HERE!
MIKEY'S... *INSIDE* THE ROBOT?!
LOOKS THAT WAY!
THAT'S THE *TRUE* PERIL OF THE *TURTLE CATCHER 3000!* NOW IF YOU ATTACK MY ROBOT, YOU *ALSO* ATTACK YOUR BROTHER! *HAHAHA!*

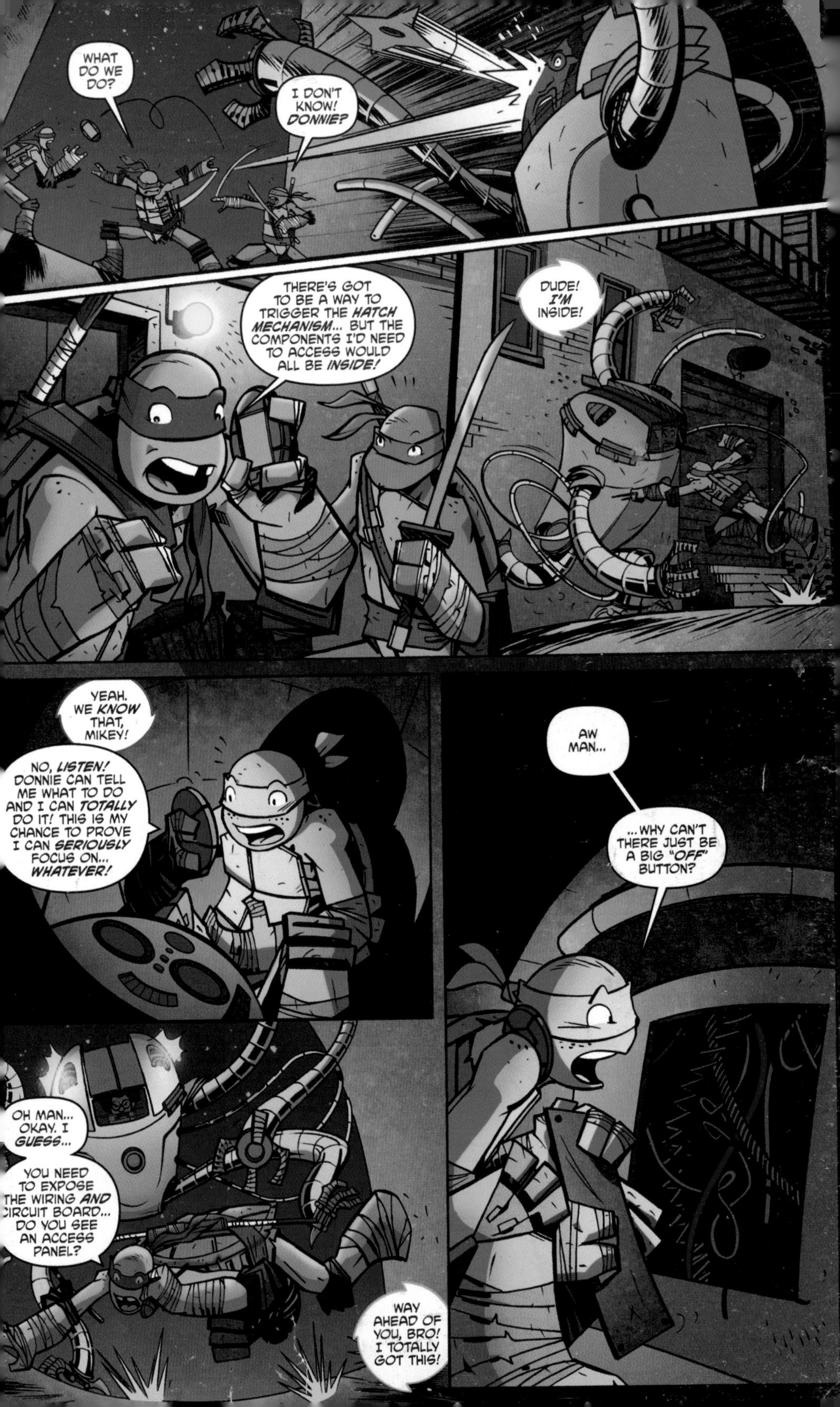
WHAT DO WE DO?
I DON'T KNOW! DONNIE?
THERE'S GOT TO BE A WAY TO TRIGGER THE HATCH MECHANISM... BUT THE COMPONENTS I'D NEED TO ACCESS WOULD ALL BE INSIDE!
DUDE! I'M INSIDE!
YEAH. WE KNOW THAT, MIKEY!
NO, LISTEN! DONNIE CAN TELL ME WHAT TO DO AND I CAN TOTALLY DO IT! THIS IS MY CHANCE TO PROVE I CAN SERIOUSLY FOCUS ON... WHATEVER!
OH MAN... OKAY. I GUESS...
YOU NEED TO EXPOSE THE WIRING AND CIRCUIT BOARD... DO YOU SEE AN ACCESS PANEL?
WAY AHEAD OF YOU, BRO! I TOTALLY GOT THIS!
AW MAN...
...WHY CAN'T THERE JUST BE A BIG "OFF" BUTTON?

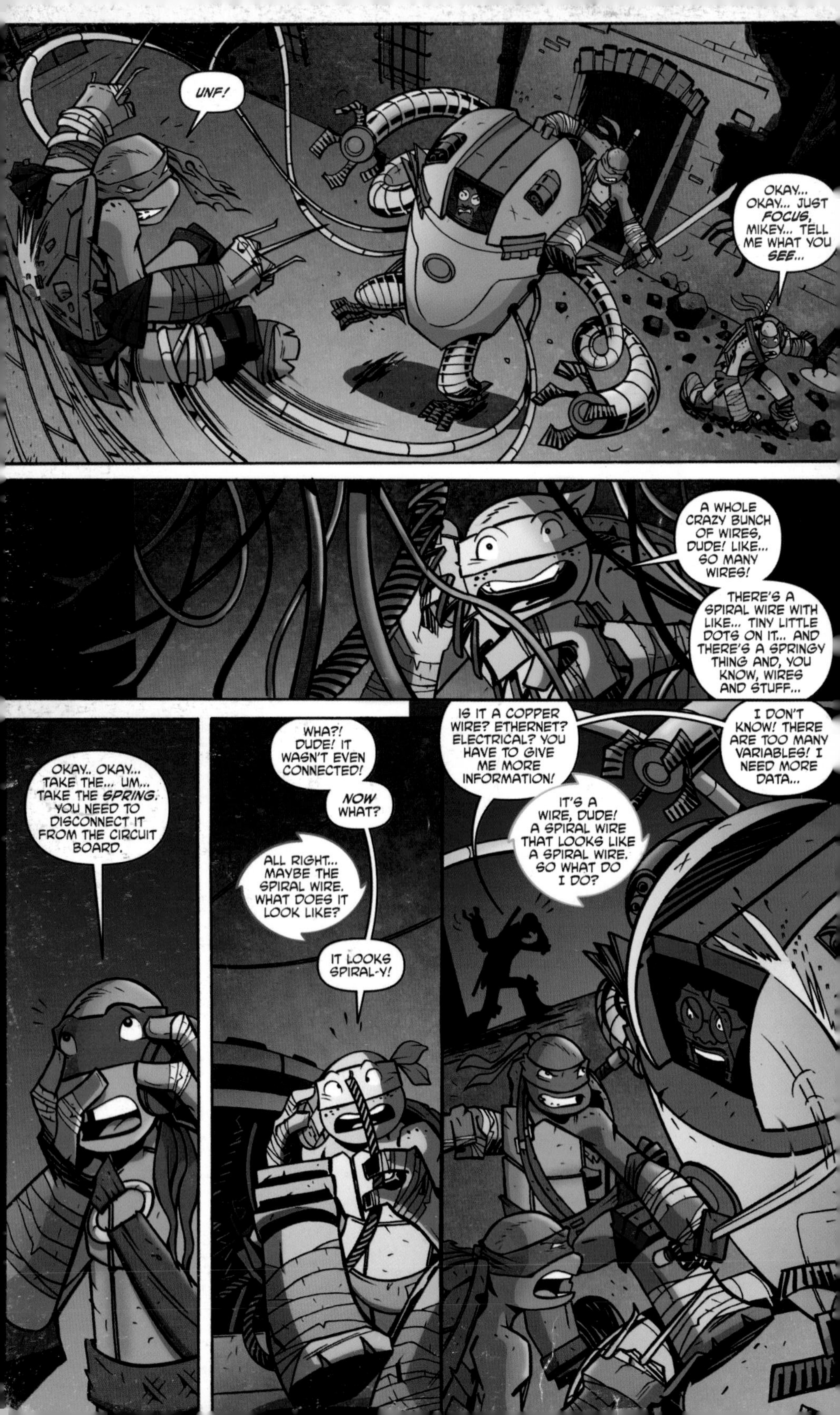
UNF!
OKAY... OKAY... JUST FOCUS, MIKEY... TELL ME WHAT YOU SEE...
A WHOLE CRAZY BUNCH OF WIRES, DUDE! LIKE... SO MANY WIRES!
THERE'S A SPIRAL WIRE WITH LIKE... TINY LITTLE DOTS ON IT... AND THERE'S A SPRINGY THING AND, YOU KNOW, WIRES AND STUFF...
OKAY.. OKAY... TAKE THE... UM... TAKE THE SPRING. YOU NEED TO DISCONNECT IT FROM THE CIRCUIT BOARD.
WHA?! DUDE! IT WASN'T EVEN CONNECTED!
NOW WHAT?
ALL RIGHT... MAYBE THE SPIRAL WIRE. WHAT DOES IT LOOK LIKE?
IT LOOKS SPIRAL-Y!
IS IT A COPPER WIRE? ETHERNET? ELECTRICAL? YOU HAVE TO GIVE ME MORE INFORMATION!
I DON'T KNOW! THERE ARE TOO MANY VARIABLES! I NEED MORE DATA...
IT'S A WIRE, DUDE! A SPIRAL WIRE THAT LOOKS LIKE A SPIRAL WIRE. SO WHAT DO I DO?

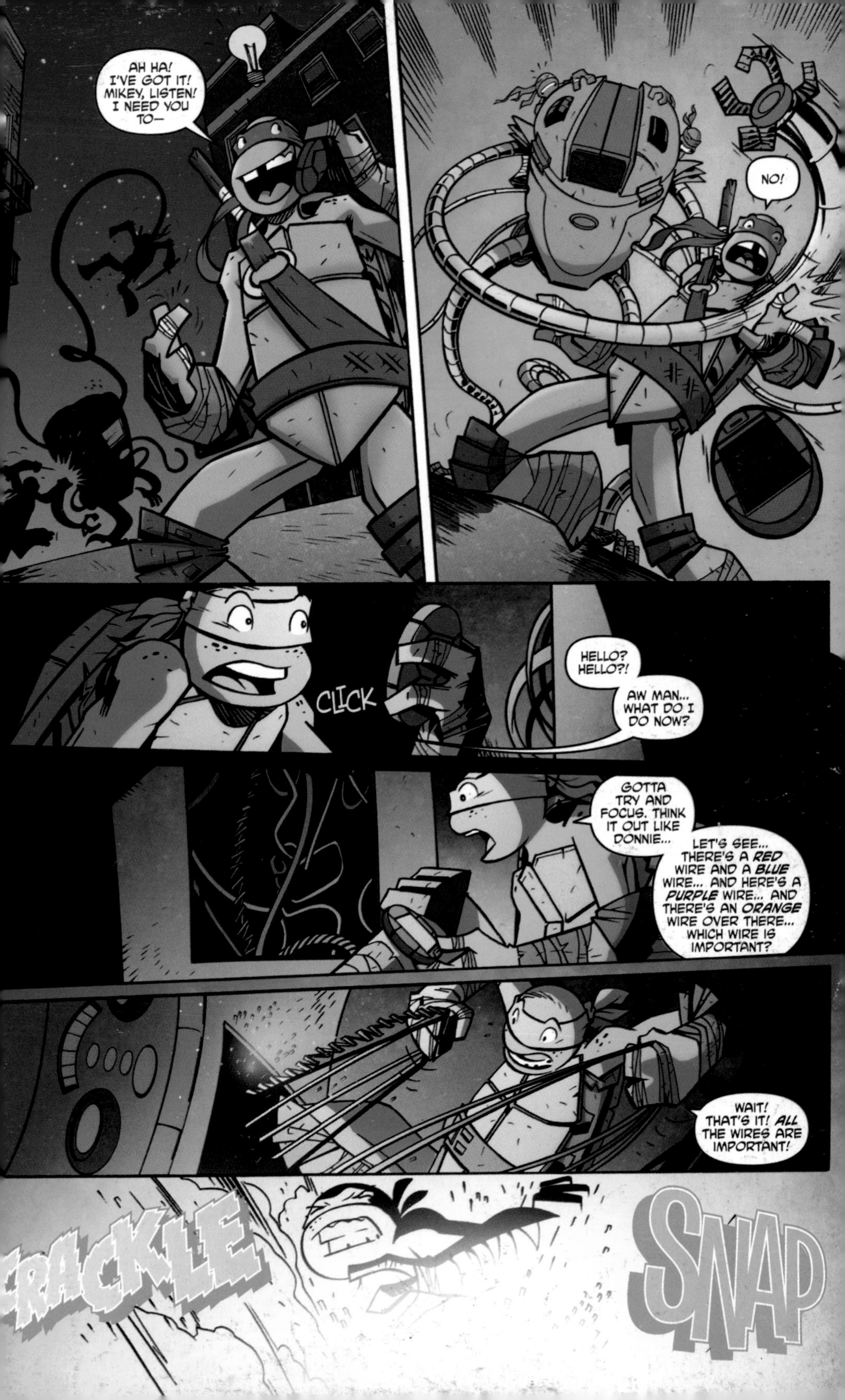
AH HA! I'VE GOT IT! MIKEY, LISTEN! I NEED YOU TO—
NO!
HELLO? HELLO?!
CLICK
AW MAN... WHAT DO I DO NOW?
GOTTA TRY AND FOCUS. THINK IT OUT LIKE DONNIE...
LET'S SEE... THERE'S A RED WIRE AND A BLUE WIRE... AND HERE'S A PURPLE WIRE... AND THERE'S AN ORANGE WIRE OVER THERE... WHICH WIRE IS IMPORTANT?
WAIT! THAT'S IT! ALL THE WIRES ARE IMPORTANT!
CRACKLE
SNAP

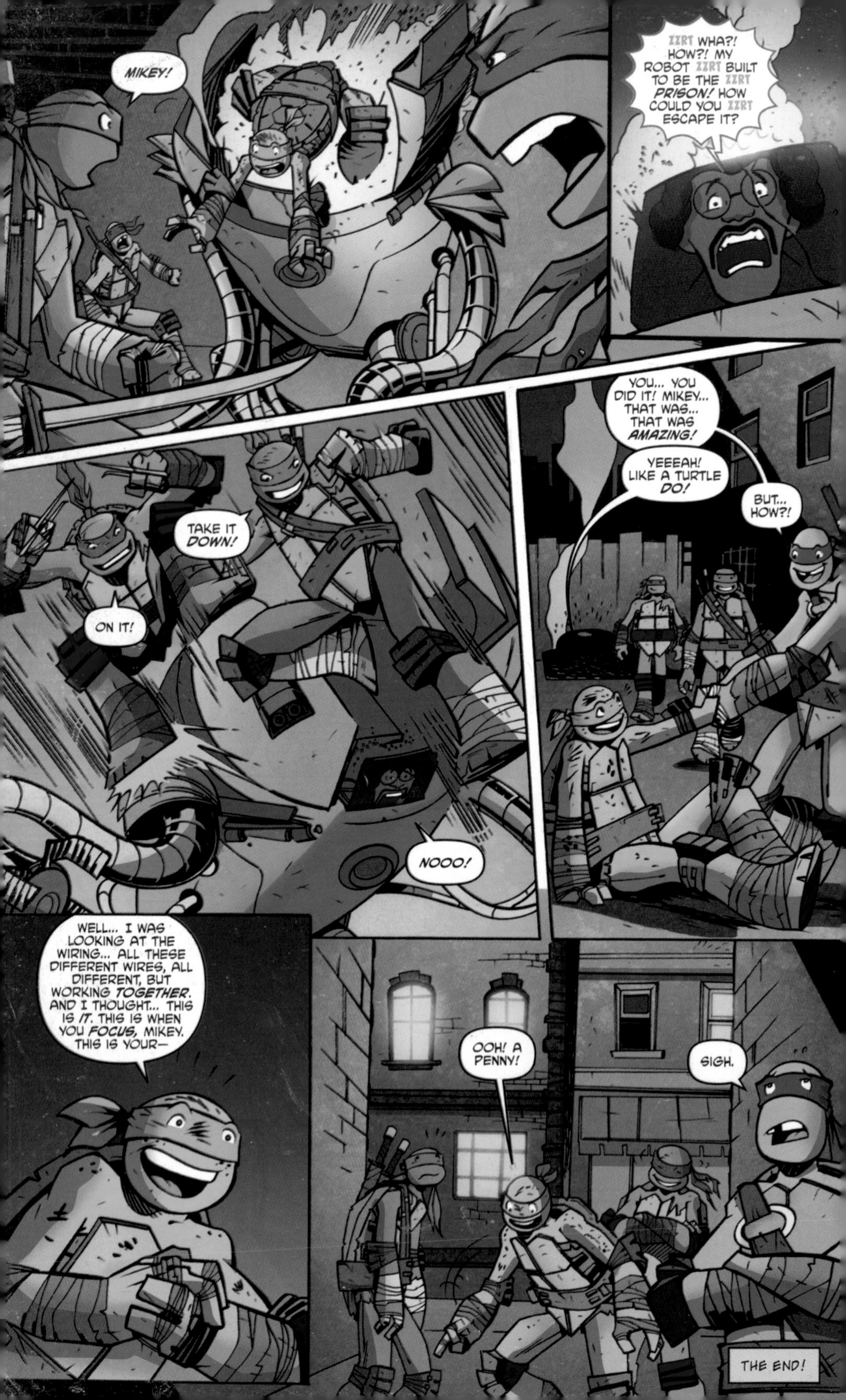
MIKEY!
ZZRT WHA?! HOW?! MY ROBOT ZZRT BUILT TO BE THE ZZRT PRISON! HOW COULD YOU ZZRT ESCAPE IT?
TAKE IT DOWN!
ON IT!
NOOO!
YOU... YOU DID IT! MIKEY... THAT WAS... THAT WAS AMAZING!
YEEEAH! LIKE A TURTLE DO!
BUT... HOW?!
WELL... I WAS LOOKING AT THE WIRING... ALL THESE DIFFERENT WIRES, ALL DIFFERENT, BUT WORKING TOGETHER. AND I THOUGHT... THIS IS IT. THIS IS WHEN YOU FOCUS, MIKEY. THIS IS YOUR—
OOH! A PENNY!
SIGH.
THE END!

Cover by JENNIFER MEYER

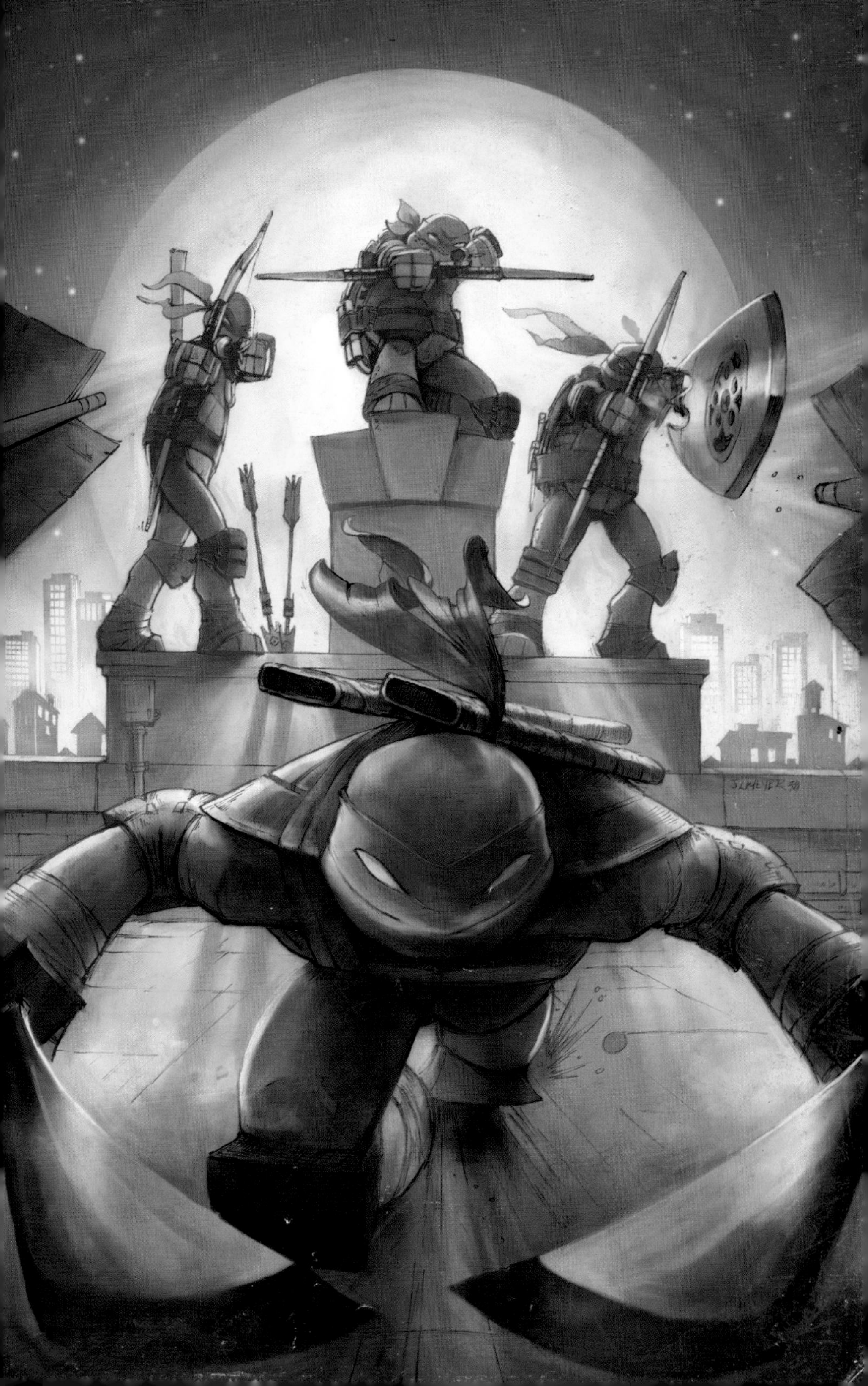
JLMEYER

Cover by **DARIO BRIZUELA**

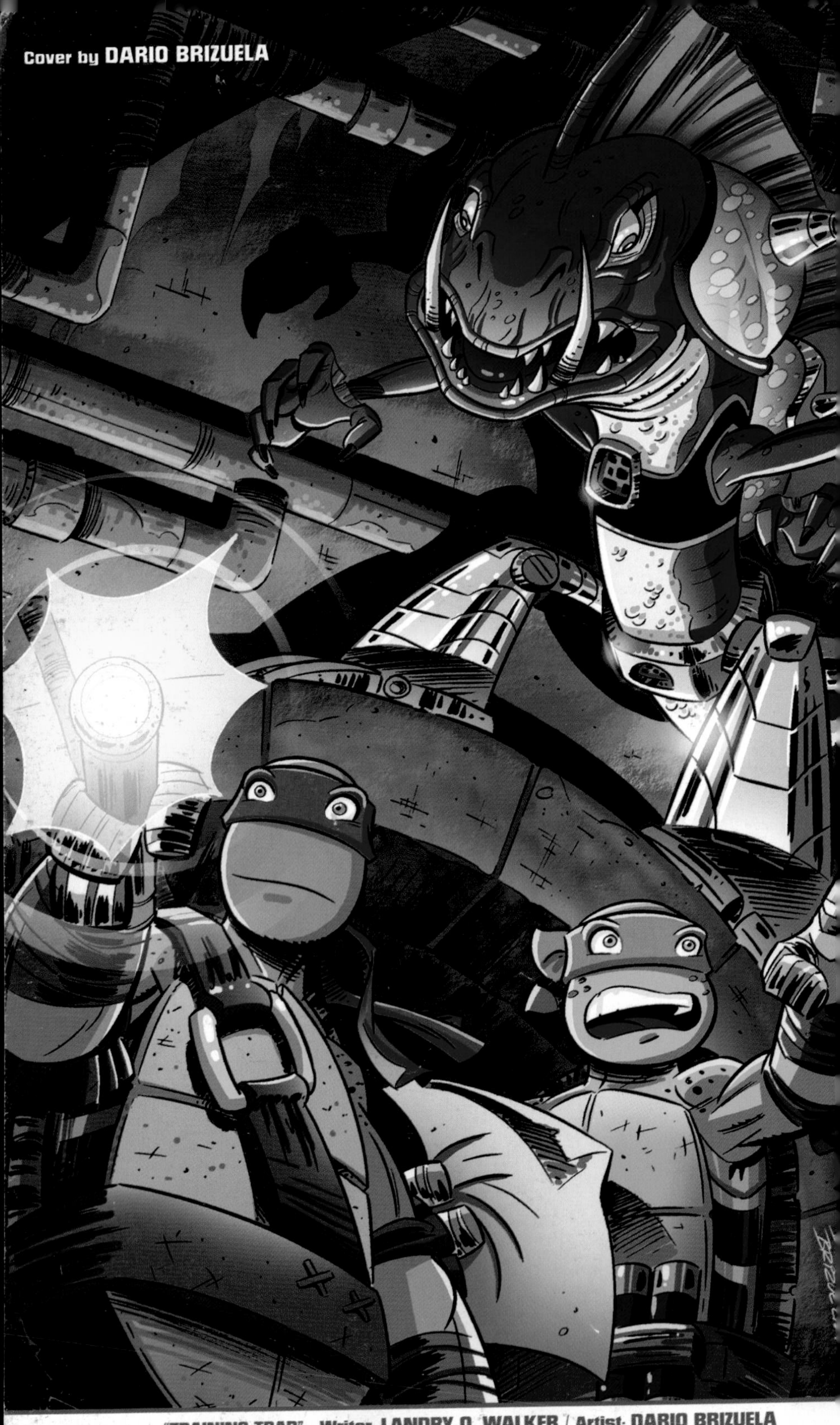

"TRAINING TRAP" - Writer: **LANDRY Q. WALKER** / Artist: **DARIO BRIZUELA**
"THE ADVENTURES OF ICE CREAM KITTY" - Writer: **MATTHEW K. MANNING** / Artist: **MARCELO FE**
"SPLINTER'S GAME" - Writer: **BOBBY CURNOW** / Artist: **CHAD THOMAS**

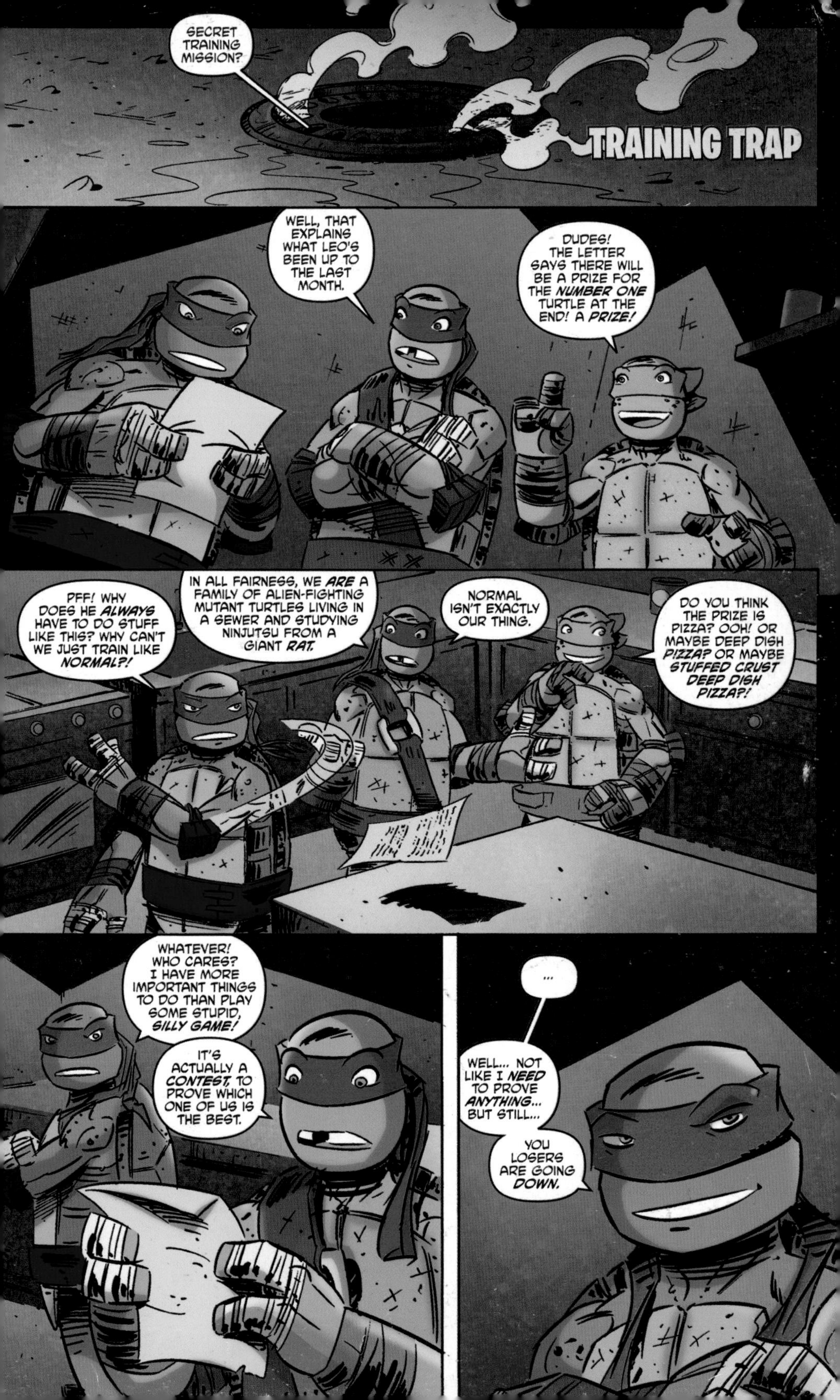
SECRET TRAINING MISSION?
TRAINING TRAP
WELL, THAT EXPLAINS WHAT LEO'S BEEN UP TO THE LAST MONTH.
DUDES! THE LETTER SAYS THERE WILL BE A PRIZE FOR THE NUMBER ONE TURTLE AT THE END! A PRIZE!
PFF! WHY DOES HE ALWAYS HAVE TO DO STUFF LIKE THIS? WHY CAN'T WE JUST TRAIN LIKE NORMAL?!
IN ALL FAIRNESS, WE ARE A FAMILY OF ALIEN-FIGHTING MUTANT TURTLES LIVING IN A SEWER AND STUDYING NINJUTSU FROM A GIANT RAT.
NORMAL ISN'T EXACTLY OUR THING.
DO YOU THINK THE PRIZE IS PIZZA? OOH! OR MAYBE DEEP DISH PIZZA? OR MAYBE STUFFED CRUST DEEP DISH PIZZA?!
WHATEVER! WHO CARES? I HAVE MORE IMPORTANT THINGS TO DO THAN PLAY SOME STUPID, SILLY GAME!
IT'S ACTUALLY A CONTEST, TO PROVE WHICH ONE OF US IS THE BEST.
...
WELL... NOT LIKE I NEED TO PROVE ANYTHING... BUT STILL...
YOU LOSERS ARE GOING DOWN.

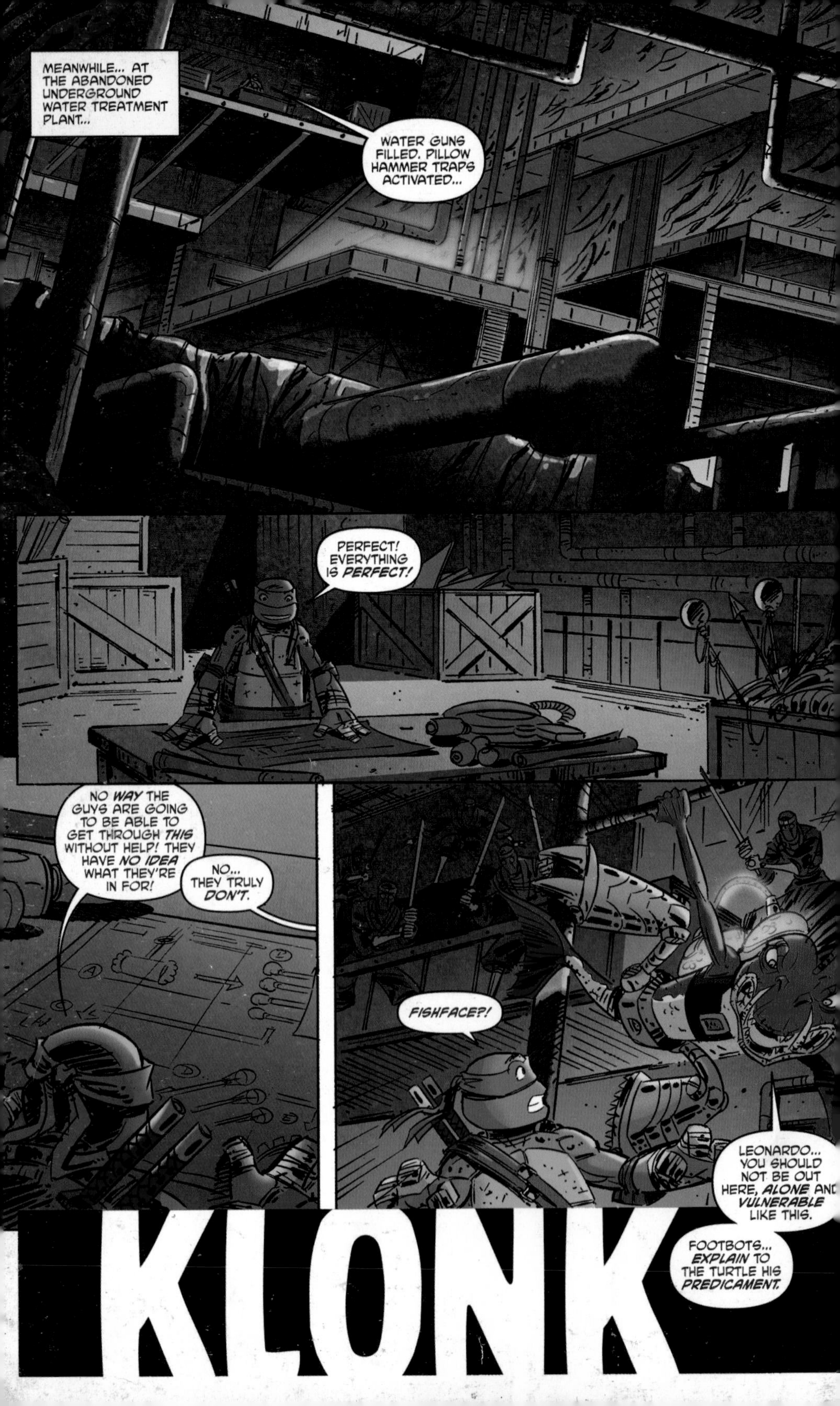
MEANWHILE... AT THE ABANDONED UNDERGROUND WATER TREATMENT PLANT...
WATER GUNS FILLED. PILLOW HAMMER TRAPS ACTIVATED...
PERFECT! EVERYTHING IS PERFECT!
NO WAY THE GUYS ARE GOING TO BE ABLE TO GET THROUGH THIS WITHOUT HELP! THEY HAVE NO IDEA WHAT THEY'RE IN FOR!
NO... THEY TRULY DON'T.
FISHFACE?!
LEONARDO... YOU SHOULD NOT BE OUT HERE, ALONE AND VULNERABLE LIKE THIS.
KLONK
FOOTBOTS... EXPLAIN TO THE TURTLE HIS PREDICAMENT.

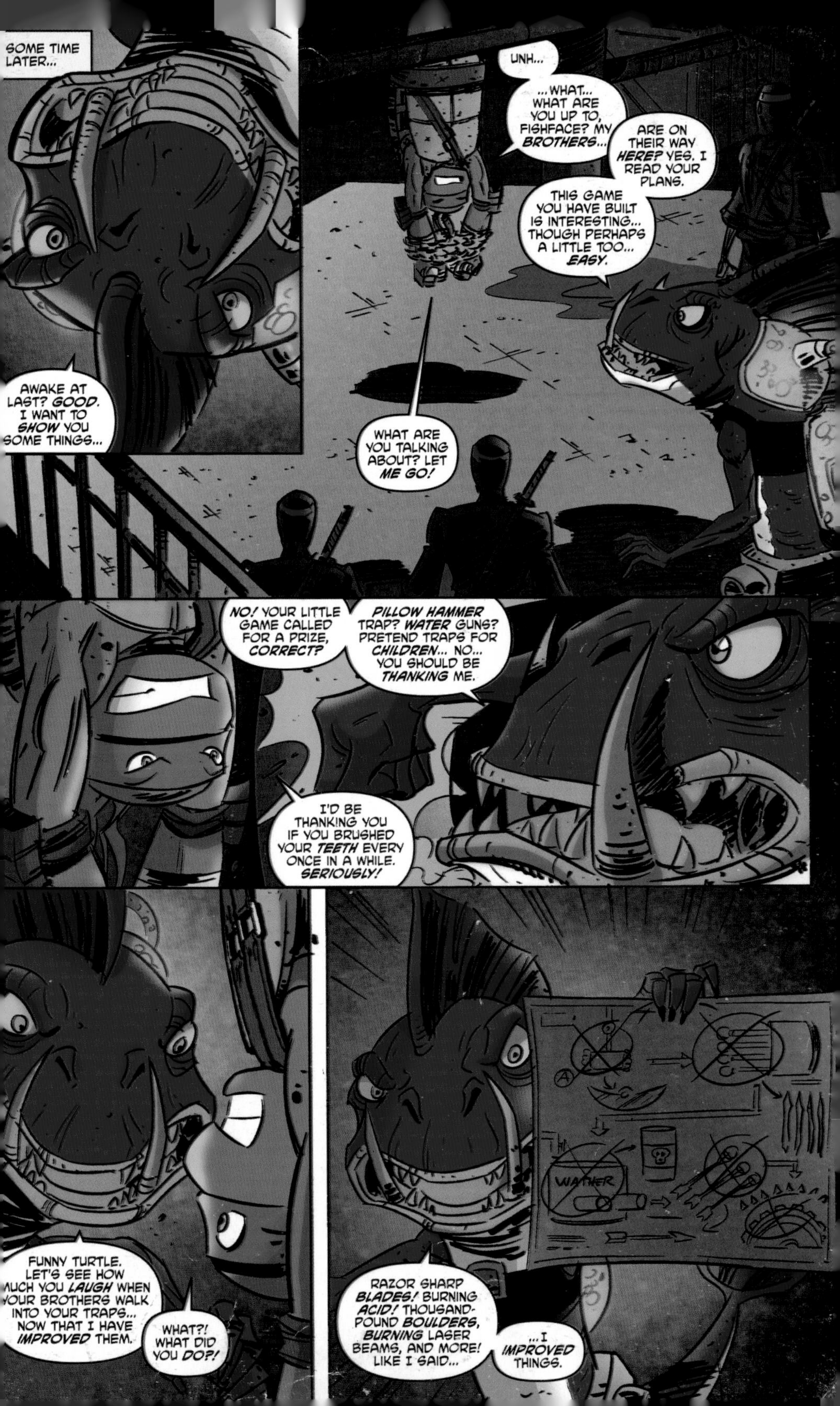
SOME TIME LATER...
AWAKE AT LAST? GOOD. I WANT TO SHOW YOU SOME THINGS...
UNH...
...WHAT... WHAT ARE YOU UP TO, FISHFACE? MY BROTHERS...
ARE ON THEIR WAY HERE? YES. I READ YOUR PLANS.
THIS GAME YOU HAVE BUILT IS INTERESTING... THOUGH PERHAPS A LITTLE TOO... EASY.
WHAT ARE YOU TALKING ABOUT? LET ME GO!
NO! YOUR LITTLE GAME CALLED FOR A PRIZE, CORRECT?
PILLOW HAMMER TRAP? WATER GUNS? PRETEND TRAPS FOR CHILDREN... NO... YOU SHOULD BE THANKING ME.
I'D BE THANKING YOU IF YOU BRUSHED YOUR TEETH EVERY ONCE IN A WHILE. SERIOUSLY!
FUNNY TURTLE. LET'S SEE HOW MUCH YOU LAUGH WHEN YOUR BROTHERS WALK INTO YOUR TRAPS... NOW THAT I HAVE IMPROVED THEM.
WHAT?! WHAT DID YOU DO?!
WATHER
RAZOR SHARP BLADES! BURNING ACID! THOUSAND-POUND BOULDERS, BURNING LASER BEAMS, AND MORE! LIKE I SAID...
...I IMPROVED THINGS.

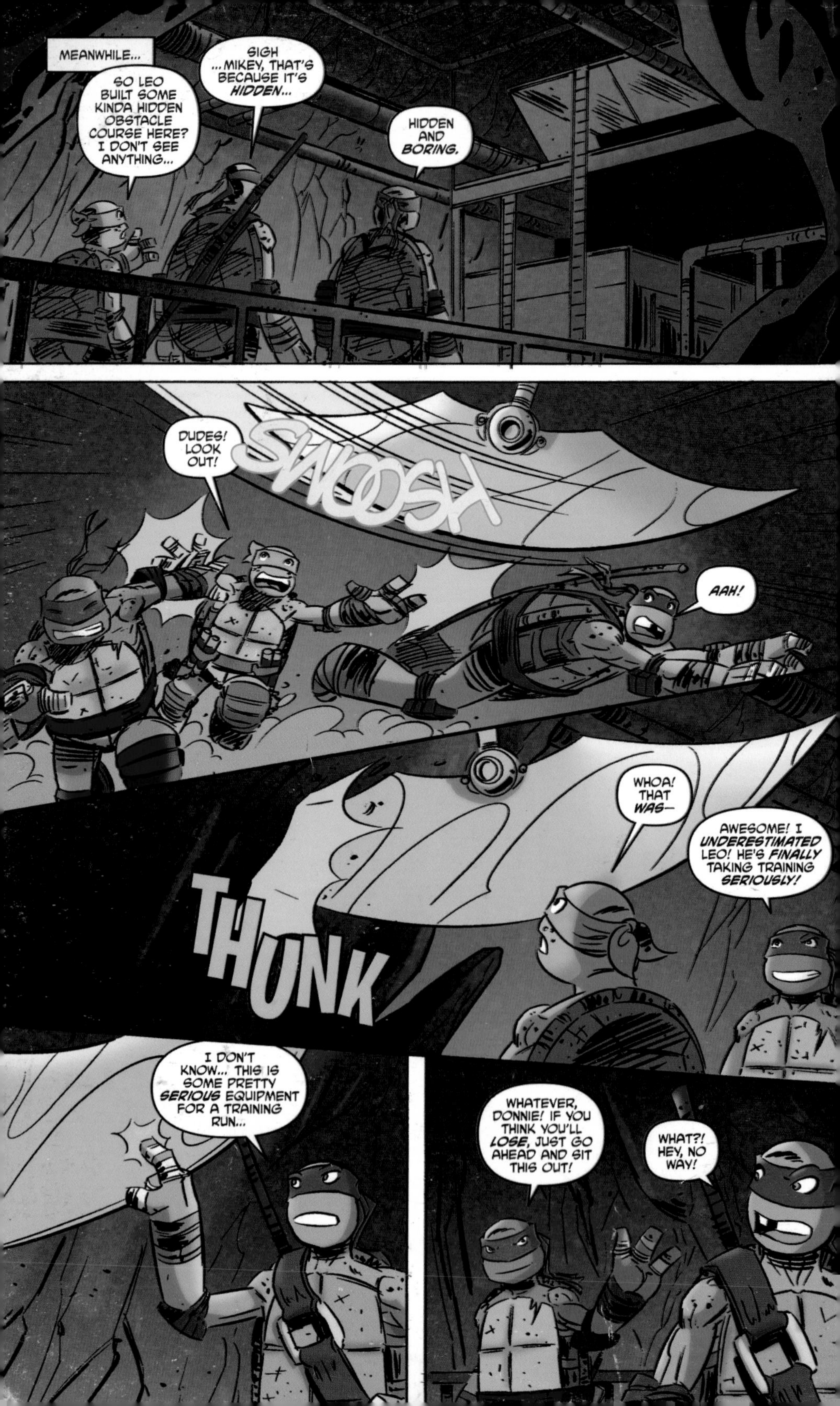

MEANWHILE...
SO LEO BUILT SOME KINDA HIDDEN OBSTACLE COURSE HERE? I DON'T SEE ANYTHING...
SIGH ...MIKEY, THAT'S BECAUSE IT'S *HIDDEN*...
HIDDEN AND *BORING.*
DUDES! LOOK OUT!
SWOOSH
AAH!
WHOA! THAT *WAS*—
AWESOME! I *UNDERESTIMATED* LEO! HE'S *FINALLY* TAKING TRAINING *SERIOUSLY!*
THUNK
I DON'T KNOW... THIS IS SOME PRETTY *SERIOUS* EQUIPMENT FOR A TRAINING RUN...
WHATEVER, DONNIE! IF YOU THINK YOU'LL *LOSE*, JUST GO AHEAD AND SIT THIS OUT!
WHAT?! HEY, NO WAY!

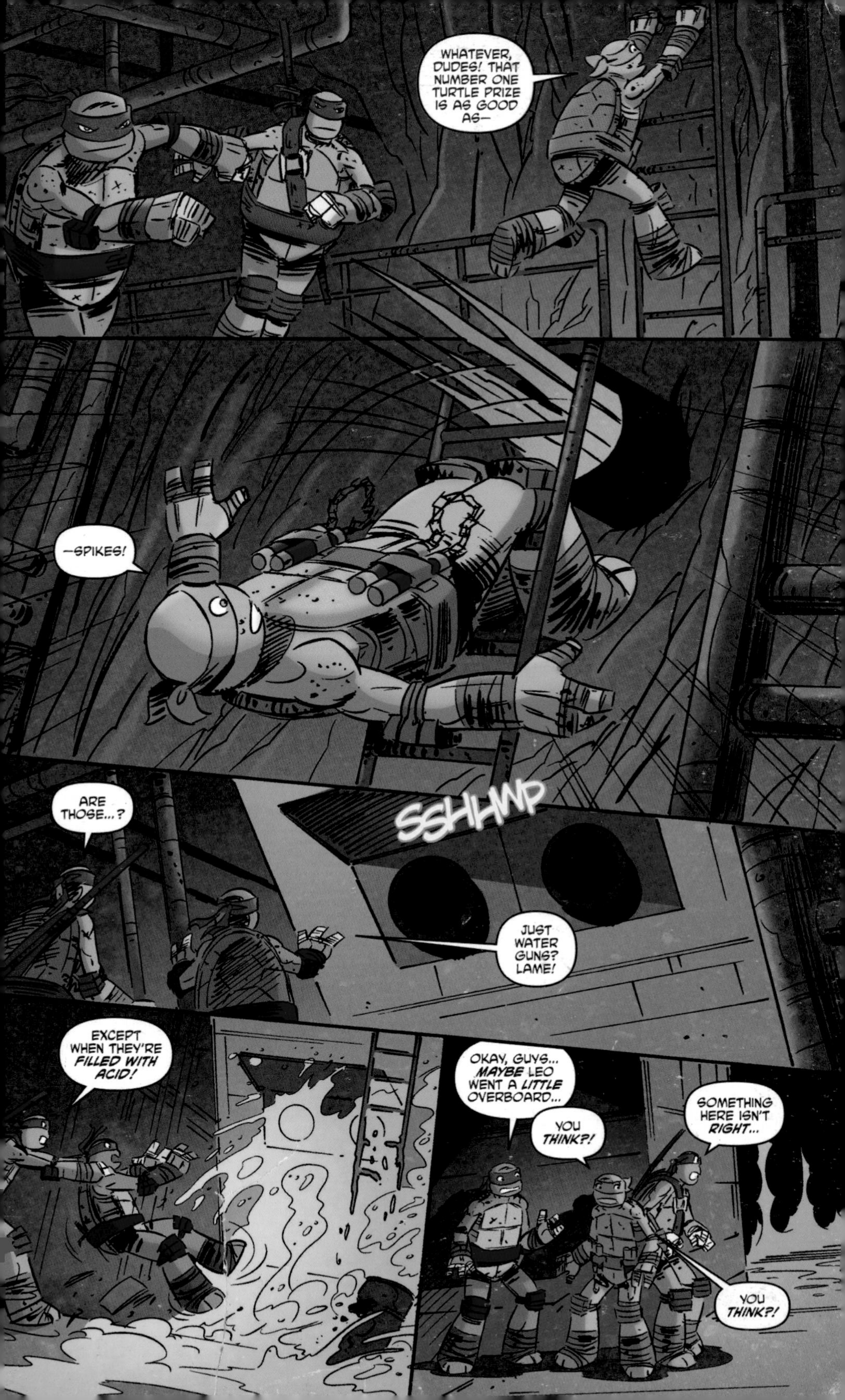
WHATEVER, DUDES! THAT NUMBER ONE TURTLE PRIZE IS AS GOOD AS—
—SPIKES!
ARE THOSE...?
SSHLWP
JUST WATER GUNS? LAME!
EXCEPT WHEN THEY'RE *FILLED WITH ACID!*
OKAY, GUYS... *MAYBE* LEO WENT A *LITTLE* OVERBOARD...
YOU *THINK?!*
SOMETHING HERE ISN'T *RIGHT*...
YOU *THINK?!*

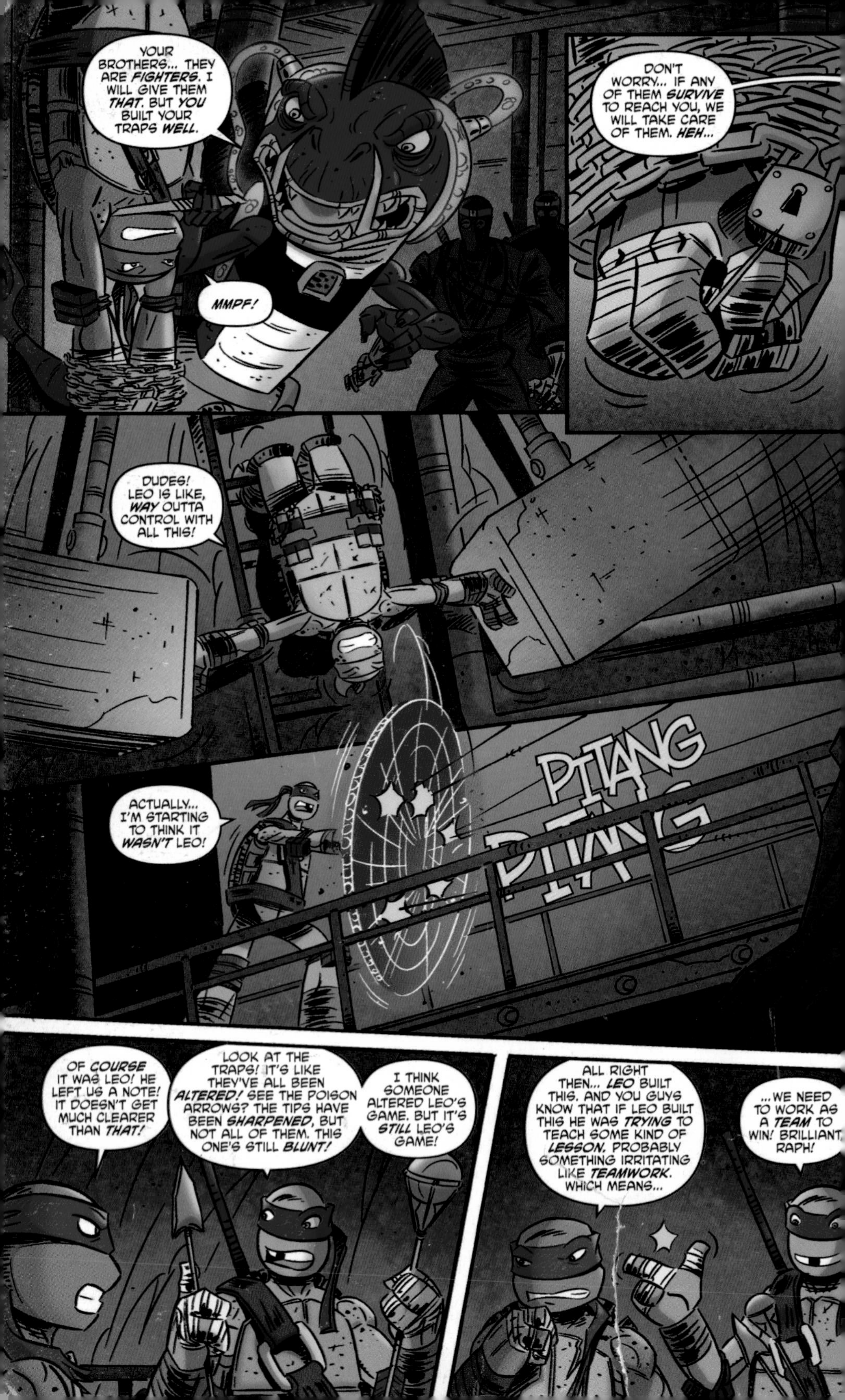
YOUR BROTHERS... THEY ARE FIGHTERS. I WILL GIVE THEM THAT. BUT YOU BUILT YOUR TRAPS WELL.
MMPF!
DON'T WORRY... IF ANY OF THEM SURVIVE TO REACH YOU, WE WILL TAKE CARE OF THEM. HEH...
DUDES! LEO IS LIKE, WAY OUTTA CONTROL WITH ALL THIS!
PTANG
ACTUALLY... I'M STARTING TO THINK IT WASN'T LEO!
PTANG
OF COURSE IT WAS LEO! HE LEFT US A NOTE! IT DOESN'T GET MUCH CLEARER THAN THAT!
LOOK AT THE TRAPS! IT'S LIKE THEY'VE ALL BEEN ALTERED! SEE THE POISON ARROWS? THE TIPS HAVE BEEN SHARPENED, BUT NOT ALL OF THEM. THIS ONE'S STILL BLUNT!
I THINK SOMEONE ALTERED LEO'S GAME. BUT IT'S STILL LEO'S GAME!
ALL RIGHT THEN... LEO BUILT THIS. AND YOU GUYS KNOW THAT IF LEO BUILT THIS HE WAS TRYING TO TEACH SOME KIND OF LESSON. PROBABLY SOMETHING IRRITATING LIKE TEAMWORK. WHICH MEANS...
...WE NEED TO WORK AS A TEAM TO WIN! BRILLIANT, RAPH!

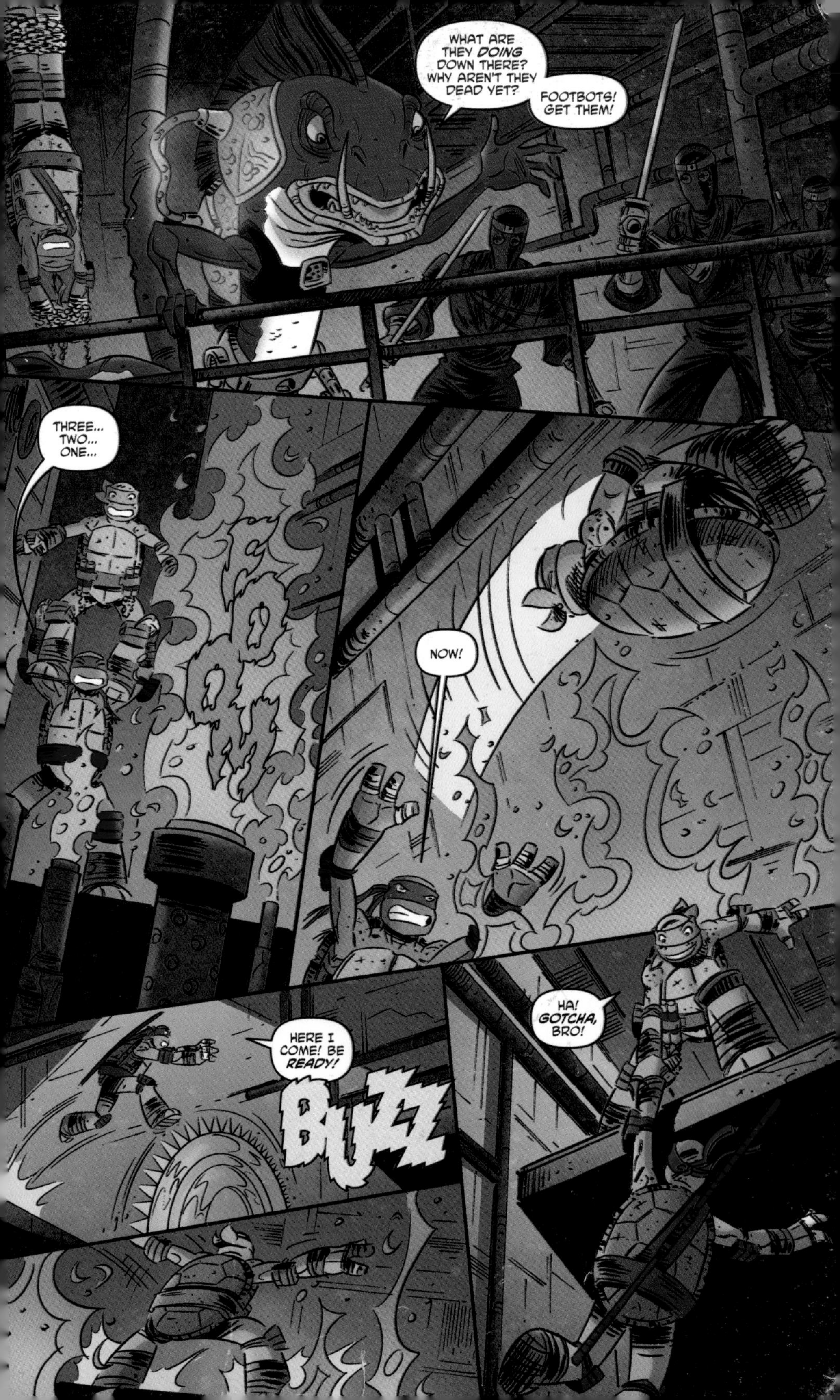
WHAT ARE THEY *DOING* DOWN THERE? WHY AREN'T THEY DEAD YET?
FOOTBOTS! GET THEM!
THREE... TWO... ONE...
NOW!
HERE I COME! BE *READY!*
BUZZ
HA! *GOTCHA,* BRO!

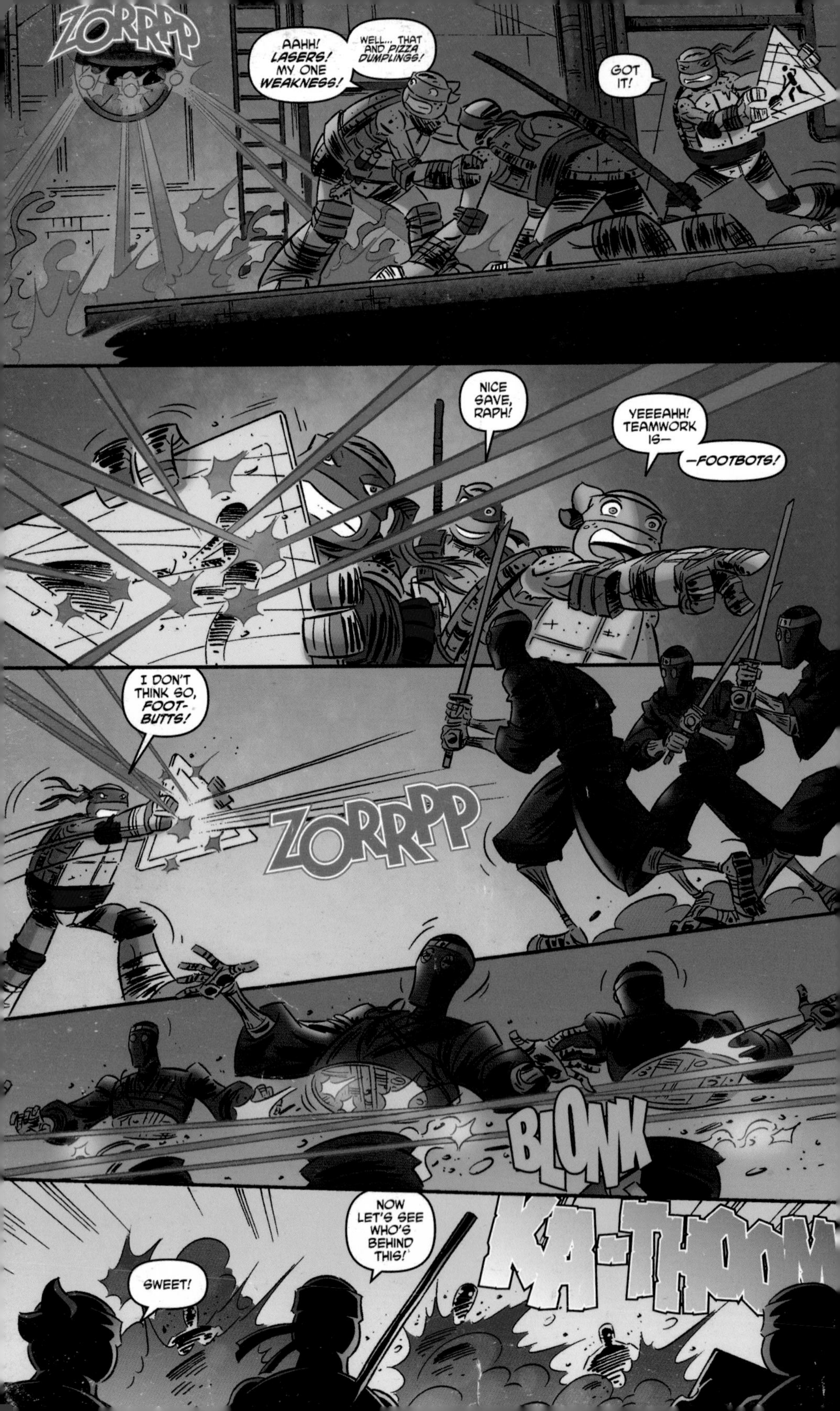
ZORRPP
AAHH! LASERS! MY ONE WEAKNESS!
WELL... THAT AND PIZZA DUMPLINGS!
GOT IT!
NICE SAVE, RAPH!
YEEEAHH! TEAMWORK IS—
—FOOTBOTS!
I DON'T THINK SO, FOOT-BUTTS!
ZORRPP
BLONK
NOW LET'S SEE WHO'S BEHIND THIS!
SWEET!
KA-THOOM

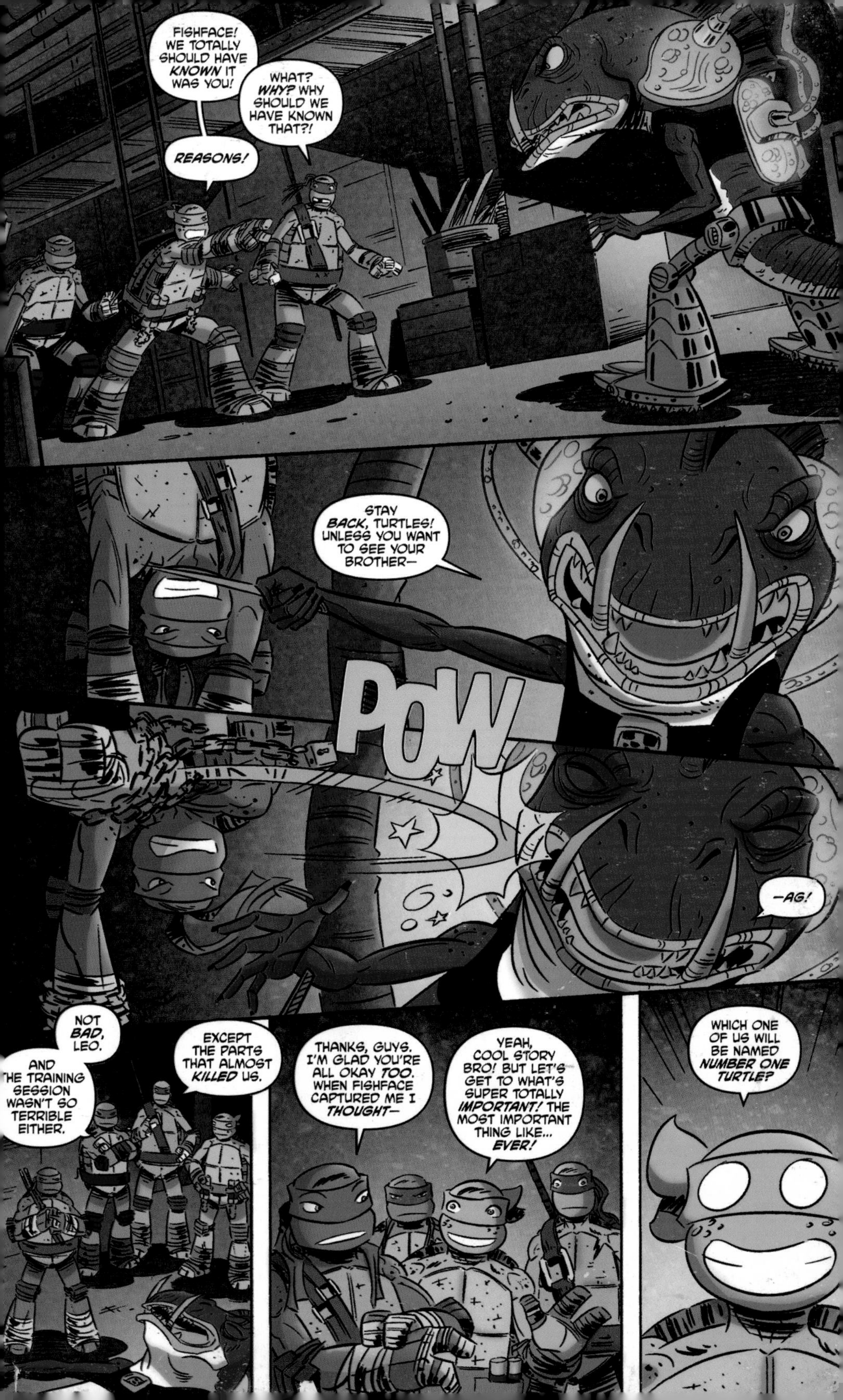

FISHFACE! WE TOTALLY SHOULD HAVE KNOWN IT WAS YOU!
WHAT? WHY? WHY SHOULD WE HAVE KNOWN THAT?!
REASONS!
STAY BACK, TURTLES! UNLESS YOU WANT TO SEE YOUR BROTHER—
POW
—AG!
NOT BAD, LEO.
AND THE TRAINING SESSION WASN'T SO TERRIBLE EITHER.
EXCEPT THE PARTS THAT ALMOST KILLED US.
THANKS, GUYS. I'M GLAD YOU'RE ALL OKAY TOO. WHEN FISHFACE CAPTURED ME I THOUGHT—
YEAH, COOL STORY BRO! BUT LET'S GET TO WHAT'S SUPER TOTALLY IMPORTANT! THE MOST IMPORTANT THING LIKE... EVER!
WHICH ONE OF US WILL BE NAMED NUMBER ONE TURTLE?

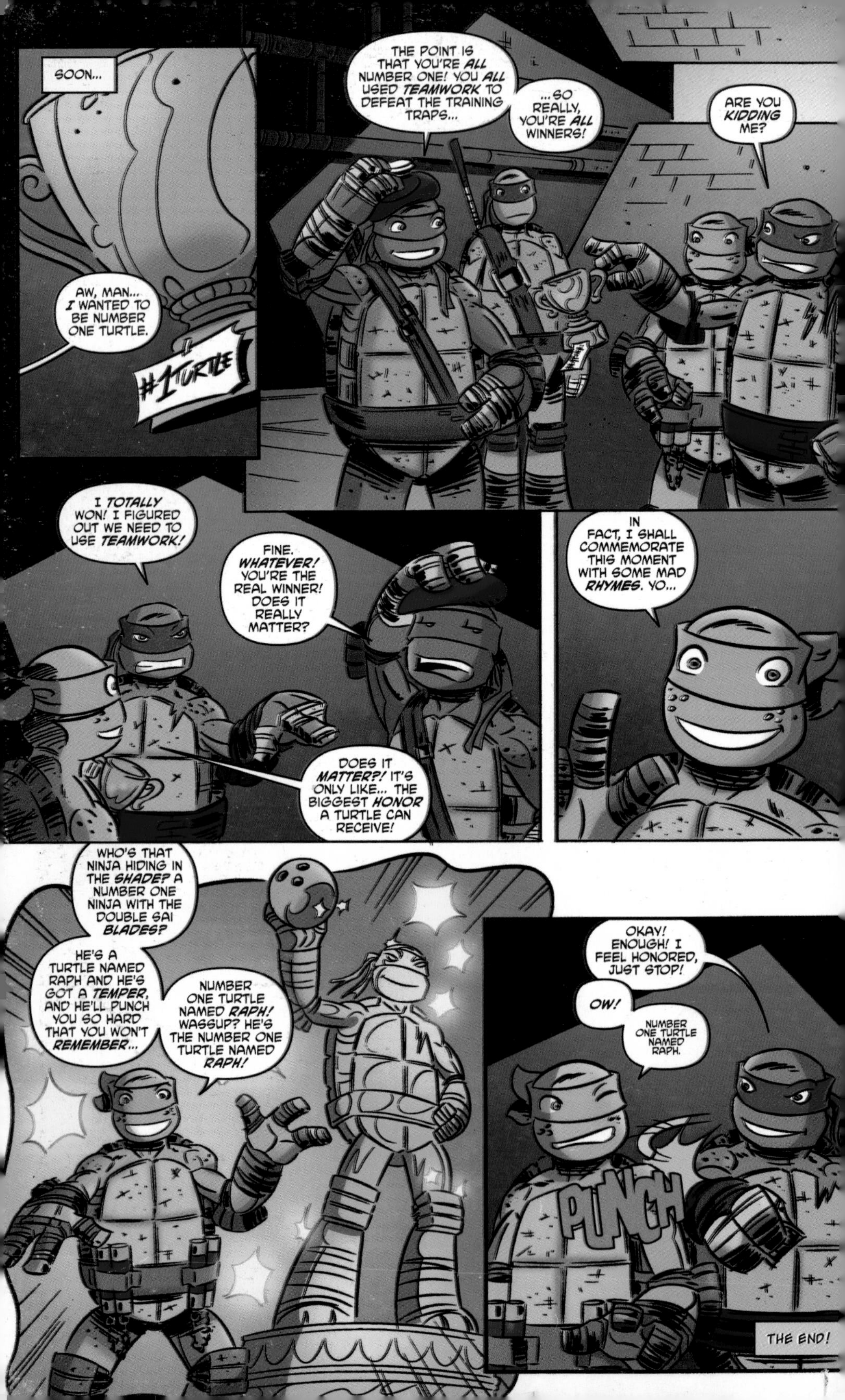
SOON...
AW, MAN... I WANTED TO BE NUMBER ONE TURTLE.
#1 TURTLE
THE POINT IS THAT YOU'RE ALL NUMBER ONE! YOU ALL USED TEAMWORK TO DEFEAT THE TRAINING TRAPS...
...SO REALLY, YOU'RE ALL WINNERS!
ARE YOU KIDDING ME?
I TOTALLY WON! I FIGURED OUT WE NEED TO USE TEAMWORK!
FINE. WHATEVER! YOU'RE THE REAL WINNER! DOES IT REALLY MATTER?
DOES IT MATTER?! IT'S ONLY LIKE... THE BIGGEST HONOR A TURTLE CAN RECEIVE!
IN FACT, I SHALL COMMEMORATE THIS MOMENT WITH SOME MAD RHYMES. YO...
WHO'S THAT NINJA HIDING IN THE SHADE? A NUMBER ONE NINJA WITH THE DOUBLE SAI BLADES?
HE'S A TURTLE NAMED RAPH AND HE'S GOT A TEMPER, AND HE'LL PUNCH YOU SO HARD THAT YOU WON'T REMEMBER...
NUMBER ONE TURTLE NAMED RAPH! WASSUP? HE'S THE NUMBER ONE TURTLE NAMED RAPH!
OKAY! ENOUGH! I FEEL HONORED, JUST STOP!
OW!
NUMBER ONE TURTLE NAMED RAPH.
PUNCH
THE END!

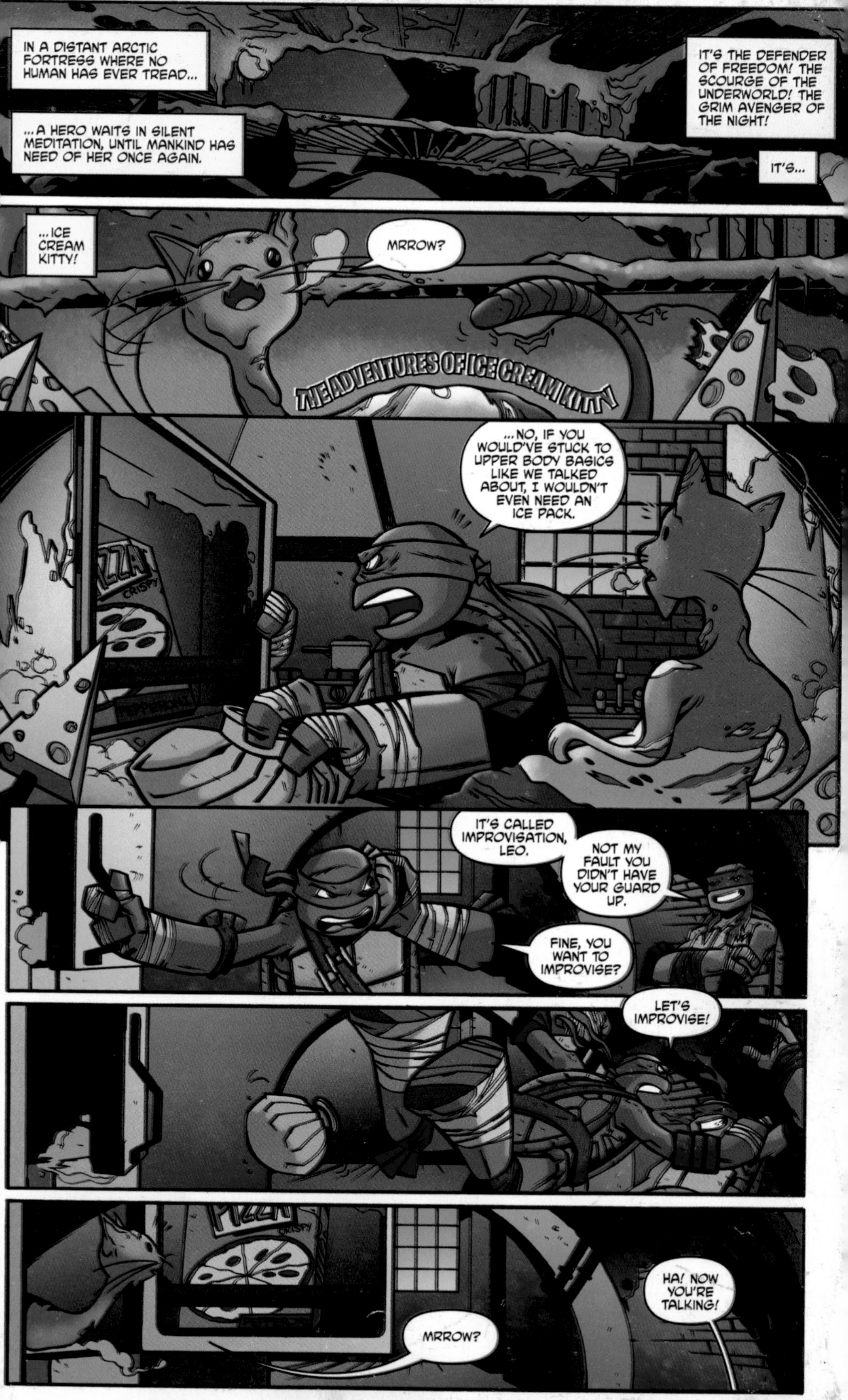

IN A DISTANT ARCTIC FORTRESS WHERE NO HUMAN HAS EVER TREAD...
...A HERO WAITS IN SILENT MEDITATION, UNTIL MANKIND HAS NEED OF HER ONCE AGAIN.
IT'S THE DEFENDER OF FREEDOM! THE SCOURGE OF THE UNDERWORLD! THE GRIM AVENGER OF THE NIGHT!
IT'S...
...ICE CREAM KITTY!
MRROW?
THE ADVENTURES OF ICE CREAM KITTY
...NO, IF YOU WOULD'VE STUCK TO UPPER BODY BASICS LIKE WE TALKED ABOUT, I WOULDN'T EVEN NEED AN ICE PACK.
PIZZA
CRISPY
IT'S CALLED IMPROVISATION, LEO.
NOT MY FAULT YOU DIDN'T HAVE YOUR GUARD UP.
FINE, YOU WANT TO IMPROVISE?
LET'S IMPROVISE!
PIZZA
CRISPY
HA! NOW YOU'RE TALKING!
MRROW?

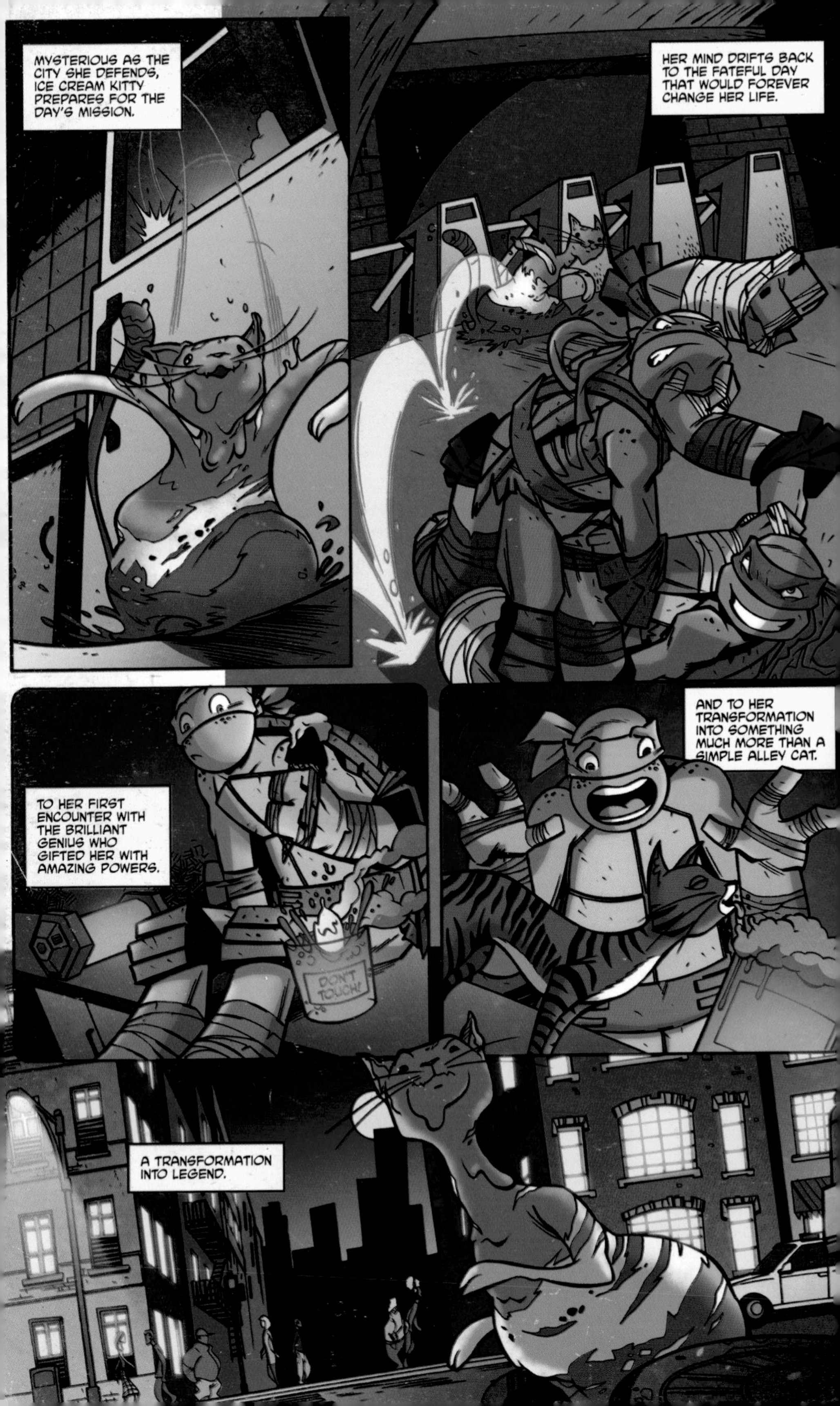
MYSTERIOUS AS THE CITY SHE DEFENDS, ICE CREAM KITTY PREPARES FOR THE DAY'S MISSION.
HER MIND DRIFTS BACK TO THE FATEFUL DAY THAT WOULD FOREVER CHANGE HER LIFE.
TO HER FIRST ENCOUNTER WITH THE BRILLIANT GENIUS WHO GIFTED HER WITH AMAZING POWERS.
DON'T TOUCH!
AND TO HER TRANSFORMATION INTO SOMETHING MUCH MORE THAN A SIMPLE ALLEY CAT.
A TRANSFORMATION INTO LEGEND.

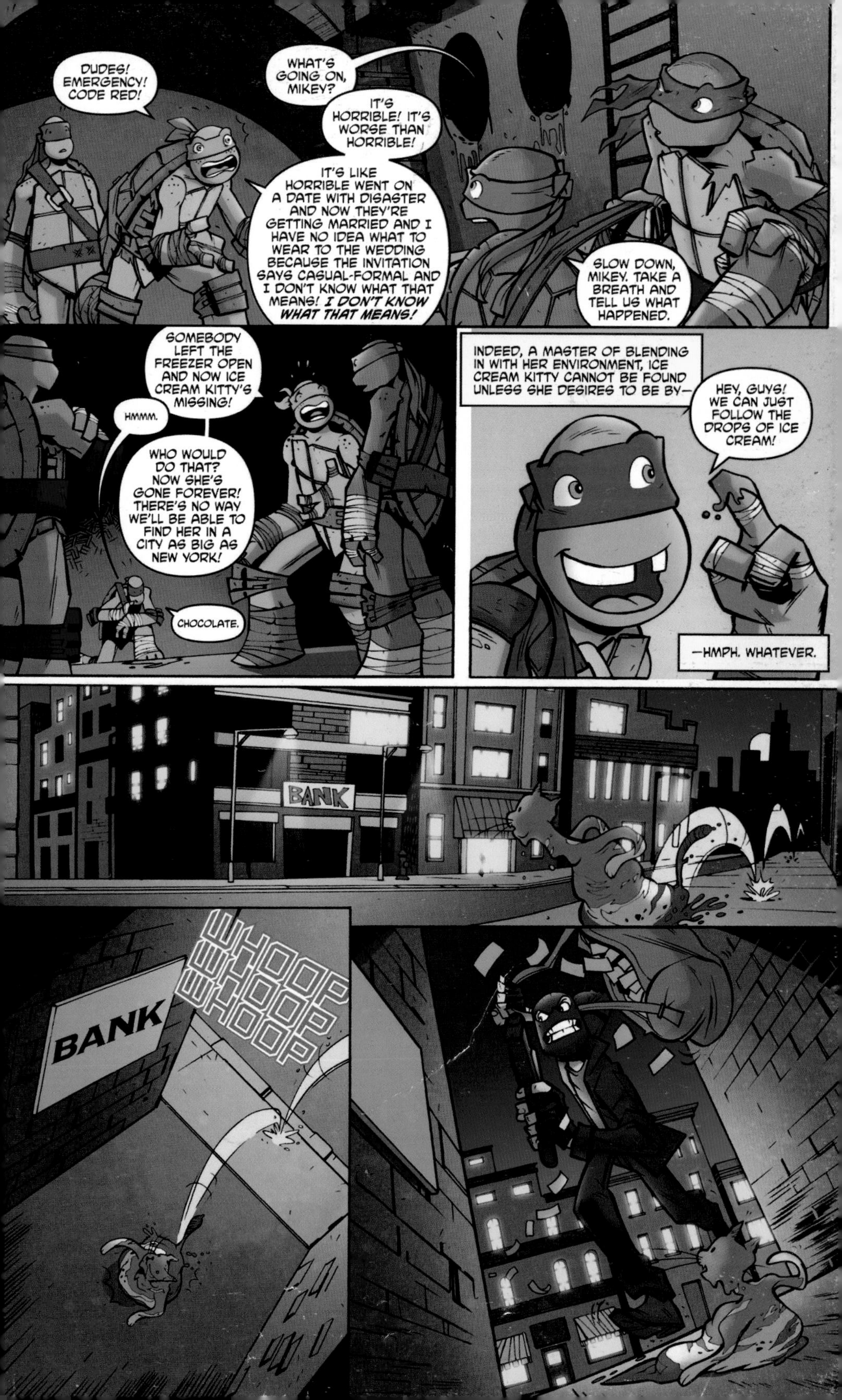
DUDES! EMERGENCY! CODE RED!
WHAT'S GOING ON, MIKEY?
IT'S HORRIBLE! IT'S WORSE THAN HORRIBLE!
IT'S LIKE HORRIBLE WENT ON A DATE WITH DISASTER AND NOW THEY'RE GETTING MARRIED AND I HAVE NO IDEA WHAT TO WEAR TO THE WEDDING BECAUSE THE INVITATION SAYS CASUAL-FORMAL AND I DON'T KNOW WHAT THAT MEANS! I DON'T KNOW WHAT THAT MEANS!
SLOW DOWN, MIKEY. TAKE A BREATH AND TELL US WHAT HAPPENED.
SOMEBODY LEFT THE FREEZER OPEN AND NOW ICE CREAM KITTY'S MISSING!
HMMM.
WHO WOULD DO THAT? NOW SHE'S GONE FOREVER! THERE'S NO WAY WE'LL BE ABLE TO FIND HER IN A CITY AS BIG AS NEW YORK!
CHOCOLATE.
INDEED, A MASTER OF BLENDING IN WITH HER ENVIRONMENT, ICE CREAM KITTY CANNOT BE FOUND UNLESS SHE DESIRES TO BE BY—
HEY, GUYS! WE CAN JUST FOLLOW THE DROPS OF ICE CREAM!
—HMPH. WHATEVER.
BANK
BANK
WHOOP WHOOP WHOOP

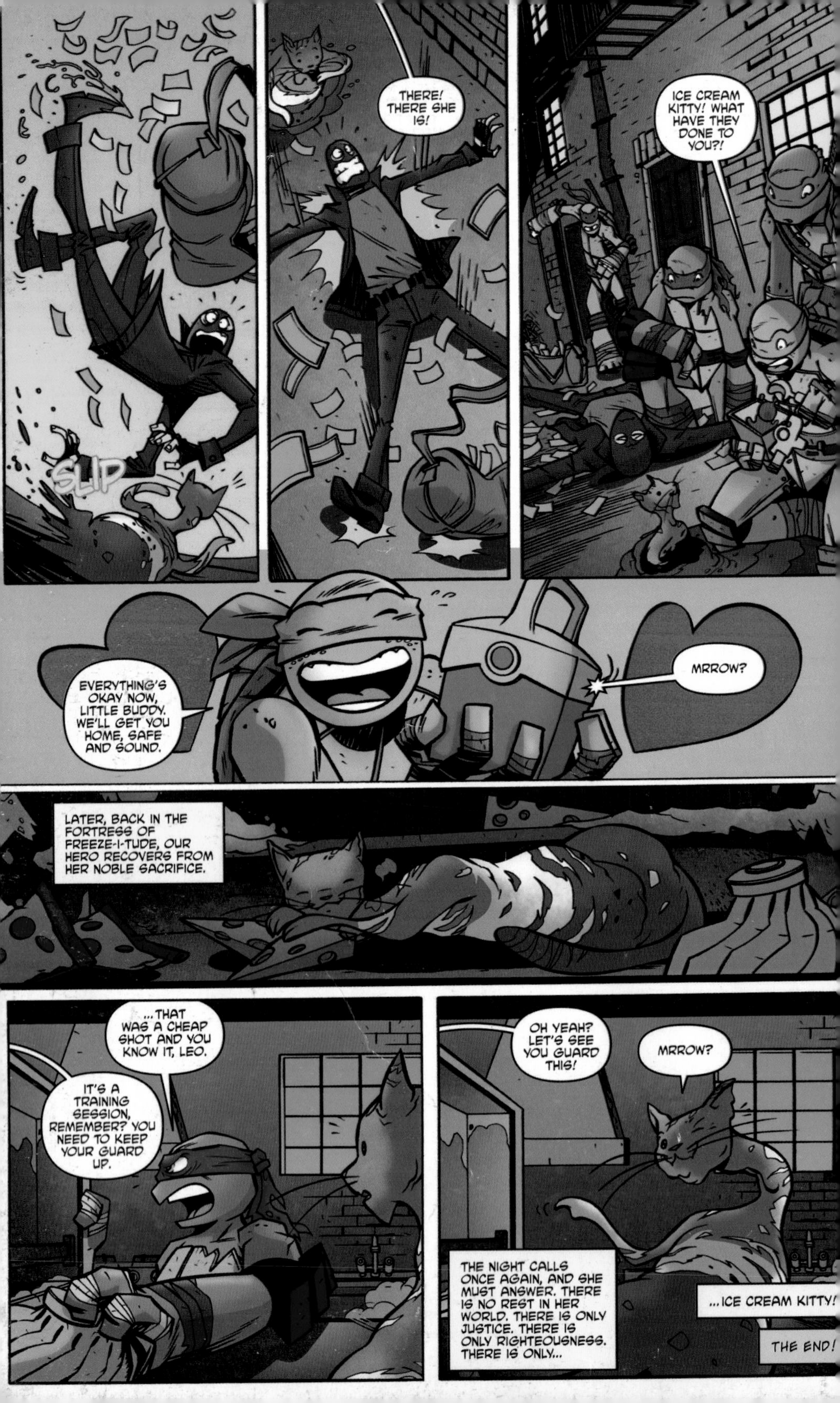
SLIP
THERE! THERE SHE IS!
ICE CREAM KITTY! WHAT HAVE THEY DONE TO YOU?!
EVERYTHING'S OKAY NOW, LITTLE BUDDY. WE'LL GET YOU HOME, SAFE AND SOUND.
MRROW?
LATER, BACK IN THE FORTRESS OF FREEZE-I-TUDE, OUR HERO RECOVERS FROM HER NOBLE SACRIFICE.
...THAT WAS A CHEAP SHOT AND YOU KNOW IT, LEO.
IT'S A TRAINING SESSION, REMEMBER? YOU NEED TO KEEP YOUR GUARD UP.
OH YEAH? LET'S SEE YOU GUARD THIS!
MRROW?
THE NIGHT CALLS ONCE AGAIN, AND SHE MUST ANSWER. THERE IS NO REST IN HER WORLD. THERE IS ONLY JUSTICE. THERE IS ONLY RIGHTEOUSNESS. THERE IS ONLY...
...ICE CREAM KITTY!
THE END!

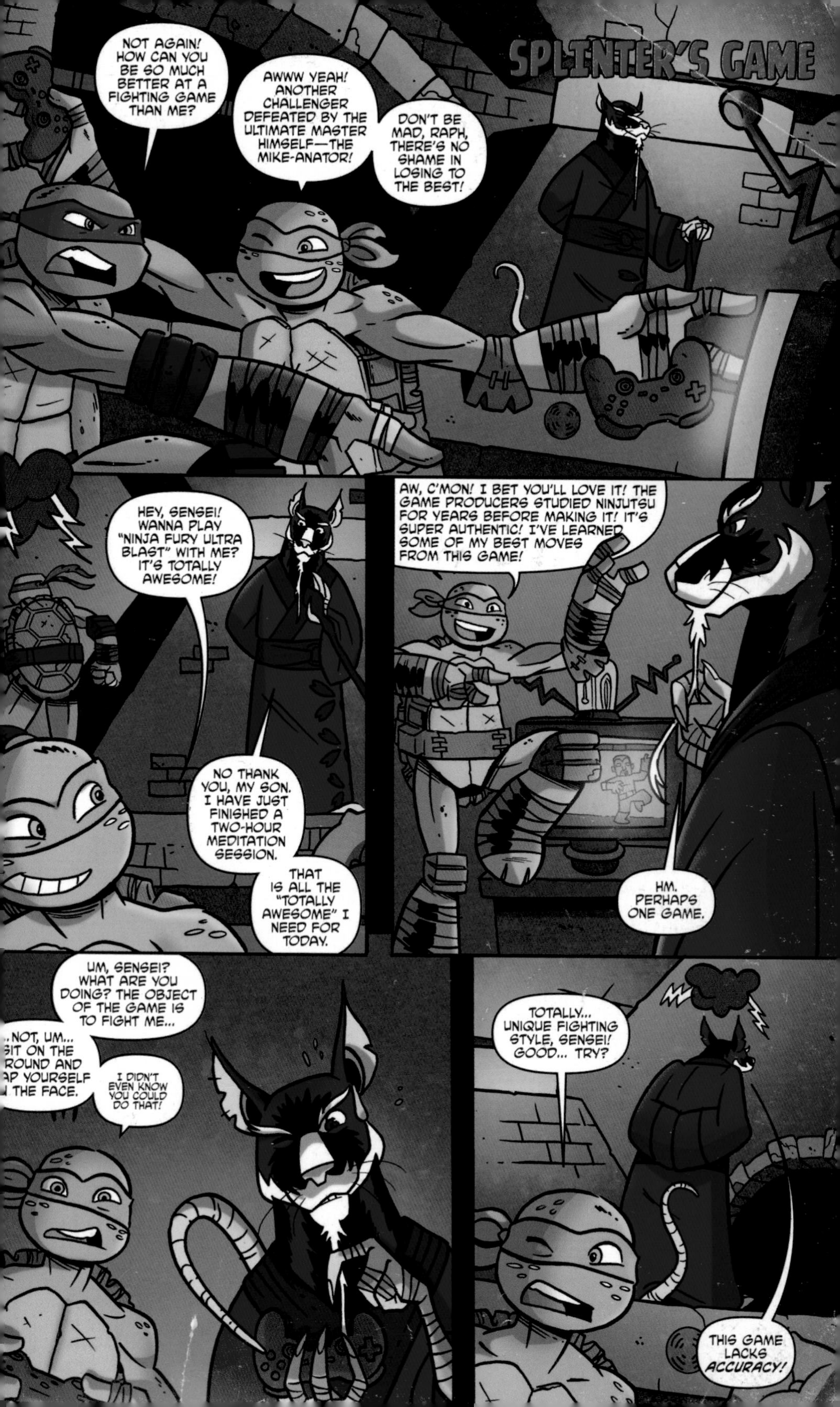
SPLINTER'S GAME
NOT AGAIN! HOW CAN YOU BE SO MUCH BETTER AT A FIGHTING GAME THAN ME?
AWWW YEAH! ANOTHER CHALLENGER DEFEATED BY THE ULTIMATE MASTER HIMSELF—THE MIKE-ANATOR!
DON'T BE MAD, RAPH, THERE'S NO SHAME IN LOSING TO THE BEST!
HEY, SENSEI! WANNA PLAY "NINJA FURY ULTRA BLAST" WITH ME? IT'S TOTALLY AWESOME!
NO THANK YOU, MY SON. I HAVE JUST FINISHED A TWO-HOUR MEDITATION SESSION.
THAT IS ALL THE "TOTALLY AWESOME" I NEED FOR TODAY.
AW, C'MON! I BET YOU'LL LOVE IT! THE GAME PRODUCERS STUDIED NINJUTSU FOR YEARS BEFORE MAKING IT! IT'S SUPER AUTHENTIC! I'VE LEARNED SOME OF MY BEST MOVES FROM THIS GAME!
HM. PERHAPS ONE GAME.
UM, SENSEI? WHAT ARE YOU DOING? THE OBJECT OF THE GAME IS TO FIGHT ME...
..NOT, UM... SIT ON THE ROUND AND AP YOURSELF THE FACE.
I DIDN'T EVEN KNOW YOU COULD DO THAT!
TOTALLY... UNIQUE FIGHTING STYLE, SENSEI! GOOD... TRY?
THIS GAME LACKS ACCURACY!

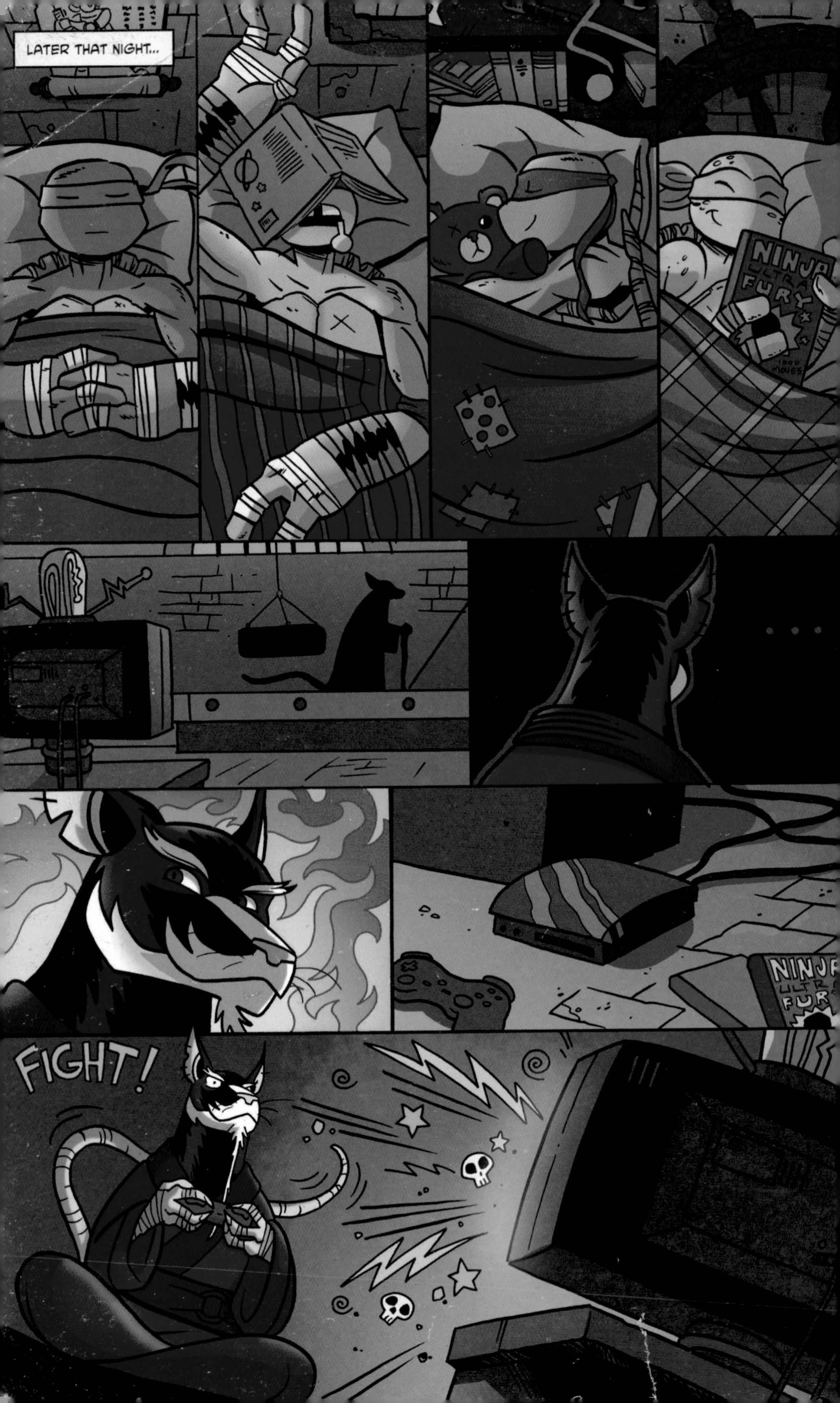

LATER THAT NIGHT...
NINJA ULTRA FURY
...
NINJA ULTRA FURY
FIGHT!

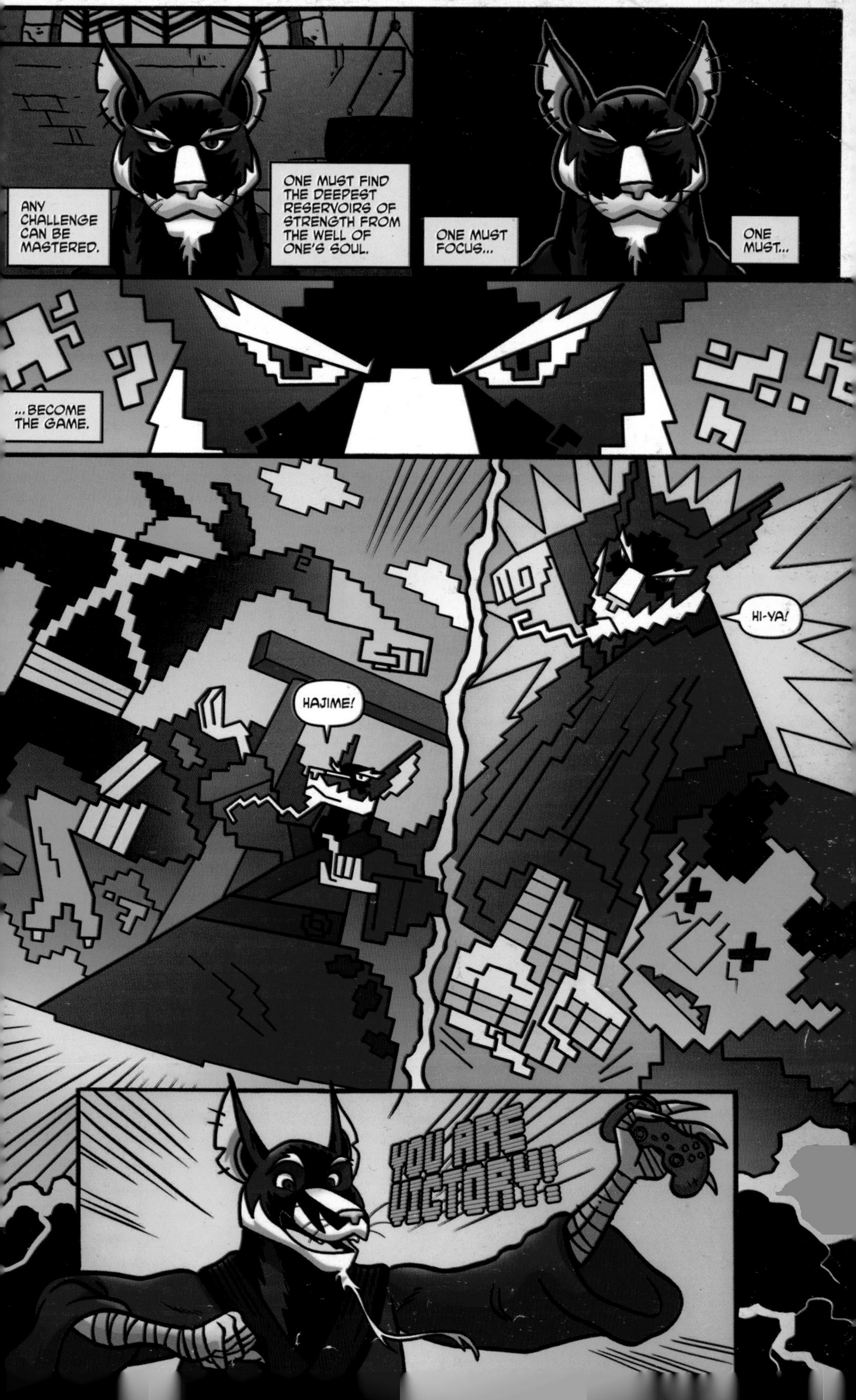
ANY CHALLENGE CAN BE MASTERED.
ONE MUST FIND THE DEEPEST RESERVOIRS OF STRENGTH FROM THE WELL OF ONE'S SOUL.
ONE MUST FOCUS...
ONE MUST...
...BECOME THE GAME.
HAJIME!
HI-YA!
YOU ARE VICTORY!

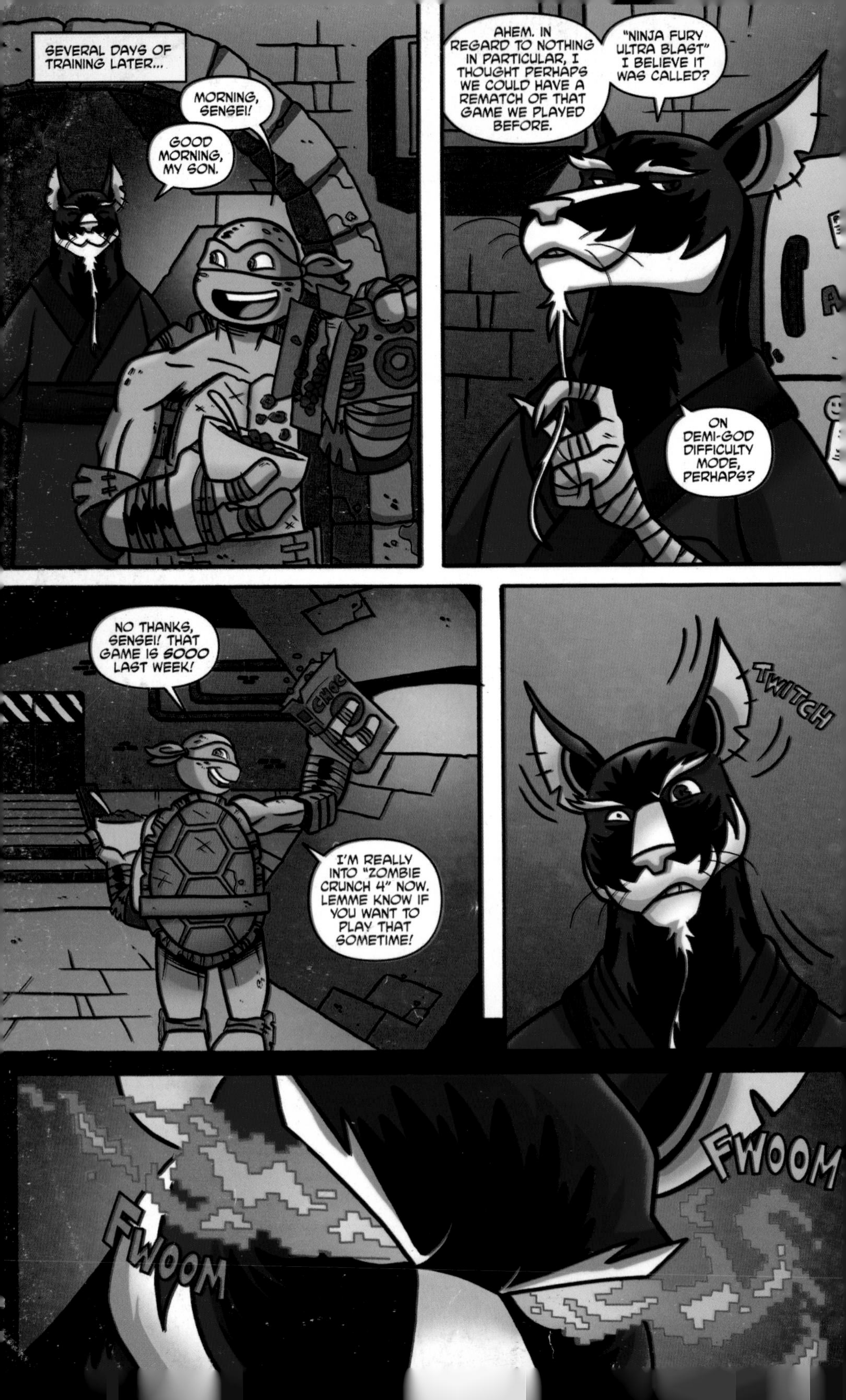
SEVERAL DAYS OF TRAINING LATER...
MORNING, SENSEI!
GOOD MORNING, MY SON.
AHEM. IN REGARD TO NOTHING IN PARTICULAR, I THOUGHT PERHAPS WE COULD HAVE A REMATCH OF THAT GAME WE PLAYED BEFORE.
"NINJA FURY ULTRA BLAST" I BELIEVE IT WAS CALLED?
ON DEMI-GOD DIFFICULTY MODE, PERHAPS?
NO THANKS, SENSEI! THAT GAME IS SOOO LAST WEEK!
I'M REALLY INTO "ZOMBIE CRUNCH 4" NOW. LEMME KNOW IF YOU WANT TO PLAY THAT SOMETIME!
TWITCH
FWOOM
FWOOM

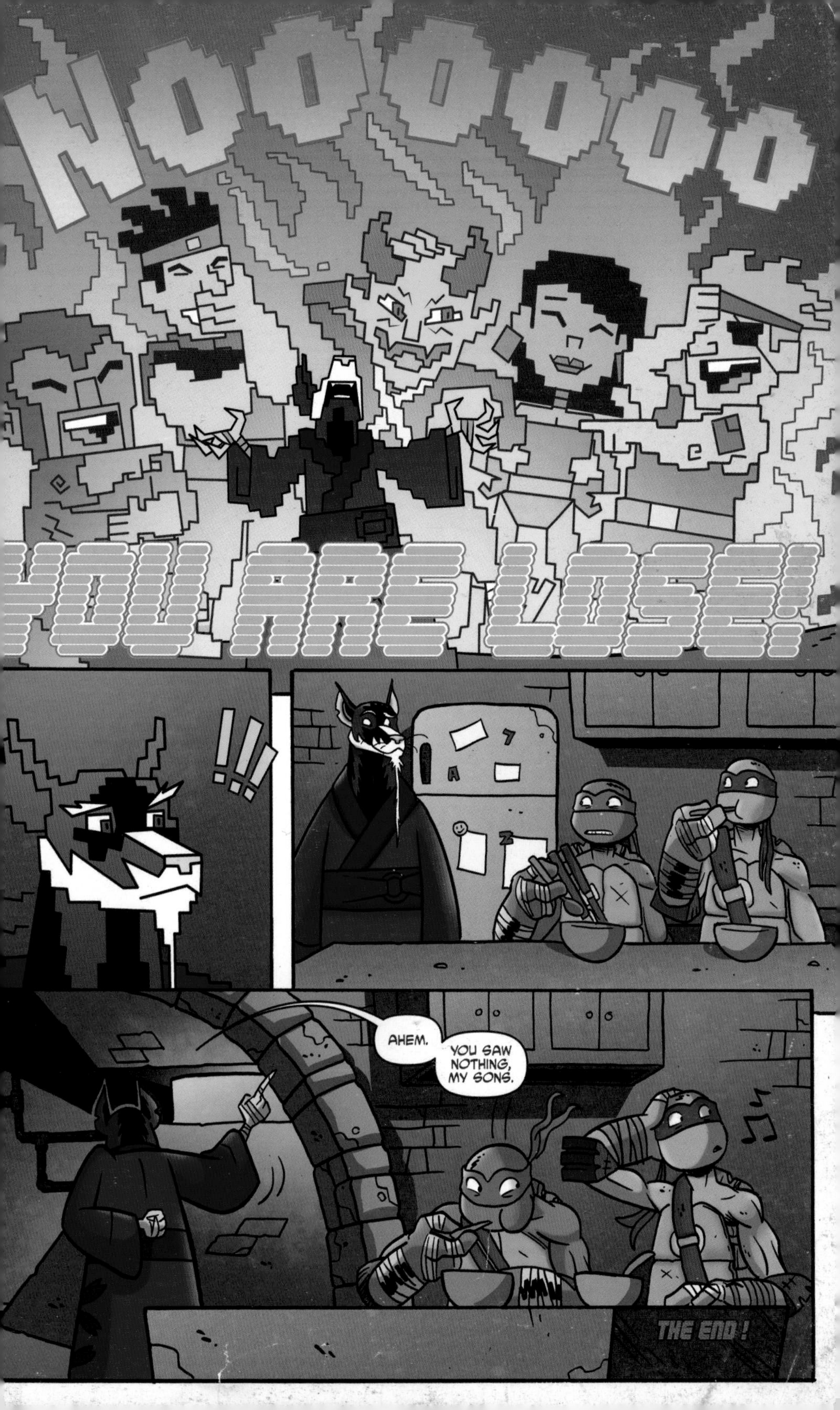
HOOOOOOO
YOU ARE LOSE!
!!!
AHEM.
YOU SAW NOTHING, MY SONS.
THE END!

Cover by **DARIO BRIZUELA**

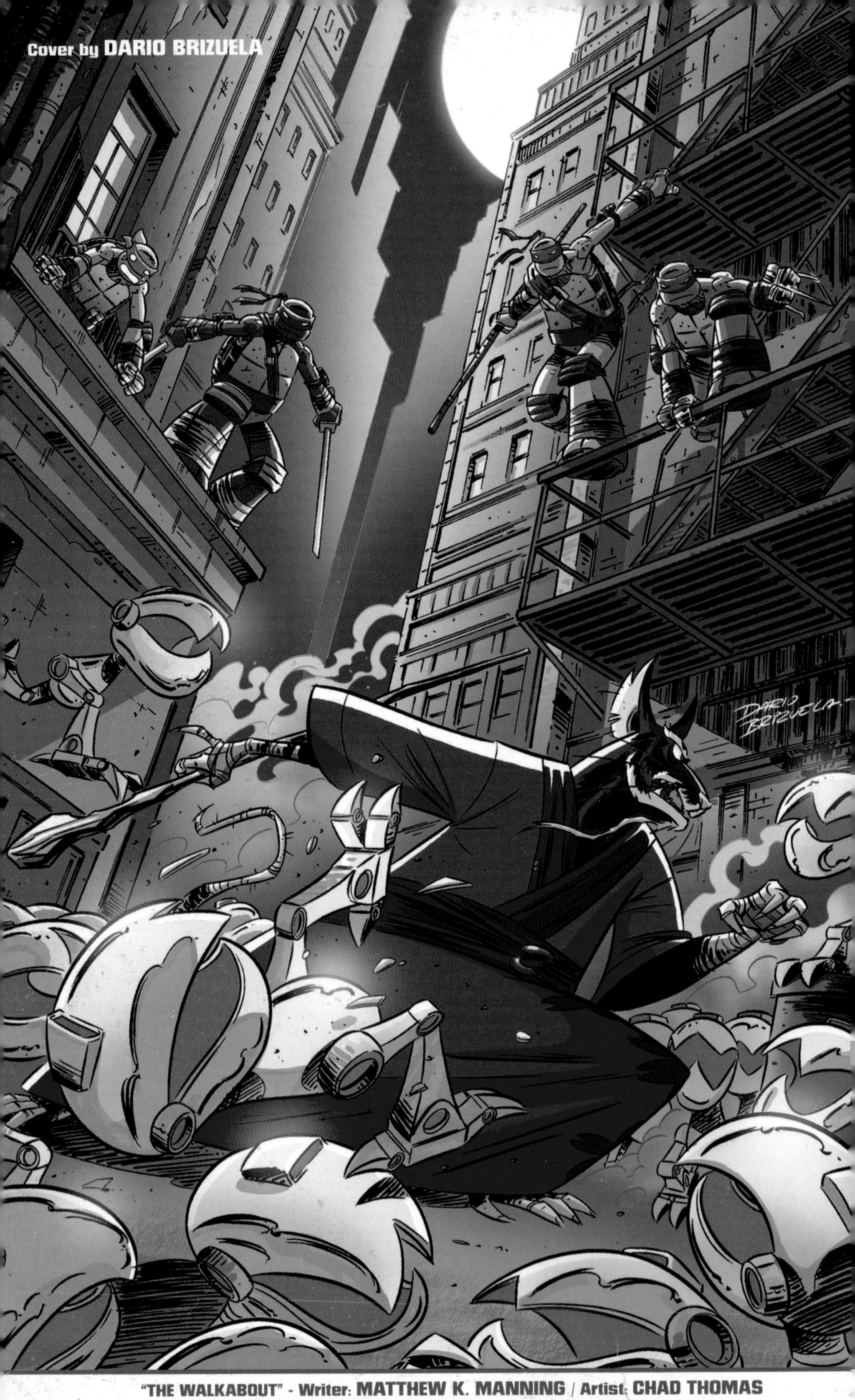
DARIO BRIZUELA

"THE WALKABOUT" - Writer: **MATTHEW K. MANNING** / Artist: **CHAD THOMAS**
"BREAKDOWN" - Writer: **PAUL ALLOR** / Artist: **MARCELO FERREIRA**

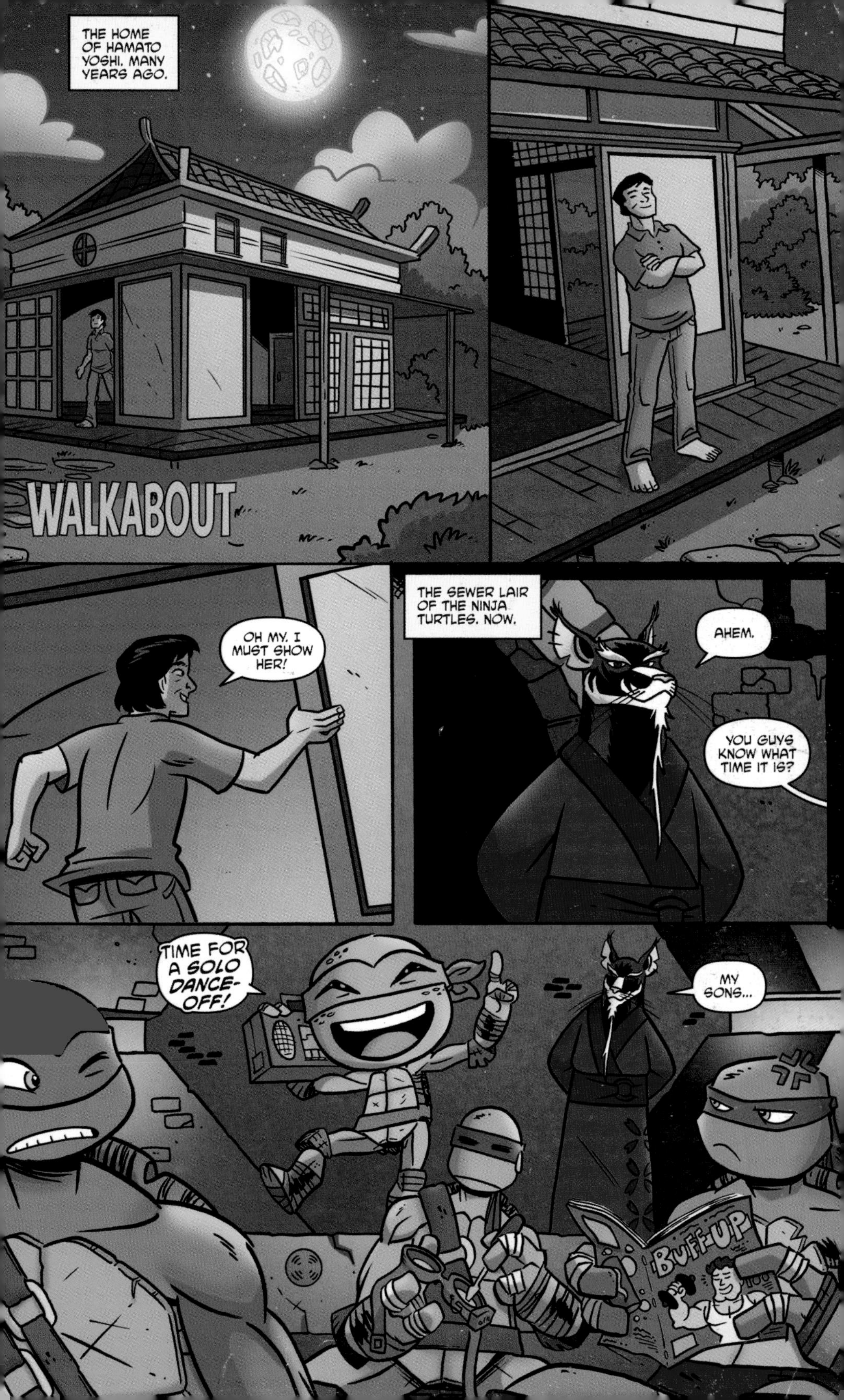
THE HOME OF HAMATO YOSHI. MANY YEARS AGO.
WALKABOUT
OH MY. I MUST SHOW HER!
THE SEWER LAIR OF THE NINJA TURTLES. NOW.
AHEM.
YOU GUYS KNOW WHAT TIME IT IS?
TIME FOR A SOLO DANCE-OFF!
MY SONS...
BUFF-UP

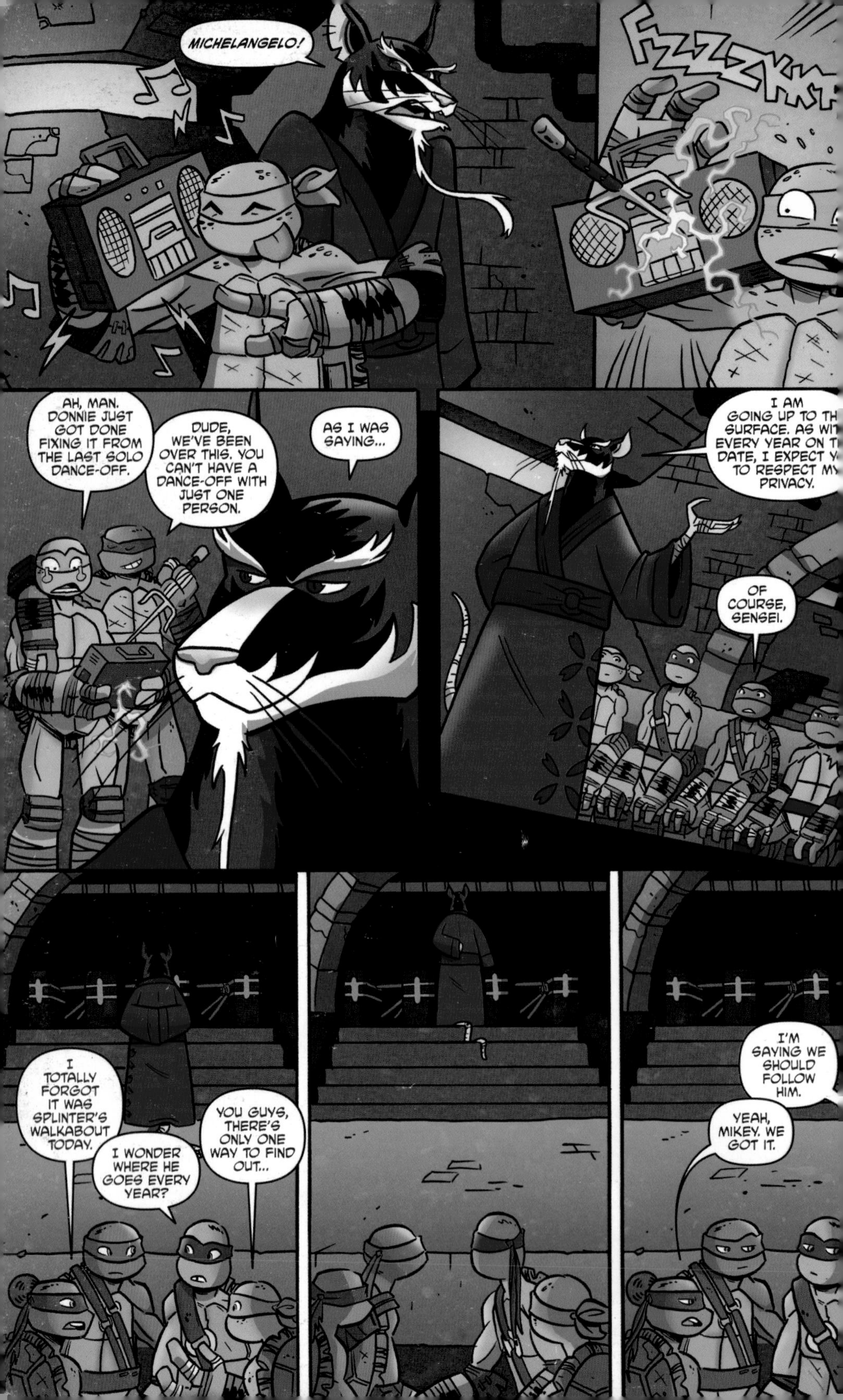

MICHELANGELO!
AH, MAN. DONNIE JUST GOT DONE FIXING IT FROM THE LAST SOLO DANCE-OFF.
DUDE, WE'VE BEEN OVER THIS. YOU CAN'T HAVE A DANCE-OFF WITH JUST ONE PERSON.
AS I WAS SAYING...
I AM GOING UP TO TH SURFACE. AS WIT EVERY YEAR ON T DATE, I EXPECT Y TO RESPECT MY PRIVACY.
OF COURSE, SENSEI.
I TOTALLY FORGOT IT WAS SPLINTER'S WALKABOUT TODAY.
I WONDER WHERE HE GOES EVERY YEAR?
YOU GUYS, THERE'S ONLY ONE WAY TO FIND OUT...
I'M SAYING WE SHOULD FOLLOW HIM.
YEAH, MIKEY. WE GOT IT.

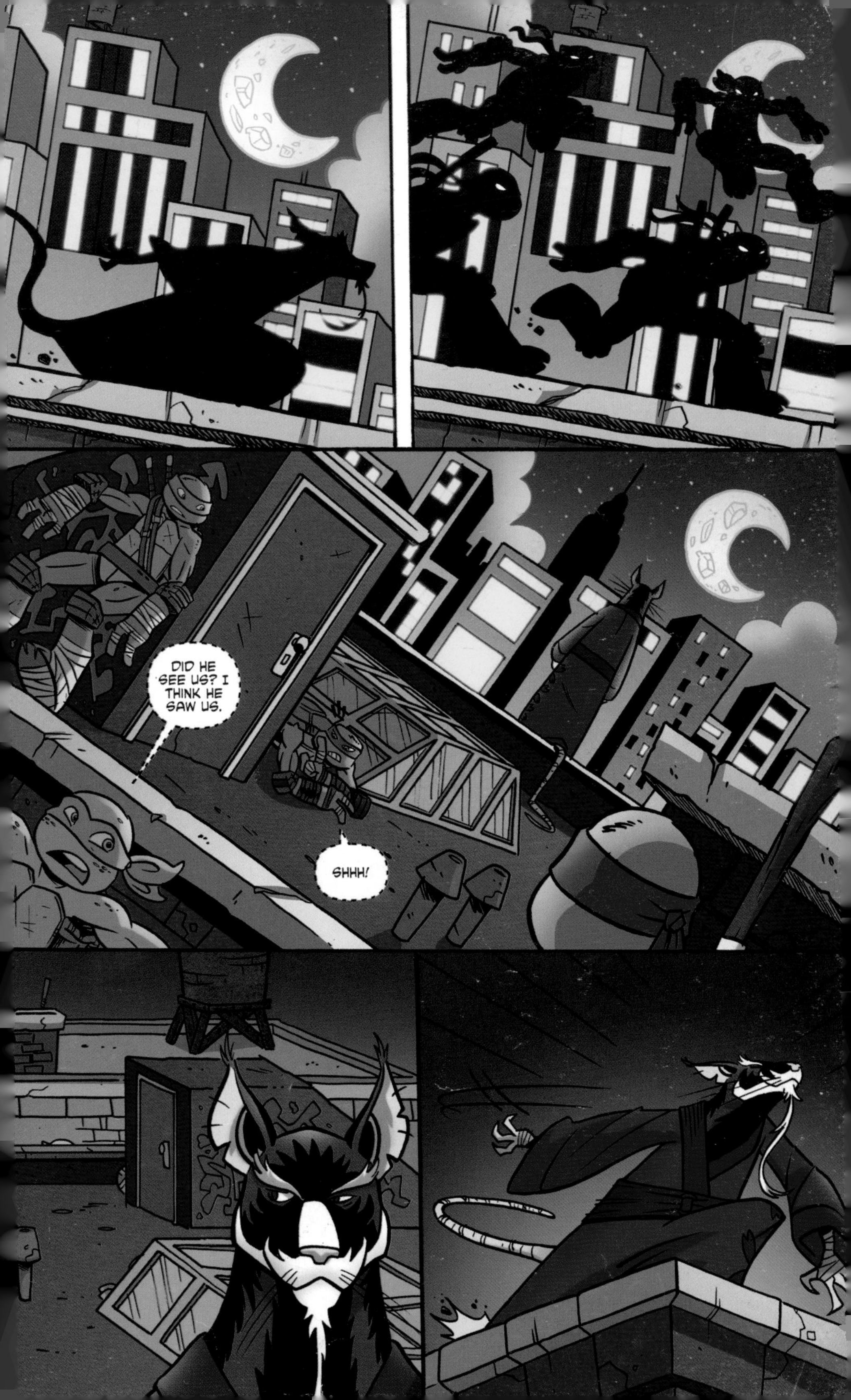
DID HE SEE US? I THINK HE SAW US.
SHHH!

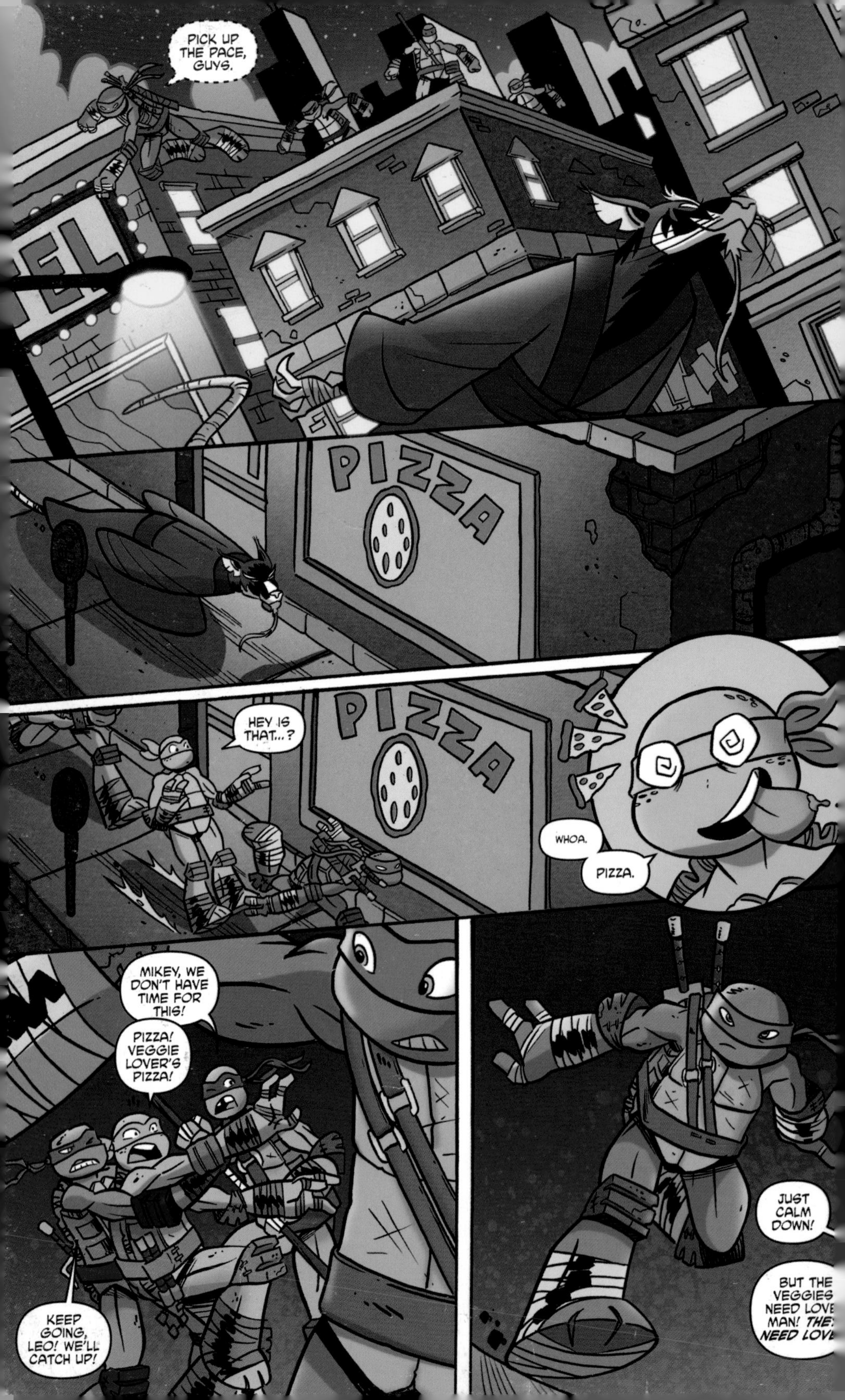
PICK UP THE PACE, GUYS.
PIZZA
PIZZA
HEY IS THAT...?
WHOA.
PIZZA.
MIKEY, WE DON'T HAVE TIME FOR THIS!
PIZZA! VEGGIE LOVER'S PIZZA!
KEEP GOING, LEO! WE'LL CATCH UP!
JUST CALM DOWN!
BUT THE VEGGIES NEED LOVE, MAN! THEY NEED LOVE

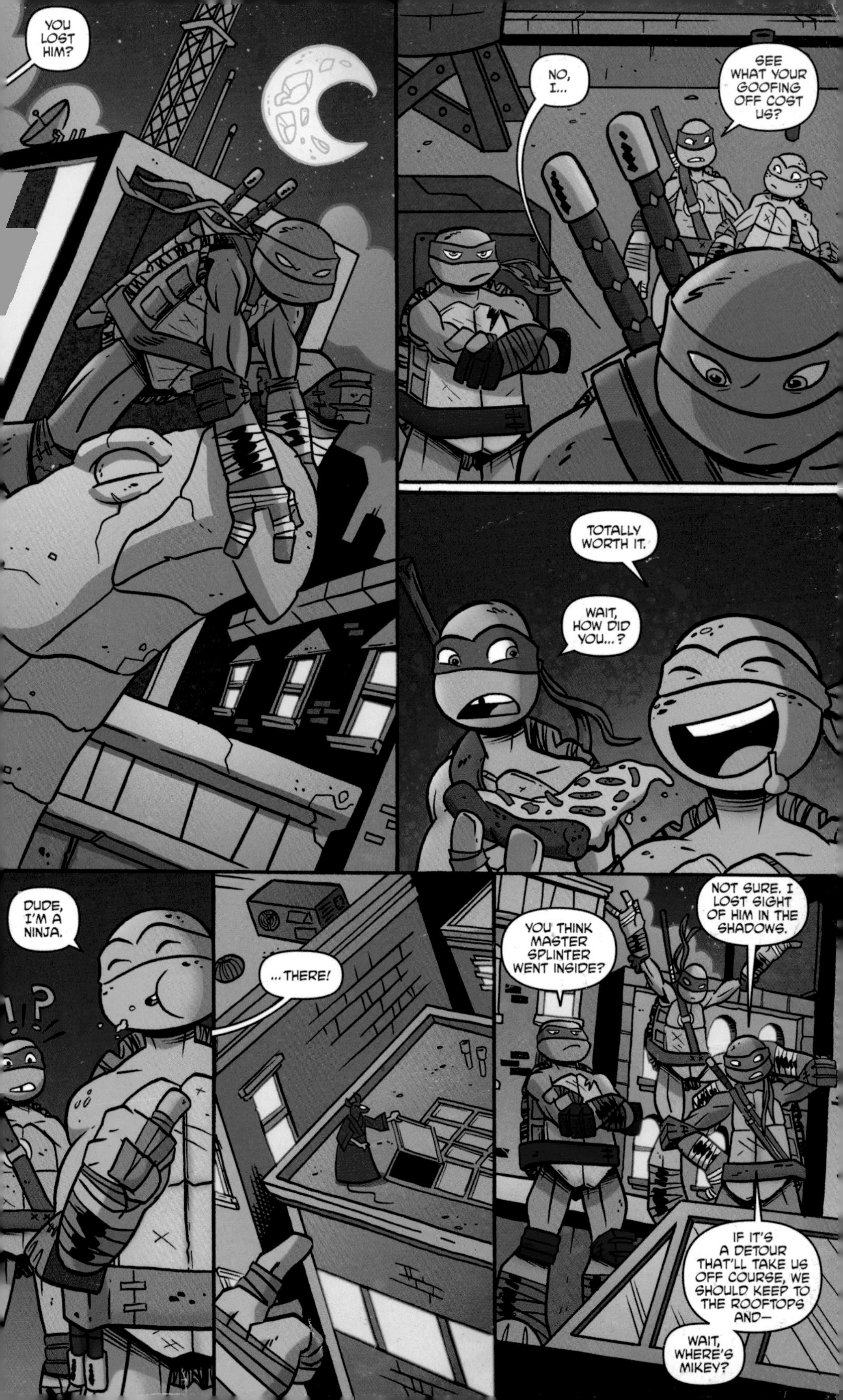
YOU LOST HIM?
NO, I...
SEE WHAT YOUR GOOFING OFF COST US?
TOTALLY WORTH IT.
WAIT, HOW DID YOU...?
DUDE, I'M A NINJA.
!?
...THERE!
YOU THINK MASTER SPLINTER WENT INSIDE?
NOT SURE. I LOST SIGHT OF HIM IN THE SHADOWS.
IF IT'S A DETOUR THAT'LL TAKE US OFF COURSE, WE SHOULD KEEP TO THE ROOFTOPS AND—
WAIT, WHERE'S MIKEY?

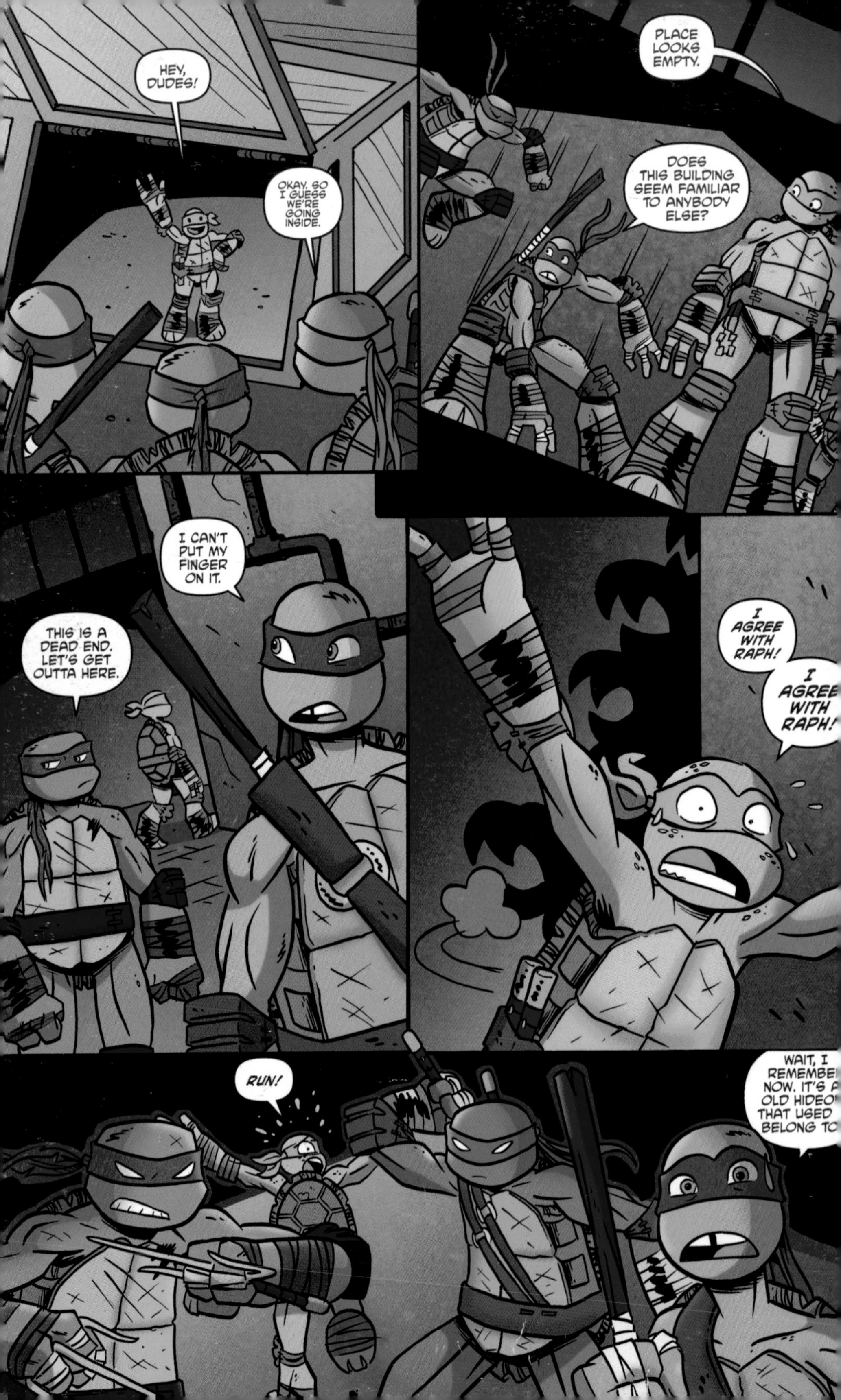
HEY, DUDES!
OKAY. SO I GUESS WE'RE GOING INSIDE.
PLACE LOOKS EMPTY.
DOES THIS BUILDING SEEM FAMILIAR TO ANYBODY ELSE?
I CAN'T PUT MY FINGER ON IT.
THIS IS A DEAD END. LET'S GET OUTTA HERE.
I AGREE WITH RAPH!
I AGREE WITH RAPH!
RUN!
WAIT, I REMEMBE NOW. IT'S A OLD HIDEO THAT USED BELONG TO

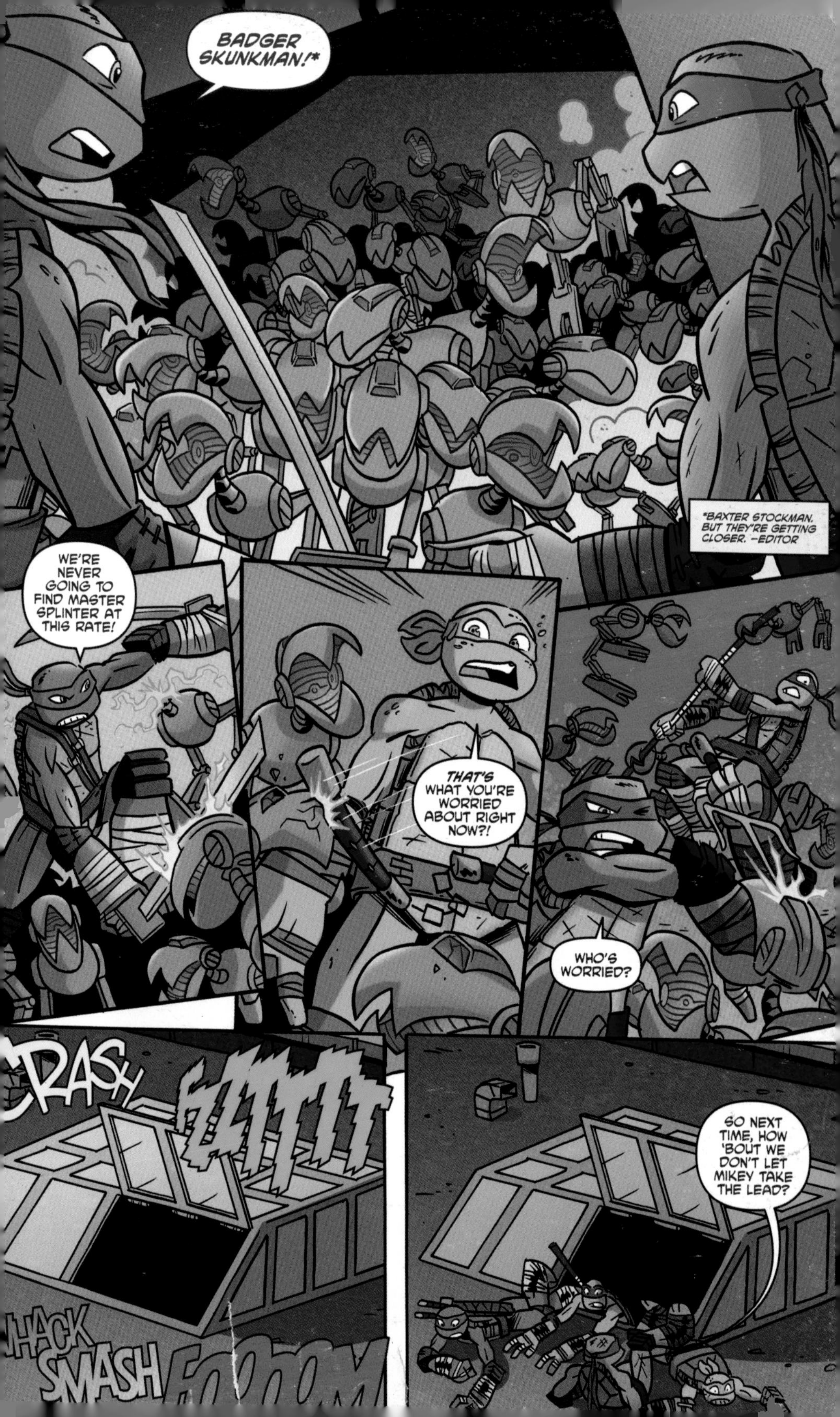
BADGER SKUNKMAN!*
*BAXTER STOCKMAN. BUT THEY'RE GETTING CLOSER. –EDITOR
WE'RE NEVER GOING TO FIND MASTER SPLINTER AT THIS RATE!
THAT'S WHAT YOU'RE WORRIED ABOUT RIGHT NOW?!
WHO'S WORRIED?
CRASH
FZZTTTT
WHACK
SMASH
FOOOOM
SO NEXT TIME, HOW 'BOUT WE DON'T LET MIKEY TAKE THE LEAD?

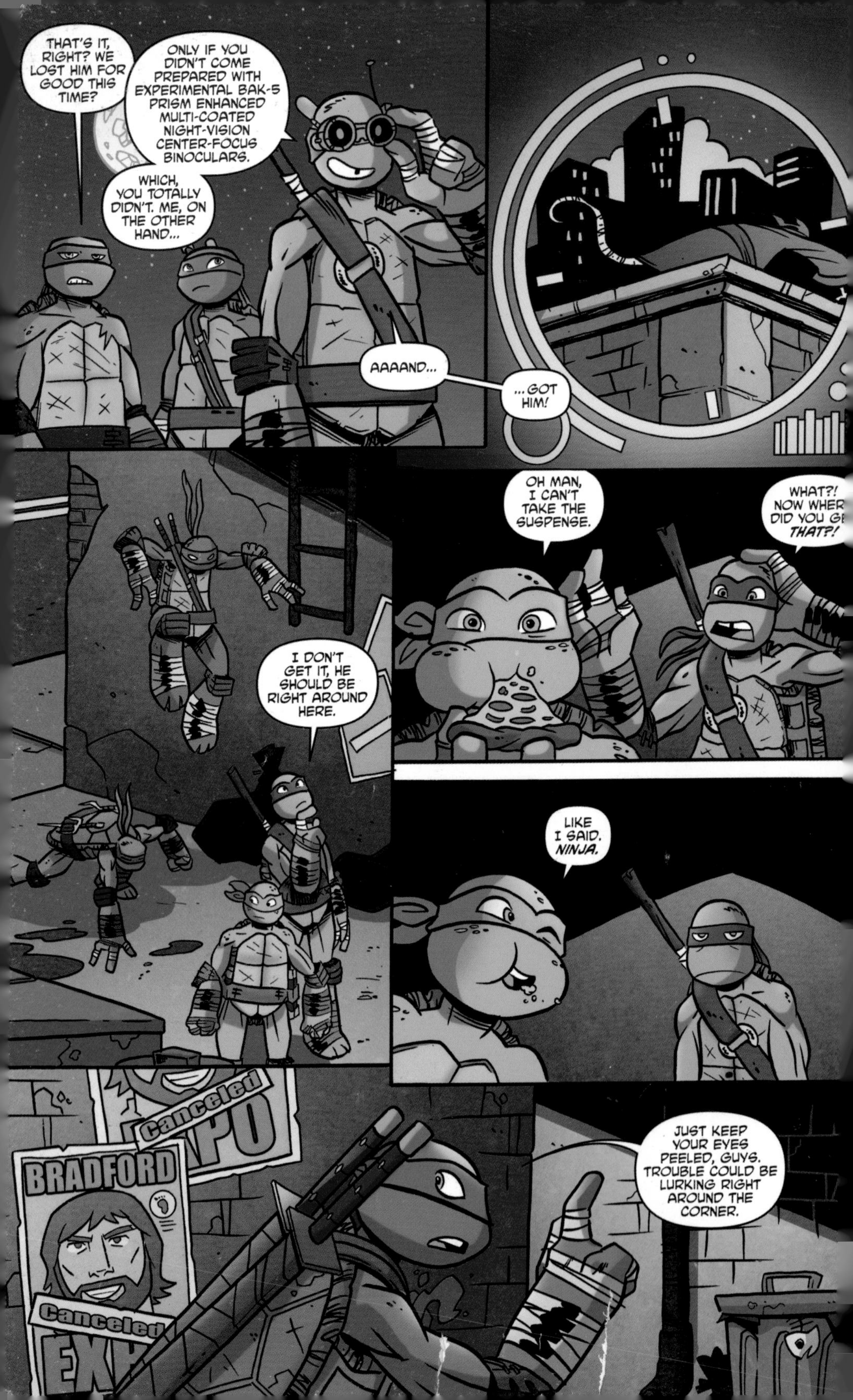
THAT'S IT, RIGHT? WE LOST HIM FOR GOOD THIS TIME?
ONLY IF YOU DIDN'T COME PREPARED WITH EXPERIMENTAL BAK-5 PRISM ENHANCED MULTI-COATED NIGHT-VISION CENTER-FOCUS BINOCULARS.
WHICH, YOU TOTALLY DIDN'T. ME, ON THE OTHER HAND...
AAAAND...
...GOT HIM!
I DON'T GET IT, HE SHOULD BE RIGHT AROUND HERE.
OH MAN, I CAN'T TAKE THE SUSPENSE.
WHAT?! NOW WHER DID YOU G THAT?!
LIKE I SAID. *NINJA.*
BRADFORD
Canceled
Canceled
PO
EXH
JUST KEEP YOUR EYES PEELED, GUYS. TROUBLE COULD BE LURKING RIGHT AROUND THE CORNER.

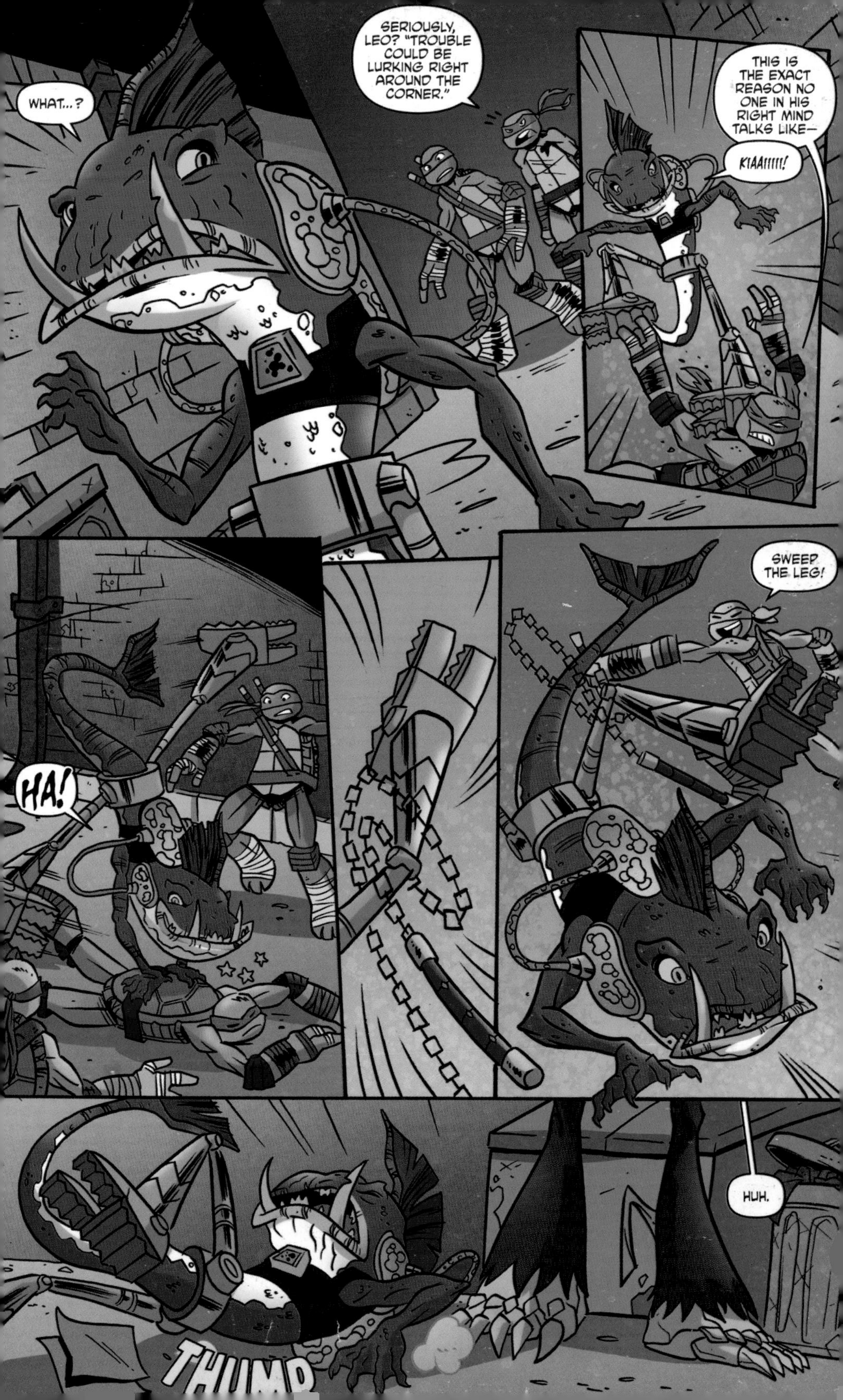
WHAT...?
SERIOUSLY, LEO? "TROUBLE COULD BE LURKING RIGHT AROUND THE CORNER."
THIS IS THE EXACT REASON NO ONE IN HIS RIGHT MIND TALKS LIKE—
KIAAIIIII!
HA!
SWEEP THE LEG!
HUH.
THUMP

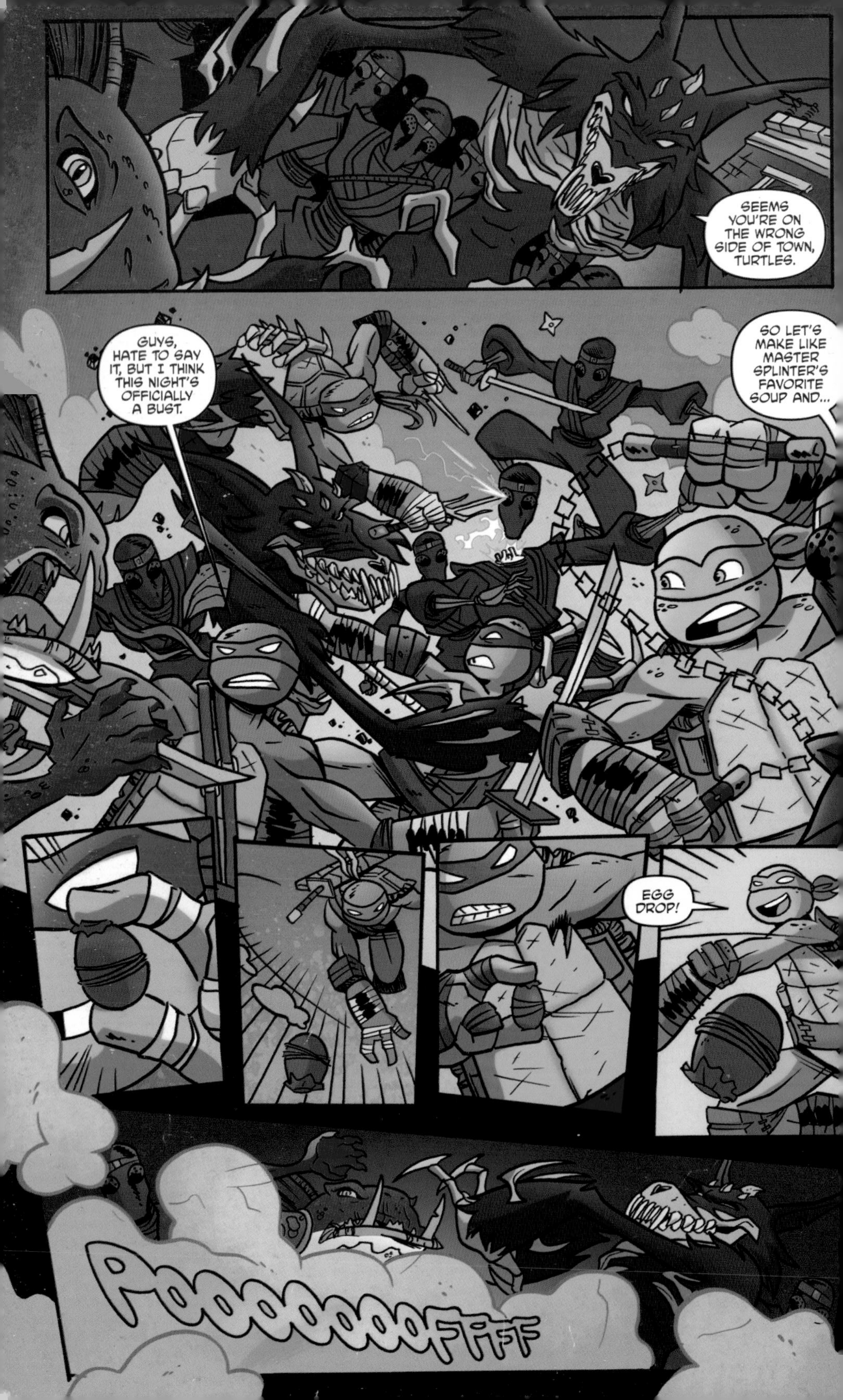
SEEMS YOU'RE ON THE WRONG SIDE OF TOWN, TURTLES.
GUYS, HATE TO SAY IT, BUT I THINK THIS NIGHT'S OFFICIALLY A BUST.
SO LET'S MAKE LIKE MASTER SPLINTER'S FAVORITE SOUP AND...
EGG DROP!
POOOOOOOOFFFF

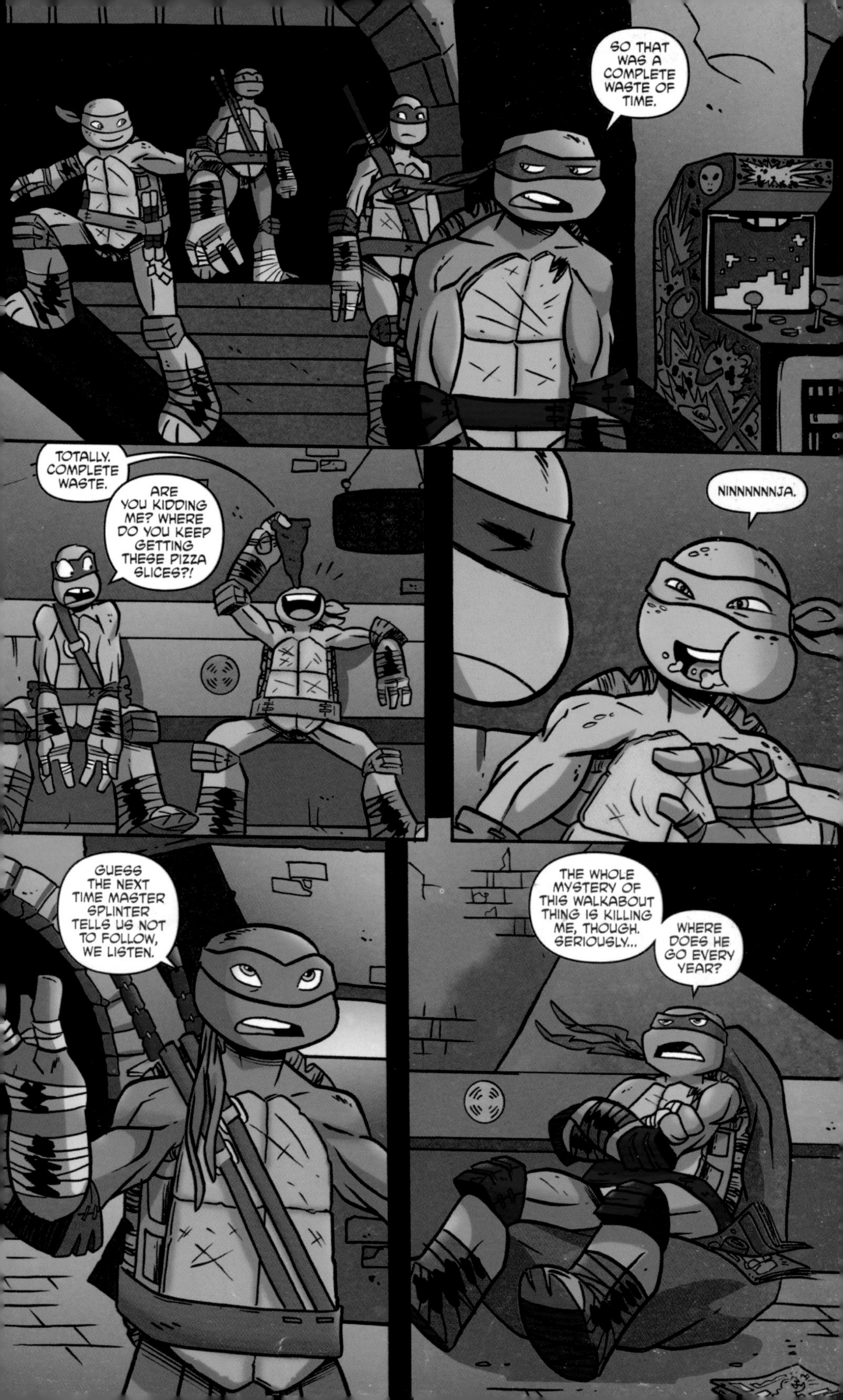
SO THAT WAS A COMPLETE WASTE OF TIME.
TOTALLY. COMPLETE WASTE.
ARE YOU KIDDING ME? WHERE DO YOU KEEP GETTING THESE PIZZA SLICES?!
NINNNNNNNJA.
GUESS THE NEXT TIME MASTER SPLINTER TELLS US NOT TO FOLLOW, WE LISTEN.
THE WHOLE MYSTERY OF THIS WALKABOUT THING IS KILLING ME, THOUGH. SERIOUSLY...
WHERE DOES HE GO EVERY YEAR?

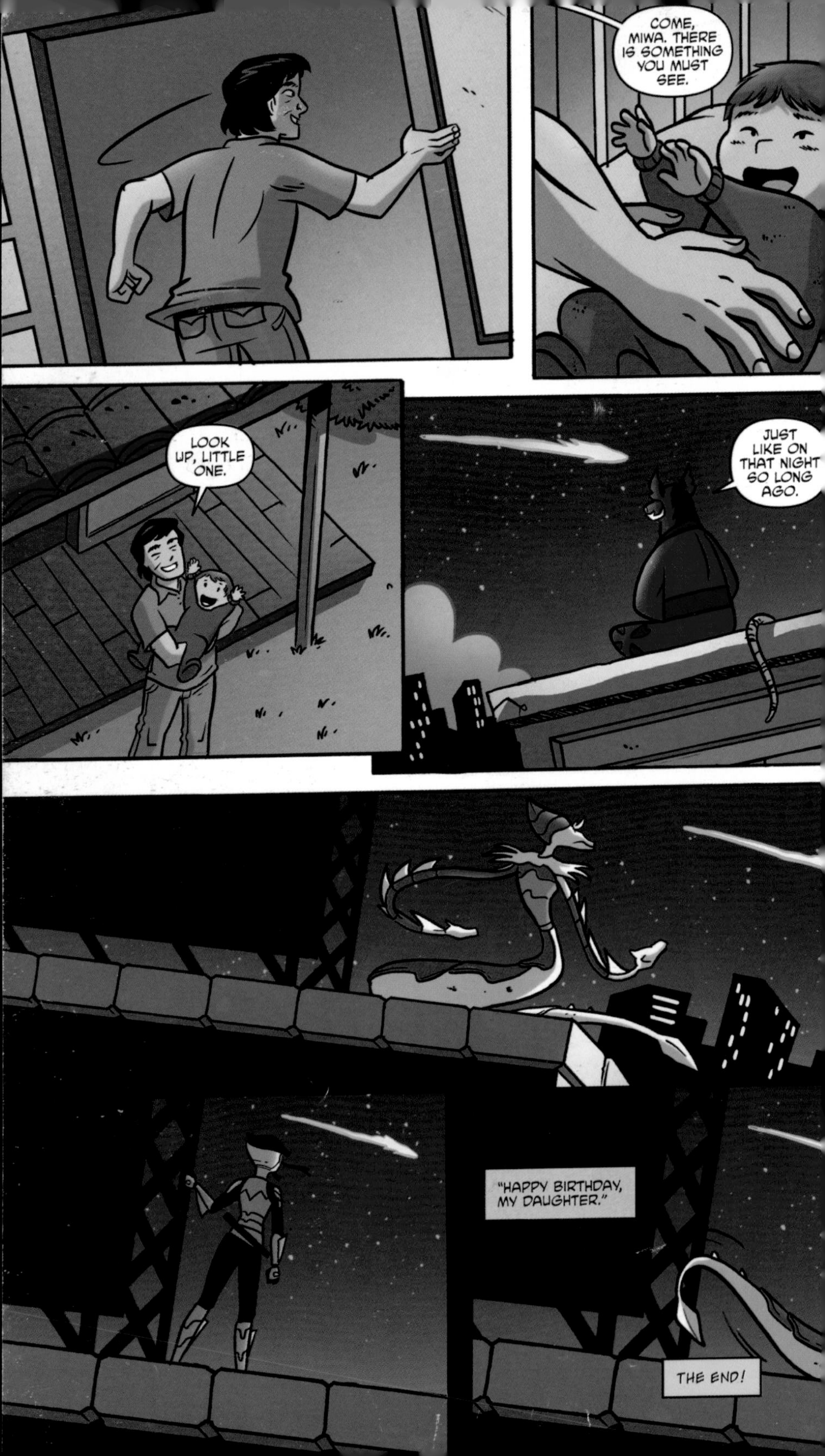
COME, MIWA. THERE IS SOMETHING YOU MUST SEE.
LOOK UP, LITTLE ONE.
JUST LIKE ON THAT NIGHT SO LONG AGO.
"HAPPY BIRTHDAY, MY DAUGHTER."
THE END!

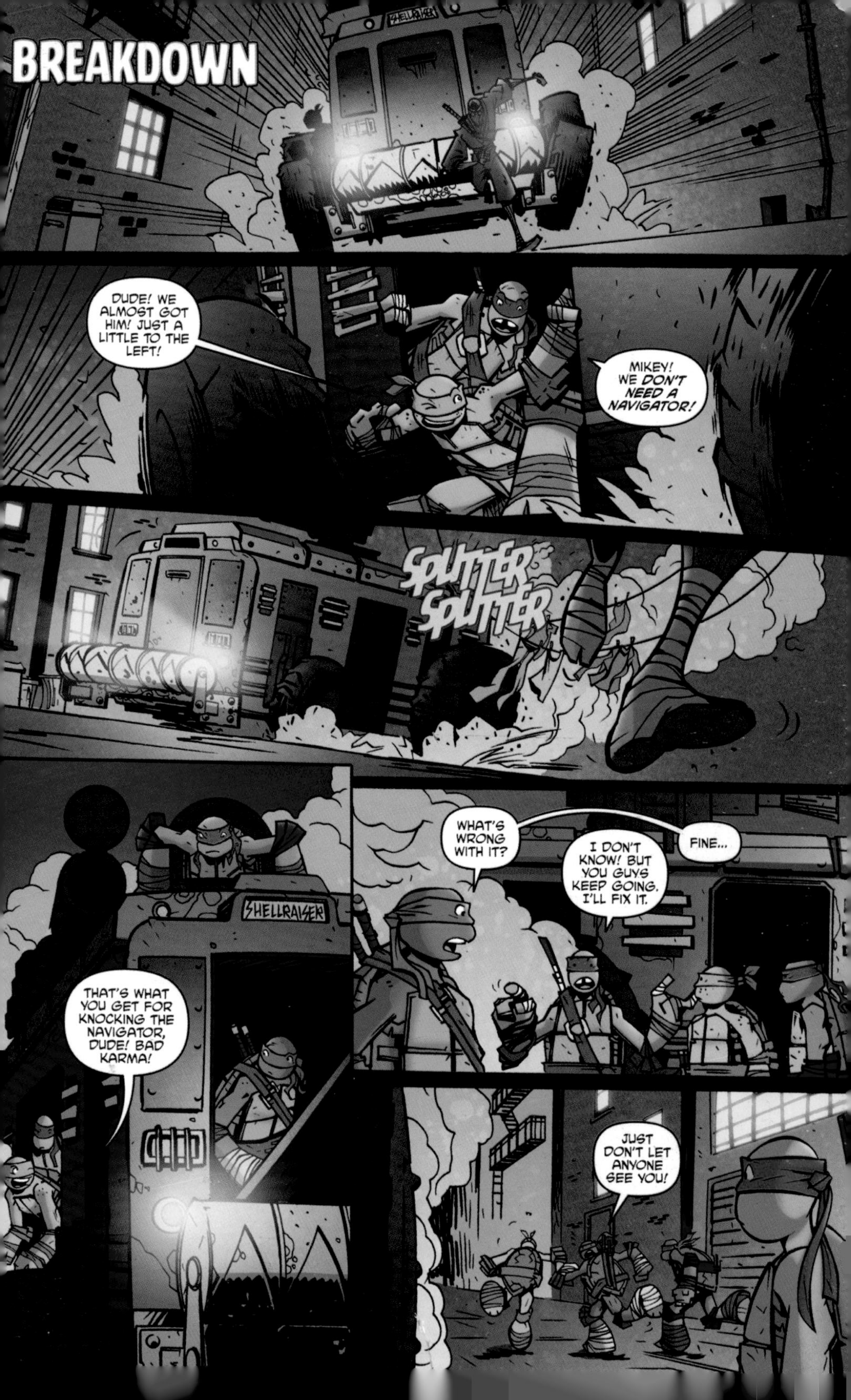
BREAKDOWN
SHELLRAISER
DUDE! WE ALMOST GOT HIM! JUST A LITTLE TO THE LEFT!
MIKEY! WE DON'T NEED A NAVIGATOR!
SPUTTER SPUTTER
SHELLRAISER
THAT'S WHAT YOU GET FOR KNOCKING THE NAVIGATOR, DUDE! BAD KARMA!
WHAT'S WRONG WITH IT?
I DON'T KNOW! BUT YOU GUYS KEEP GOING. I'LL FIX IT.
FINE...
JUST DON'T LET ANYONE SEE YOU!

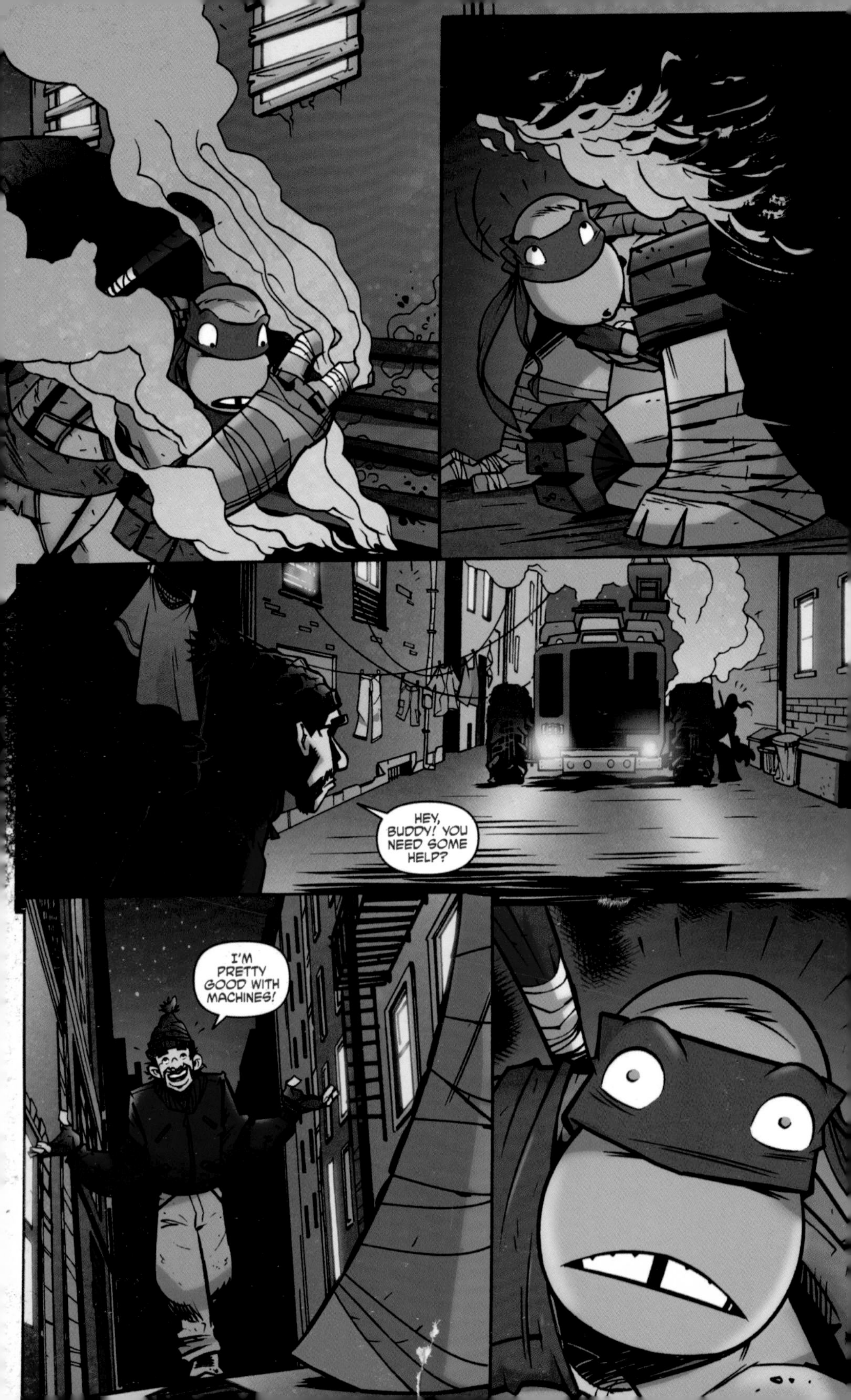
HEY, BUDDY! YOU NEED SOME HELP?
I'M PRETTY GOOD WITH MACHINES!

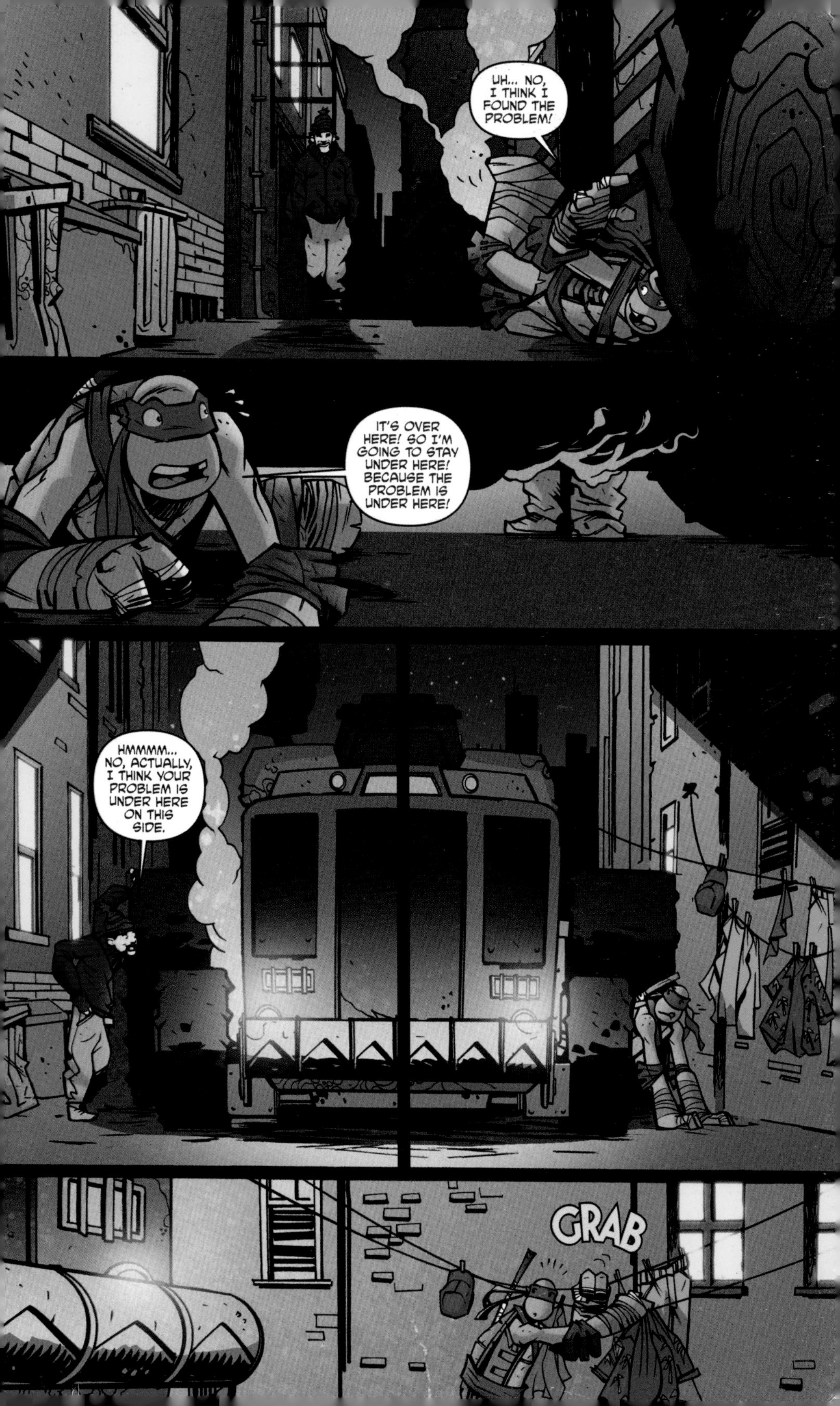
UH... NO, I THINK I FOUND THE PROBLEM!
IT'S OVER HERE! SO I'M GOING TO STAY UNDER HERE! BECAUSE THE PROBLEM IS UNDER HERE!
HMMMM... NO, ACTUALLY, I THINK YOUR PROBLEM IS UNDER HERE ON THIS SIDE.
GRAB

HEY, DON'T TOUCH THAT!

FUNNY GLOVES YOU GOT THERE.

ZOINK

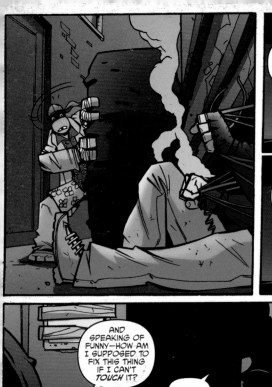

AND SPEAKING OF FUNNY—HOW AM I SUPPOSED TO FIX THIS THING IF I CAN'T *TOUCH* IT?

YOU'RE *NOT!*

I'M FINE! EVERYTHING IS FINE!

WE DON'T NEED ANY HELP.

BZZT BZZT

DONNIE, WE NEED SOME HELP!

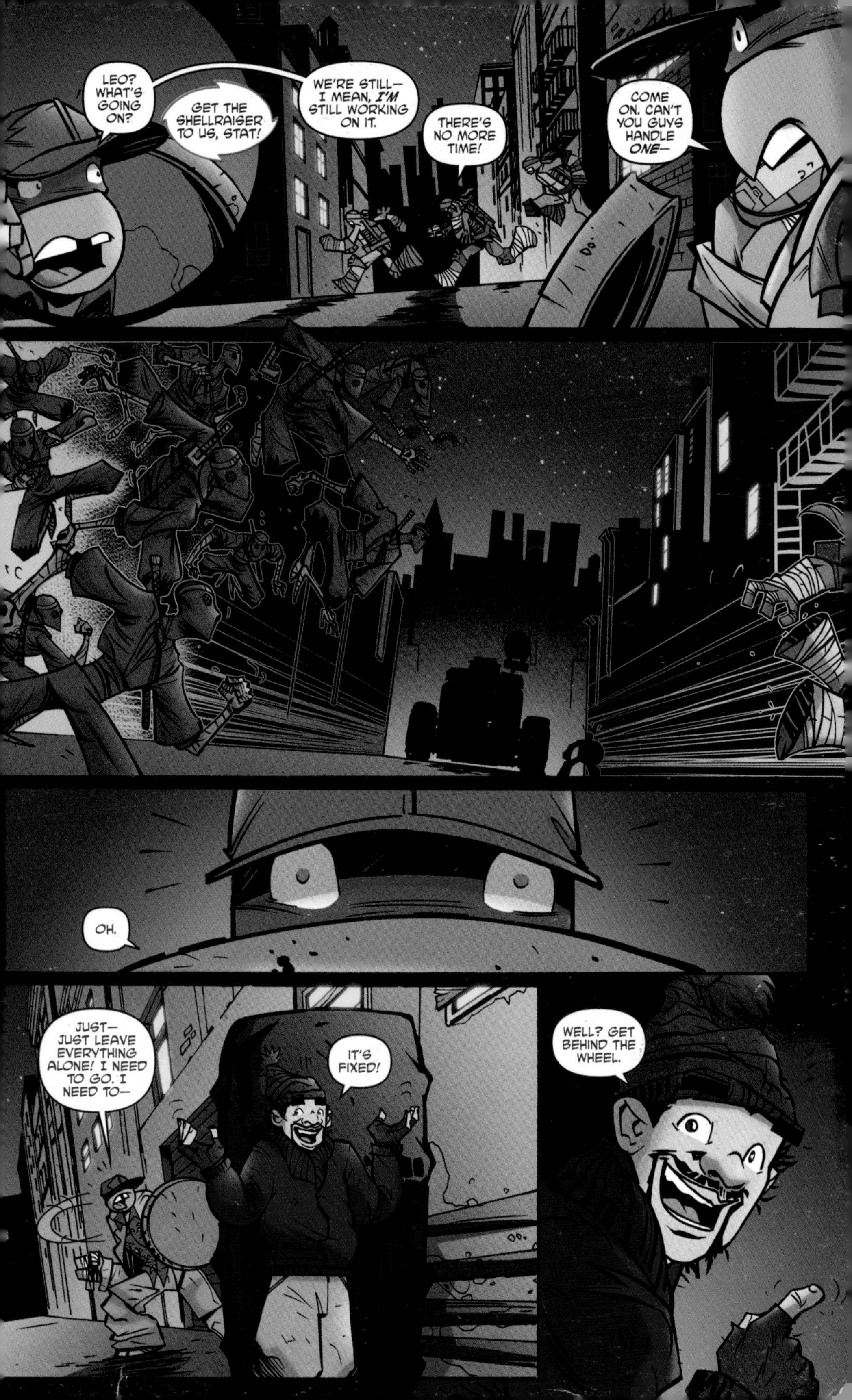
LEO? WHAT'S GOING ON?
GET THE SHELLRAISER TO US, STAT!
WE'RE STILL— I MEAN, I'M STILL WORKING ON IT.
THERE'S NO MORE TIME!
COME ON. CAN'T YOU GUYS HANDLE ONE—
OH.
JUST— JUST LEAVE EVERYTHING ALONE! I NEED TO GO. I NEED TO—
IT'S FIXED!
WELL? GET BEHIND THE WHEEL.

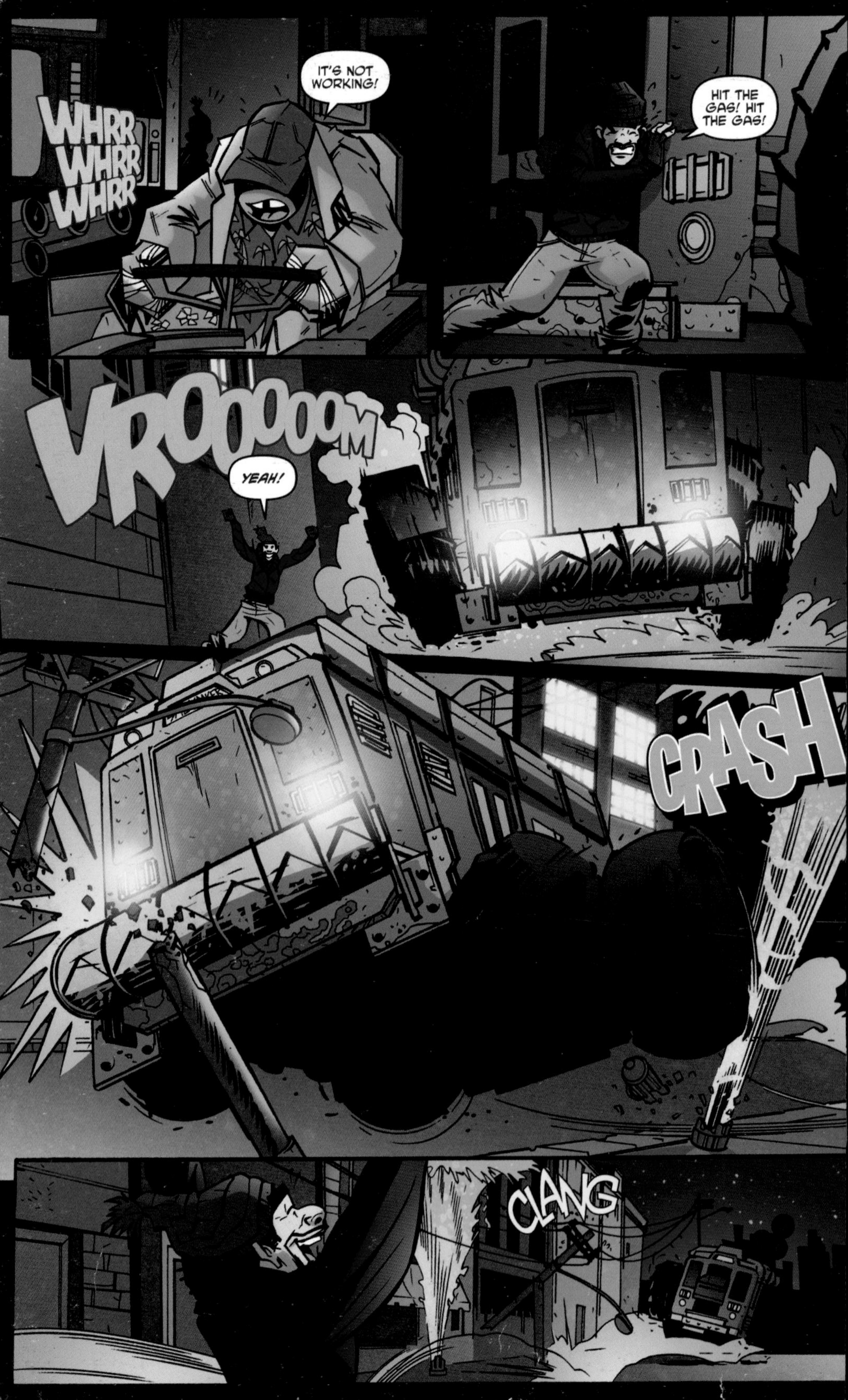
WHRR WHRR WHRR
IT'S NOT WORKING!
HIT THE GAS! HIT THE GAS!
VROOOOOM
YEAH!
CRASH
CLANG

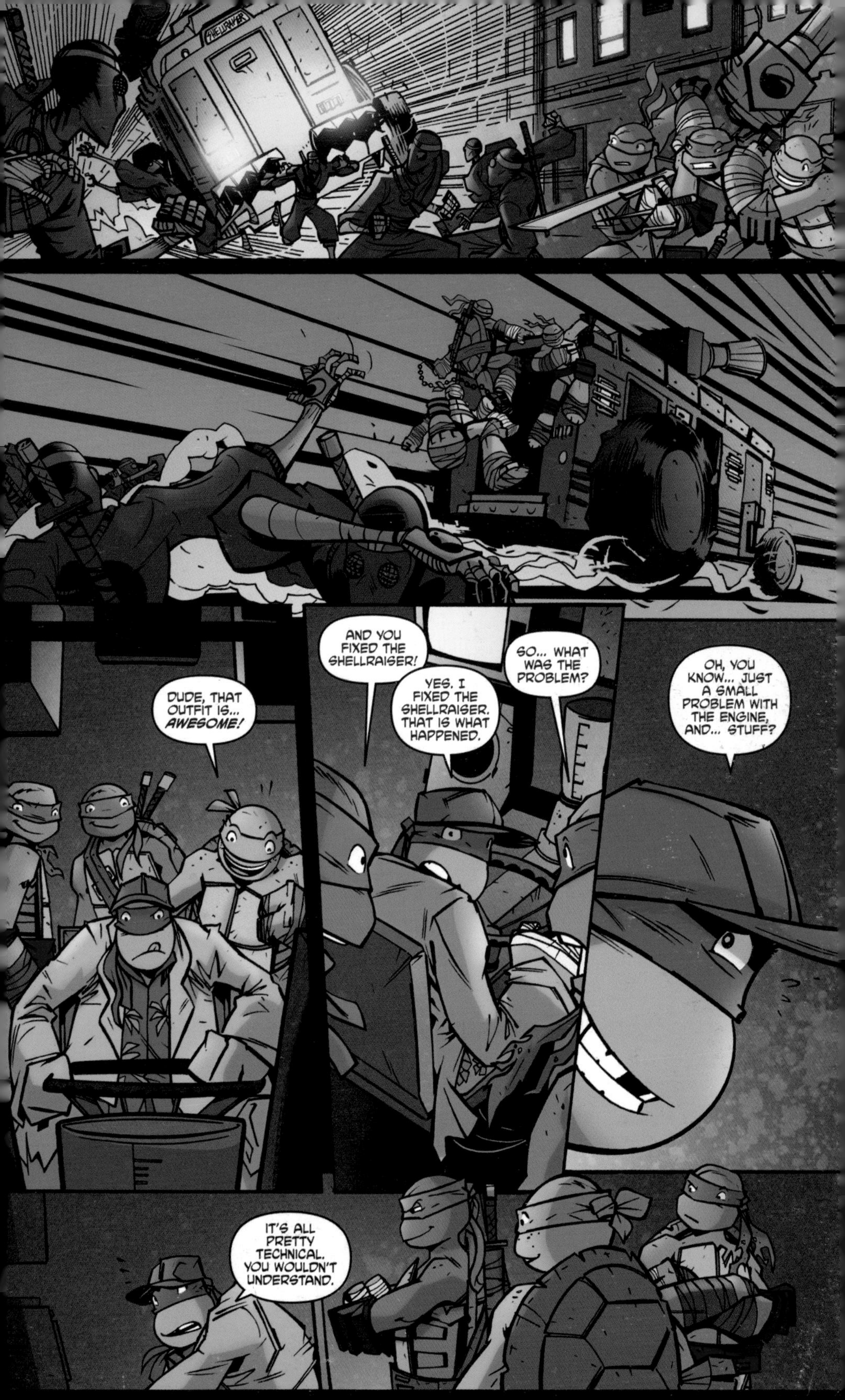
DUDE, THAT OUTFIT IS... *AWESOME!*
AND YOU FIXED THE SHELLRAISER!
YES. I FIXED THE SHELLRAISER. THAT IS WHAT HAPPENED.
SO... WHAT WAS THE PROBLEM?
OH, YOU KNOW... JUST A SMALL PROBLEM WITH THE ENGINE, AND... STUFF?
IT'S ALL PRETTY TECHNICAL. YOU WOULDN'T UNDERSTAND.

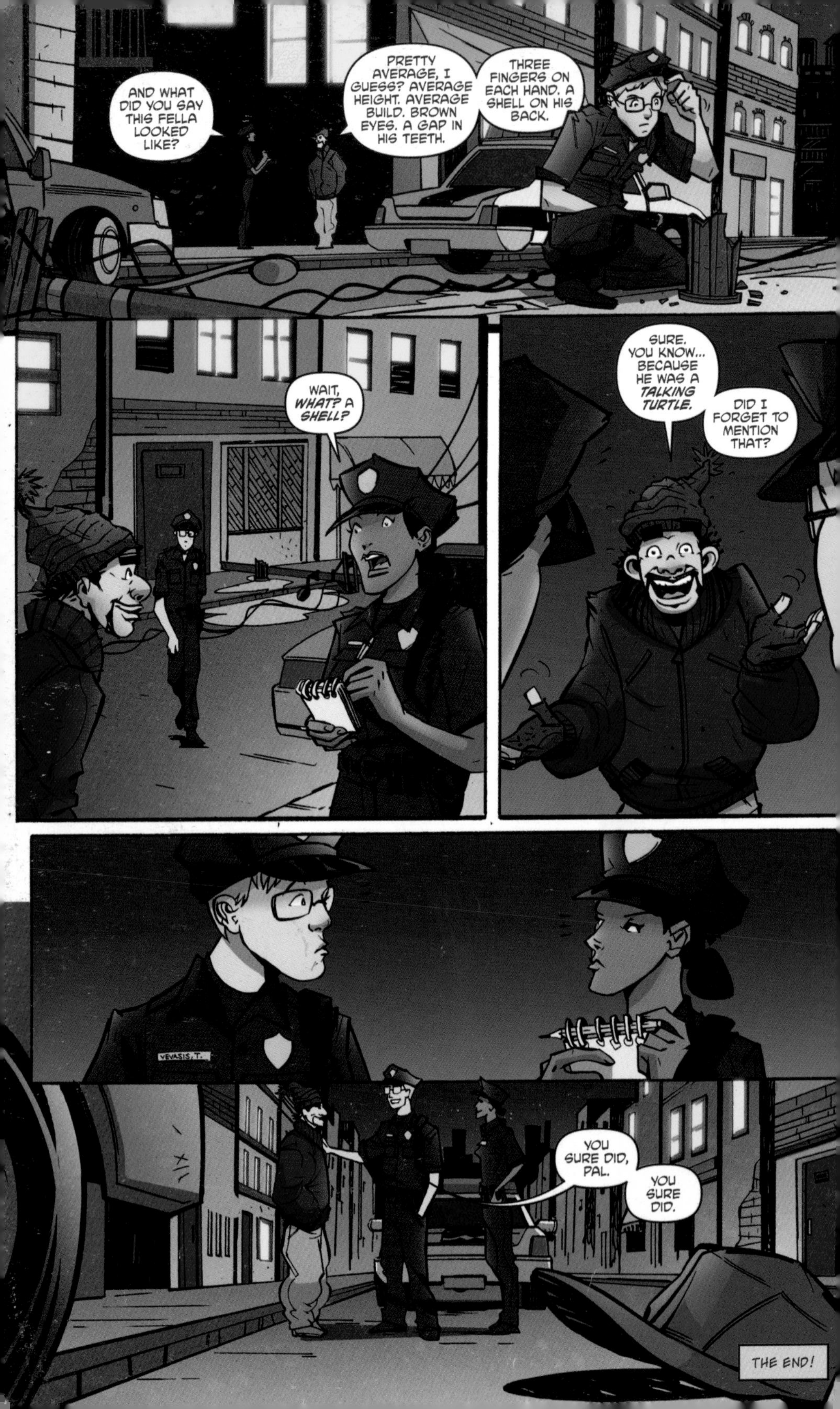
AND WHAT DID YOU SAY THIS FELLA LOOKED LIKE?
PRETTY AVERAGE, I GUESS? AVERAGE HEIGHT. AVERAGE BUILD. BROWN EYES. A GAP IN HIS TEETH.
THREE FINGERS ON EACH HAND. A SHELL ON HIS BACK.
WAIT, WHAT? A SHELL?
SURE. YOU KNOW... BECAUSE HE WAS A TALKING TURTLE.
DID I FORGET TO MENTION THAT?
VEVASIS, T.
YOU SURE DID, PAL.
YOU SURE DID.
THE END!

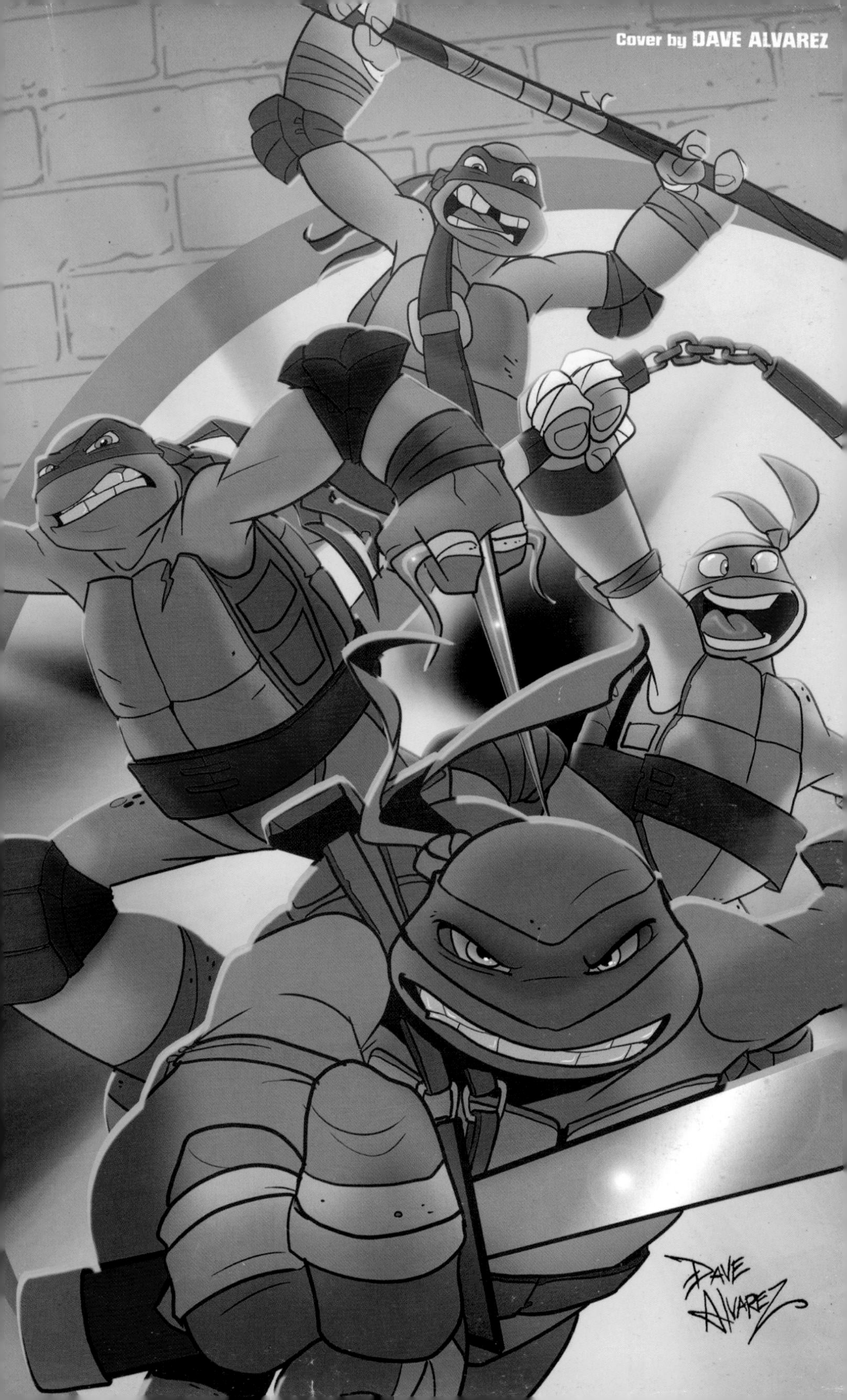
DAVE
ALVAREZ
Cover by **DAVE ALVAREZ**

Cover by **DARIO BRIZUELA**

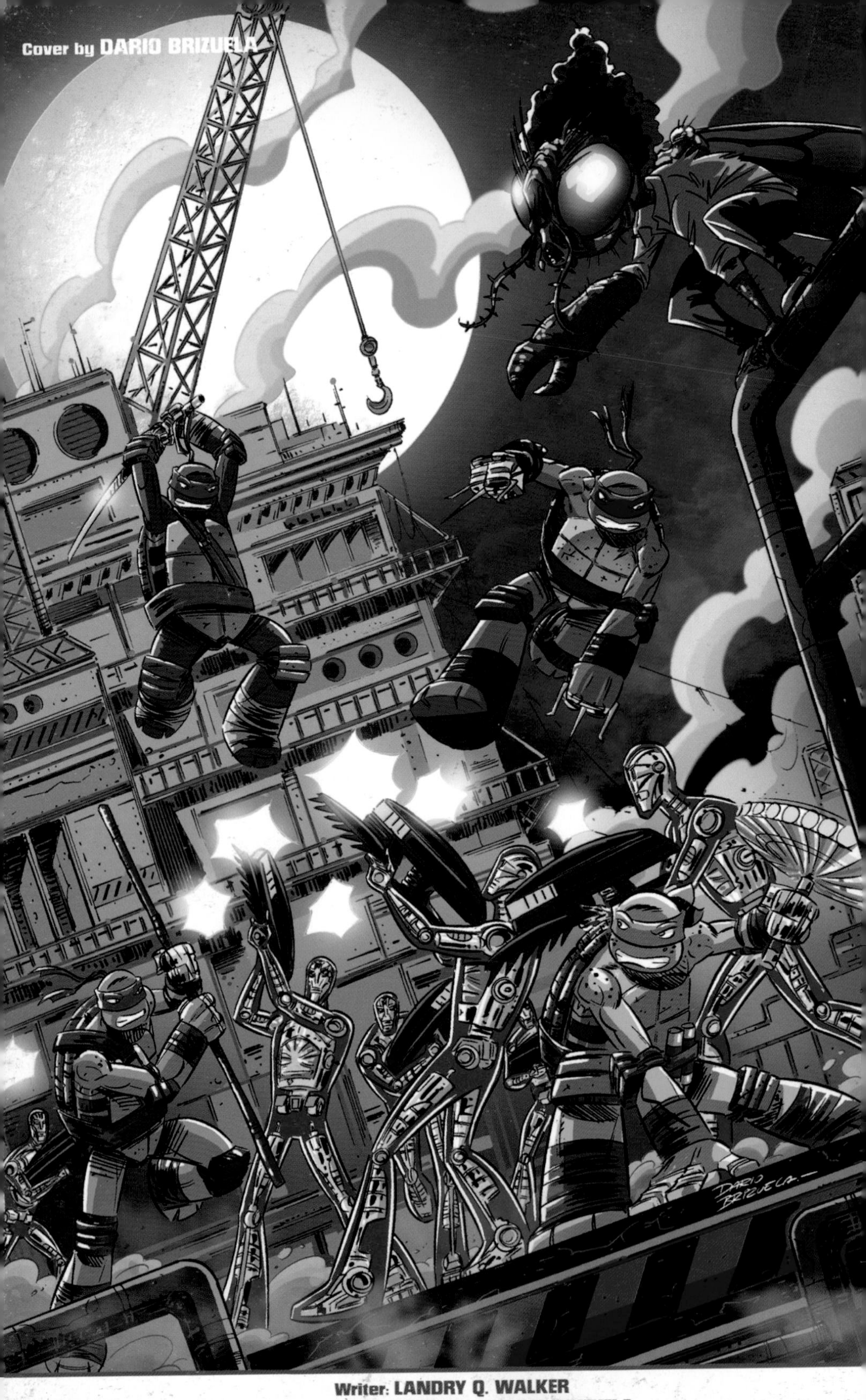
DARIO BRIZUELA

Writer: LANDRY Q. WALKER
Artists: CHAD THOMAS & DARIO BRIZUELA

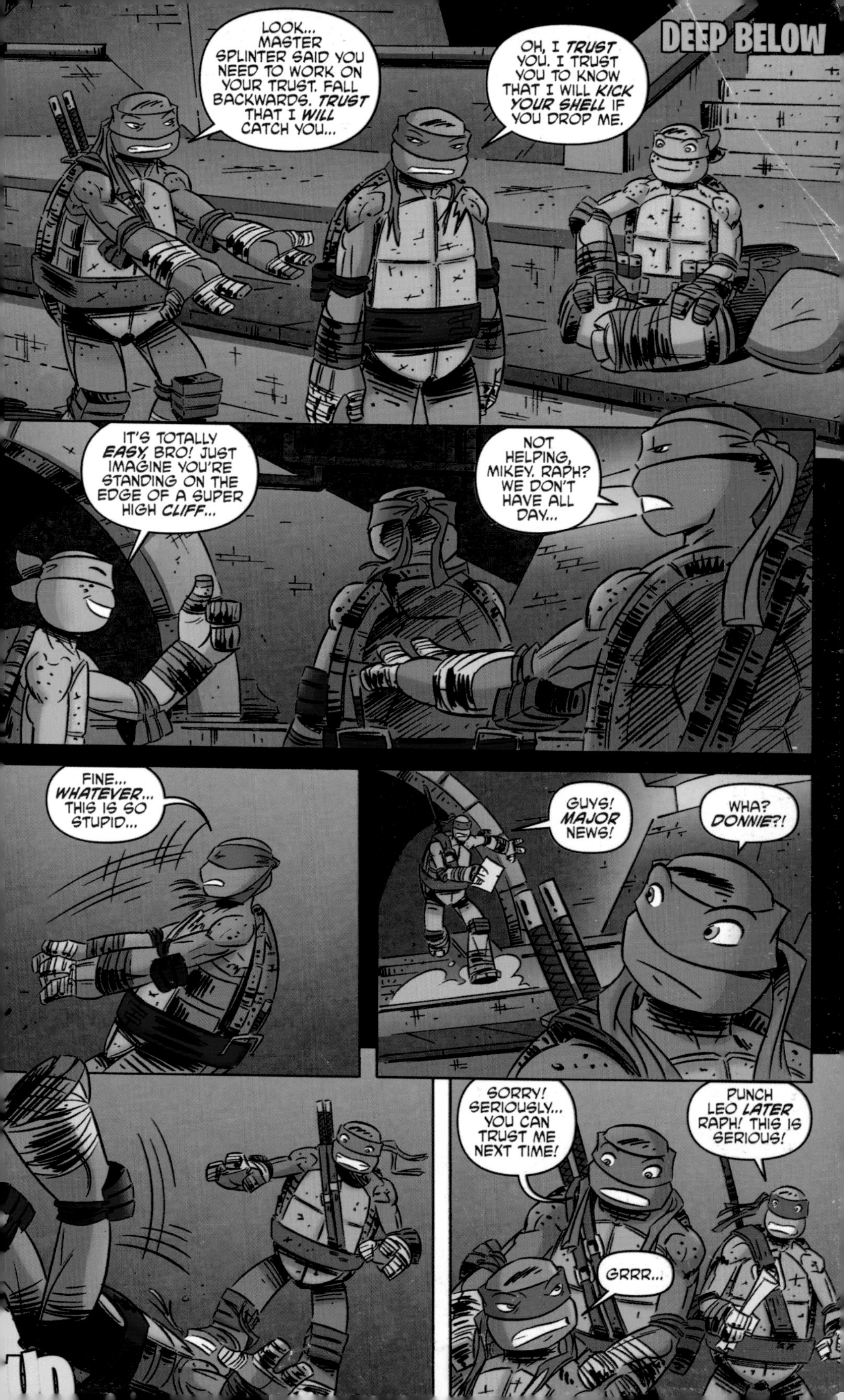
DEEP BELOW
LOOK... MASTER SPLINTER SAID YOU NEED TO WORK ON YOUR TRUST. FALL BACKWARDS. TRUST THAT I WILL CATCH YOU...
OH, I TRUST YOU. I TRUST YOU TO KNOW THAT I WILL KICK YOUR SHELL IF YOU DROP ME.
IT'S TOTALLY EASY, BRO! JUST IMAGINE YOU'RE STANDING ON THE EDGE OF A SUPER HIGH CLIFF...
NOT HELPING, MIKEY. RAPH? WE DON'T HAVE ALL DAY...
FINE... WHATEVER... THIS IS SO STUPID...
GUYS! MAJOR NEWS!
WHA? DONNIE?!
SORRY! SERIOUSLY... YOU CAN TRUST ME NEXT TIME!
PUNCH LEO LATER RAPH! THIS IS SERIOUS!
GRRR...

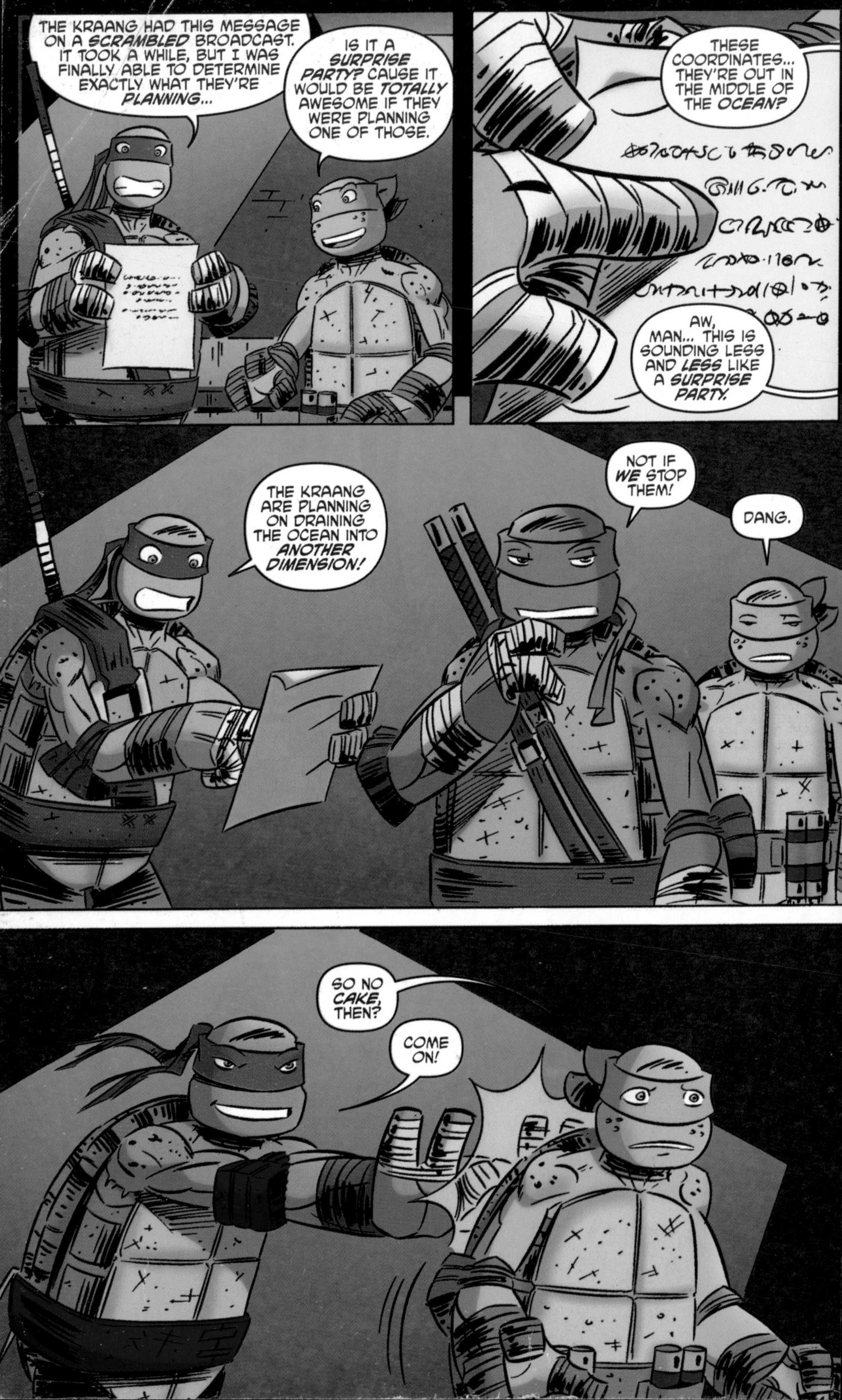
THE KRAANG HAD THIS MESSAGE ON A SCRAMBLED BROADCAST. IT TOOK A WHILE, BUT I WAS FINALLY ABLE TO DETERMINE EXACTLY WHAT THEY'RE PLANNING...
IS IT A SURPRISE PARTY? CAUSE IT WOULD BE TOTALLY AWESOME IF THEY WERE PLANNING ONE OF THOSE.
THESE COORDINATES... THEY'RE OUT IN THE MIDDLE OF THE OCEAN?
AW, MAN... THIS IS SOUNDING LESS AND LESS LIKE A SURPRISE PARTY.
THE KRAANG ARE PLANNING ON DRAINING THE OCEAN INTO ANOTHER DIMENSION!
NOT IF WE STOP THEM!
DANG.
SO NO CAKE, THEN?
COME ON!

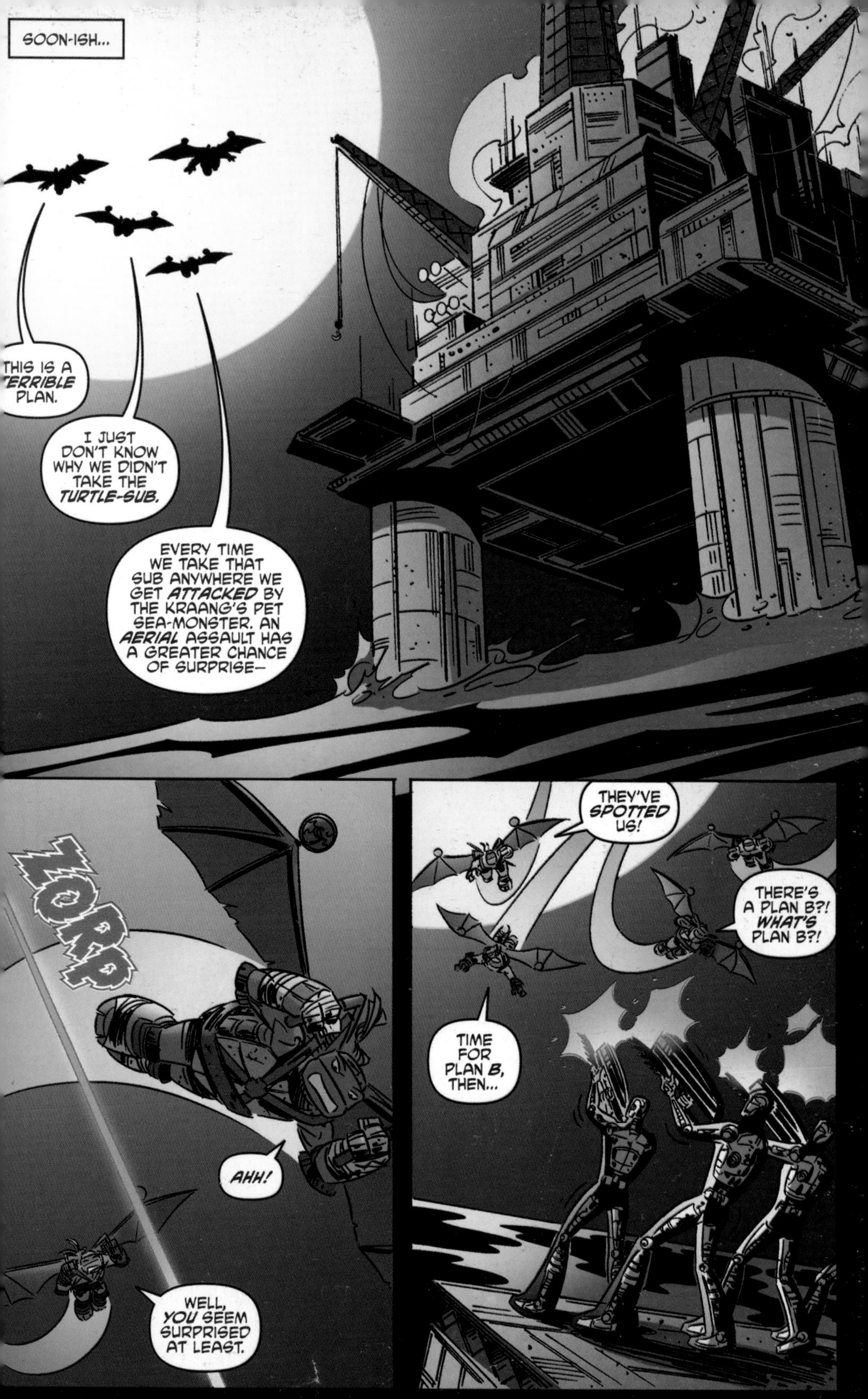
SOON-ISH...
THIS IS A ERRIBLE PLAN.
I JUST DON'T KNOW WHY WE DIDN'T TAKE THE TURTLE-SUB.
EVERY TIME WE TAKE THAT SUB ANYWHERE WE GET ATTACKED BY THE KRAANG'S PET SEA-MONSTER. AN AERIAL ASSAULT HAS A GREATER CHANCE OF SURPRISE–
ZORP
AHH!
WELL, YOU SEEM SURPRISED AT LEAST.
THEY'VE SPOTTED US!
THERE'S A PLAN B?! WHAT'S PLAN B?!
TIME FOR PLAN B, THEN...

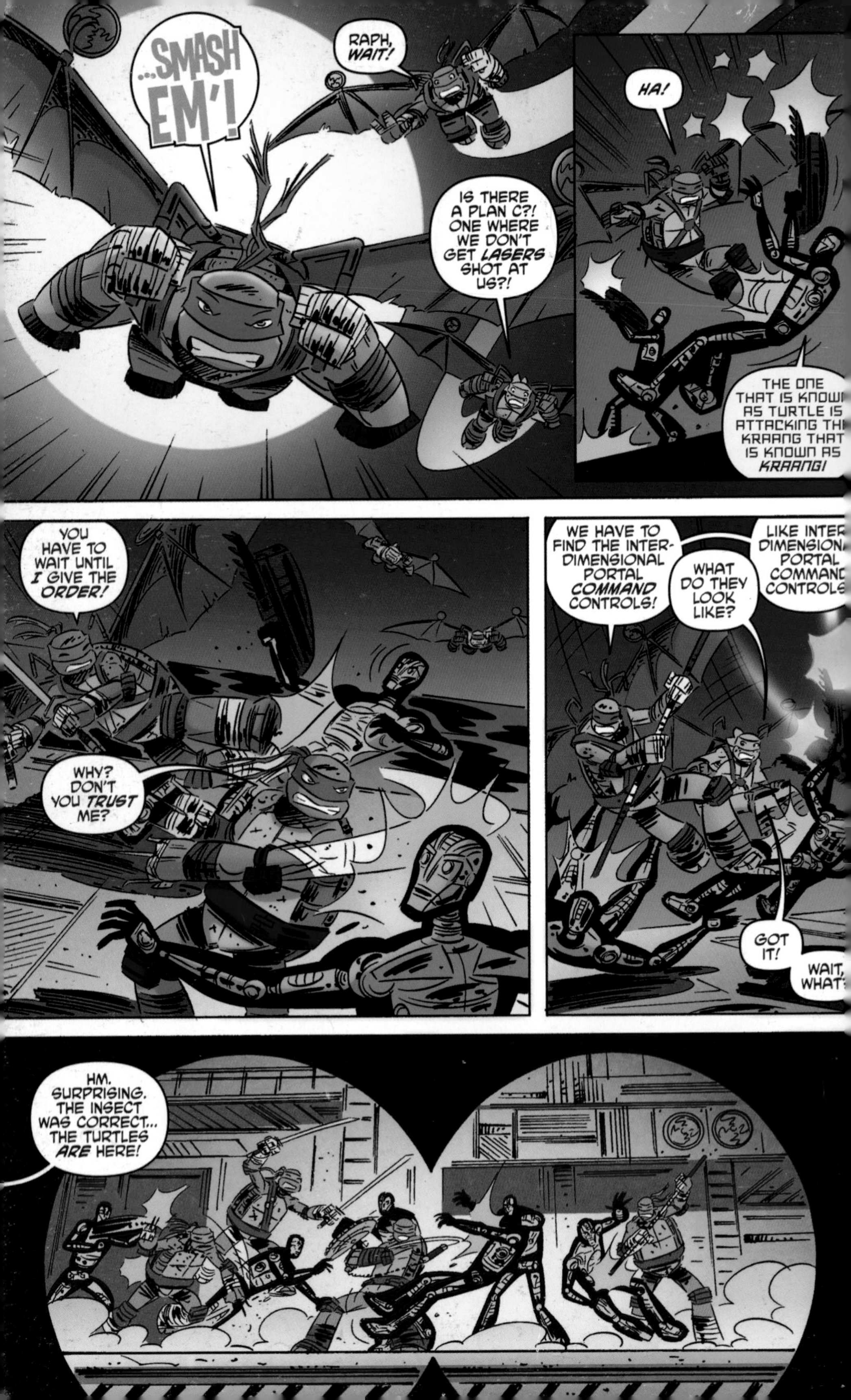
...SMASH EM'!
RAPH, WAIT!
IS THERE A PLAN C?! ONE WHERE WE DON'T GET LASERS SHOT AT US?!
HA!
THE ONE THAT IS KNOWN AS TURTLE IS ATTACKING THE KRAANG THAT IS KNOWN AS KRAANG!
YOU HAVE TO WAIT UNTIL I GIVE THE ORDER!
WHY? DON'T YOU TRUST ME?
WE HAVE TO FIND THE INTER-DIMENSIONAL PORTAL COMMAND CONTROLS!
WHAT DO THEY LOOK LIKE?
LIKE INTER-DIMENSIONAL PORTAL COMMAND CONTROLS!
GOT IT!
WAIT, WHAT?
HM. SURPRISING. THE INSECT WAS CORRECT... THE TURTLES ARE HERE!

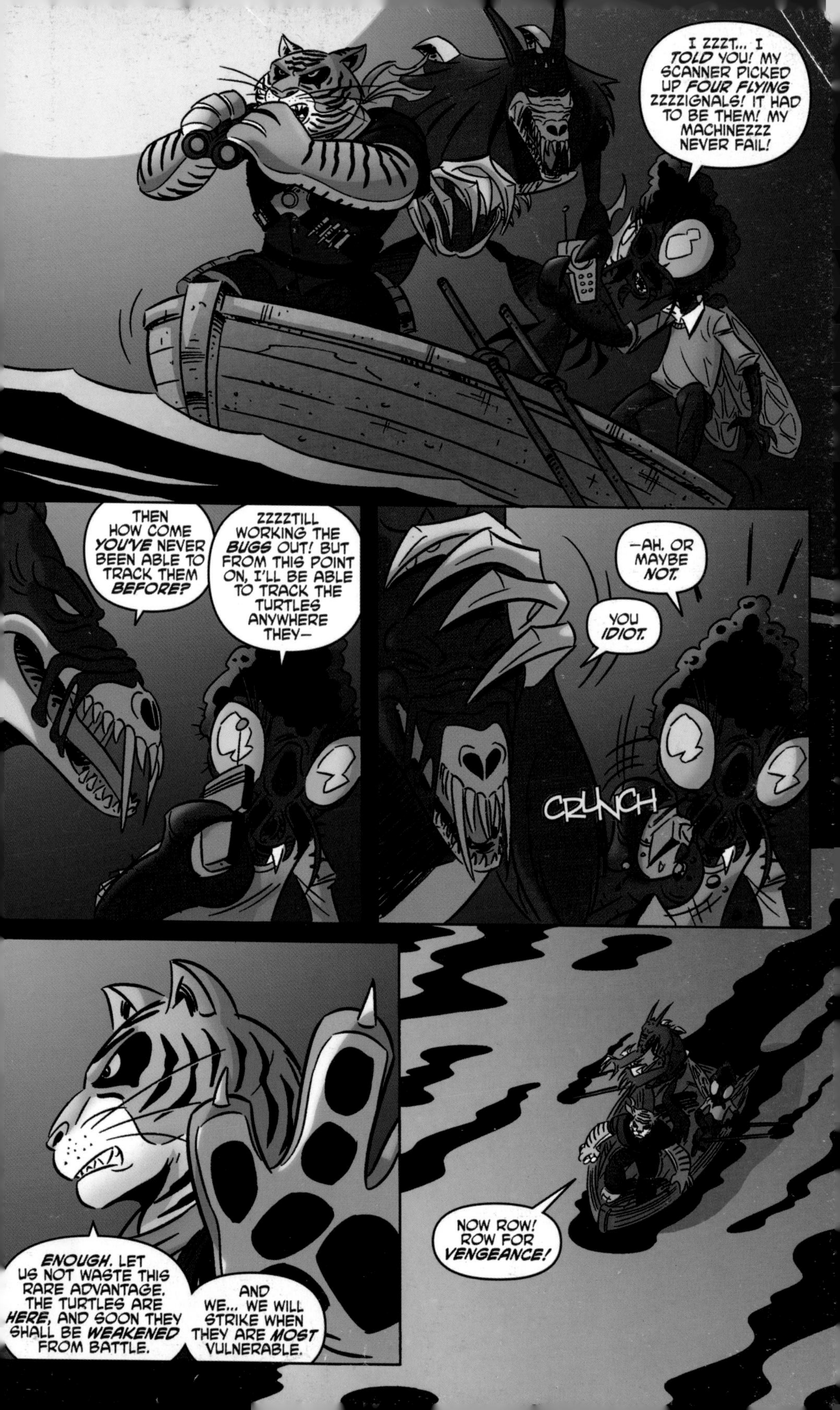

I ZZZT... I TOLD YOU! MY SCANNER PICKED UP FOUR FLYING ZZZIGNALS! IT HAD TO BE THEM! MY MACHINEZZZ NEVER FAIL!
THEN HOW COME YOU'VE NEVER BEEN ABLE TO TRACK THEM BEFORE?
ZZZZTILL WORKING THE BUGS OUT! BUT FROM THIS POINT ON, I'LL BE ABLE TO TRACK THE TURTLES ANYWHERE THEY—
—AH, OR MAYBE NOT.
YOU IDIOT.
CRUNCH
ENOUGH. LET US NOT WASTE THIS RARE ADVANTAGE. THE TURTLES ARE HERE, AND SOON THEY SHALL BE WEAKENED FROM BATTLE.
AND WE... WE WILL STRIKE WHEN THEY ARE MOST VULNERABLE.
NOW ROW! ROW FOR VENGEANCE!

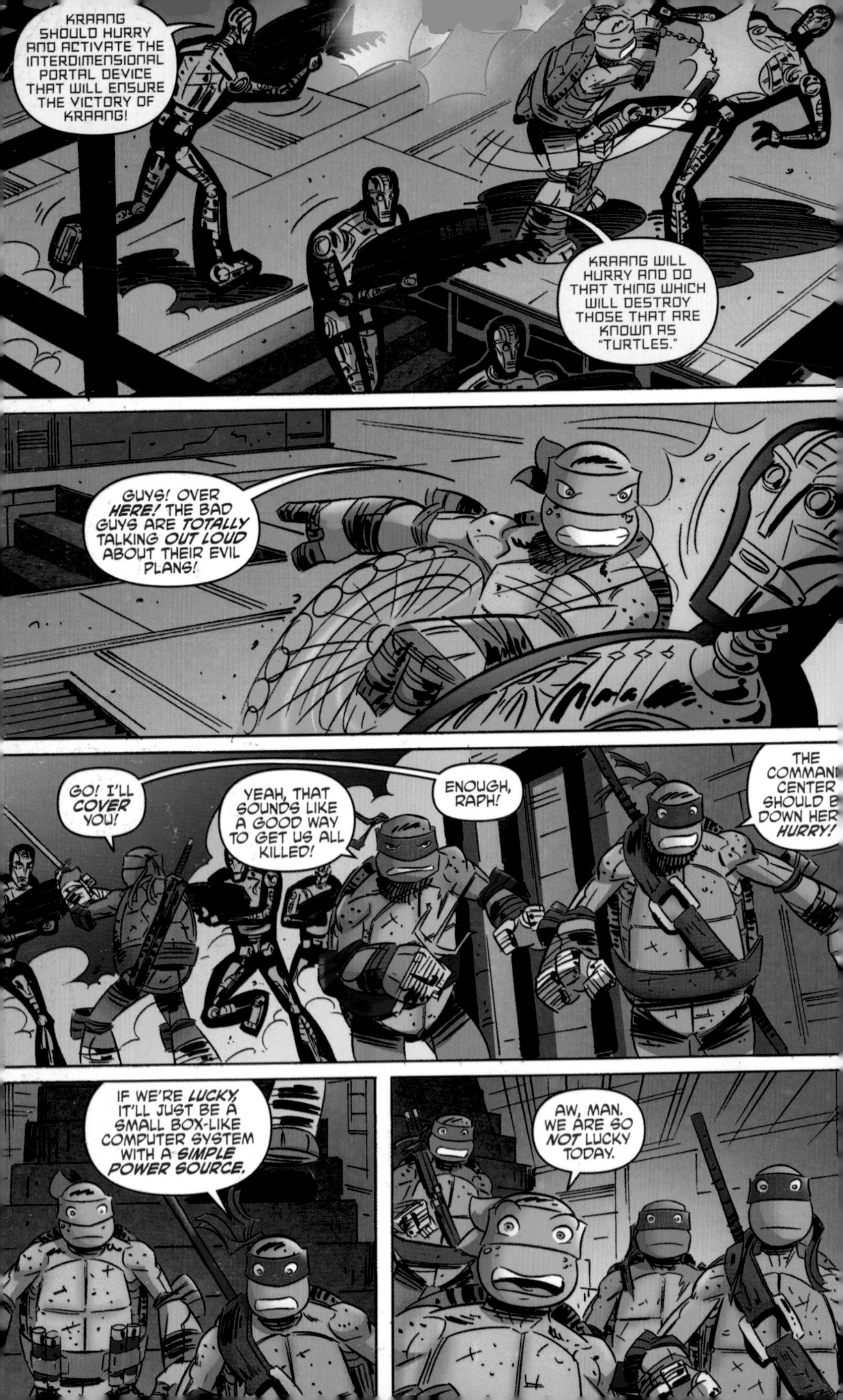

KRAANG SHOULD HURRY AND ACTIVATE THE INTERDIMENSIONAL PORTAL DEVICE THAT WILL ENSURE THE VICTORY OF KRAANG!
KRAANG WILL HURRY AND DO THAT THING WHICH WILL DESTROY THOSE THAT ARE KNOWN AS "TURTLES."
GUYS! OVER HERE! THE BAD GUYS ARE TOTALLY TALKING OUT LOUD ABOUT THEIR EVIL PLANS!
GO! I'LL COVER YOU!
YEAH, THAT SOUNDS LIKE A GOOD WAY TO GET US ALL KILLED!
ENOUGH, RAPH!
THE COMMAN CENTER SHOULD B DOWN HER HURRY!
IF WE'RE LUCKY, IT'LL JUST BE A SMALL BOX-LIKE COMPUTER SYSTEM WITH A SIMPLE POWER SOURCE.
AW, MAN. WE ARE SO NOT LUCKY TODAY.

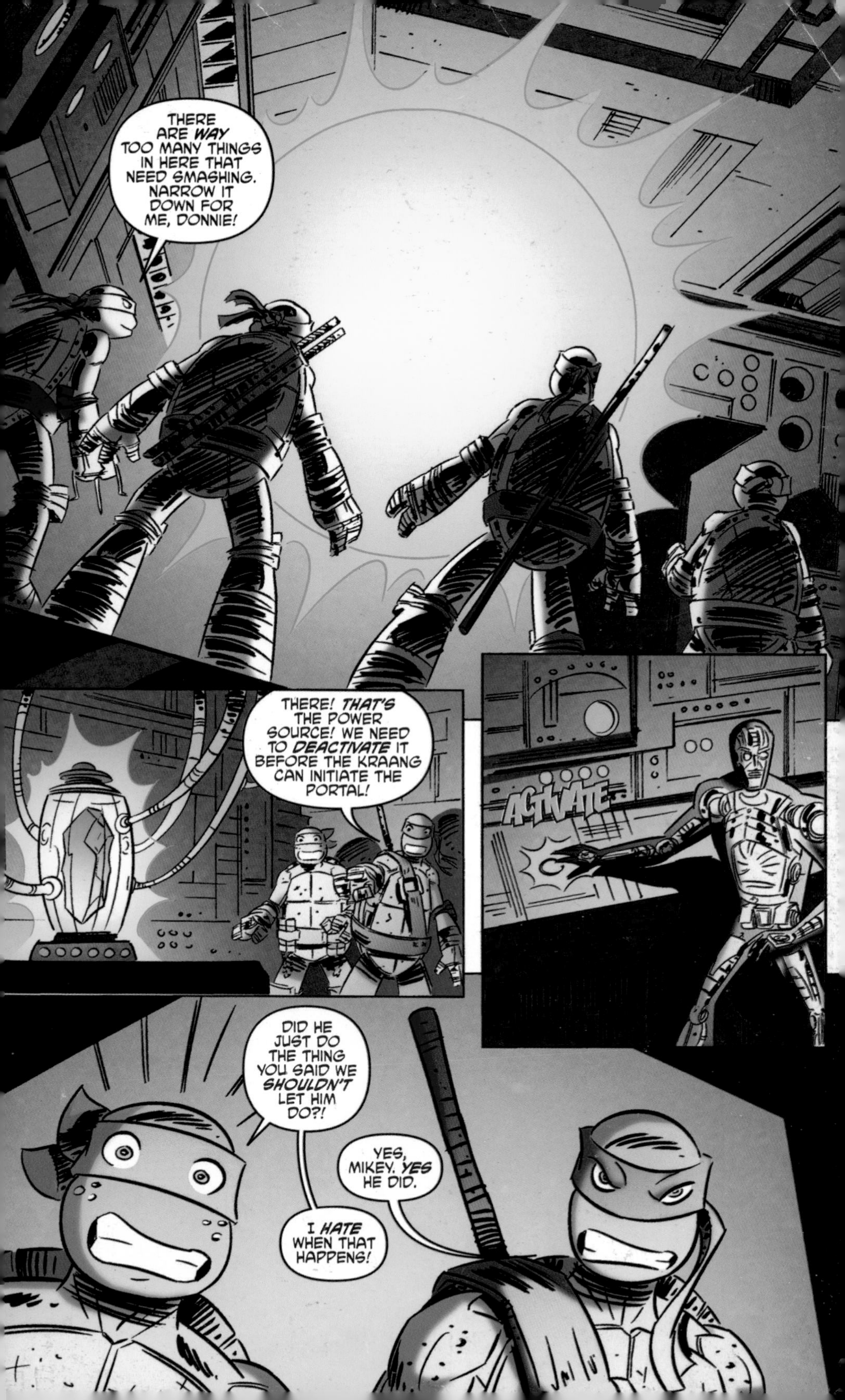
THERE ARE *WAY* TOO MANY THINGS IN HERE THAT NEED SMASHING. NARROW IT DOWN FOR ME, DONNIE!
THERE! *THAT'S* THE POWER SOURCE! WE NEED TO *DEACTIVATE* IT BEFORE THE KRAANG CAN INITIATE THE PORTAL!
ACTIVATE
DID HE JUST DO THE THING YOU SAID WE *SHOULDN'T* LET HIM DO?!
YES, MIKEY. *YES* HE DID.
I *HATE* WHEN THAT HAPPENS!

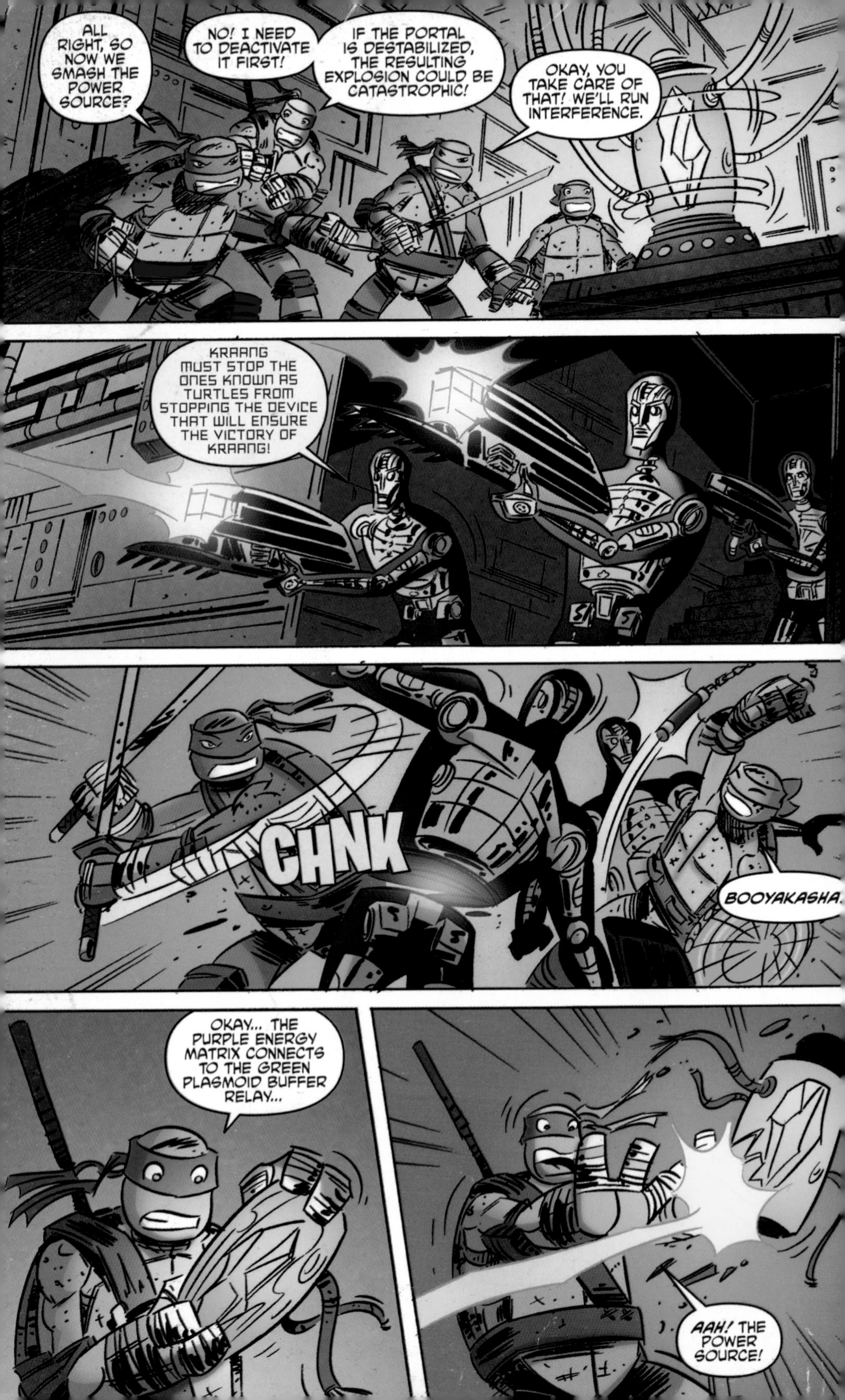
ALL RIGHT, SO NOW WE SMASH THE POWER SOURCE?
NO! I NEED TO DEACTIVATE IT FIRST!
IF THE PORTAL IS DESTABILIZED, THE RESULTING EXPLOSION COULD BE CATASTROPHIC!
OKAY, YOU TAKE CARE OF THAT! WE'LL RUN INTERFERENCE.
KRAANG MUST STOP THE ONES KNOWN AS TURTLES FROM STOPPING THE DEVICE THAT WILL ENSURE THE VICTORY OF KRAANG!
CHNK
BOOYAKASHA!
OKAY... THE PURPLE ENERGY MATRIX CONNECTS TO THE GREEN PLASMOID BUFFER RELAY...
AAH! THE POWER SOURCE!

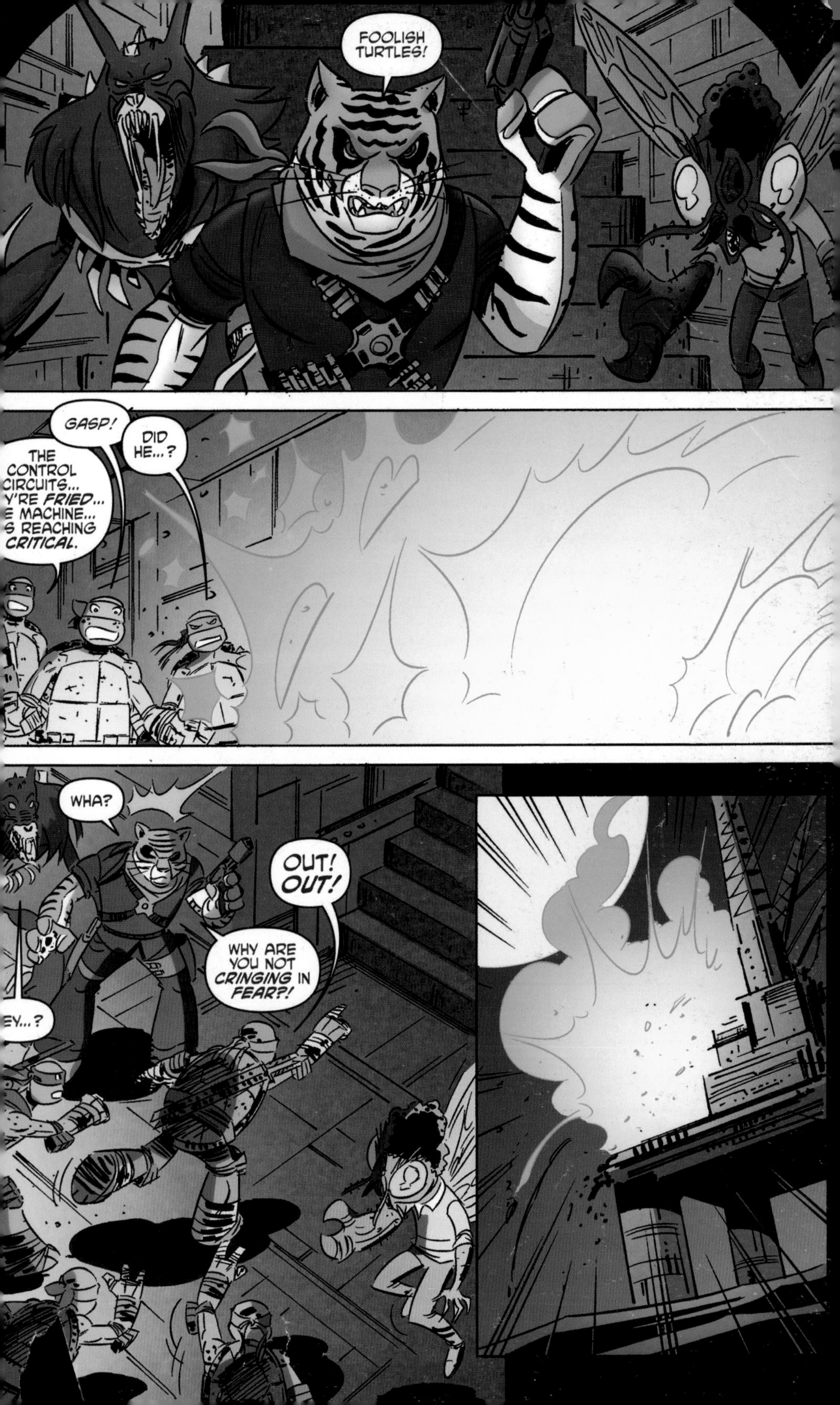

FOOLISH TURTLES!
GASP!
DID HE...?
THE CONTROL CIRCUITS... Y'RE FRIED... E MACHINE... S REACHING CRITICAL.
WHA?
OUT! OUT!
WHY ARE YOU NOT CRINGING IN FEAR?!
EY...?

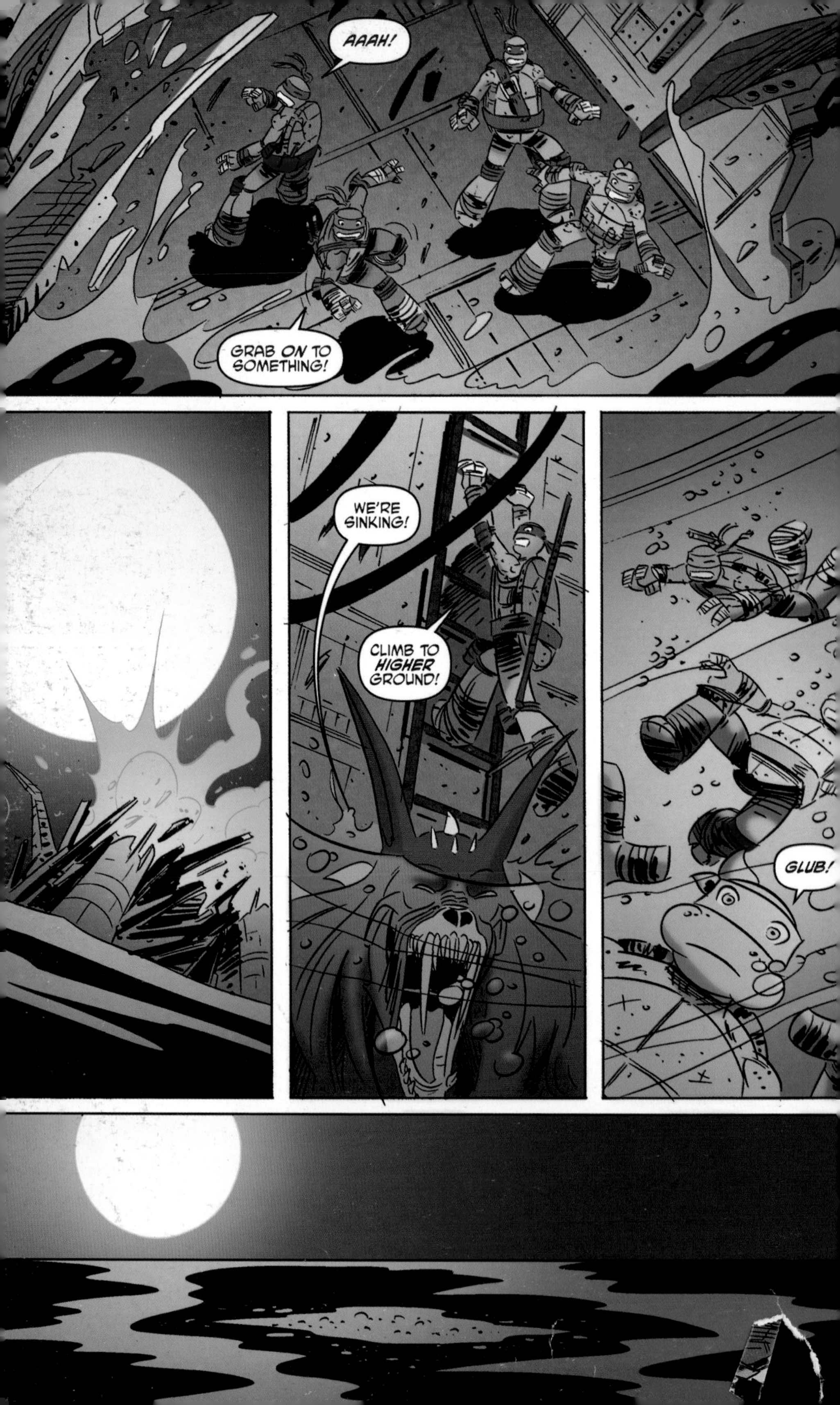
AAAH!
GRAB ON TO SOMETHING!
WE'RE SINKING!
CLIMB TO HIGHER GROUND!
GLUB!

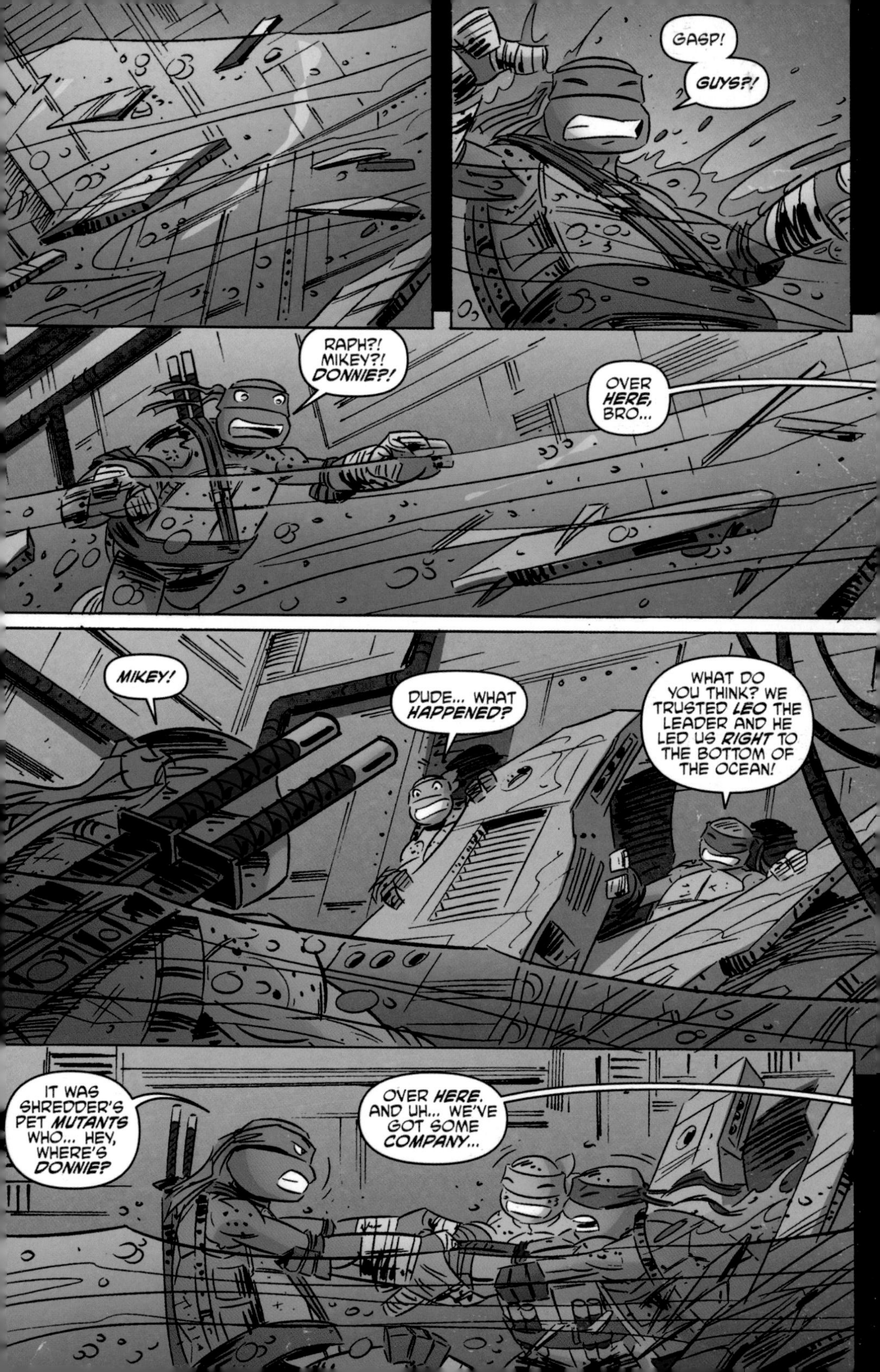
GASP!
GUYS?!
RAPH?! MIKEY?! DONNIE?!
OVER HERE, BRO...
MIKEY!
DUDE... WHAT HAPPENED?
WHAT DO YOU THINK? WE TRUSTED LEO THE LEADER AND HE LED US RIGHT TO THE BOTTOM OF THE OCEAN!
IT WAS SHREDDER'S PET MUTANTS WHO... HEY, WHERE'S DONNIE?
OVER HERE. AND UH... WE'VE GOT SOME COMPANY...

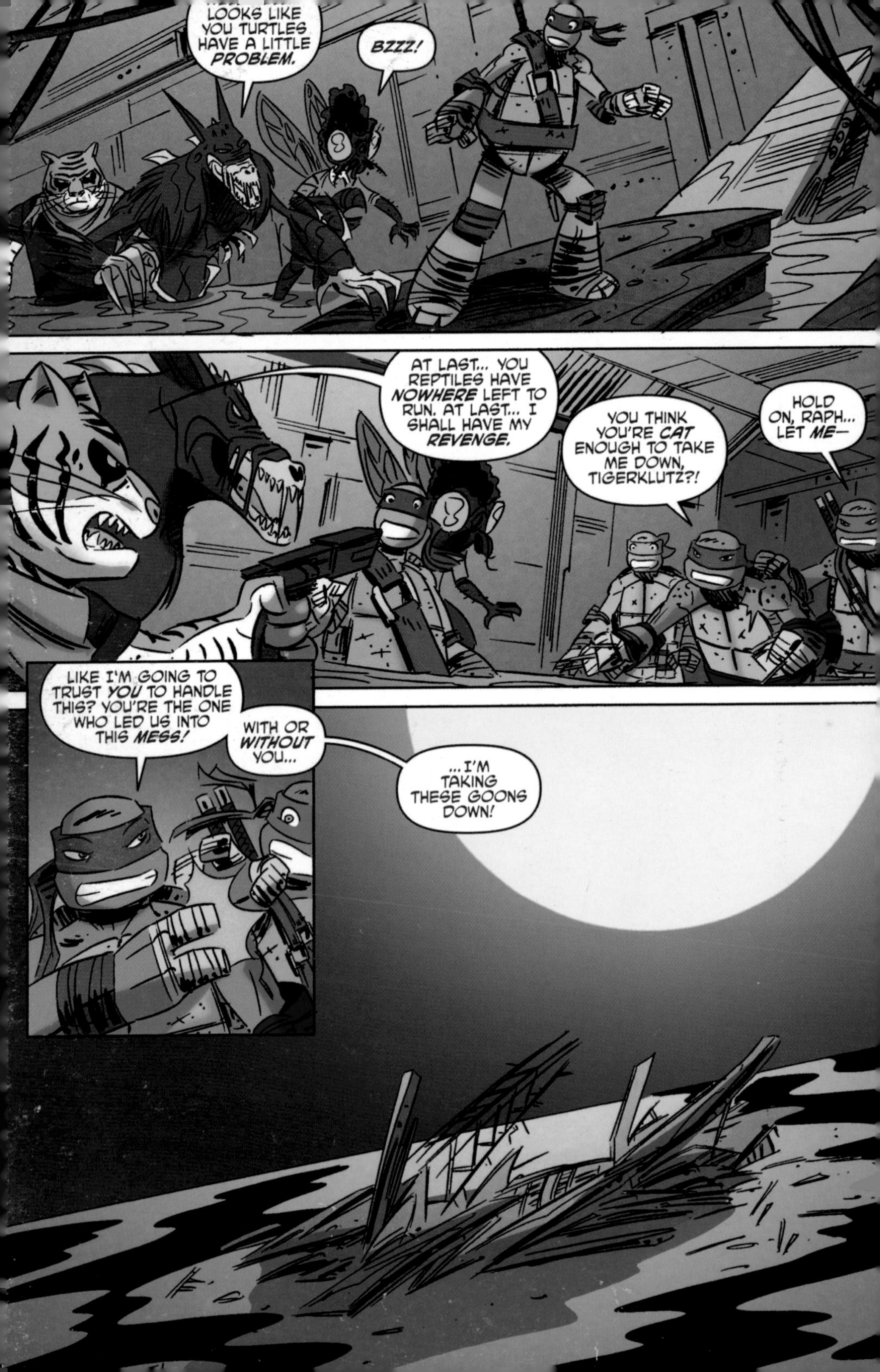
LOOKS LIKE YOU TURTLES HAVE A LITTLE *PROBLEM.*
BZZZ!
AT LAST... YOU REPTILES HAVE *NOWHERE* LEFT TO RUN. AT LAST... I SHALL HAVE MY *REVENGE.*
YOU THINK YOU'RE *CAT* ENOUGH TO TAKE ME DOWN, TIGERKLUTZ?!
HOLD ON, RAPH... LET *ME*—
LIKE I'M GOING TO TRUST *YOU* TO HANDLE THIS? YOU'RE THE ONE WHO LED US INTO THIS *MESS!*
WITH OR *WITHOUT* YOU...
...I'M TAKING THESE GOONS DOWN!

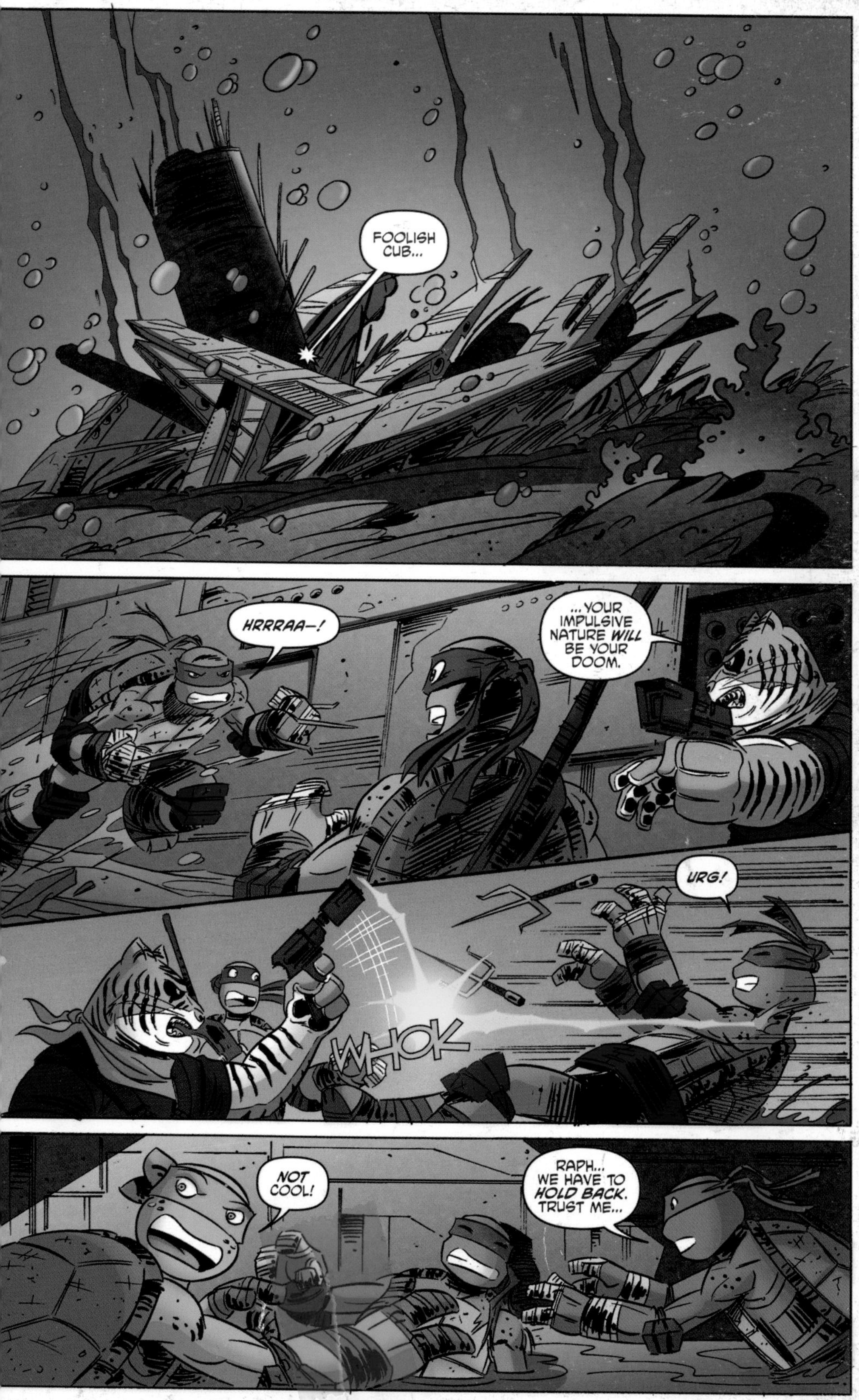
FOOLISH CUB...
HRRRAA--!
...YOUR IMPULSIVE NATURE *WILL* BE YOUR DOOM.
URG!
WHOK
NOT COOL!
RAPH... WE HAVE TO *HOLD BACK*. TRUST ME...

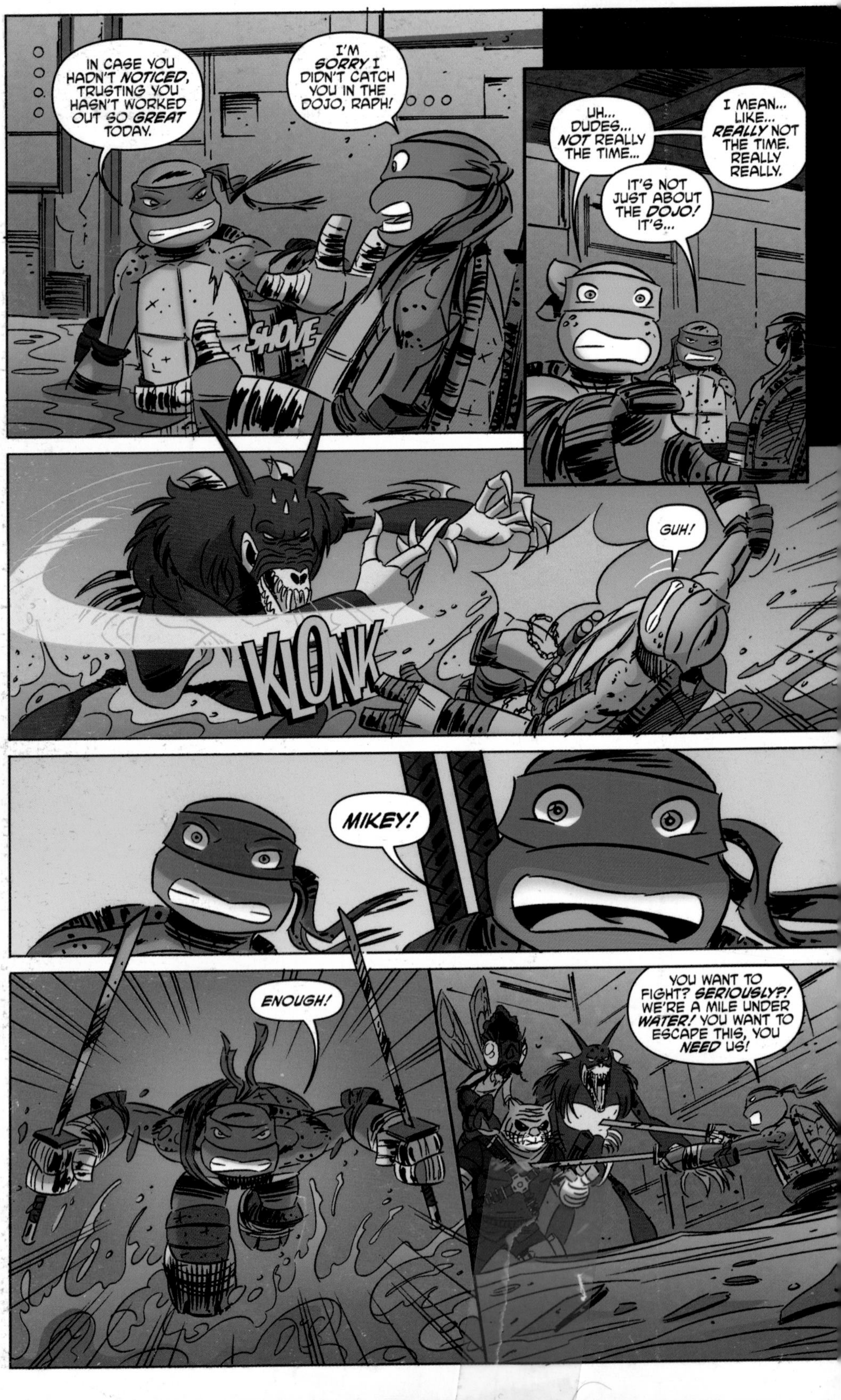
IN CASE YOU HADN'T *NOTICED*, TRUSTING YOU HASN'T WORKED OUT SO *GREAT* TODAY.
I'M *SORRY* I DIDN'T CATCH YOU IN THE DOJO, RAPH!
SHOVE
UH... DUDES... *NOT* REALLY THE TIME...
I MEAN... LIKE... *REALLY* NOT THE TIME. REALLY REALLY.
IT'S NOT JUST ABOUT THE *DOJO!* IT'S...
GUH!
KLONK
MIKEY!
ENOUGH!
YOU WANT TO FIGHT? *SERIOUSLY?!* WE'RE A MILE UNDER *WATER!* YOU WANT TO ESCAPE THIS, YOU *NEED* US!

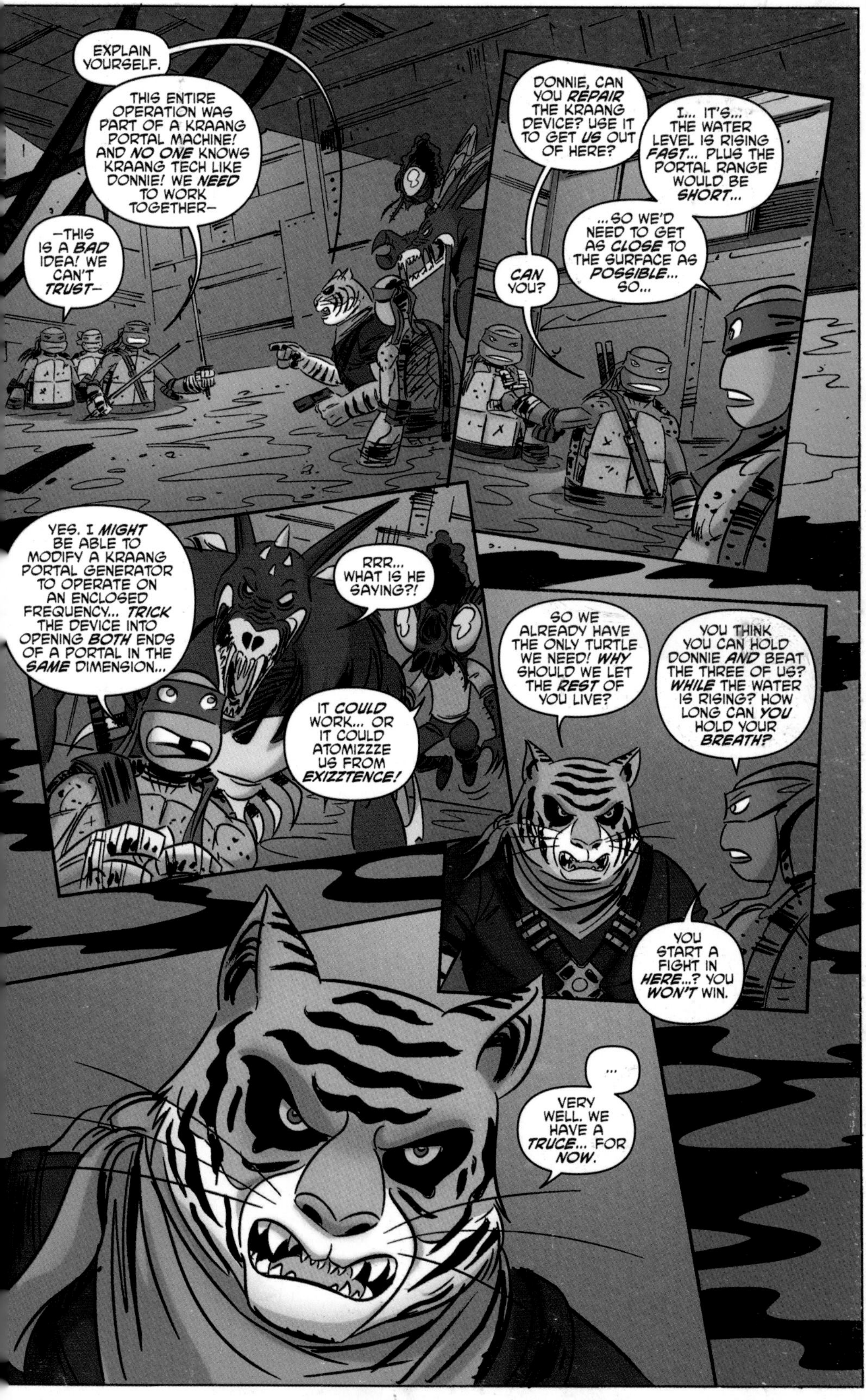
EXPLAIN YOURSELF.
THIS ENTIRE OPERATION WAS PART OF A KRAANG PORTAL MACHINE! AND NO ONE KNOWS KRAANG TECH LIKE DONNIE! WE NEED TO WORK TOGETHER—
—THIS IS A BAD IDEA! WE CAN'T TRUST—
DONNIE, CAN YOU REPAIR THE KRAANG DEVICE? USE IT TO GET US OUT OF HERE?
I... IT'S... THE WATER LEVEL IS RISING FAST... PLUS THE PORTAL RANGE WOULD BE SHORT...
...SO WE'D NEED TO GET AS CLOSE TO THE SURFACE AS POSSIBLE... SO...
CAN YOU?
YES. I MIGHT BE ABLE TO MODIFY A KRAANG PORTAL GENERATOR TO OPERATE ON AN ENCLOSED FREQUENCY... TRICK THE DEVICE INTO OPENING BOTH ENDS OF A PORTAL IN THE SAME DIMENSION...
RRR... WHAT IS HE SAYING?!
IT COULD WORK... OR IT COULD ATOMIZZZE US FROM EXIZZZTENCE!
SO WE ALREADY HAVE THE ONLY TURTLE WE NEED! WHY SHOULD WE LET THE REST OF YOU LIVE?
YOU THINK YOU CAN HOLD DONNIE AND BEAT THE THREE OF US? WHILE THE WATER IS RISING? HOW LONG CAN YOU HOLD YOUR BREATH?
YOU START A FIGHT IN HERE...? YOU WON'T WIN.
...
VERY WELL. WE HAVE A TRUCE... FOR NOW.

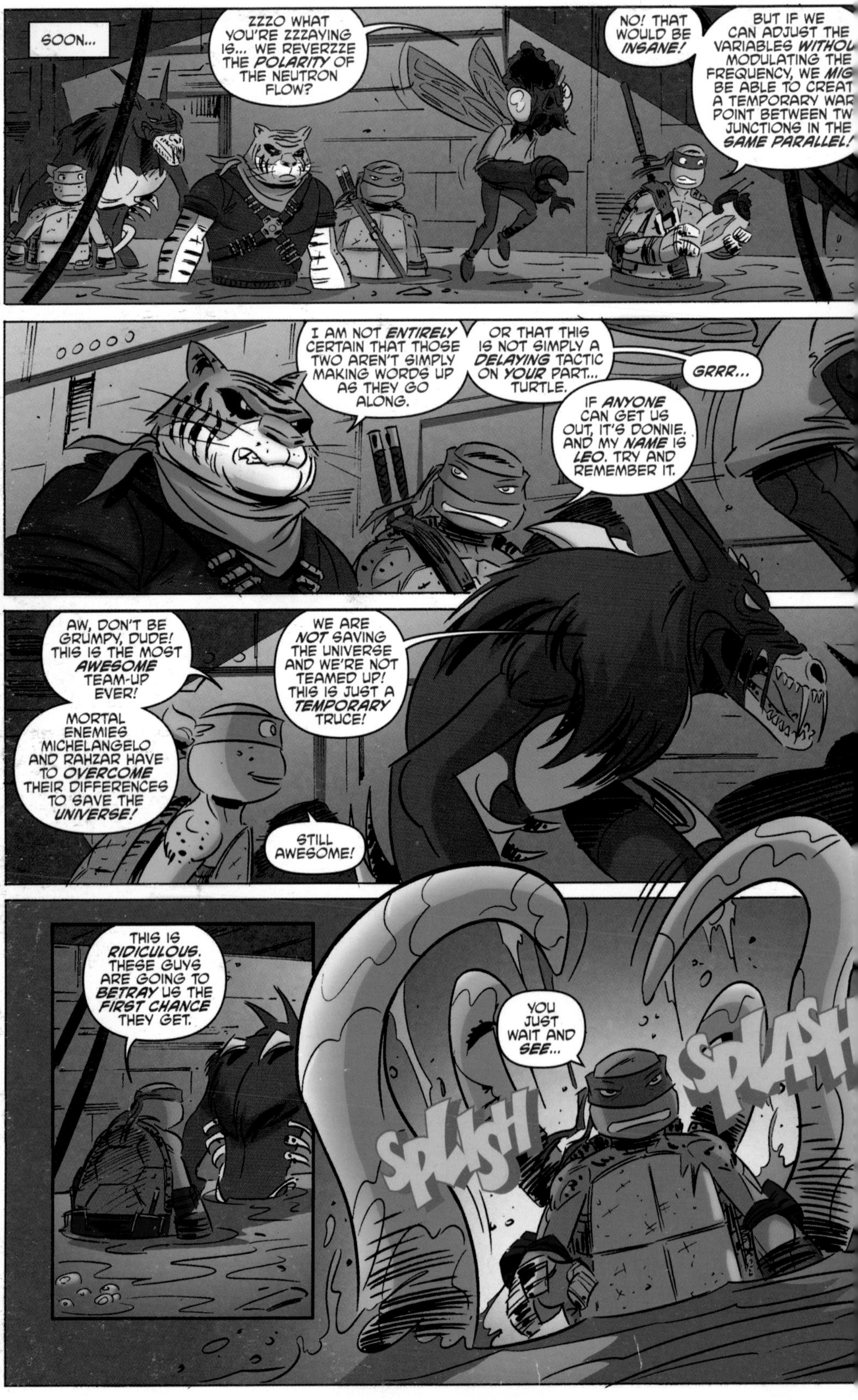
SOON...
ZZZO WHAT YOU'RE ZZZAYING IS... WE REVERZZE THE POLARITY OF THE NEUTRON FLOW?
NO! THAT WOULD BE INSANE!
BUT IF WE CAN ADJUST THE VARIABLES WITHOU MODULATING THE FREQUENCY, WE MIG BE ABLE TO CREAT A TEMPORARY WAR POINT BETWEEN TW JUNCTIONS IN THE SAME PARALLEL!
I AM NOT ENTIRELY CERTAIN THAT THOSE TWO AREN'T SIMPLY MAKING WORDS UP AS THEY GO ALONG.
OR THAT THIS IS NOT SIMPLY A DELAYING TACTIC ON YOUR PART... TURTLE.
GRRR...
IF ANYONE CAN GET US OUT, IT'S DONNIE. AND MY NAME IS LEO. TRY AND REMEMBER IT.
AW, DON'T BE GRUMPY, DUDE! THIS IS THE MOST AWESOME TEAM-UP EVER!
MORTAL ENEMIES MICHELANGELO AND RAHZAR HAVE TO OVERCOME THEIR DIFFERENCES TO SAVE THE UNIVERSE!
WE ARE NOT SAVING THE UNIVERSE AND WE'RE NOT TEAMED UP! THIS IS JUST A TEMPORARY TRUCE!
STILL AWESOME!
THIS IS RIDICULOUS. THESE GUYS ARE GOING TO BETRAY US THE FIRST CHANCE THEY GET.
YOU JUST WAIT AND SEE...
SPLISH
SPLASH

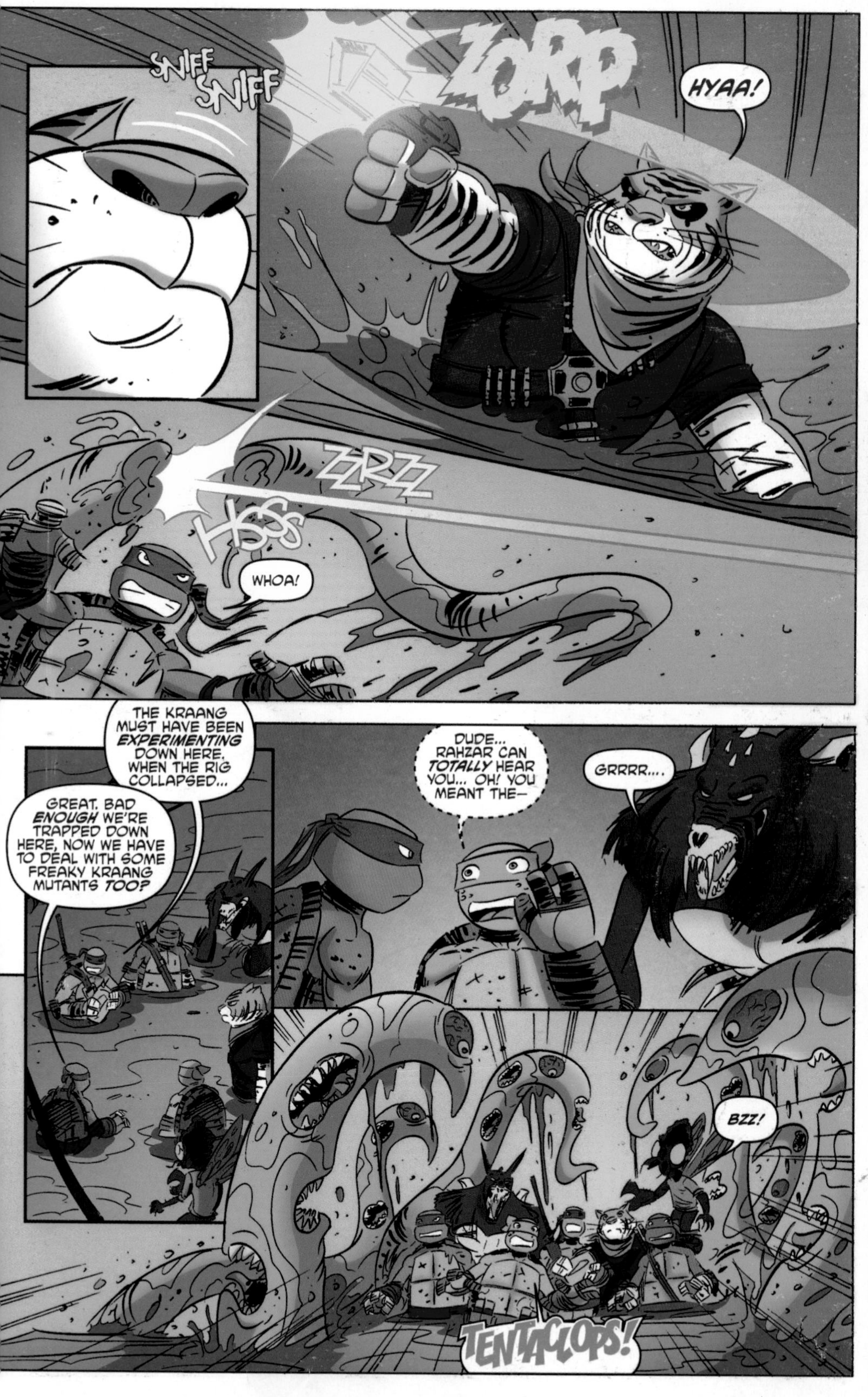
SNIFF SNIFF
ZORP
HYAA!
ZZRZZ
HSSS
WHOA!
THE KRAANG MUST HAVE BEEN EXPERIMENTING DOWN HERE. WHEN THE RIG COLLAPSED...
GREAT. BAD ENOUGH WE'RE TRAPPED DOWN HERE, NOW WE HAVE TO DEAL WITH SOME FREAKY KRAANG MUTANTS TOO?
DUDE... RAHZAR CAN TOTALLY HEAR YOU... OH! YOU MEANT THE–
GRRRR....
BZZ!
TENTACLOPS!

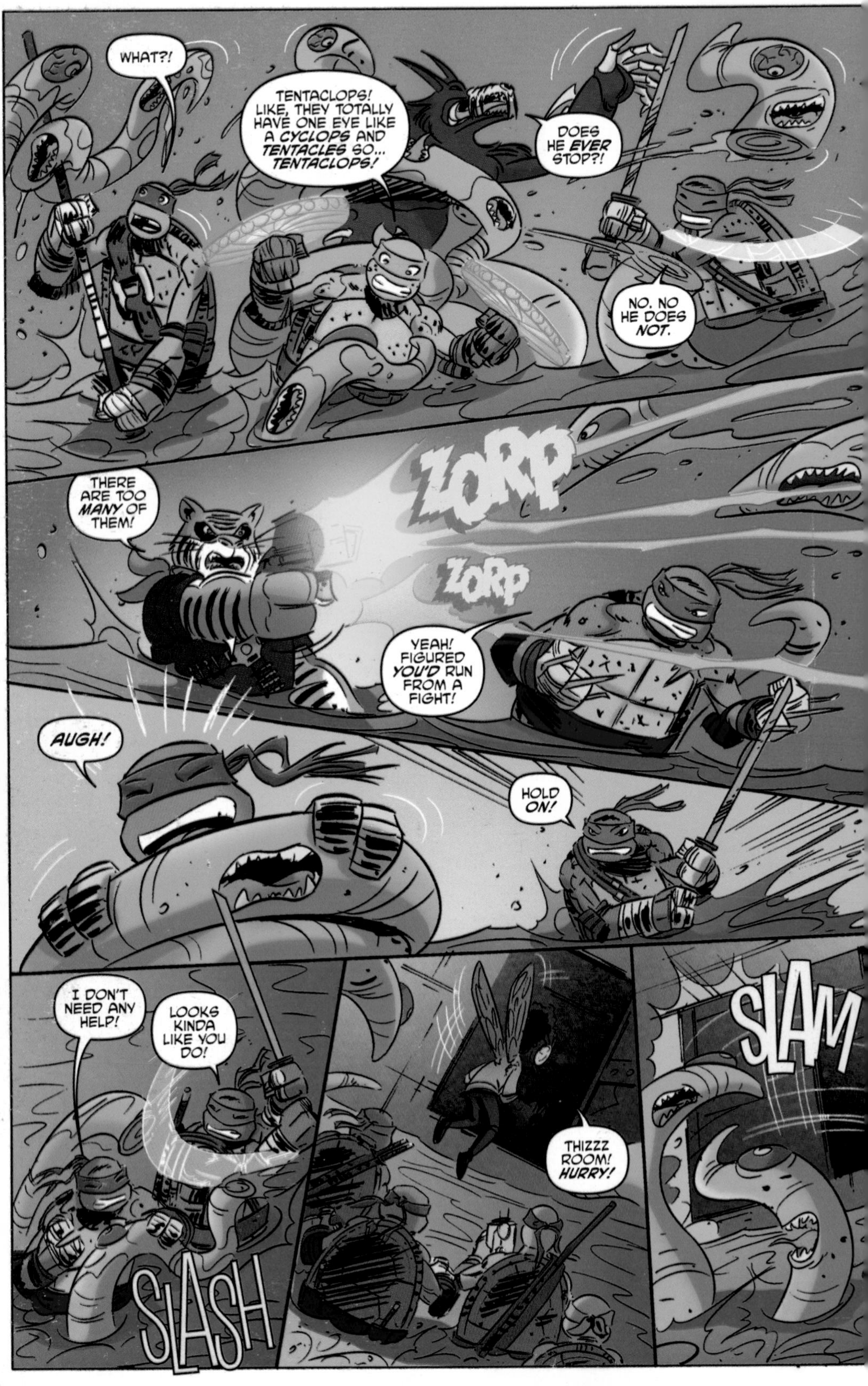
WHAT?!
TENTACLOPS! LIKE, THEY TOTALLY HAVE ONE EYE LIKE A CYCLOPS AND TENTACLES SO... TENTACLOPS!
DOES HE EVER STOP?!
NO. NO HE DOES NOT.
ZORP
THERE ARE TOO MANY OF THEM!
ZORP
YEAH! FIGURED YOU'D RUN FROM A FIGHT!
AUGH!
HOLD ON!
I DON'T NEED ANY HELP!
LOOKS KINDA LIKE YOU DO!
SLASH
THIZZZ ROOM! HURRY!
SLAM

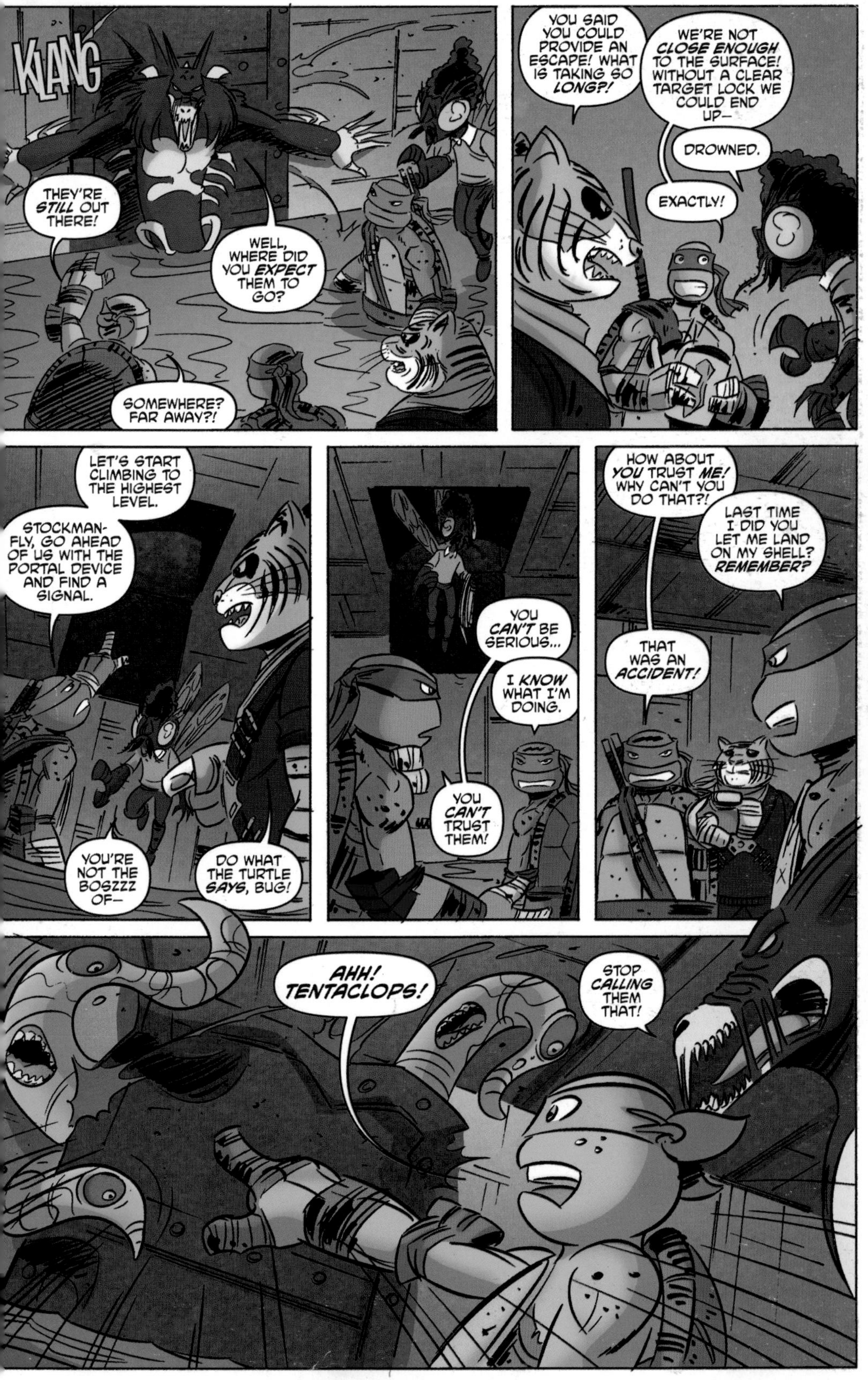
KLANG
THEY'RE STILL OUT THERE!
WELL, WHERE DID YOU EXPECT THEM TO GO?
SOMEWHERE? FAR AWAY?!
YOU SAID YOU COULD PROVIDE AN ESCAPE! WHAT IS TAKING SO LONG?!
WE'RE NOT CLOSE ENOUGH TO THE SURFACE! WITHOUT A CLEAR TARGET LOCK WE COULD END UP—
DROWNED.
EXACTLY!
LET'S START CLIMBING TO THE HIGHEST LEVEL.
STOCKMAN-FLY, GO AHEAD OF US WITH THE PORTAL DEVICE AND FIND A SIGNAL.
YOU'RE NOT THE BOSZZZ OF—
DO WHAT THE TURTLE SAYS, BUG!
YOU CAN'T BE SERIOUS...
I KNOW WHAT I'M DOING.
YOU CAN'T TRUST THEM!
HOW ABOUT YOU TRUST ME! WHY CAN'T YOU DO THAT?!
LAST TIME I DID YOU LET ME LAND ON MY SHELL? REMEMBER?
THAT WAS AN ACCIDENT!
AHH! TENTACLOPS!
STOP CALLING THEM THAT!

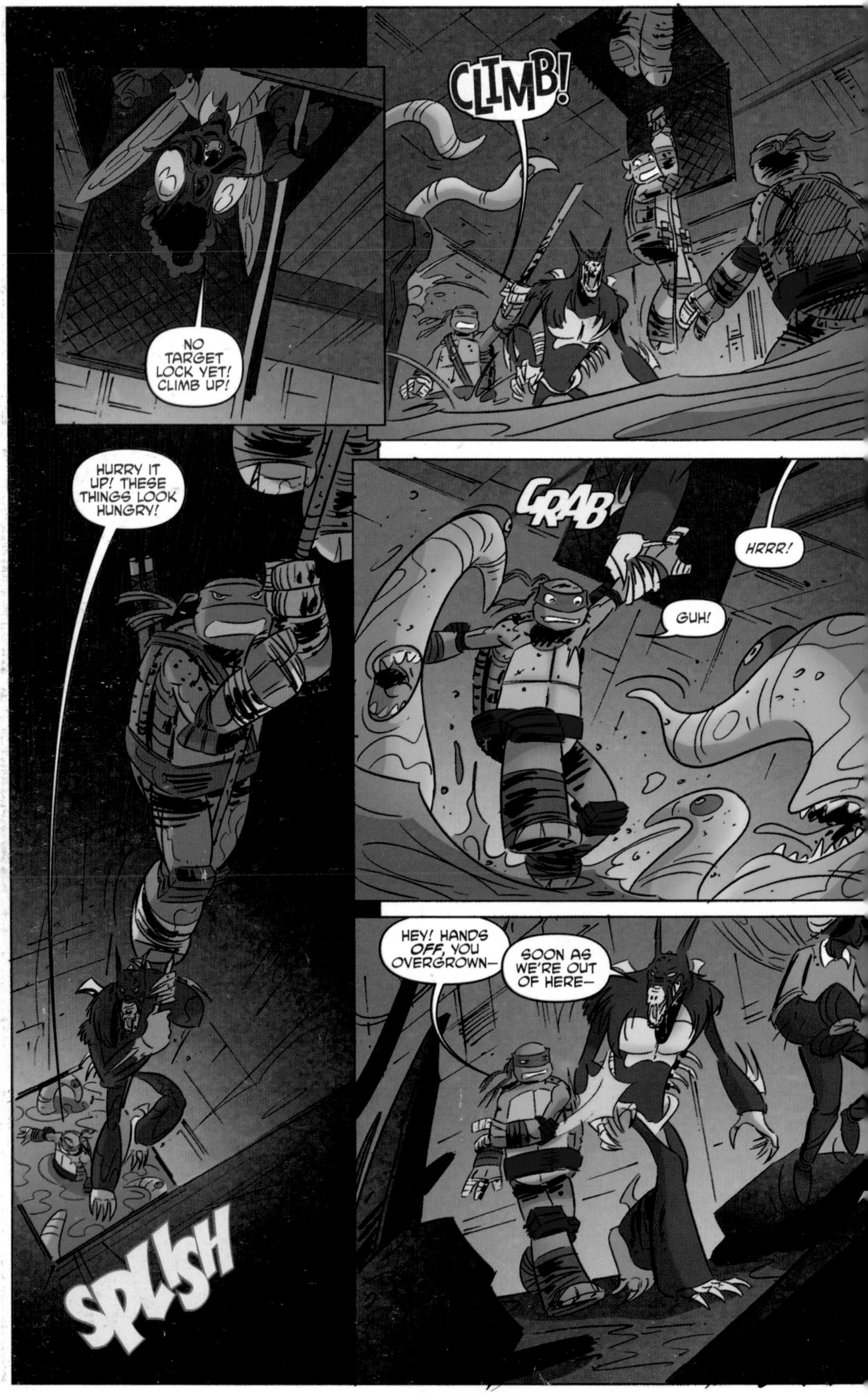
NO TARGET LOCK YET! CLIMB UP!
CLIMB!
HURRY IT UP! THESE THINGS LOOK HUNGRY!
SPLISH
GRAB
HRRR!
GUH!
HEY! HANDS OFF, YOU OVERGROWN—
SOON AS WE'RE OUT OF HERE—

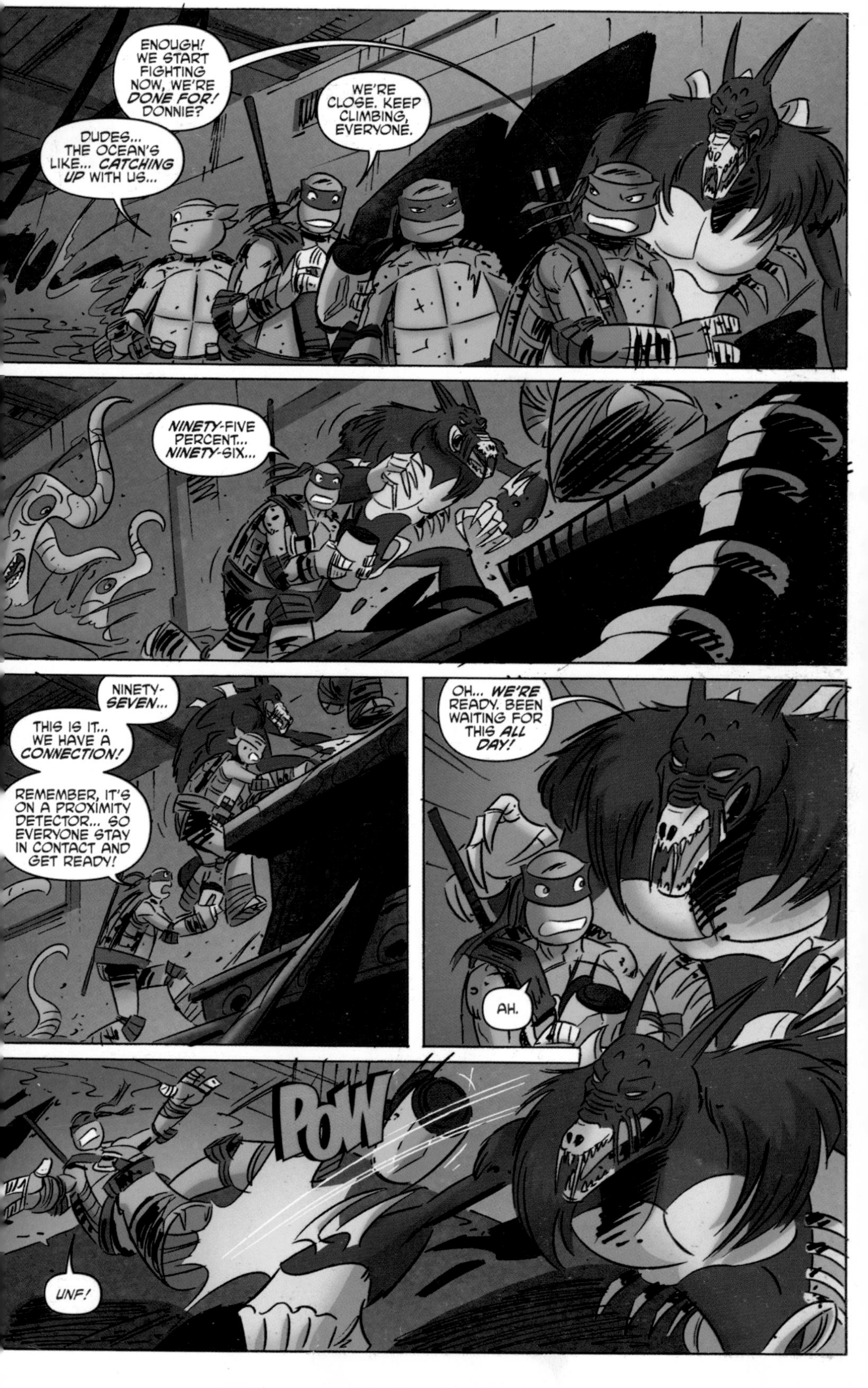
ENOUGH! WE START FIGHTING NOW, WE'RE DONE FOR! DONNIE?
DUDES... THE OCEAN'S LIKE... CATCHING UP WITH US...
WE'RE CLOSE. KEEP CLIMBING, EVERYONE.
NINETY-FIVE PERCENT... NINETY-SIX...
NINETY-SEVEN...
THIS IS IT... WE HAVE A CONNECTION!
REMEMBER, IT'S ON A PROXIMITY DETECTOR... SO EVERYONE STAY IN CONTACT AND GET READY!
OH... WE'RE READY. BEEN WAITING FOR THIS ALL DAY!
AH.
POW
UNF!

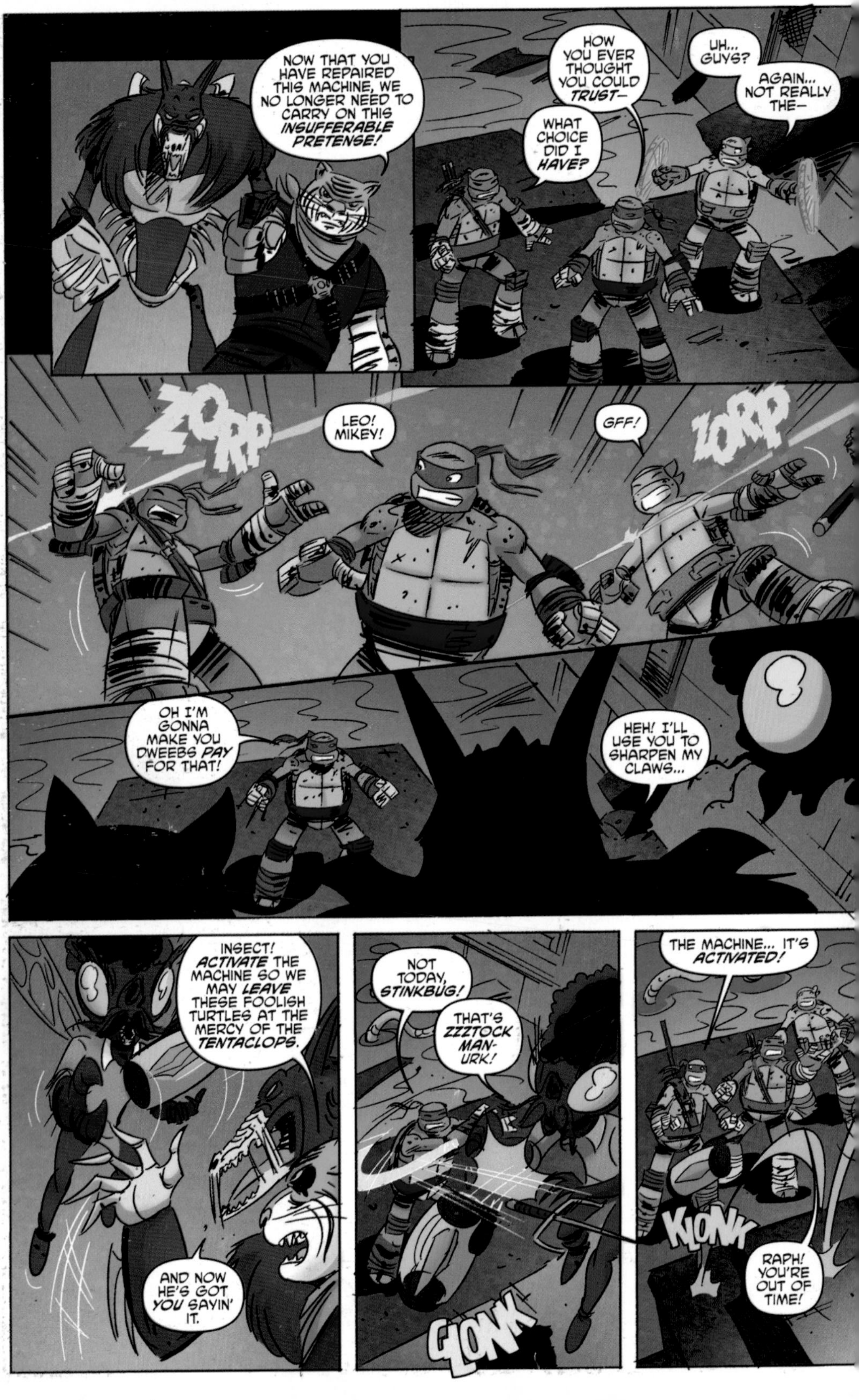
NOW THAT YOU HAVE REPAIRED THIS MACHINE, WE NO LONGER NEED TO CARRY ON THIS INSUFFERABLE PRETENSE!
HOW YOU EVER THOUGHT YOU COULD TRUST—
WHAT CHOICE DID I HAVE?
UH... GUYS?
AGAIN... NOT REALLY THE—
ZORP
LEO! MIKEY!
GFF!
ZORP
OH I'M GONNA MAKE YOU DWEEBS PAY FOR THAT!
HEH! I'LL USE YOU TO SHARPEN MY CLAWS...
INSECT! ACTIVATE THE MACHINE SO WE MAY LEAVE THESE FOOLISH TURTLES AT THE MERCY OF THE TENTACLOPS.
AND NOW HE'S GOT YOU SAYIN' IT.
NOT TODAY, STINKBUG!
THAT'S ZZZTOCK MAN-URK!
GLONK
THE MACHINE... IT'S ACTIVATED!
KLONK
RAPH! YOU'RE OUT OF TIME!

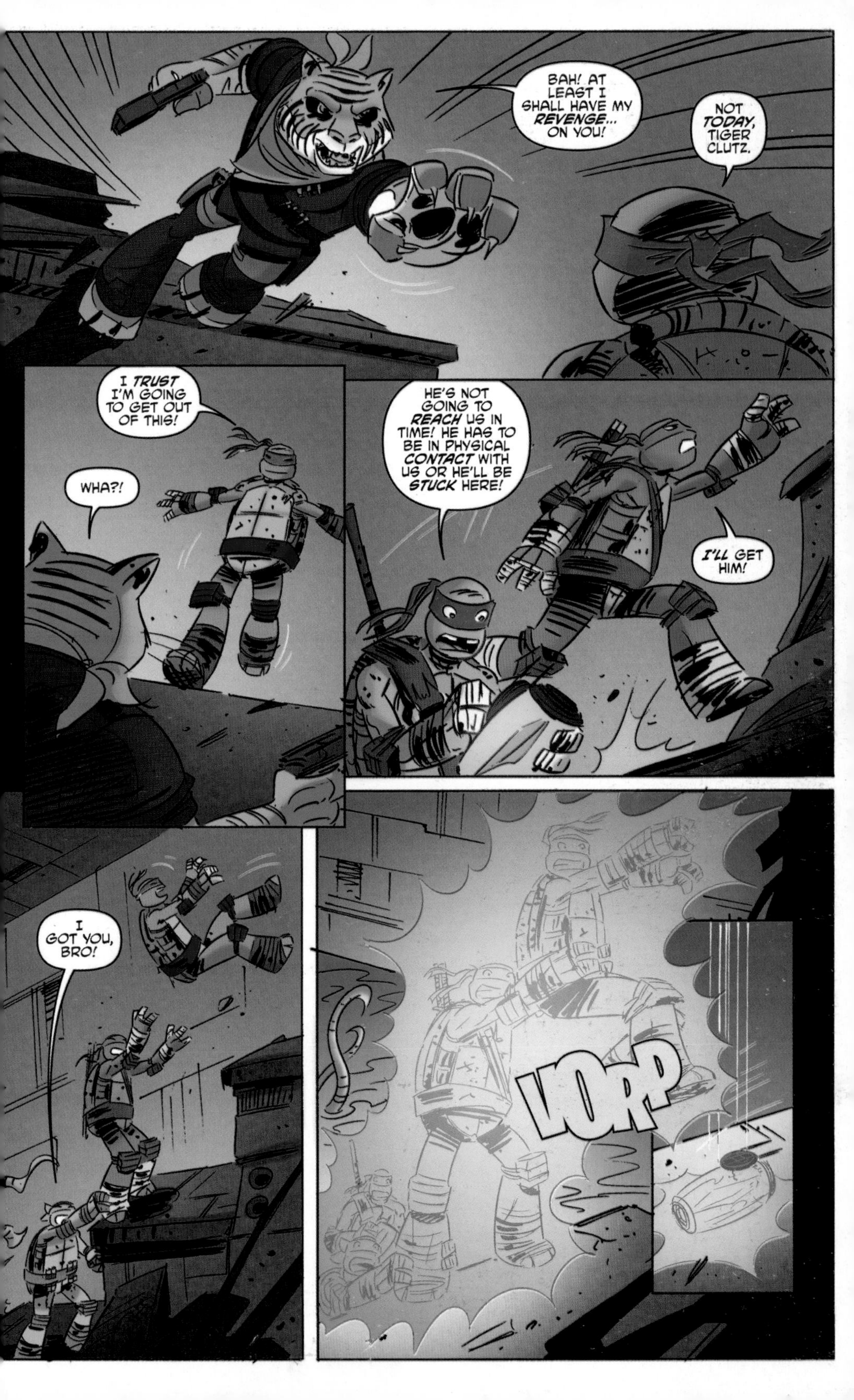
BAH! AT LEAST I SHALL HAVE MY REVENGE... ON YOU!
NOT TODAY, TIGER CLUTZ.
I TRUST I'M GOING TO GET OUT OF THIS!
WHA?!
HE'S NOT GOING TO REACH US IN TIME! HE HAS TO BE IN PHYSICAL CONTACT WITH US OR HE'LL BE STUCK HERE!
I'LL GET HIM!
I GOT YOU, BRO!
VORP

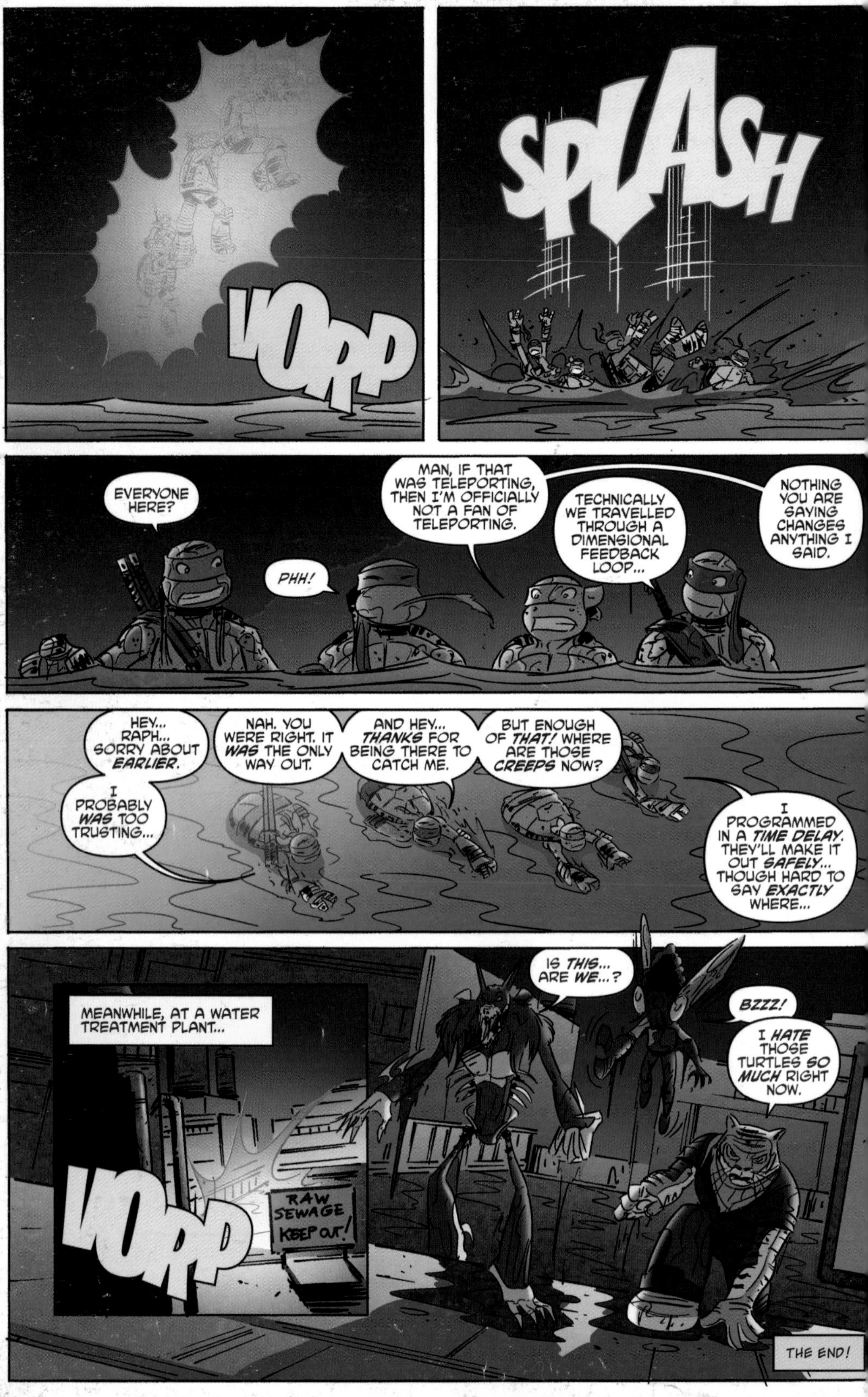
VORP
SPLASH
EVERYONE HERE?
PHH!
MAN, IF THAT WAS TELEPORTING, THEN I'M OFFICIALLY NOT A FAN OF TELEPORTING.
TECHNICALLY WE TRAVELLED THROUGH A DIMENSIONAL FEEDBACK LOOP...
NOTHING YOU ARE SAYING CHANGES ANYTHING I SAID.
HEY... RAPH... SORRY ABOUT EARLIER.
I PROBABLY WAS TOO TRUSTING...
NAH. YOU WERE RIGHT. IT WAS THE ONLY WAY OUT.
AND HEY... THANKS FOR BEING THERE TO CATCH ME.
BUT ENOUGH OF THAT! WHERE ARE THOSE CREEPS NOW?
I PROGRAMMED IN A TIME DELAY. THEY'LL MAKE IT OUT SAFELY... THOUGH HARD TO SAY EXACTLY WHERE...
MEANWHILE, AT A WATER TREATMENT PLANT...
IS THIS... ARE WE...?
BZZZ!
I HATE THOSE TURTLES SO MUCH RIGHT NOW.
VORP
RAW SEWAGE KEEP OUT!
THE END!

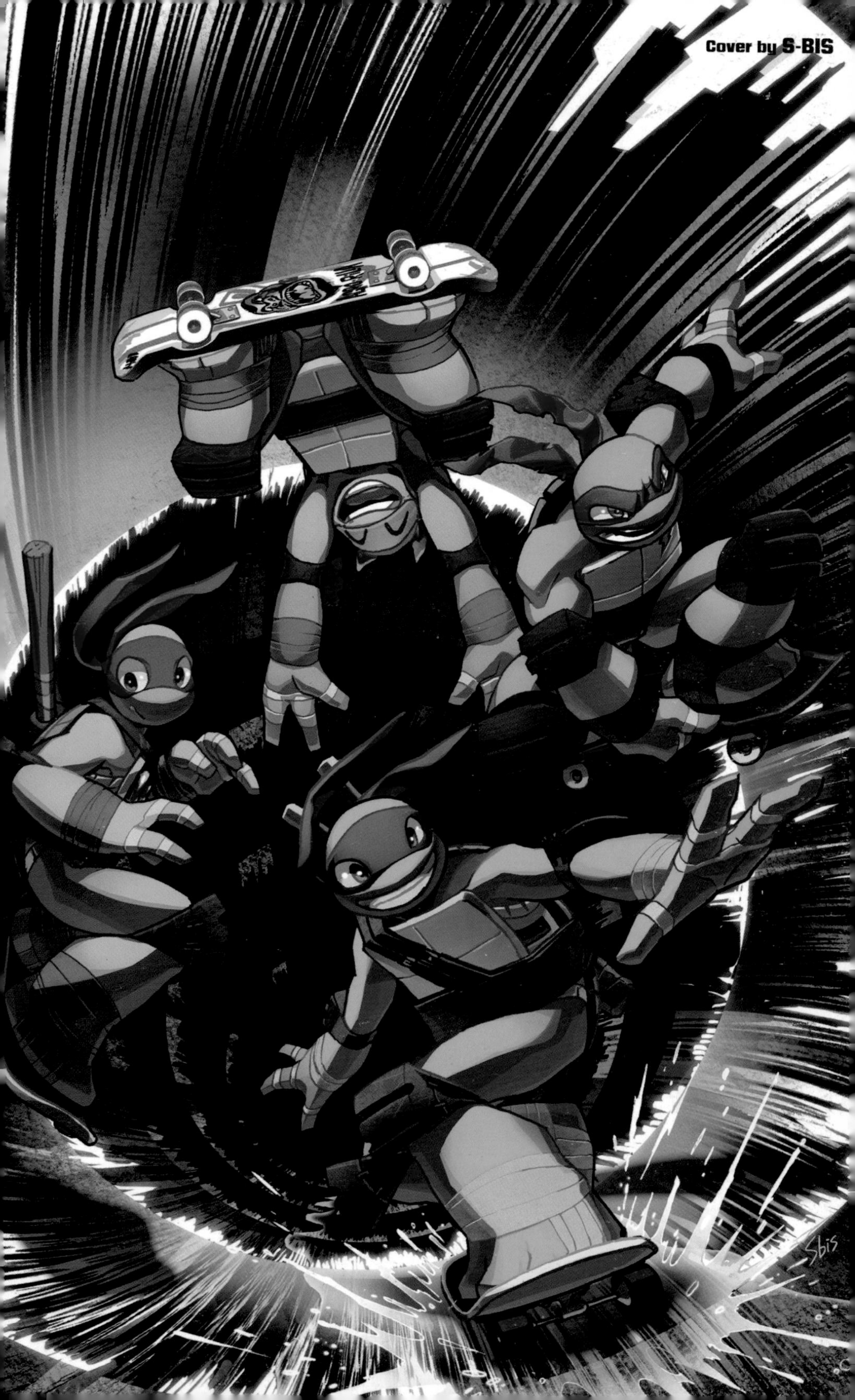
Sbis
Cover by S-BIS

Cover by **TANNA TUCKER**

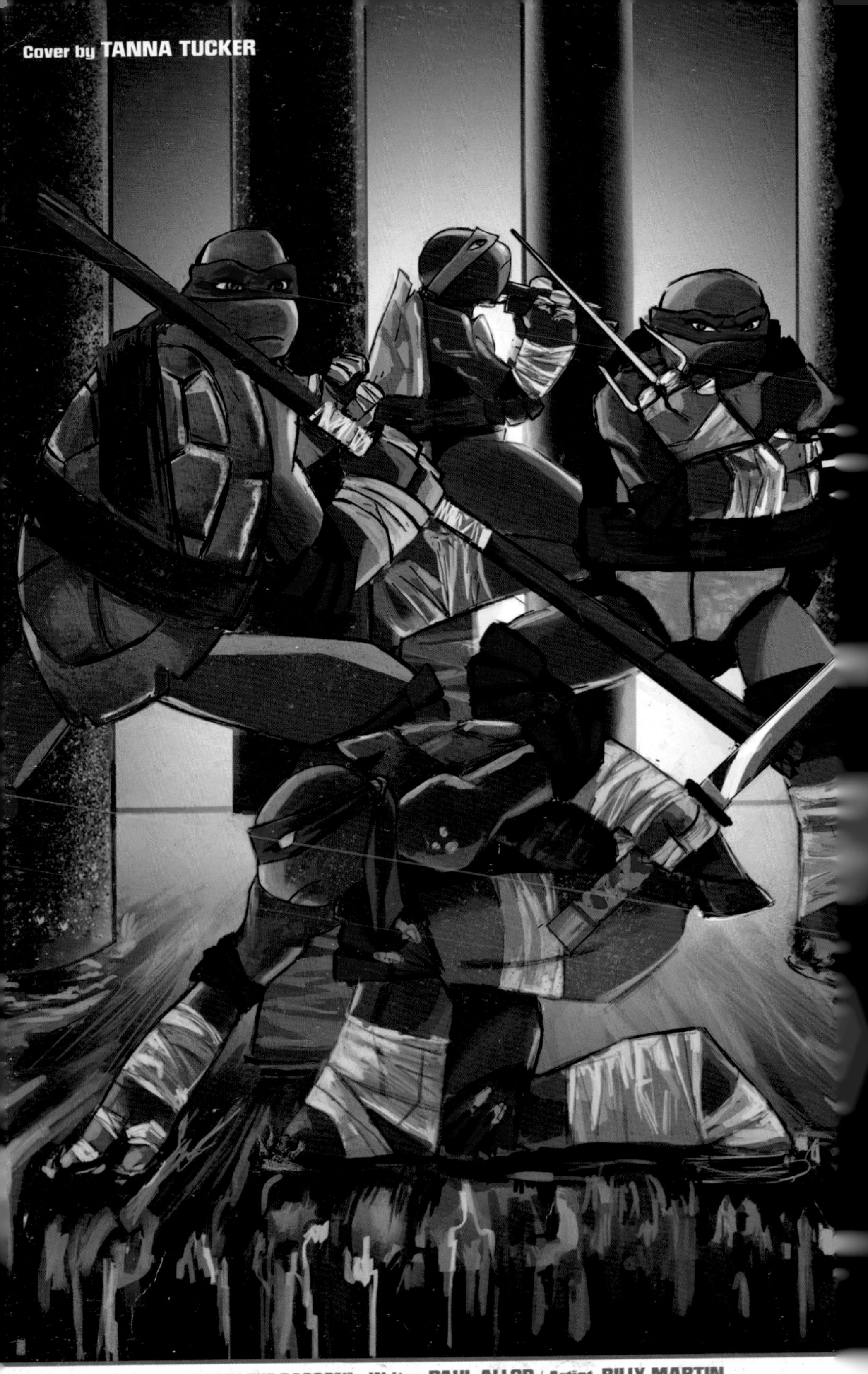

"CASEY THE RACOON" - Writer: **PAUL ALLOR** / Artist: **BILLY MARTIN**
"SECRET SANTA" - Writer: **LANDRY Q. WALKER** / Artist & Colorist: **PAULINA GANUCHEAU**

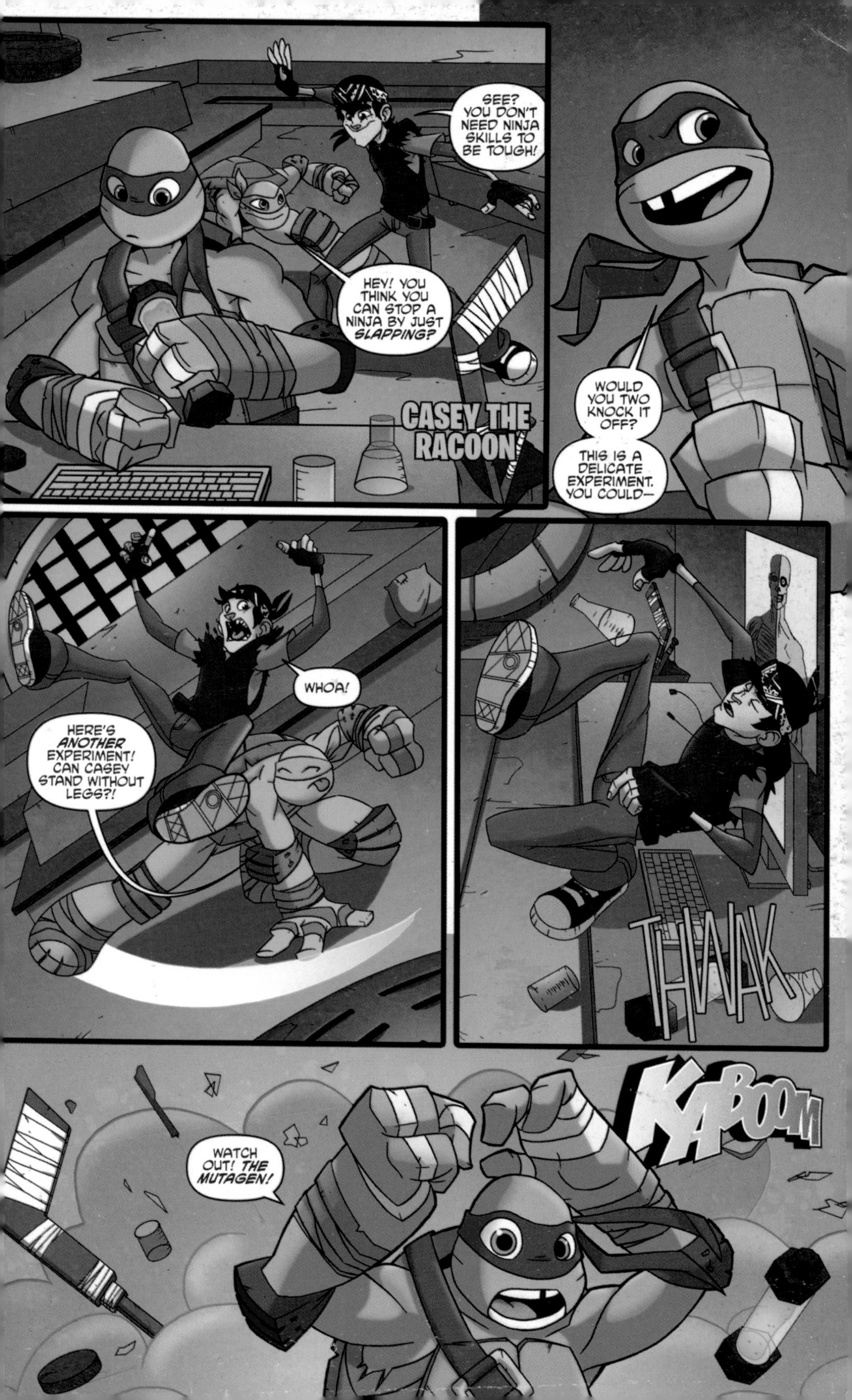
SEE? YOU DON'T NEED NINJA SKILLS TO BE TOUGH!
HEY! YOU THINK YOU CAN STOP A NINJA BY JUST *SLAPPING*?
CASEY THE RACOON
WOULD YOU TWO KNOCK IT OFF?
THIS IS A DELICATE EXPERIMENT. YOU COULD—
WHOA!
HERE'S *ANOTHER* EXPERIMENT! CAN CASEY STAND WITHOUT LEGS?!
THWAK
KABOOM
WATCH OUT! *THE MUTAGEN!*

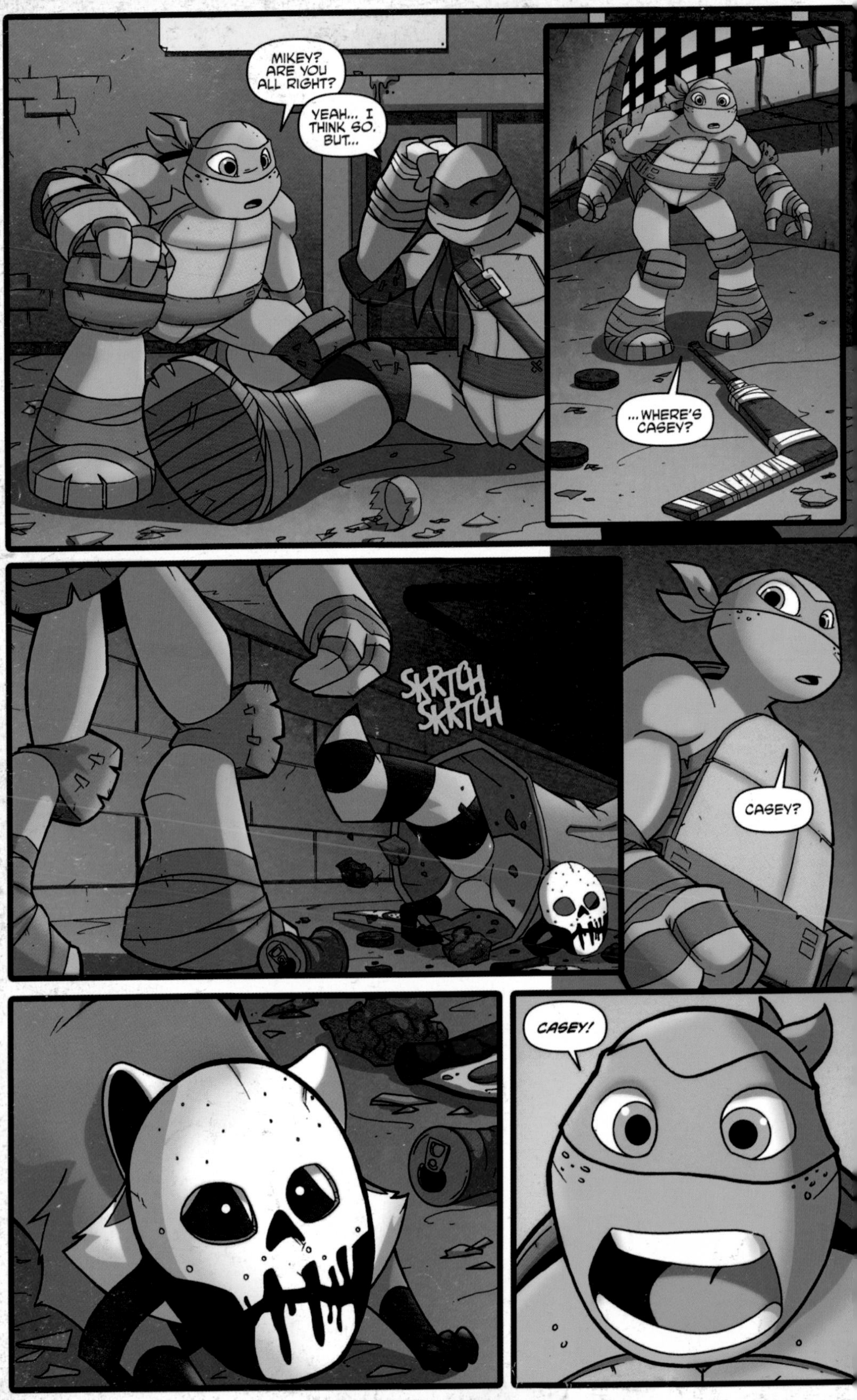
MIKEY? ARE YOU ALL RIGHT?
YEAH... I THINK SO. BUT...
...WHERE'S CASEY?
SKRTCH SKRTCH
CASEY?
CASEY!

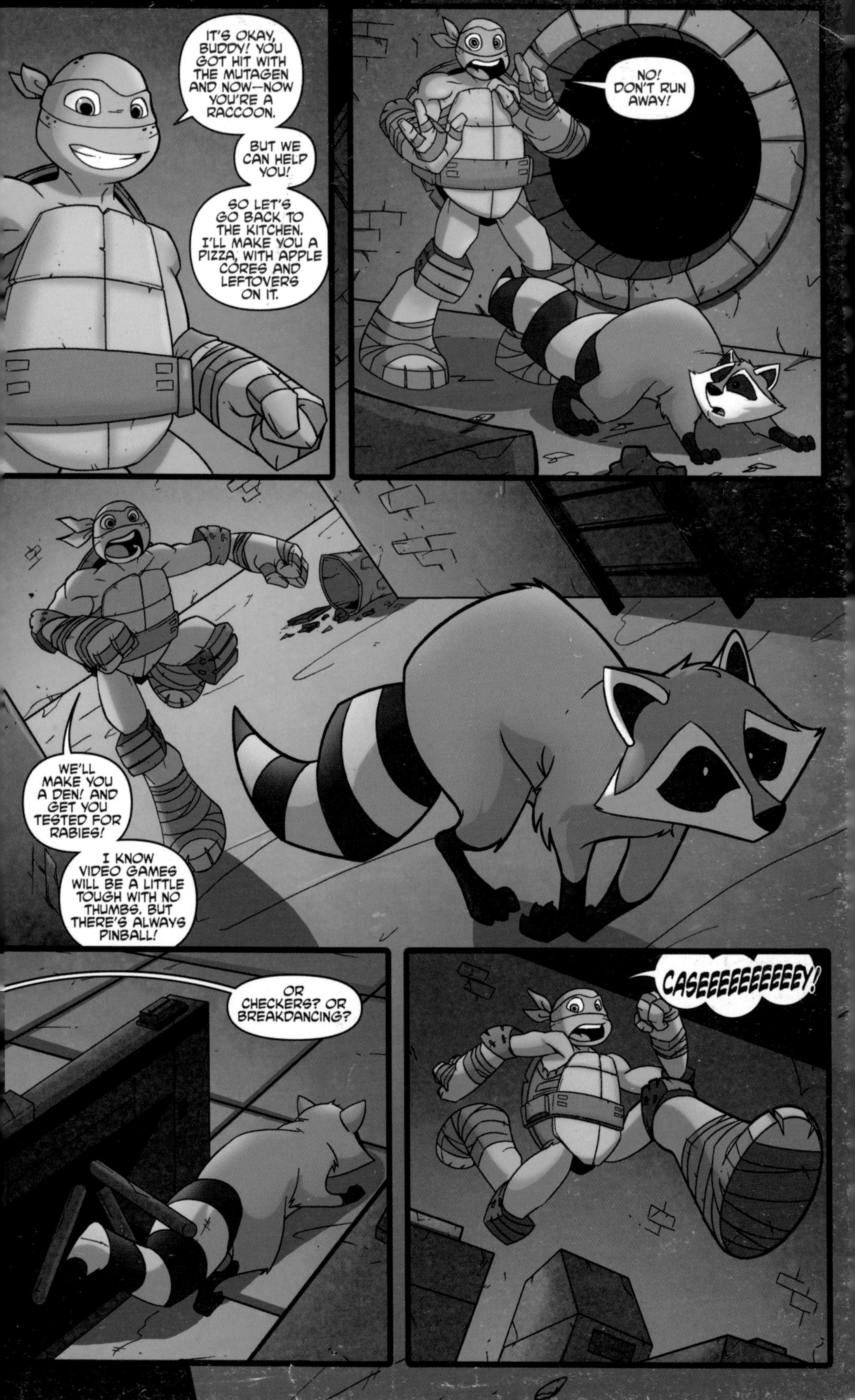
IT'S OKAY, BUDDY! YOU GOT HIT WITH THE MUTAGEN AND NOW—NOW YOU'RE A RACCOON.
BUT WE CAN HELP YOU!
SO LET'S GO BACK TO THE KITCHEN. I'LL MAKE YOU A PIZZA, WITH APPLE CORES AND LEFTOVERS ON IT.
NO! DON'T RUN AWAY!
WE'LL MAKE YOU A DEN! AND GET YOU TESTED FOR RABIES!
I KNOW VIDEO GAMES WILL BE A LITTLE TOUGH WITH NO THUMBS. BUT THERE'S ALWAYS PINBALL!
OR CHECKERS? OR BREAKDANCING?
CASEEEEEEEEEEEY!

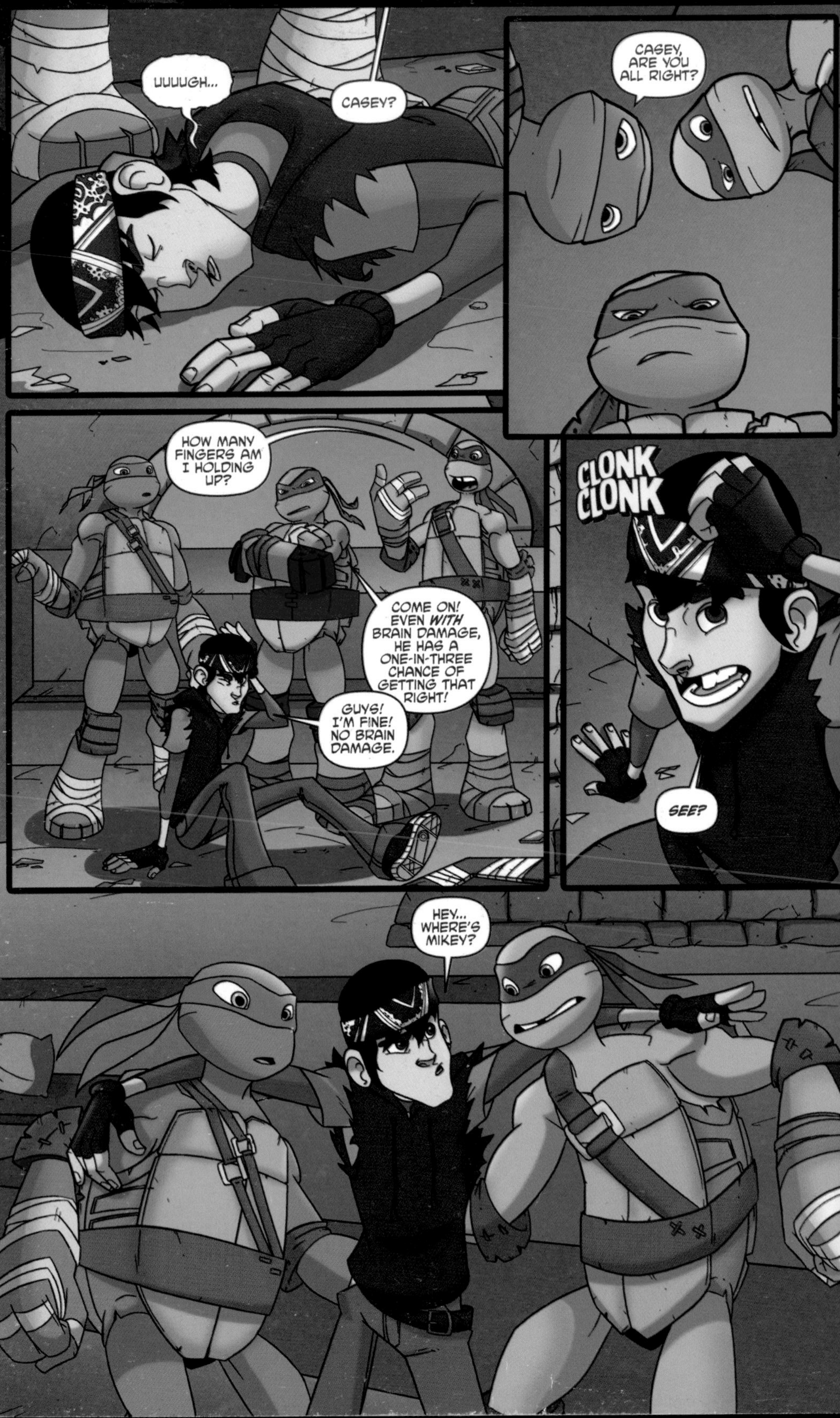
UUUUGH...
CASEY?
CASEY, ARE YOU ALL RIGHT?
HOW MANY FINGERS AM I HOLDING UP?
COME ON! EVEN *WITH* BRAIN DAMAGE, HE HAS A ONE-IN-THREE CHANCE OF GETTING THAT RIGHT!
GUYS! I'M FINE! NO BRAIN DAMAGE.
CLONK CLONK
SEE?
HEY... WHERE'S MIKEY?

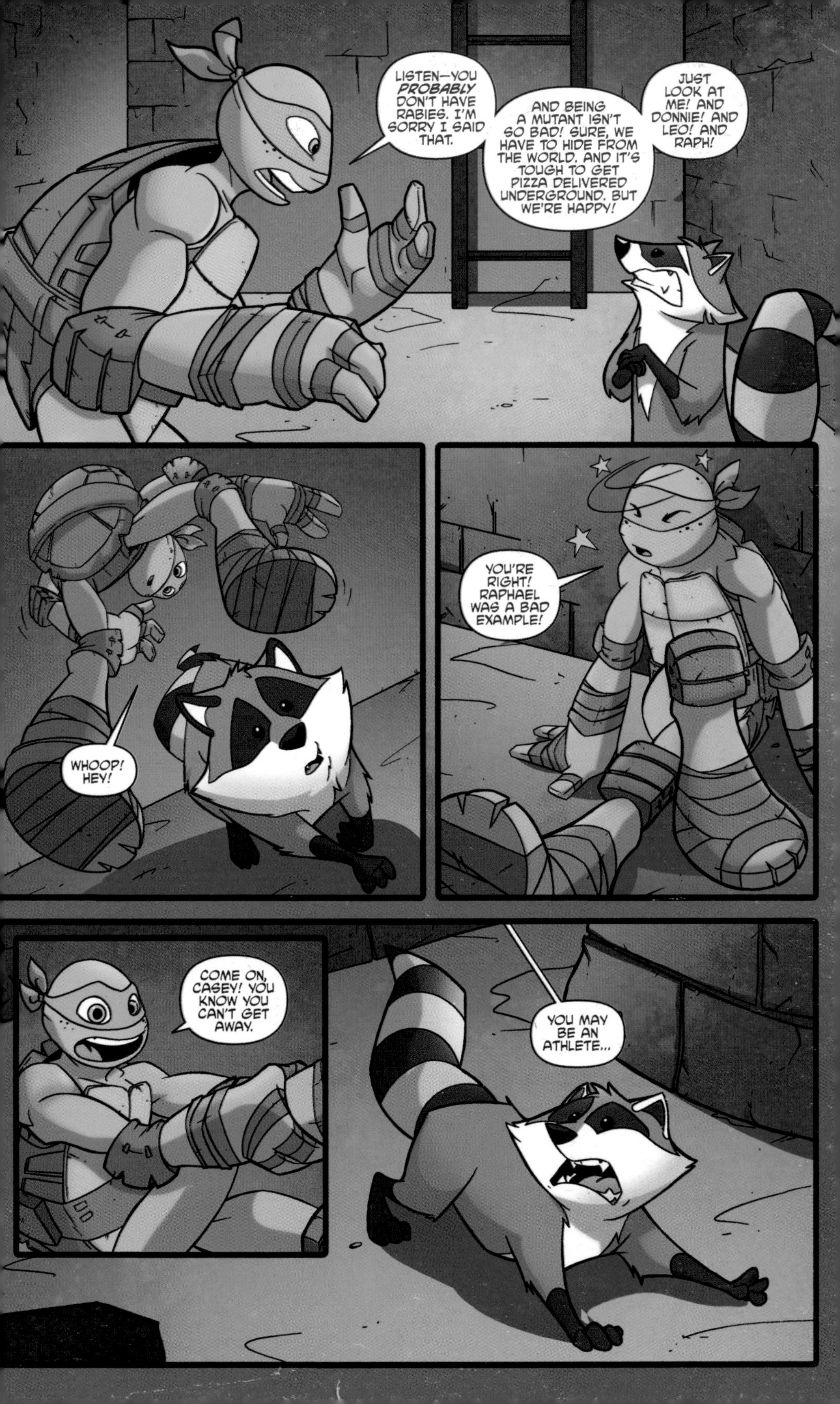

LISTEN—YOU *PROBABLY* DON'T HAVE RABIES. I'M SORRY I SAID THAT.
AND BEING A MUTANT ISN'T SO BAD! SURE, WE HAVE TO HIDE FROM THE WORLD. AND IT'S TOUGH TO GET PIZZA DELIVERED UNDERGROUND. BUT WE'RE HAPPY!
JUST LOOK AT ME! AND DONNIE! AND LEO! AND RAPH!
WHOOP! HEY!
YOU'RE RIGHT! RAPHAEL WAS A BAD EXAMPLE!
COME ON, CASEY! YOU KNOW YOU CAN'T GET AWAY.
YOU MAY BE AN ATHLETE...

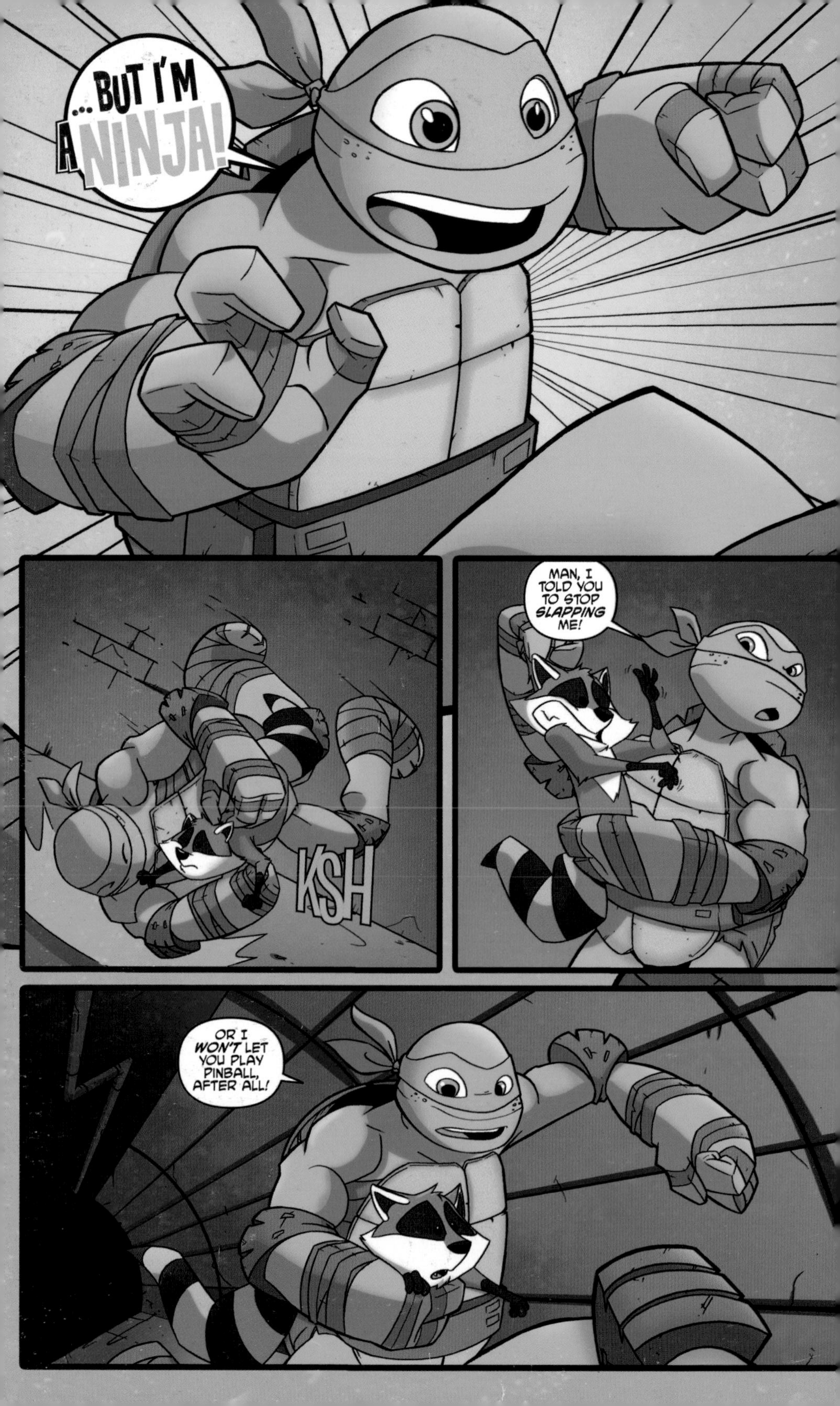
...BUT I'M A NINJA!
KSH
MAN, I TOLD YOU TO STOP SLAPPING ME!
OR I WON'T LET YOU PLAY PINBALL, AFTER ALL!

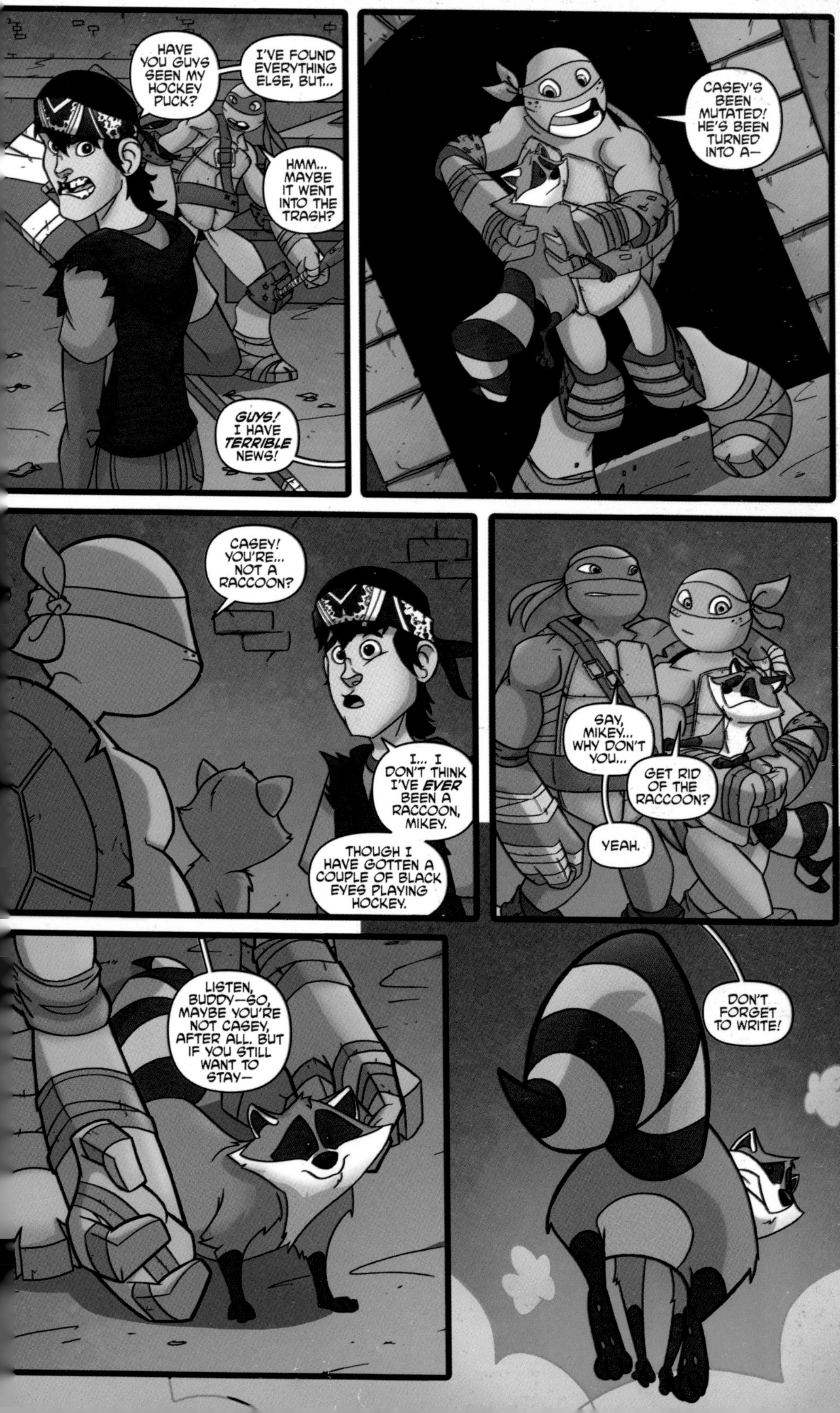
HAVE YOU GUYS SEEN MY HOCKEY PUCK?
I'VE FOUND EVERYTHING ELSE, BUT...
HMM... MAYBE IT WENT INTO THE TRASH?
GUYS! I HAVE *TERRIBLE* NEWS!
CASEY'S BEEN MUTATED! HE'S BEEN TURNED INTO A—
CASEY! YOU'RE... NOT A RACCOON?
I... I DON'T THINK I'VE *EVER* BEEN A RACCOON, MIKEY.
THOUGH I HAVE GOTTEN A COUPLE OF BLACK EYES PLAYING HOCKEY.
SAY, MIKEY... WHY DON'T YOU...
GET RID OF THE RACCOON?
YEAH.
LISTEN, BUDDY—SO, MAYBE YOU'RE NOT CASEY, AFTER ALL. BUT IF YOU STILL WANT TO STAY—
DON'T FORGET TO WRITE!

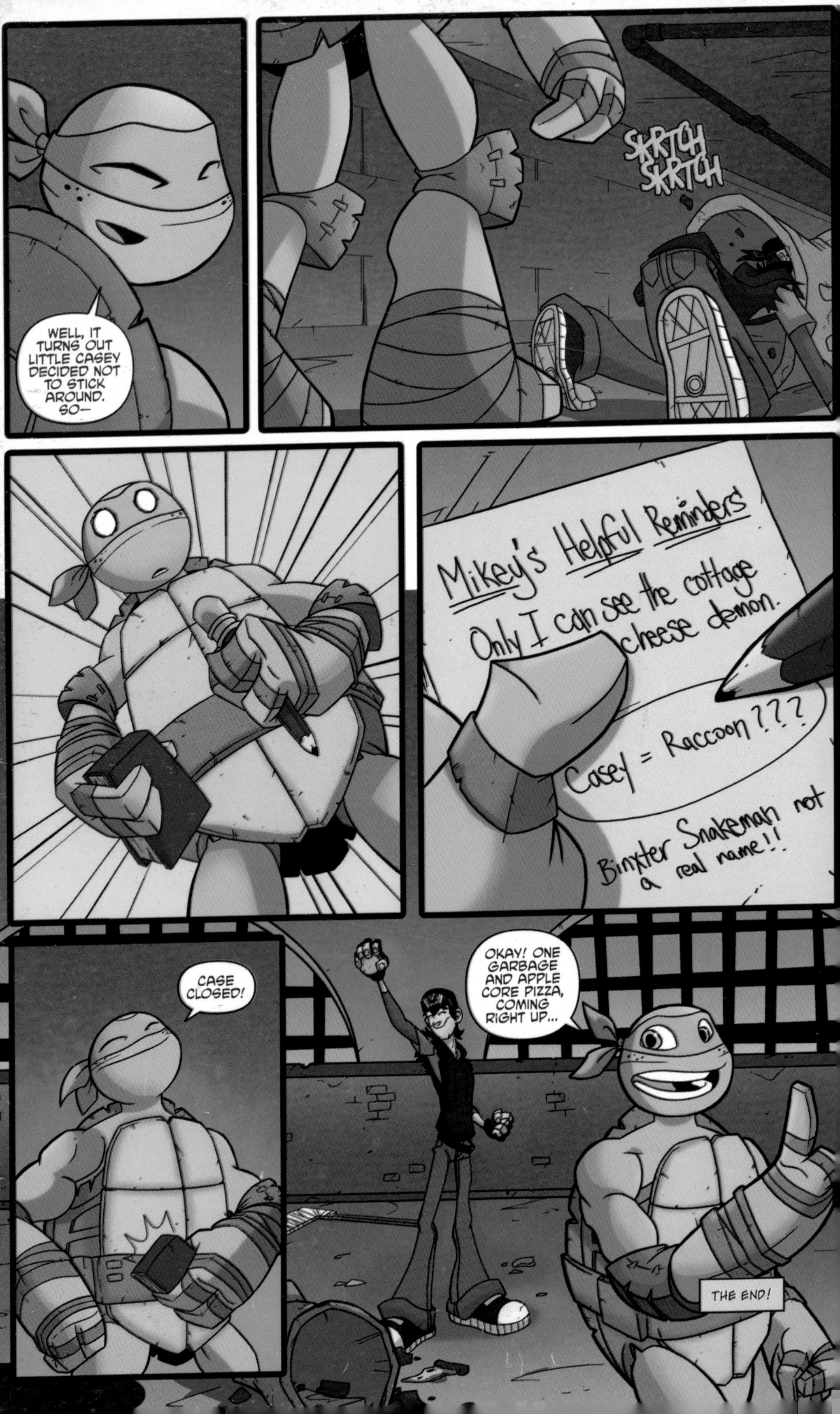
WELL, IT TURNS OUT LITTLE CASEY DECIDED NOT TO STICK AROUND. SO—
SKRTCH SKRTCH
Mikey's Helpful Reminders
Only I can see the cottage cheese demon.
Casey = Raccoon???
Binxter Snakeman not a real name!!
CASE CLOSED!
OKAY! ONE GARBAGE AND APPLE CORE PIZZA, COMING RIGHT UP...
THE END!

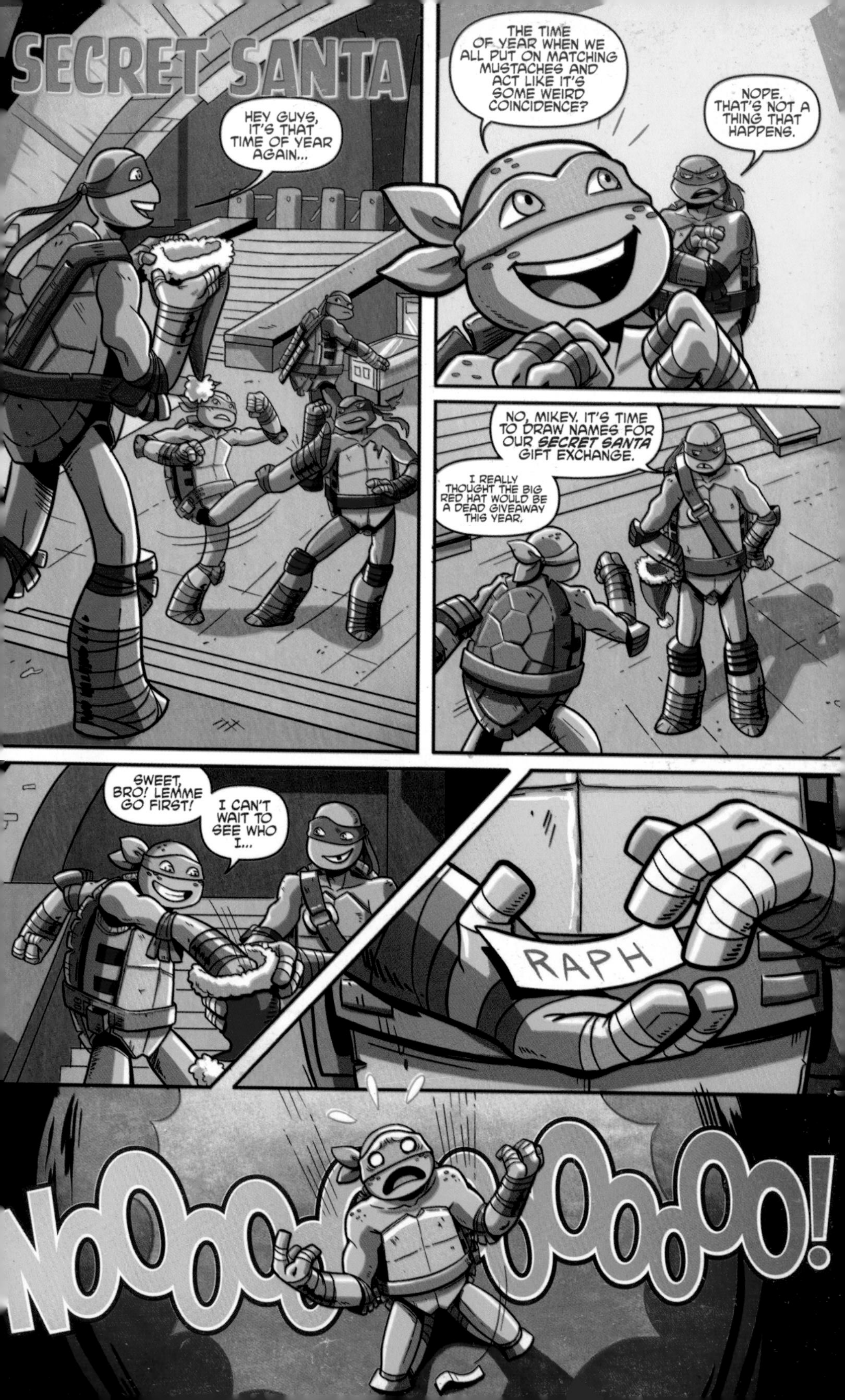
SECRET SANTA
HEY GUYS, IT'S THAT TIME OF YEAR AGAIN...
THE TIME OF YEAR WHEN WE ALL PUT ON MATCHING MUSTACHES AND ACT LIKE IT'S SOME WEIRD COINCIDENCE?
NOPE. THAT'S NOT A THING THAT HAPPENS.
NO, MIKEY. IT'S TIME TO DRAW NAMES FOR OUR SECRET SANTA GIFT EXCHANGE.
I REALLY THOUGHT THE BIG RED HAT WOULD BE A DEAD GIVEAWAY THIS YEAR.
SWEET, BRO! LEMME GO FIRST!
I CAN'T WAIT TO SEE WHO I...
RAPH
NOOOOOOOOOOOOO!

YOU GOTTA SWITCH WITH ME, DONNIE! I GOT—

LA LA LA LA LA LA!

LA LA! I CAN'T HEAR YOU BECAUSE SECRET SANTA IS SECRET!

BUT—

IT'S RIGHT THERE IN THE NAME. LA LA LA!

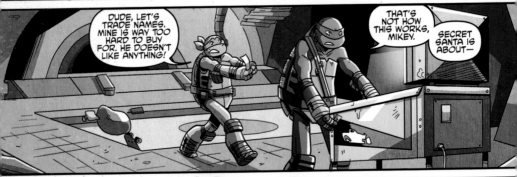

DUDE, LET'S TRADE NAMES. MINE IS WAY TOO HARD TO BUY FOR. HE DOESN'T LIKE ANYTHING!

THAT'S NOT HOW THIS WORKS, MIKEY.

SECRET SANTA IS ABOUT—

HA!

HEY!

GRAB

"MIKEY."

AH, MAN. I CAN'T BE MY OWN SECRET SANTA. I'M A TERRIBLE GIFT GIVER.

MIKEY

LOOKS LIKE YOU'RE STUCK WITH RAPH. BUT YOU CAN TOTALLY DO THIS.

YOU JUST NEED SOME IMAGINATION, A LITTLE HOLIDAY SPIRIT...

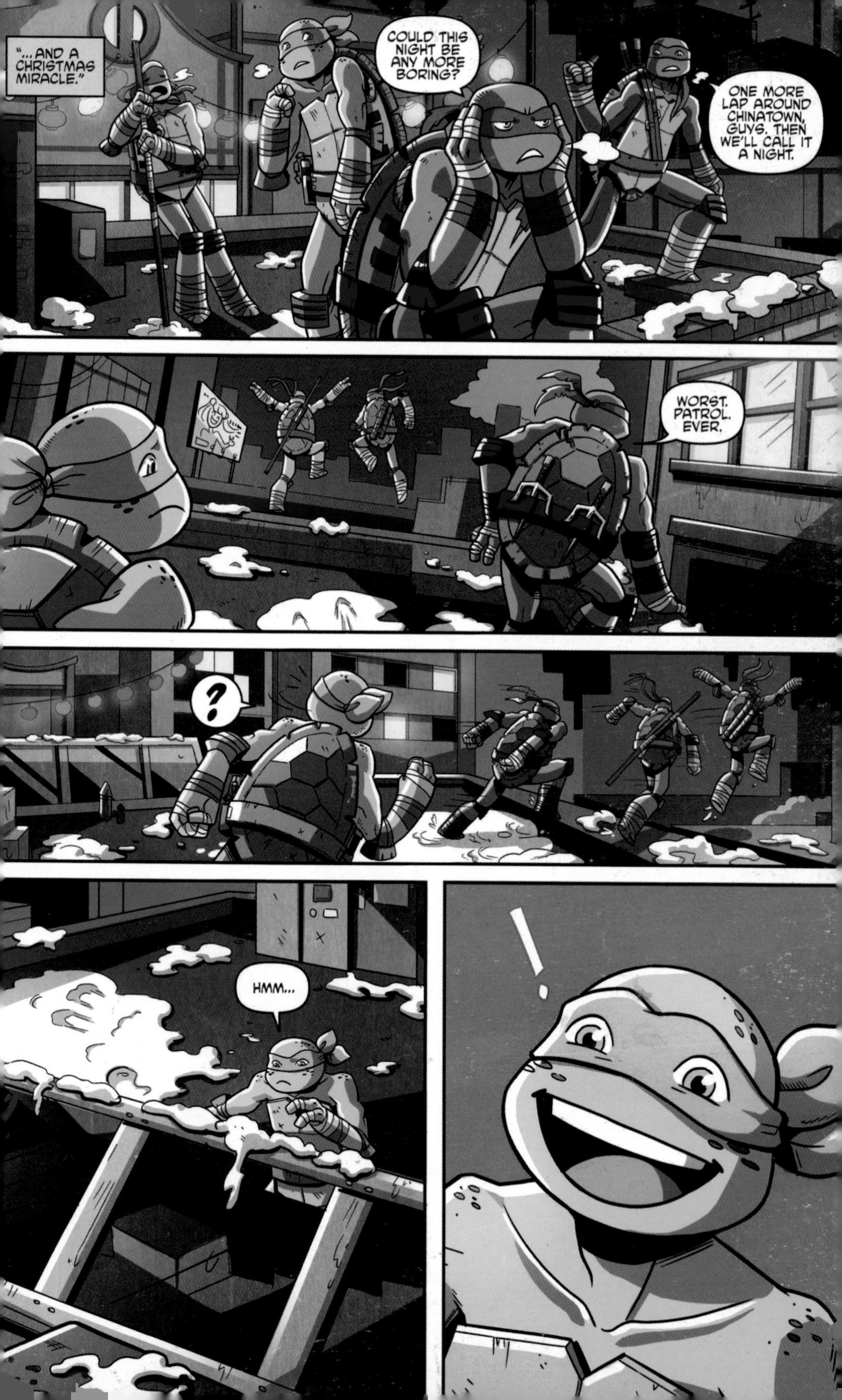
"...AND A CHRISTMAS MIRACLE."
COULD THIS NIGHT BE ANY MORE BORING?
ONE MORE LAP AROUND CHINATOWN, GUYS. THEN WE'LL CALL IT A NIGHT.
WORST. PATROL. EVER.
?
HMM...
!

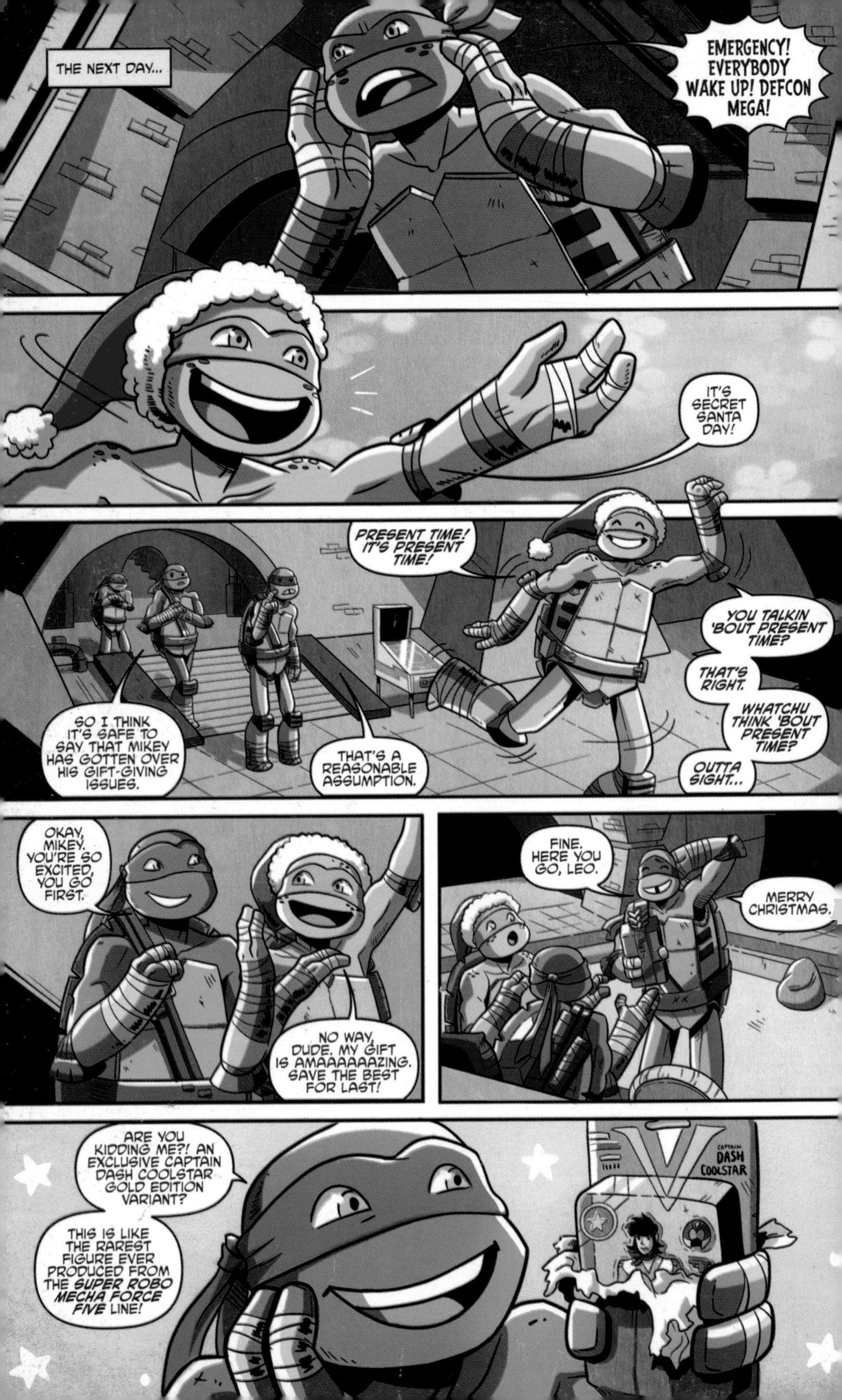
THE NEXT DAY...
EMERGENCY! EVERYBODY WAKE UP! DEFCON MEGA!
IT'S SECRET SANTA DAY!
PRESENT TIME! IT'S PRESENT TIME!
YOU TALKIN 'BOUT PRESENT TIME?
THAT'S RIGHT.
WHATCHU THINK 'BOUT PRESENT TIME?
OUTTA SIGHT...
SO I THINK IT'S SAFE TO SAY THAT MIKEY HAS GOTTEN OVER HIS GIFT-GIVING ISSUES.
THAT'S A REASONABLE ASSUMPTION.
OKAY, MIKEY. YOU'RE SO EXCITED, YOU GO FIRST.
NO WAY, DUDE. MY GIFT IS AMAAAAAAAZING. SAVE THE BEST FOR LAST!
FINE. HERE YOU GO, LEO.
MERRY CHRISTMAS.
ARE YOU KIDDING ME?! AN EXCLUSIVE CAPTAIN DASH COOLSTAR GOLD EDITION VARIANT?
THIS IS LIKE THE RAREST FIGURE EVER PRODUCED FROM THE *SUPER ROBO MECHA FORCE FIVE* LINE!
CAPTAIN DASH COOLSTAR

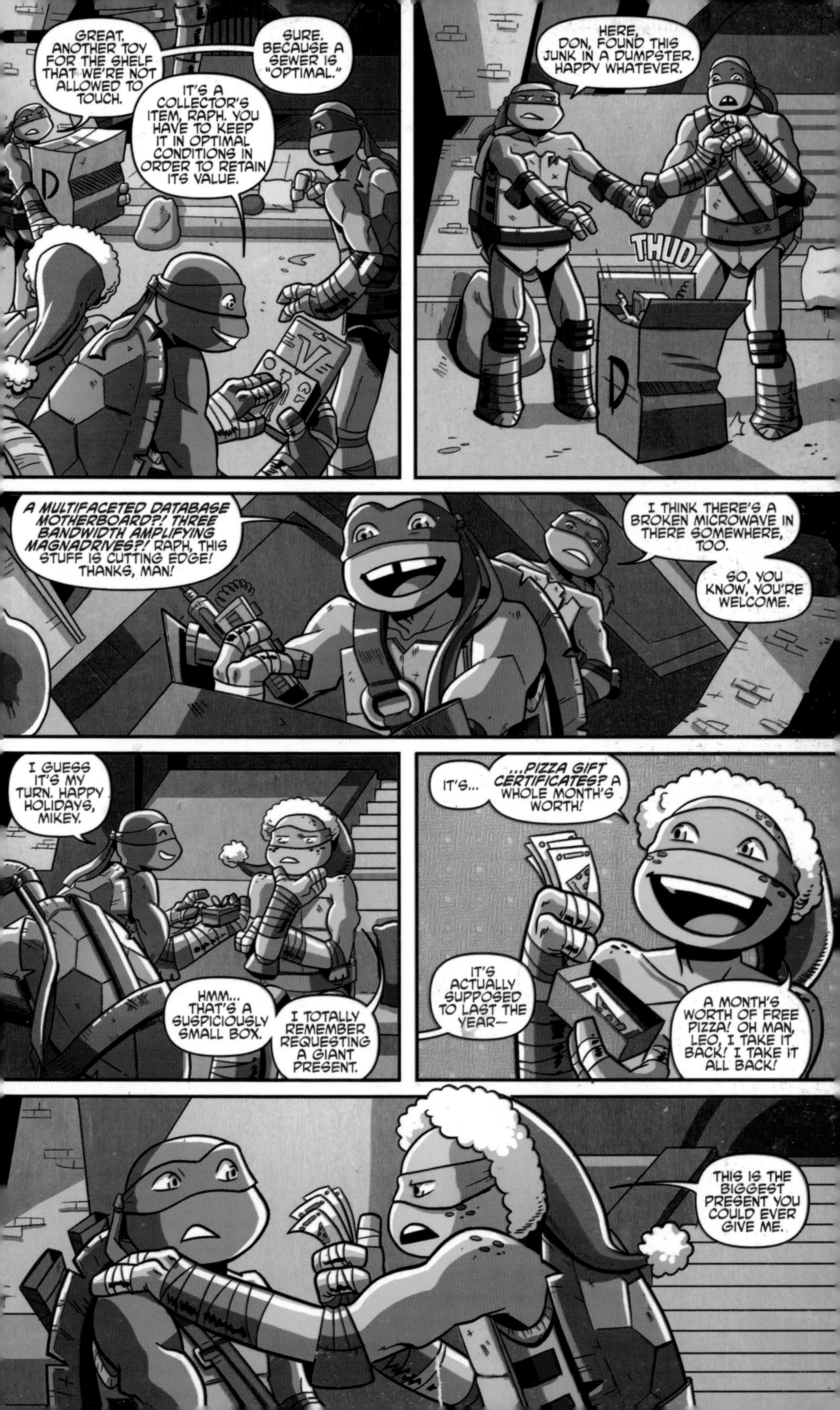
GREAT. ANOTHER TOY FOR THE SHELF THAT WE'RE NOT ALLOWED TO TOUCH.
SURE. BECAUSE A SEWER IS "OPTIMAL."
IT'S A COLLECTOR'S ITEM, RAPH. YOU HAVE TO KEEP IT IN OPTIMAL CONDITIONS IN ORDER TO RETAIN ITS VALUE.
HERE, DON, FOUND THIS JUNK IN A DUMPSTER. HAPPY WHATEVER.
THUD
A MULTIFACETED DATABASE MOTHERBOARD?! THREE BANDWIDTH AMPLIFYING MAGNADRIVES?! RAPH, THIS STUFF IS CUTTING EDGE! THANKS, MAN!
I THINK THERE'S A BROKEN MICROWAVE IN THERE SOMEWHERE, TOO.
SO, YOU KNOW, YOU'RE WELCOME.
I GUESS IT'S MY TURN. HAPPY HOLIDAYS, MIKEY.
HMM... THAT'S A SUSPICIOUSLY SMALL BOX.
I TOTALLY REMEMBER REQUESTING A GIANT PRESENT.
IT'S...
...PIZZA GIFT CERTIFICATES? A WHOLE MONTH'S WORTH!
IT'S ACTUALLY SUPPOSED TO LAST THE YEAR—
A MONTH'S WORTH OF FREE PIZZA! OH MAN, LEO, I TAKE IT BACK! I TAKE IT ALL BACK!
THIS IS THE BIGGEST PRESENT YOU COULD EVER GIVE ME.

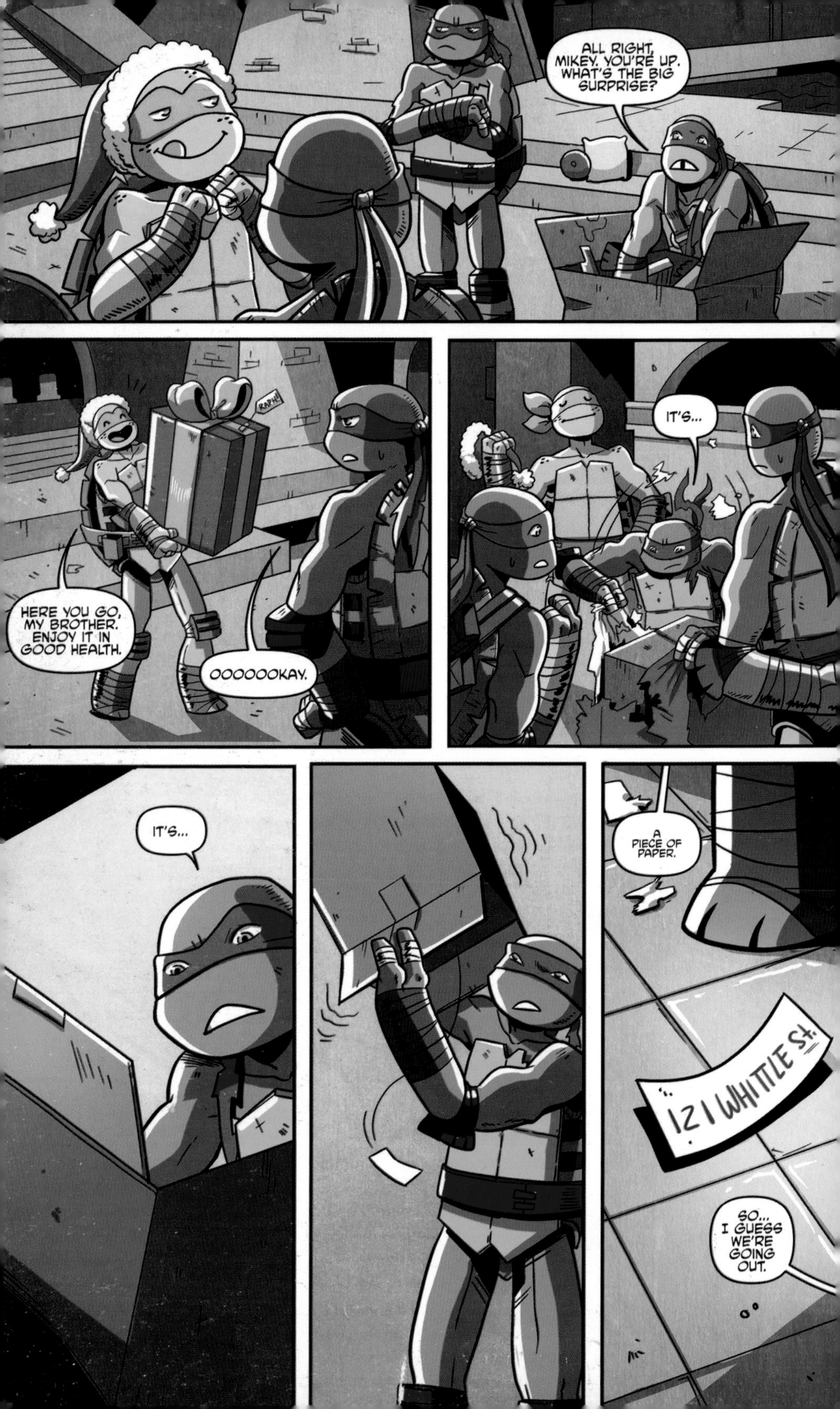
ALL RIGHT, MIKEY. YOU'RE UP. WHAT'S THE BIG SURPRISE?
RAPH!
HERE YOU GO, MY BROTHER. ENJOY IT IN GOOD HEALTH.
OOOOOOKAY.
IT'S...
IT'S...
A PIECE OF PAPER.
121 WHITTLE St.
SO... I GUESS WE'RE GOING OUT.

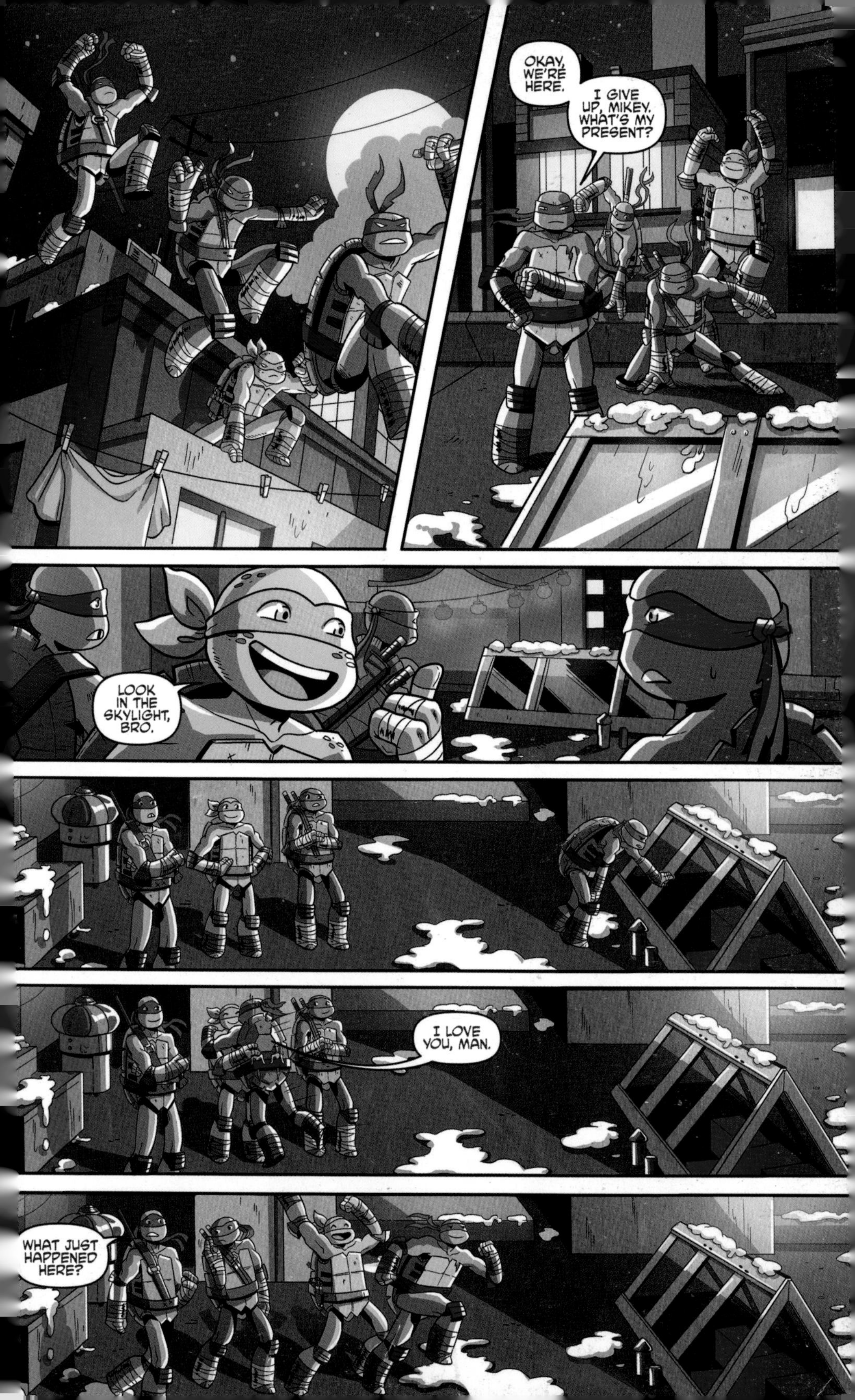
OKAY, WE'RE HERE.
I GIVE UP, MIKEY. WHAT'S MY PRESENT?
LOOK IN THE SKYLIGHT, BRO.
I LOVE YOU, MAN.
WHAT JUST HAPPENED HERE?

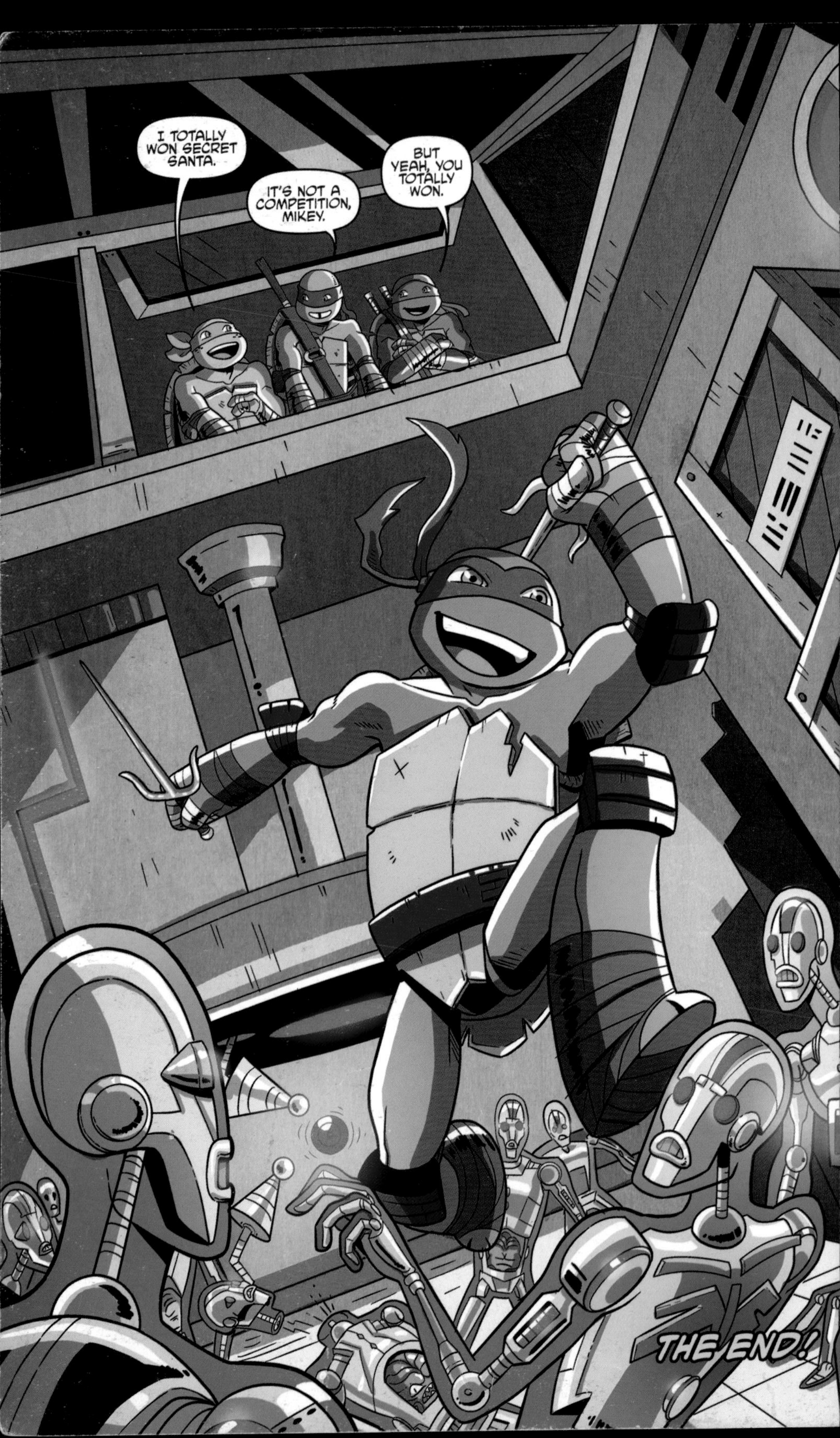
I TOTALLY WON SECRET SANTA.
IT'S NOT A COMPETITION, MIKEY.
BUT YEAH, YOU TOTALLY WON.
THE END!

Cover by **JEFFREY CRUZ**

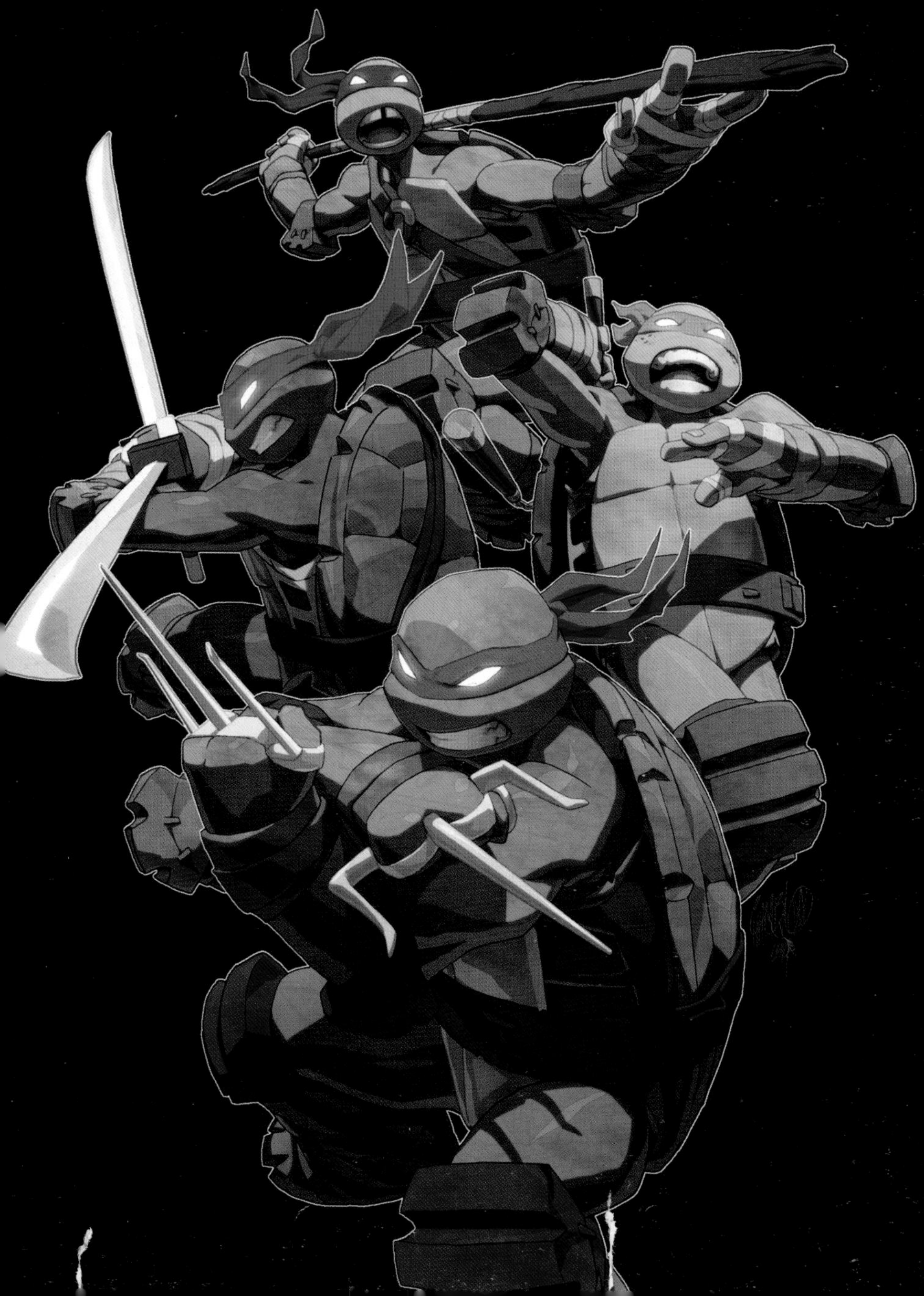

Cover by DARIO BRIZUELA

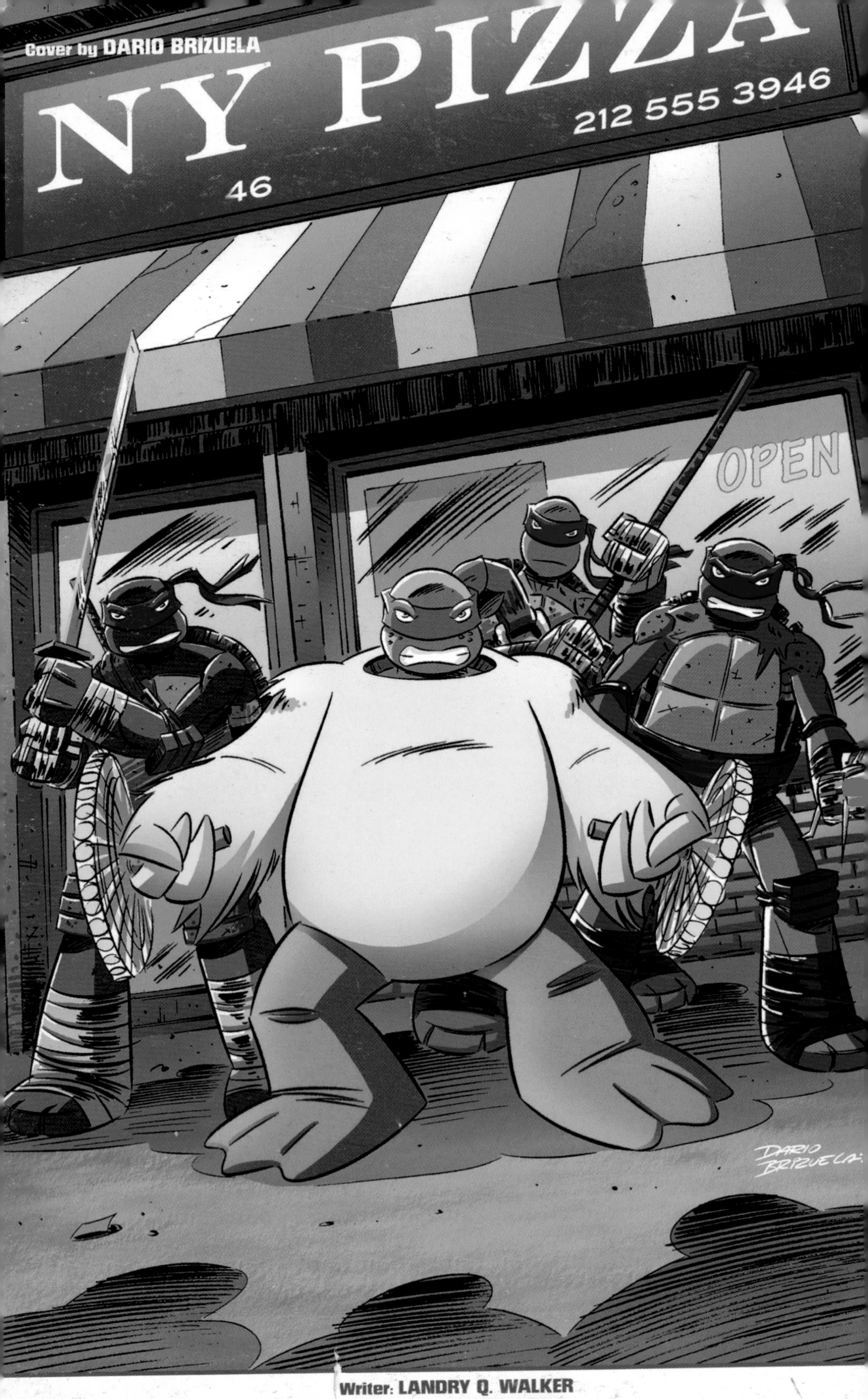
NY PIZZA
212 555 3946
46
OPEN
DARIO BRIZUELA

Writer: LANDRY Q. WALKER
Artist: CHAD THOMAS

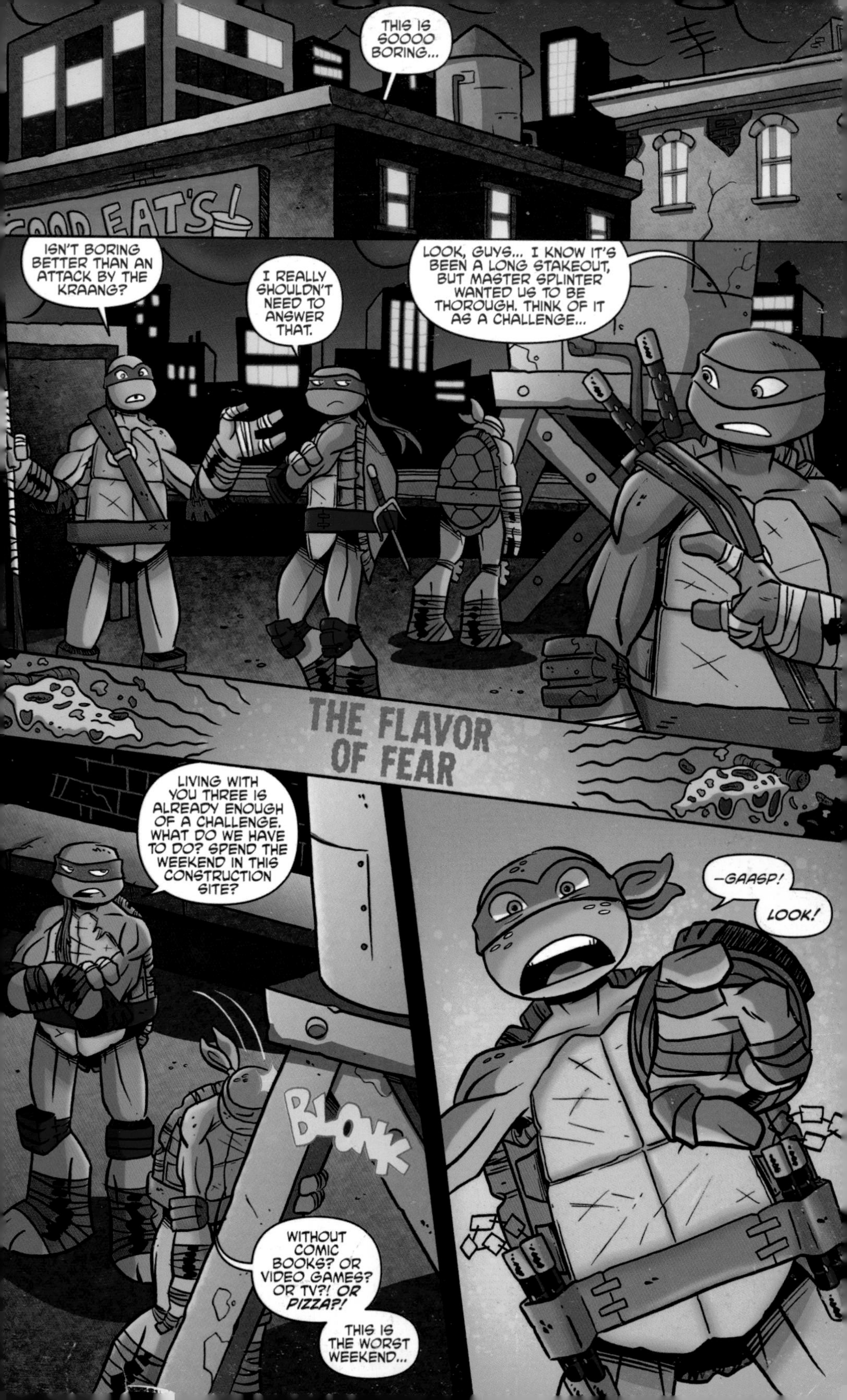
THIS IS SOOOO BORING...
GOOD EATS
ISN'T BORING BETTER THAN AN ATTACK BY THE KRAANG?
I REALLY SHOULDN'T NEED TO ANSWER THAT.
LOOK, GUYS... I KNOW IT'S BEEN A LONG STAKEOUT, BUT MASTER SPLINTER WANTED US TO BE THOROUGH. THINK OF IT AS A CHALLENGE...
THE FLAVOR OF FEAR
LIVING WITH YOU THREE IS ALREADY ENOUGH OF A CHALLENGE. WHAT DO WE HAVE TO DO? SPEND THE WEEKEND IN THIS CONSTRUCTION SITE?
BLONK
WITHOUT COMIC BOOKS? OR VIDEO GAMES? OR TV?! OR PIZZA?!
THIS IS THE WORST WEEKEND...
—GAASP!
LOOK!

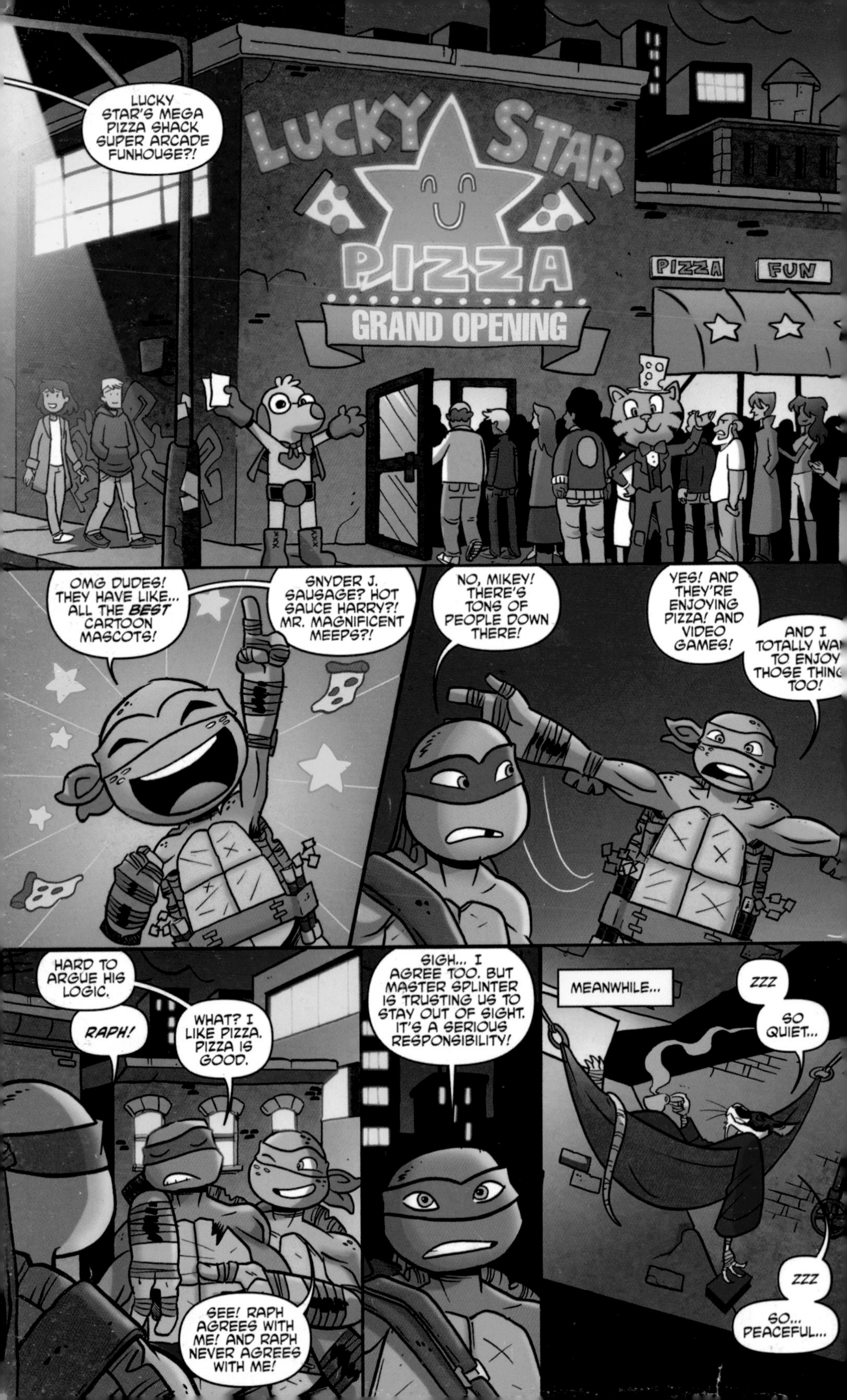

LUCKY STAR'S MEGA PIZZA SHACK SUPER ARCADE FUNHOUSE?!
LUCKY STAR
PIZZA
GRAND OPENING
PIZZA
FUN
OMG DUDES! THEY HAVE LIKE... ALL THE BEST CARTOON MASCOTS!
SNYDER J. SAUSAGE? HOT SAUCE HARRY?! MR. MAGNIFICENT MEEPS?!
NO, MIKEY! THERE'S TONS OF PEOPLE DOWN THERE!
YES! AND THEY'RE ENJOYING PIZZA! AND VIDEO GAMES!
AND I TOTALLY WAN TO ENJOY THOSE THING TOO!
HARD TO ARGUE HIS LOGIC.
RAPH!
WHAT? I LIKE PIZZA. PIZZA IS GOOD.
SEE! RAPH AGREES WITH ME! AND RAPH NEVER AGREES WITH ME!
SIGH... I AGREE TOO. BUT MASTER SPLINTER IS TRUSTING US TO STAY OUT OF SIGHT. IT'S A SERIOUS RESPONSIBILITY!
MEANWHILE...
ZZZ
SO QUIET...
ZZZ
SO... PEACEFUL...

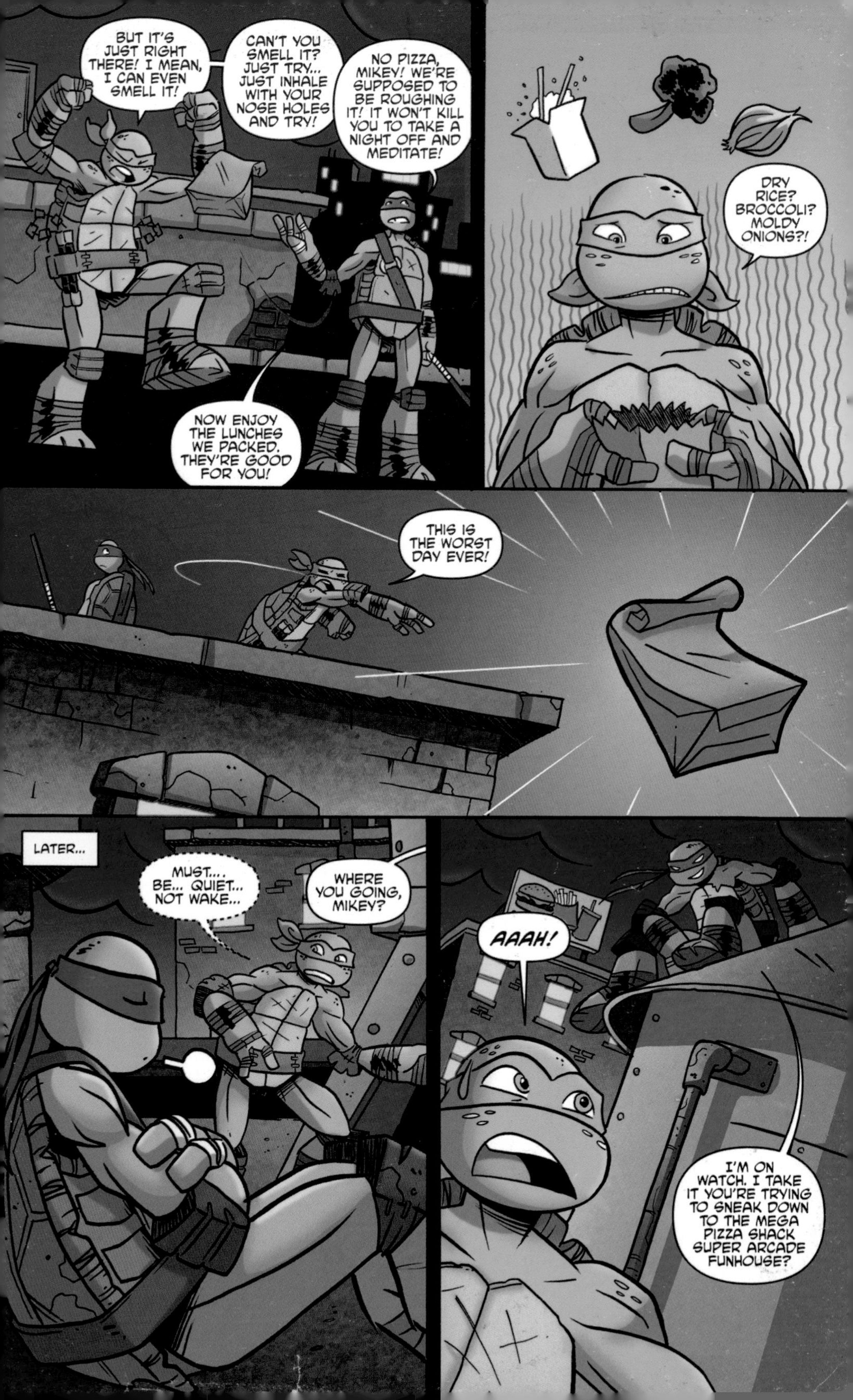
BUT IT'S JUST RIGHT THERE! I MEAN, I CAN EVEN SMELL IT!
CAN'T YOU SMELL IT? JUST TRY... JUST INHALE WITH YOUR NOSE HOLES AND TRY!
NO PIZZA, MIKEY! WE'RE SUPPOSED TO BE ROUGHING IT! IT WON'T KILL YOU TO TAKE A NIGHT OFF AND MEDITATE!
NOW ENJOY THE LUNCHES WE PACKED. THEY'RE GOOD FOR YOU!
DRY RICE? BROCCOLI? MOLDY ONIONS?!
THIS IS THE WORST DAY EVER!
LATER...
MUST.... BE... QUIET... NOT WAKE...
WHERE YOU GOING, MIKEY?
AAAH!
I'M ON WATCH. I TAKE IT YOU'RE TRYING TO SNEAK DOWN TO THE MEGA PIZZA SHACK SUPER ARCADE FUNHOUSE?

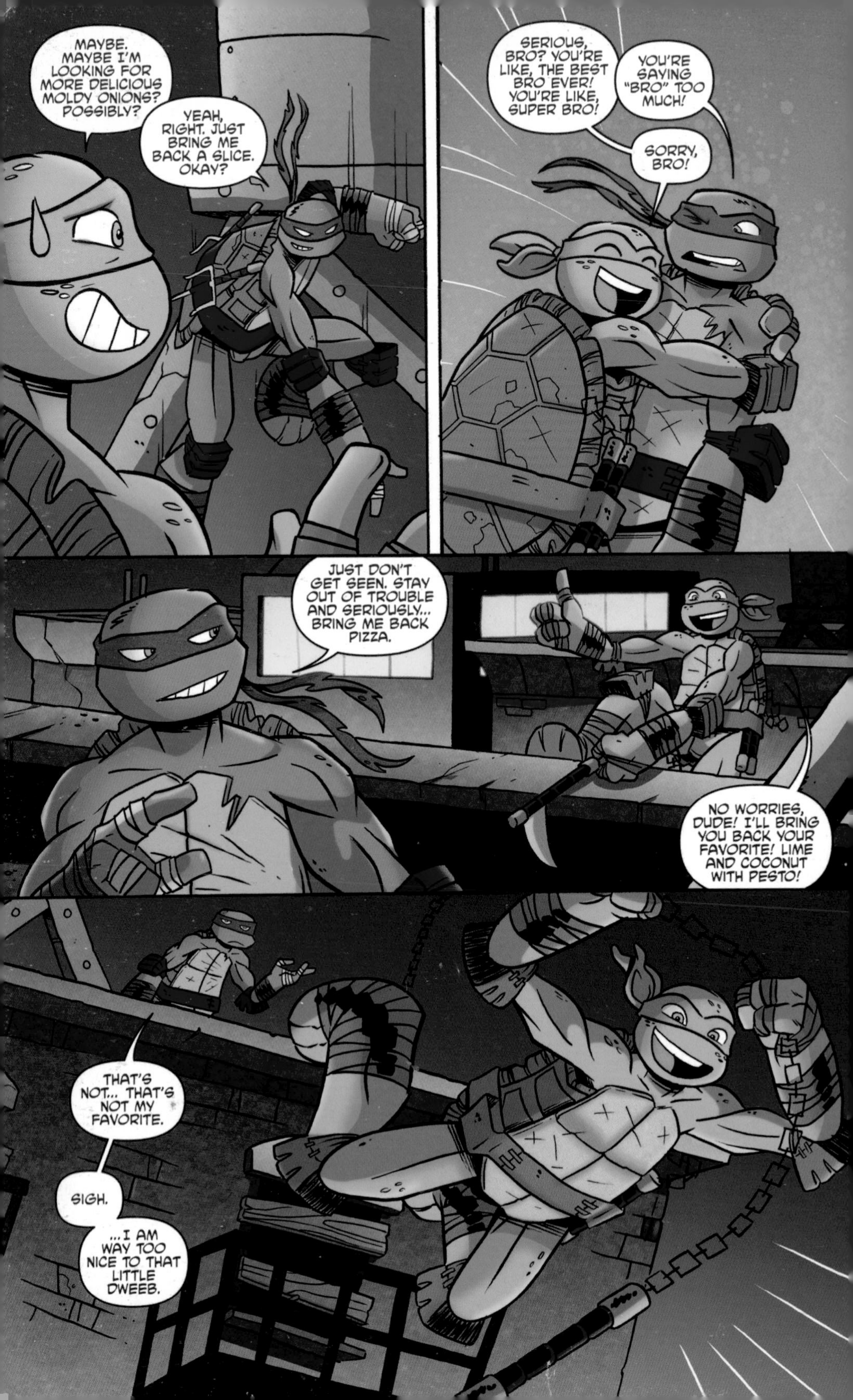
MAYBE. MAYBE I'M LOOKING FOR MORE DELICIOUS MOLDY ONIONS? POSSIBLY?
YEAH, RIGHT. JUST BRING ME BACK A SLICE. OKAY?
SERIOUS, BRO? YOU'RE LIKE, THE BEST BRO EVER! YOU'RE LIKE, SUPER BRO!
YOU'RE SAYING "BRO" TOO MUCH!
SORRY, BRO!
JUST DON'T GET SEEN. STAY OUT OF TROUBLE AND SERIOUSLY... BRING ME BACK PIZZA.
NO WORRIES, DUDE! I'LL BRING YOU BACK YOUR FAVORITE! LIME AND COCONUT WITH PESTO!
THAT'S NOT... THAT'S NOT MY FAVORITE.
SIGH.
...I AM WAY TOO NICE TO THAT LITTLE DWEEB.

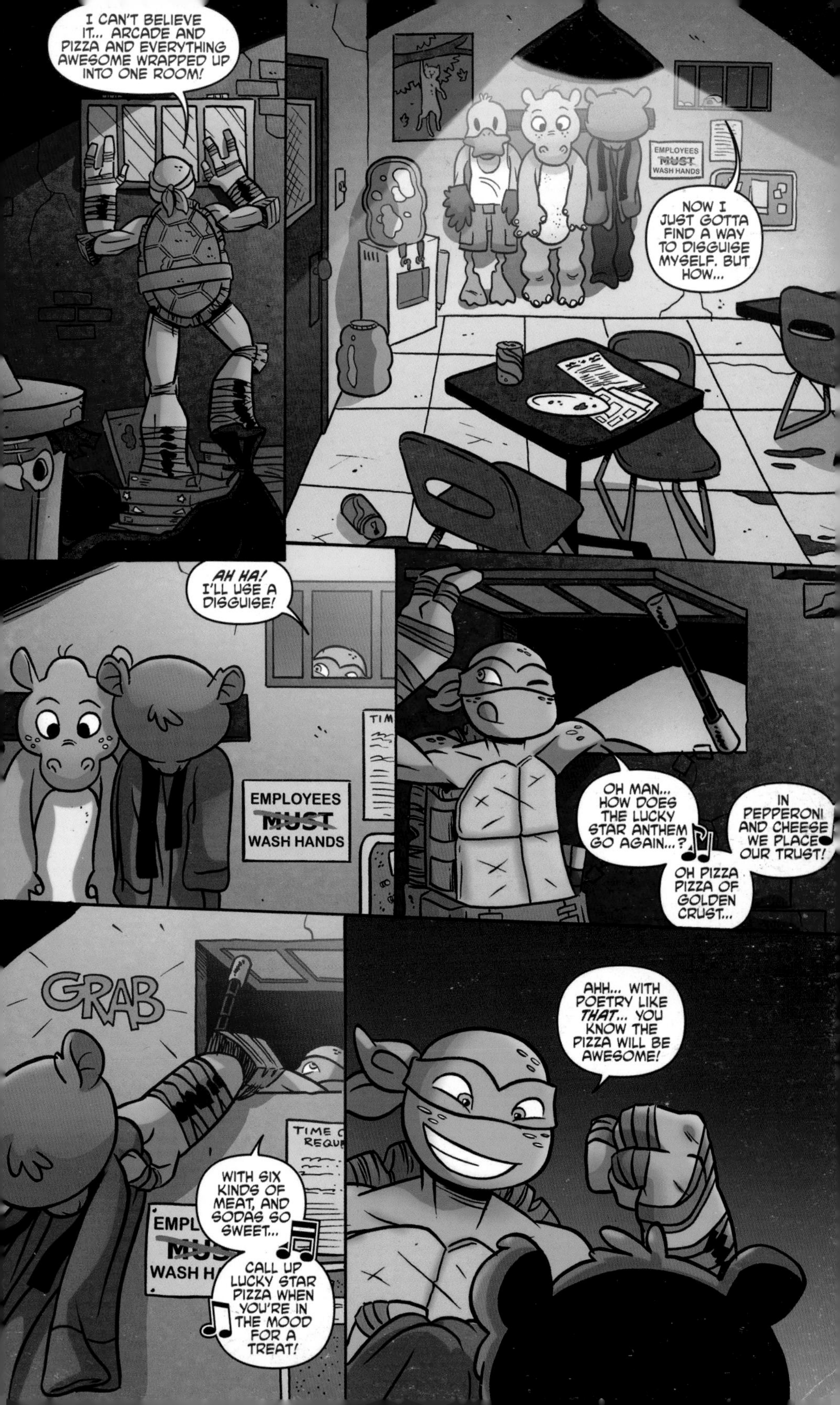
I CAN'T BELIEVE IT... ARCADE AND PIZZA AND EVERYTHING AWESOME WRAPPED UP INTO ONE ROOM!
EMPLOYEES MUST WASH HANDS
NOW I JUST GOTTA FIND A WAY TO DISGUISE MYSELF. BUT HOW...
AH HA! I'LL USE A DISGUISE!
EMPLOYEES MUST WASH HANDS
OH MAN... HOW DOES THE LUCKY STAR ANTHEM GO AGAIN...?
OH PIZZA PIZZA OF GOLDEN CRUST...
IN PEPPERONI AND CHEESE WE PLACE OUR TRUST!
GRAB
WITH SIX KINDS OF MEAT, AND SODAS SO SWEET...
CALL UP LUCKY STAR PIZZA WHEN YOU'RE IN THE MOOD FOR A TREAT!
AHH... WITH POETRY LIKE THAT... YOU KNOW THE PIZZA WILL BE AWESOME!

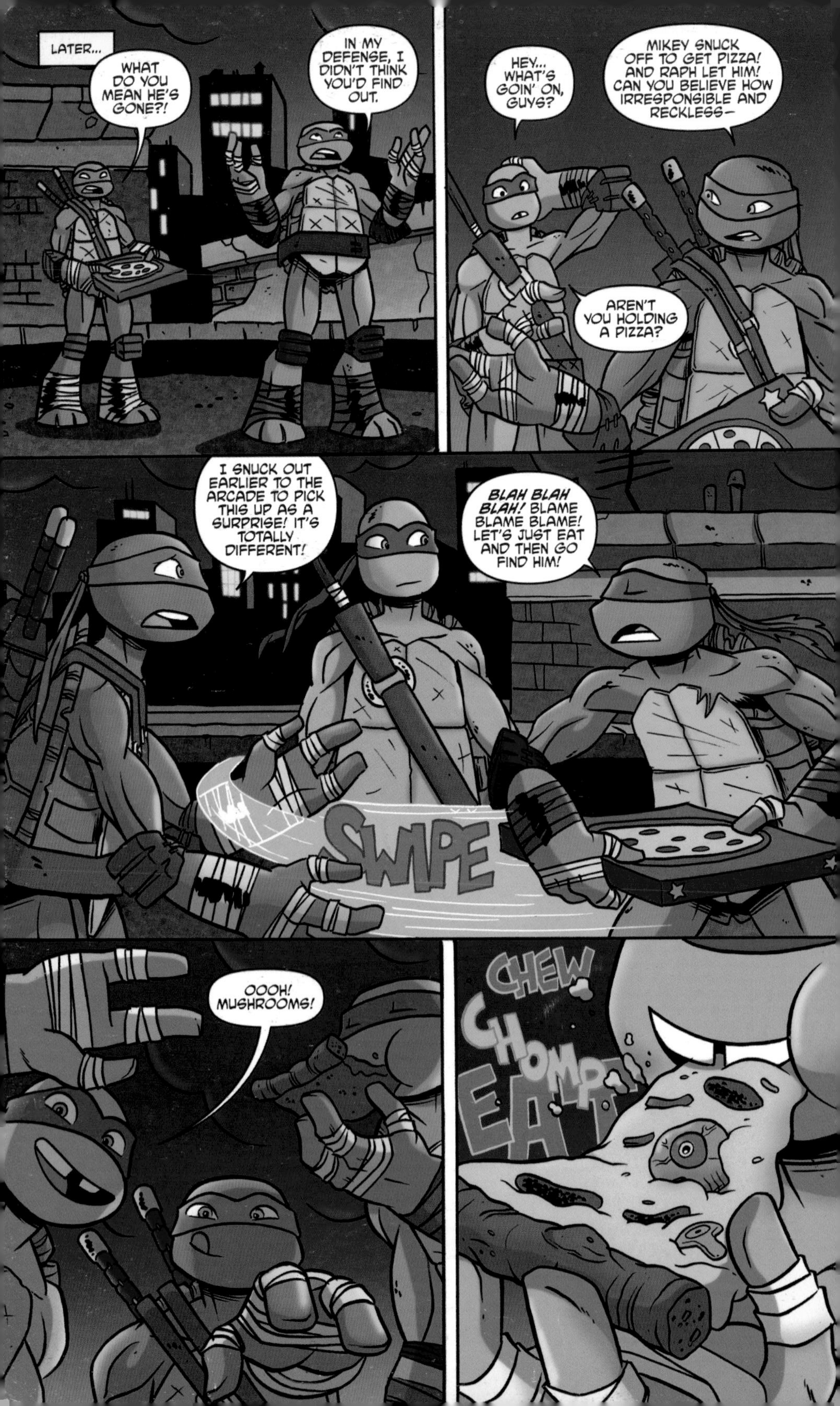

LATER...
WHAT DO YOU MEAN HE'S GONE?!
IN MY DEFENSE, I DIDN'T THINK YOU'D FIND OUT.
HEY... WHAT'S GOIN' ON, GUYS?
MIKEY SNUCK OFF TO GET PIZZA! AND RAPH LET HIM! CAN YOU BELIEVE HOW IRRESPONSIBLE AND RECKLESS—
AREN'T YOU HOLDING A PIZZA?
I SNUCK OUT EARLIER TO THE ARCADE TO PICK THIS UP AS A SURPRISE! IT'S TOTALLY DIFFERENT!
BLAH BLAH BLAH! BLAME BLAME BLAME! LET'S JUST EAT AND THEN GO FIND HIM!
SWIPE
OOOH! MUSHROOMS!
CHEW
CHOMP
EAT

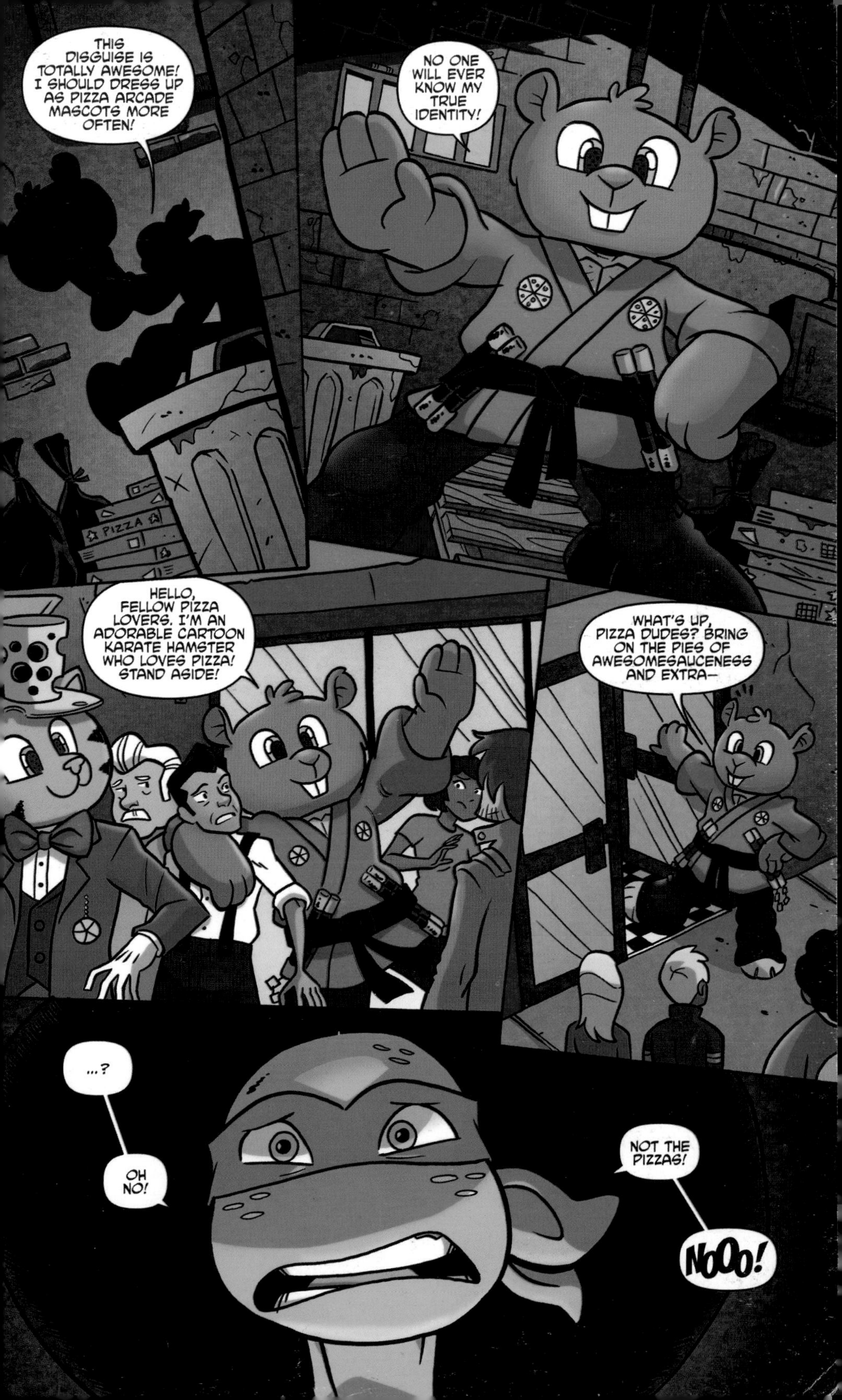

THIS DISGUISE IS TOTALLY AWESOME! I SHOULD DRESS UP AS PIZZA ARCADE MASCOTS MORE OFTEN!
NO ONE WILL EVER KNOW MY TRUE IDENTITY!
PIZZA
HELLO, FELLOW PIZZA LOVERS. I'M AN ADORABLE CARTOON KARATE HAMSTER WHO LOVES PIZZA! STAND ASIDE!
WHAT'S UP, PIZZA DUDES? BRING ON THE PIES OF AWESOMESAUCENESS AND EXTRA—
...?
OH NO!
NOT THE PIZZAS!
NOOO!

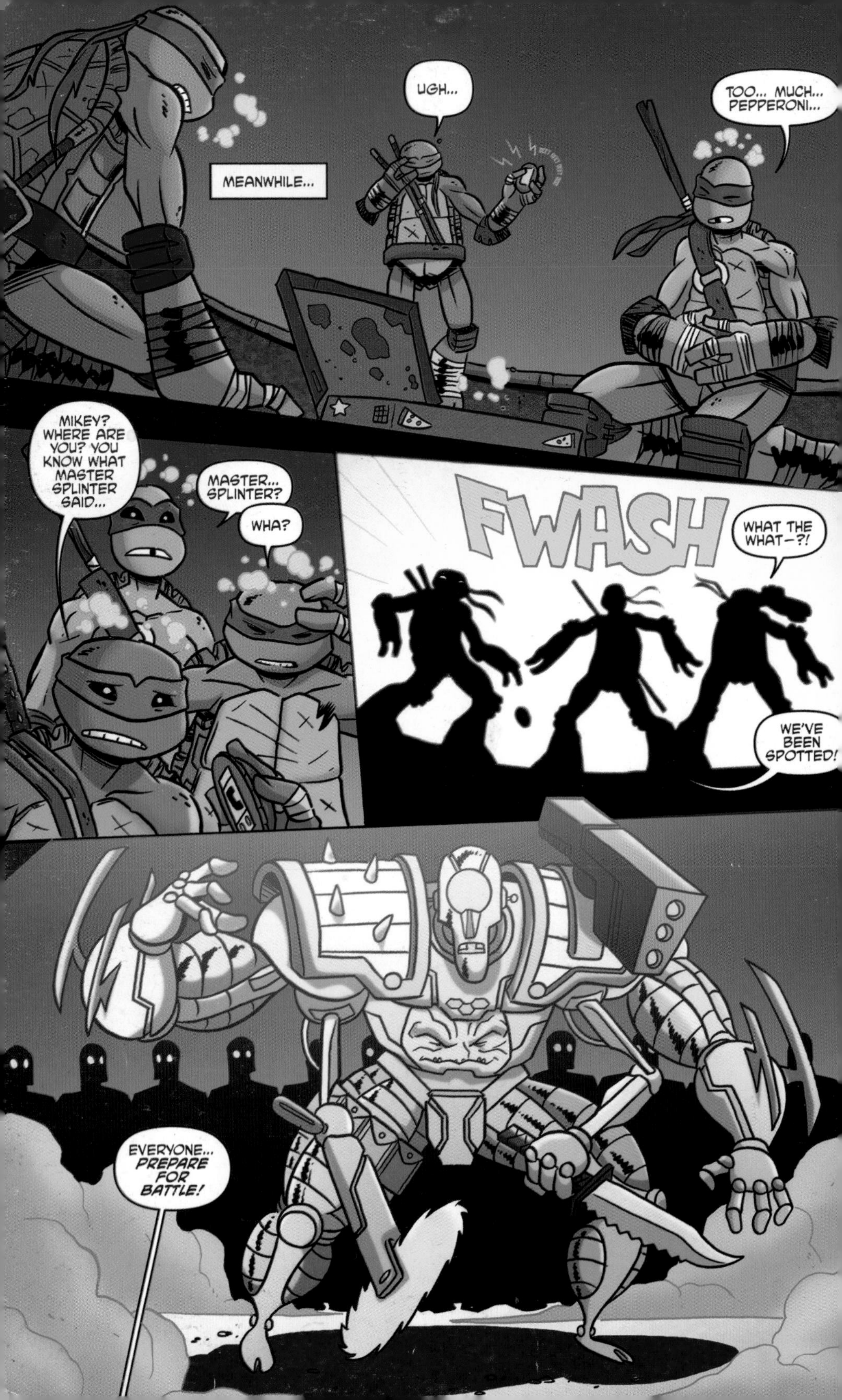
MEANWHILE...
UGH...
TOO... MUCH... PEPPERONI...
MIKEY? WHERE ARE YOU? YOU KNOW WHAT MASTER SPLINTER SAID...
MASTER... SPLINTER?
WHA?
FWASH
WHAT THE WHAT—?!
WE'VE BEEN SPOTTED!
EVERYONE... PREPARE FOR BATTLE!

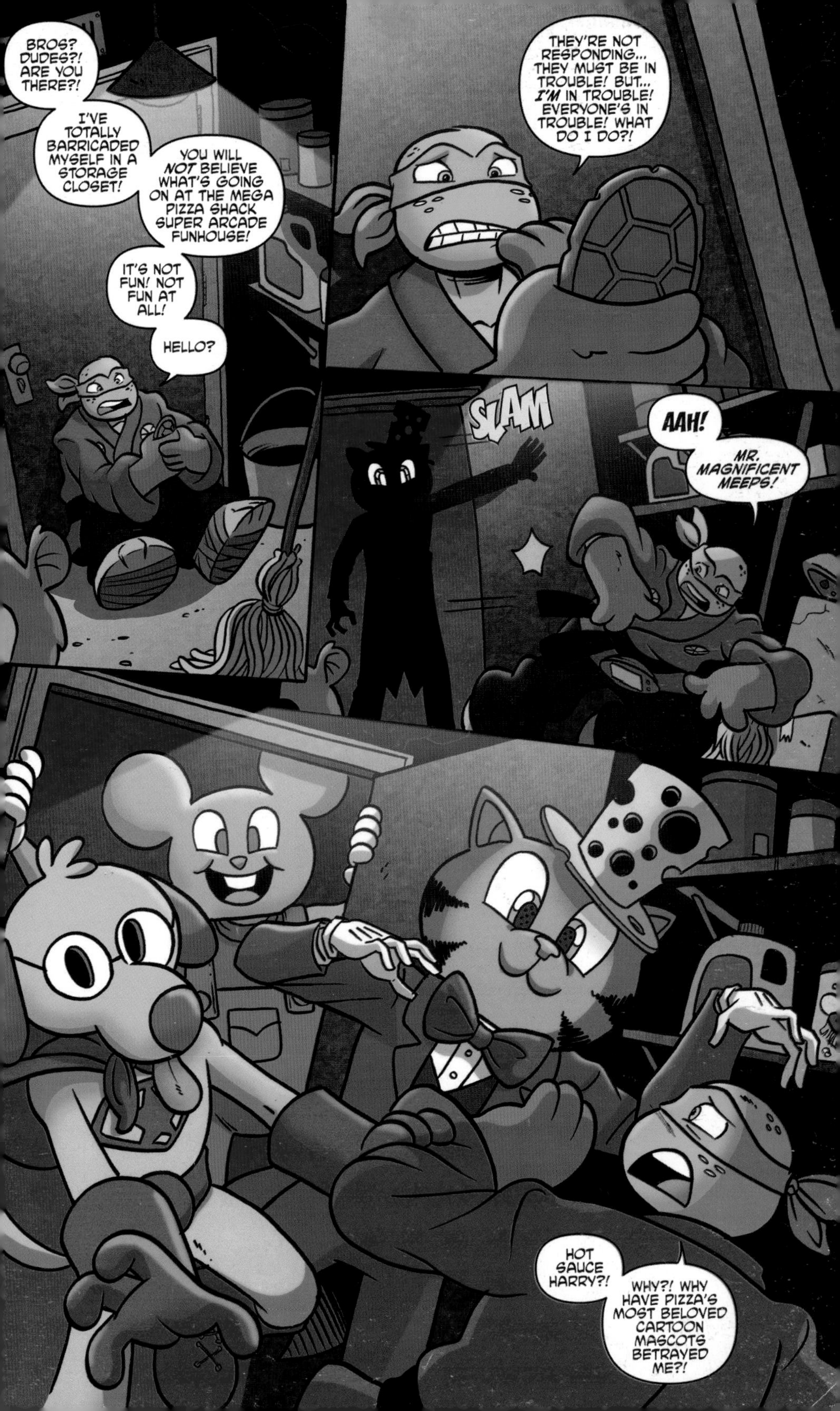
BROS? DUDES?! ARE YOU THERE?!
I'VE TOTALLY BARRICADED MYSELF IN A STORAGE CLOSET!
YOU WILL *NOT* BELIEVE WHAT'S GOING ON AT THE MEGA PIZZA SHACK SUPER ARCADE FUNHOUSE!
IT'S NOT FUN! NOT FUN AT ALL!
HELLO?
THEY'RE NOT RESPONDING... THEY MUST BE IN TROUBLE! BUT... *I'M* IN TROUBLE! EVERYONE'S IN TROUBLE! WHAT DO I DO?!
SLAM
AAH!
MR. MAGNIFICENT MEEPS!
HOT SAUCE HARRY?!
WHY?! WHY HAVE PIZZA'S MOST BELOVED CARTOON MASCOTS BETRAYED ME?!

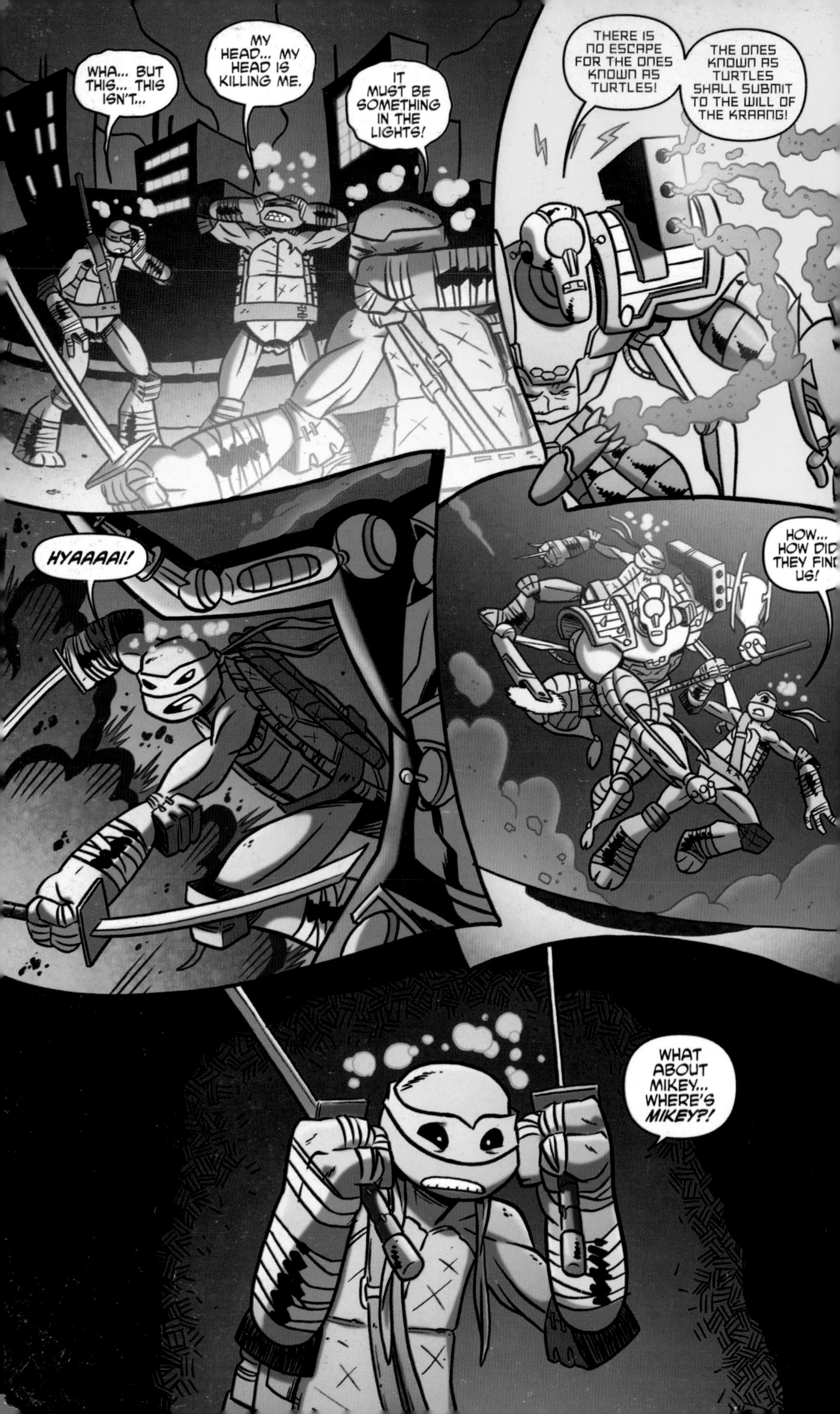
WHA... BUT THIS... THIS ISN'T...
MY HEAD... MY HEAD IS KILLING ME.
IT MUST BE SOMETHING IN THE LIGHTS!
THERE IS NO ESCAPE FOR THE ONES KNOWN AS TURTLES!
THE ONES KNOWN AS TURTLES SHALL SUBMIT TO THE WILL OF THE KRAANG!
HYAAAAI!
HOW... HOW DID THEY FIND US!
WHAT ABOUT MIKEY... WHERE'S MIKEY?!

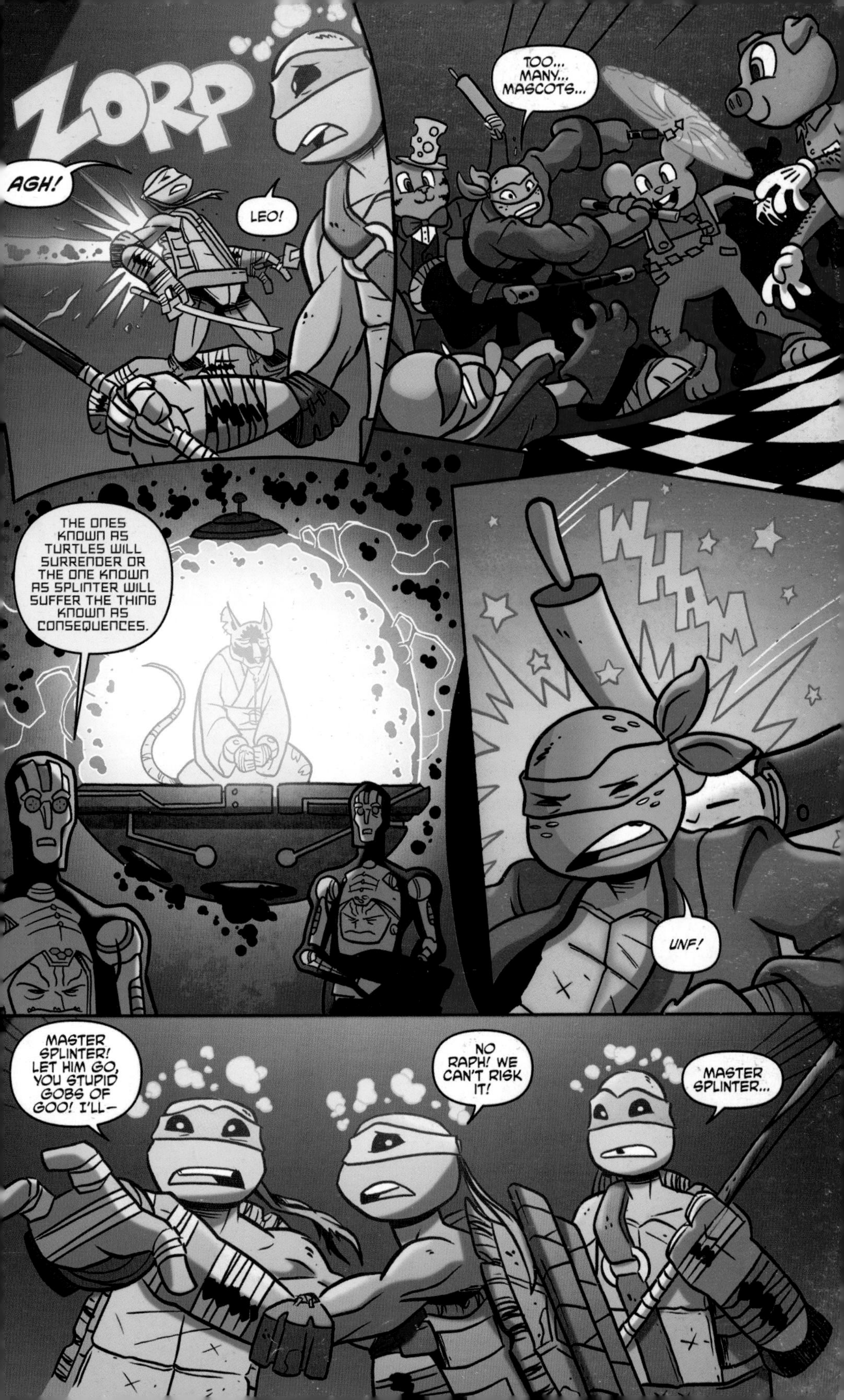
ZORP
AGH!
LEO!
TOO... MANY... MASCOTS...
THE ONES KNOWN AS TURTLES WILL SURRENDER OR THE ONE KNOWN AS SPLINTER WILL SUFFER THE THING KNOWN AS CONSEQUENCES.
WHAM
UNF!
MASTER SPLINTER! LET HIM GO, YOU STUPID GOBS OF GOO! I'LL—
NO RAPH! WE CAN'T RISK IT!
MASTER SPLINTER...

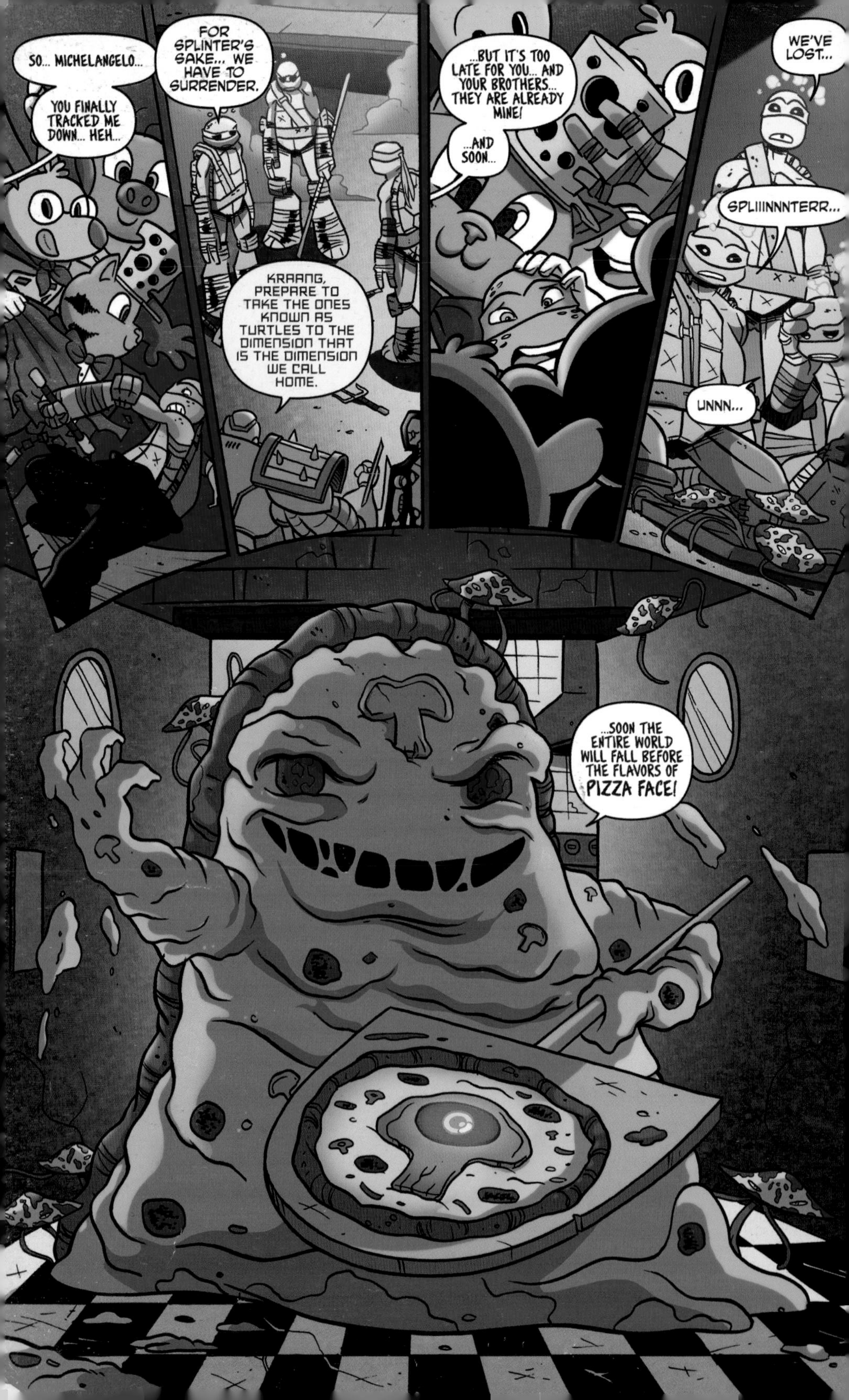
SO... MICHELANGELO...
YOU FINALLY TRACKED ME DOWN... HEH...
FOR SPLINTER'S SAKE... WE HAVE TO SURRENDER.
KRAANG, PREPARE TO TAKE THE ONES KNOWN AS TURTLES TO THE DIMENSION THAT IS THE DIMENSION WE CALL HOME.
...BUT IT'S TOO LATE FOR YOU... AND YOUR BROTHERS... THEY ARE ALREADY MINE!
...AND SOON...
WE'VE LOST...
SPLIIINNNTERR...
UNNN...
...SOON THE ENTIRE WORLD WILL FALL BEFORE THE FLAVORS OF PIZZA FACE!

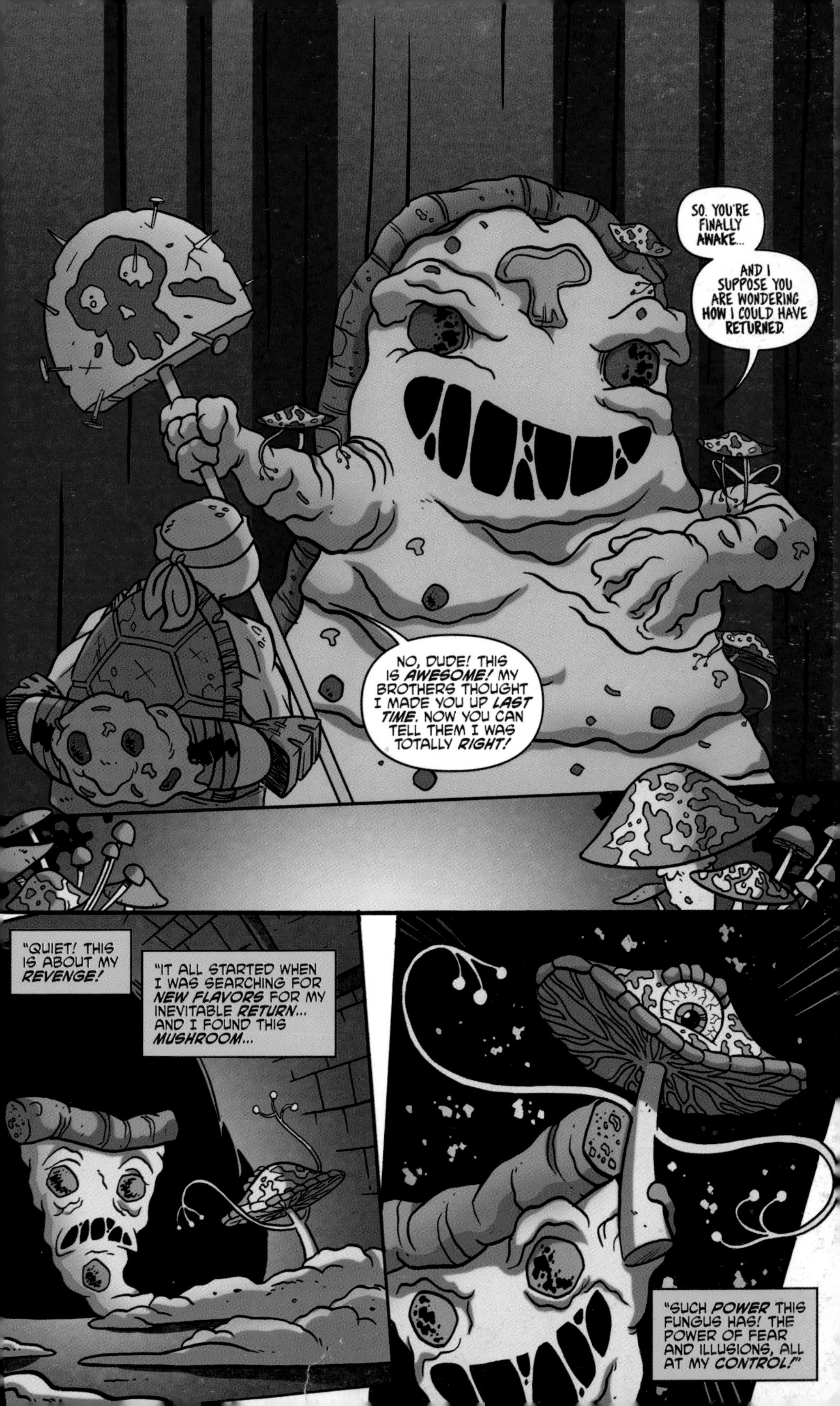

SO. YOU'RE FINALLY AWAKE...
AND I SUPPOSE YOU ARE WONDERING HOW I COULD HAVE RETURNED.
NO, DUDE! THIS IS AWESOME! MY BROTHERS THOUGHT I MADE YOU UP LAST TIME. NOW YOU CAN TELL THEM I WAS TOTALLY RIGHT!
"QUIET! THIS IS ABOUT MY REVENGE!
"IT ALL STARTED WHEN I WAS SEARCHING FOR NEW FLAVORS FOR MY INEVITABLE RETURN... AND I FOUND THIS MUSHROOM...
"SUCH POWER THIS FUNGUS HAS! THE POWER OF FEAR AND ILLUSIONS, ALL AT MY CONTROL!"

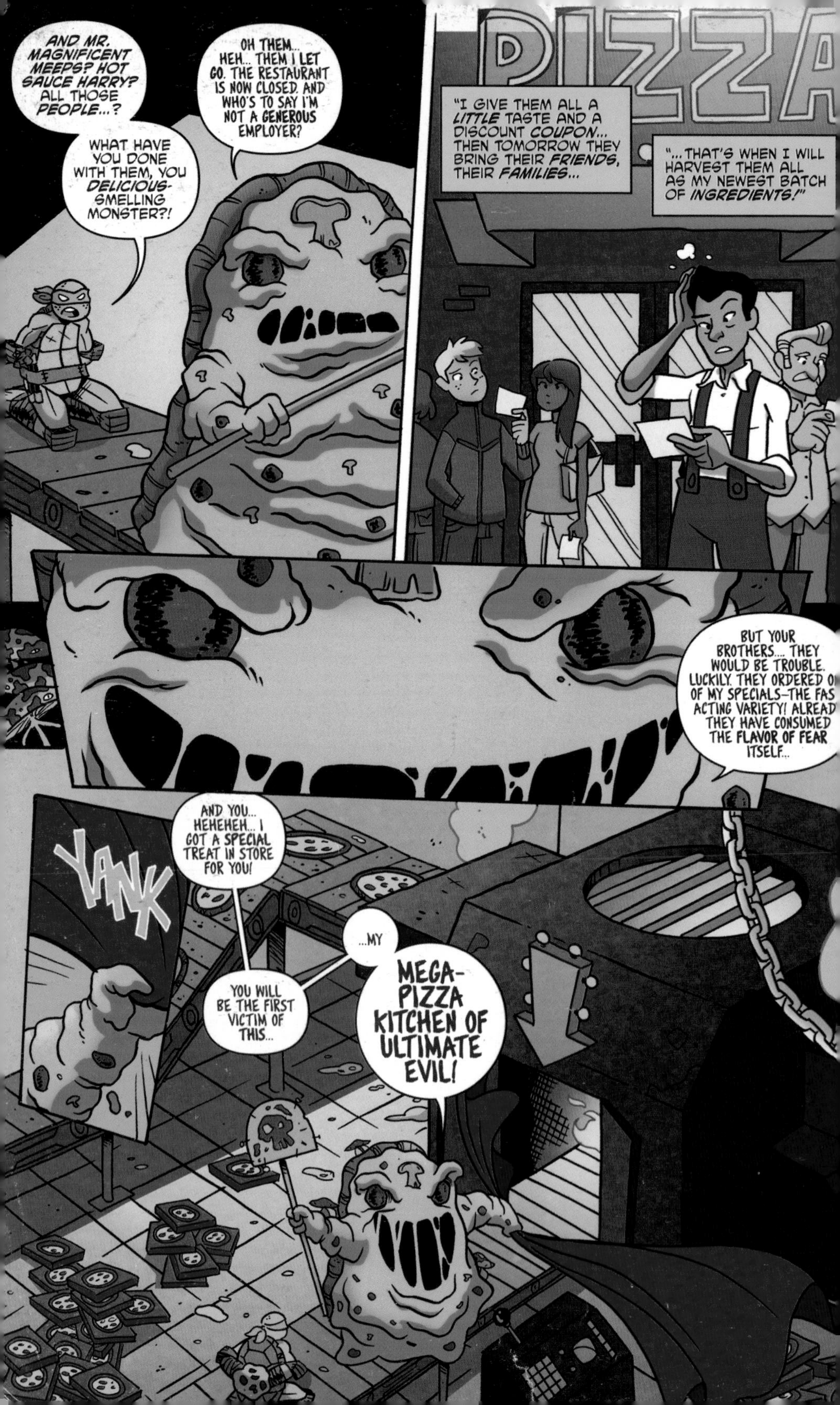

AND MR. MAGNIFICENT MEEPS? HOT SAUCE HARRY? ALL THOSE PEOPLE...?
WHAT HAVE YOU DONE WITH THEM, YOU DELICIOUS-SMELLING MONSTER?!
OH THEM... HEH... THEM I LET GO. THE RESTAURANT IS NOW CLOSED. AND WHO'S TO SAY I'M NOT A GENEROUS EMPLOYER?
PIZZA
"I GIVE THEM ALL A LITTLE TASTE AND A DISCOUNT COUPON... THEN TOMORROW THEY BRING THEIR FRIENDS, THEIR FAMILIES...
"...THAT'S WHEN I WILL HARVEST THEM ALL AS MY NEWEST BATCH OF INGREDIENTS!"
BUT YOUR BROTHERS.... THEY WOULD BE TROUBLE. LUCKILY, THEY ORDERED O OF MY SPECIALS—THE FAS ACTING VARIETY! ALREAD THEY HAVE CONSUMED THE FLAVOR OF FEAR ITSELF...
YANK
AND YOU... HEHEHEH... I GOT A SPECIAL TREAT IN STORE FOR YOU!
YOU WILL BE THE FIRST VICTIM OF THIS...
...MY
MEGA-PIZZA KITCHEN OF ULTIMATE EVIL!

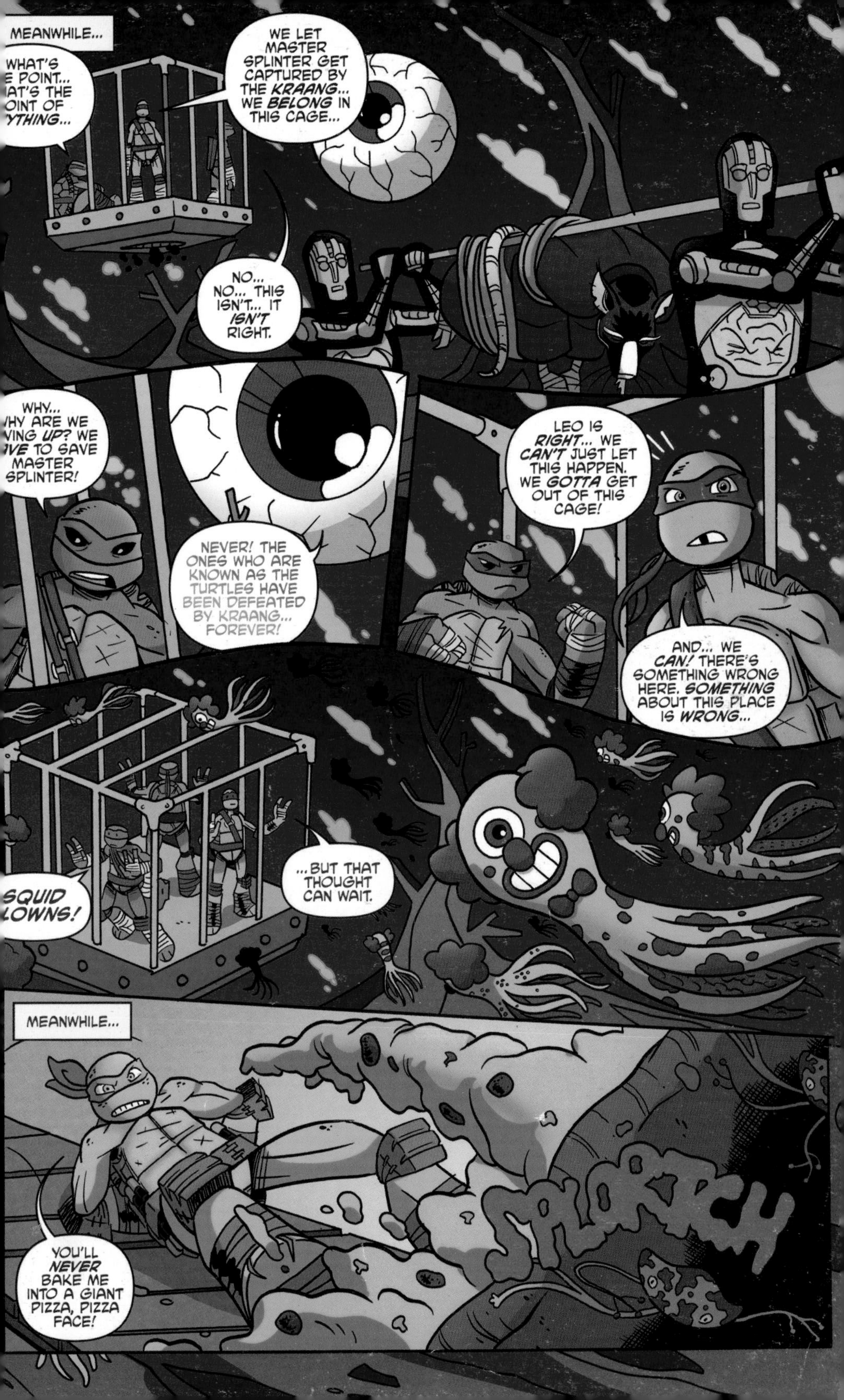
MEANWHILE...
WHAT'S E POINT... AT'S THE OINT OF YTHING...
WE LET MASTER SPLINTER GET CAPTURED BY THE KRAANG... WE BELONG IN THIS CAGE...
NO... NO... THIS ISN'T... IT ISN'T RIGHT.
WHY... HY ARE WE VING UP? WE VE TO SAVE MASTER SPLINTER!
NEVER! THE ONES WHO ARE KNOWN AS THE TURTLES HAVE BEEN DEFEATED BY KRAANG... FOREVER!
LEO IS RIGHT... WE CAN'T JUST LET THIS HAPPEN. WE GOTTA GET OUT OF THIS CAGE!
AND... WE CAN! THERE'S SOMETHING WRONG HERE. SOMETHING ABOUT THIS PLACE IS WRONG...
SQUID LOWNS!
...BUT THAT THOUGHT CAN WAIT.
MEANWHILE...
YOU'LL NEVER BAKE ME INTO A GIANT PIZZA, PIZZA FACE!
SPLORCH

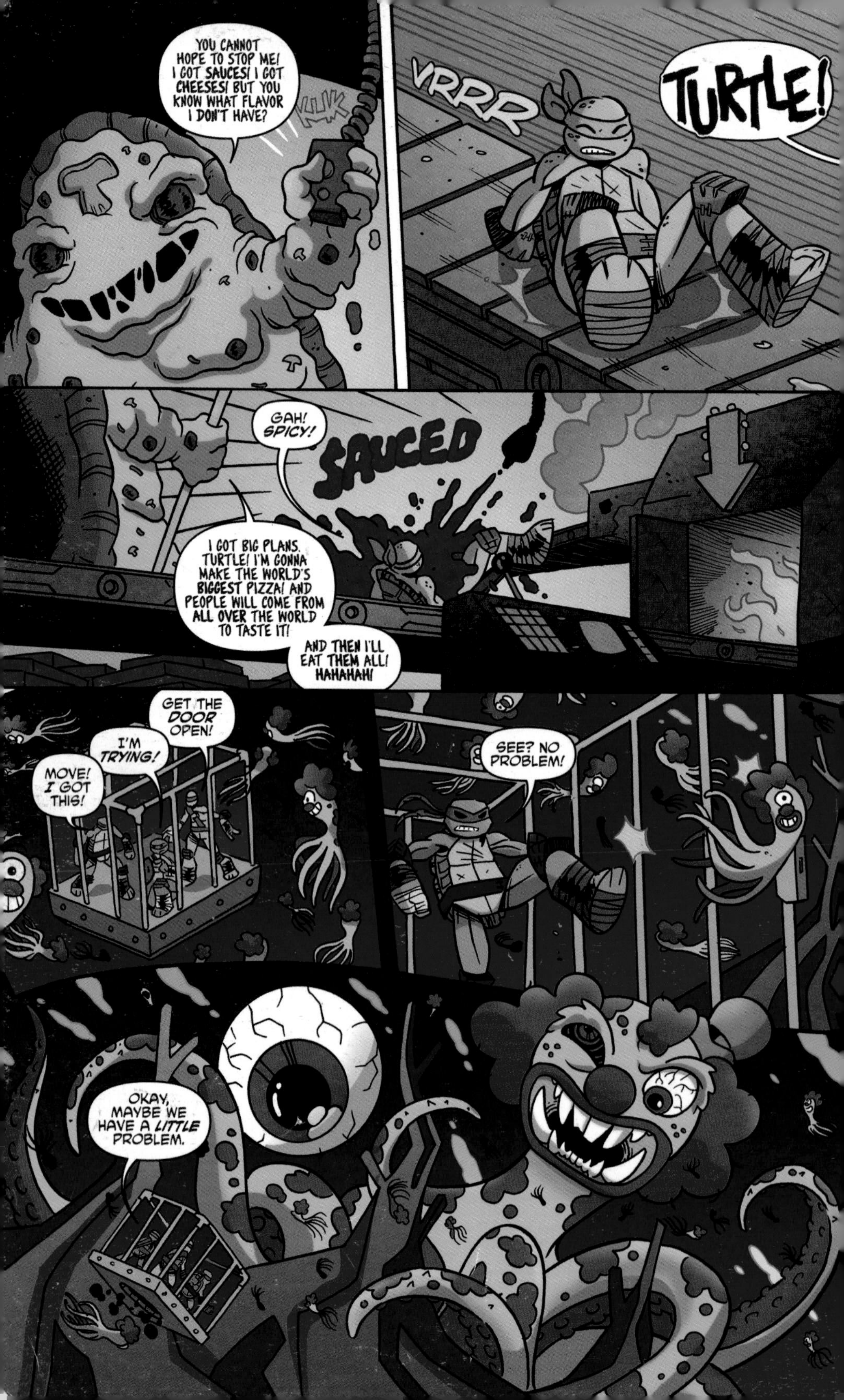
YOU CANNOT HOPE TO STOP ME! I GOT SAUCES! I GOT CHEESES! BUT YOU KNOW WHAT FLAVOR I DON'T HAVE?
KLIK
VRRR
TURTLE!
GAH! SPICY!
SAUCED
I GOT BIG PLANS, TURTLE! I'M GONNA MAKE THE WORLD'S BIGGEST PIZZA! AND PEOPLE WILL COME FROM ALL OVER THE WORLD TO TASTE IT!
AND THEN I'LL EAT THEM ALL! HAHAHAH!
GET THE DOOR OPEN!
I'M TRYING!
MOVE! I GOT THIS!
SEE? NO PROBLEM!
OKAY, MAYBE WE HAVE A LITTLE PROBLEM.

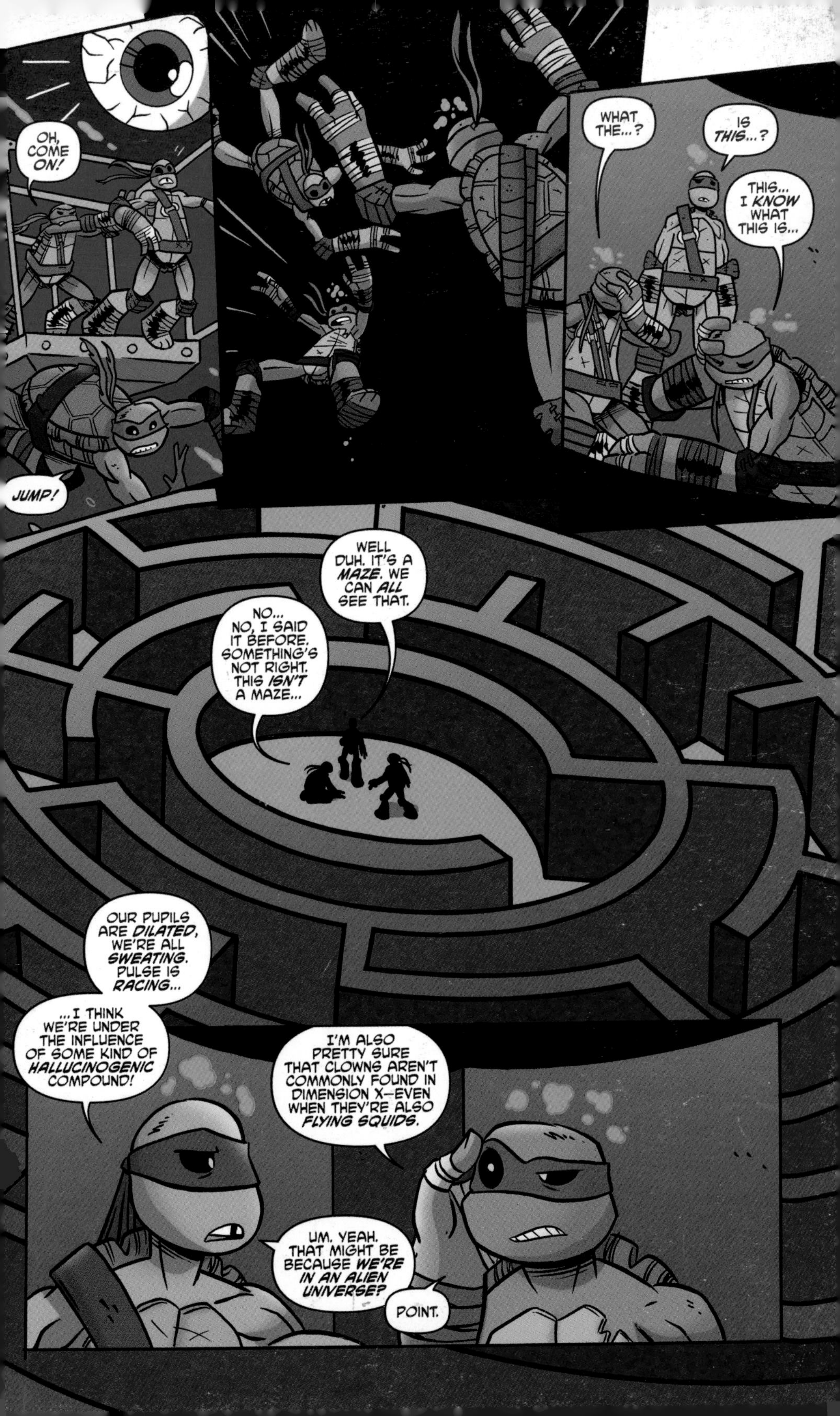
OH, COME ON!
JUMP!
WHAT THE...?
IS THIS...?
THIS... I KNOW WHAT THIS IS...
WELL DUH. IT'S A MAZE. WE CAN ALL SEE THAT.
NO... NO, I SAID IT BEFORE. SOMETHING'S NOT RIGHT. THIS ISN'T A MAZE...
OUR PUPILS ARE DILATED, WE'RE ALL SWEATING. PULSE IS RACING...
...I THINK WE'RE UNDER THE INFLUENCE OF SOME KIND OF HALLUCINOGENIC COMPOUND!
I'M ALSO PRETTY SURE THAT CLOWNS AREN'T COMMONLY FOUND IN DIMENSION X—EVEN WHEN THEY'RE ALSO FLYING SQUIDS.
UM. YEAH. THAT MIGHT BE BECAUSE WE'RE IN AN ALIEN UNIVERSE?
POINT.

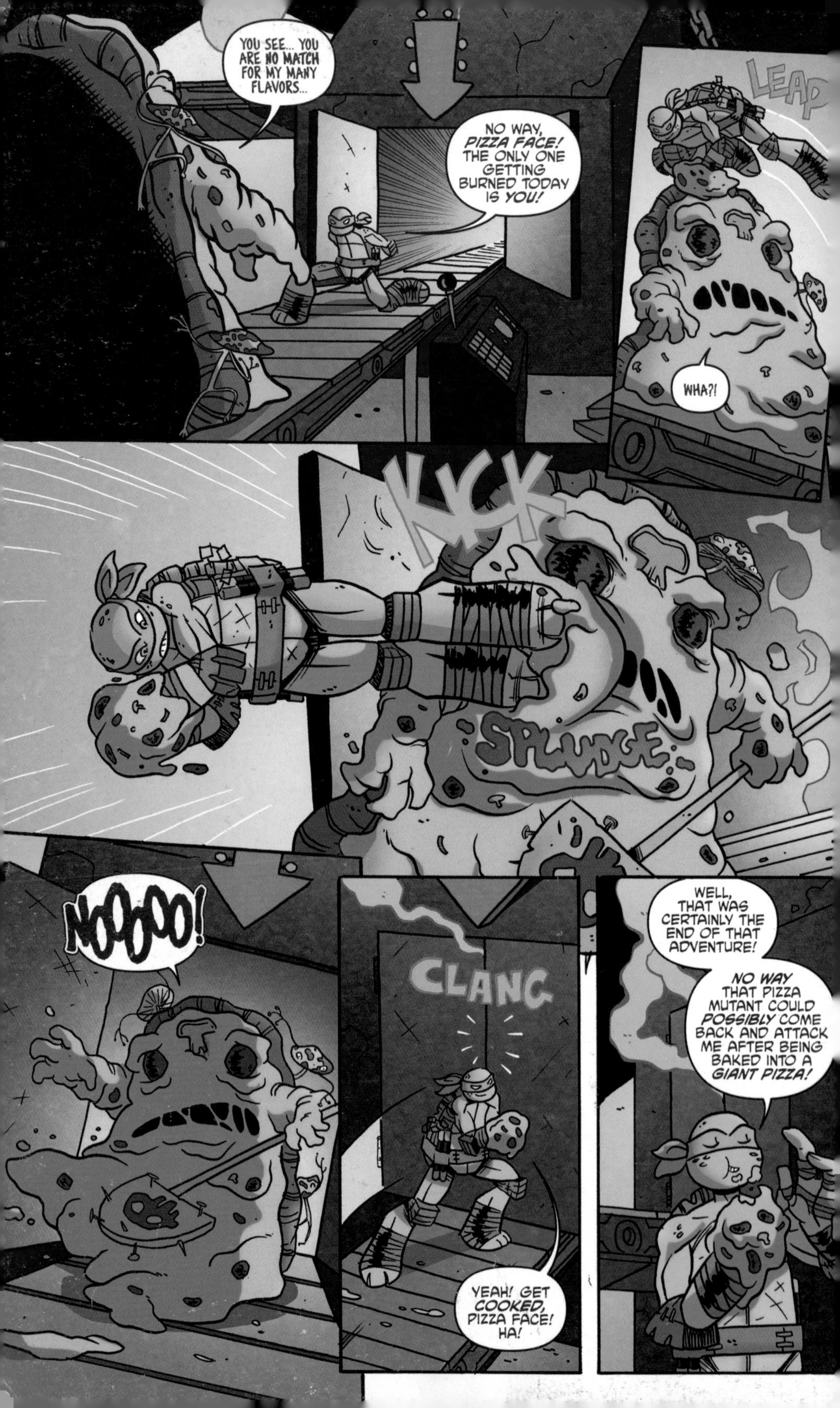
YOU SEE... YOU ARE NO MATCH FOR MY MANY FLAVORS...
NO WAY, PIZZA FACE! THE ONLY ONE GETTING BURNED TODAY IS YOU!
LEAP
WHA?!
KICK
SPLUDGE
NOOOOO!
CLANG
YEAH! GET COOKED, PIZZA FACE! HA!
WELL, THAT WAS CERTAINLY THE END OF THAT ADVENTURE!
NO WAY THAT PIZZA MUTANT COULD POSSIBLY COME BACK AND ATTACK ME AFTER BEING BAKED INTO A GIANT PIZZA!

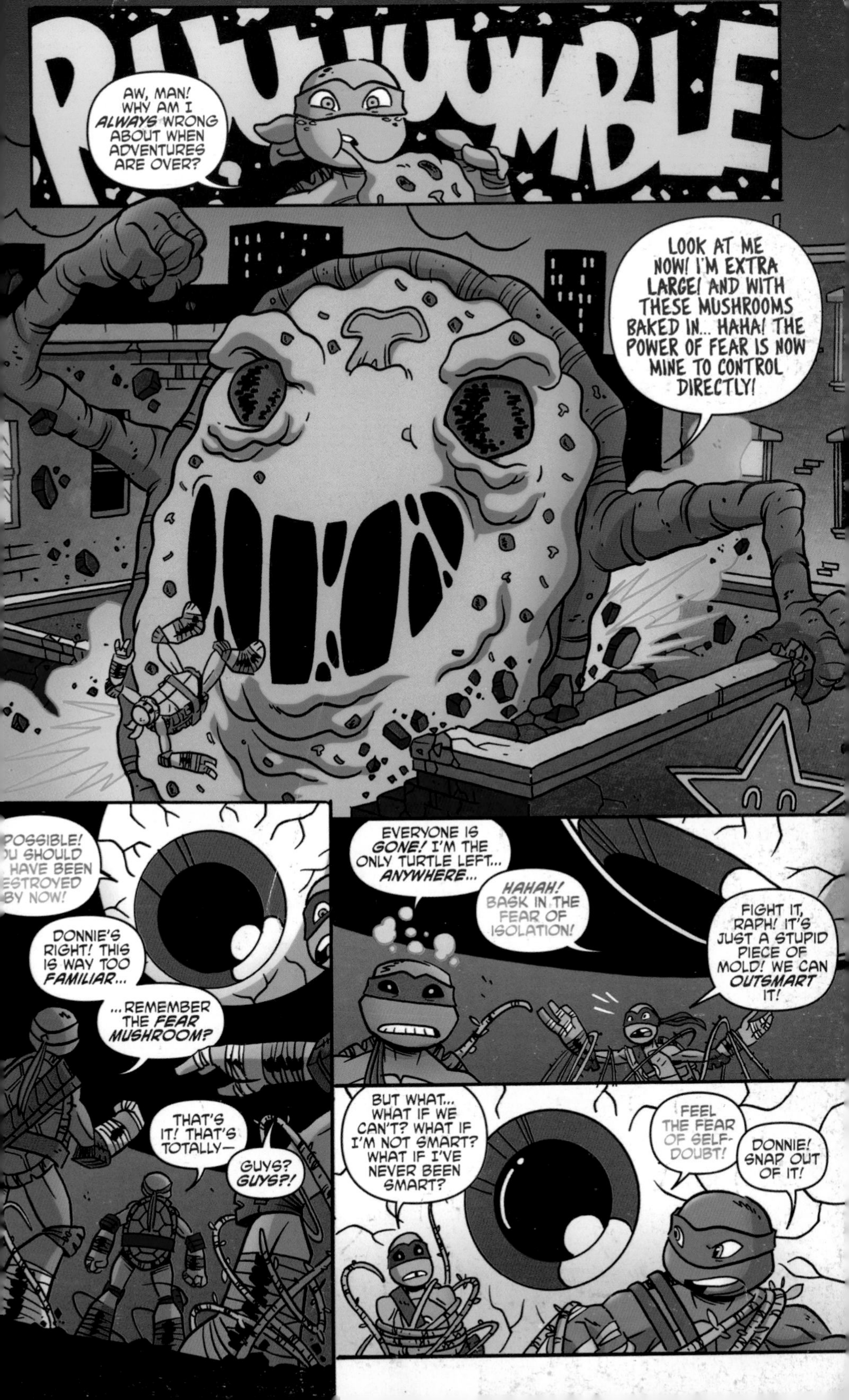
RUUUUUMBLE
AW, MAN! WHY AM I ALWAYS WRONG ABOUT WHEN ADVENTURES ARE OVER?
LOOK AT ME NOW! I'M EXTRA LARGE! AND WITH THESE MUSHROOMS BAKED IN... HAHA! THE POWER OF FEAR IS NOW MINE TO CONTROL DIRECTLY!
POSSIBLE! U SHOULD HAVE BEEN ESTROYED BY NOW!
DONNIE'S RIGHT! THIS IS WAY TOO FAMILIAR...
...REMEMBER THE FEAR MUSHROOM?
THAT'S IT! THAT'S TOTALLY—
GUYS? GUYS?!
EVERYONE IS GONE! I'M THE ONLY TURTLE LEFT... ANYWHERE...
HAHAH! BASK IN THE FEAR OF ISOLATION!
FIGHT IT, RAPH! IT'S JUST A STUPID PIECE OF MOLD! WE CAN OUTSMART IT!
BUT WHAT... WHAT IF WE CAN'T? WHAT IF I'M NOT SMART? WHAT IF I'VE NEVER BEEN SMART?
FEEL THE FEAR OF SELF-DOUBT!
DONNIE! SNAP OUT OF IT!

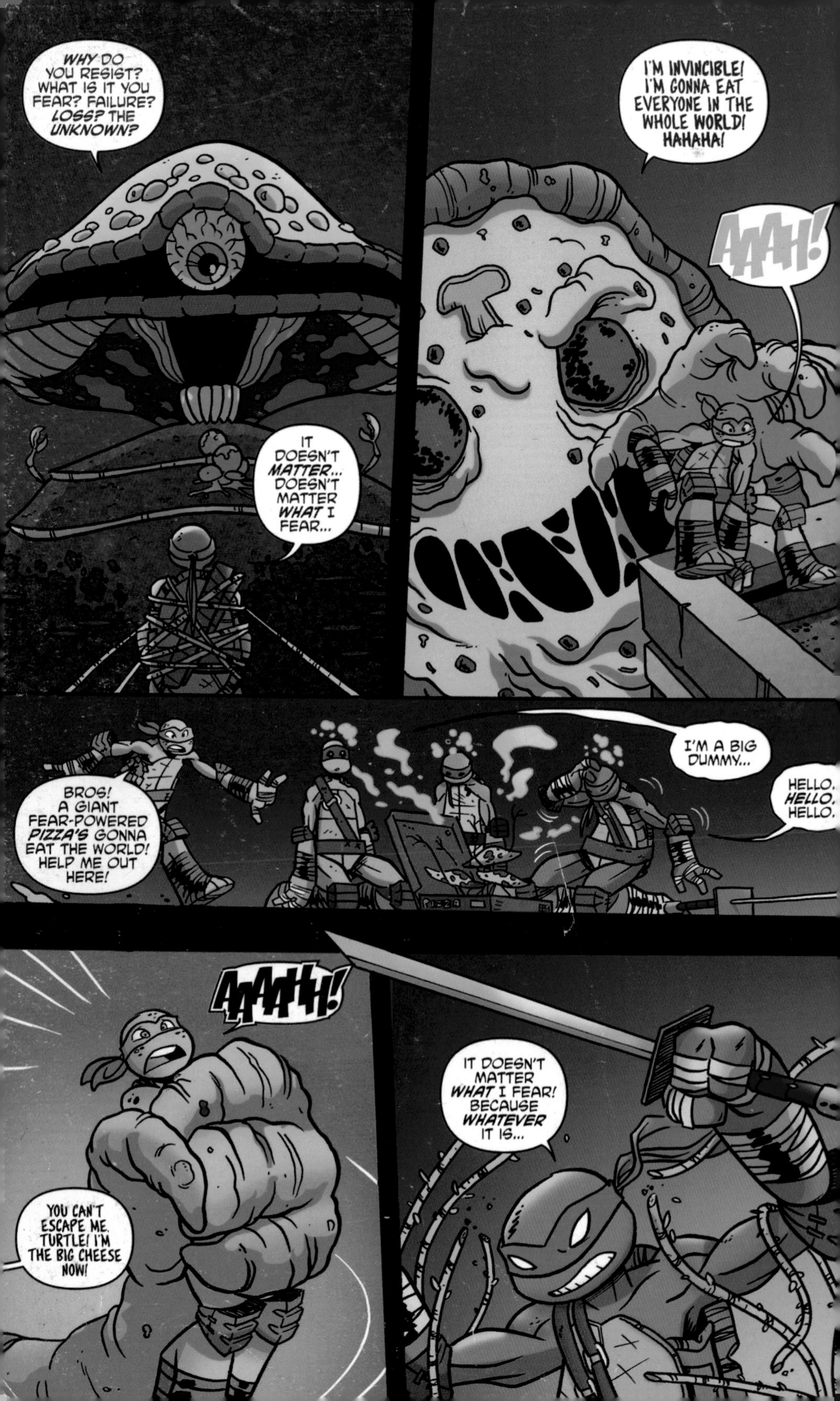
WHY DO YOU RESIST? WHAT IS IT YOU FEAR? FAILURE? LOSS? THE UNKNOWN?
IT DOESN'T MATTER... DOESN'T MATTER WHAT I FEAR...
I'M INVINCIBLE! I'M GONNA EAT EVERYONE IN THE WHOLE WORLD! HAHAHA!
AAAAH!
BROS! A GIANT FEAR-POWERED PIZZA'S GONNA EAT THE WORLD! HELP ME OUT HERE!
I'M A BIG DUMMY...
HELLO. HELLO. HELLO.
AAAAHH!
YOU CAN'T ESCAPE ME, TURTLE! I'M THE BIG CHEESE NOW!
IT DOESN'T MATTER WHAT I FEAR! BECAUSE WHATEVER IT IS...

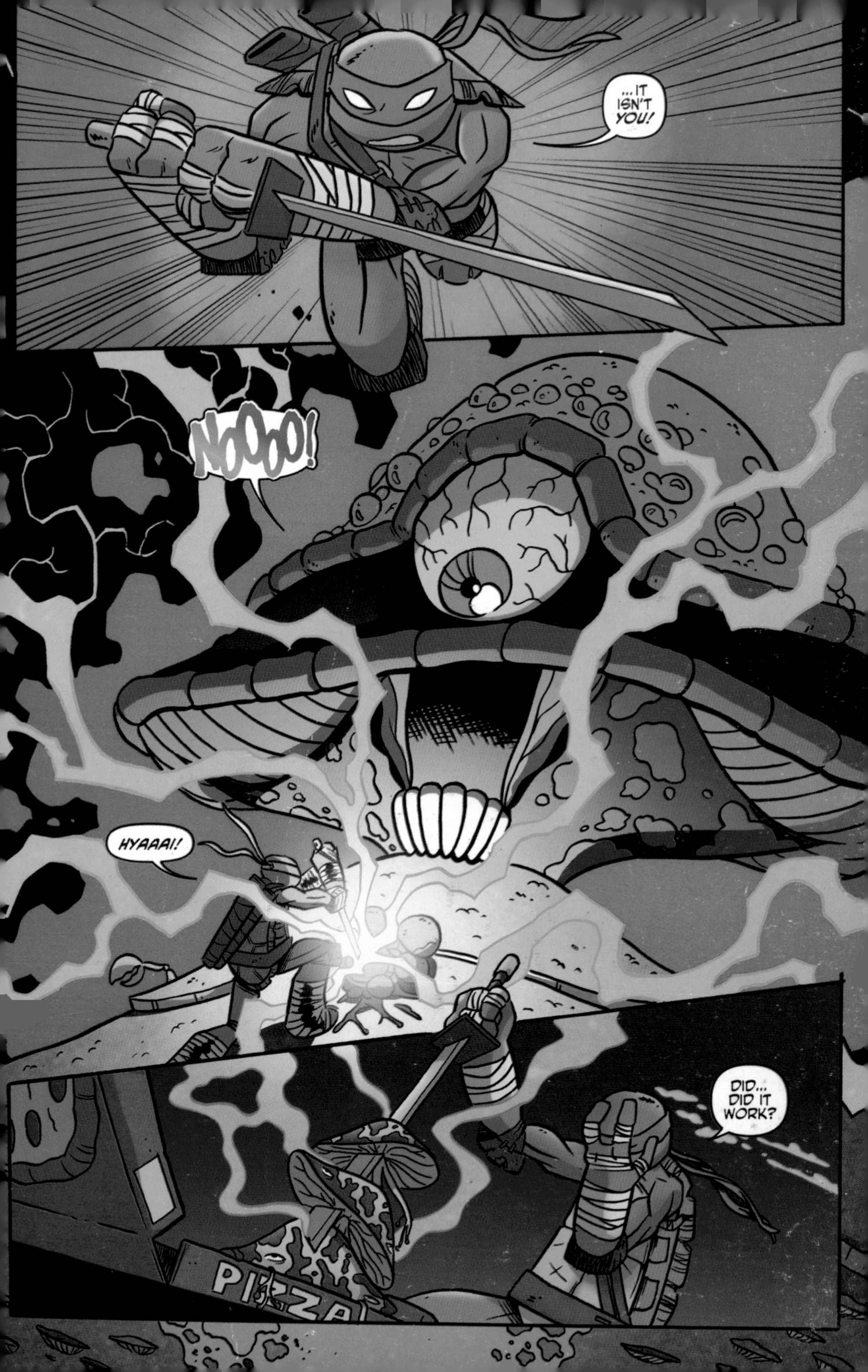
...IT ISN'T YOU!
NOOOO!
HYAAAI!
DID... DID IT WORK?
PIZZA

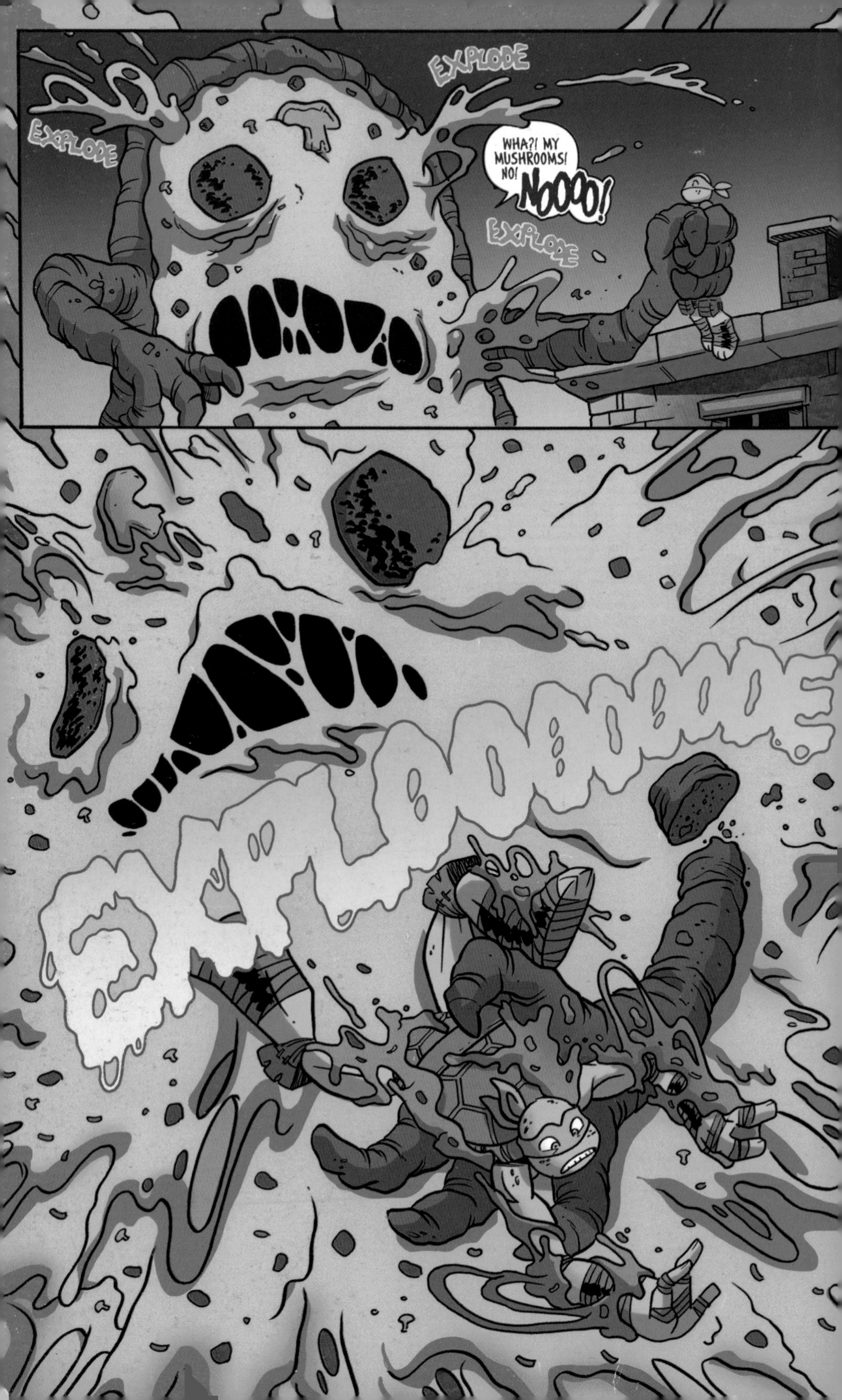
EXPLODE
EXPLODE
WHA?! MY MUSHROOMS! NO! NOOOO!
EXPLODE

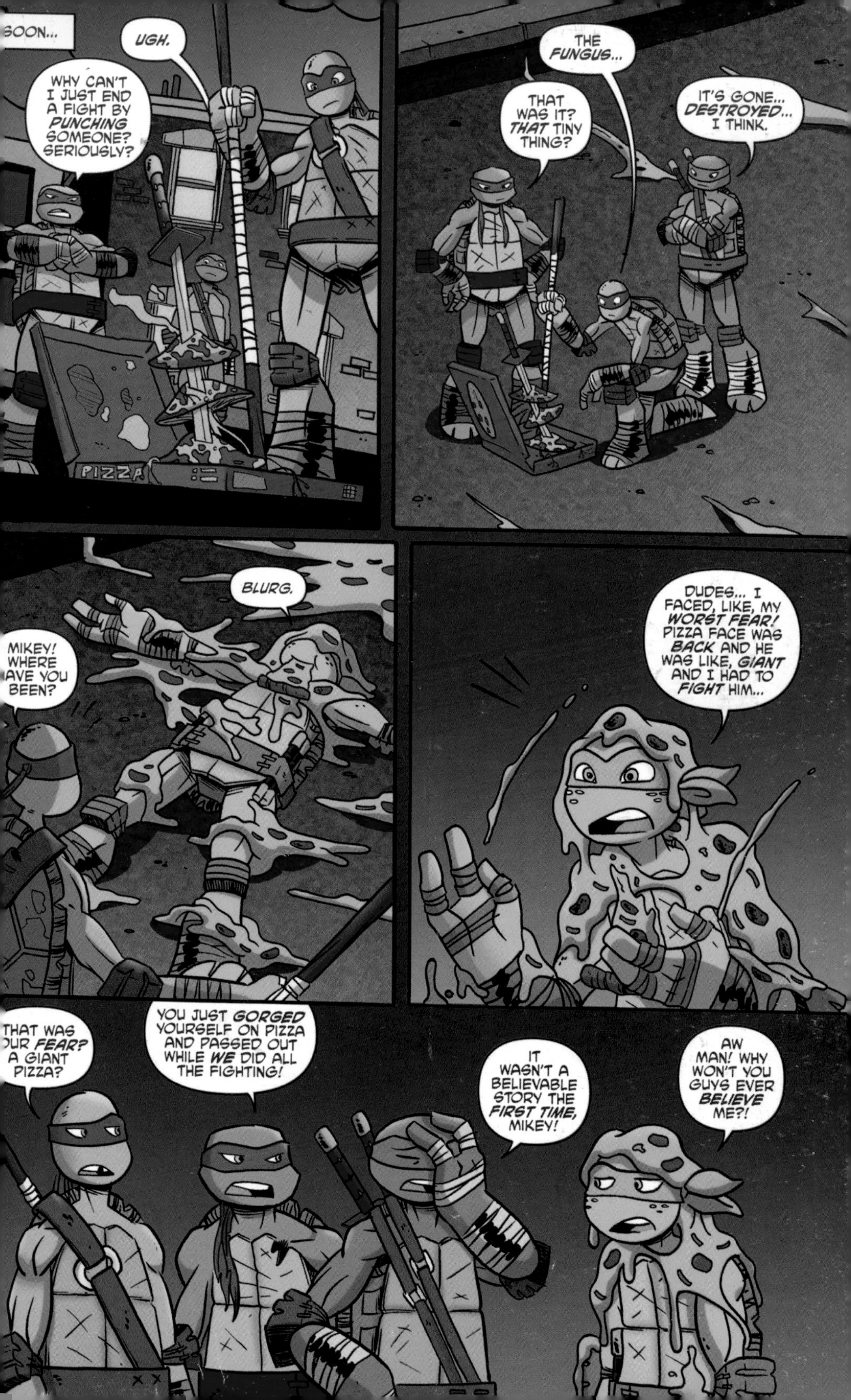
SOON...
UGH.
WHY CAN'T I JUST END A FIGHT BY PUNCHING SOMEONE? SERIOUSLY?
THE FUNGUS...
THAT WAS IT? THAT TINY THING?
IT'S GONE... DESTROYED... I THINK.
PIZZA
BLURG.
MIKEY! WHERE AVE YOU BEEN?
DUDES... I FACED, LIKE, MY WORST FEAR! PIZZA FACE WAS BACK AND HE WAS LIKE, GIANT AND I HAD TO FIGHT HIM...
THAT WAS UR FEAR? A GIANT PIZZA?
YOU JUST GORGED YOURSELF ON PIZZA AND PASSED OUT WHILE WE DID ALL THE FIGHTING!
IT WASN'T A BELIEVABLE STORY THE FIRST TIME, MIKEY!
AW MAN! WHY WON'T YOU GUYS EVER BELIEVE ME?!

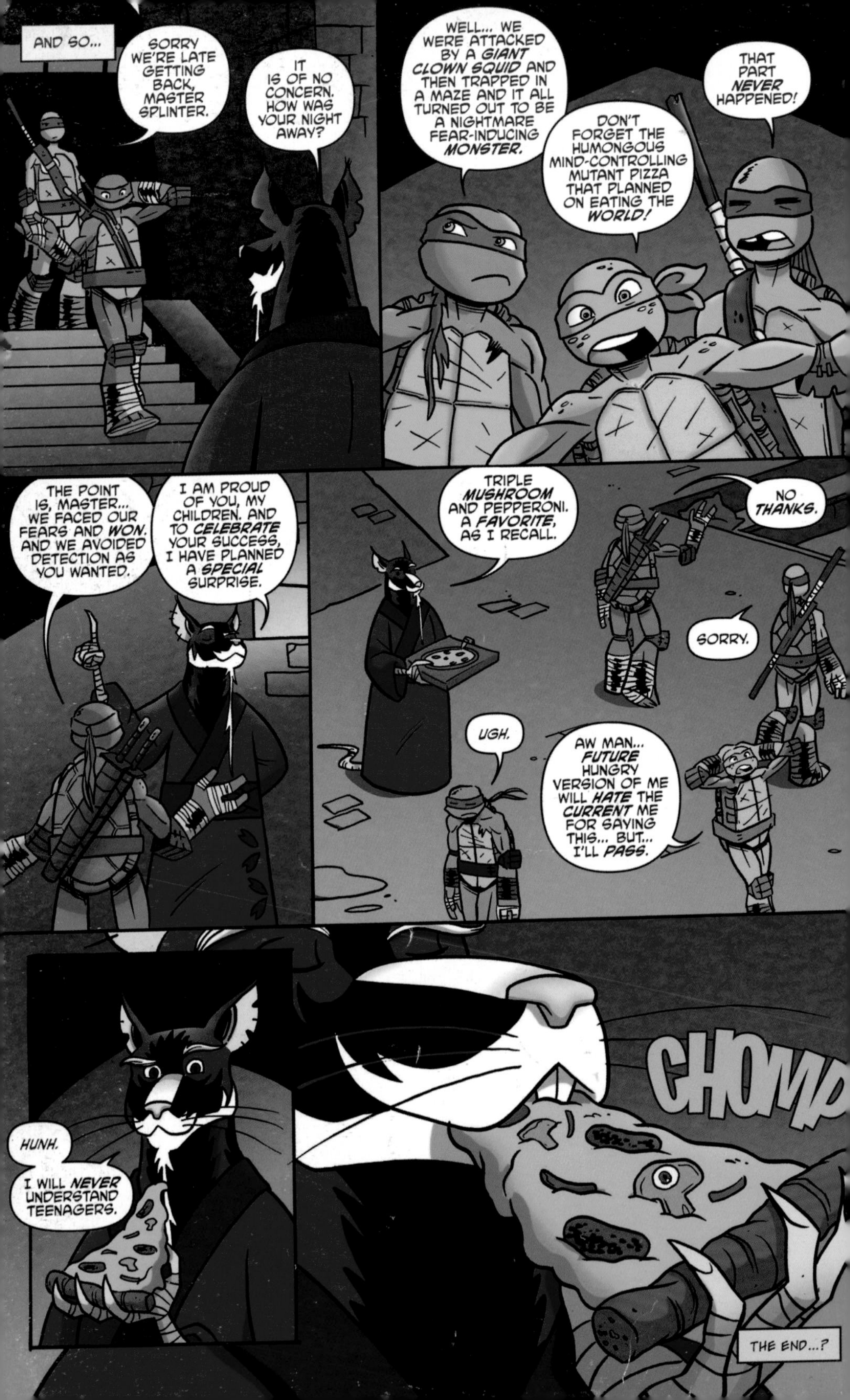
AND SO...
SORRY WE'RE LATE GETTING BACK, MASTER SPLINTER.
IT IS OF NO CONCERN. HOW WAS YOUR NIGHT AWAY?
WELL... WE WERE ATTACKED BY A GIANT CLOWN SQUID AND THEN TRAPPED IN A MAZE AND IT ALL TURNED OUT TO BE A NIGHTMARE FEAR-INDUCING MONSTER.
DON'T FORGET THE HUMONGOUS MIND-CONTROLLING MUTANT PIZZA THAT PLANNED ON EATING THE WORLD!
THAT PART NEVER HAPPENED!
THE POINT IS, MASTER... WE FACED OUR FEARS AND WON. AND WE AVOIDED DETECTION AS YOU WANTED.
I AM PROUD OF YOU, MY CHILDREN. AND TO CELEBRATE YOUR SUCCESS, I HAVE PLANNED A SPECIAL SURPRISE.
TRIPLE MUSHROOM AND PEPPERONI. A FAVORITE, AS I RECALL.
NO THANKS.
SORRY.
UGH.
AW MAN... FUTURE HUNGRY VERSION OF ME WILL HATE THE CURRENT ME FOR SAYING THIS... BUT... I'LL PASS.
HUNH.
I WILL NEVER UNDERSTAND TEENAGERS.
CHOMP
THE END...?

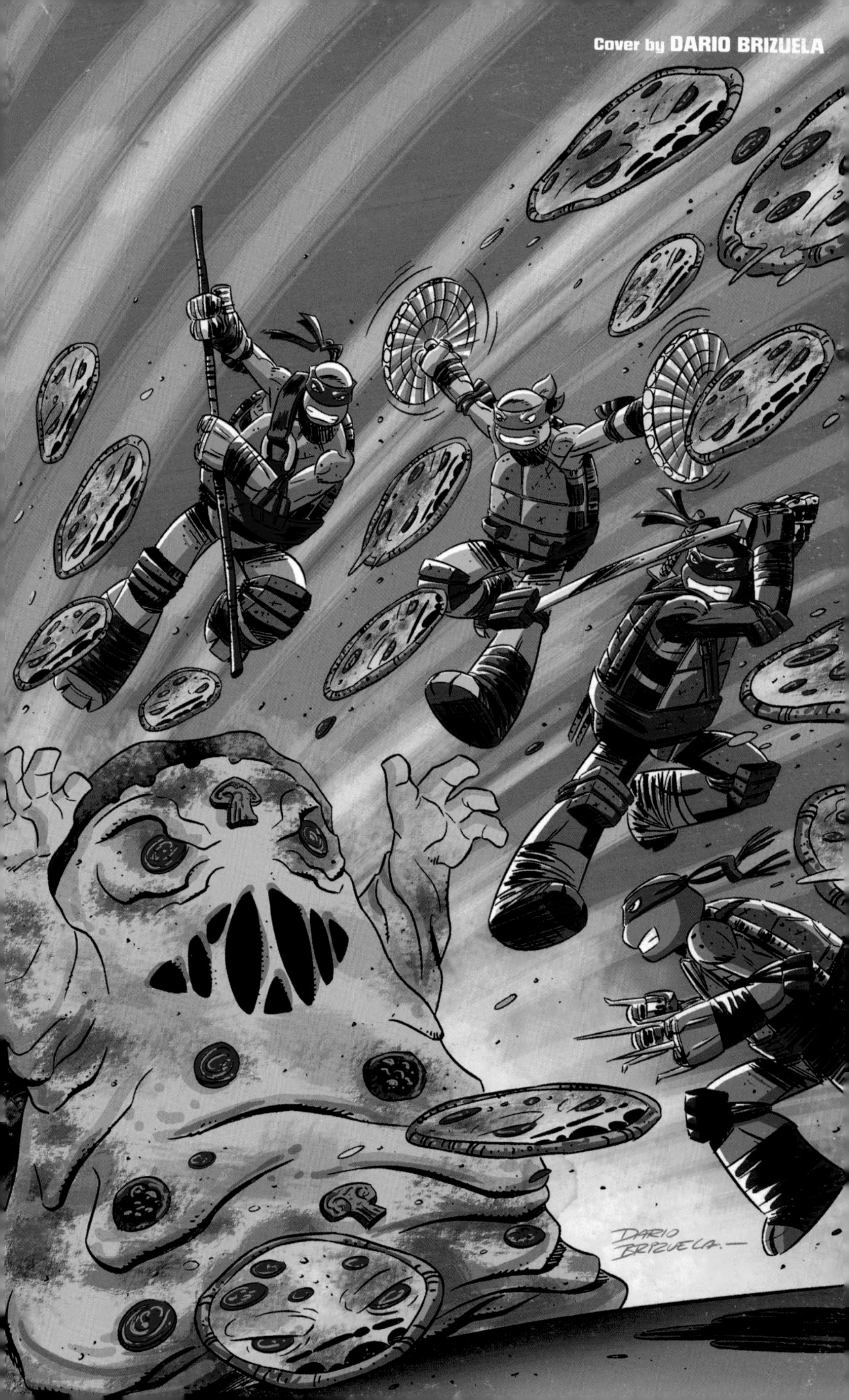
DARIO
BRIZUELA

Cover by DARIO BRIZUELA

Cover by **JAKE TABULA**

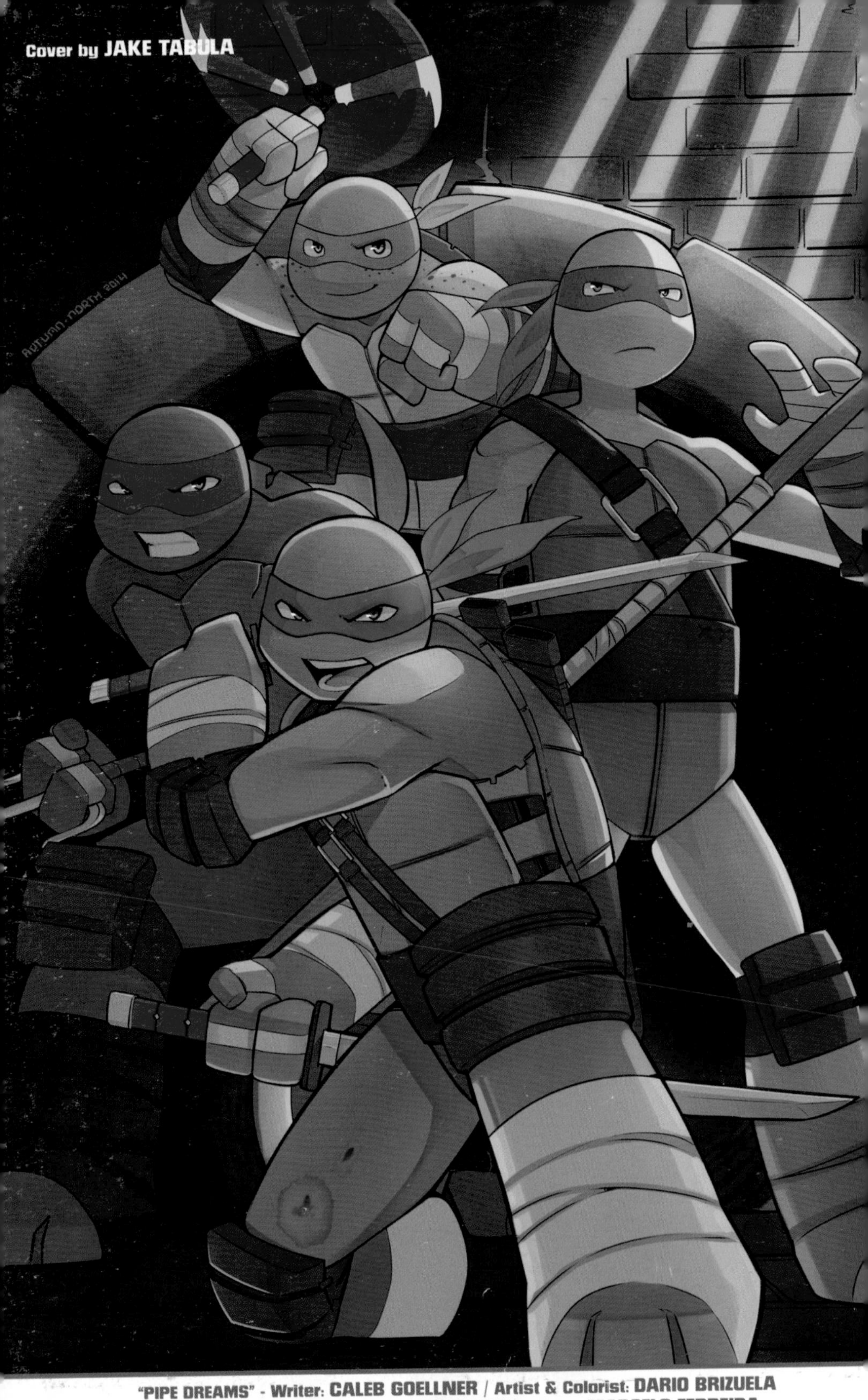
AUTUMN-NORTH 2014

"PIPE DREAMS" - Writer: **CALEB GOELLNER** / Artist & Colorist: **DARIO BRIZUELA**
"WHO'S 'ZA-SOME" - Writer: **CALEB GOELLNER** / Artist: **MARCELO FERREIRA**

PIPE DREAMS

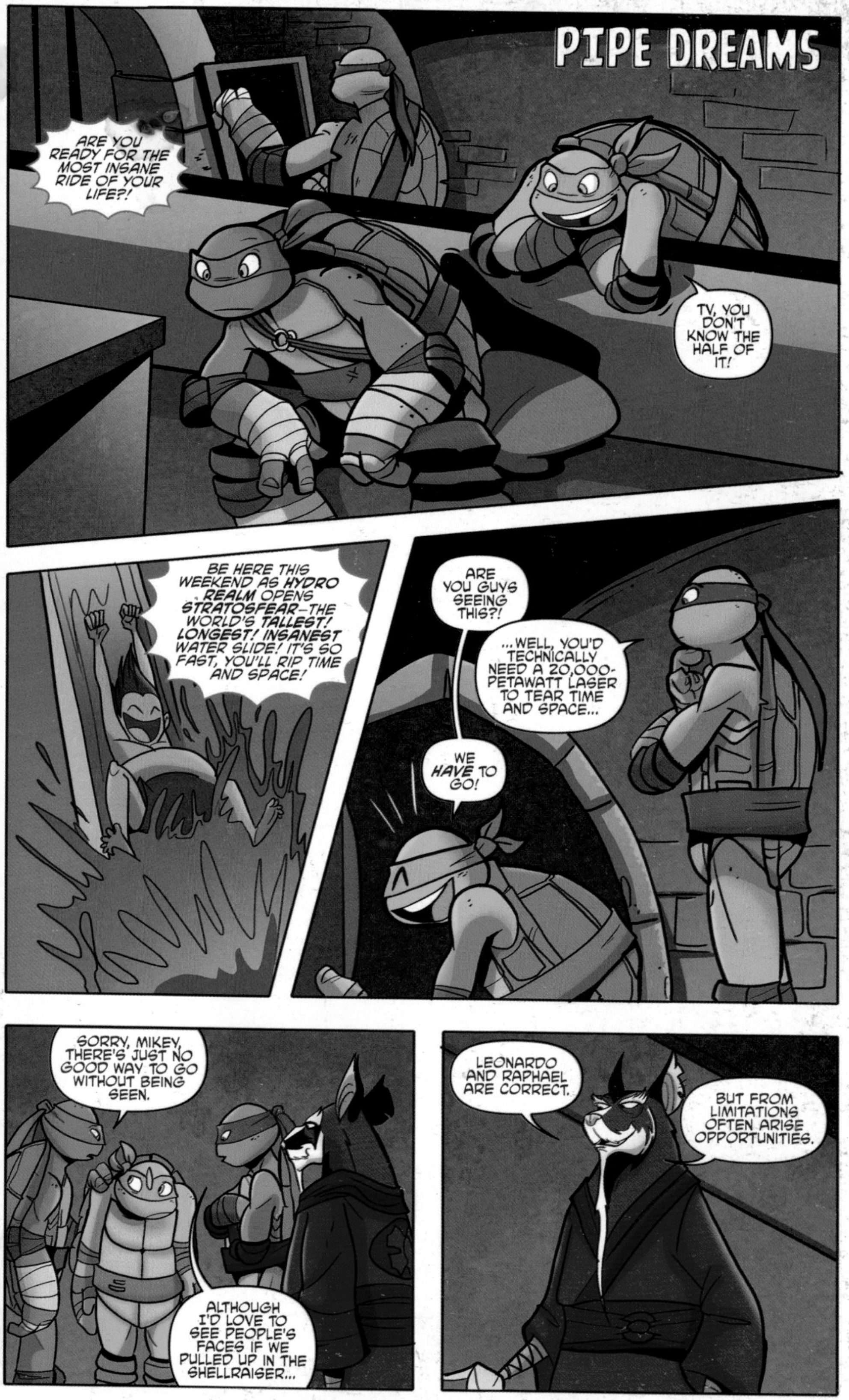
PIPE DREAMS
ARE YOU READY FOR THE MOST INSANE RIDE OF YOUR LIFE?!
TV, YOU DON'T KNOW THE HALF OF IT!
BE HERE THIS WEEKEND AS HYDRO REALM OPENS STRATOSFEAR—THE WORLD'S TALLEST! LONGEST! INSANEST WATER SLIDE! IT'S SO FAST, YOU'LL RIP TIME AND SPACE!
ARE YOU GUYS SEEING THIS?!
...WELL, YOU'D TECHNICALLY NEED A 20,000-PETAWATT LASER TO TEAR TIME AND SPACE...
WE HAVE TO GO!
SORRY, MIKEY, THERE'S JUST NO GOOD WAY TO GO WITHOUT BEING SEEN.
ALTHOUGH I'D LOVE TO SEE PEOPLE'S FACES IF WE PULLED UP IN THE SHELLRAISER...
LEONARDO AND RAPHAEL ARE CORRECT.
BUT FROM LIMITATIONS OFTEN ARISE OPPORTUNITIES.

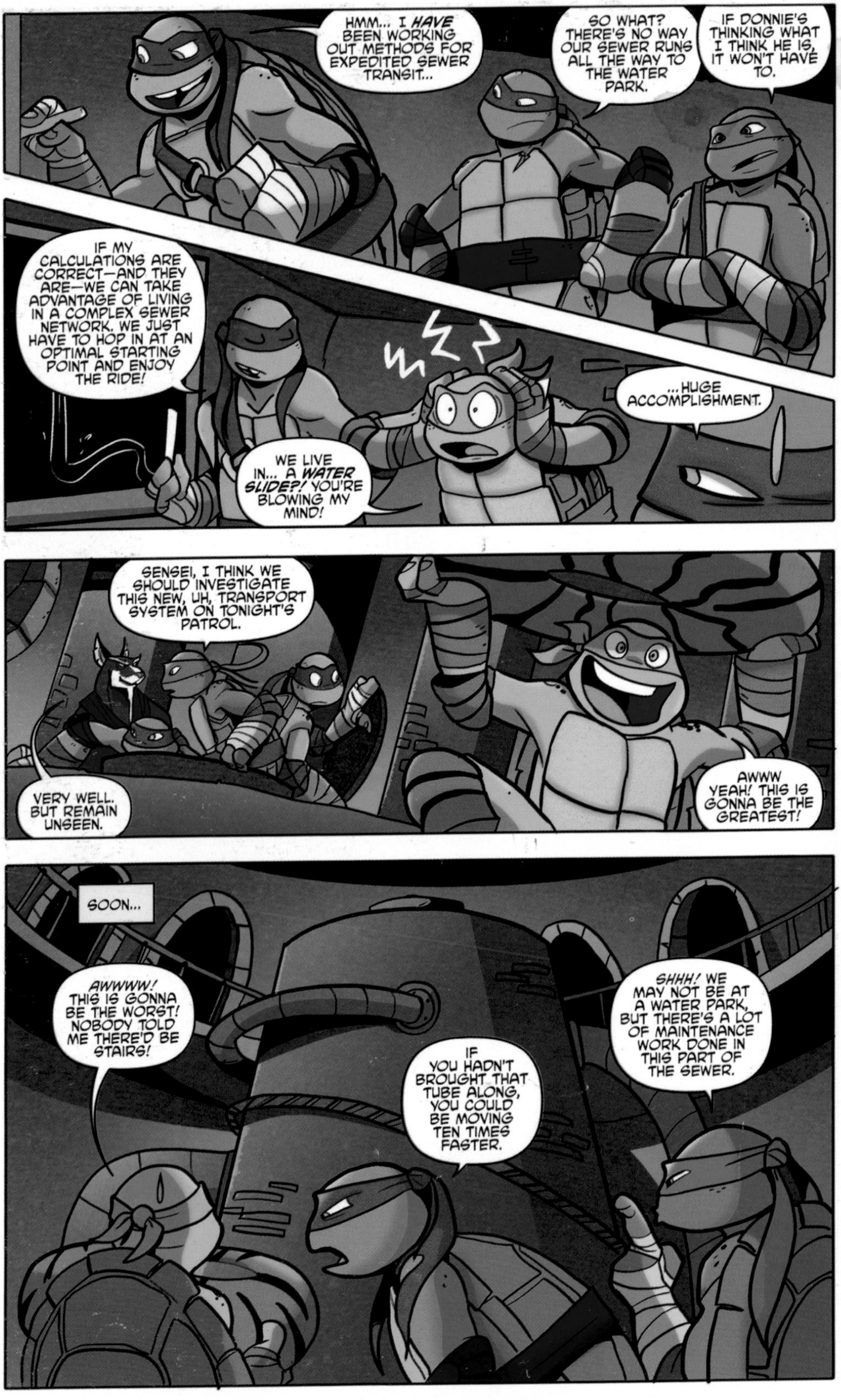
HMM... I *HAVE* BEEN WORKING OUT METHODS FOR EXPEDITED SEWER TRANSIT...
SO WHAT? THERE'S NO WAY OUR SEWER RUNS ALL THE WAY TO THE WATER PARK.
IF DONNIE'S THINKING WHAT I THINK HE IS, IT WON'T HAVE TO.
IF MY CALCULATIONS ARE CORRECT—AND THEY ARE—WE CAN TAKE ADVANTAGE OF LIVING IN A COMPLEX SEWER NETWORK. WE JUST HAVE TO HOP IN AT AN OPTIMAL STARTING POINT AND ENJOY THE RIDE!
WE LIVE IN... A *WATER SLIDE?!* YOU'RE BLOWING MY MIND!
...HUGE ACCOMPLISHMENT.
SENSEI, I THINK WE SHOULD INVESTIGATE THIS NEW, UH, TRANSPORT SYSTEM ON TONIGHT'S PATROL.
VERY WELL. BUT REMAIN UNSEEN.
AWWW YEAH! THIS IS GONNA BE THE GREATEST!
SOON...
AWWWW! THIS IS GONNA BE THE WORST! NOBODY TOLD ME THERE'D BE STAIRS!
IF YOU HADN'T BROUGHT THAT TUBE ALONG, YOU COULD BE MOVING TEN TIMES FASTER.
SHHH! WE MAY NOT BE AT A WATER PARK, BUT THERE'S A LOT OF MAINTENANCE WORK DONE IN THIS PART OF THE SEWER.

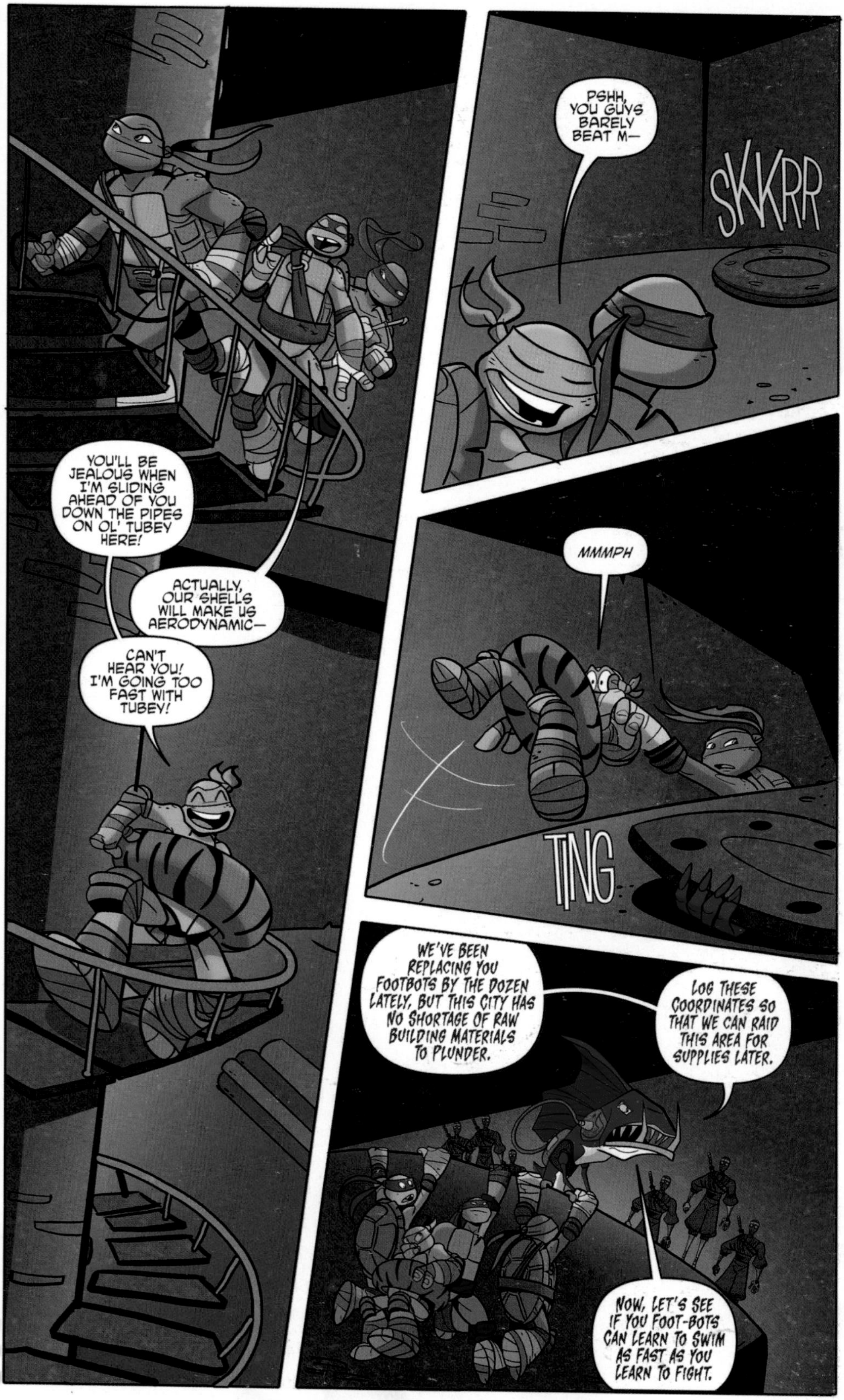

YOU'LL BE JEALOUS WHEN I'M SLIDING AHEAD OF YOU DOWN THE PIPES ON OL' TUBEY HERE!
ACTUALLY, OUR SHELLS WILL MAKE US AERODYNAMIC—
CAN'T HEAR YOU! I'M GOING TOO FAST WITH TUBEY!
PSHH, YOU GUYS BARELY BEAT M—
SKKRR
MMMPH
TING
WE'VE BEEN REPLACING YOU FOOTBOTS BY THE DOZEN LATELY, BUT THIS CITY HAS NO SHORTAGE OF RAW BUILDING MATERIALS TO PLUNDER.
LOG THESE COORDINATES SO THAT WE CAN RAID THIS AREA FOR SUPPLIES LATER.
NOW, LET'S SEE IF YOU FOOT-BOTS CAN LEARN TO SWIM AS FAST AS YOU LEARN TO FIGHT.

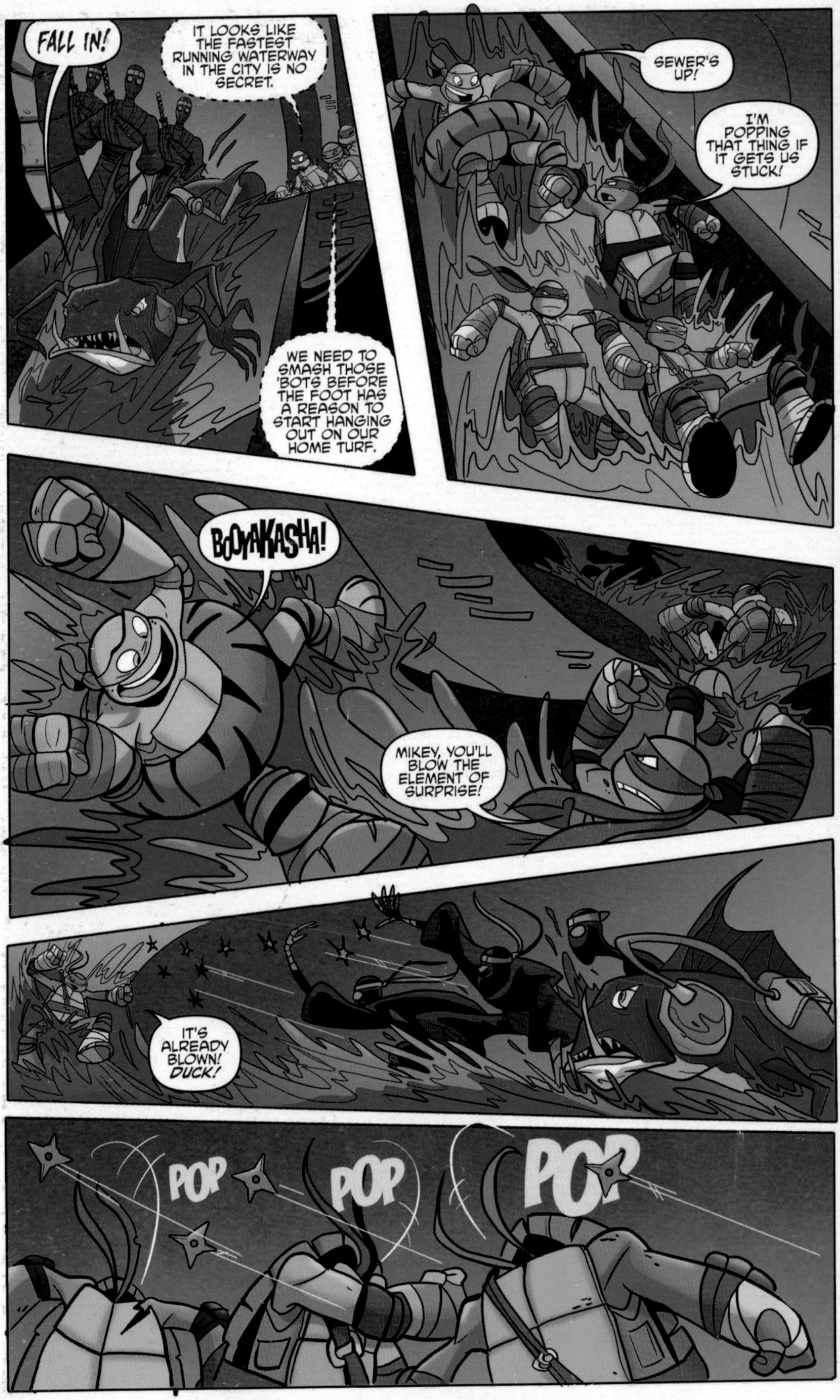
FALL IN!
IT LOOKS LIKE THE FASTEST RUNNING WATERWAY IN THE CITY IS NO SECRET.
WE NEED TO SMASH THOSE 'BOTS BEFORE THE FOOT HAS A REASON TO START HANGING OUT ON OUR HOME TURF.
SEWER'S UP!
I'M POPPING THAT THING IF IT GETS US STUCK!
BOOYAKASHA!
MIKEY, YOU'LL BLOW THE ELEMENT OF SURPRISE!
IT'S ALREADY BLOWN! DUCK!
POP
POP
POP

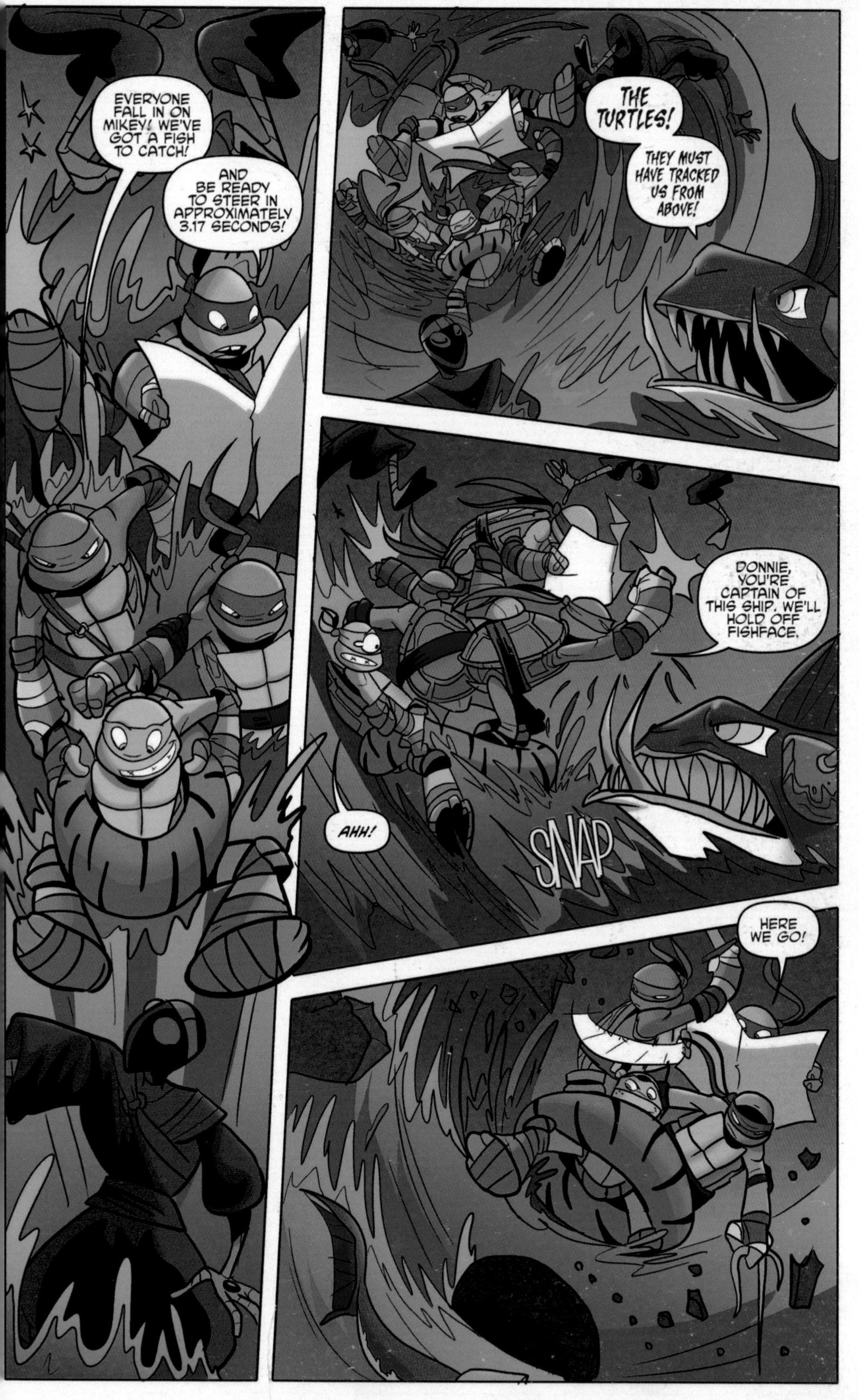
EVERYONE FALL IN ON MIKEY! WE'VE GOT A FISH TO CATCH!
AND BE READY TO STEER IN APPROXIMATELY 3.17 SECONDS!
THE TURTLES!
THEY MUST HAVE TRACKED US FROM ABOVE!
DONNIE, YOU'RE CAPTAIN OF THIS SHIP. WE'LL HOLD OFF FISHFACE.
AHH!
SNAP
HERE WE GO!

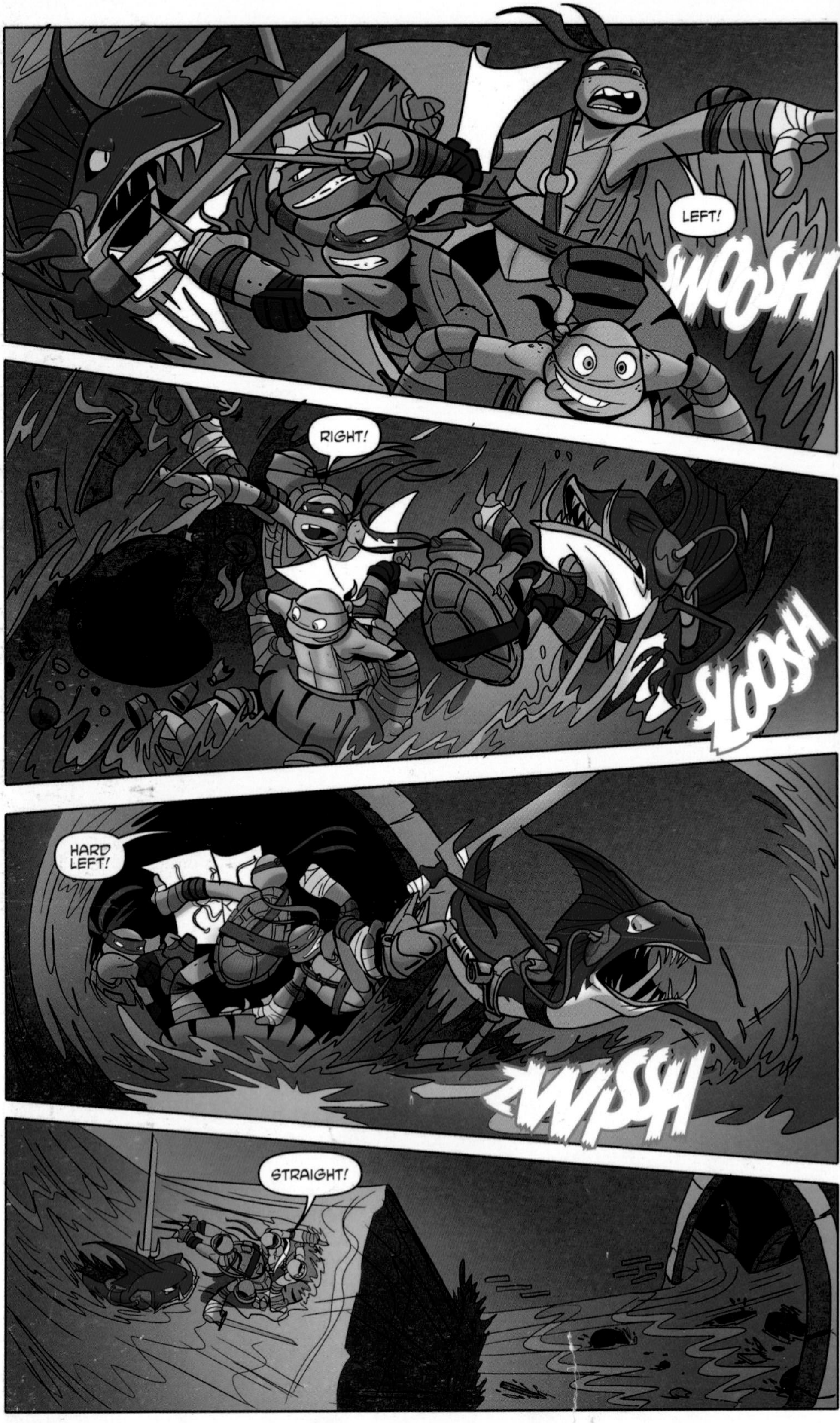
LEFT!
SWOOSH
RIGHT!
SLOOSH
HARD LEFT!
ZWSSH
STRAIGHT!

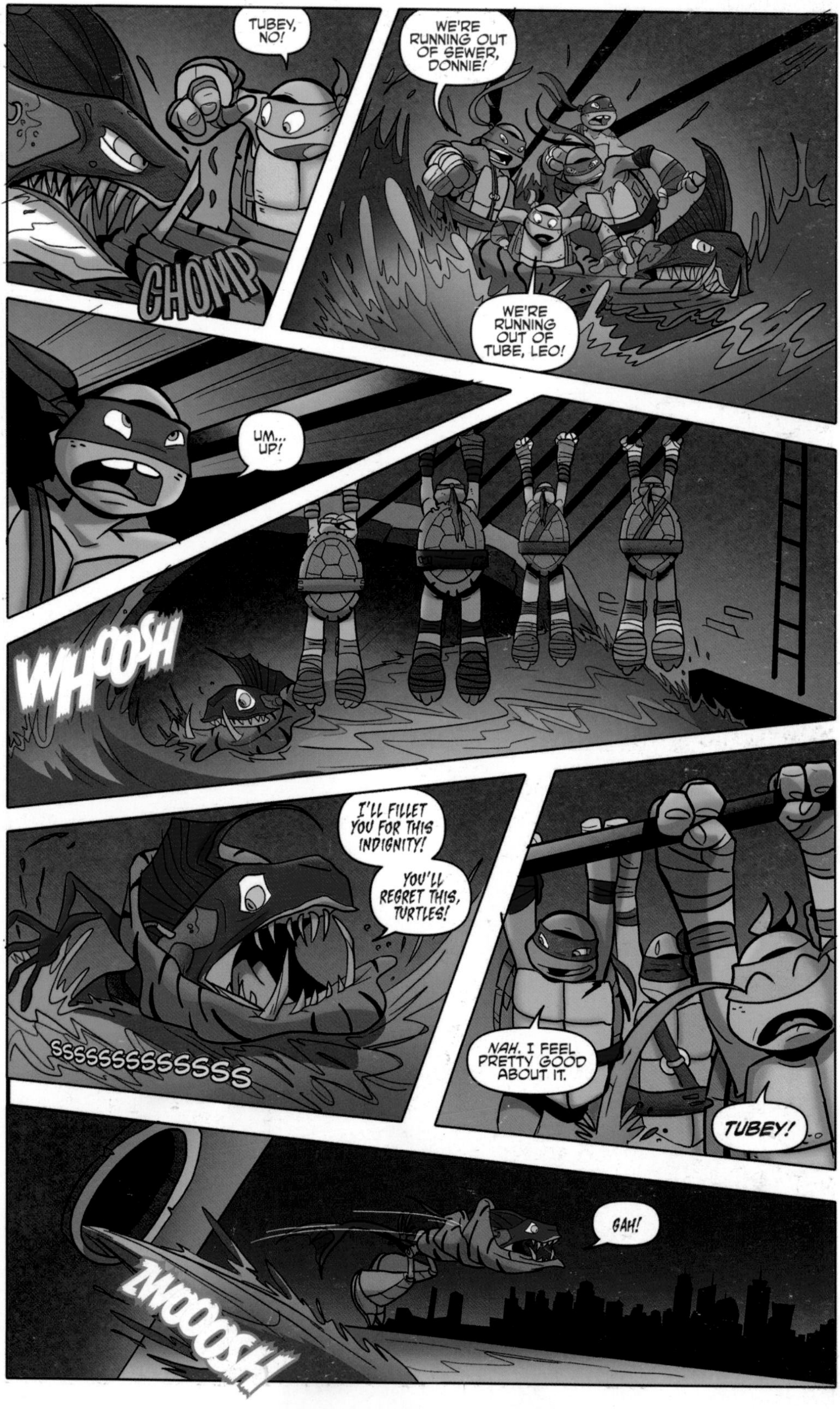
TUBEY, NO!
CHOMP
WE'RE RUNNING OUT OF SEWER, DONNIE!
WE'RE RUNNING OUT OF TUBE, LEO!
UM... UP!
WHOOSH
I'LL FILLET YOU FOR THIS INDIGNITY!
YOU'LL REGRET THIS, TURTLES!
SSSSSSSSSSSSSS
NAH. I FEEL PRETTY GOOD ABOUT IT.
TUBEY!
GAH!
ZWOOOOSH

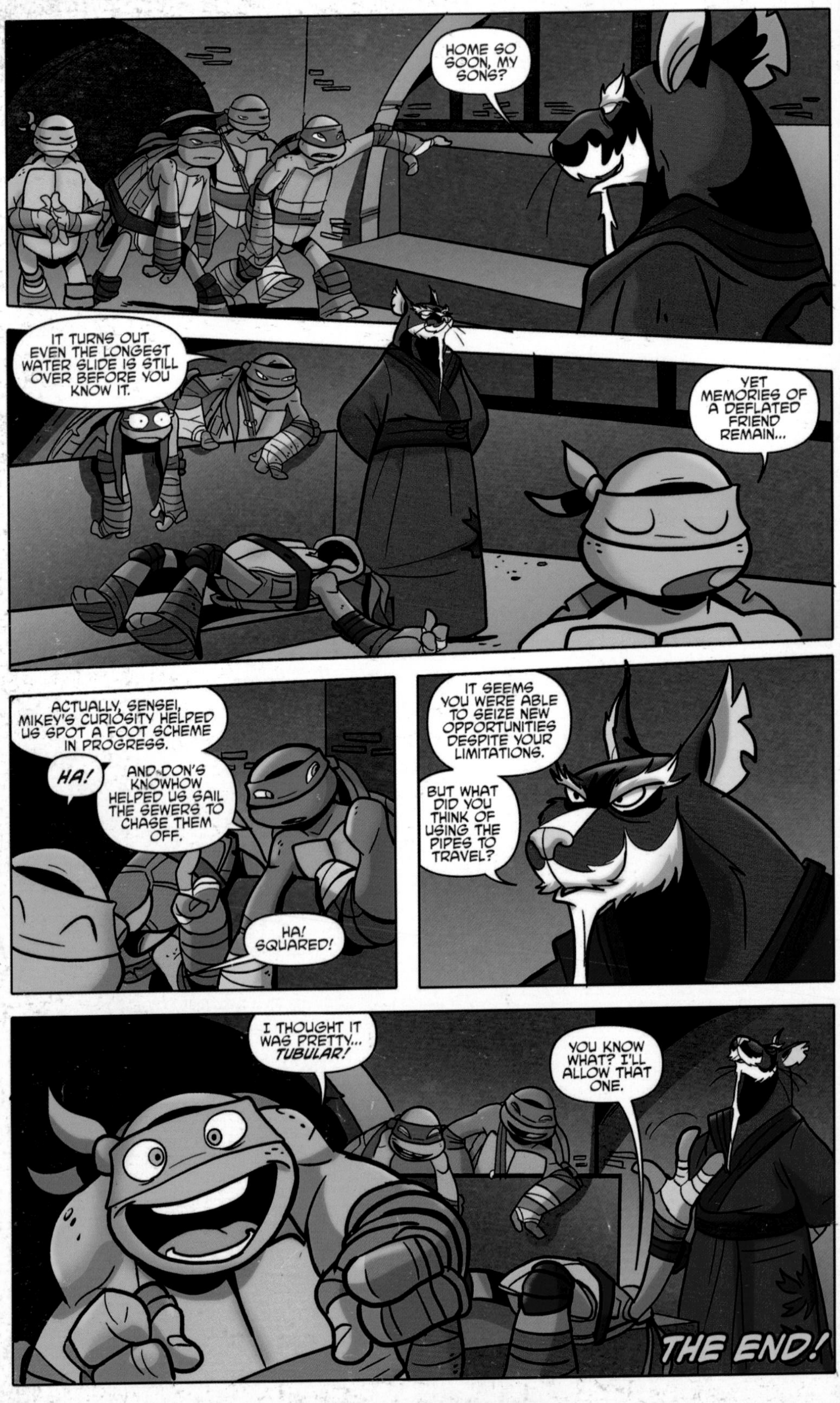
HOME SO SOON, MY SONS?
IT TURNS OUT EVEN THE LONGEST WATER SLIDE IS STILL OVER BEFORE YOU KNOW IT.
YET MEMORIES OF A DEFLATED FRIEND REMAIN...
ACTUALLY, SENSEI, MIKEY'S CURIOSITY HELPED US SPOT A FOOT SCHEME IN PROGRESS.
HA!
AND DON'S KNOWHOW HELPED US SAIL THE SEWERS TO CHASE THEM OFF.
HA! SQUARED!
IT SEEMS YOU WERE ABLE TO SEIZE NEW OPPORTUNITIES DESPITE YOUR LIMITATIONS.
BUT WHAT DID YOU THINK OF USING THE PIPES TO TRAVEL?
I THOUGHT IT WAS PRETTY... *TUBULAR!*
YOU KNOW WHAT? I'LL ALLOW THAT ONE.
THE END!

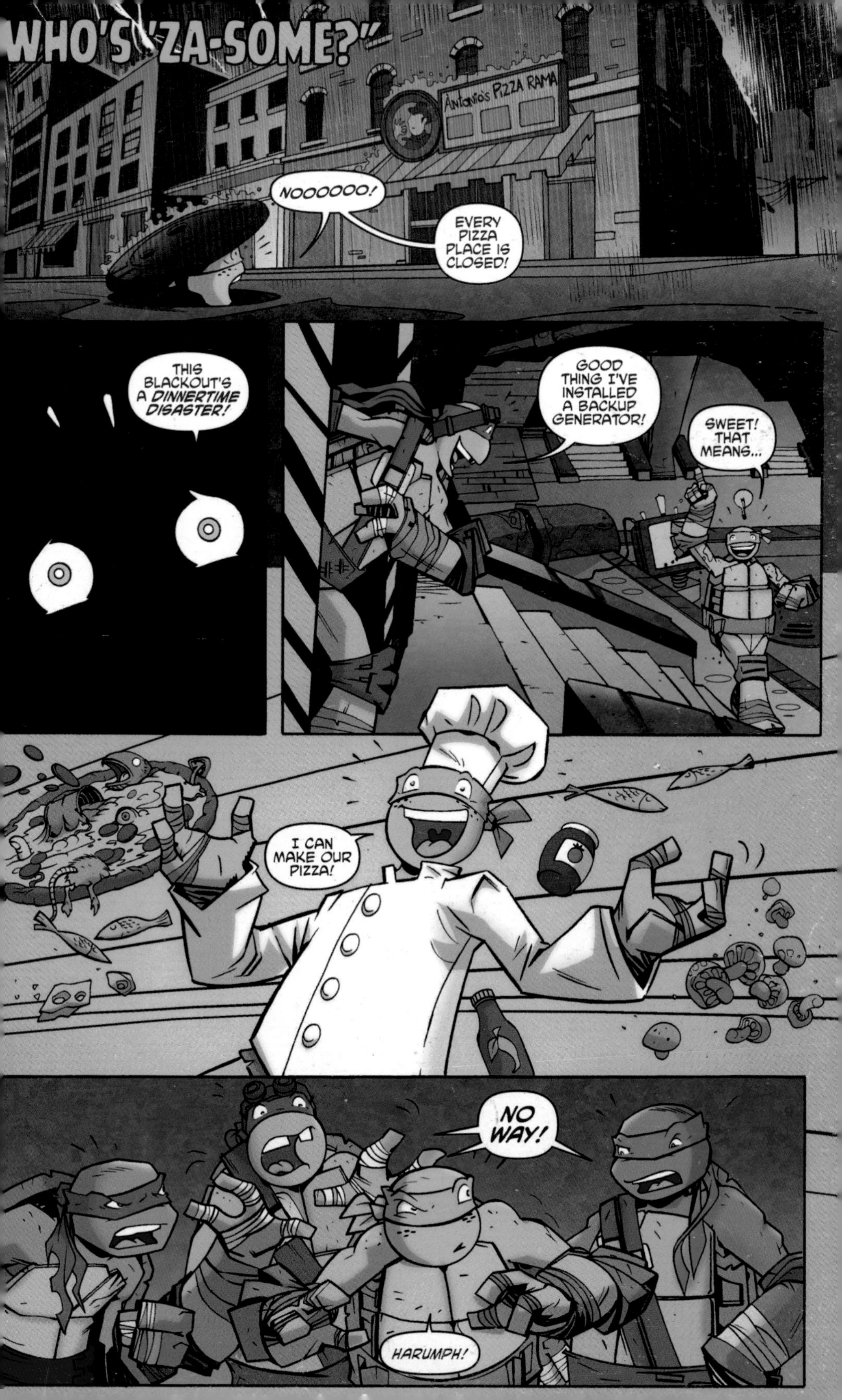
WHO'S "ZA-SOME?"
Antonio's PIZZA RAMA
NOOOOOO!
EVERY PIZZA PLACE IS CLOSED!
THIS BLACKOUT'S A DINNERTIME DISASTER!
GOOD THING I'VE INSTALLED A BACKUP GENERATOR!
SWEET! THAT MEANS...
I CAN MAKE OUR PIZZA!
NO WAY!
HARUMPH!

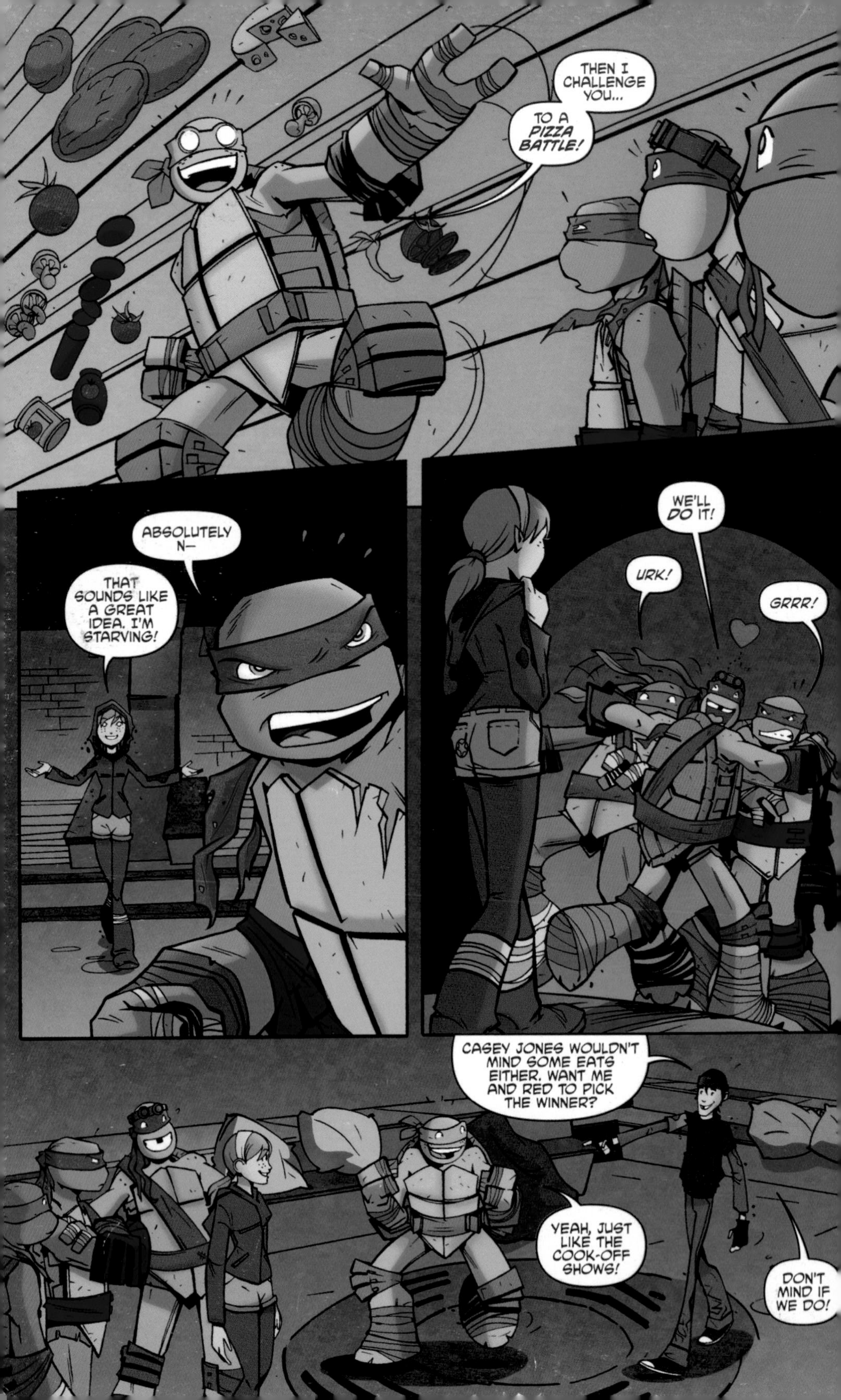
THEN I CHALLENGE YOU...
TO A PIZZA BATTLE!
ABSOLUTELY N—
THAT SOUNDS LIKE A GREAT IDEA. I'M STARVING!
WE'LL DO IT!
URK!
GRRR!
CASEY JONES WOULDN'T MIND SOME EATS EITHER. WANT ME AND RED TO PICK THE WINNER?
YEAH, JUST LIKE THE COOK-OFF SHOWS!
DON'T MIND IF WE DO!

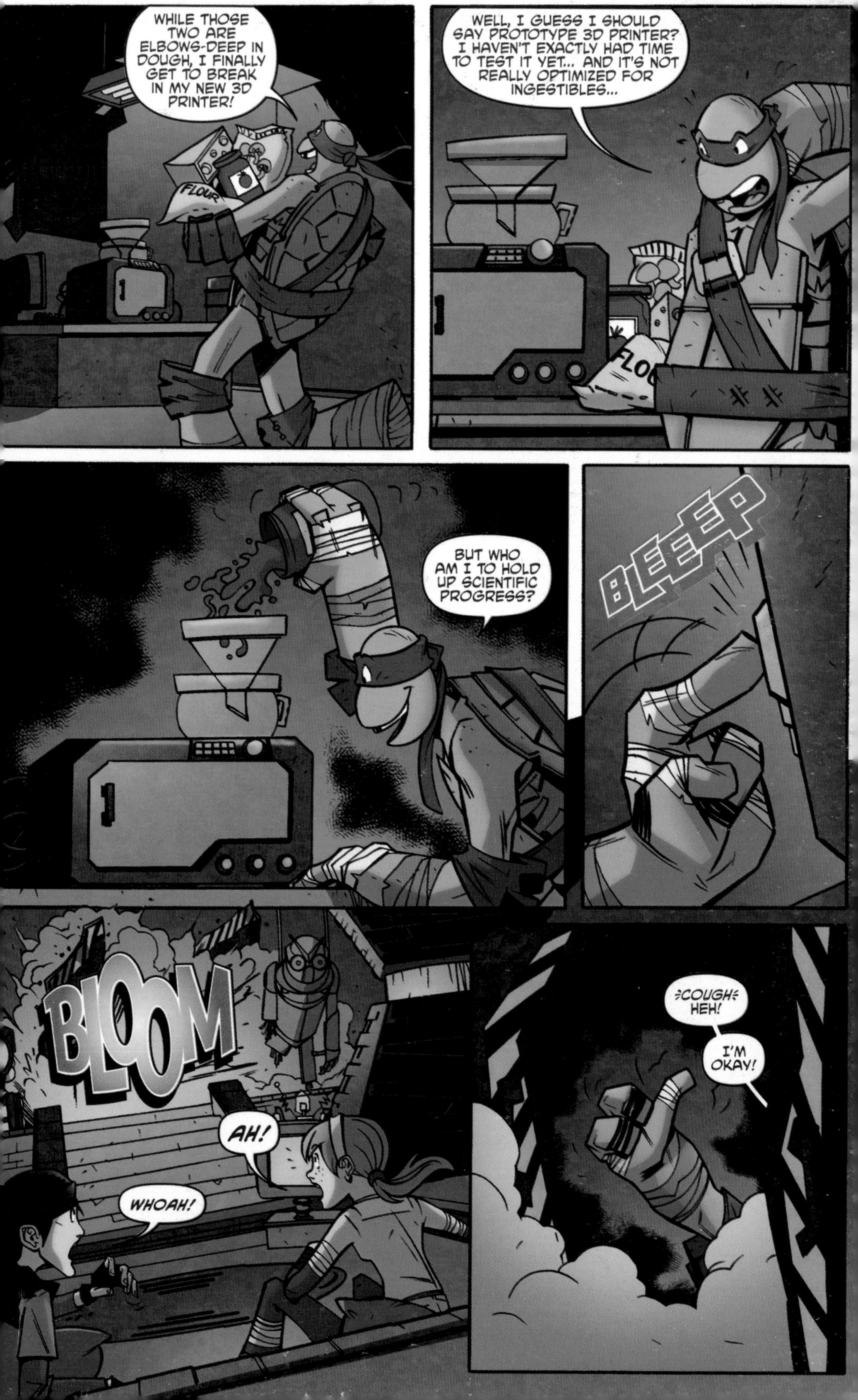

WHILE THOSE TWO ARE ELBOWS-DEEP IN DOUGH, I FINALLY GET TO BREAK IN MY NEW 3D PRINTER!
FLOUR
WELL, I GUESS I SHOULD SAY PROTOTYPE 3D PRINTER? I HAVEN'T EXACTLY HAD TIME TO TEST IT YET... AND IT'S NOT REALLY OPTIMIZED FOR INGESTIBLES...
BUT WHO AM I TO HOLD UP SCIENTIFIC PROGRESS?
BLEEEP
BLOOM
AH!
WHOAH!
COUGH HEH!
I'M OKAY!

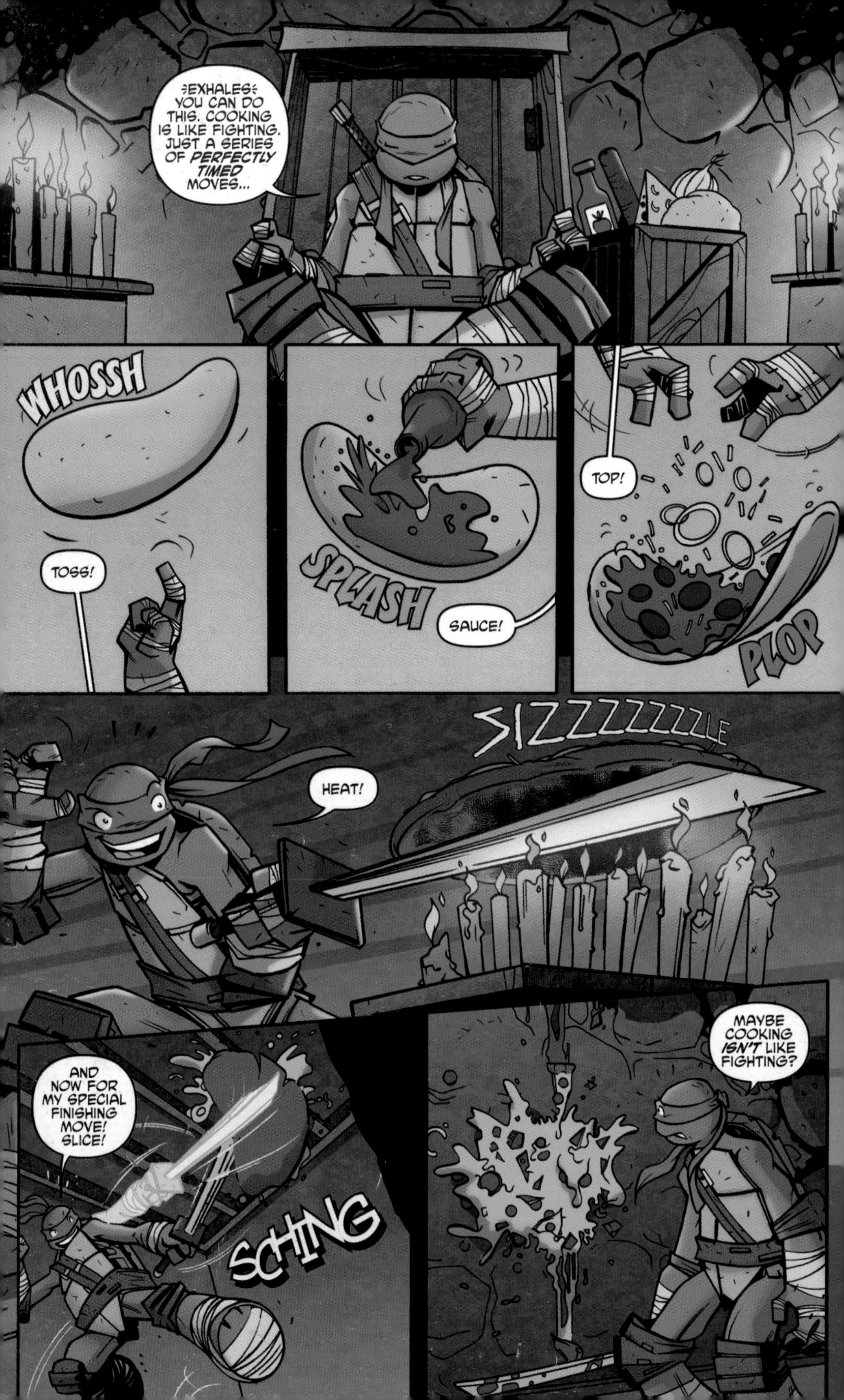

⸗EXHALES⸗ YOU CAN DO THIS. COOKING IS LIKE FIGHTING. JUST A SERIES OF *PERFECTLY TIMED* MOVES...
WHOSSH
TOSS!
SPLASH
SAUCE!
TOP!
PLOP
SIZZZZZZZZLE
HEAT!
AND NOW FOR MY SPECIAL FINISHING MOVE! SLICE!
SCHING
MAYBE COOKING *ISN'T* LIKE FIGHTING?

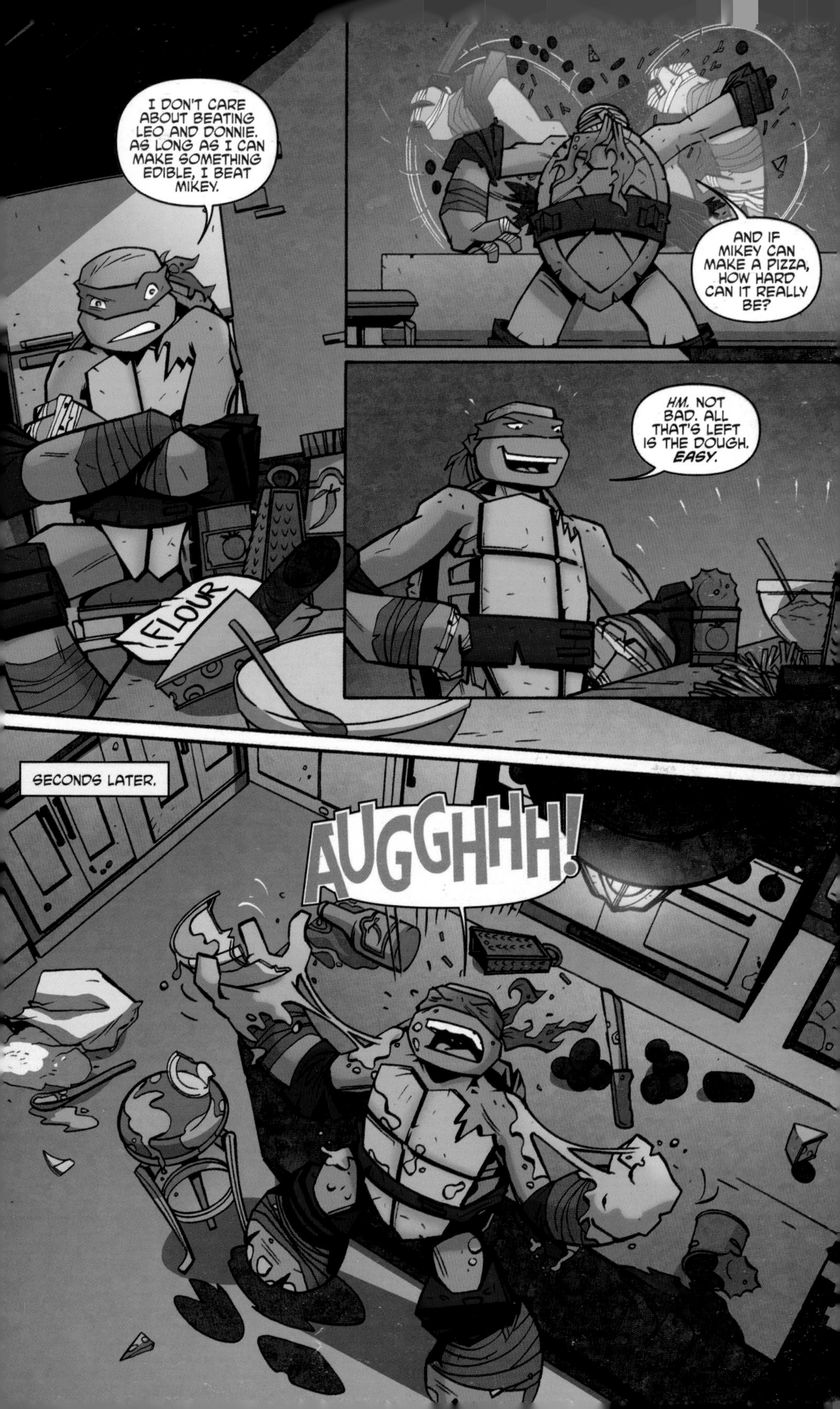
I DON'T CARE ABOUT BEATING LEO AND DONNIE. AS LONG AS I CAN MAKE SOMETHING EDIBLE, I BEAT MIKEY.
AND IF MIKEY CAN MAKE A PIZZA, HOW HARD CAN IT REALLY BE?
FLOUR
HM. NOT BAD. ALL THAT'S LEFT IS THE DOUGH. EASY.
SECONDS LATER.
AUGGHHH!

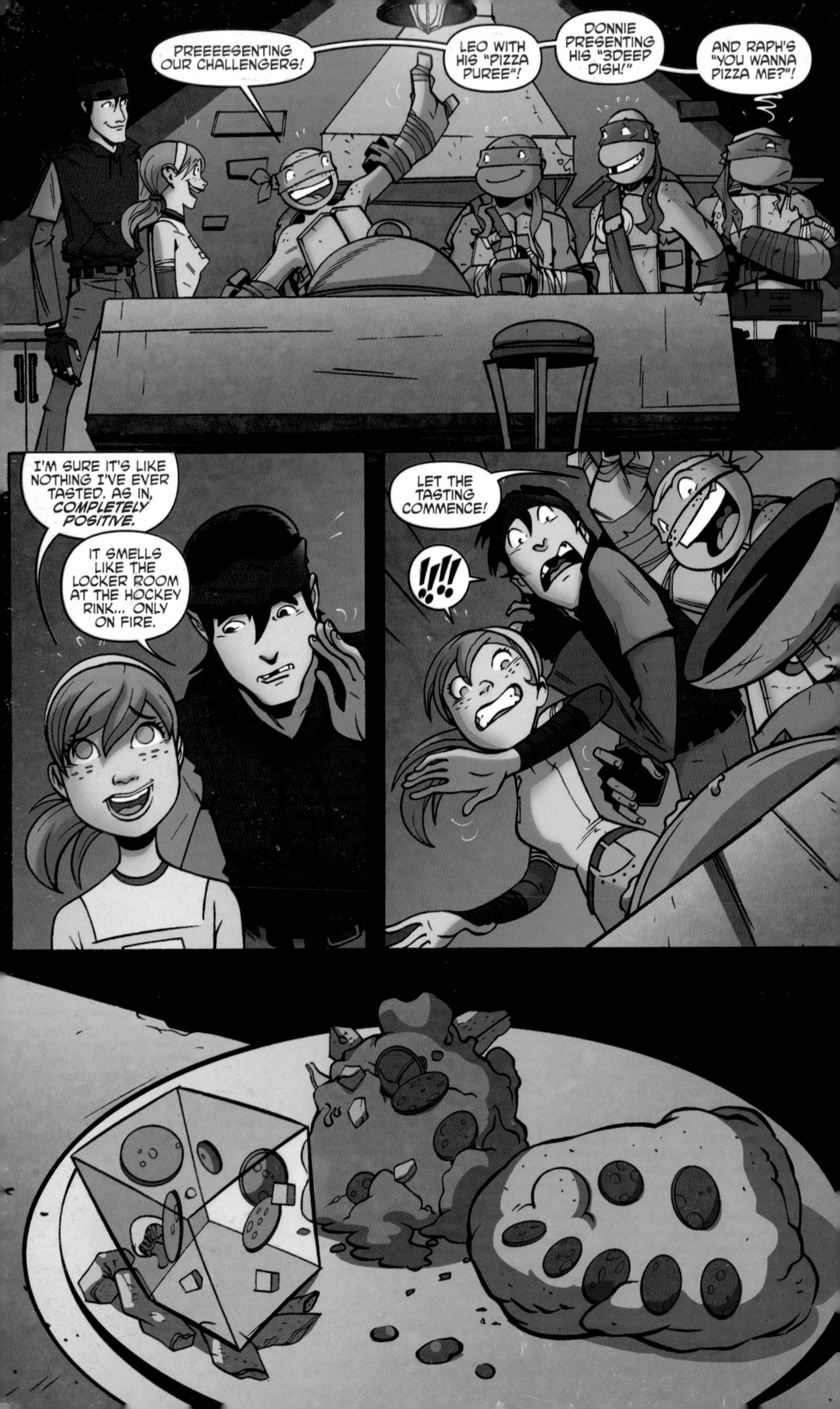
PREEEESENTING OUR CHALLENGERS!
LEO WITH HIS "PIZZA PUREE"!
DONNIE PRESENTING HIS "3DEEP DISH!"
AND RAPH'S "YOU WANNA PIZZA ME?"!
I'M SURE IT'S LIKE NOTHING I'VE EVER TASTED. AS IN, *COMPLETELY POSITIVE.*
IT SMELLS LIKE THE LOCKER ROOM AT THE HOCKEY RINK... ONLY ON FIRE.
LET THE TASTING COMMENCE!
!!!!

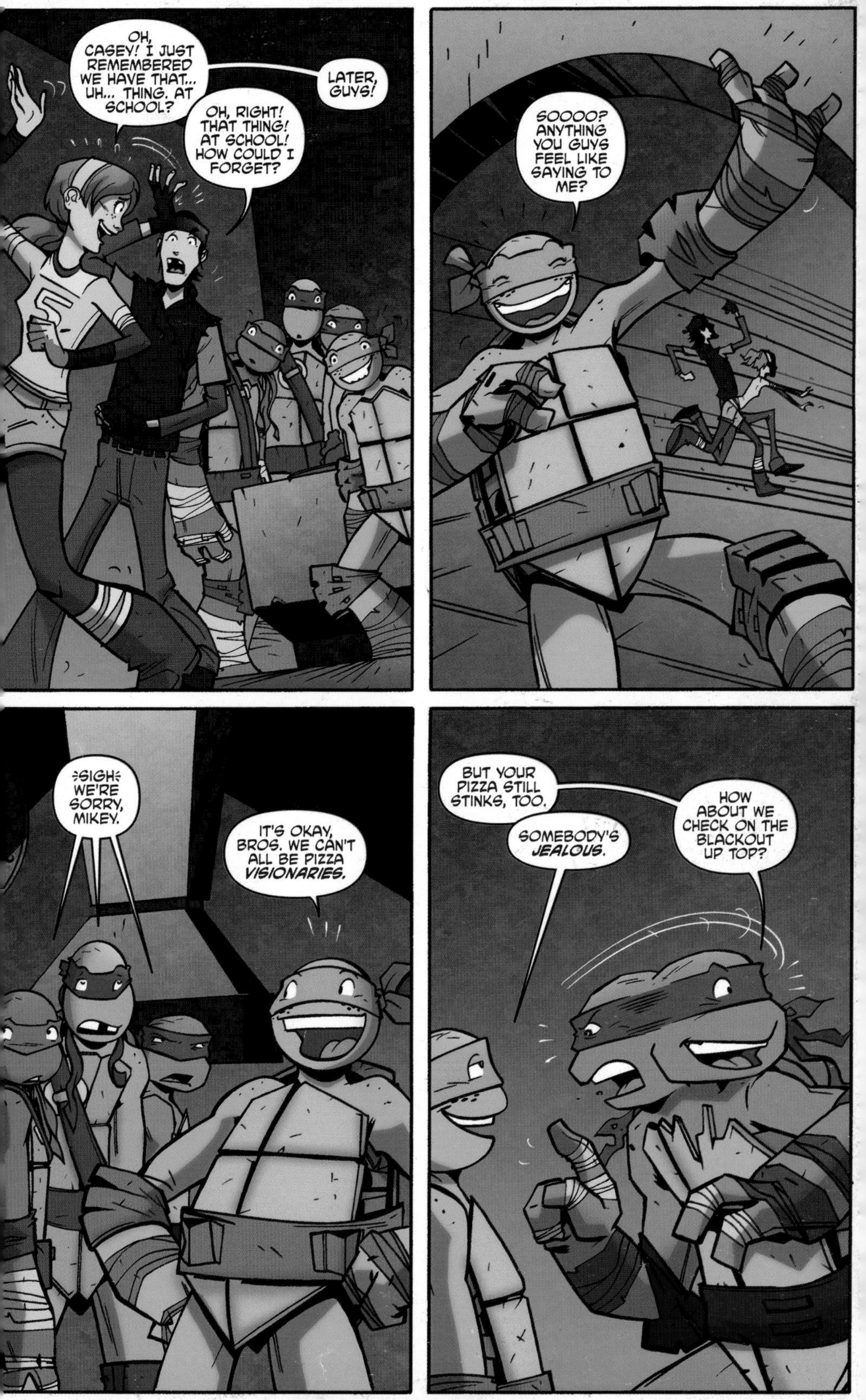
OH, CASEY! I JUST REMEMBERED WE HAVE THAT... UH... THING. AT SCHOOL?
LATER, GUYS!
OH, RIGHT! THAT THING! AT SCHOOL! HOW COULD I FORGET?
SOOOO? ANYTHING YOU GUYS FEEL LIKE SAYING TO ME?
SIGH WE'RE SORRY, MIKEY.
IT'S OKAY, BROS. WE CAN'T ALL BE PIZZA VISIONARIES.
BUT YOUR PIZZA STILL STINKS, TOO.
SOMEBODY'S JEALOUS.
HOW ABOUT WE CHECK ON THE BLACKOUT UP TOP?

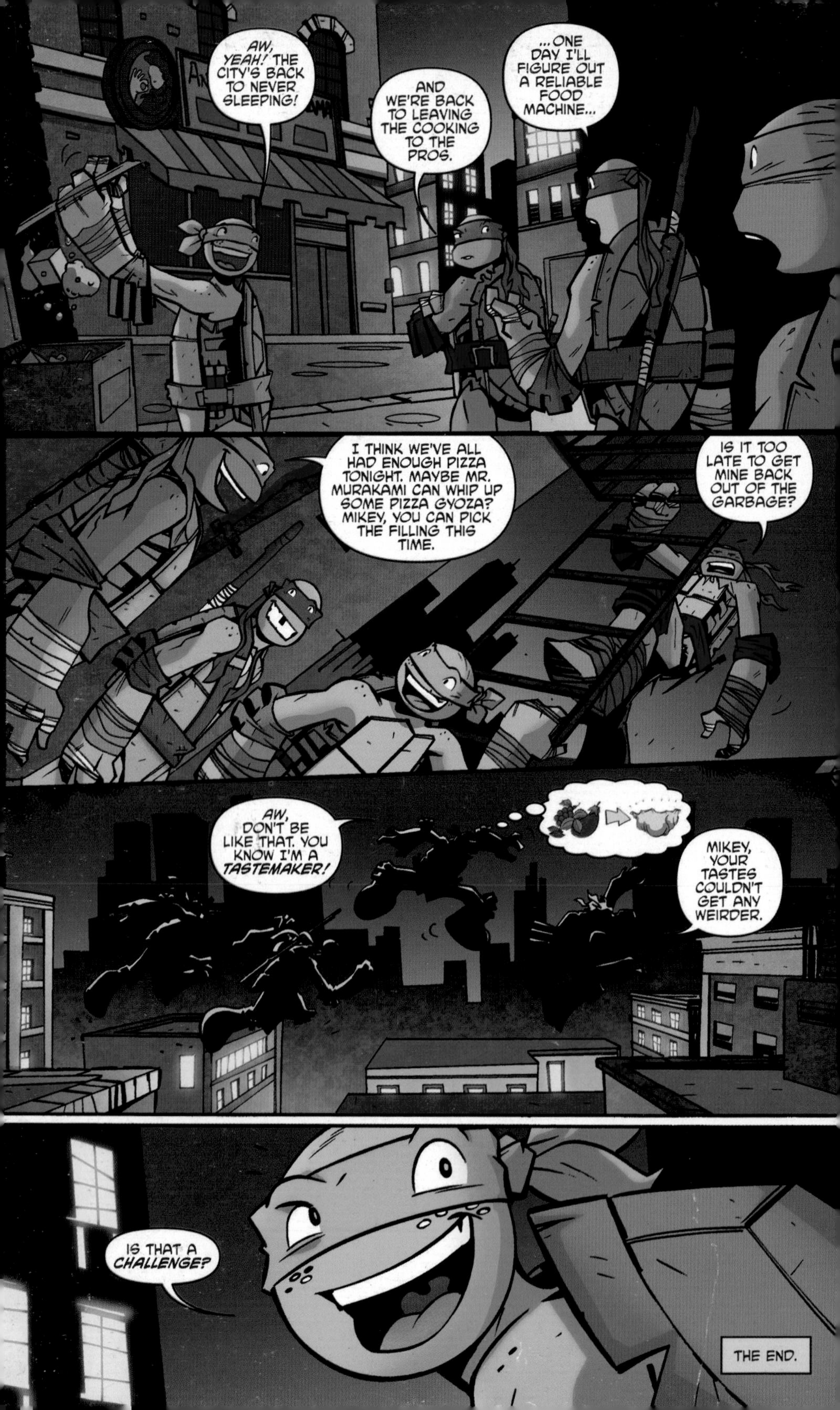
AW, YEAH! THE CITY'S BACK TO NEVER SLEEPING!
AND WE'RE BACK TO LEAVING THE COOKING TO THE PROS.
...ONE DAY I'LL FIGURE OUT A RELIABLE FOOD MACHINE...
I THINK WE'VE ALL HAD ENOUGH PIZZA TONIGHT. MAYBE MR. MURAKAMI CAN WHIP UP SOME PIZZA GYOZA? MIKEY, YOU CAN PICK THE FILLING THIS TIME.
IS IT TOO LATE TO GET MINE BACK OUT OF THE GARBAGE?
AW, DON'T BE LIKE THAT. YOU KNOW I'M A TASTEMAKER!
MIKEY, YOUR TASTES COULDN'T GET ANY WEIRDER.
IS THAT A CHALLENGE?
THE END.

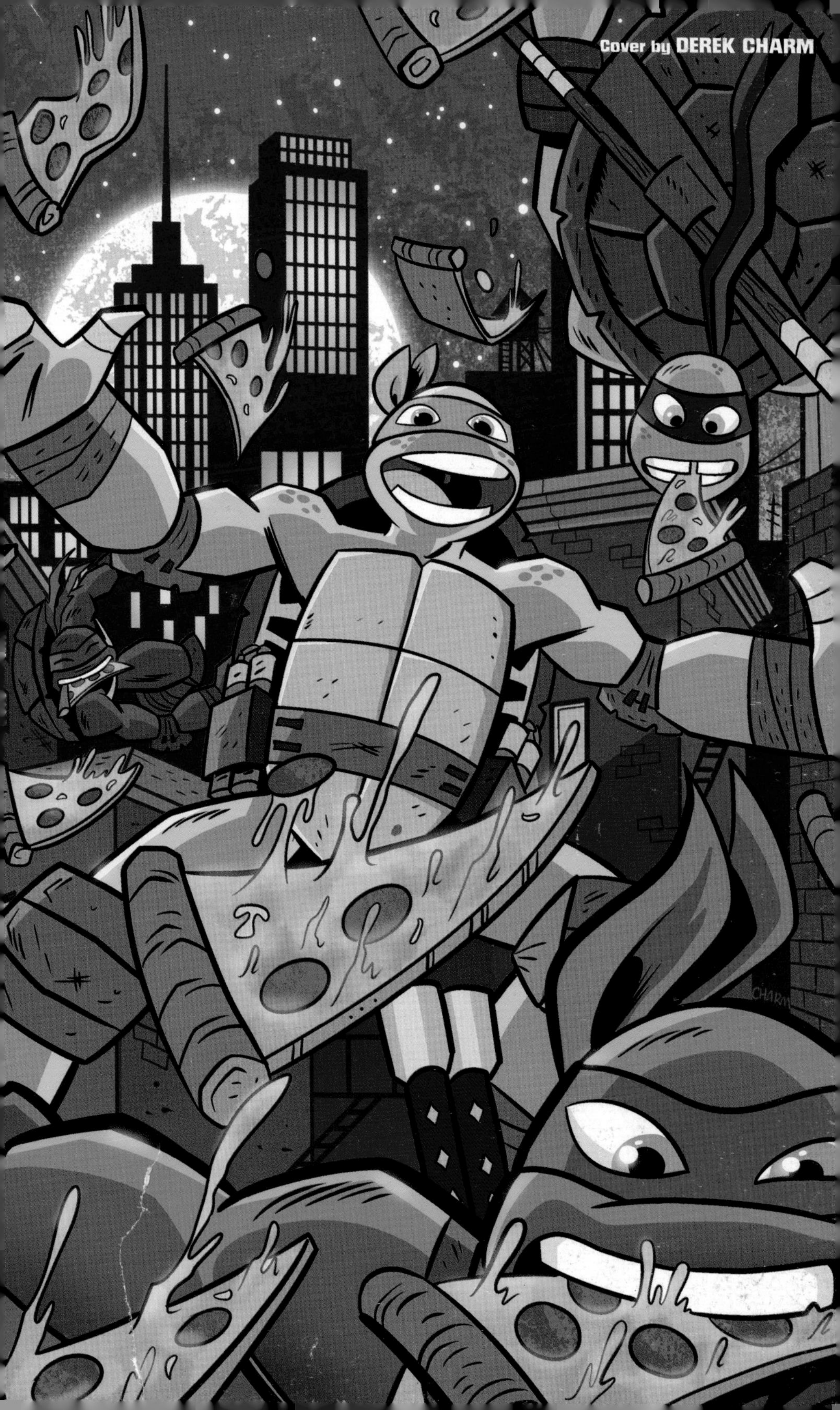
Cover by DEREK CHARM
CHARM

Cover by **DARIO BRIZUELA**

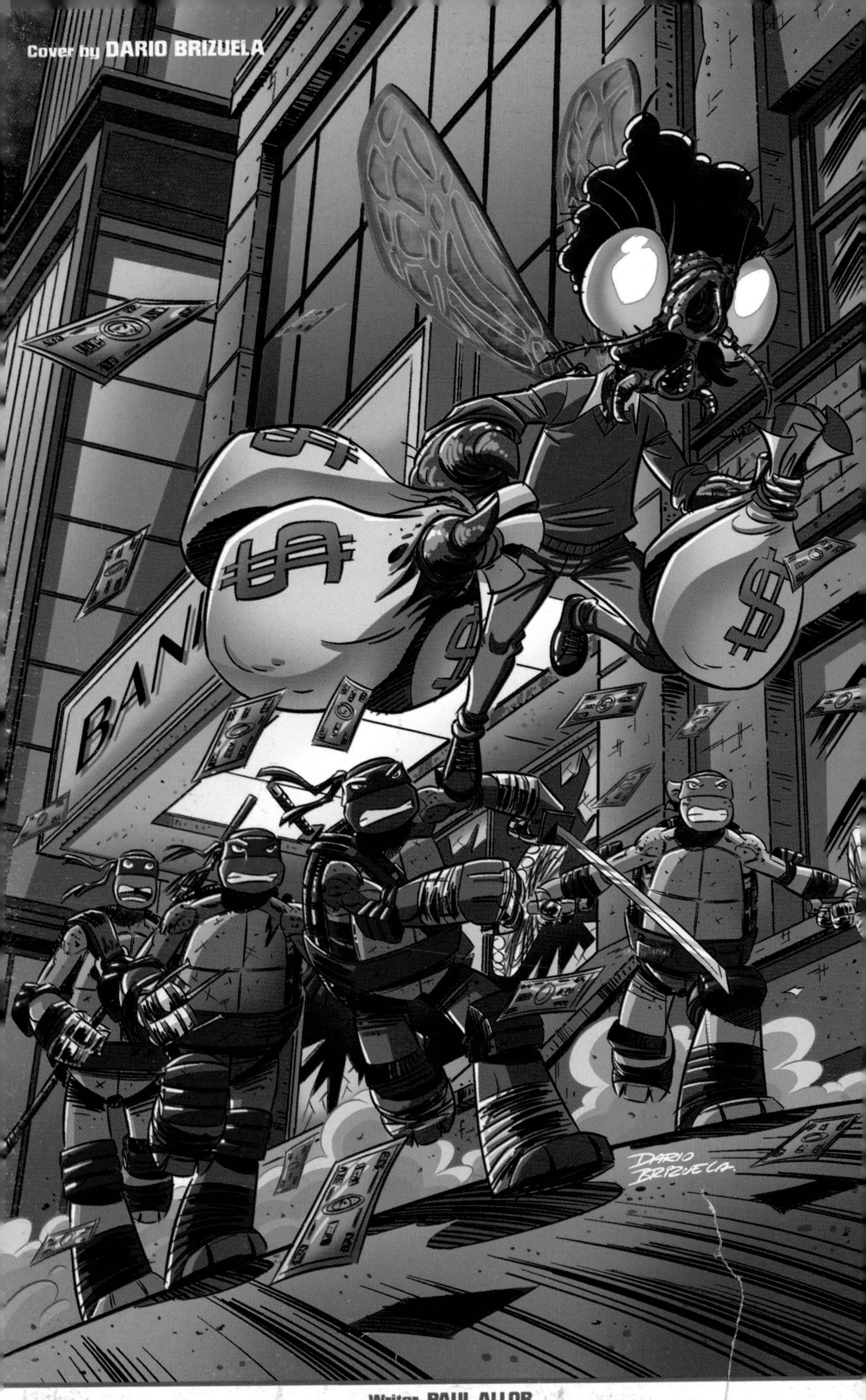
BAN
DARIO BRIZUELA

Writer: PAUL ALLOR
Artist: DARIO BRIZUELA

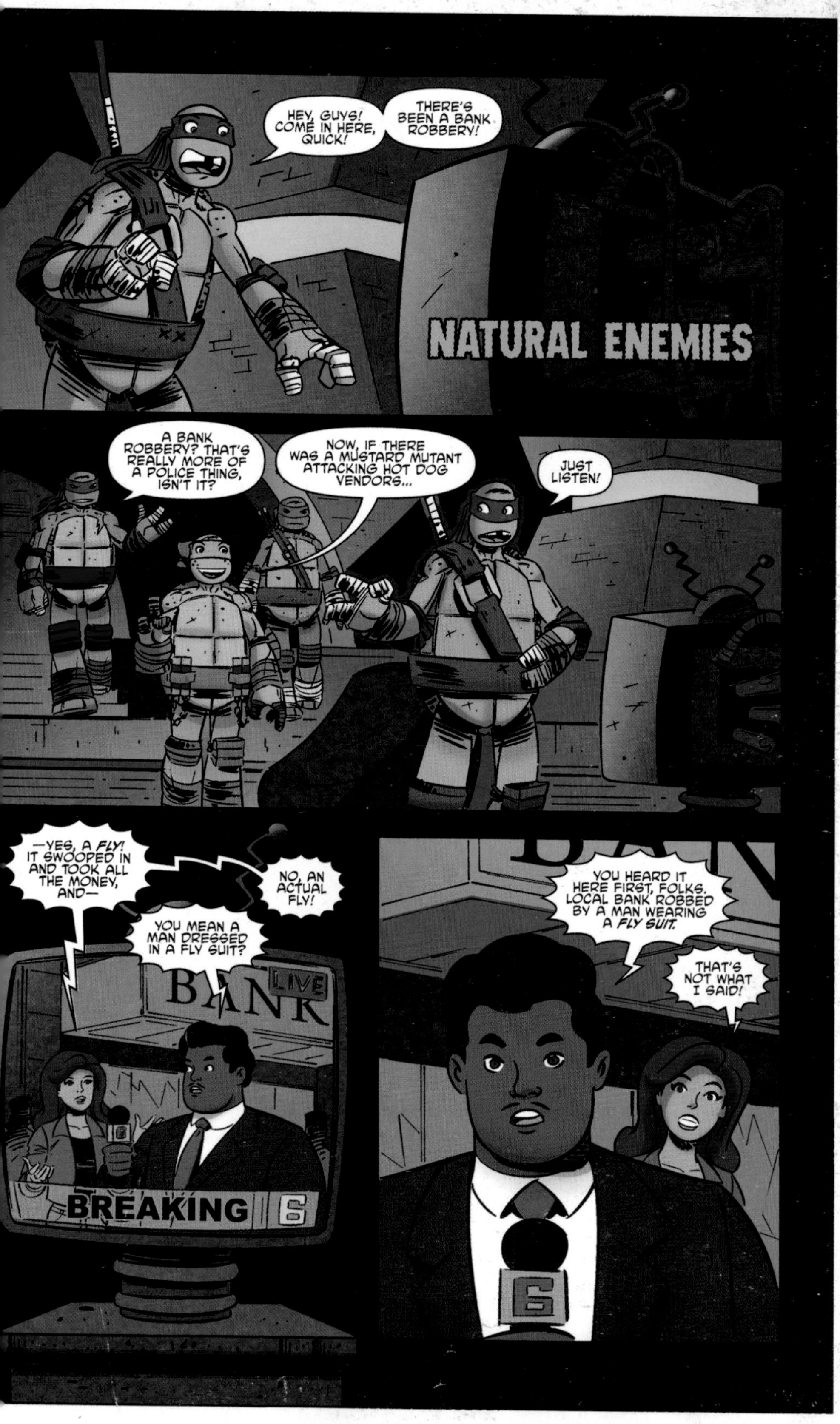
HEY, GUYS! COME IN HERE, QUICK!
THERE'S BEEN A BANK ROBBERY!
NATURAL ENEMIES
A BANK ROBBERY? THAT'S REALLY MORE OF A POLICE THING, ISN'T IT?
NOW, IF THERE WAS A MUSTARD MUTANT ATTACKING HOT DOG VENDORS...
JUST LISTEN!
—YES, A FLY! IT SWOOPED IN AND TOOK ALL THE MONEY, AND—
NO, AN ACTUAL FLY!
YOU MEAN A MAN DRESSED IN A FLY SUIT?
BANK
LIVE
BREAKING
6
YOU HEARD IT HERE FIRST, FOLKS. LOCAL BANK ROBBED BY A MAN WEARING A FLY SUIT.
THAT'S NOT WHAT I SAID!
6

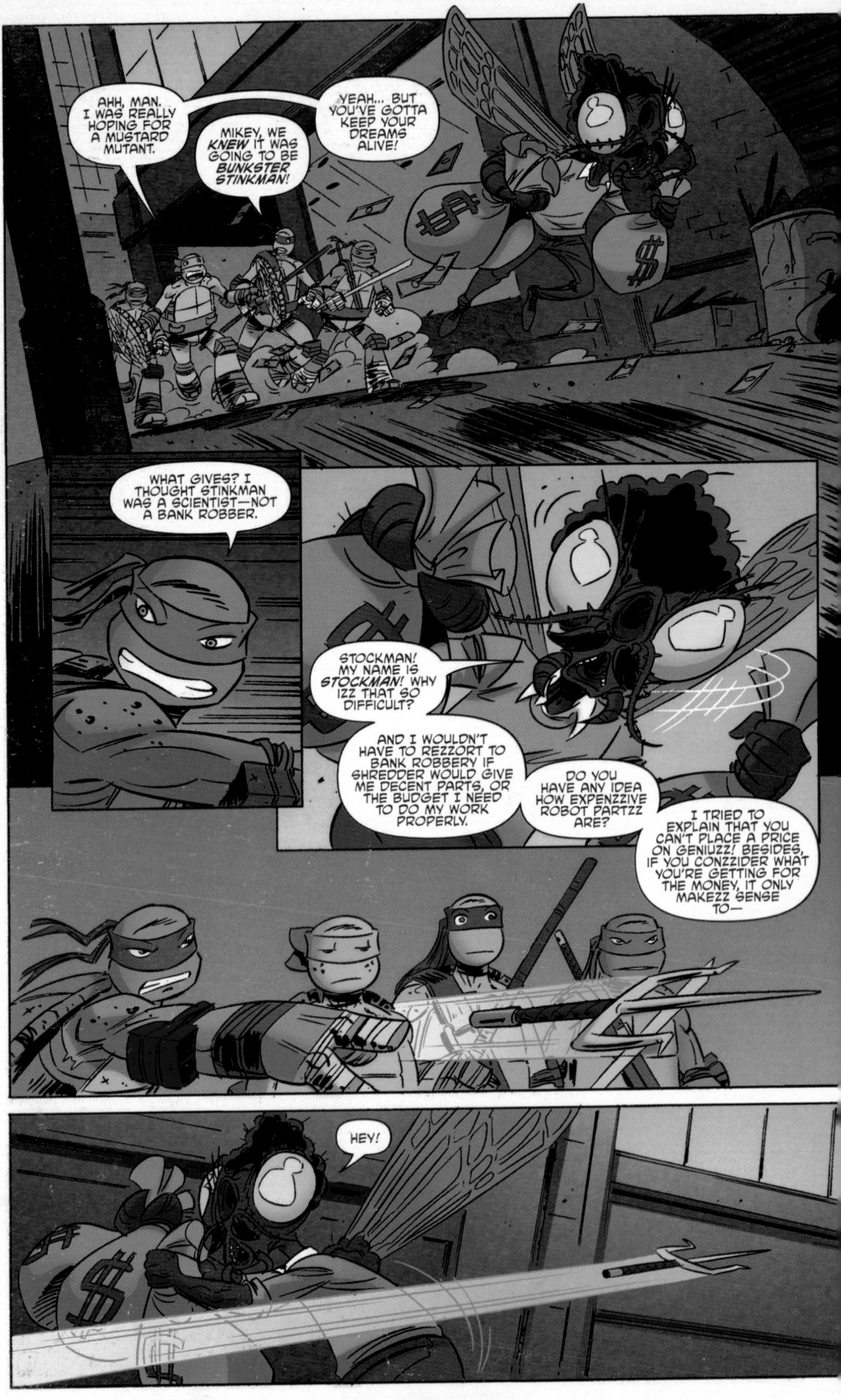
AHH, MAN. I WAS REALLY HOPING FOR A MUSTARD MUTANT.
MIKEY, WE *KNEW* IT WAS GOING TO BE *BUNKSTER STINKMAN!*
YEAH... BUT YOU'VE GOTTA KEEP YOUR DREAMS ALIVE!
WHAT GIVES? I THOUGHT STINKMAN WAS A SCIENTIST—NOT A BANK ROBBER.
STOCKMAN! MY NAME IS *STOCKMAN!* WHY IZZ THAT SO DIFFICULT?
AND I WOULDN'T HAVE TO REZZORT TO BANK ROBBERY IF SHREDDER WOULD GIVE ME DECENT PARTS, OR THE BUDGET I NEED TO DO MY WORK PROPERLY.
DO YOU HAVE ANY IDEA HOW EXPENZZIVE ROBOT PARTZZ ARE?
I TRIED TO EXPLAIN THAT YOU CAN'T PLACE A PRICE ON GENIUZZ! BESIDES, IF YOU CONZZIDER WHAT YOU'RE GETTING FOR THE MONEY, IT ONLY MAKEZZ SENSE TO—
HEY!

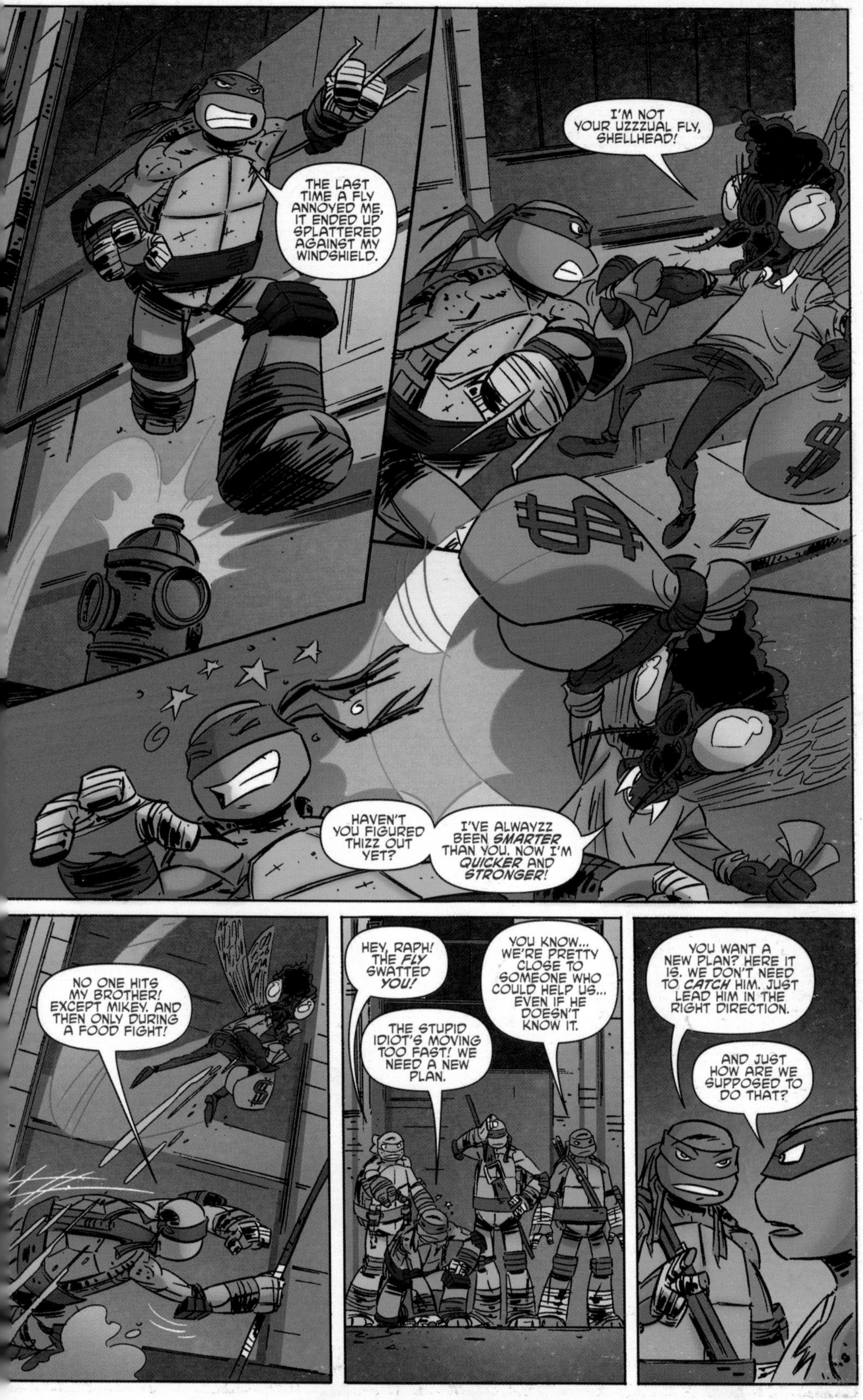
THE LAST TIME A FLY ANNOYED ME, IT ENDED UP SPLATTERED AGAINST MY WINDSHIELD.
I'M NOT YOUR UZZZUAL FLY, SHELLHEAD!
HAVEN'T YOU FIGURED THIZZ OUT YET?
I'VE ALWAYZZ BEEN SMARTER THAN YOU. NOW I'M QUICKER AND STRONGER!
NO ONE HITS MY BROTHER! EXCEPT MIKEY. AND THEN ONLY DURING A FOOD FIGHT!
HEY, RAPH! THE FLY SWATTED YOU!
THE STUPID IDIOT'S MOVING TOO FAST! WE NEED A NEW PLAN.
YOU KNOW... WE'RE PRETTY CLOSE TO SOMEONE WHO COULD HELP US... EVEN IF HE DOESN'T KNOW IT.
YOU WANT A NEW PLAN? HERE IT IS. WE DON'T NEED TO CATCH HIM. JUST LEAD HIM IN THE RIGHT DIRECTION.
AND JUST HOW ARE WE SUPPOSED TO DO THAT?

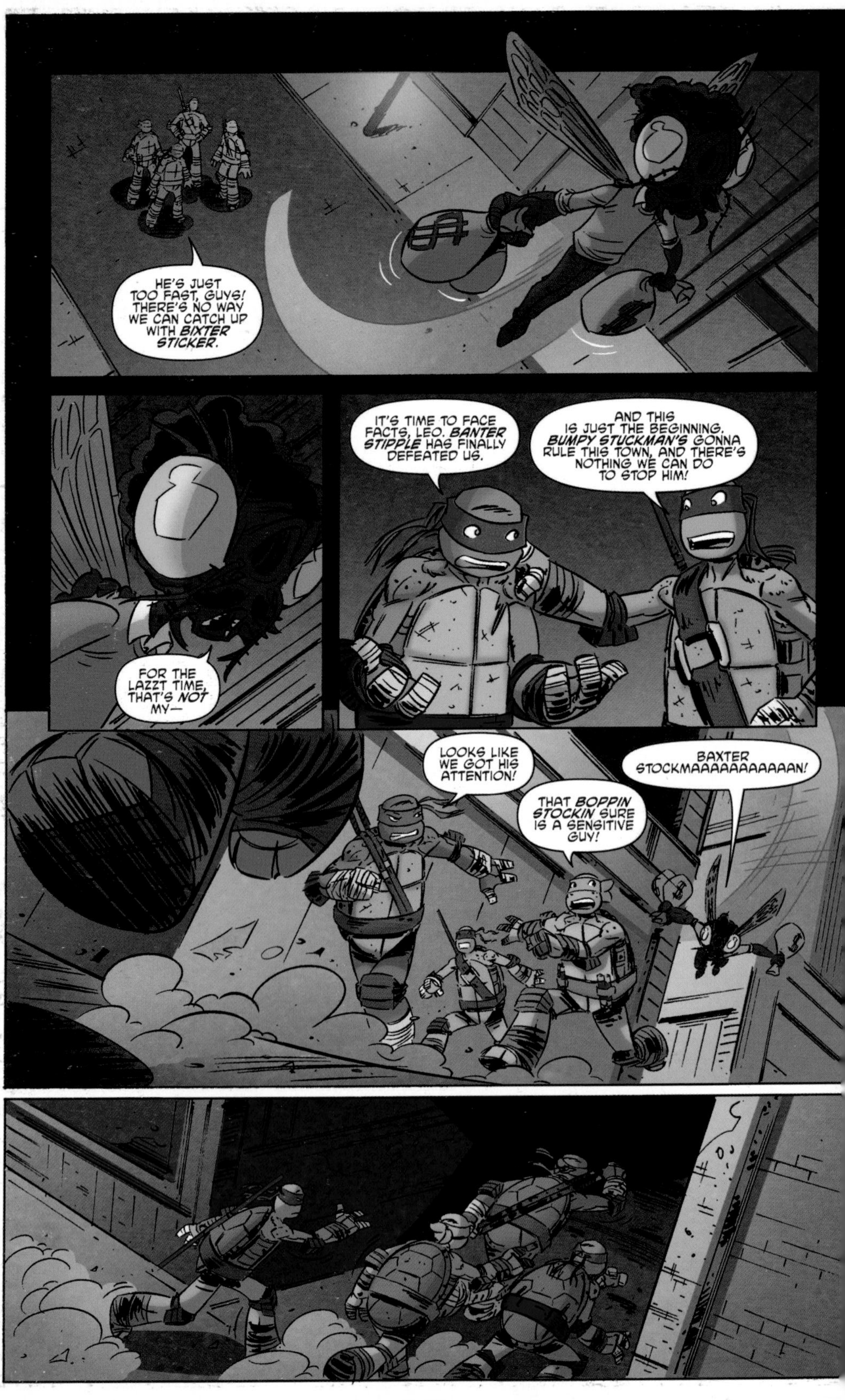
HE'S JUST TOO FAST, GUYS! THERE'S NO WAY WE CAN CATCH UP WITH BIXTER STICKER.
FOR THE LAZZT TIME, THAT'S NOT MY—
IT'S TIME TO FACE FACTS, LEO. BANTER STIPPLE HAS FINALLY DEFEATED US.
AND THIS IS JUST THE BEGINNING. BUMPY STUCKMAN'S GONNA RULE THIS TOWN, AND THERE'S NOTHING WE CAN DO TO STOP HIM!
LOOKS LIKE WE GOT HIS ATTENTION!
THAT BOPPIN STOCKIN SURE IS A SENSITIVE GUY!
BAXTER STOCKMAAAAAAAAAAAAN!

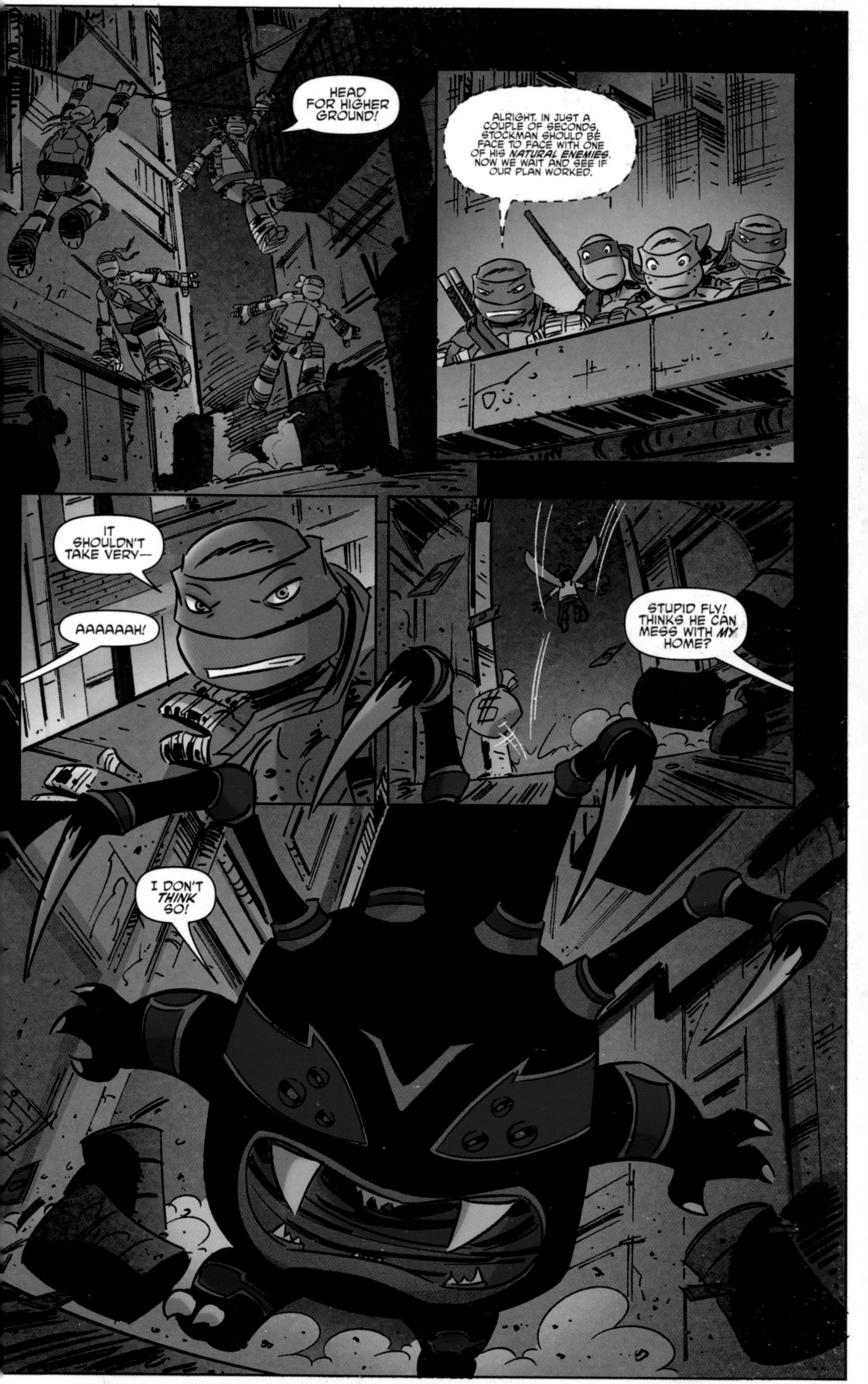
HEAD FOR HIGHER GROUND!
ALRIGHT. IN JUST A COUPLE OF SECONDS, STOCKMAN SHOULD BE FACE TO FACE WITH ONE OF HIS NATURAL ENEMIES. NOW WE WAIT AND SEE IF OUR PLAN WORKED.
IT SHOULDN'T TAKE VERY—
AAAAAAH!
STUPID FLY! THINKS HE CAN MESS WITH MY HOME?
I DON'T THINK SO!

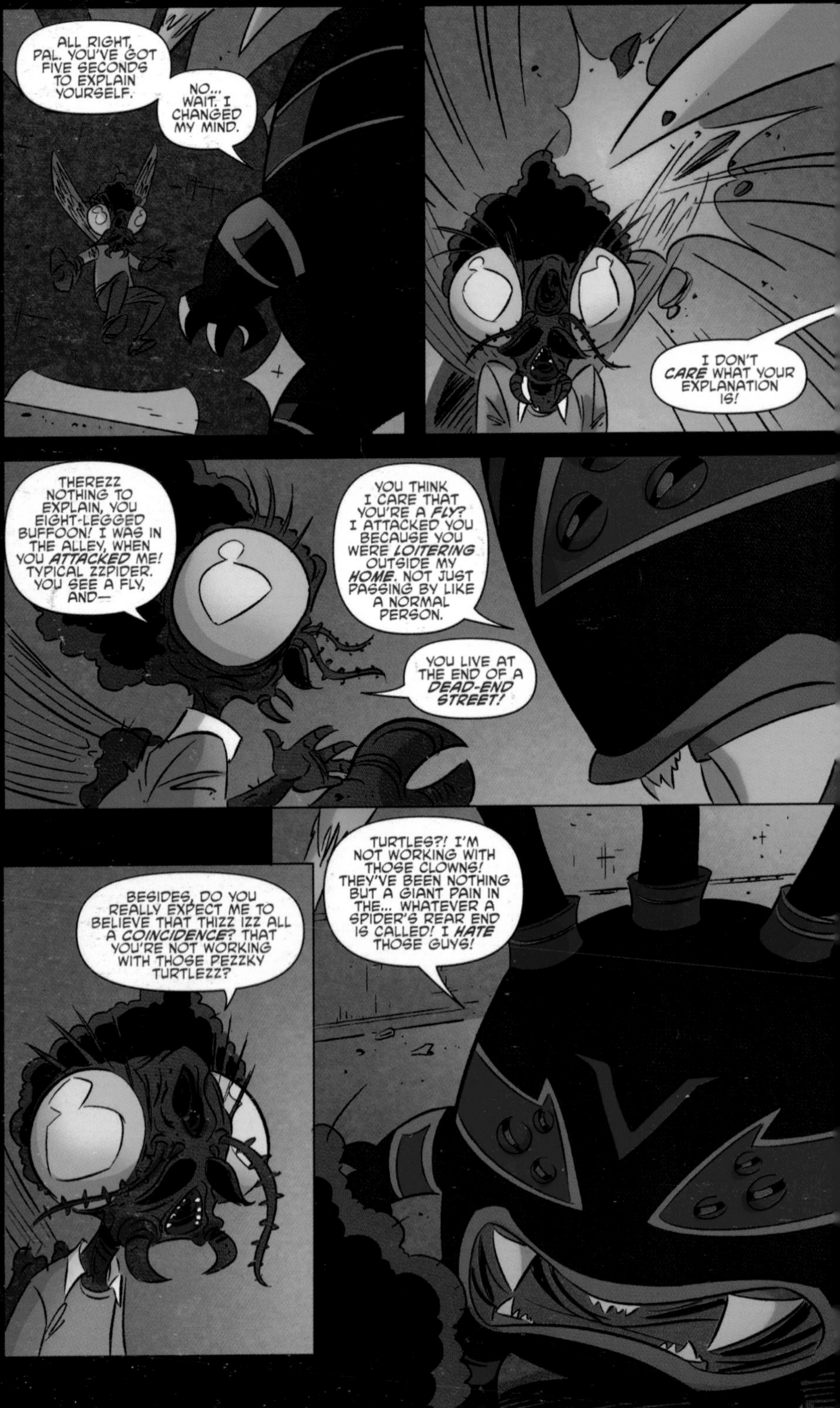

ALL RIGHT, PAL. YOU'VE GOT FIVE SECONDS TO EXPLAIN YOURSELF.
NO... WAIT. I CHANGED MY MIND.
I DON'T CARE WHAT YOUR EXPLANATION IS!
THEREZZ NOTHING TO EXPLAIN, YOU EIGHT-LEGGED BUFFOON! I WAS IN THE ALLEY, WHEN YOU ATTACKED ME! TYPICAL ZZPIDER. YOU SEE A FLY, AND—
YOU THINK I CARE THAT YOU'RE A FLY? I ATTACKED YOU BECAUSE YOU WERE LOITERING OUTSIDE MY HOME. NOT JUST PASSING BY LIKE A NORMAL PERSON.
YOU LIVE AT THE END OF A DEAD-END STREET!
BESIDES, DO YOU REALLY EXPECT ME TO BELIEVE THAT THIZZ IZZ ALL A COINCIDENCE? THAT YOU'RE NOT WORKING WITH THOSE PEZZKY TURTLEZZ?
TURTLES?! I'M NOT WORKING WITH THOSE CLOWNS! THEY'VE BEEN NOTHING BUT A GIANT PAIN IN THE... WHATEVER A SPIDER'S REAR END IS CALLED! I HATE THOSE GUYS!

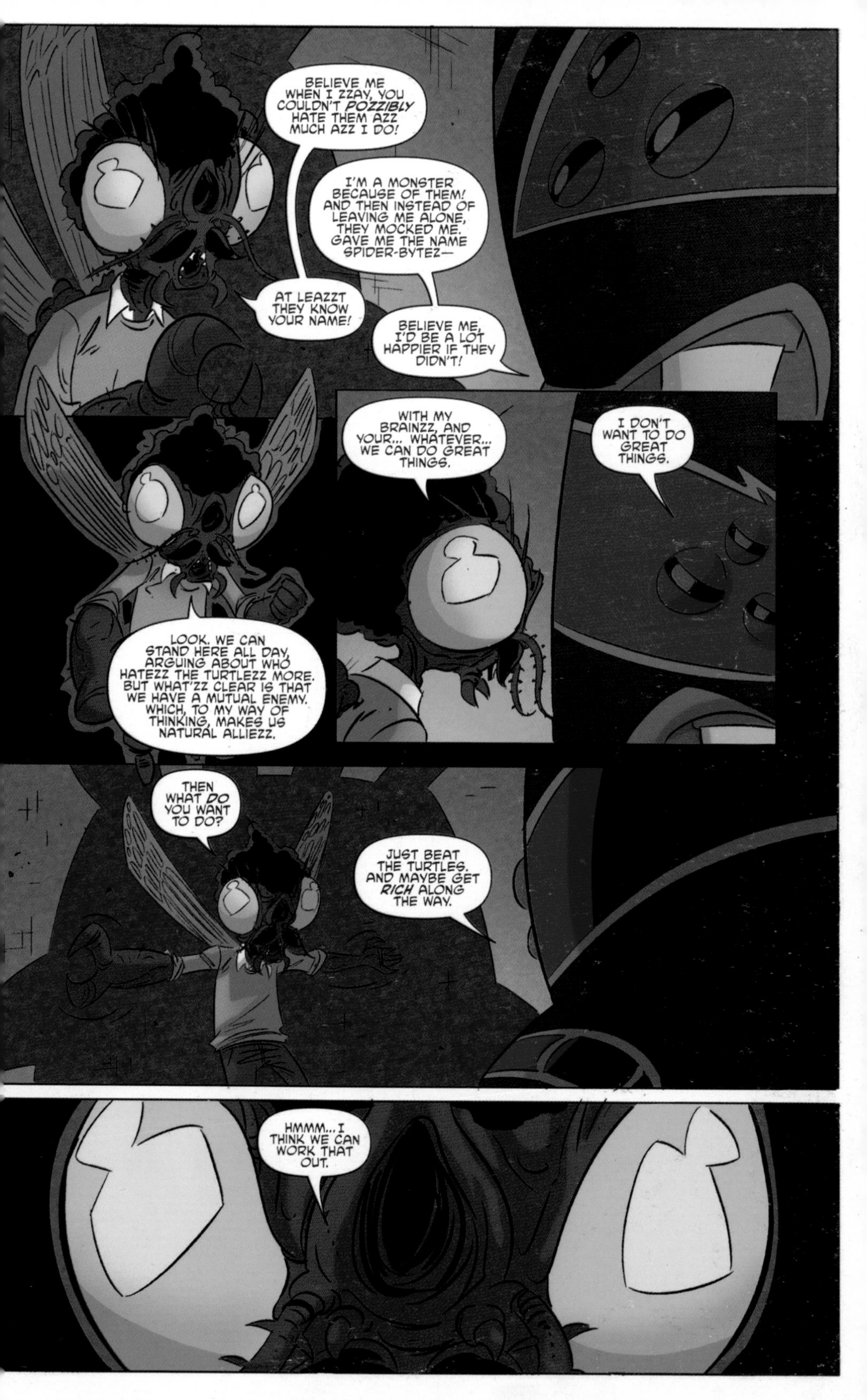
BELIEVE ME WHEN I ZZAY, YOU COULDN'T POZZIBLY HATE THEM AZZ MUCH AZZ I DO!
I'M A MONSTER BECAUSE OF THEM! AND THEN INSTEAD OF LEAVING ME ALONE, THEY MOCKED ME. GAVE ME THE NAME SPIDER-BYTEZ—
AT LEAZZT THEY KNOW YOUR NAME!
BELIEVE ME, I'D BE A LOT HAPPIER IF THEY DIDN'T!
LOOK. WE CAN STAND HERE ALL DAY, ARGUING ABOUT WHO HATEZZ THE TURTLEZZ MORE. BUT WHAT'ZZ CLEAR IS THAT WE HAVE A MUTUAL ENEMY. WHICH, TO MY WAY OF THINKING, MAKES US NATURAL ALLIEZZ.
WITH MY BRAINZZ, AND YOUR... WHATEVER... WE CAN DO GREAT THINGS.
I DON'T WANT TO DO GREAT THINGS.
THEN WHAT DO YOU WANT TO DO?
JUST BEAT THE TURTLES. AND MAYBE GET RICH ALONG THE WAY.
HMMM... I THINK WE CAN WORK THAT OUT.

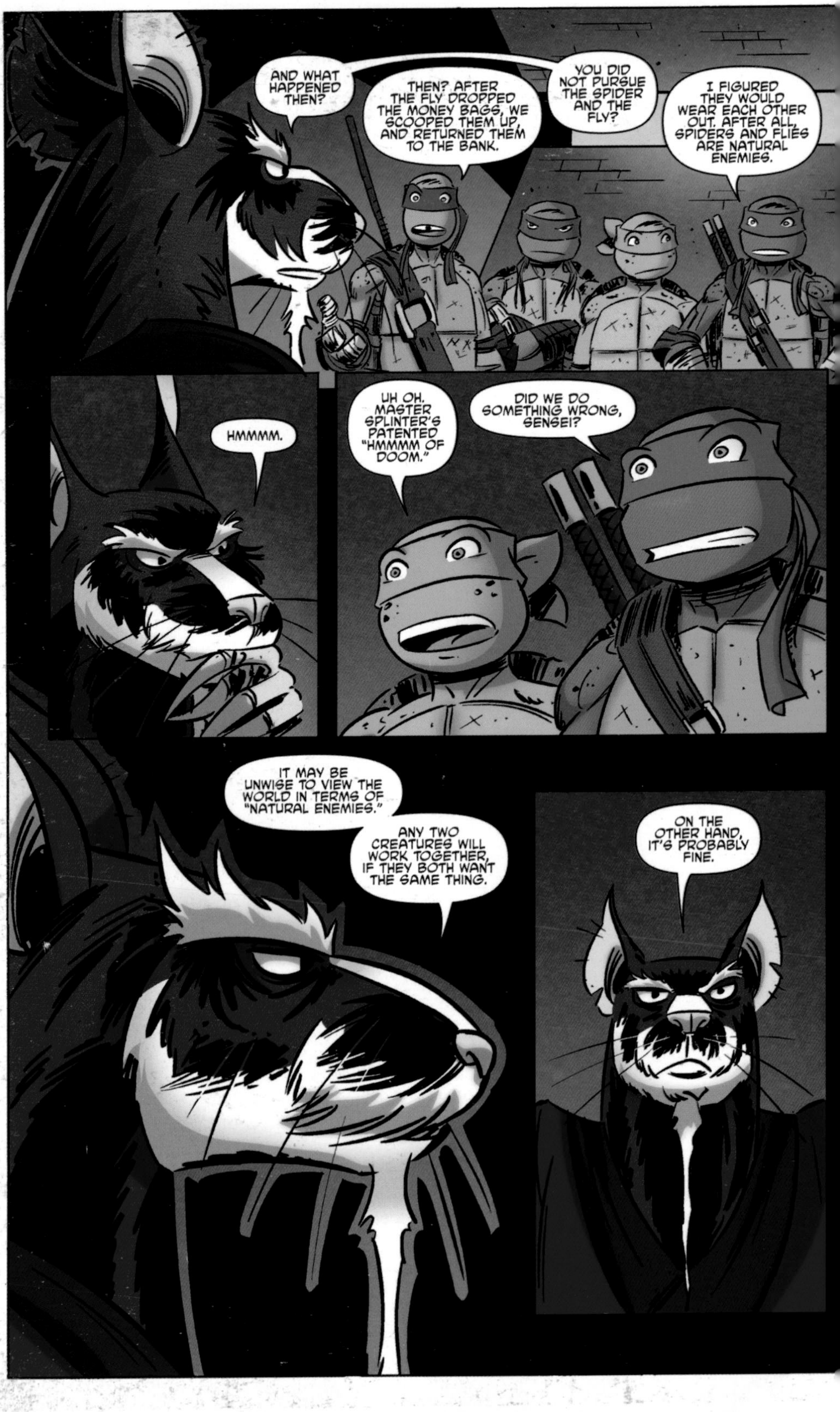
AND WHAT HAPPENED THEN?
THEN? AFTER THE FLY DROPPED THE MONEY BAGS, WE SCOOPED THEM UP, AND RETURNED THEM TO THE BANK.
YOU DID NOT PURSUE THE SPIDER AND THE FLY?
I FIGURED THEY WOULD WEAR EACH OTHER OUT. AFTER ALL, SPIDERS AND FLIES ARE NATURAL ENEMIES.
HMMMM.
UH OH. MASTER SPLINTER'S PATENTED "HMMMM OF DOOM."
DID WE DO SOMETHING WRONG, SENSEI?
IT MAY BE UNWISE TO VIEW THE WORLD IN TERMS OF "NATURAL ENEMIES."
ANY TWO CREATURES WILL WORK TOGETHER, IF THEY BOTH WANT THE SAME THING.
ON THE OTHER HAND, IT'S PROBABLY FINE.

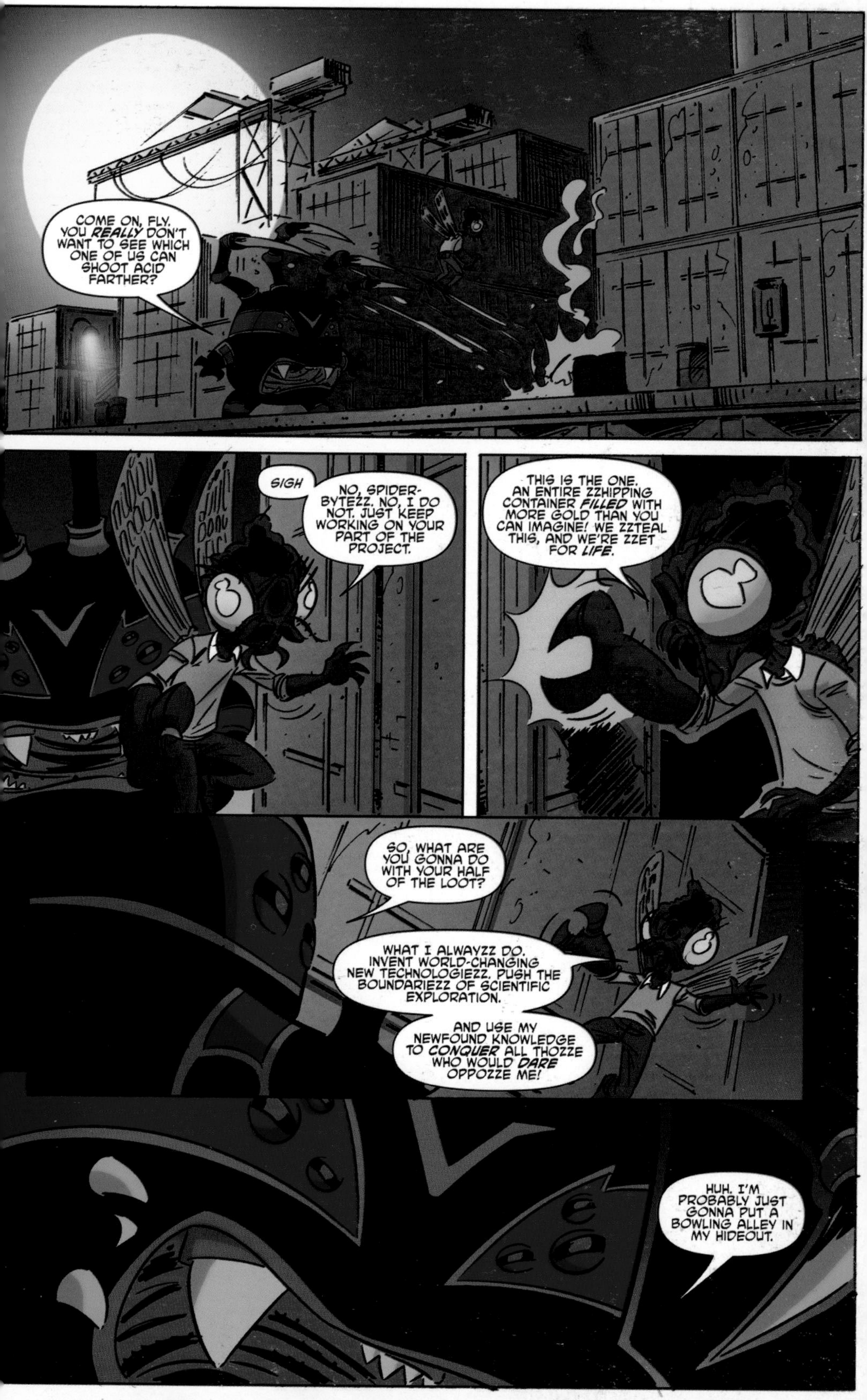
COME ON, FLY. YOU *REALLY* DON'T WANT TO SEE WHICH ONE OF US CAN SHOOT ACID FARTHER?
SIGH
NO, SPIDER-BYTEZZ. NO, I DO NOT. JUST KEEP WORKING ON YOUR PART OF THE PROJECT.
THIS IS THE ONE. AN ENTIRE ZZHIPPING CONTAINER *FILLED* WITH MORE GOLD THAN YOU CAN IMAGINE! WE ZZTEAL THIS, AND WE'RE ZZET FOR *LIFE*.
SO, WHAT ARE YOU GONNA DO WITH YOUR HALF OF THE LOOT?
WHAT I ALWAYZZ DO. INVENT WORLD-CHANGING NEW TECHNOLOGIEZZ. PUSH THE BOUNDARIEZZ OF SCIENTIFIC EXPLORATION.
AND USE MY NEWFOUND KNOWLEDGE TO *CONQUER* ALL THOZZE WHO WOULD *DARE* OPPOZZE ME!
HUH. I'M PROBABLY JUST GONNA PUT A BOWLING ALLEY IN MY HIDEOUT.

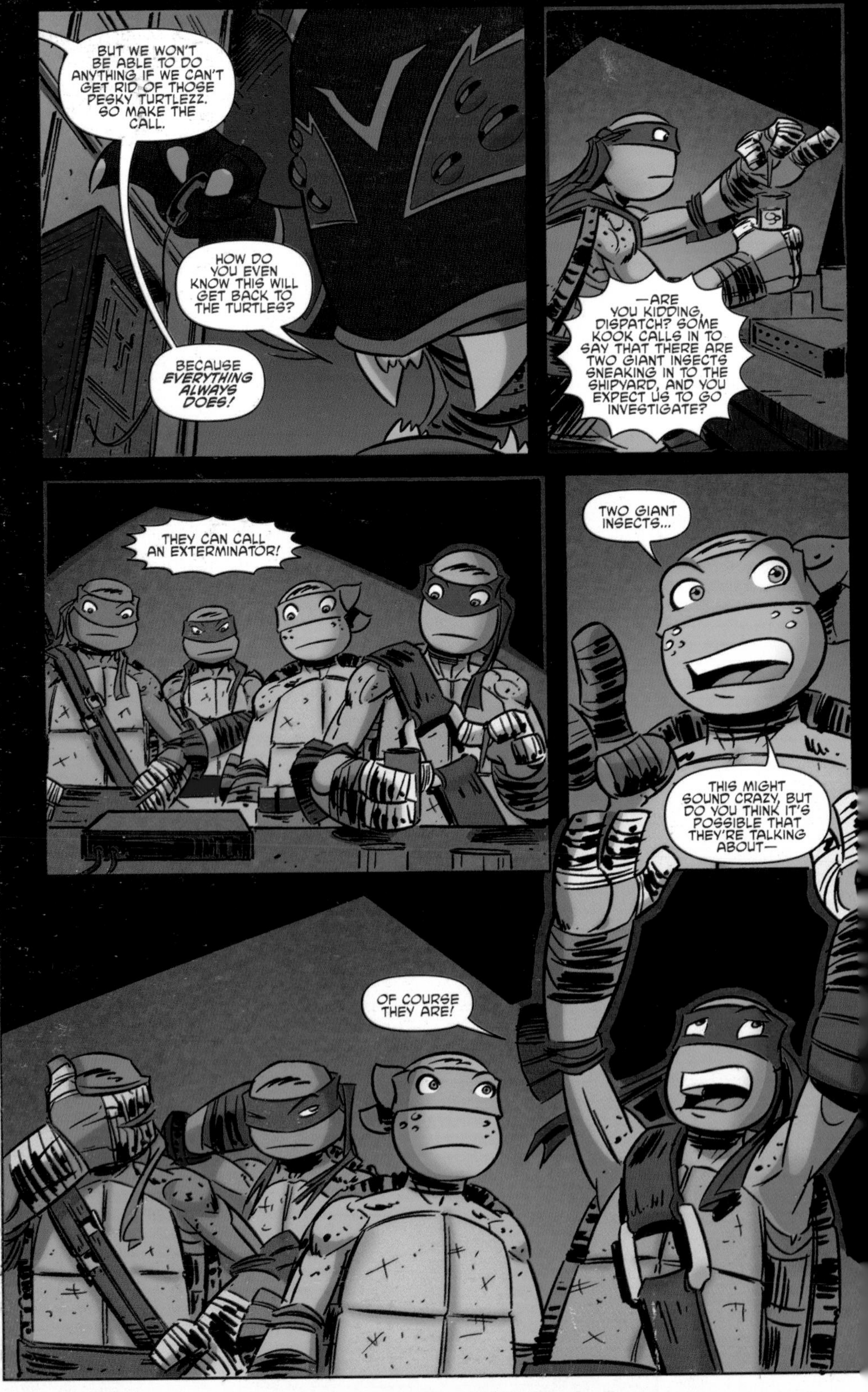
BUT WE WON'T BE ABLE TO DO ANYTHING IF WE CAN'T GET RID OF THOSE PESKY TURTLEZZ. SO MAKE THE CALL.
HOW DO YOU EVEN KNOW THIS WILL GET BACK TO THE TURTLES?
BECAUSE *EVERYTHING ALWAYS* DOES!
—ARE YOU KIDDING, DISPATCH? SOME KOOK CALLS IN TO SAY THAT THERE ARE TWO GIANT INSECTS SNEAKING IN TO THE SHIPYARD, AND YOU EXPECT US TO GO INVESTIGATE?
THEY CAN CALL AN EXTERMINATOR!
TWO GIANT INSECTS...
THIS MIGHT SOUND CRAZY, BUT DO YOU THINK IT'S POSSIBLE THAT THEY'RE TALKING ABOUT—
OF COURSE THEY ARE!

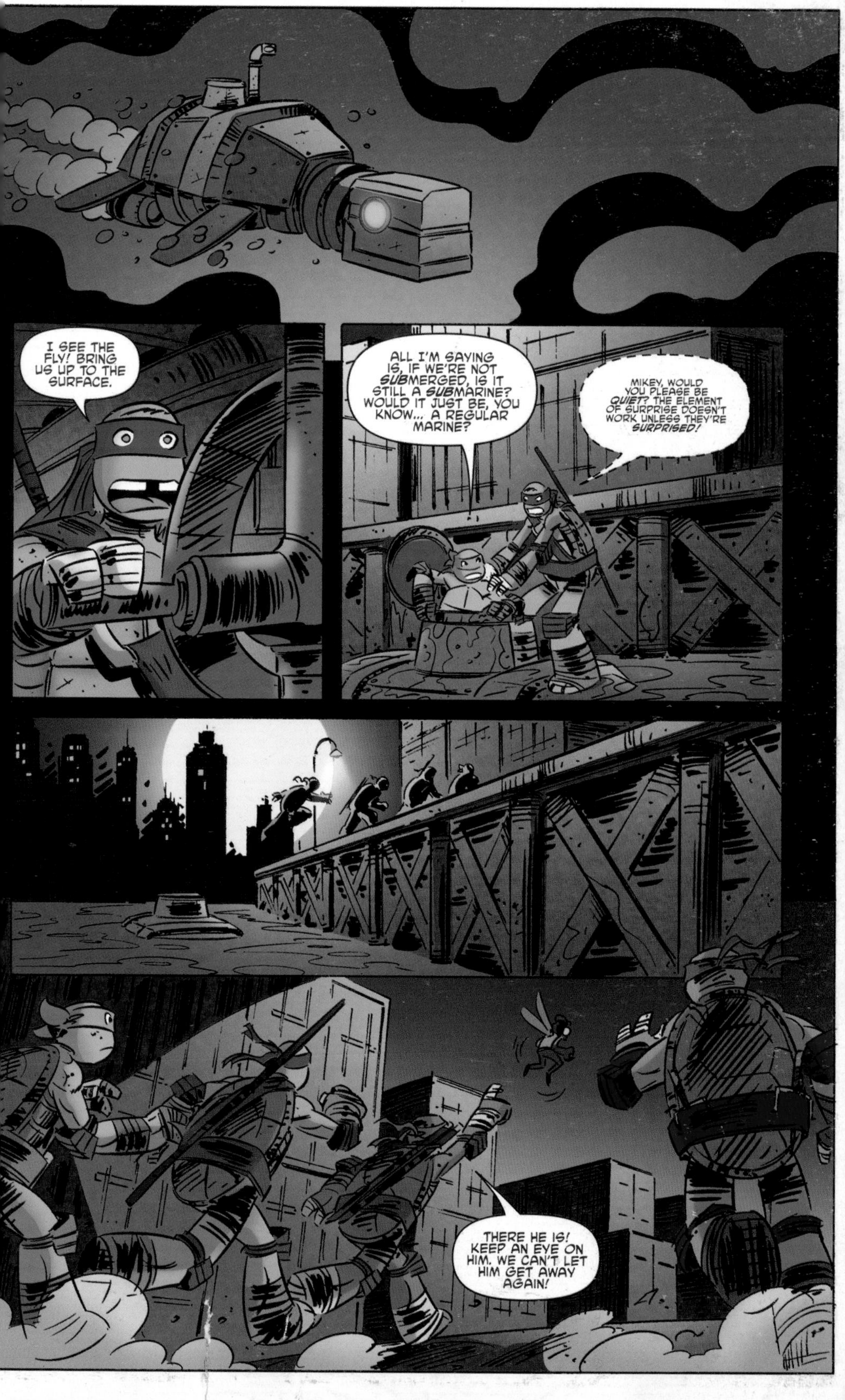
I SEE THE FLY! BRING US UP TO THE SURFACE.
ALL I'M SAYING IS, IF WE'RE NOT SUBMERGED, IS IT STILL A SUBMARINE? WOULD IT JUST BE, YOU KNOW... A REGULAR MARINE?
MIKEY, WOULD YOU PLEASE BE QUIET? THE ELEMENT OF SURPRISE DOESN'T WORK UNLESS THEY'RE SURPRISED!
THERE HE IS! KEEP AN EYE ON HIM. WE CAN'T LET HIM GET AWAY AGAIN!

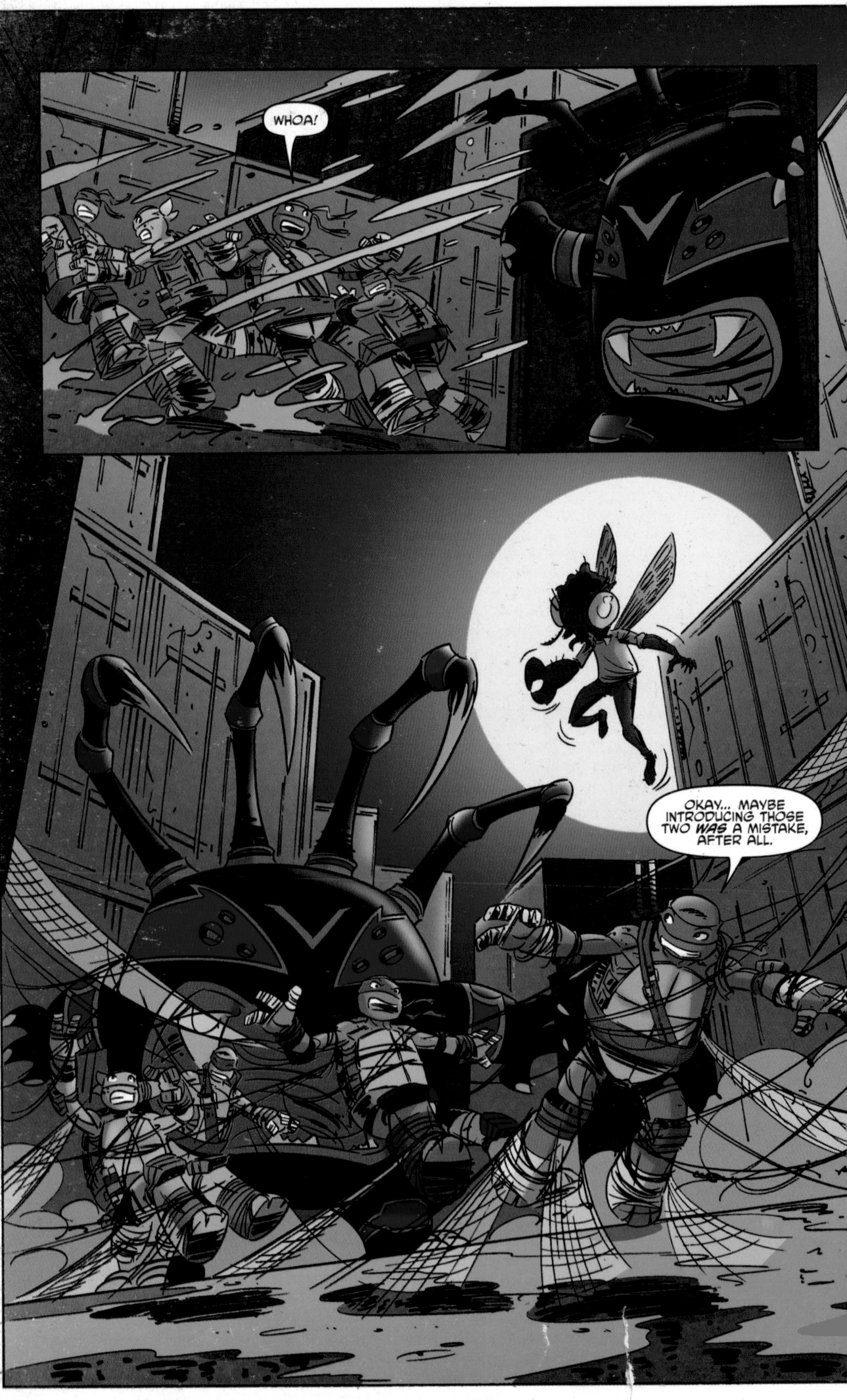
WHOA!
OKAY... MAYBE INTRODUCING THOSE TWO WAS A MISTAKE, AFTER ALL.

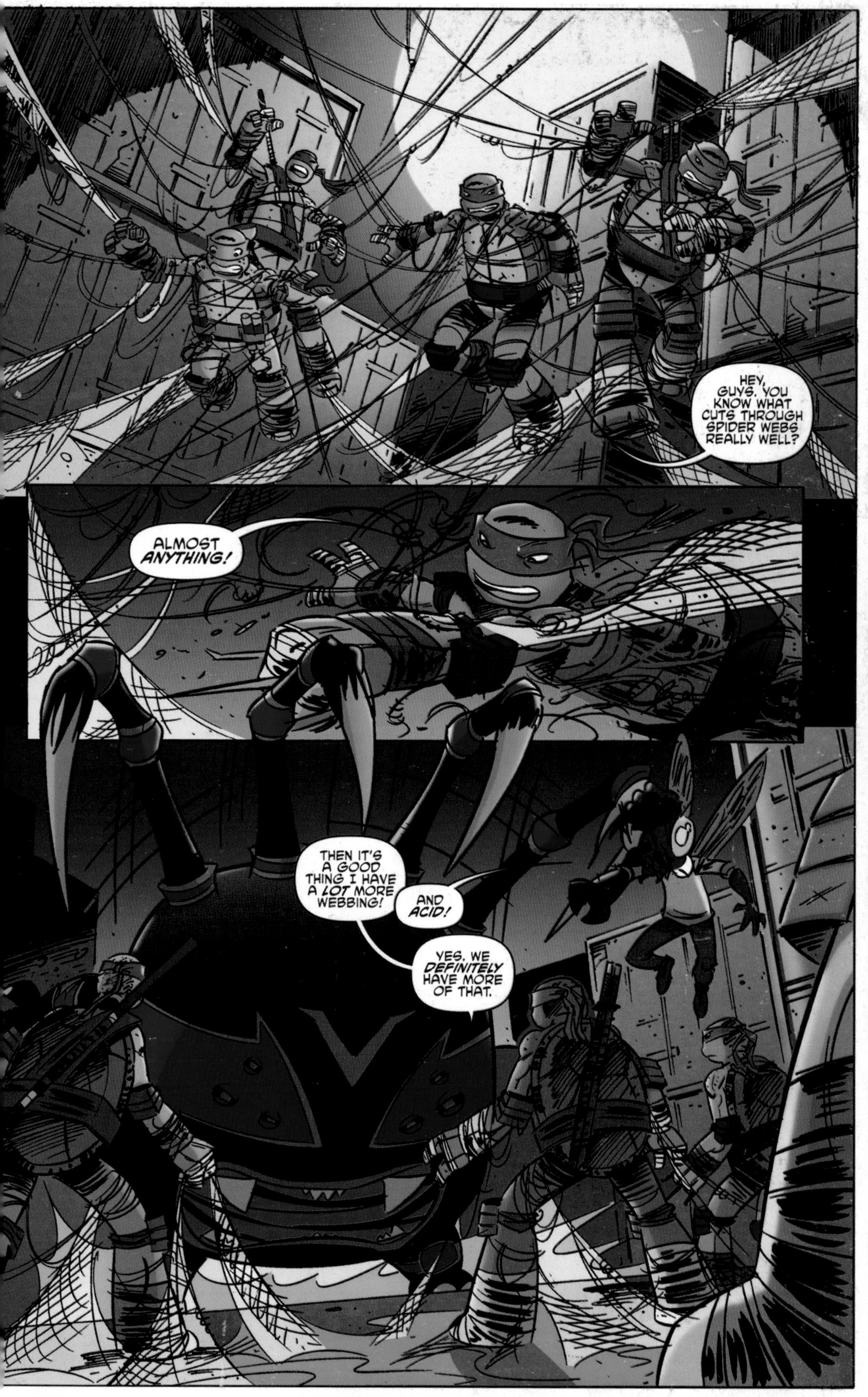
HEY, GUYS, YOU KNOW WHAT CUTS THROUGH SPIDER WEBS REALLY WELL?
ALMOST ANYTHING!
THEN IT'S A GOOD THING I HAVE A LOT MORE WEBBING!
AND ACID!
YES. WE DEFINITELY HAVE MORE OF THAT.

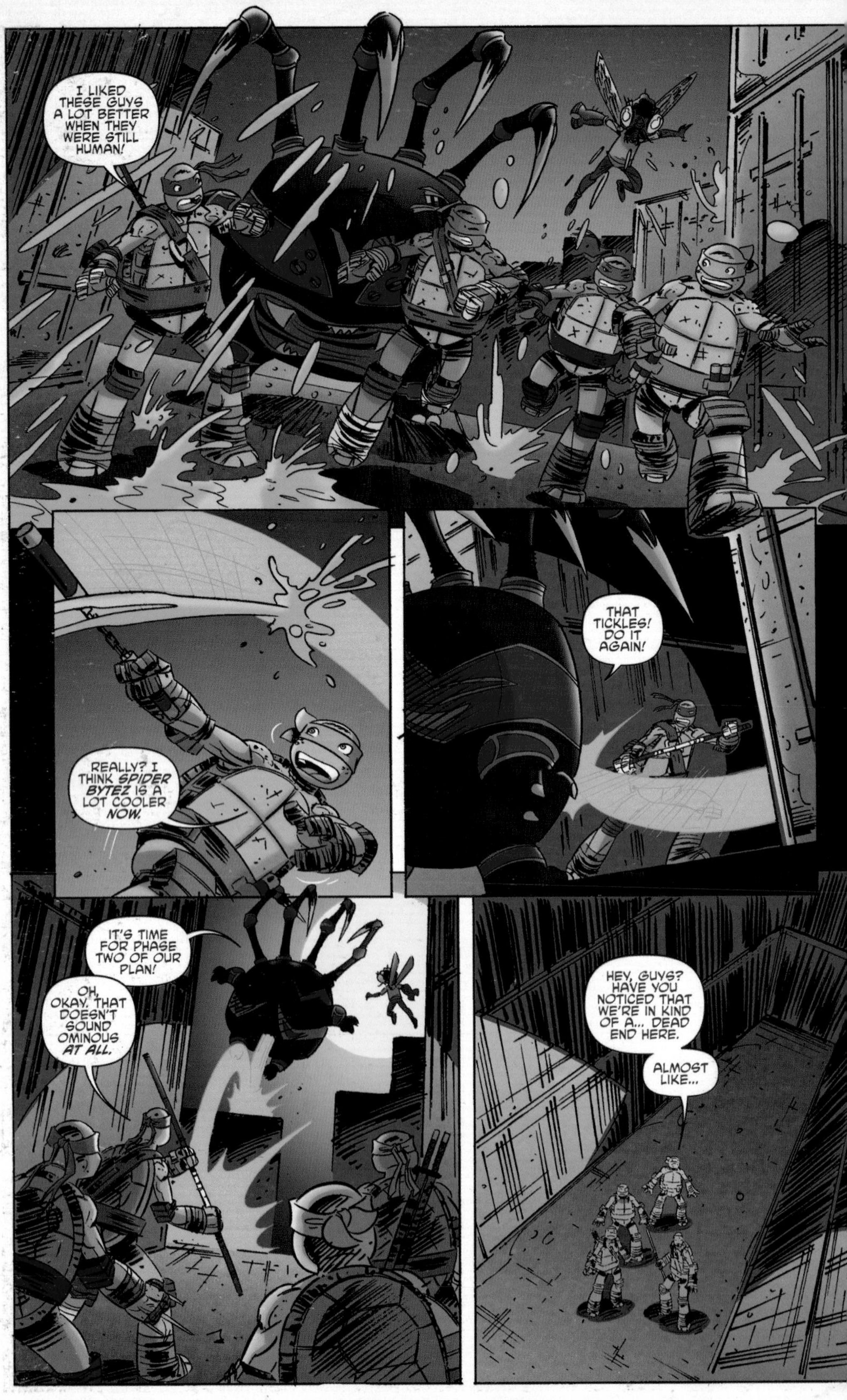
I LIKED THESE GUYS A LOT BETTER WHEN THEY WERE STILL HUMAN!
REALLY? I THINK SPIDER BYTEZ IS A LOT COOLER NOW.
THAT TICKLES! DO IT AGAIN!
IT'S TIME FOR PHASE TWO OF OUR PLAN!
OH, OKAY. THAT DOESN'T SOUND OMINOUS AT ALL.
HEY, GUYS? HAVE YOU NOTICED THAT WE'RE IN KIND OF A... DEAD END HERE.
ALMOST LIKE...

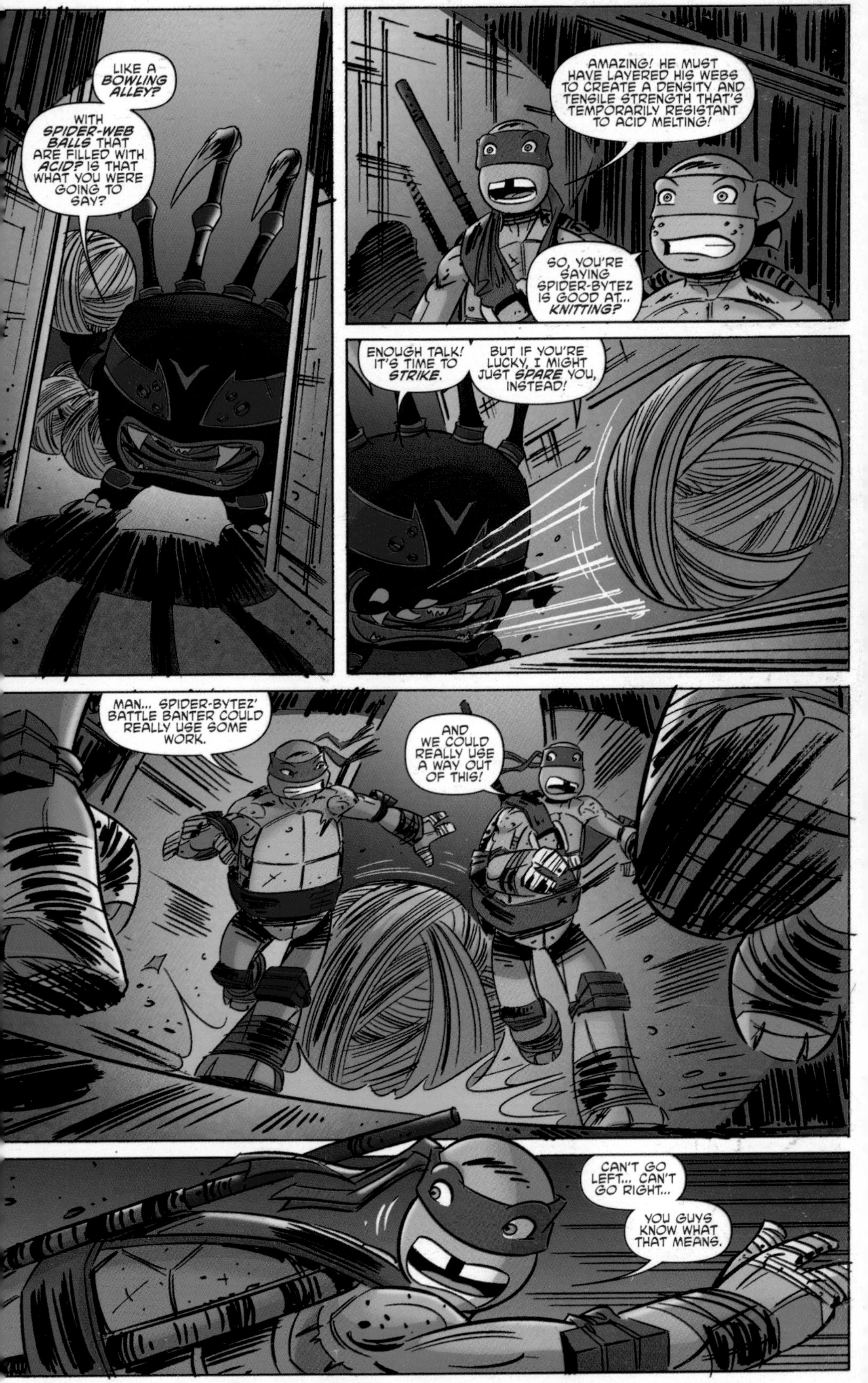
LIKE A BOWLING ALLEY?
WITH SPIDER-WEB BALLS THAT ARE FILLED WITH ACID? IS THAT WHAT YOU WERE GOING TO SAY?
AMAZING! HE MUST HAVE LAYERED HIS WEBS TO CREATE A DENSITY AND TENSILE STRENGTH THAT'S TEMPORARILY RESISTANT TO ACID MELTING!
SO, YOU'RE SAYING SPIDER-BYTEZ IS GOOD AT... KNITTING?
ENOUGH TALK! IT'S TIME TO STRIKE.
BUT IF YOU'RE LUCKY, I MIGHT JUST SPARE YOU, INSTEAD!
MAN... SPIDER-BYTEZ' BATTLE BANTER COULD REALLY USE SOME WORK.
AND WE COULD REALLY USE A WAY OUT OF THIS!
CAN'T GO LEFT... CAN'T GO RIGHT...
YOU GUYS KNOW WHAT THAT MEANS.

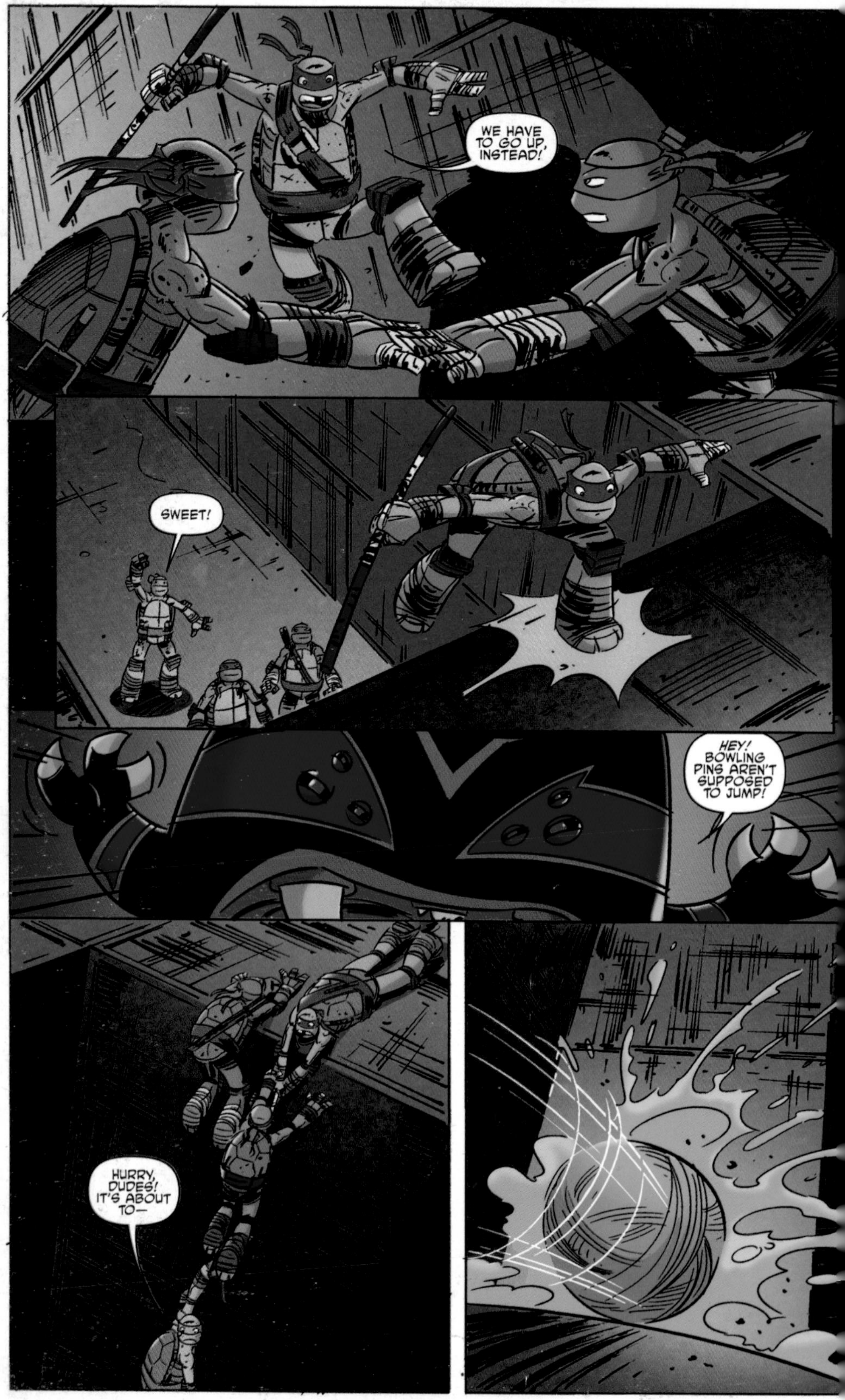
WE HAVE TO GO UP, INSTEAD!
SWEET!
HEY! BOWLING PINS AREN'T SUPPOSED TO JUMP!
HURRY, DUDES! IT'S ABOUT TO—

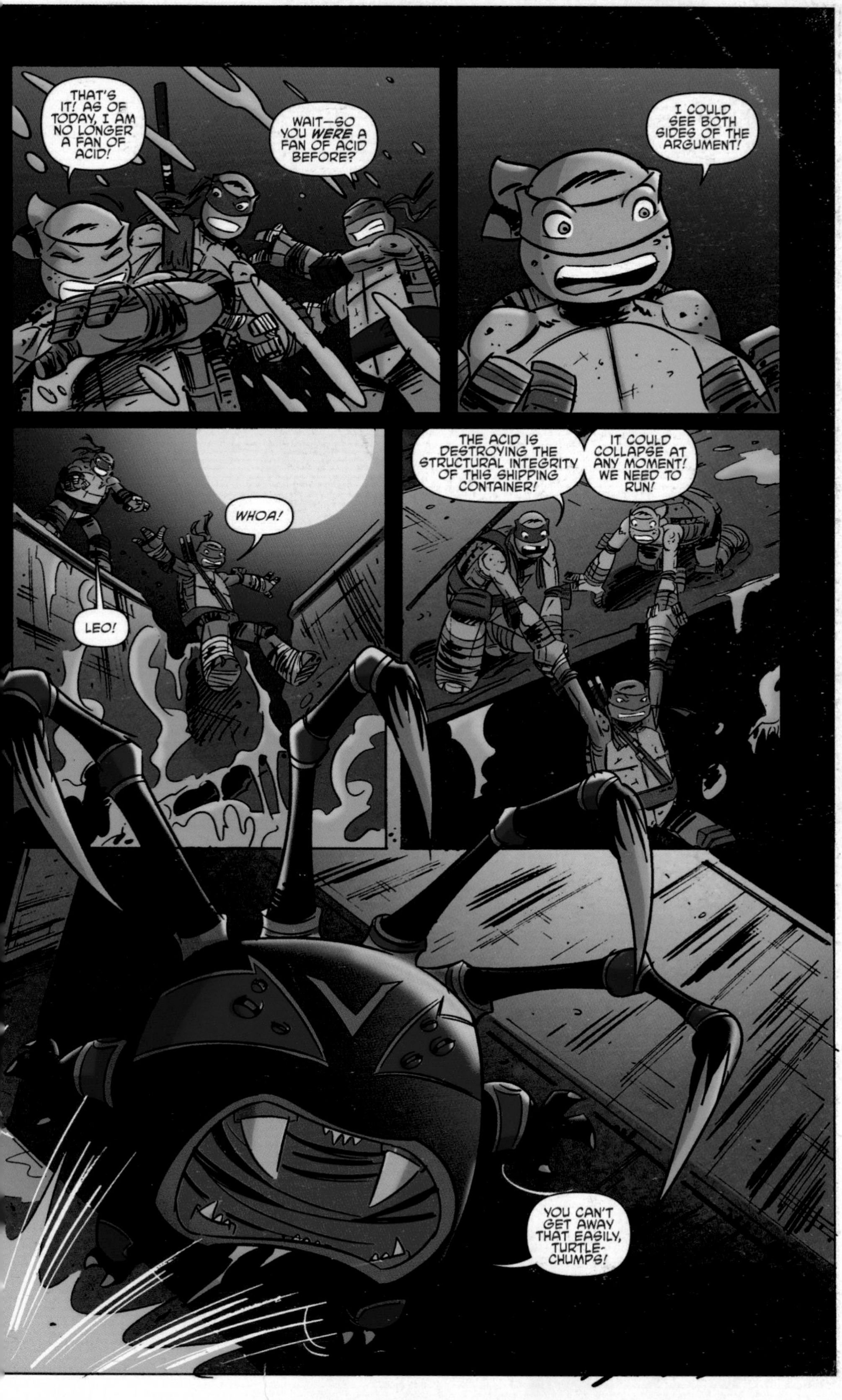
THAT'S IT! AS OF TODAY, I AM NO LONGER A FAN OF ACID!
WAIT—SO YOU *WERE* A FAN OF ACID BEFORE?
I COULD SEE BOTH SIDES OF THE ARGUMENT!
WHOA!
LEO!
THE ACID IS DESTROYING THE STRUCTURAL INTEGRITY OF THIS SHIPPING CONTAINER!
IT COULD COLLAPSE AT ANY MOMENT! WE NEED TO RUN!
YOU CAN'T GET AWAY THAT EASILY, TURTLE-CHUMPS!

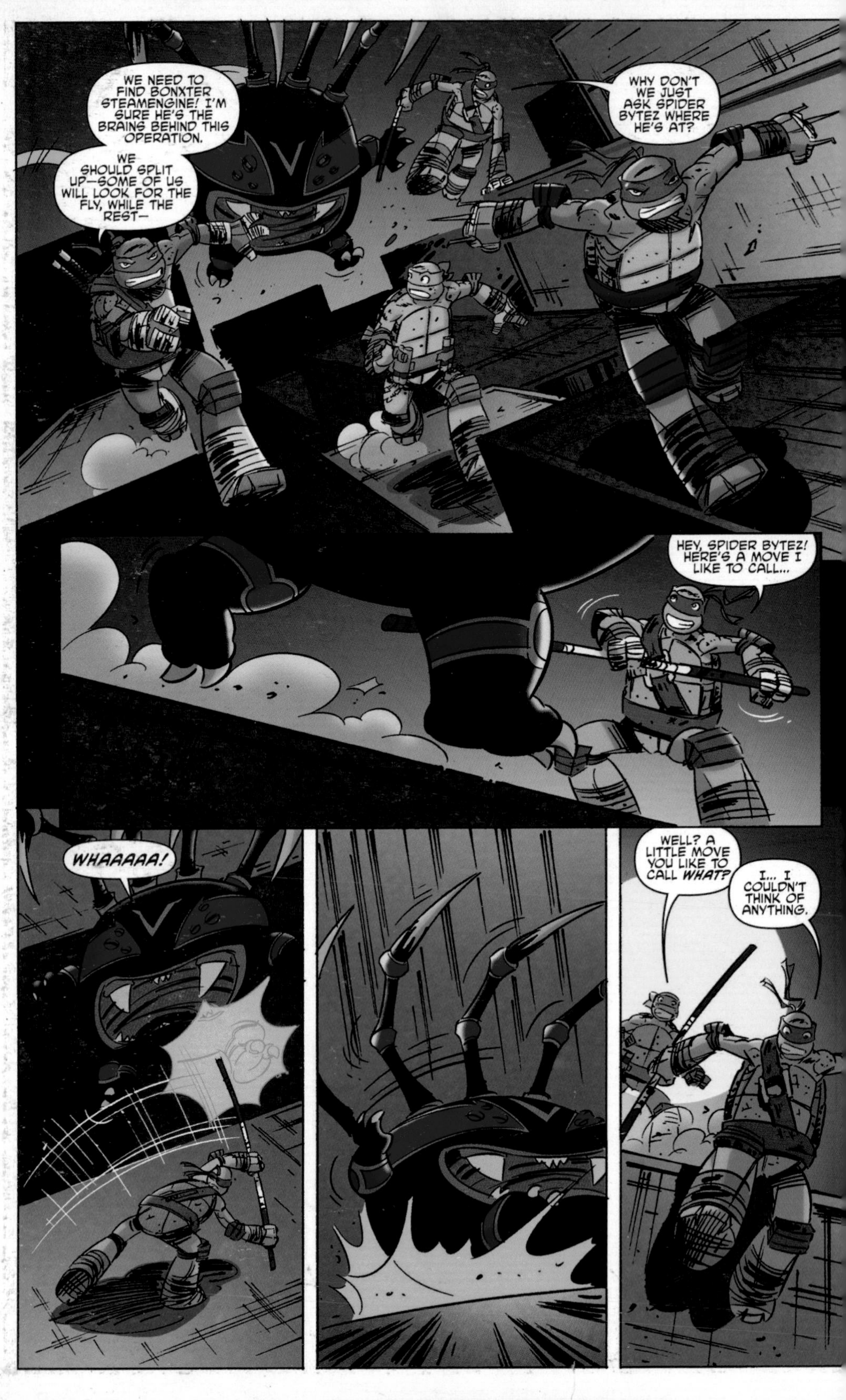
WE NEED TO FIND BONXTER STEAMENGINE! I'M SURE HE'S THE BRAINS BEHIND THIS OPERATION.
WE SHOULD SPLIT UP—SOME OF US WILL LOOK FOR THE FLY, WHILE THE REST—
WHY DON'T WE JUST ASK SPIDER BYTEZ WHERE HE'S AT?
HEY, SPIDER BYTEZ! HERE'S A MOVE I LIKE TO CALL...
WHAAAAAA!
WELL? A LITTLE MOVE YOU LIKE TO CALL WHAT?
I... I COULDN'T THINK OF ANYTHING.

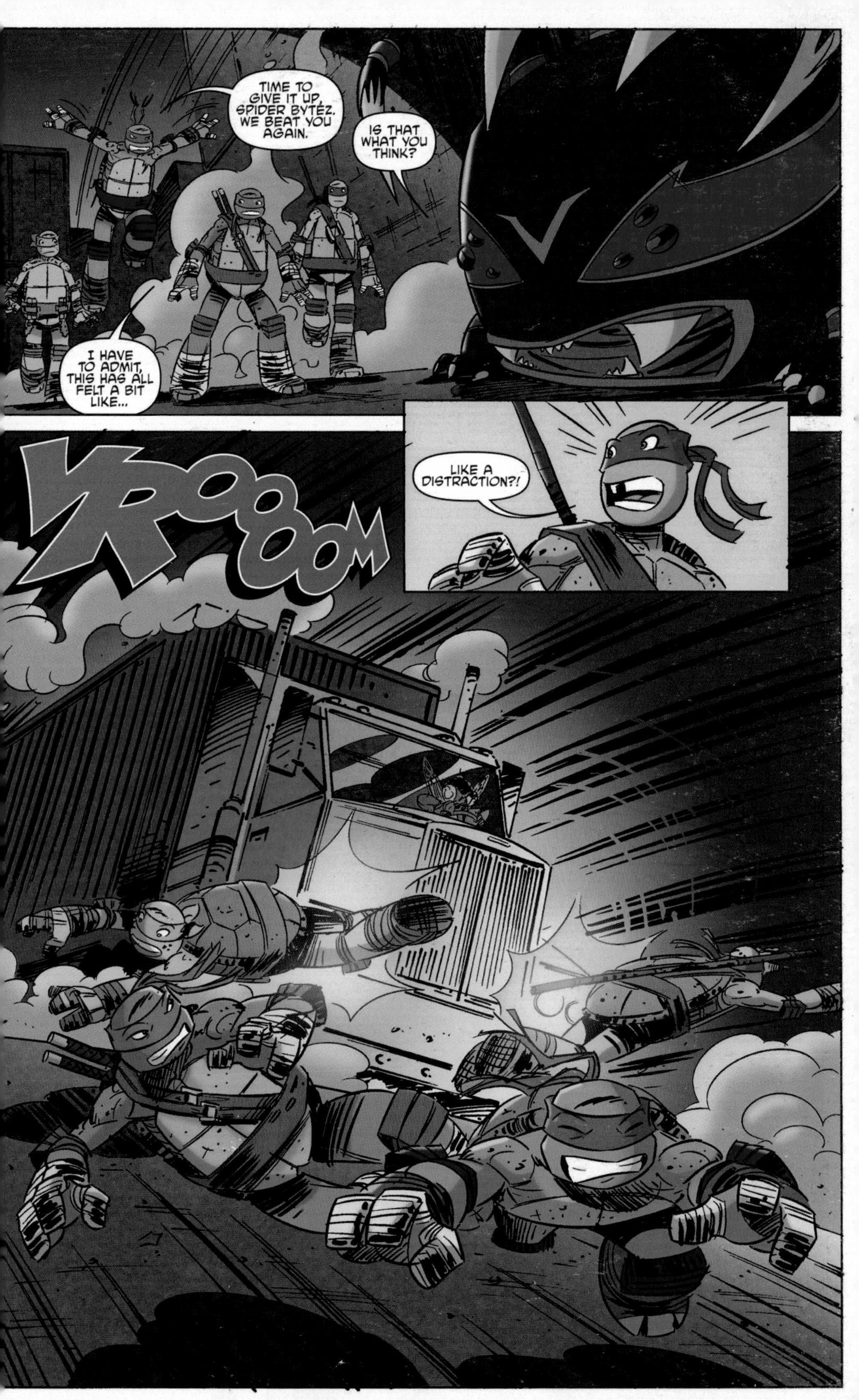
TIME TO GIVE IT UP, SPIDER BYTEZ. WE BEAT YOU AGAIN.
IS THAT WHAT YOU THINK?
I HAVE TO ADMIT, THIS HAS ALL FELT A BIT LIKE...
LIKE A DISTRACTION?!
VROOOOOM

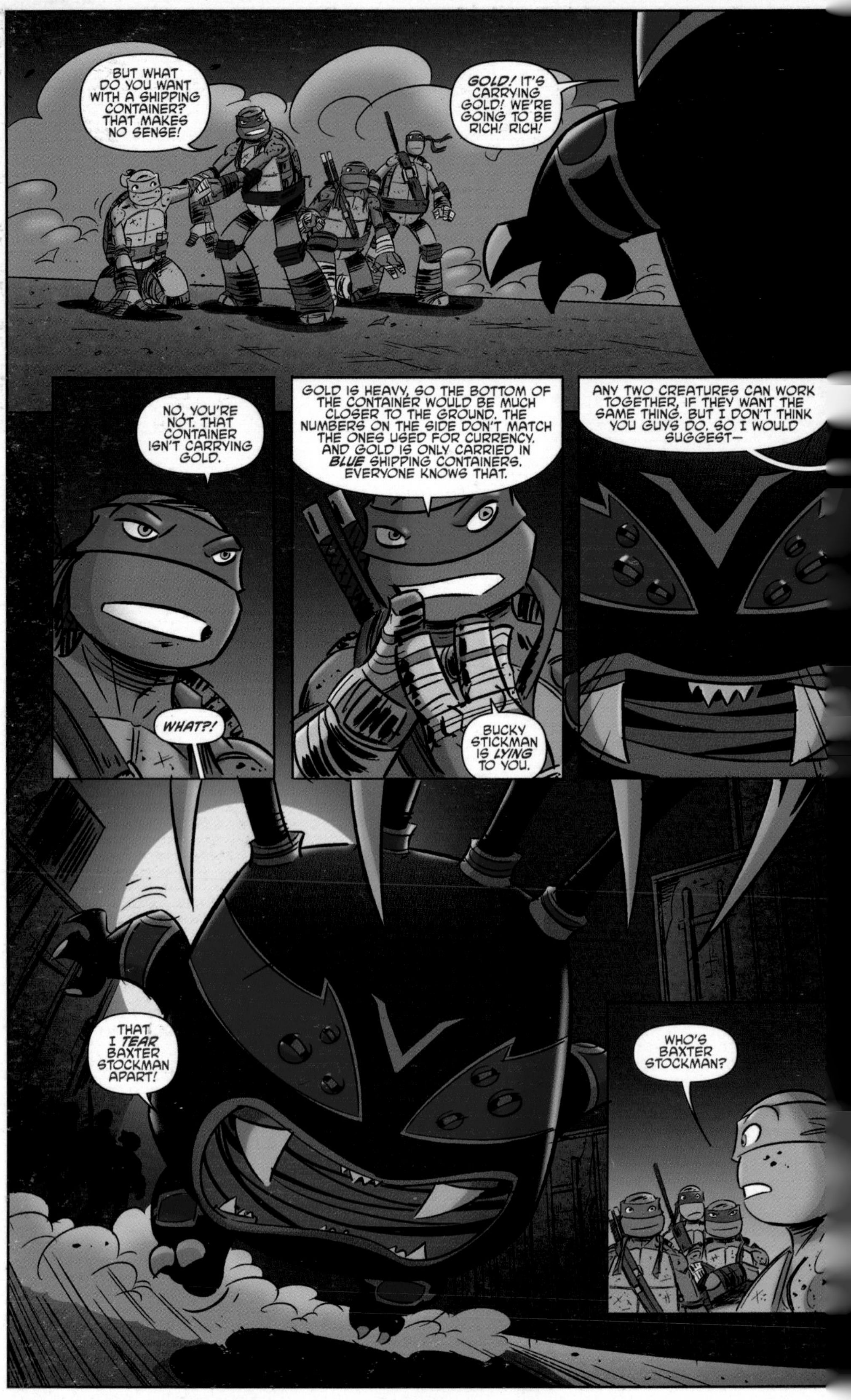
BUT WHAT DO YOU WANT WITH A SHIPPING CONTAINER? THAT MAKES NO SENSE!
GOLD! IT'S CARRYING GOLD! WE'RE GOING TO BE RICH! RICH!
NO, YOU'RE NOT. THAT CONTAINER ISN'T CARRYING GOLD.
WHAT?!
GOLD IS HEAVY, SO THE BOTTOM OF THE CONTAINER WOULD BE MUCH CLOSER TO THE GROUND. THE NUMBERS ON THE SIDE DON'T MATCH THE ONES USED FOR CURRENCY. AND GOLD IS ONLY CARRIED IN BLUE SHIPPING CONTAINERS. EVERYONE KNOWS THAT.
BUCKY STICKMAN IS LYING TO YOU.
ANY TWO CREATURES CAN WORK TOGETHER, IF THEY WANT THE SAME THING. BUT I DON'T THINK YOU GUYS DO. SO I WOULD SUGGEST—
THAT I TEAR BAXTER STOCKMAN APART!
WHO'S BAXTER STOCKMAN?

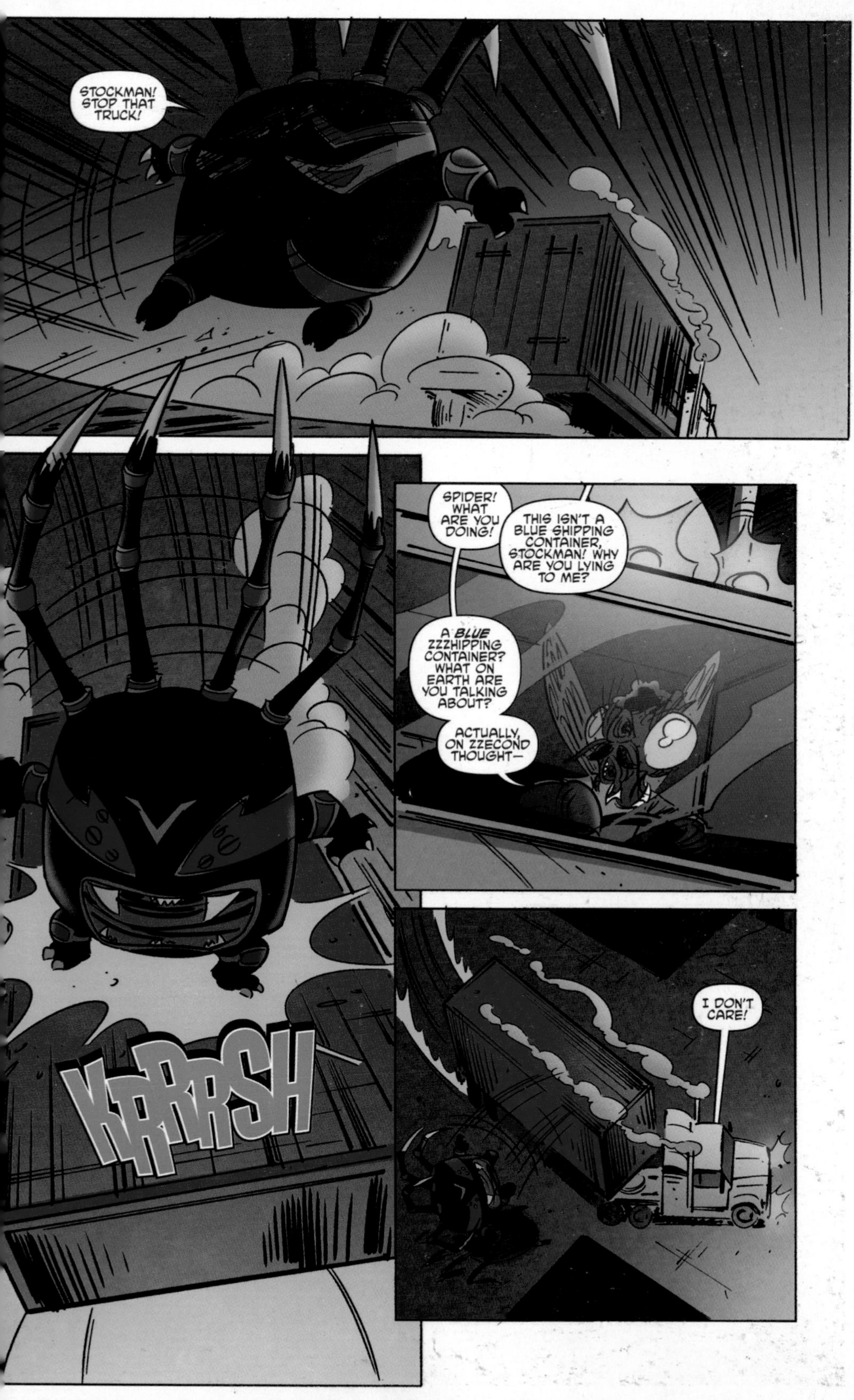
STOCKMAN! STOP THAT TRUCK!
KRRRSH
SPIDER! WHAT ARE YOU DOING!
THIS ISN'T A BLUE SHIPPING CONTAINER, STOCKMAN! WHY ARE YOU LYING TO ME?
A BLUE ZZZHIPPING CONTAINER? WHAT ON EARTH ARE YOU TALKING ABOUT?
ACTUALLY, ON ZZECOND THOUGHT—
I DON'T CARE!

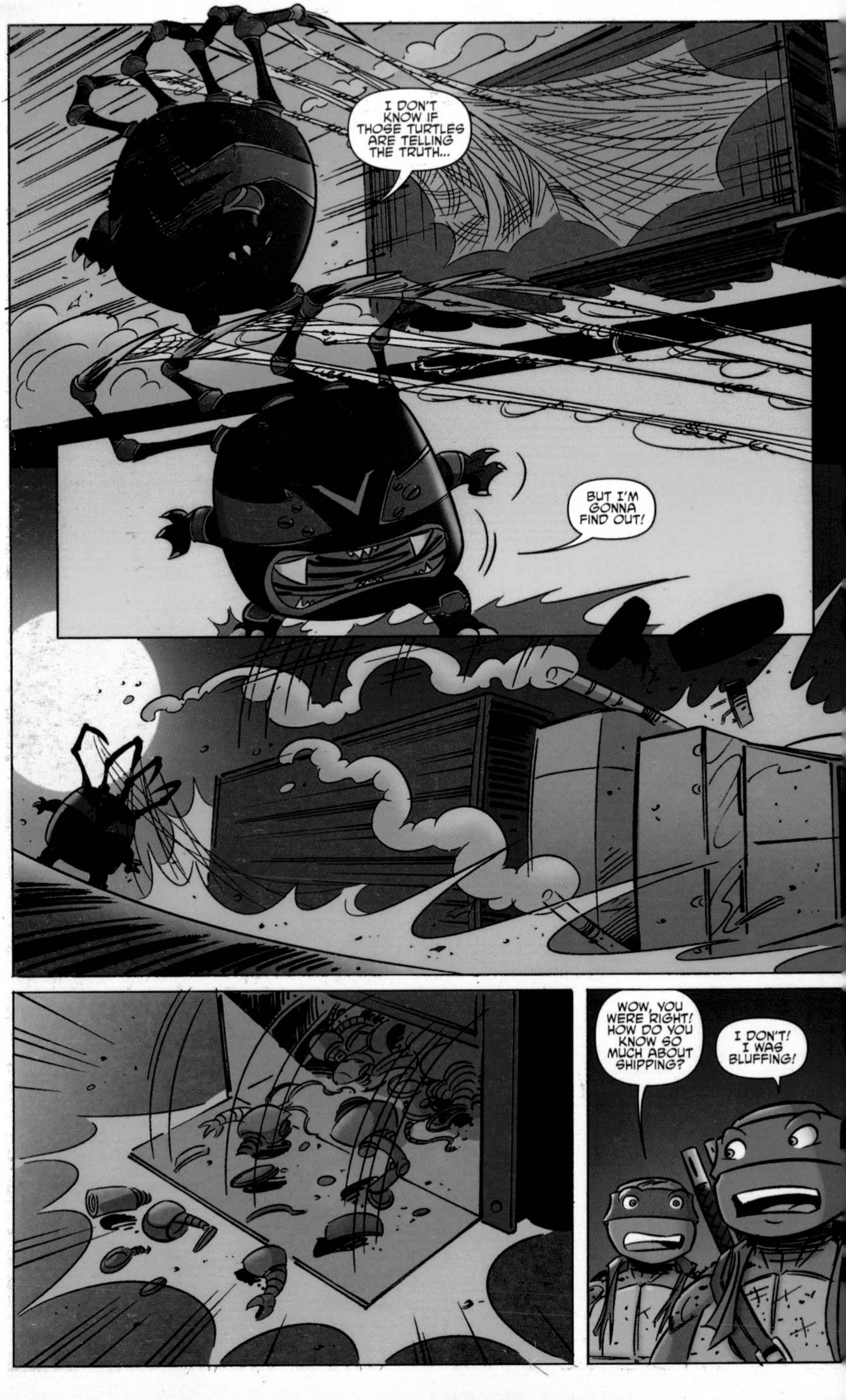
I DON'T KNOW IF THOSE TURTLES ARE TELLING THE TRUTH...
BUT I'M GONNA FIND OUT!
WOW, YOU WERE RIGHT! HOW DO YOU KNOW SO MUCH ABOUT SHIPPING?
I DON'T! I WAS BLUFFING!

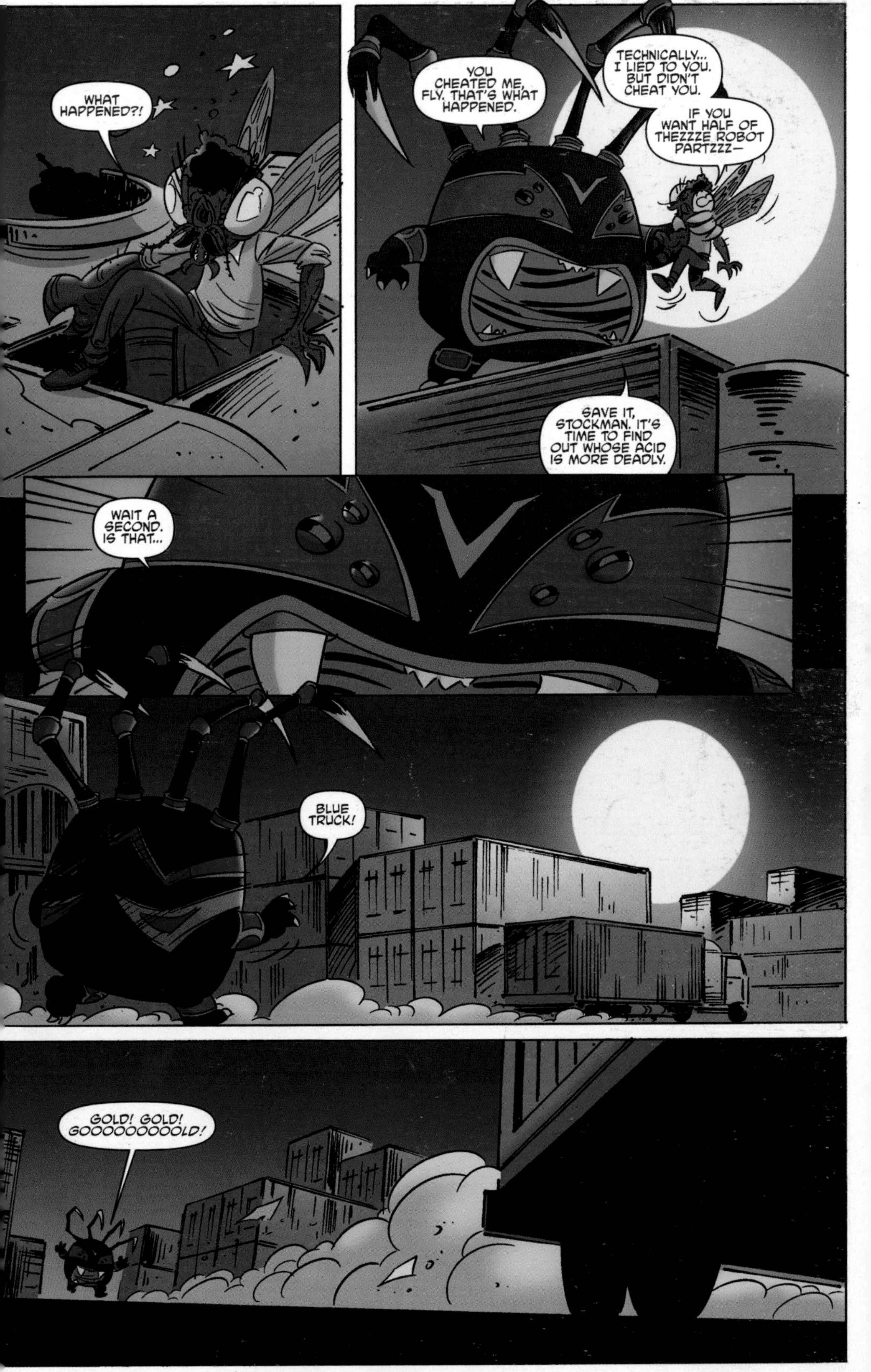

WHAT HAPPENED?!
YOU CHEATED ME, FLY. THAT'S WHAT HAPPENED.
TECHNICALLY... I LIED TO YOU. BUT DIDN'T CHEAT YOU.
IF YOU WANT HALF OF THEZZZE ROBOT PARTZZZ—
SAVE IT, STOCKMAN. IT'S TIME TO FIND OUT WHOSE ACID IS MORE DEADLY.
WAIT A SECOND. IS THAT...
BLUE TRUCK!
GOLD! GOLD! GOOOOOOOOOOLD!

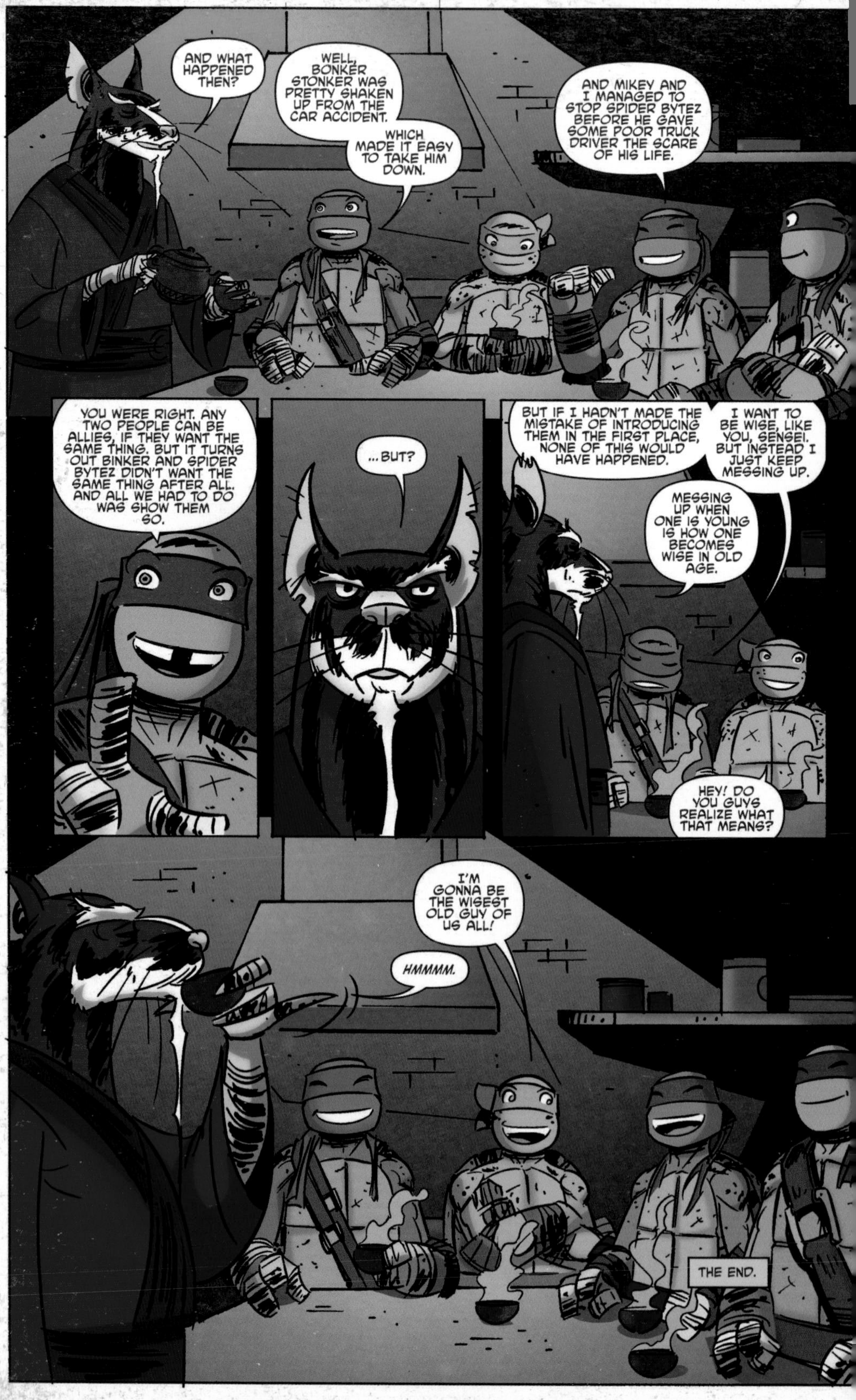
AND WHAT HAPPENED THEN?
WELL, BONKER STONKER WAS PRETTY SHAKEN UP FROM THE CAR ACCIDENT.
WHICH MADE IT EASY TO TAKE HIM DOWN.
AND MIKEY AND I MANAGED TO STOP SPIDER BYTEZ BEFORE HE GAVE SOME POOR TRUCK DRIVER THE SCARE OF HIS LIFE.
YOU WERE RIGHT. ANY TWO PEOPLE CAN BE ALLIES, IF THEY WANT THE SAME THING. BUT IT TURNS OUT BINKER AND SPIDER BYTEZ DIDN'T WANT THE SAME THING AFTER ALL. AND ALL WE HAD TO DO WAS SHOW THEM SO.
...BUT?
BUT IF I HADN'T MADE THE MISTAKE OF INTRODUCING THEM IN THE FIRST PLACE, NONE OF THIS WOULD HAVE HAPPENED.
I WANT TO BE WISE, LIKE YOU, SENSEI. BUT INSTEAD I JUST KEEP MESSING UP.
MESSING UP WHEN ONE IS YOUNG IS HOW ONE BECOMES WISE IN OLD AGE.
HEY! DO YOU GUYS REALIZE WHAT THAT MEANS?
I'M GONNA BE THE WISEST OLD GUY OF US ALL!
HMMMM.
THE END.

Cover by **DARIO BRIZUELA**

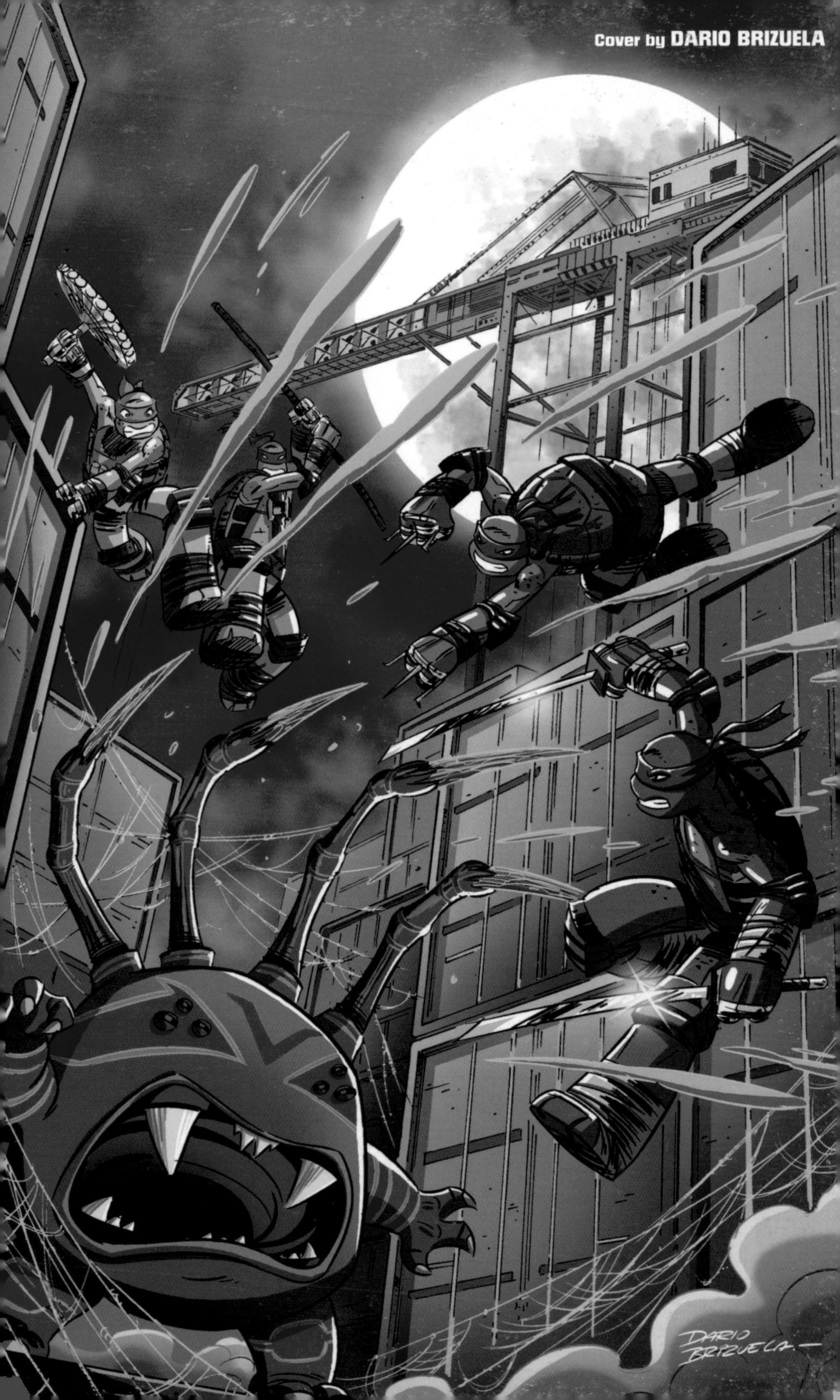
DARIO BRIZUELA

Cover by **JON SOMMARIVA**

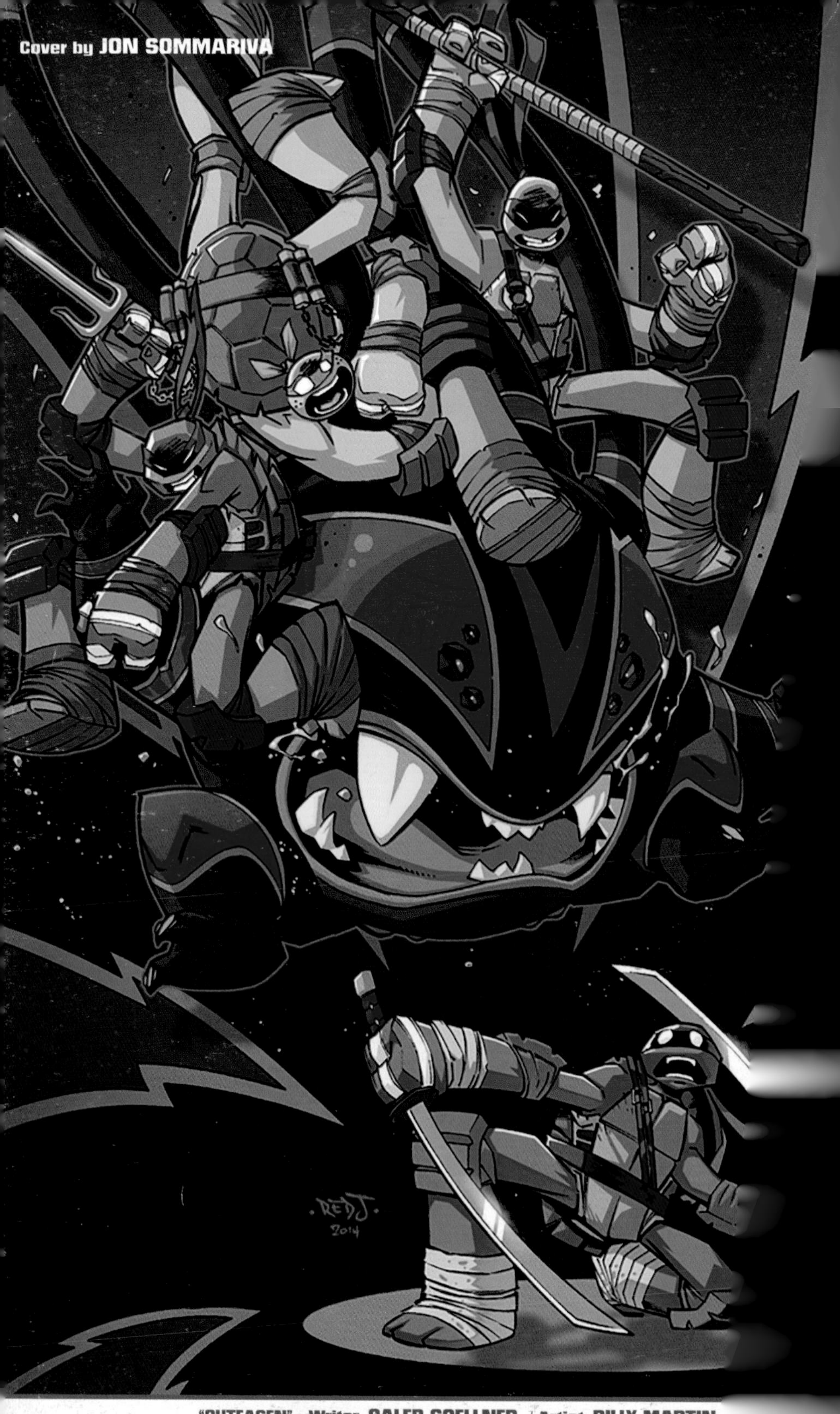

"CUTEAGEN" - Writer: **CALEB GOELLNER** / Artist: **BILLY MARTIN**
"TAG!" - Writer: **MATTHEW K. MANNING** / Artist: **MARCELO FERRE**

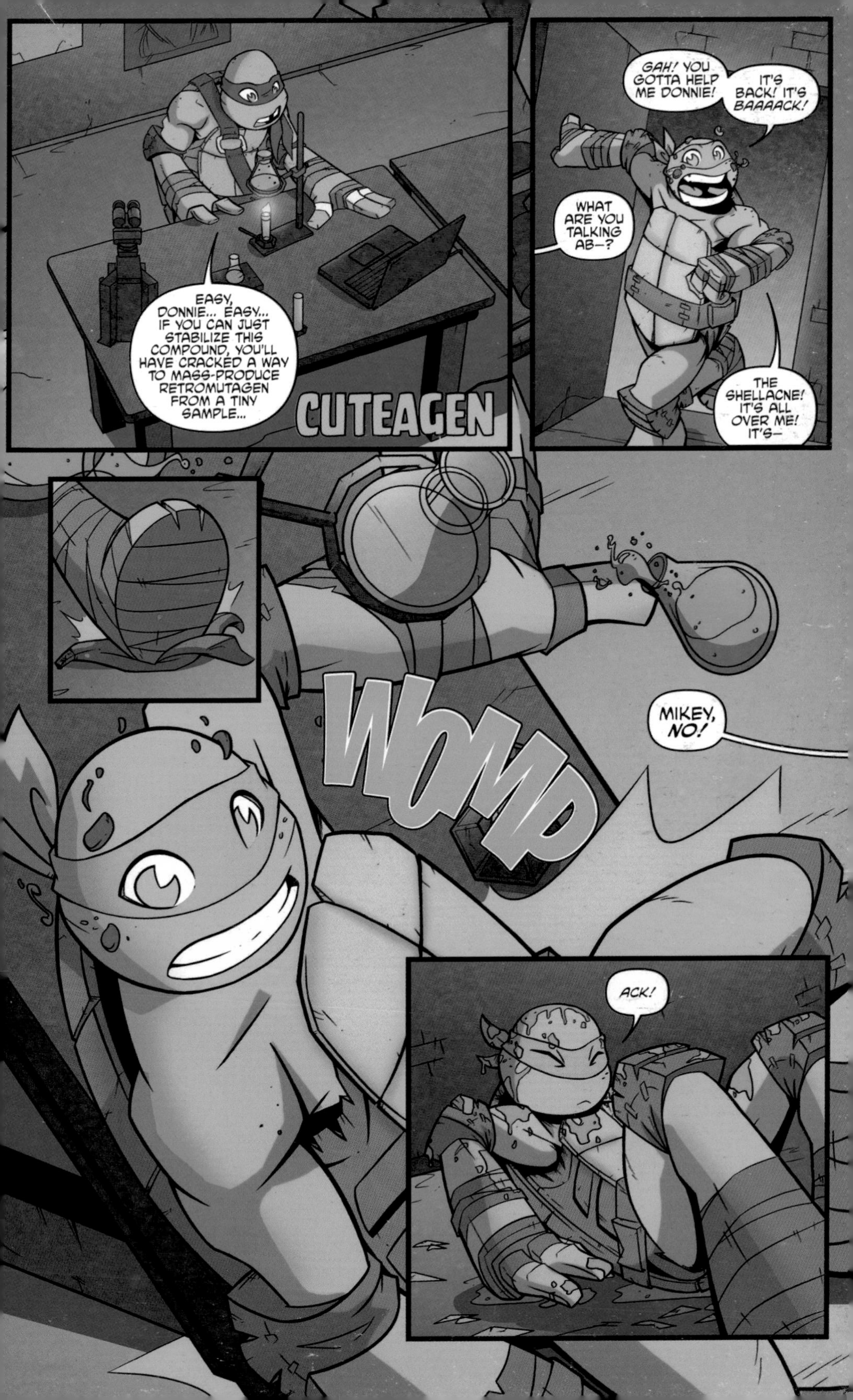
CUTEAGEN
EASY, DONNIE... EASY... IF YOU CAN JUST STABILIZE THIS COMPOUND, YOU'LL HAVE CRACKED A WAY TO MASS-PRODUCE RETROMUTAGEN FROM A TINY SAMPLE...
GAH! YOU GOTTA HELP ME DONNIE!
IT'S BACK! IT'S BAAAACK!
WHAT ARE YOU TALKING AB–?
THE SHELLACNE! IT'S ALL OVER ME! IT'S—
WOMP
MIKEY, NO!
ACK!

MIKEY! ARE YOU OKAY?

HA! I GUESS IT WASN'T SHELLACNE!

I JUST FELL ASLEEP ON A SLICE OF PIZZA AGAIN. HILARIOUS, RIGHT?

YUP, GUESS I'LL JUST, UM... LET YOU GET BACK TO YOUR SCIENCE... HEH.

HEH, HE, HAHA, WHEEE!

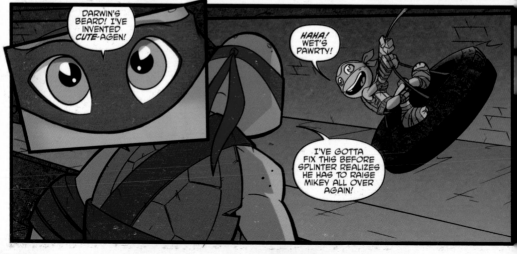

DARWIN'S BEARD! I'VE INVENTED CUTE-AGEN!

HAHA! WET'S PAWRTY!

I'VE GOTTA FIX THIS BEFORE SPLINTER REALIZES HE HAS TO RAISE MIKEY ALL OVER AGAIN!

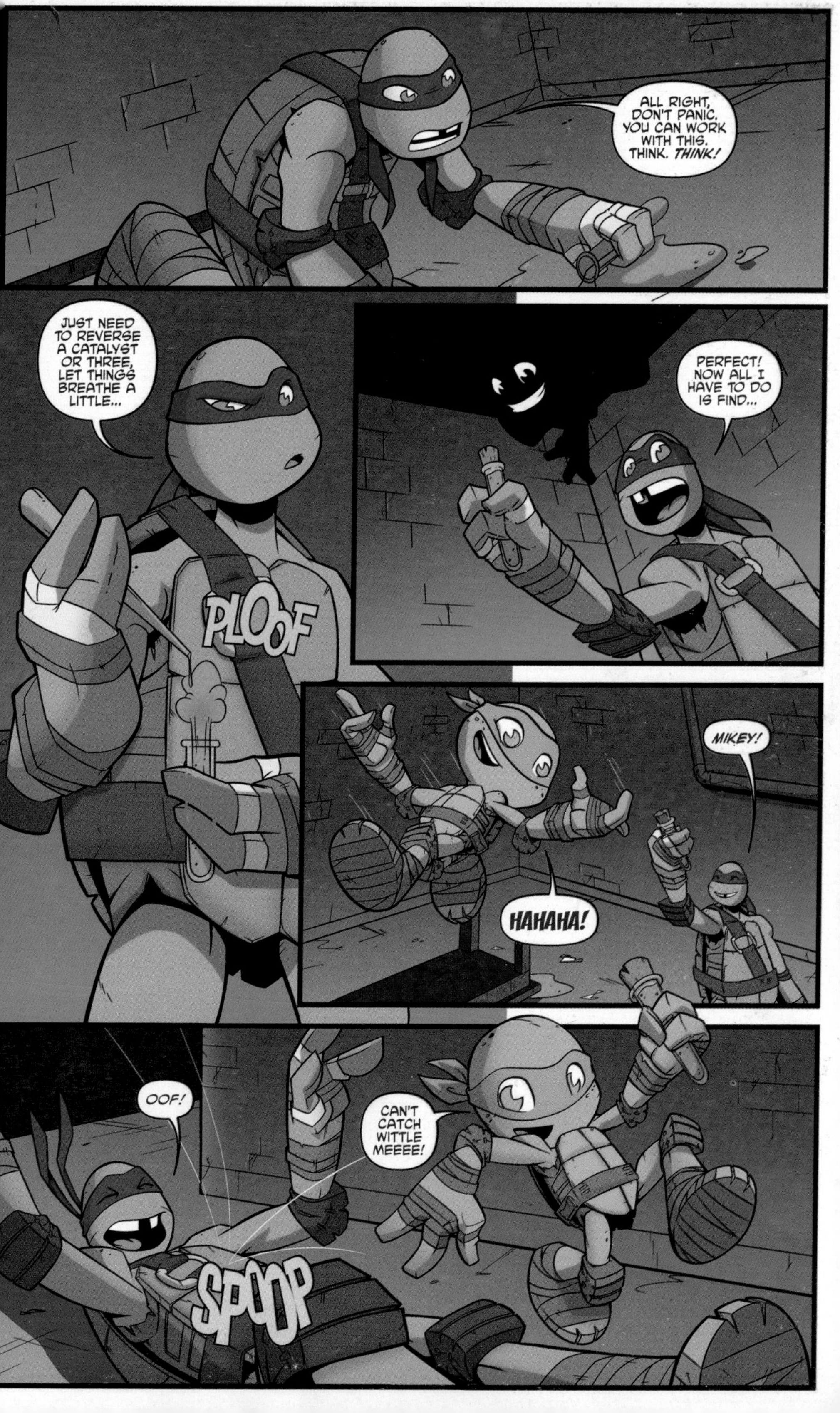

ALL RIGHT, DON'T PANIC. YOU CAN WORK WITH THIS. THINK. *THINK!*
JUST NEED TO REVERSE A CATALYST OR THREE, LET THINGS BREATHE A LITTLE...
PLOOF
PERFECT! NOW ALL I HAVE TO DO IS FIND...
MIKEY!
HAHAHA!
OOF!
CAN'T CATCH WITTLE MEEEE!
SPOOP

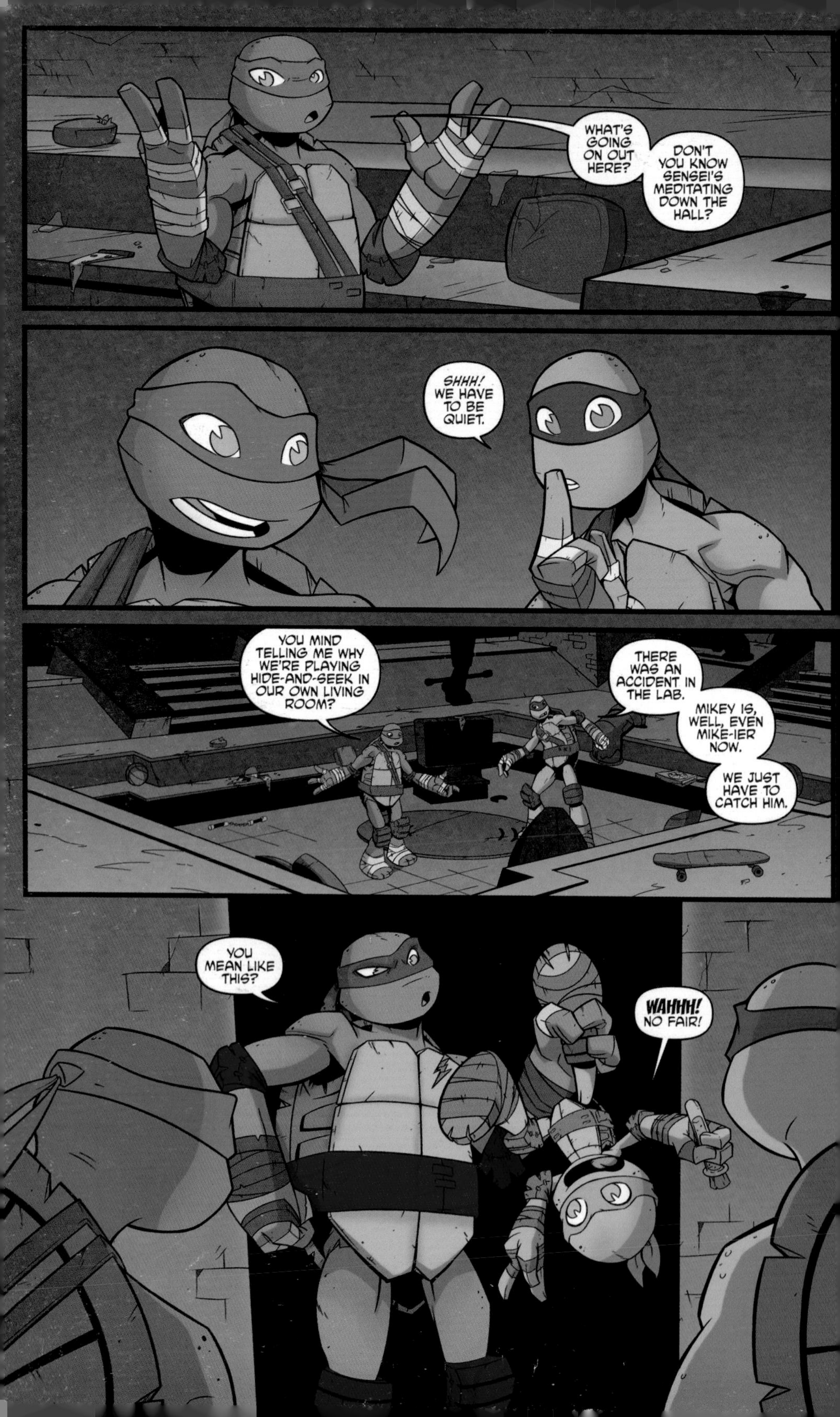
WHAT'S GOING ON OUT HERE?
DON'T YOU KNOW SENSEI'S MEDITATING DOWN THE HALL?
SHHH! WE HAVE TO BE QUIET.
YOU MIND TELLING ME WHY WE'RE PLAYING HIDE-AND-SEEK IN OUR OWN LIVING ROOM?
THERE WAS AN ACCIDENT IN THE LAB.
MIKEY IS, WELL, EVEN MIKE-IER NOW.
WE JUST HAVE TO CATCH HIM.
YOU MEAN LIKE THIS?
WAHHH! NO FAIR!

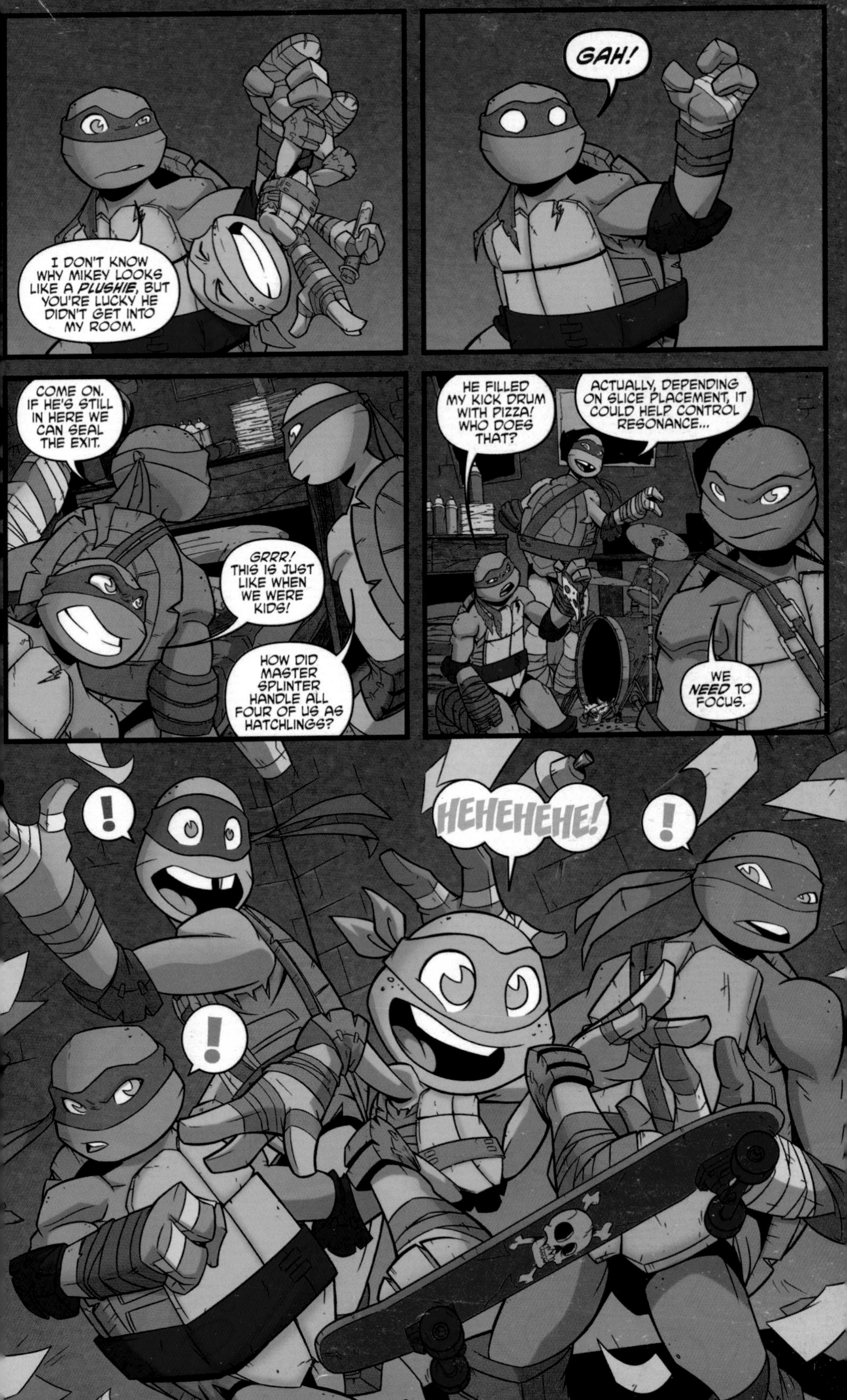
I DON'T KNOW WHY MIKEY LOOKS LIKE A *PLUSHIE*, BUT YOU'RE LUCKY HE DIDN'T GET INTO MY ROOM.
GAH!
COME ON. IF HE'S STILL IN HERE WE CAN SEAL THE EXIT.
GRRR! THIS IS JUST LIKE WHEN WE WERE KIDS!
HOW DID MASTER SPLINTER HANDLE ALL FOUR OF US AS HATCHLINGS?
HE FILLED MY KICK DRUM WITH PIZZA! WHO DOES THAT?
ACTUALLY, DEPENDING ON SLICE PLACEMENT, IT COULD HELP CONTROL RESONANCE...
WE *NEED* TO FOCUS.
!
HEHEHEHE!
!
!

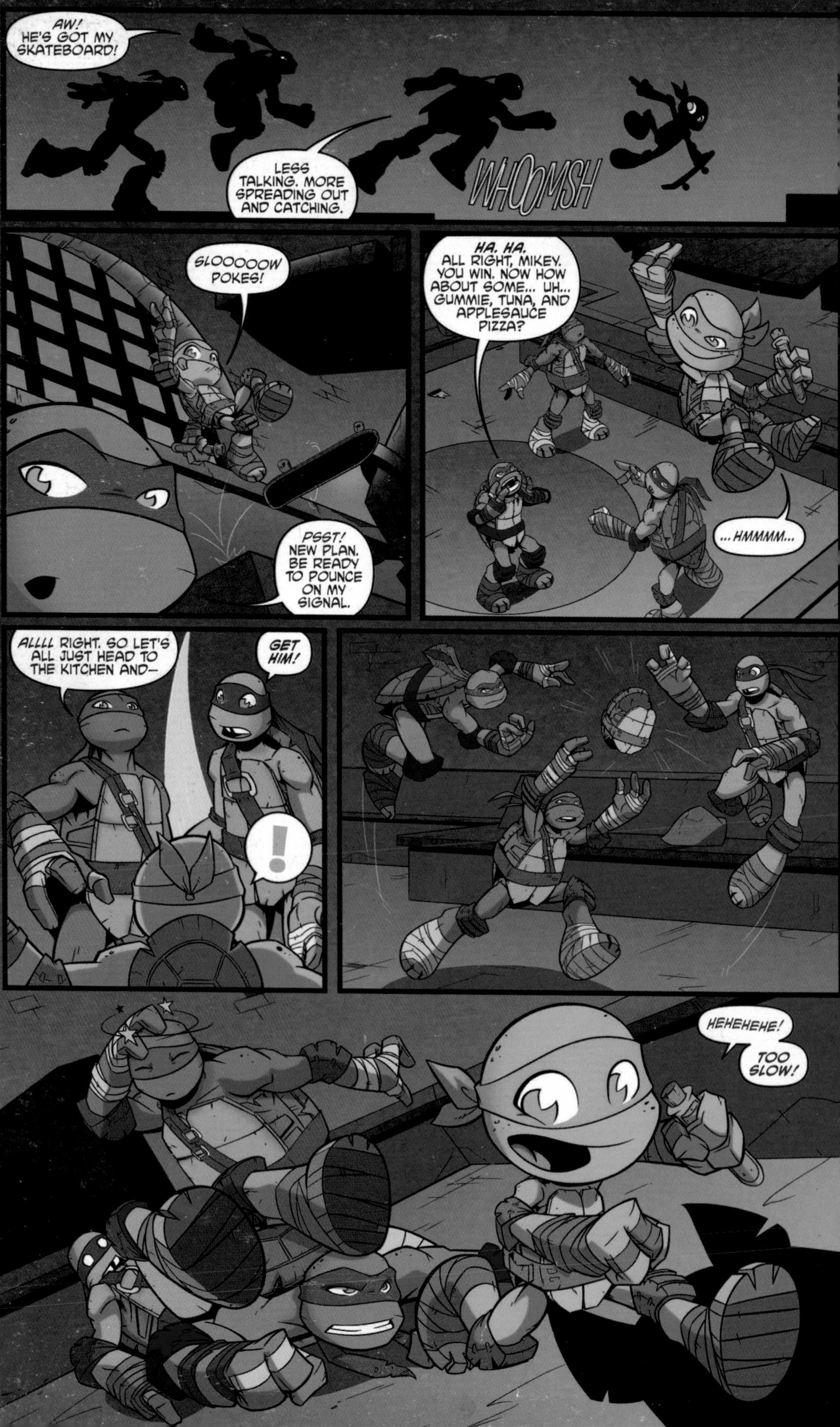
AW! HE'S GOT MY SKATEBOARD!
LESS TALKING. MORE SPREADING OUT AND CATCHING.
WHOOMSH
SLOOOOOW POKES!
PSST! NEW PLAN. BE READY TO POUNCE ON MY SIGNAL.
HA. HA. ALL RIGHT, MIKEY. YOU WIN. NOW HOW ABOUT SOME... UH... GUMMIE, TUNA, AND APPLESAUCE PIZZA?
...HMMMM...
ALLLL RIGHT. SO LET'S ALL JUST HEAD TO THE KITCHEN AND—
GET HIM!
!
HEHEHEHE!
TOO SLOW!

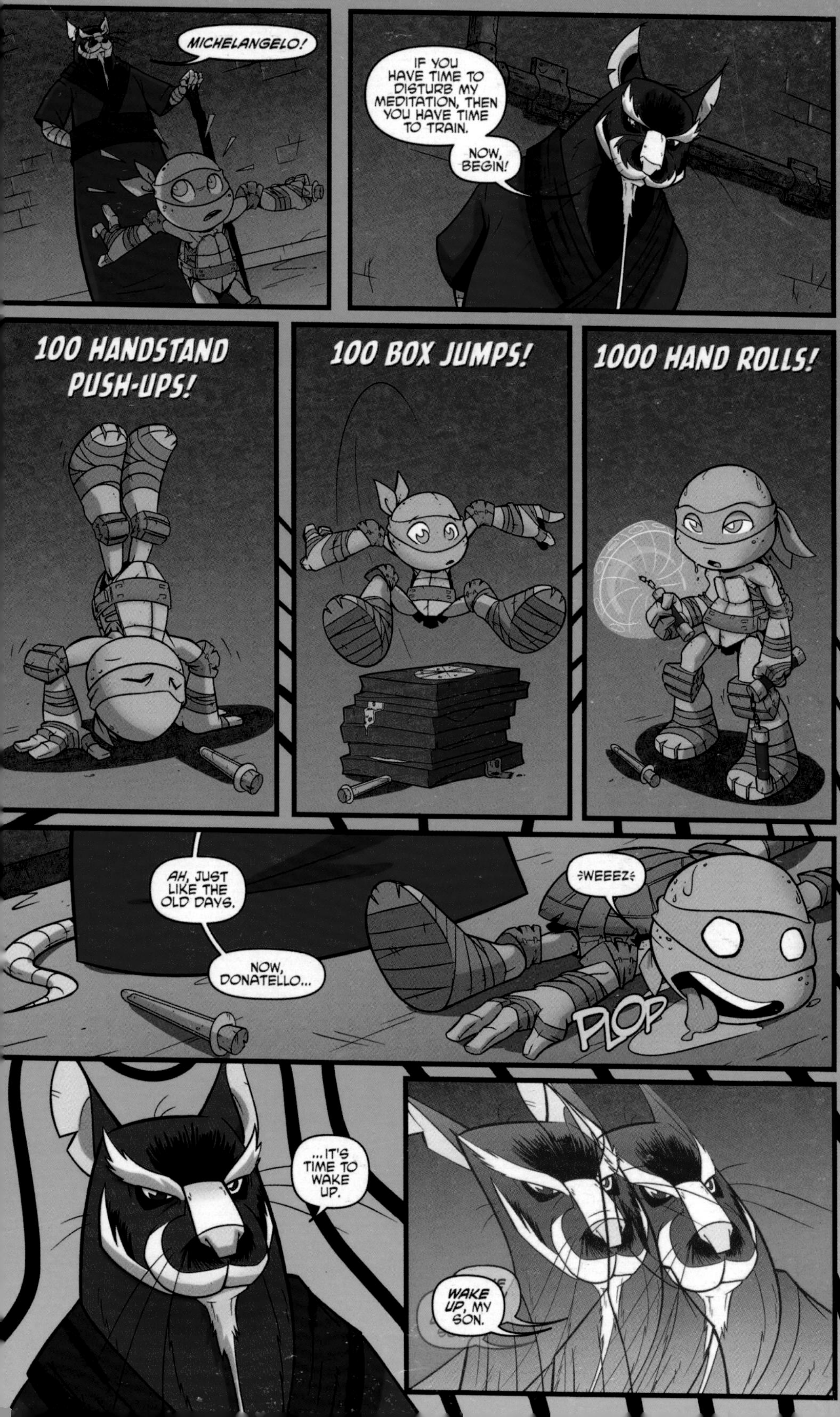
MICHELANGELO!
IF YOU HAVE TIME TO DISTURB MY MEDITATION, THEN YOU HAVE TIME TO TRAIN.
NOW, BEGIN!
100 HANDSTAND PUSH-UPS!
100 BOX JUMPS!
1000 HAND ROLLS!
AH, JUST LIKE THE OLD DAYS.
NOW, DONATELLO...
WEEEZ
PLOP
...IT'S TIME TO WAKE UP.
WAKE UP, MY SON.

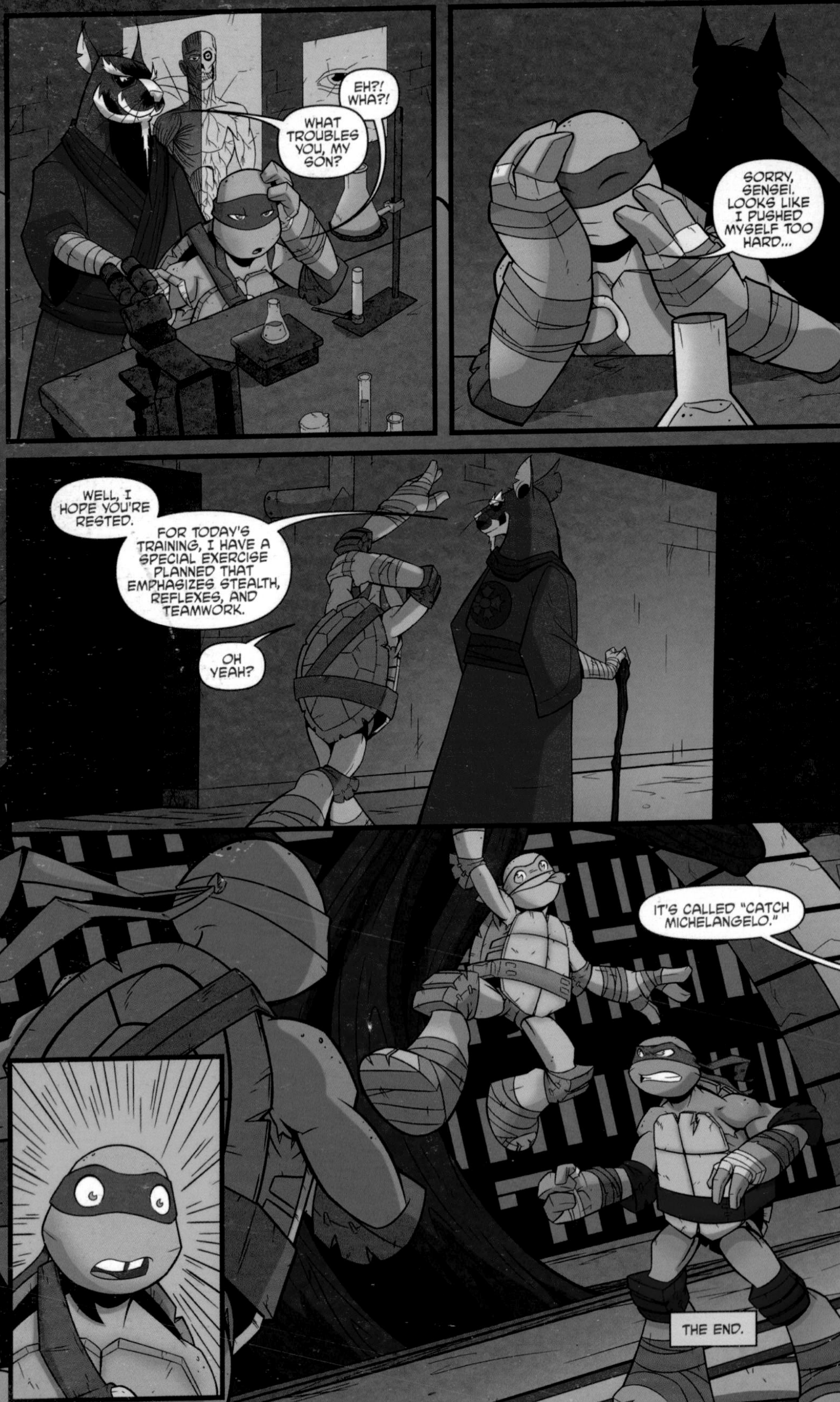
WHAT TROUBLES YOU, MY SON?
EH?! WHA?!
SORRY, SENSEI. LOOKS LIKE I PUSHED MYSELF TOO HARD...
WELL, I HOPE YOU'RE RESTED.
FOR TODAY'S TRAINING, I HAVE A SPECIAL EXERCISE PLANNED THAT EMPHASIZES STEALTH, REFLEXES, AND TEAMWORK.
OH YEAH?
IT'S CALLED "CATCH MICHELANGELO."
THE END.

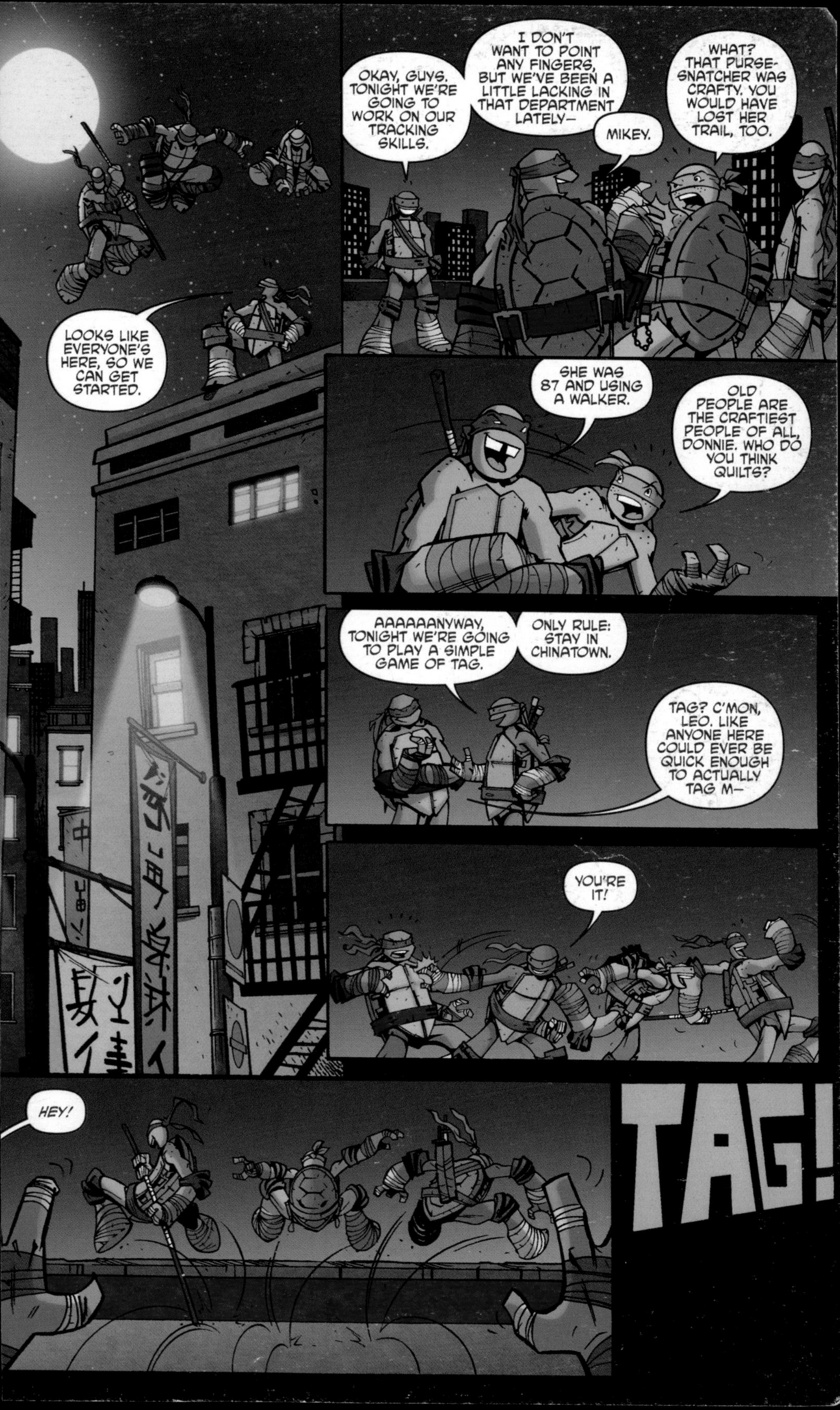

LOOKS LIKE EVERYONE'S HERE, SO WE CAN GET STARTED.
OKAY, GUYS. TONIGHT WE'RE GOING TO WORK ON OUR TRACKING SKILLS.
I DON'T WANT TO POINT ANY FINGERS, BUT WE'VE BEEN A LITTLE LACKING IN THAT DEPARTMENT LATELY—
MIKEY.
WHAT? THAT PURSE-SNATCHER WAS CRAFTY. YOU WOULD HAVE LOST HER TRAIL, TOO.
SHE WAS 87 AND USING A WALKER.
OLD PEOPLE ARE THE CRAFTIEST PEOPLE OF ALL, DONNIE. WHO DO YOU THINK QUILTS?
AAAAAAANYWAY, TONIGHT WE'RE GOING TO PLAY A SIMPLE GAME OF TAG.
ONLY RULE: STAY IN CHINATOWN.
TAG? C'MON, LEO. LIKE ANYONE HERE COULD EVER BE QUICK ENOUGH TO ACTUALLY TAG M—
YOU'RE IT!
HEY!
TAG!

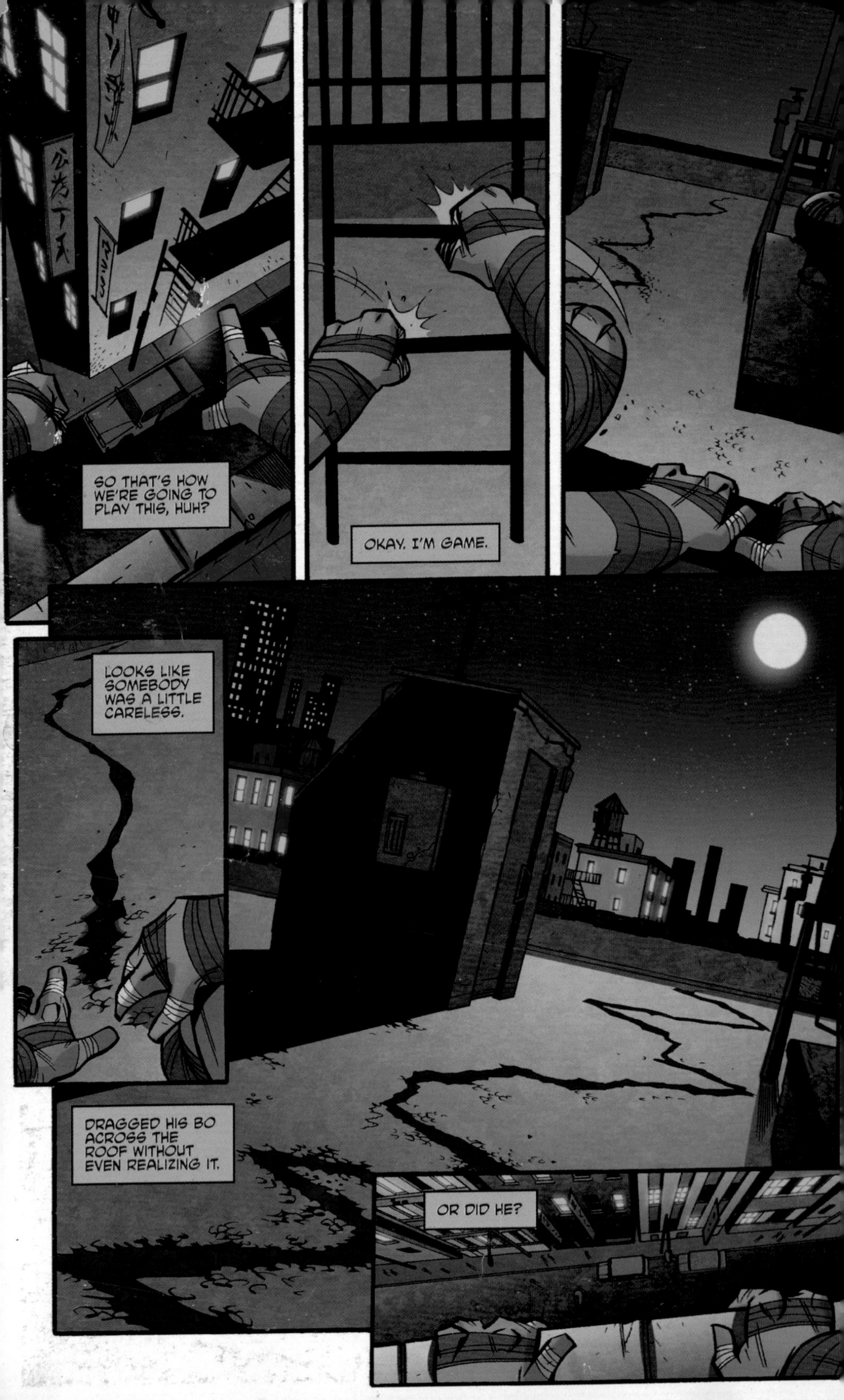
SO THAT'S HOW WE'RE GOING TO PLAY THIS, HUH?
OKAY. I'M GAME.
LOOKS LIKE SOMEBODY WAS A LITTLE CARELESS.
DRAGGED HIS BO ACROSS THE ROOF WITHOUT EVEN REALIZING IT.
OR DID HE?

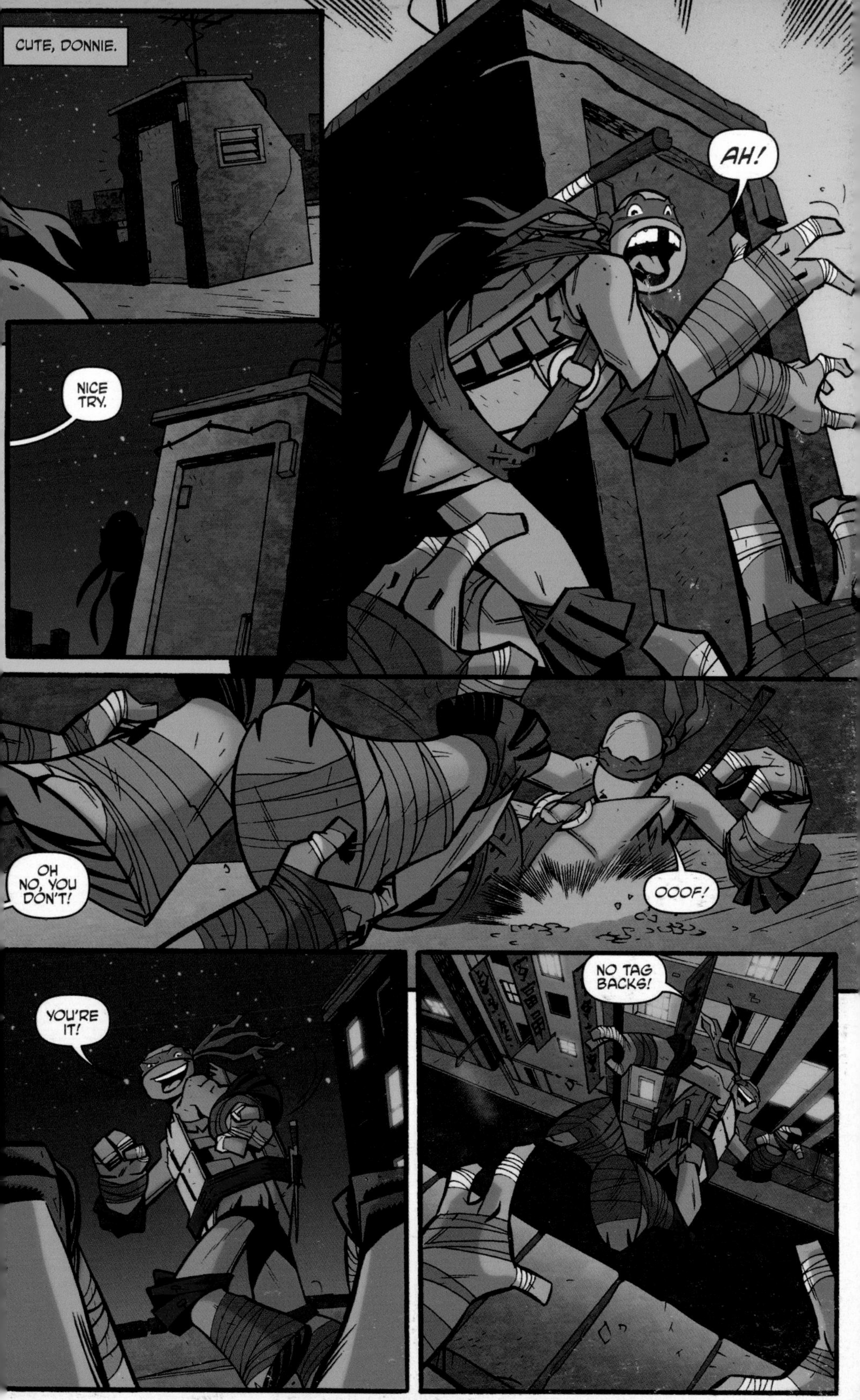
CUTE, DONNIE.
AH!
NICE TRY.
OH NO, YOU DON'T!
OOOF!
YOU'RE IT!
NO TAG BACKS!

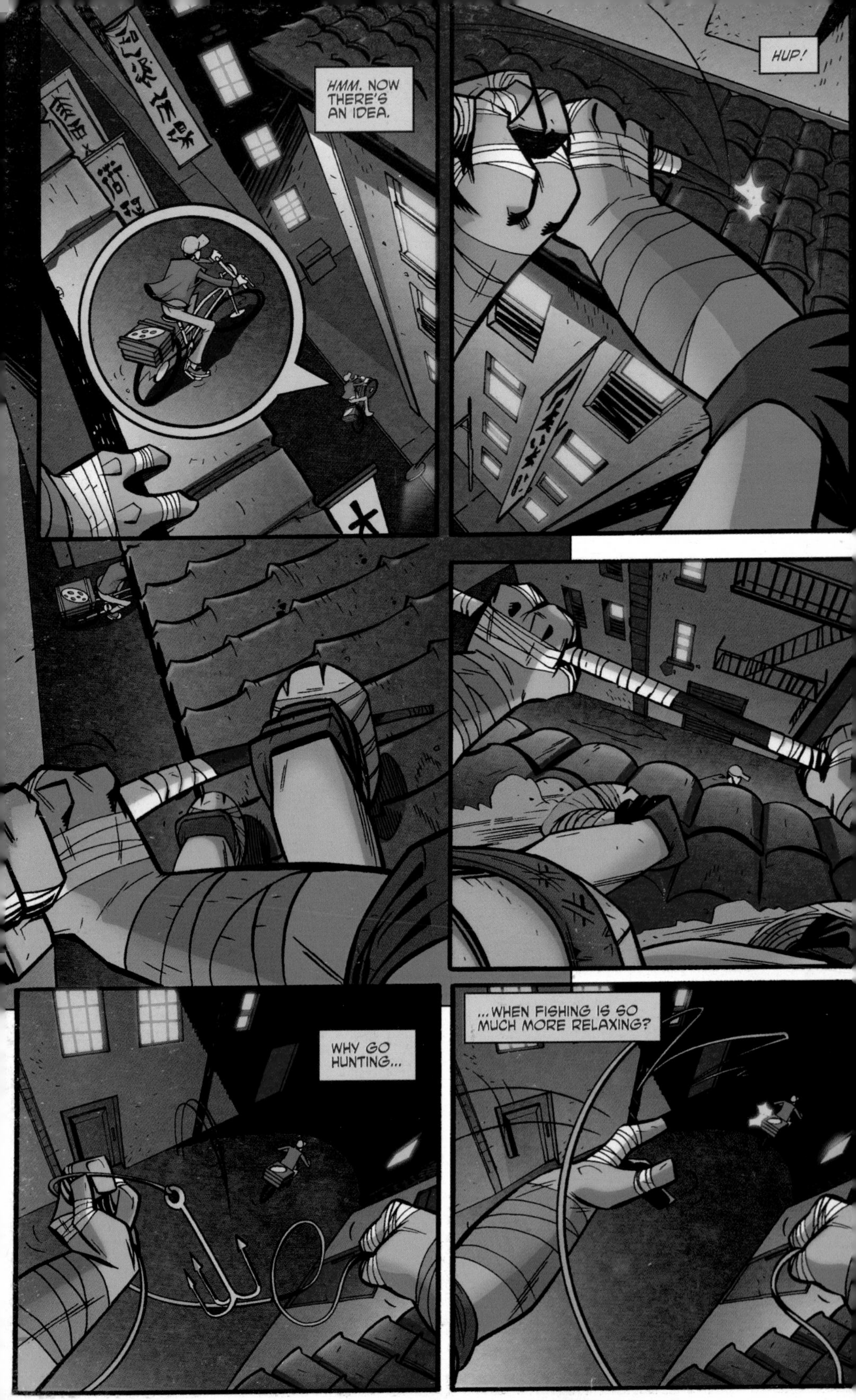
HMM. NOW THERE'S AN IDEA.
HUP!
WHY GO HUNTING...
...WHEN FISHING IS SO MUCH MORE RELAXING?

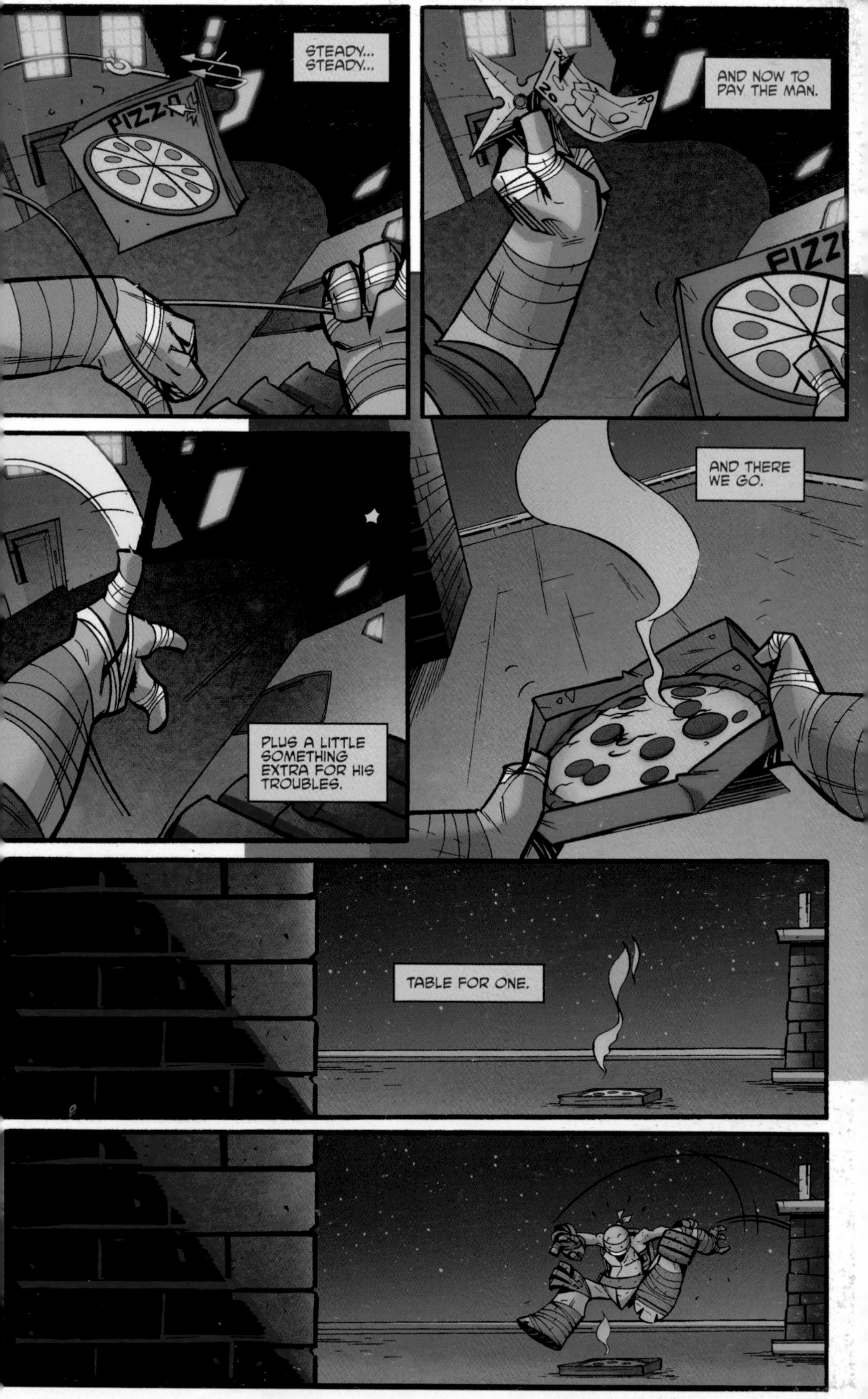
STEADY... STEADY...
PIZZA
AND NOW TO PAY THE MAN.
PIZZ
PLUS A LITTLE SOMETHING EXTRA FOR HIS TROUBLES.
AND THERE WE GO.
TABLE FOR ONE.

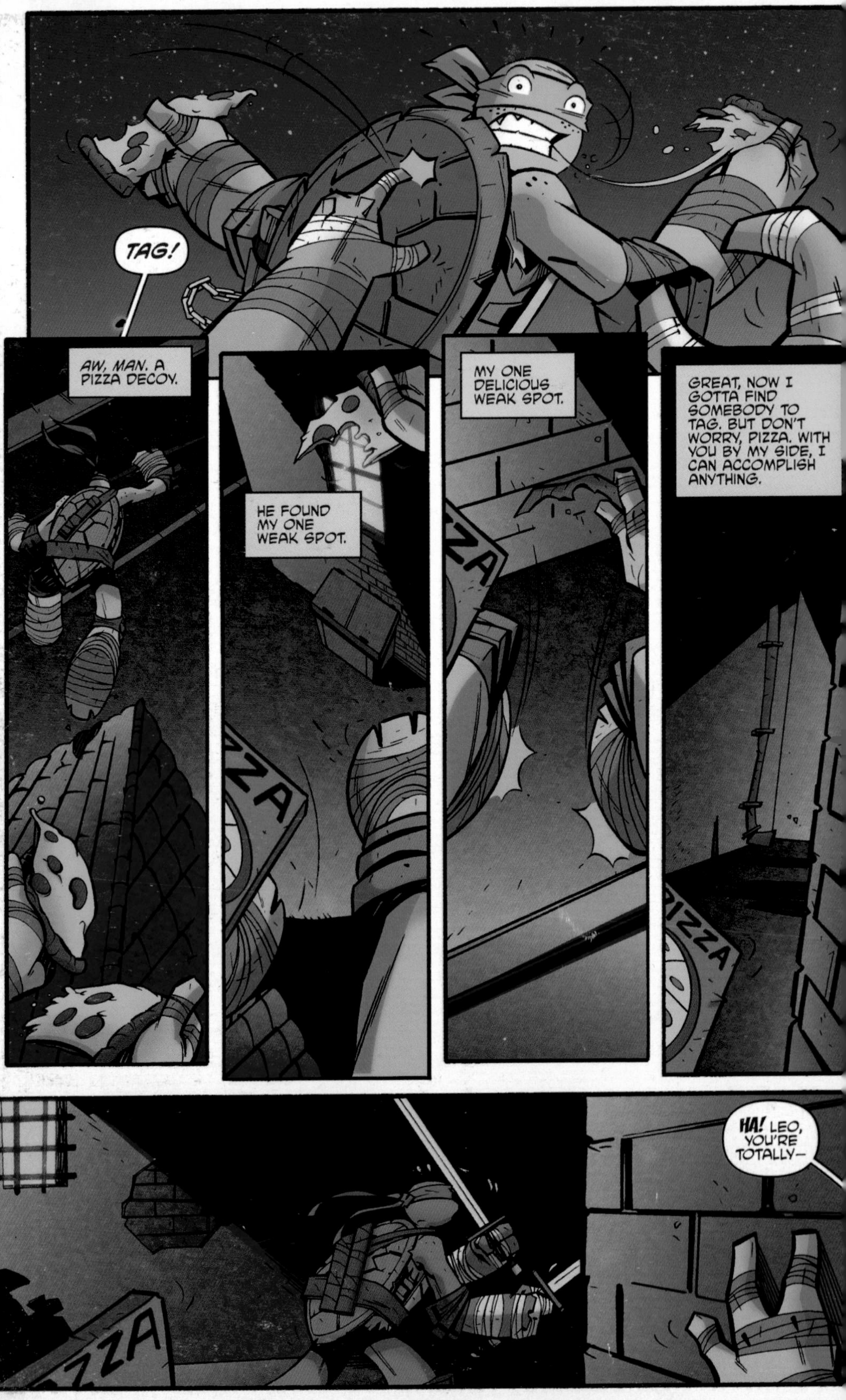
TAG!
AW, MAN. A PIZZA DECOY.
HE FOUND MY ONE WEAK SPOT.
MY ONE DELICIOUS WEAK SPOT.
GREAT, NOW I GOTTA FIND SOMEBODY TO TAG. BUT DON'T WORRY, PIZZA. WITH YOU BY MY SIDE, I CAN ACCOMPLISH ANYTHING.
HA! LEO, YOU'RE TOTALLY—
PIZZA

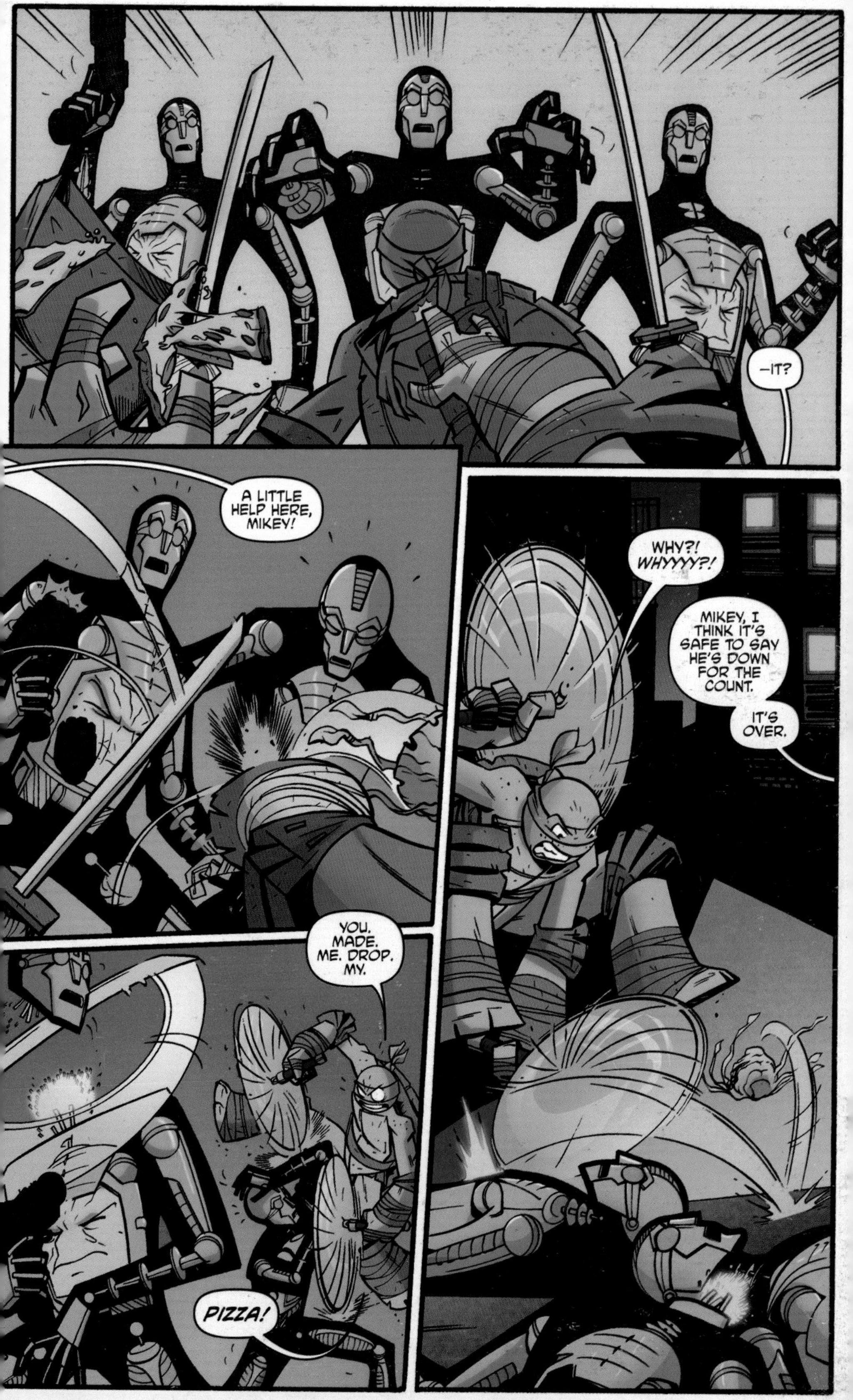

—IT?
A LITTLE HELP HERE, MIKEY!
WHY?! WHYYYY?!
MIKEY, I THINK IT'S SAFE TO SAY HE'S DOWN FOR THE COUNT.
IT'S OVER.
YOU. MADE. ME. DROP. MY.
PIZZA!

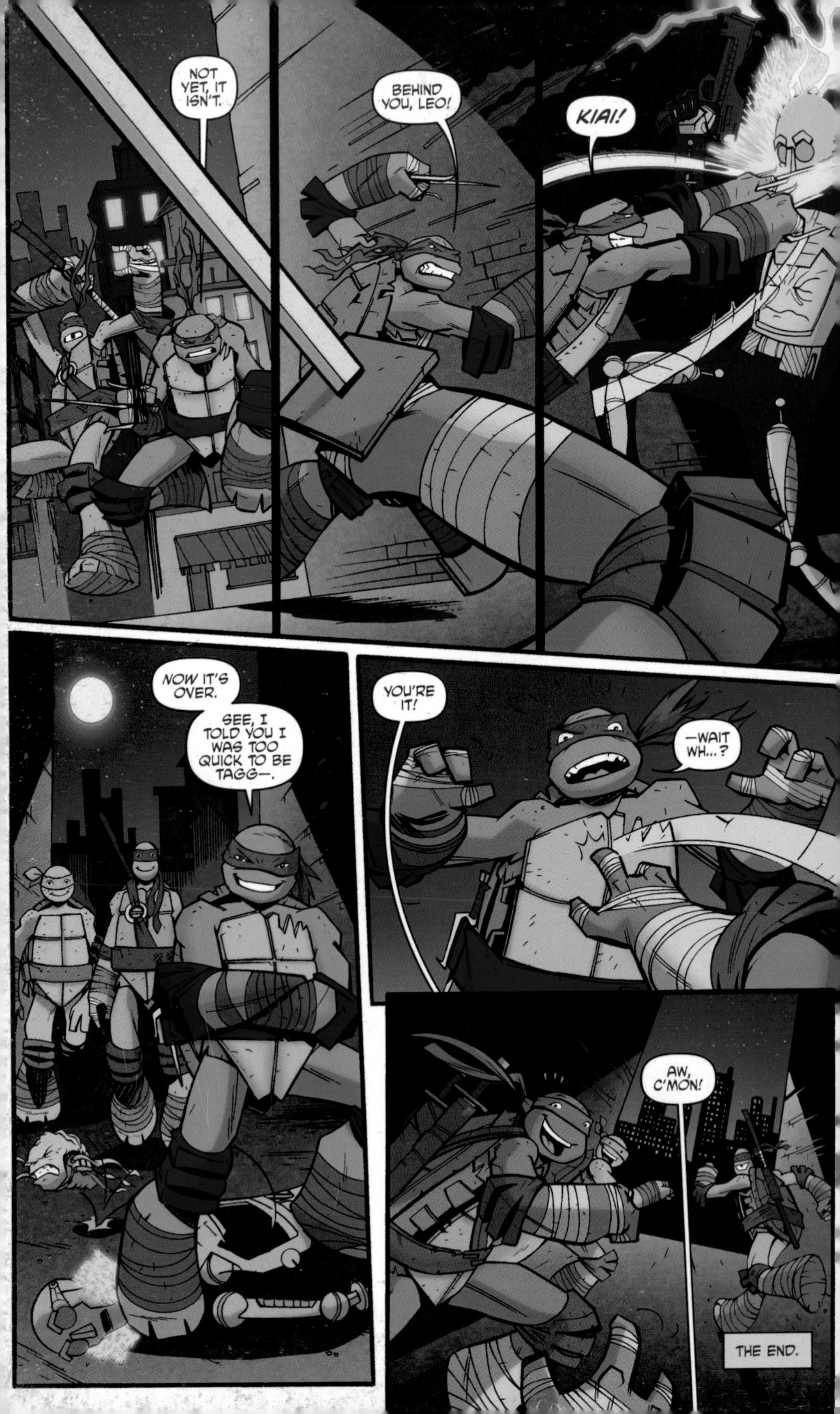
NOT YET, IT ISN'T.
BEHIND YOU, LEO!
KIAI!
NOW IT'S OVER.
SEE, I TOLD YOU I WAS TOO QUICK TO BE TAGG—.
YOU'RE IT!
—WAIT WH...?
AW, C'MON!
THE END.

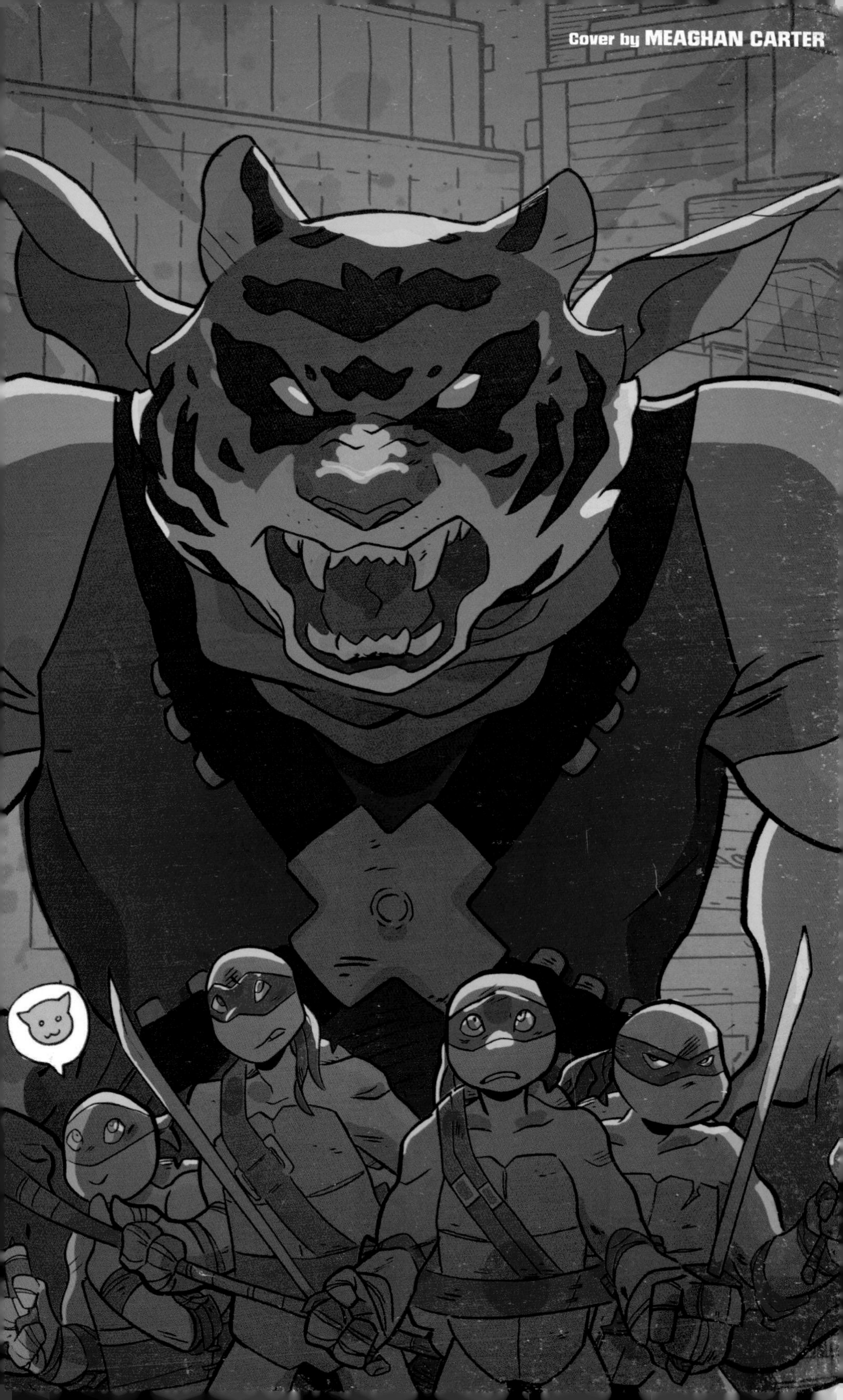

Cover by **MEAGHAN CARTER**

Cover by DARIO BRIZUELA

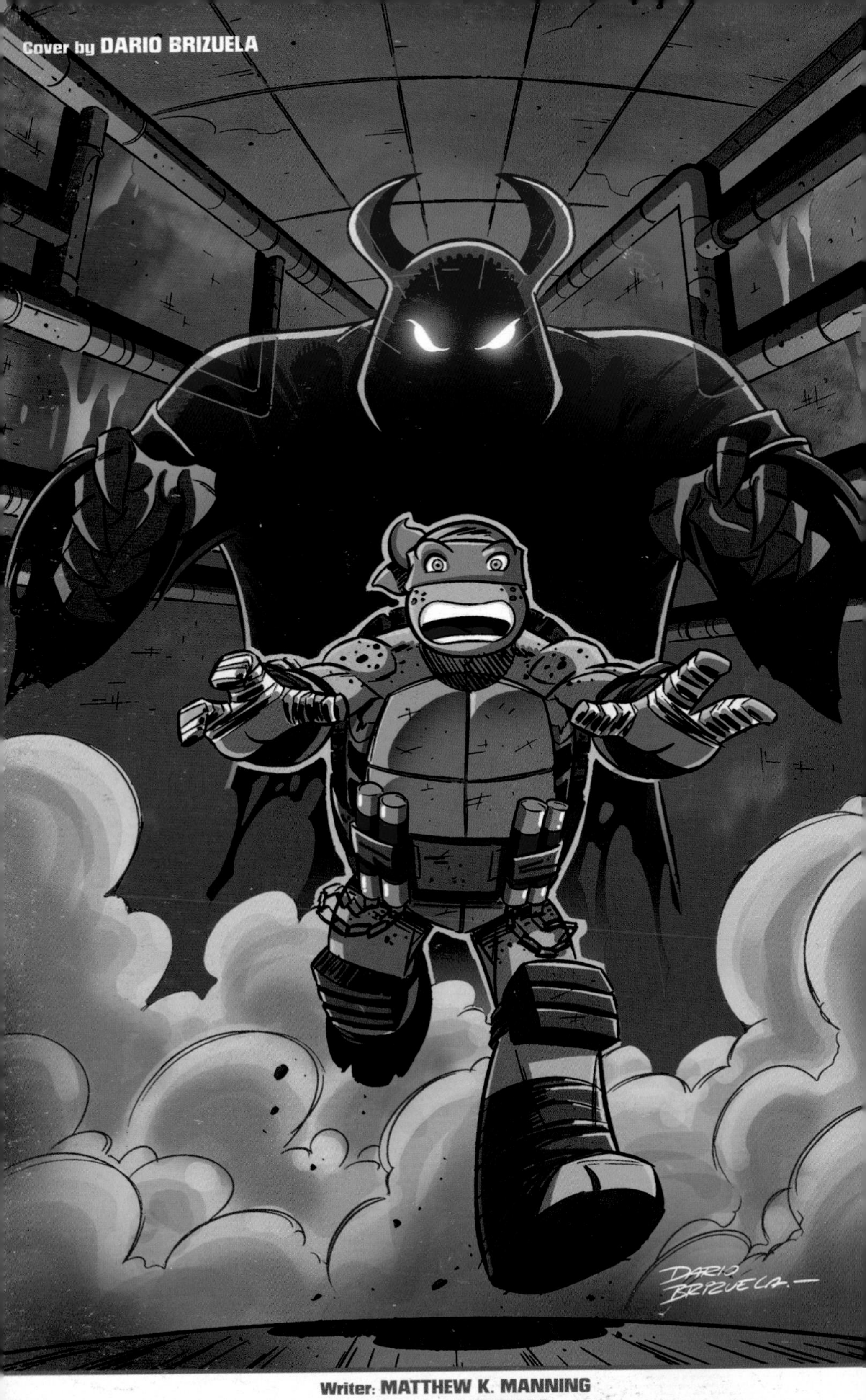
DARIO BRIZUELA

Writer: MATTHEW K. MANNING
Artist: CHAD THOMAS

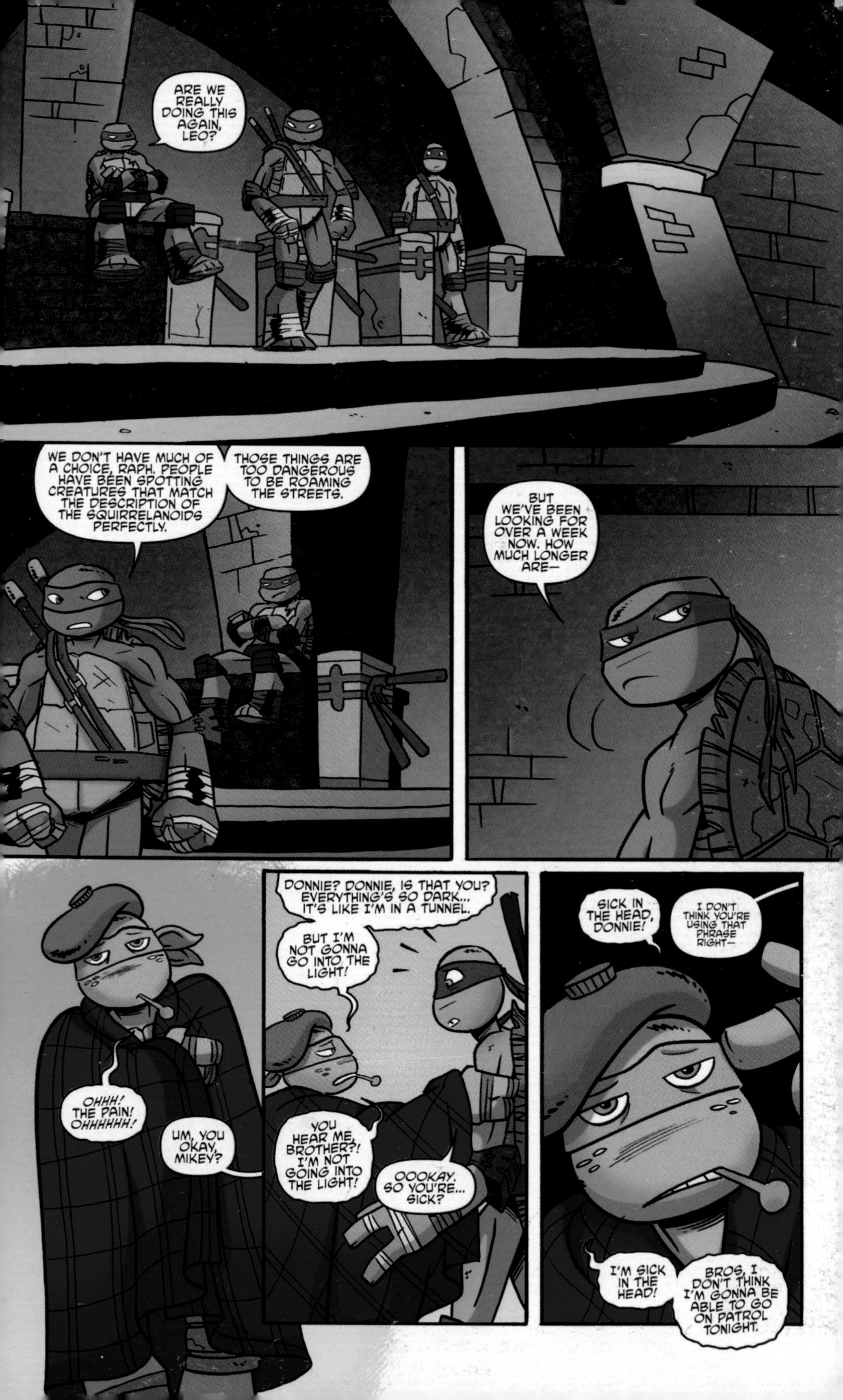
ARE WE REALLY DOING THIS AGAIN, LEO?
WE DON'T HAVE MUCH OF A CHOICE, RAPH. PEOPLE HAVE BEEN SPOTTING CREATURES THAT MATCH THE DESCRIPTION OF THE SQUIRRELANOIDS PERFECTLY.
THOSE THINGS ARE TOO DANGEROUS TO BE ROAMING THE STREETS.
BUT WE'VE BEEN LOOKING FOR OVER A WEEK NOW. HOW MUCH LONGER ARE—
OHHH! THE PAIN! OHHHHHH!
UM, YOU OKAY, MIKEY?
DONNIE? DONNIE, IS THAT YOU? EVERYTHING'S SO DARK... IT'S LIKE I'M IN A TUNNEL.
BUT I'M NOT GONNA GO INTO THE LIGHT!
YOU HEAR ME, BROTHER?! I'M NOT GOING INTO THE LIGHT!
OOOKAY. SO YOU'RE... SICK?
SICK IN THE HEAD, DONNIE!
I DON'T THINK YOU'RE USING THAT PHRASE RIGHT—
I'M SICK IN THE HEAD!
BROS, I DON'T THINK I'M GONNA BE ABLE TO GO ON PATROL TONIGHT.

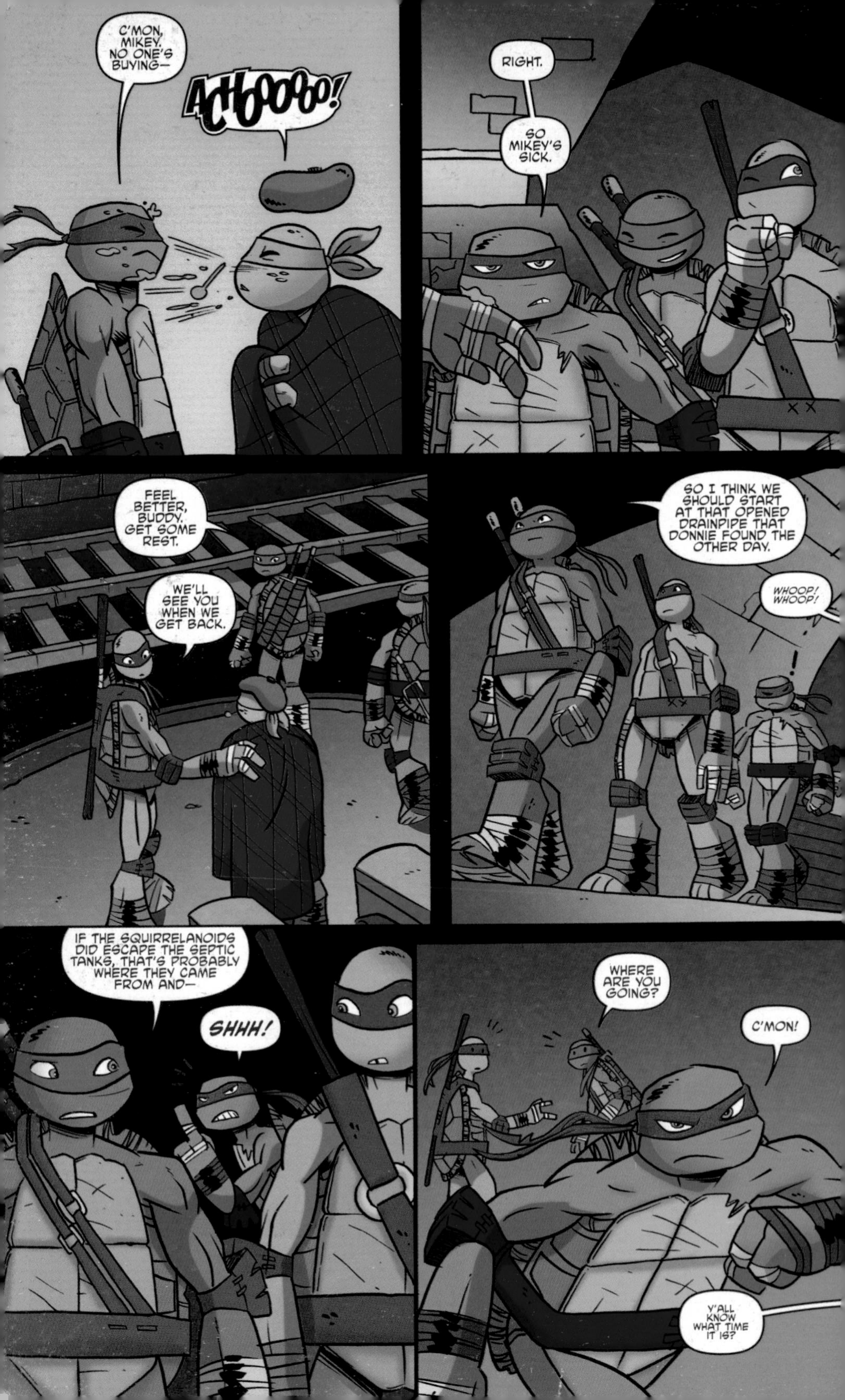
C'MON, MIKEY. NO ONE'S BUYING—
ACHOOOOO!
RIGHT.
SO MIKEY'S SICK.
FEEL BETTER, BUDDY. GET SOME REST.
WE'LL SEE YOU WHEN WE GET BACK.
SO I THINK WE SHOULD START AT THAT OPENED DRAINPIPE THAT DONNIE FOUND THE OTHER DAY.
WHOOP! WHOOP!
IF THE SQUIRRELANOIDS DID ESCAPE THE SEPTIC TANKS, THAT'S PROBABLY WHERE THEY CAME FROM AND—
SHHH!
WHERE ARE YOU GOING?
C'MON!
Y'ALL KNOW WHAT TIME IT IS?

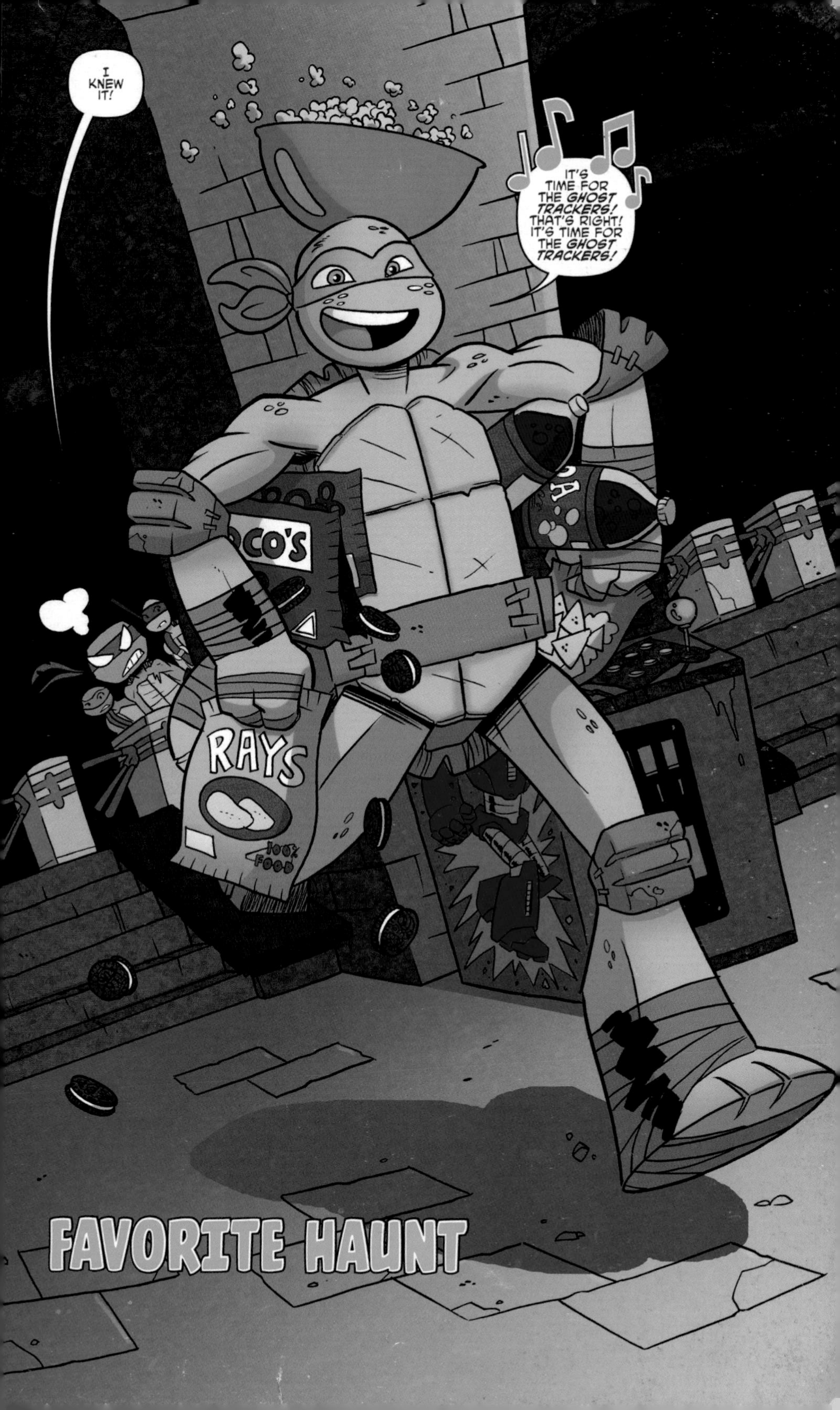
I KNEW IT!
IT'S TIME FOR THE GHOST TRACKERS! THAT'S RIGHT! IT'S TIME FOR THE GHOST TRACKERS!
OCO'S
RAYS
100% FOOD
FAVORITE HAUNT

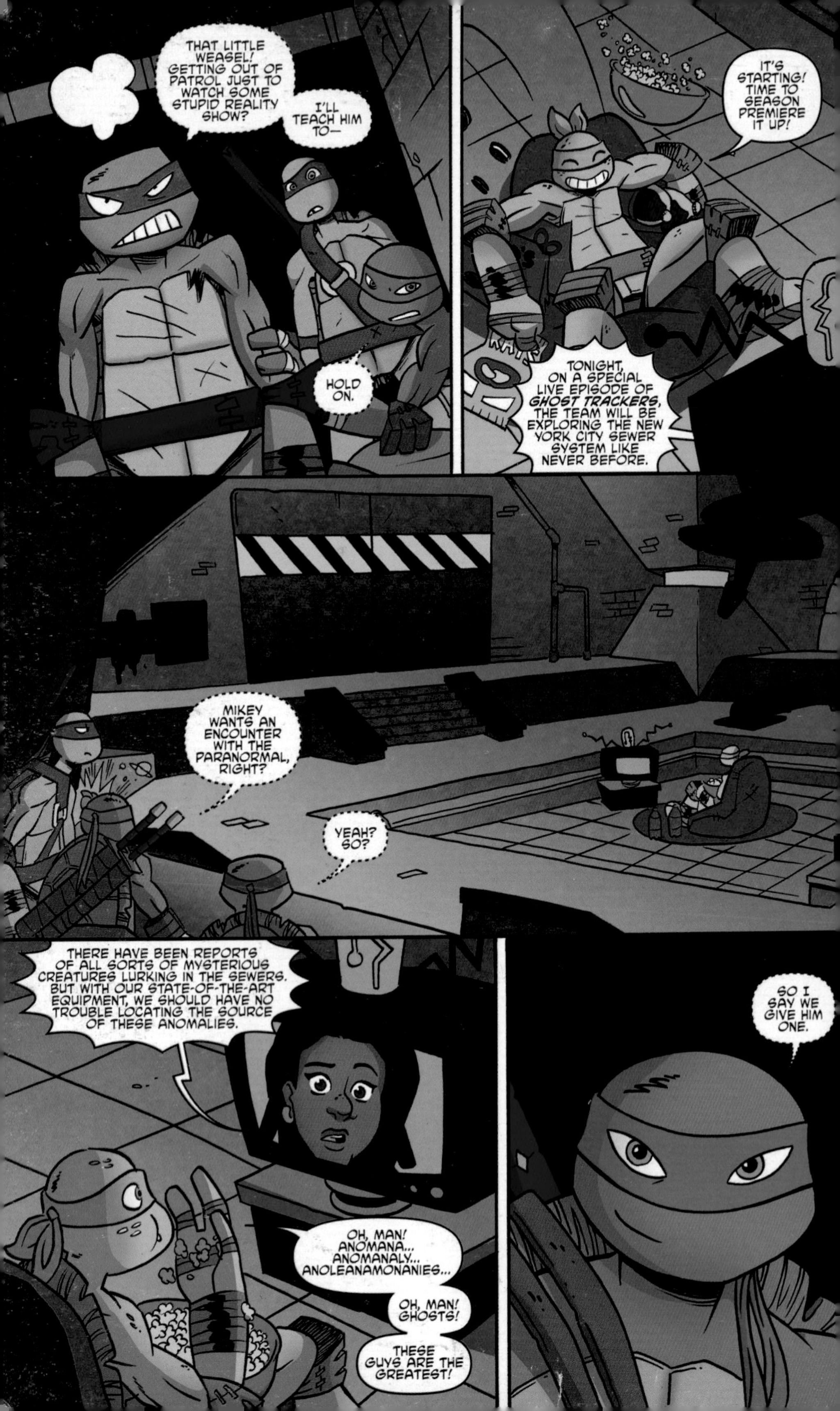

THAT LITTLE WEASEL! GETTING OUT OF PATROL JUST TO WATCH SOME STUPID REALITY SHOW?
I'LL TEACH HIM TO—
HOLD ON.
IT'S STARTING! TIME TO SEASON PREMIERE IT UP!
TONIGHT, ON A SPECIAL LIVE EPISODE OF *GHOST TRACKERS*, THE TEAM WILL BE EXPLORING THE NEW YORK CITY SEWER SYSTEM LIKE NEVER BEFORE.
MIKEY WANTS AN ENCOUNTER WITH THE PARANORMAL, RIGHT?
YEAH? SO?
THERE HAVE BEEN REPORTS OF ALL SORTS OF MYSTERIOUS CREATURES LURKING IN THE SEWERS. BUT WITH OUR STATE-OF-THE-ART EQUIPMENT, WE SHOULD HAVE NO TROUBLE LOCATING THE SOURCE OF THESE ANOMALIES.
OH, MAN! ANOMANA... ANOMANALY... ANOLEANAMONANIES...
OH, MAN! GHOSTS!
THESE GUYS ARE THE GREATEST!
SO I SAY WE GIVE HIM ONE.

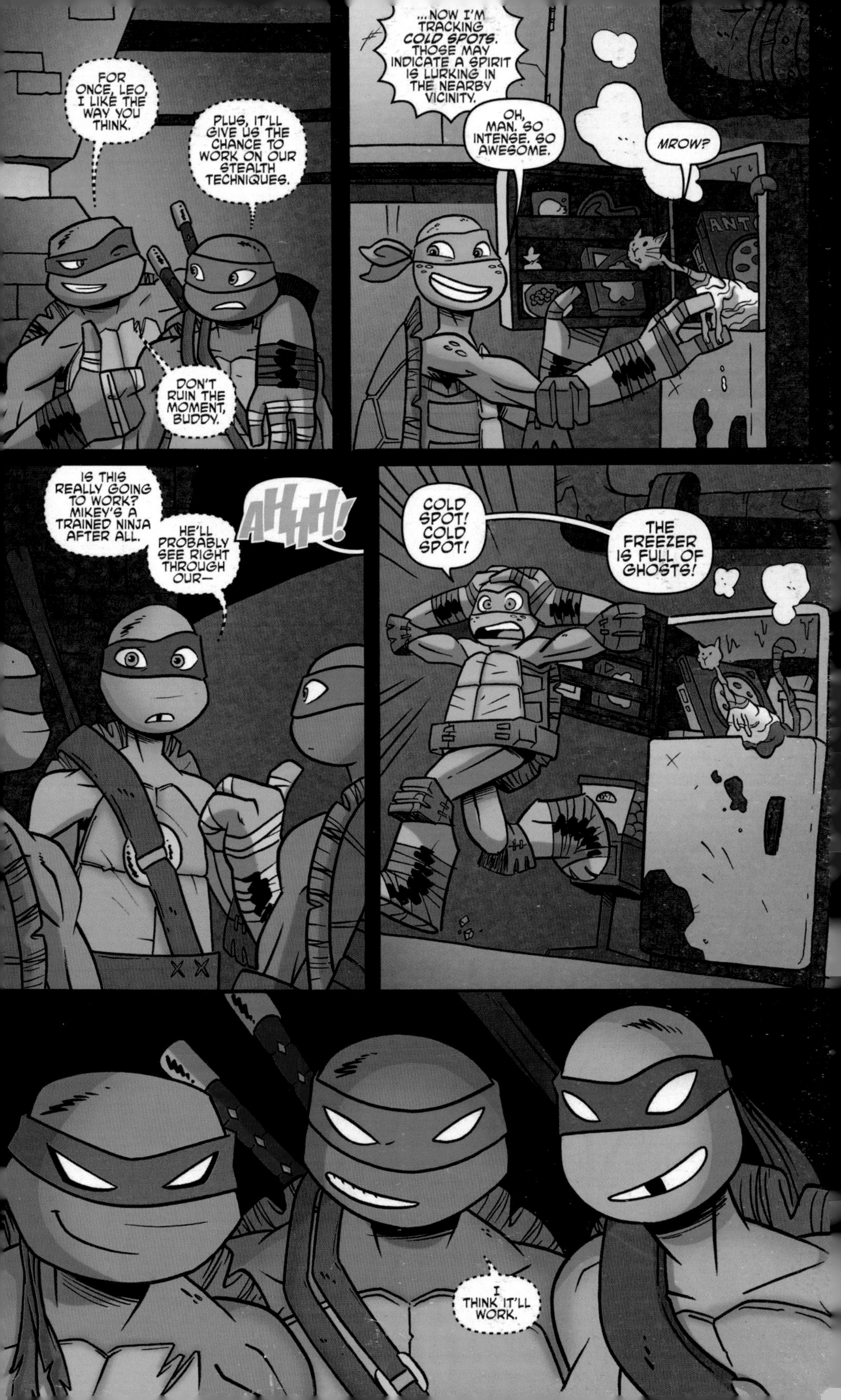
FOR ONCE, LEO, I LIKE THE WAY YOU THINK.
PLUS, IT'LL GIVE US THE CHANCE TO WORK ON OUR STEALTH TECHNIQUES.
DON'T RUIN THE MOMENT, BUDDY.
...NOW I'M TRACKING COLD SPOTS. THOSE MAY INDICATE A SPIRIT IS LURKING IN THE NEARBY VICINITY.
OH, MAN. SO INTENSE. SO AWESOME.
MROW?
IS THIS REALLY GOING TO WORK? MIKEY'S A TRAINED NINJA AFTER ALL.
HE'LL PROBABLY SEE RIGHT THROUGH OUR—
AHHH!
COLD SPOT! COLD SPOT!
THE FREEZER IS FULL OF GHOSTS!
I THINK IT'LL WORK.

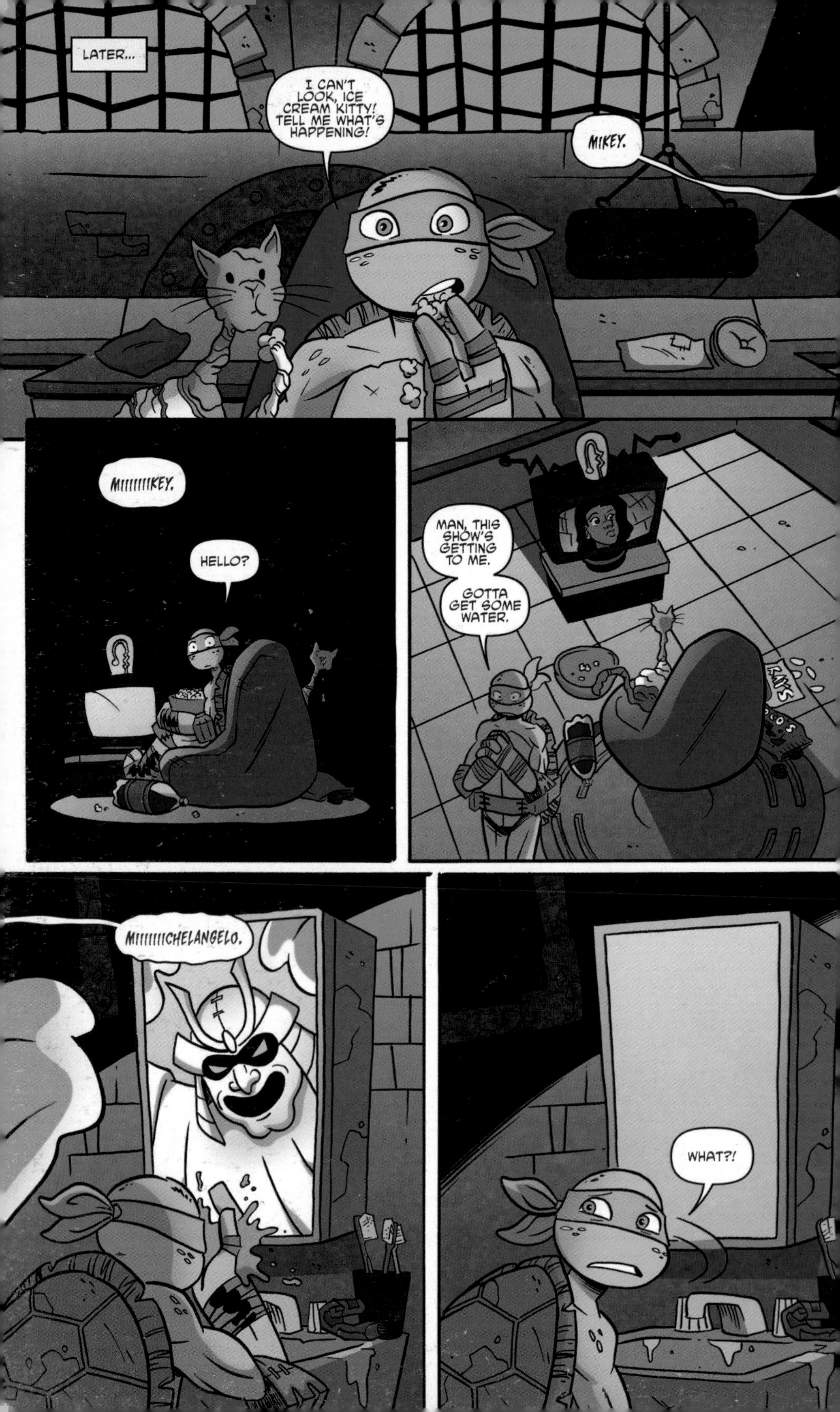
LATER...
I CAN'T LOOK, ICE CREAM KITTY! TELL ME WHAT'S HAPPENING!
MIKEY.
MIIIIIIIKEY.
HELLO?
MAN, THIS SHOW'S GETTING TO ME.
GOTTA GET SOME WATER.
MIIIIIIICHELANGELO.
WHAT?!

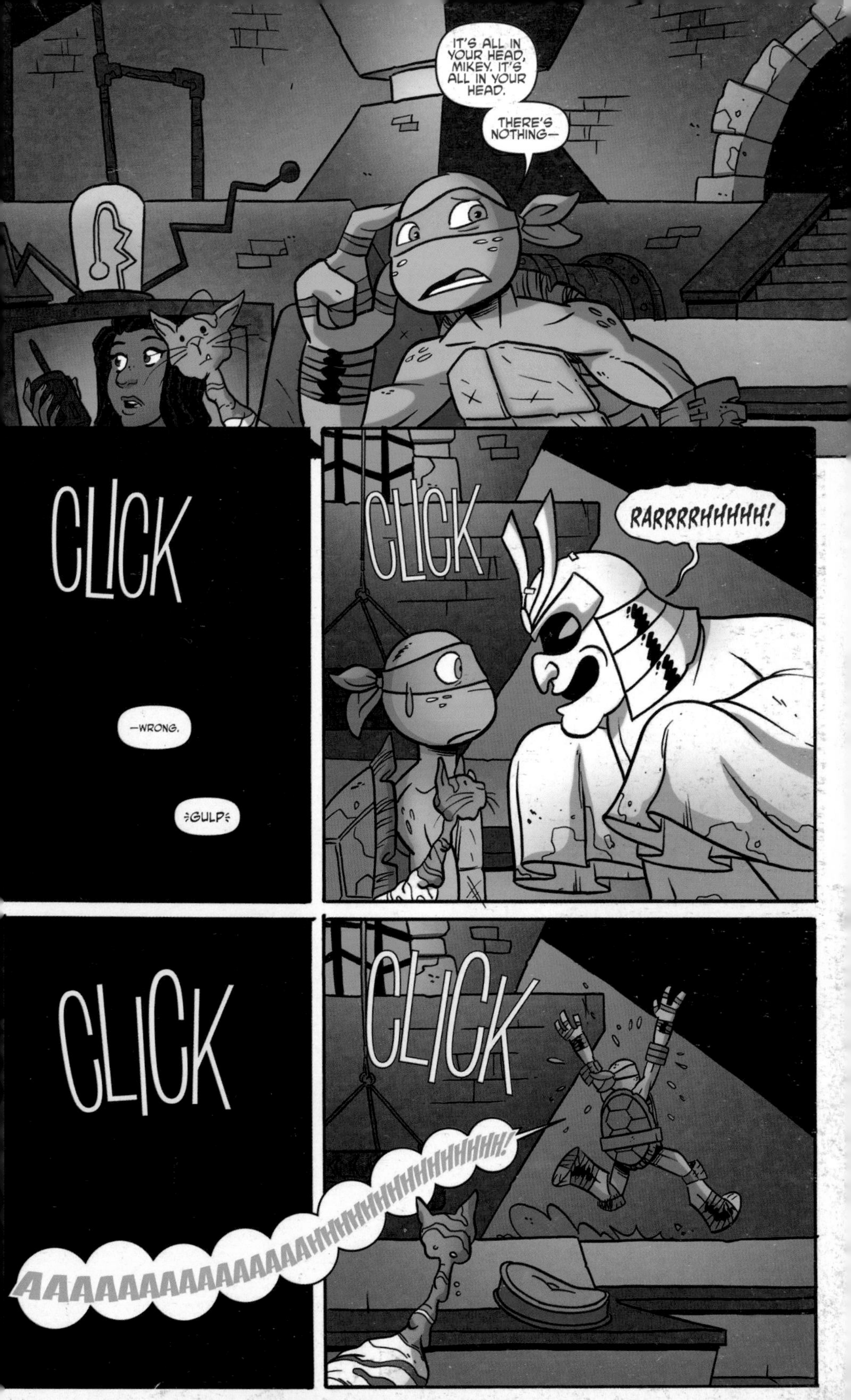
IT'S ALL IN YOUR HEAD, MIKEY. IT'S ALL IN YOUR HEAD.
THERE'S NOTHING—
CLICK
—WRONG.
GULP
CLICK
RARRRRHHHHH!
CLICK
CLICK
AAAAAAAAAAAAAAAHHHHHHHHHHHHHHH!

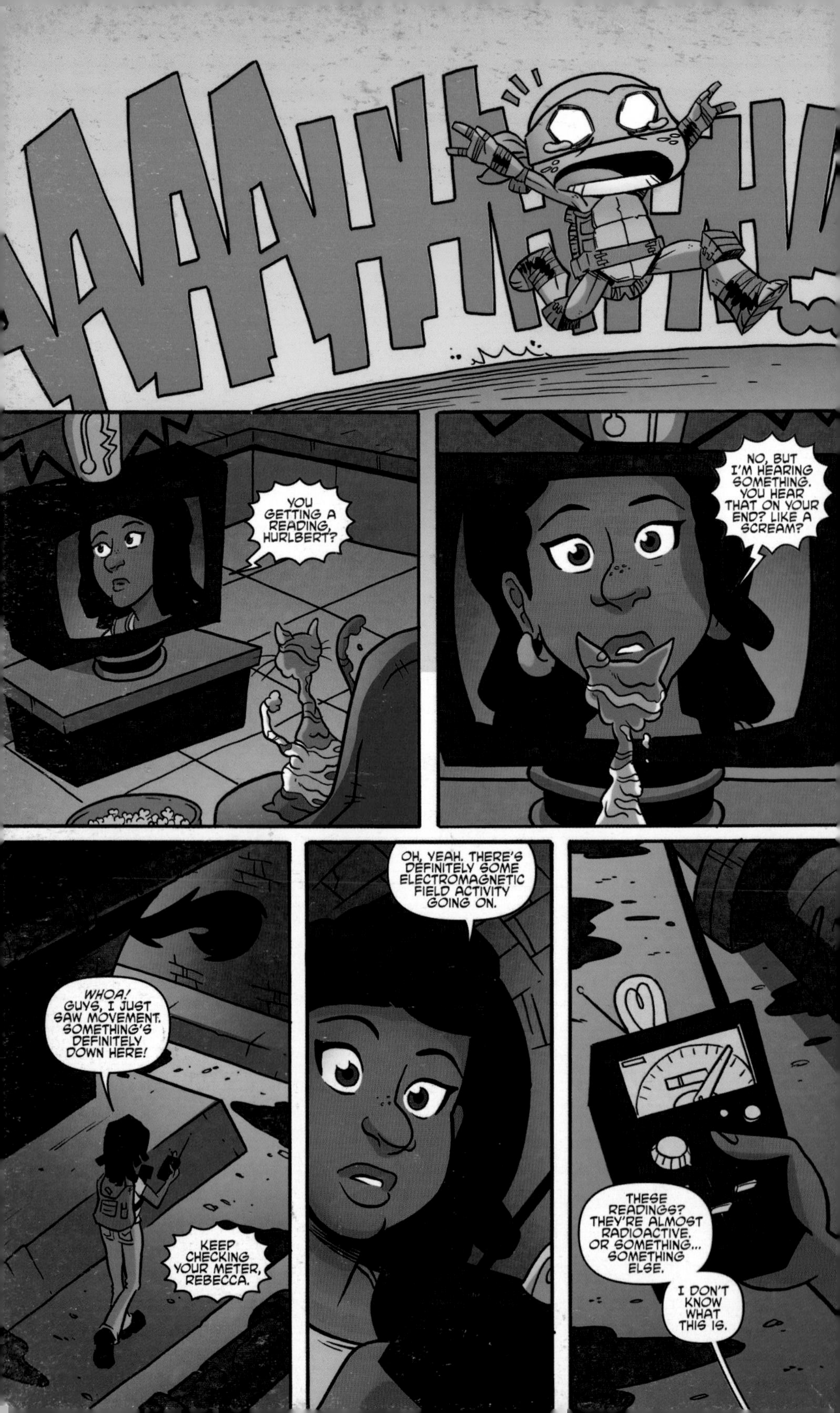
AAAAAAHHHHH
YOU GETTING A READING, HURLBERT?
NO, BUT I'M HEARING SOMETHING. YOU HEAR THAT ON YOUR END? LIKE A SCREAM?
WHOA! GUYS, I JUST SAW MOVEMENT. SOMETHING'S DEFINITELY DOWN HERE!
KEEP CHECKING YOUR METER, REBECCA.
OH, YEAH. THERE'S DEFINITELY SOME ELECTROMAGNETIC FIELD ACTIVITY GOING ON.
THESE READINGS? THEY'RE ALMOST RADIOACTIVE. OR SOMETHING... SOMETHING ELSE.
I DON'T KNOW WHAT THIS IS.

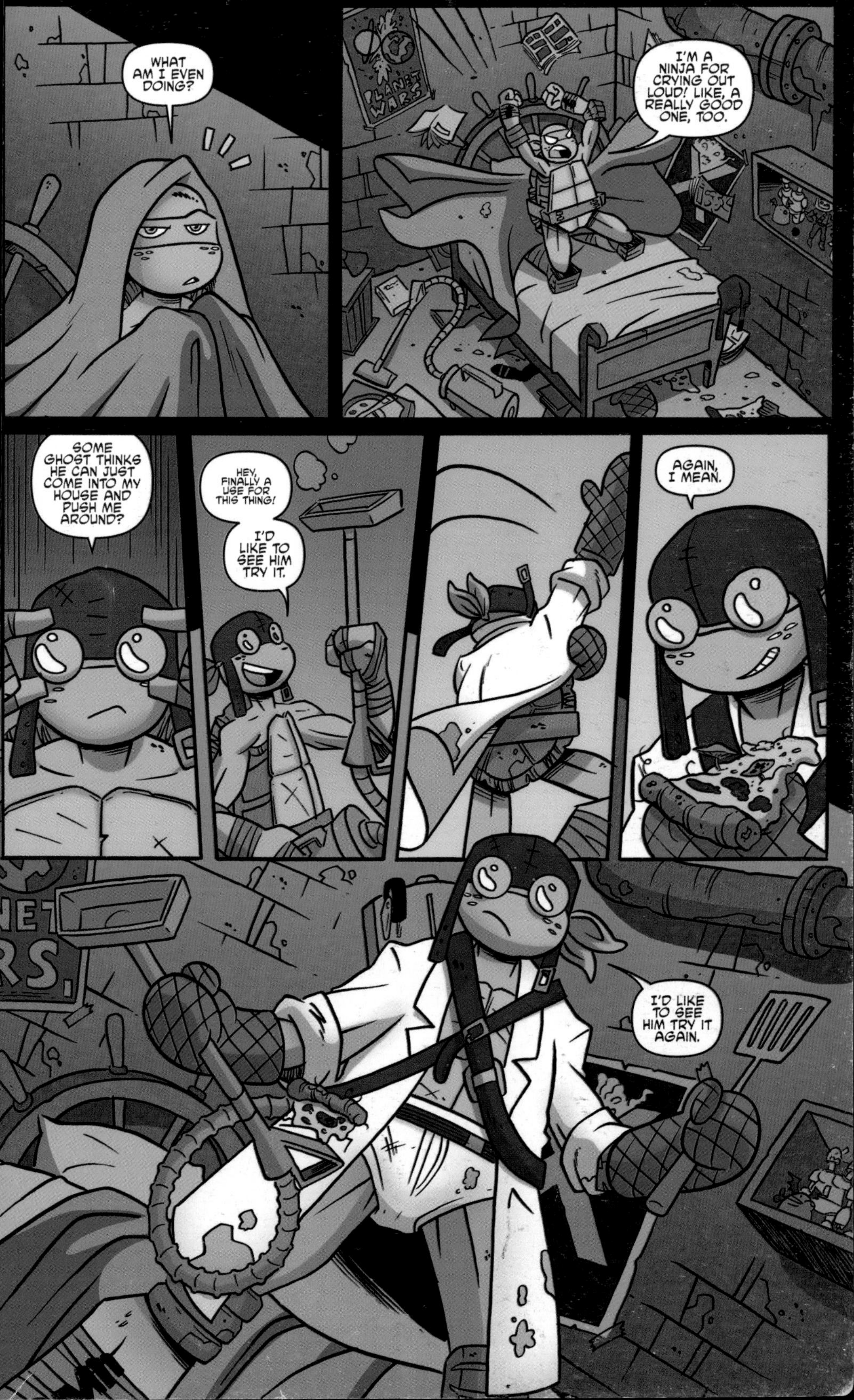

WHAT AM I EVEN DOING?
I'M A NINJA FOR CRYING OUT LOUD! LIKE, A REALLY GOOD ONE, TOO.
PLANET WARS
SOME GHOST THINKS HE CAN JUST COME INTO MY HOUSE AND PUSH ME AROUND?
HEY, FINALLY A USE FOR THIS THING!
I'D LIKE TO SEE HIM TRY IT.
AGAIN, I MEAN.
I'D LIKE TO SEE HIM TRY IT AGAIN.

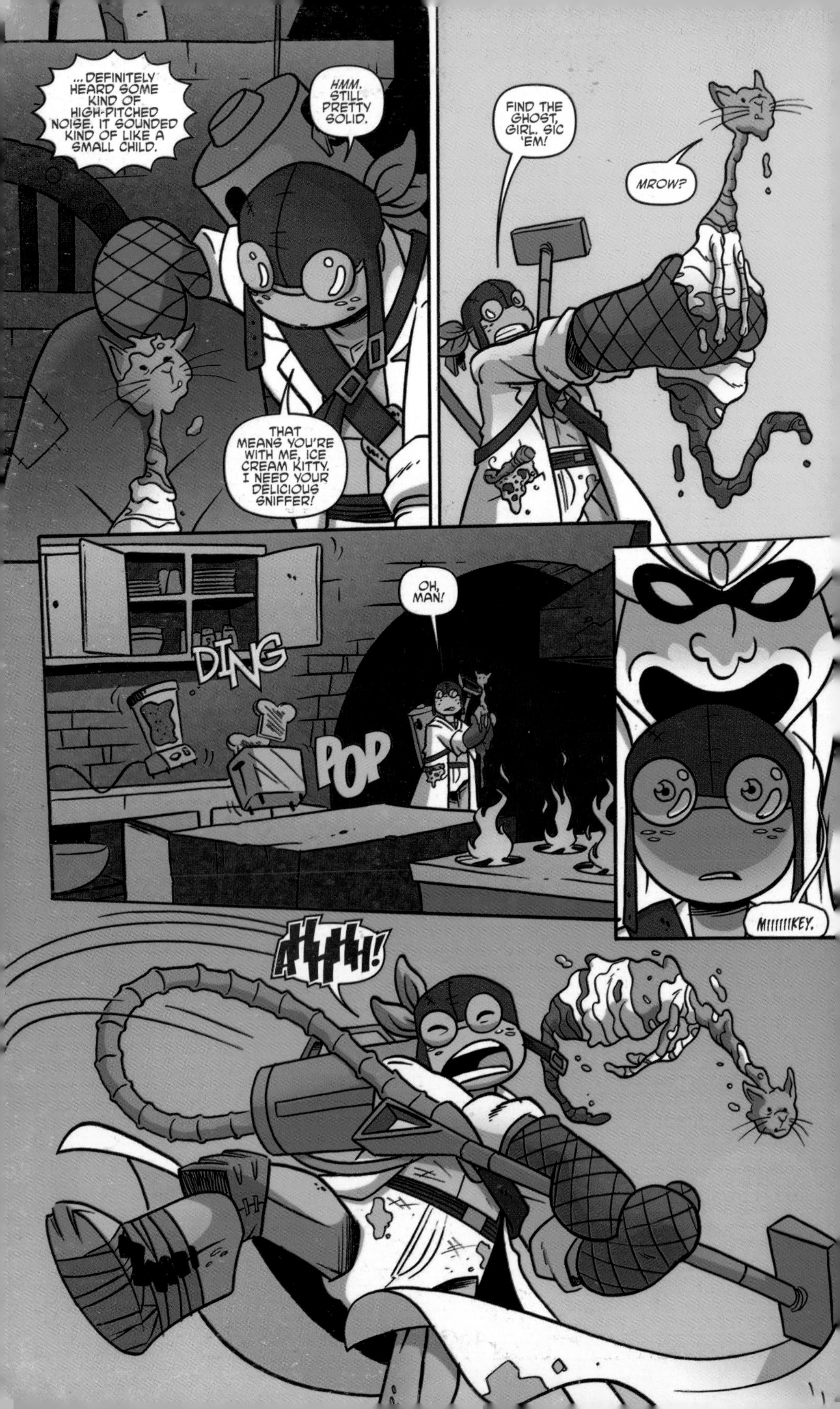
...DEFINITELY HEARD SOME KIND OF HIGH-PITCHED NOISE. IT SOUNDED KIND OF LIKE A SMALL CHILD.
HMM. STILL PRETTY SOLID.
THAT MEANS YOU'RE WITH ME, ICE CREAM KITTY. I NEED YOUR DELICIOUS SNIFFER!
FIND THE GHOST, GIRL. SIC 'EM!
MROW?
DING
POP
OH, MAN!
MIIIIIIKEY.
AHHH!

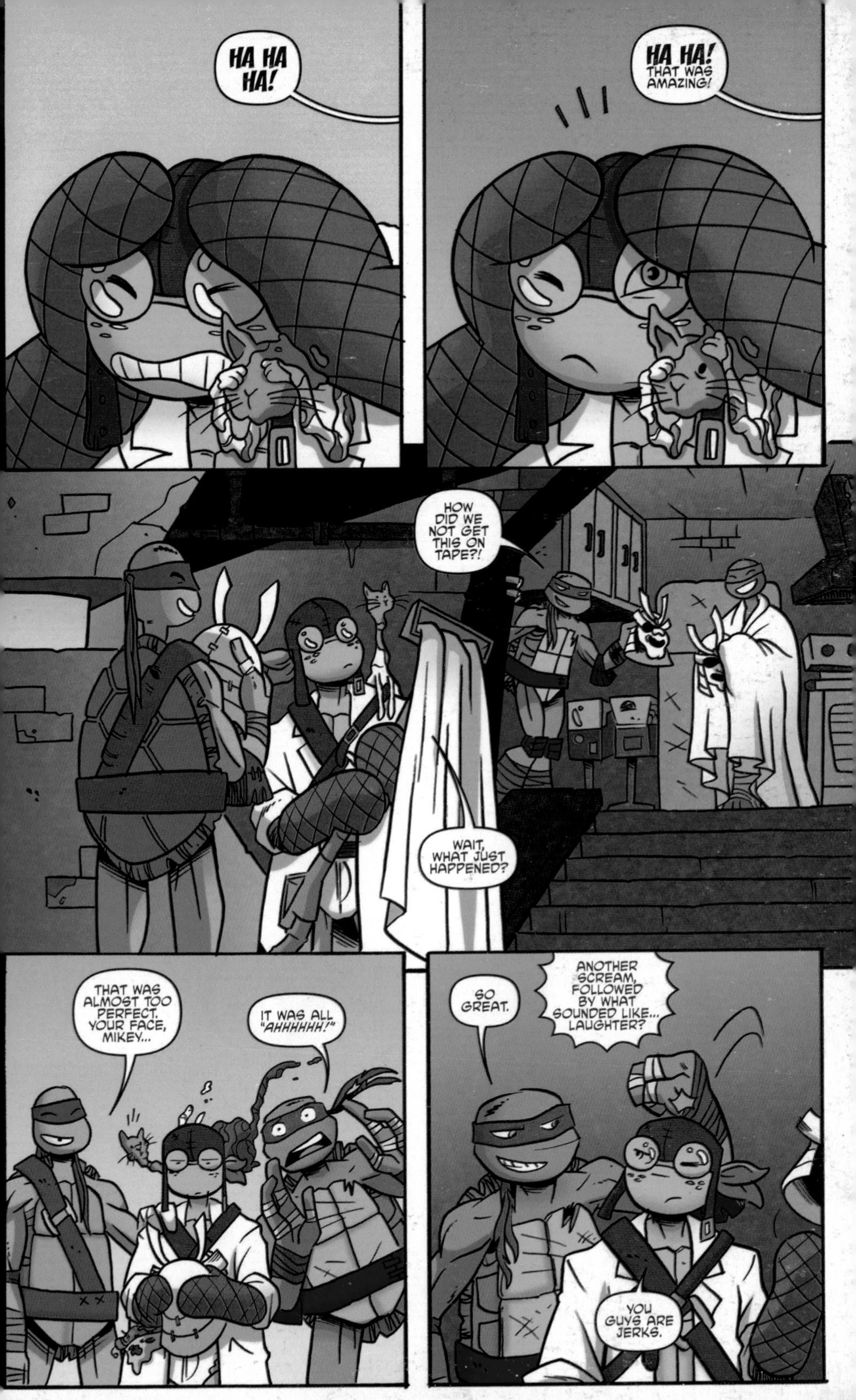

HA HA HA!
HA HA! THAT WAS AMAZING!
HOW DID WE NOT GET THIS ON TAPE?!
WAIT, WHAT JUST HAPPENED?
THAT WAS ALMOST TOO PERFECT. YOUR FACE, MIKEY...
IT WAS ALL "AHHHHHH!"
SO GREAT.
ANOTHER SCREAM, FOLLOWED BY WHAT SOUNDED LIKE... LAUGHTER?
YOU GUYS ARE JERKS.

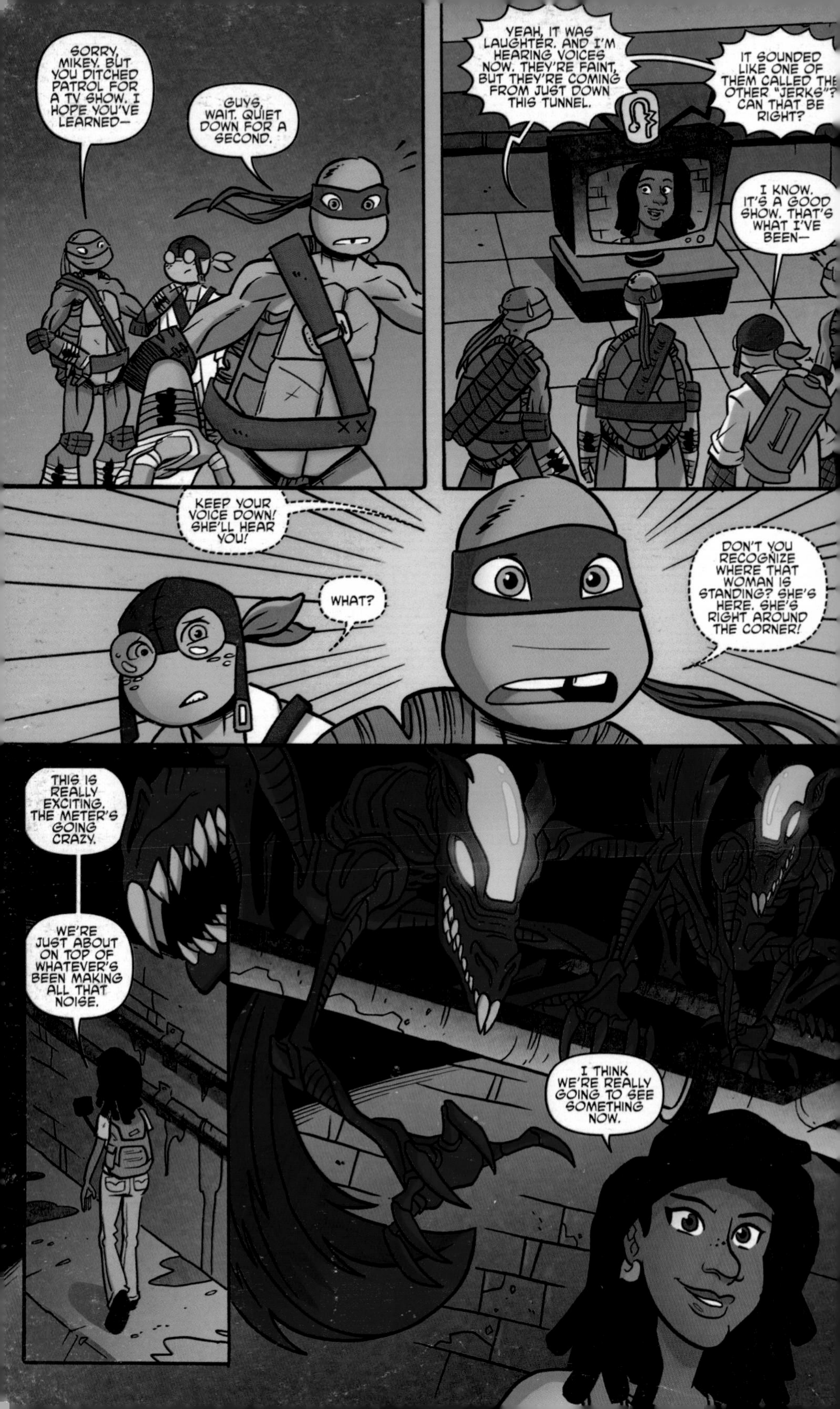

SORRY, MIKEY. BUT YOU DITCHED PATROL FOR A TV SHOW. I HOPE YOU'VE LEARNED—
GUYS, WAIT. QUIET DOWN FOR A SECOND.
YEAH, IT WAS LAUGHTER. AND I'M HEARING VOICES NOW. THEY'RE FAINT, BUT THEY'RE COMING FROM JUST DOWN THIS TUNNEL.
IT SOUNDED LIKE ONE OF THEM CALLED THE OTHER "JERKS"? CAN THAT BE RIGHT?
I KNOW. IT'S A GOOD SHOW. THAT'S WHAT I'VE BEEN—
KEEP YOUR VOICE DOWN! SHE'LL HEAR YOU!
WHAT?
DON'T YOU RECOGNIZE WHERE THAT WOMAN IS STANDING? SHE'S HERE. SHE'S RIGHT AROUND THE CORNER!
THIS IS REALLY EXCITING. THE METER'S GOING CRAZY.
WE'RE JUST ABOUT ON TOP OF WHATEVER'S BEEN MAKING ALL THAT NOISE.
I THINK WE'RE REALLY GOING TO SEE SOMETHING NOW.

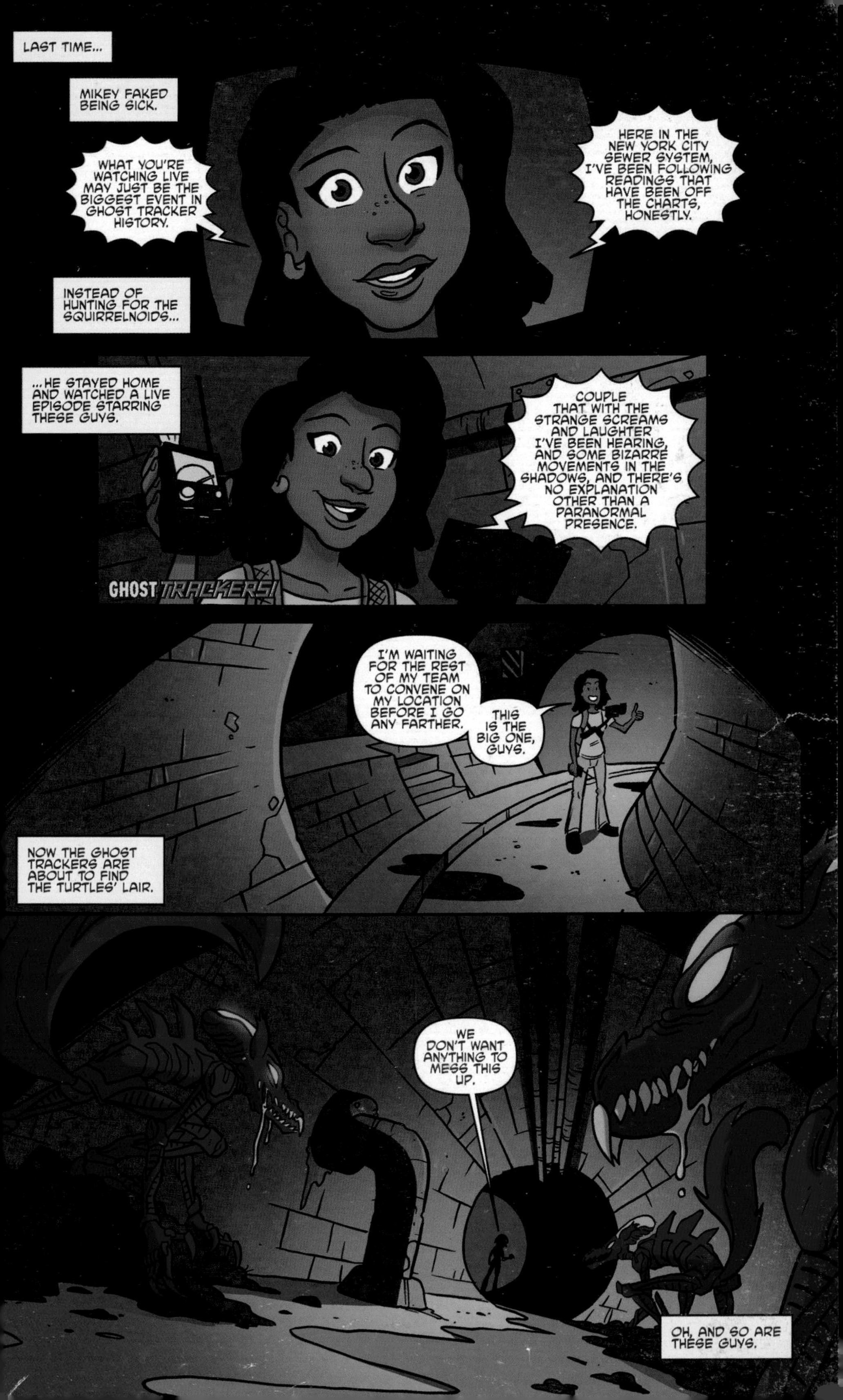
LAST TIME...
MIKEY FAKED BEING SICK.
WHAT YOU'RE WATCHING LIVE MAY JUST BE THE BIGGEST EVENT IN GHOST TRACKER HISTORY.
HERE IN THE NEW YORK CITY SEWER SYSTEM, I'VE BEEN FOLLOWING READINGS THAT HAVE BEEN OFF THE CHARTS, HONESTLY.
INSTEAD OF HUNTING FOR THE SQUIRRELNOIDS...
...HE STAYED HOME AND WATCHED A LIVE EPISODE STARRING THESE GUYS.
COUPLE THAT WITH THE STRANGE SCREAMS AND LAUGHTER I'VE BEEN HEARING, AND SOME BIZARRE MOVEMENTS IN THE SHADOWS, AND THERE'S NO EXPLANATION OTHER THAN A PARANORMAL PRESENCE.
GHOST TRACKERS!
I'M WAITING FOR THE REST OF MY TEAM TO CONVENE ON MY LOCATION BEFORE I GO ANY FARTHER.
THIS IS THE BIG ONE, GUYS.
NOW THE GHOST TRACKERS ARE ABOUT TO FIND THE TURTLES' LAIR.
WE DON'T WANT ANYTHING TO MESS THIS UP.
OH, AND SO ARE THESE GUYS.

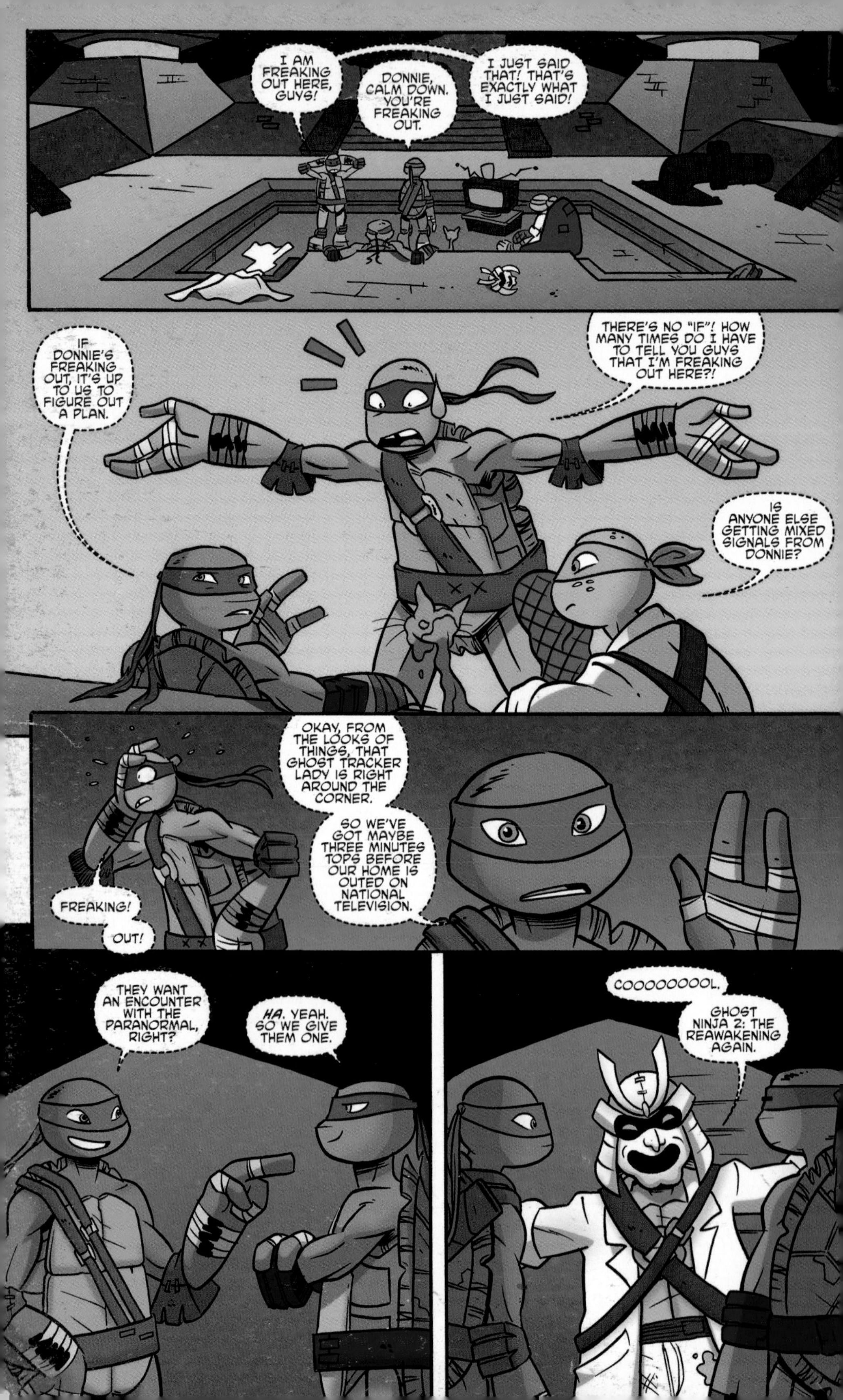
I AM FREAKING OUT HERE, GUYS!
DONNIE, CALM DOWN. YOU'RE FREAKING OUT.
I JUST SAID THAT! THAT'S EXACTLY WHAT I JUST SAID!
IF DONNIE'S FREAKING OUT, IT'S UP TO US TO FIGURE OUT A PLAN.
THERE'S NO "IF"! HOW MANY TIMES DO I HAVE TO TELL YOU GUYS THAT I'M FREAKING OUT HERE?!
IS ANYONE ELSE GETTING MIXED SIGNALS FROM DONNIE?
OKAY, FROM THE LOOKS OF THINGS, THAT GHOST TRACKER LADY IS RIGHT AROUND THE CORNER.
SO WE'VE GOT MAYBE THREE MINUTES TOPS BEFORE OUR HOME IS OUTED ON NATIONAL TELEVISION.
FREAKING!
OUT!
THEY WANT AN ENCOUNTER WITH THE PARANORMAL, RIGHT?
HA. YEAH. SO WE GIVE THEM ONE.
COOOOOOOOL.
GHOST NINJA 2: THE REAWAKENING AGAIN.

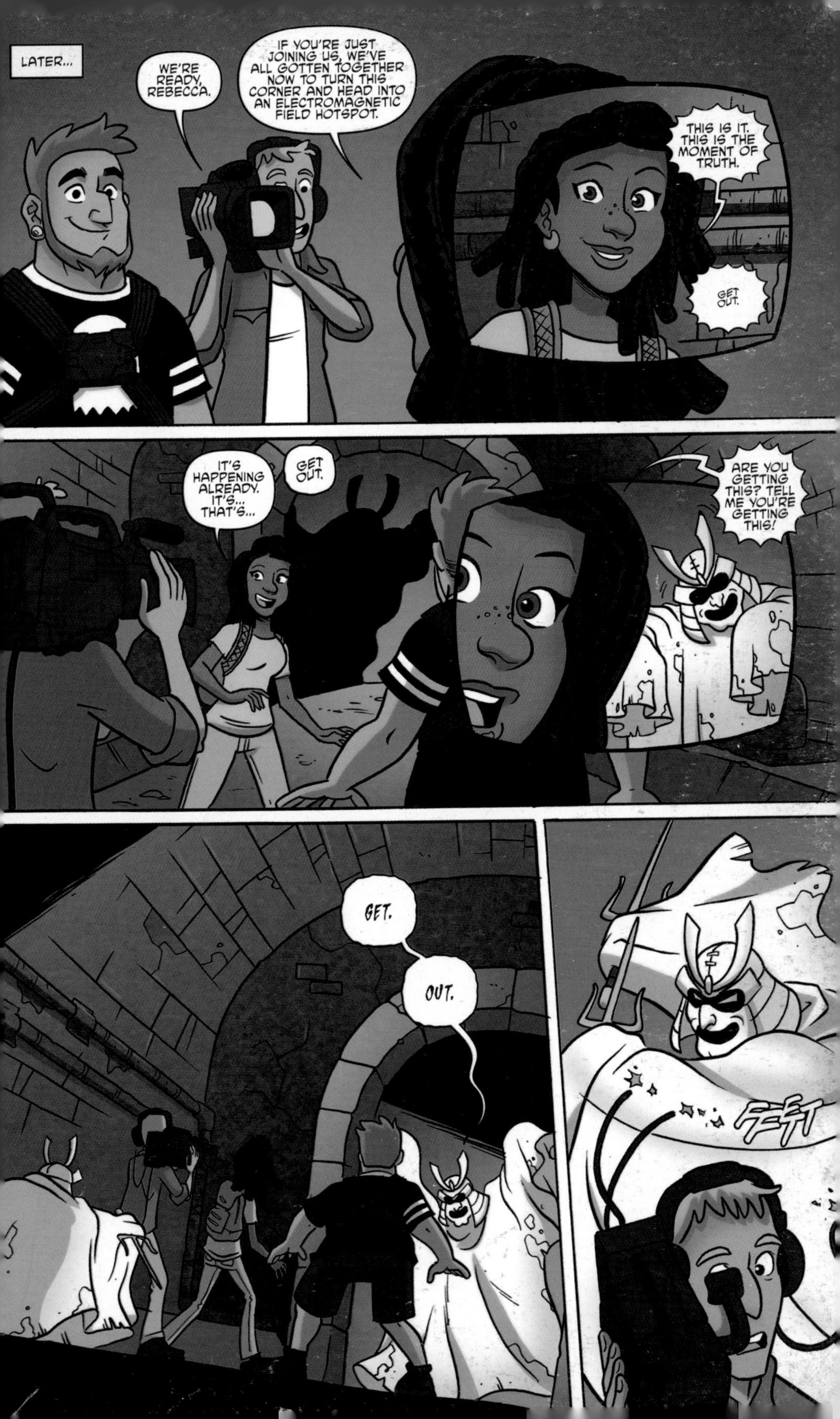
LATER...
WE'RE READY, REBECCA.
IF YOU'RE JUST JOINING US, WE'VE ALL GOTTEN TOGETHER NOW TO TURN THIS CORNER AND HEAD INTO AN ELECTROMAGNETIC FIELD HOTSPOT.
THIS IS IT. THIS IS THE MOMENT OF TRUTH.
GET OUT.
IT'S HAPPENING ALREADY. IT'S... THAT'S...
GET OUT.
ARE YOU GETTING THIS? TELL ME YOU'RE GETTING THIS!
GET.
OUT.

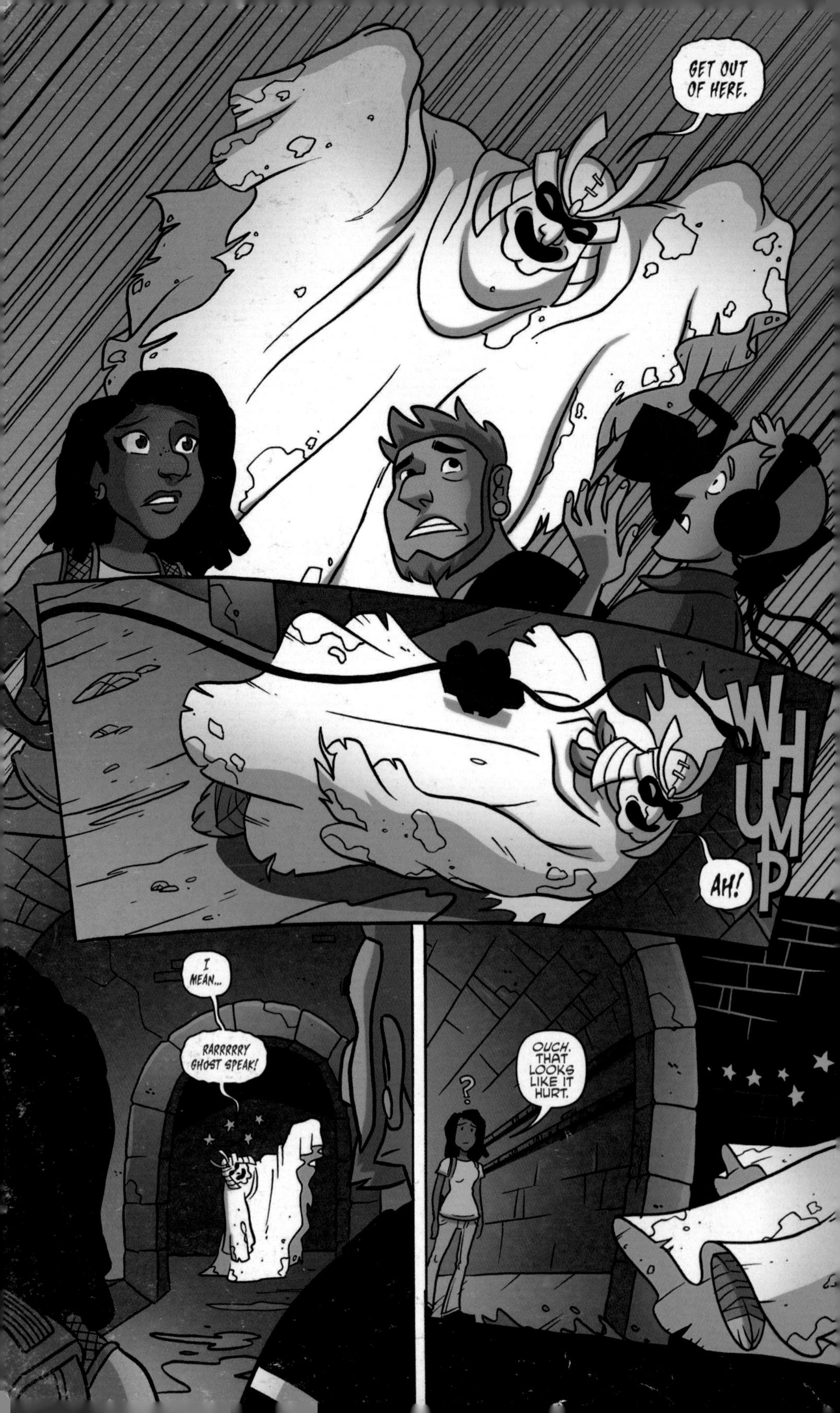

GET OUT OF HERE.
WHUMP
AH!
I MEAN...
RARRRRRY GHOST SPEAK!
?
OUCH. THAT LOOKS LIKE IT HURT.

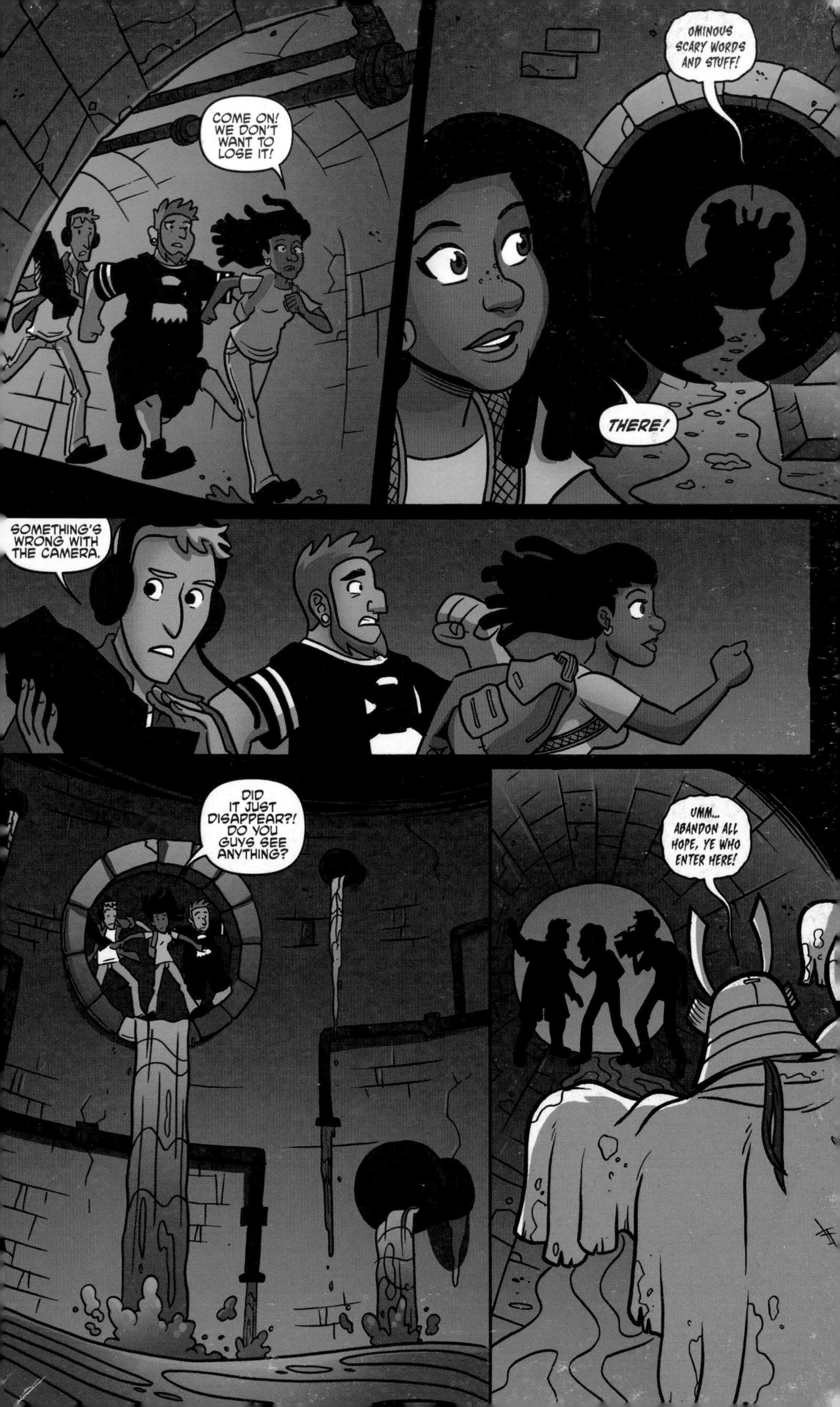
COME ON! WE DON'T WANT TO LOSE IT!
OMINOUS SCARY WORDS AND STUFF!
THERE!
SOMETHING'S WRONG WITH THE CAMERA.
DID IT JUST DISAPPEAR?! DO YOU GUYS SEE ANYTHING?
UMM... ABANDON ALL HOPE, YE WHO ENTER HERE!

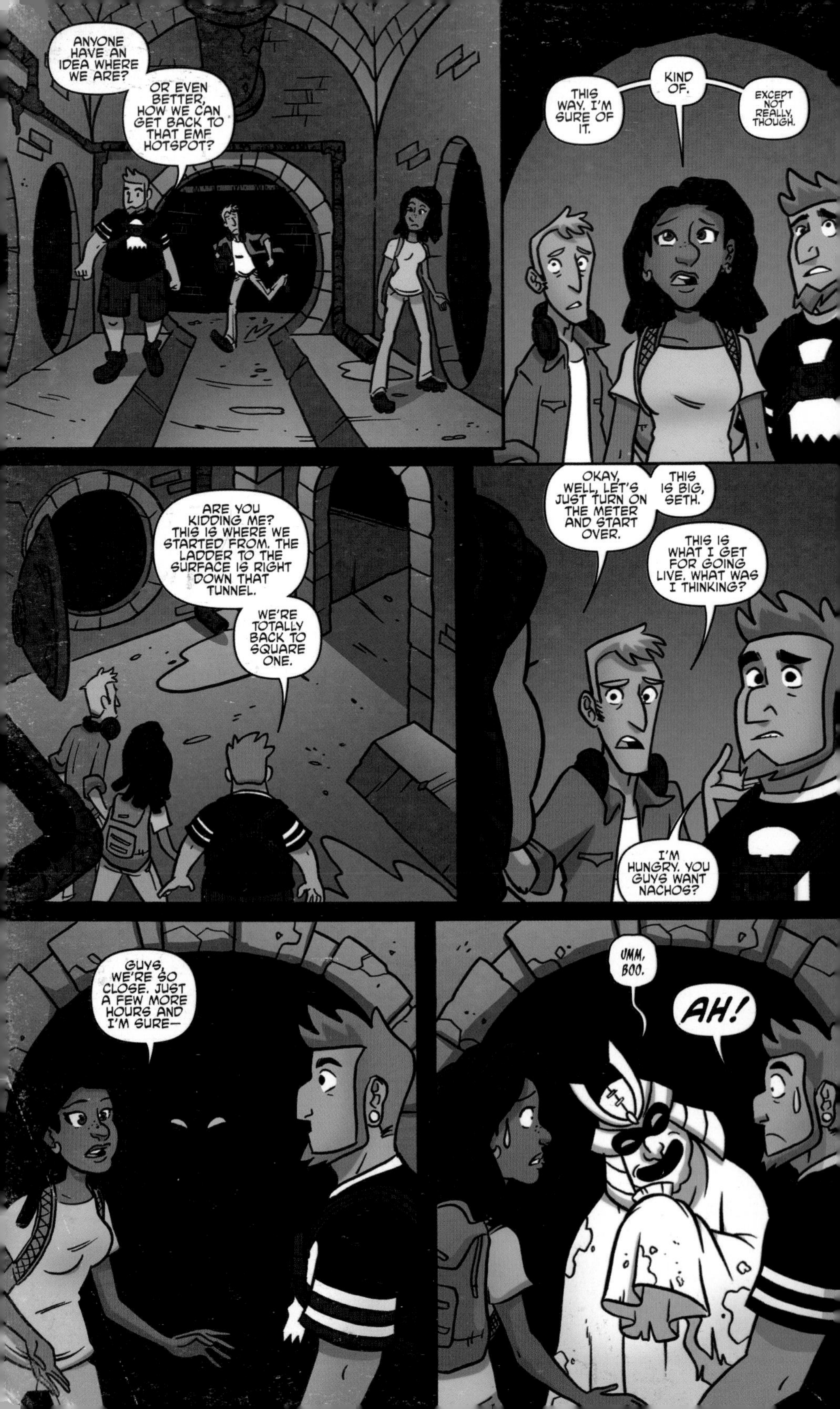
ANYONE HAVE AN IDEA WHERE WE ARE?
OR EVEN BETTER, HOW WE CAN GET BACK TO THAT EMF HOTSPOT?
THIS WAY. I'M SURE OF IT.
KIND OF.
EXCEPT NOT REALLY, THOUGH.
ARE YOU KIDDING ME? THIS IS WHERE WE STARTED FROM. THE LADDER TO THE SURFACE IS RIGHT DOWN THAT TUNNEL.
WE'RE TOTALLY BACK TO SQUARE ONE.
OKAY, WELL, LET'S JUST TURN ON THE METER AND START OVER.
THIS IS BIG, SETH.
THIS IS WHAT I GET FOR GOING LIVE. WHAT WAS I THINKING?
I'M HUNGRY. YOU GUYS WANT NACHOS?
GUYS, WE'RE SO CLOSE. JUST A FEW MORE HOURS AND I'M SURE—
UMM, BOO.
AH!

BOO-YAKASHA!
OH, MAN. LOOK AT MIKEY GO!
HE'S REALLY GETTING INTO IT!
SO THAT'S ONE PROBLEM SOLVED.
AND LOOK, GOOD NEWS, GUYS!
WE'RE RIGHT BY DONNIE'S DRAINPIPE. WE CAN START OUR PATROL FOR THE SQUIRRELNOIDS FROM HERE.
YOUR GOOD NEWS IS ALWAYS THE WORST KIND OF GOOD NEWS.
RRRRRRR RRRRRRRR RRRRR
C'MON, MIKEY. GIVE IT A REST.
RRRRRRR RRRRRRRR RRRRR
HEY! KNOCK IT OFF! YOU'RE DRIPPING ALL... OVER... MY...

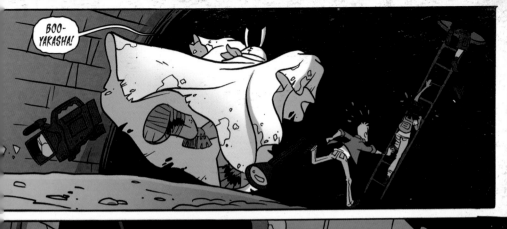

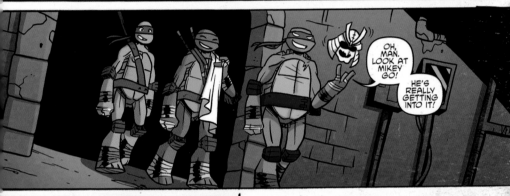

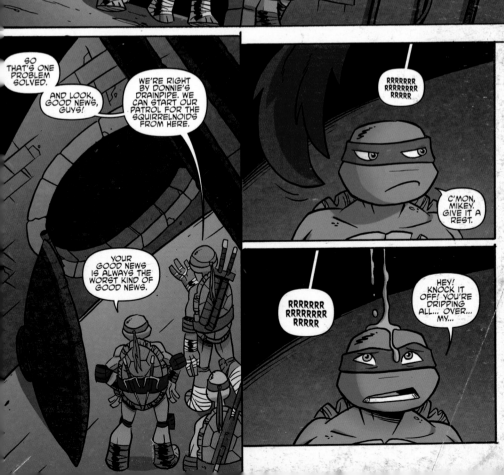

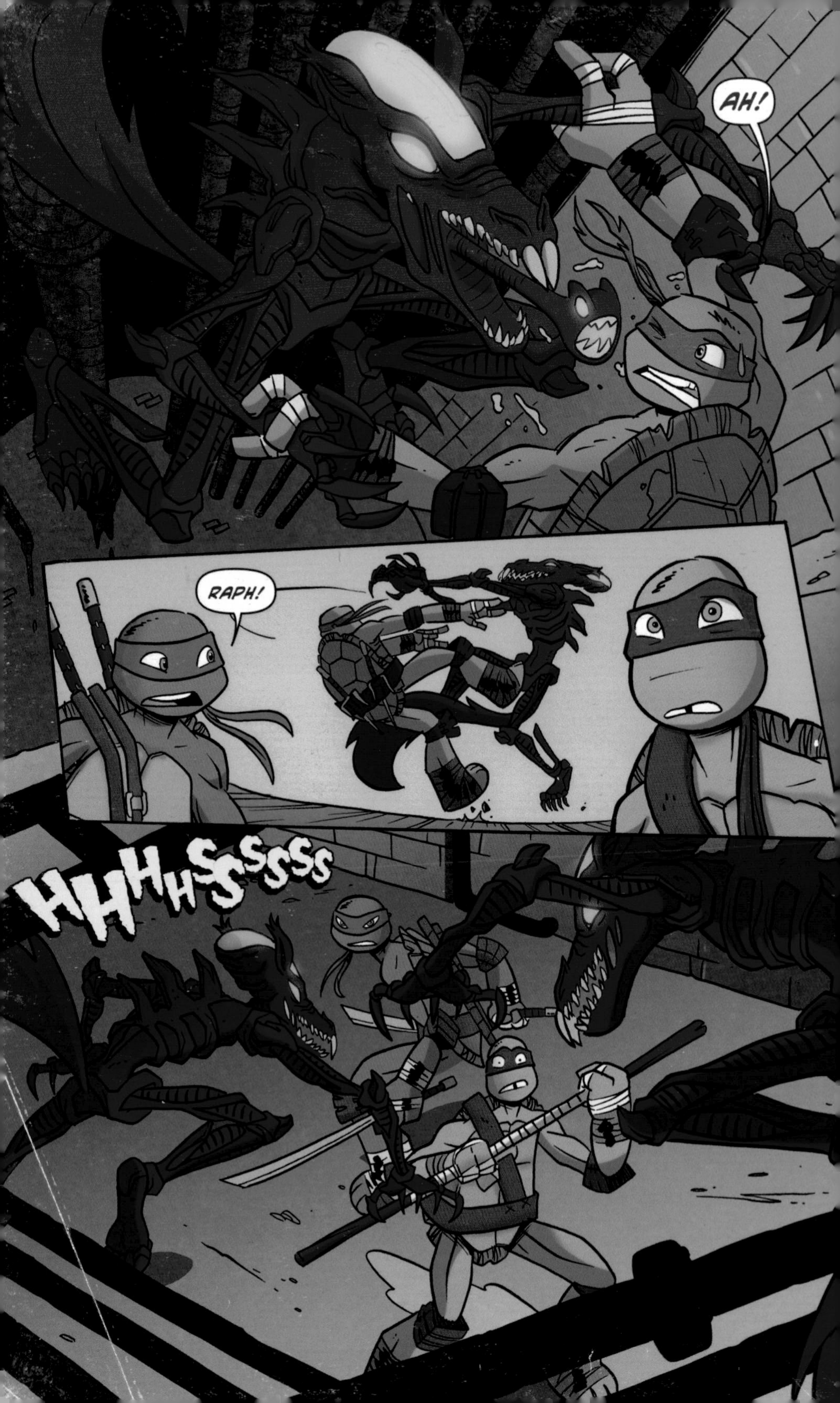
AH!
RAPH!
HHHHSSSSSS

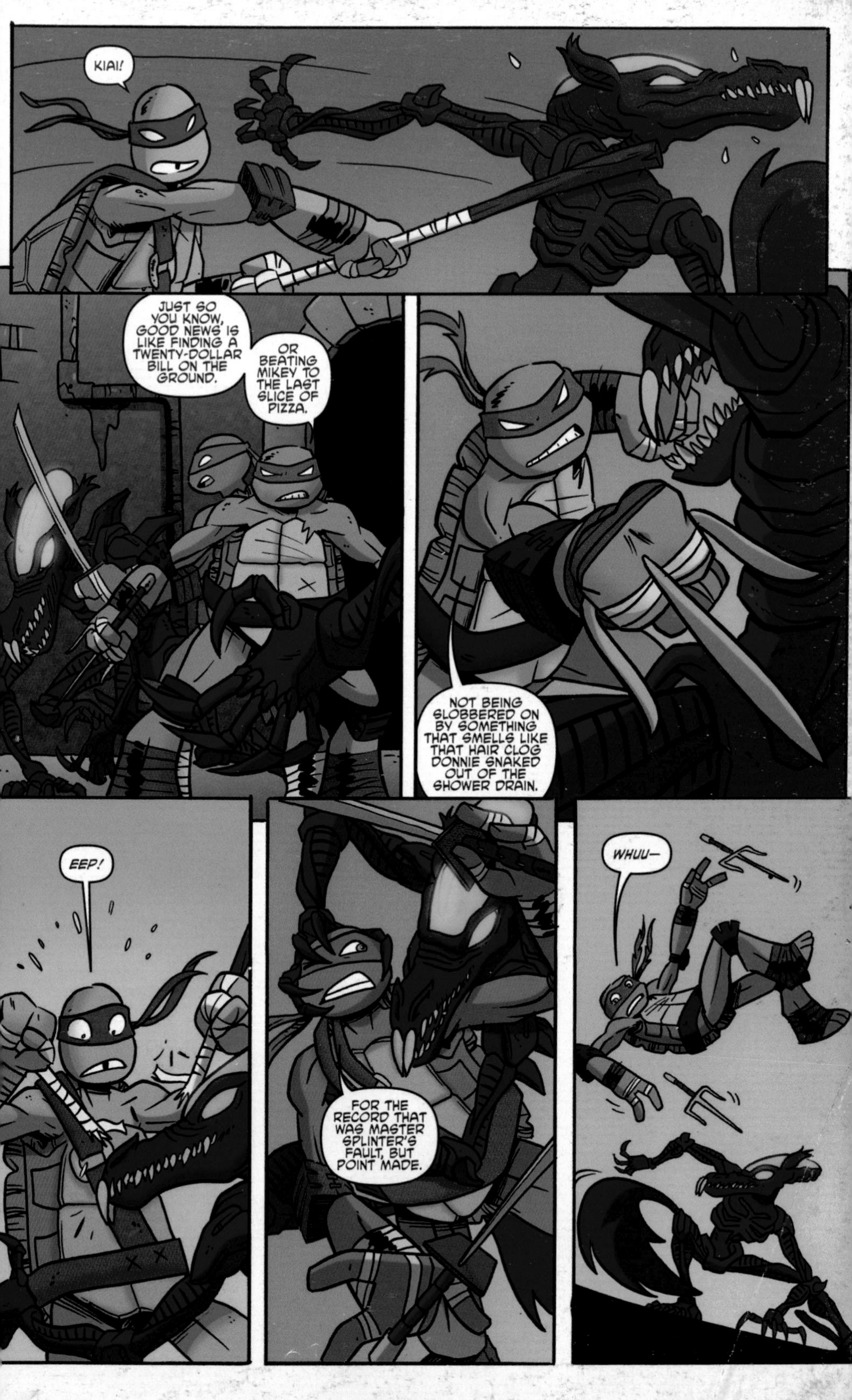
KIAI!
JUST SO YOU KNOW, GOOD NEWS IS LIKE FINDING A TWENTY-DOLLAR BILL ON THE GROUND.
OR BEATING MIKEY TO THE LAST SLICE OF PIZZA.
NOT BEING SLOBBERED ON BY SOMETHING THAT SMELLS LIKE THAT HAIR CLOG DONNIE SNAKED OUT OF THE SHOWER DRAIN.
EEP!
FOR THE RECORD THAT WAS MASTER SPLINTER'S FAULT, BUT POINT MADE.
WHUU—

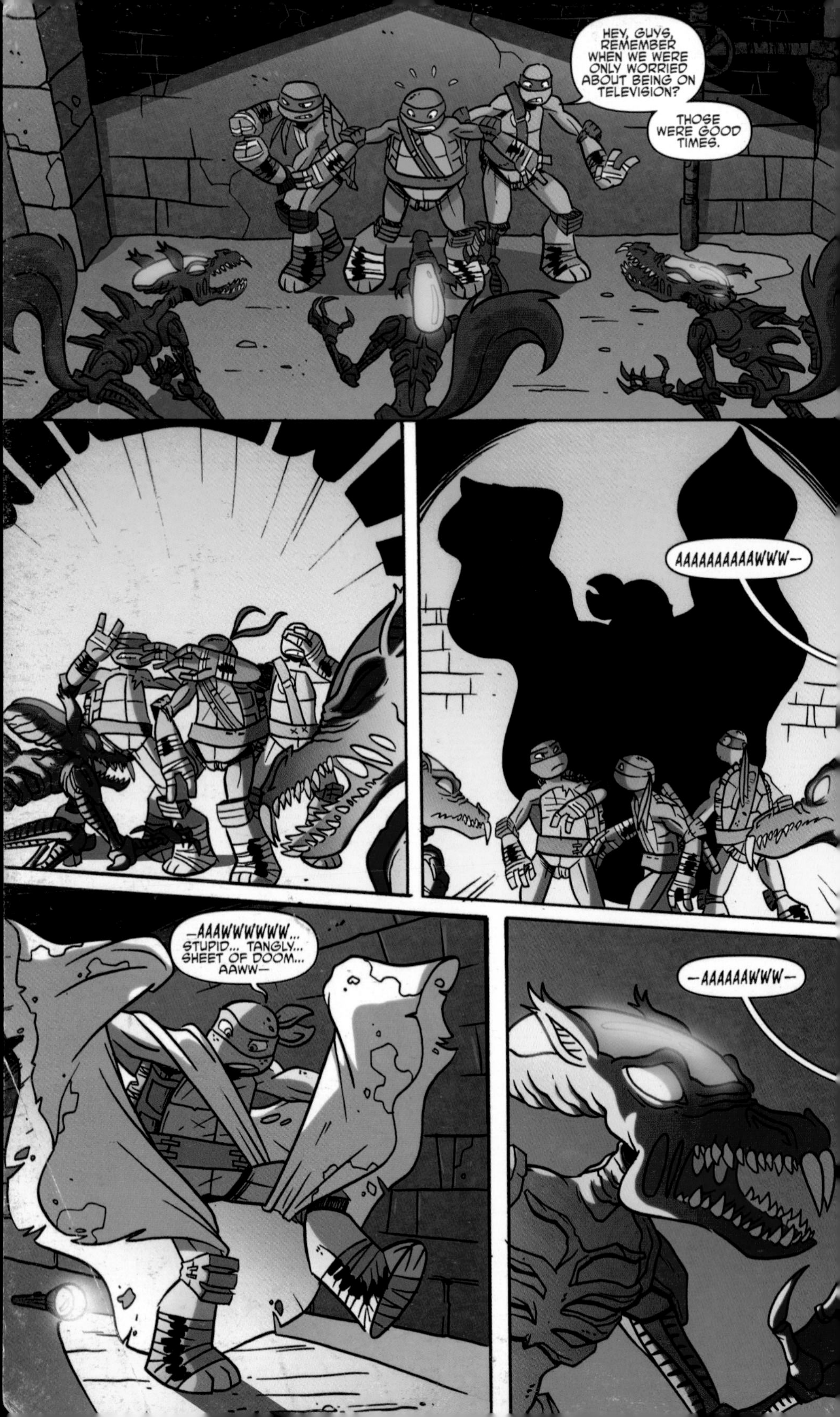
HEY, GUYS, REMEMBER WHEN WE WERE ONLY WORRIED ABOUT BEING ON TELEVISION?
THOSE WERE GOOD TIMES.
AAAAAAAAAAWWW—
—AAAWWWWWW... STUPID... TANGLY... SHEET OF DOOM... AAWW—
—AAAAAAWWW—

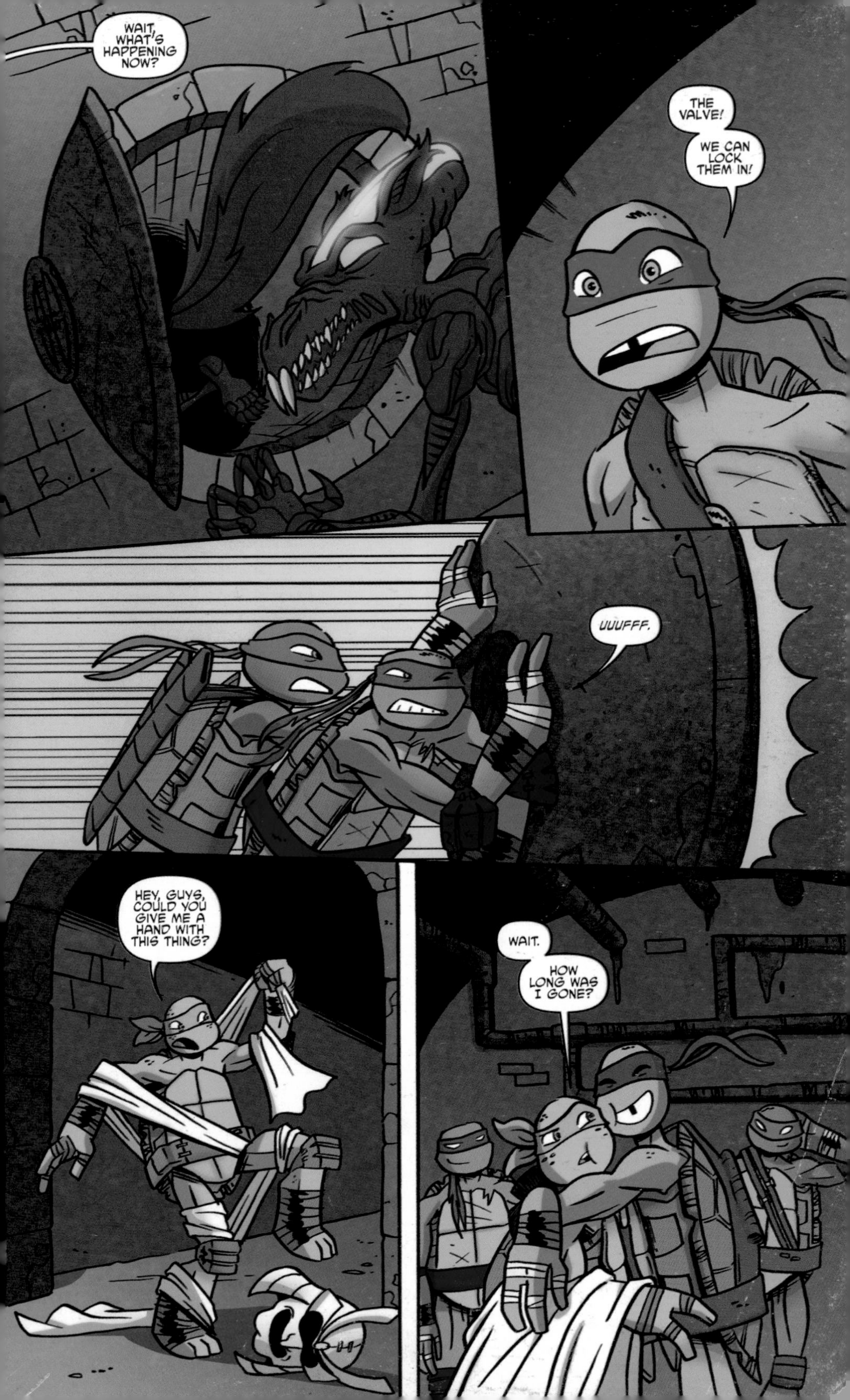
WAIT, WHAT'S HAPPENING NOW?
THE VALVE!
WE CAN LOCK THEM IN!
UUUFFF.
HEY, GUYS, COULD YOU GIVE ME A HAND WITH THIS THING?
WAIT.
HOW LONG WAS I GONE?

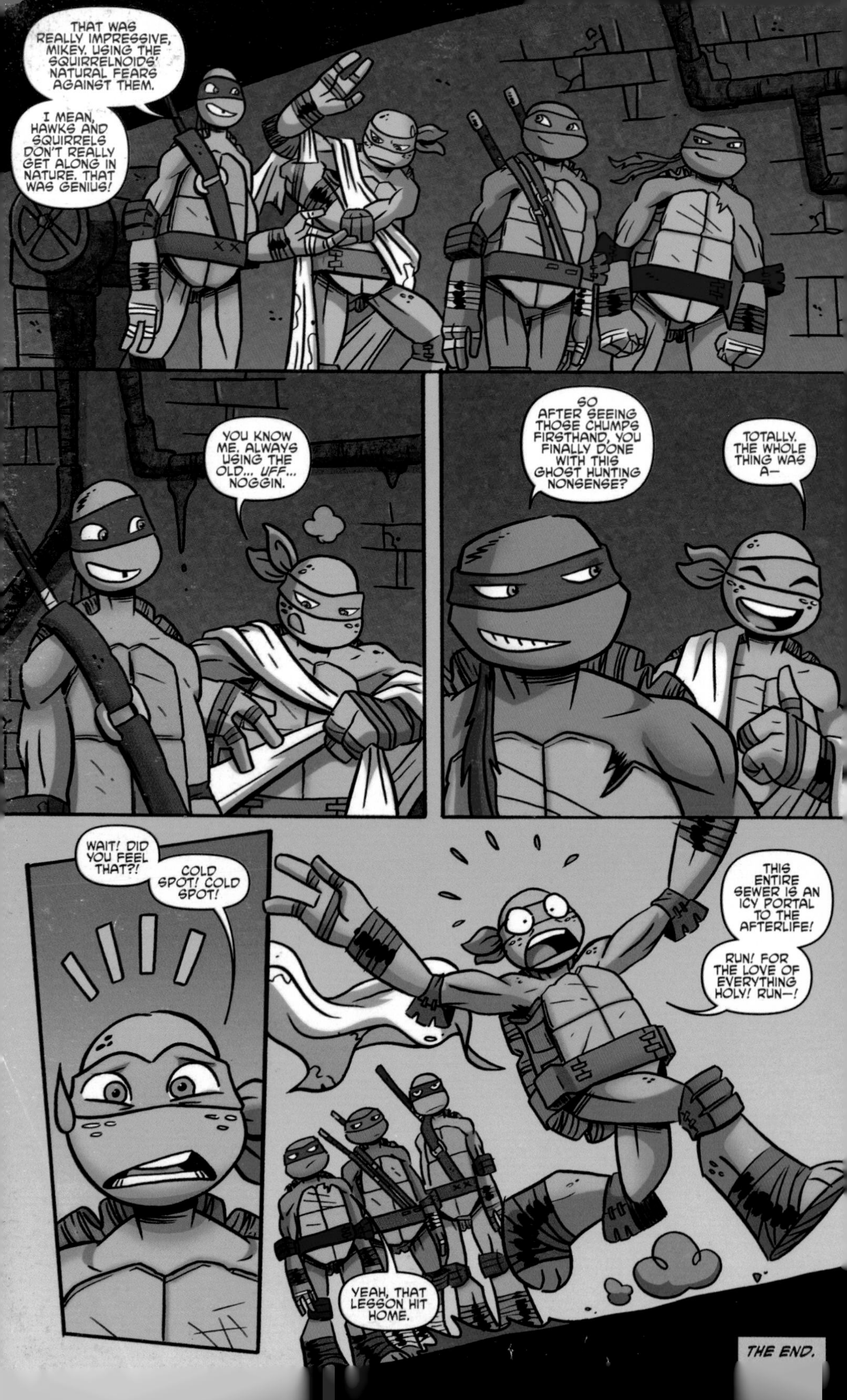

THAT WAS REALLY IMPRESSIVE, MIKEY. USING THE SQUIRRELNOIDS' NATURAL FEARS AGAINST THEM.
I MEAN, HAWKS AND SQUIRRELS DON'T REALLY GET ALONG IN NATURE. THAT WAS GENIUS!
YOU KNOW ME. ALWAYS USING THE OLD... *UFF*... NOGGIN.
SO AFTER SEEING THOSE CHUMPS FIRSTHAND, YOU FINALLY DONE WITH THIS GHOST HUNTING NONSENSE?
TOTALLY. THE WHOLE THING WAS A—
WAIT! DID YOU FEEL THAT?!
COLD SPOT! COLD SPOT!
THIS ENTIRE SEWER IS AN ICY PORTAL TO THE AFTERLIFE!
RUN! FOR THE LOVE OF EVERYTHING HOLY! RUN—!
YEAH, THAT LESSON HIT HOME.
THE END.

Cover by ELSA CHARRETIER

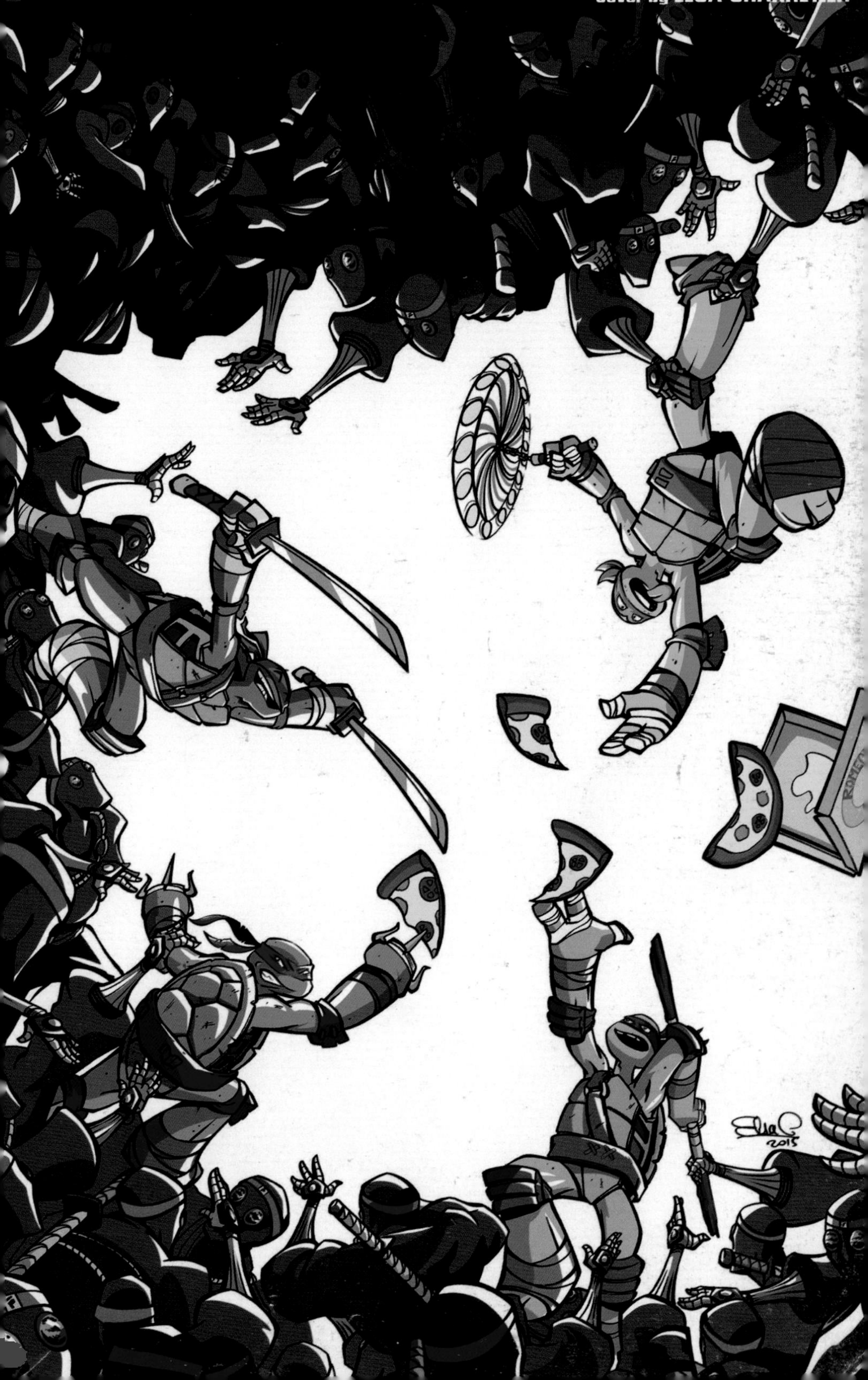

Cover by DARIO BRIZUELA

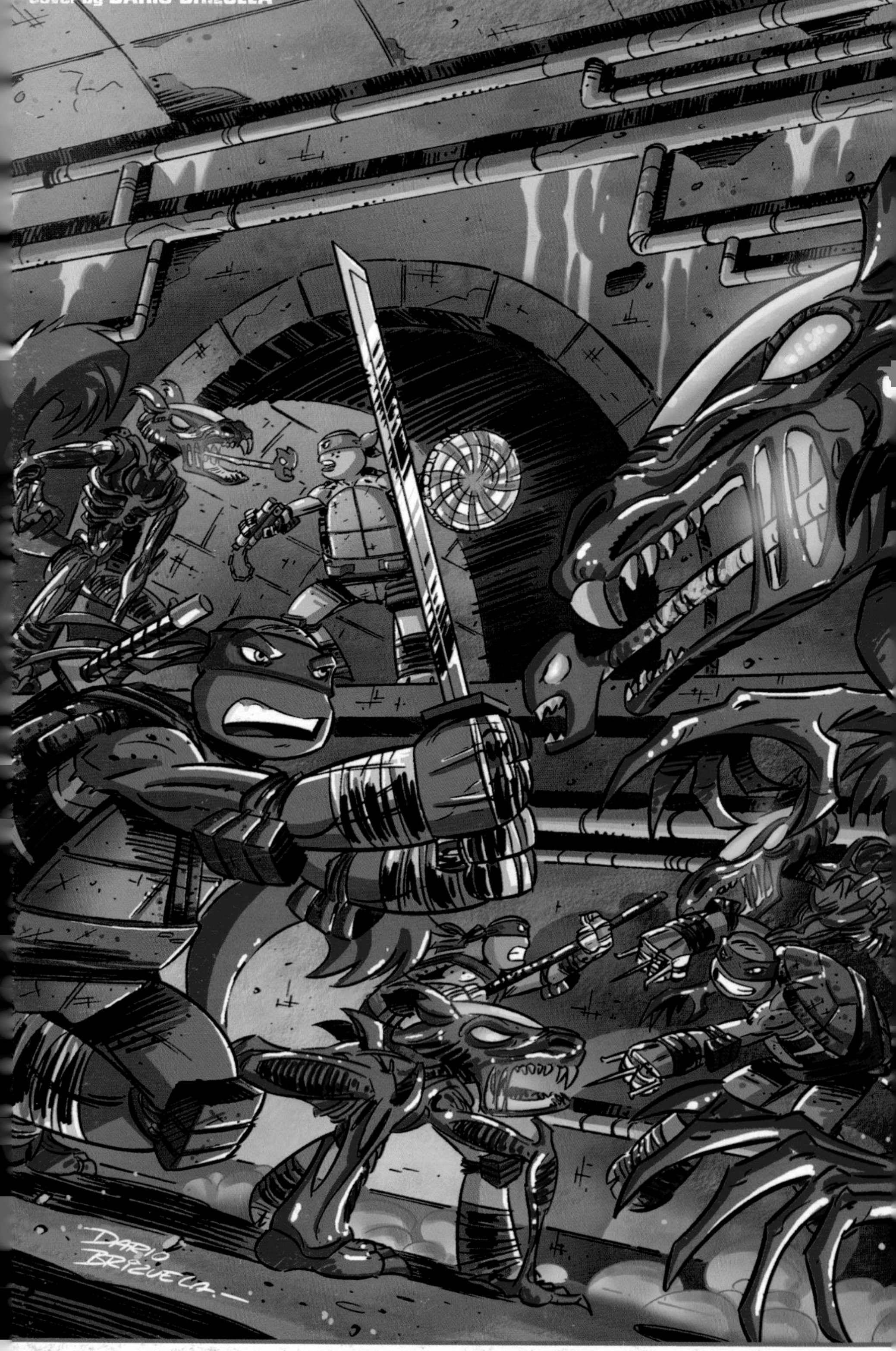
DARIO BRIZUELA

"FROM HERE TO SEWERTERNIA" - Writer: CALEB GOELLNER / Artist: CHAD THOMAS
"ACTING OUT!" - Writer: MATTHEW K. MANNING / Artist: MARCELO FERREIRA
Ink Assist: ATHILA FABBIO

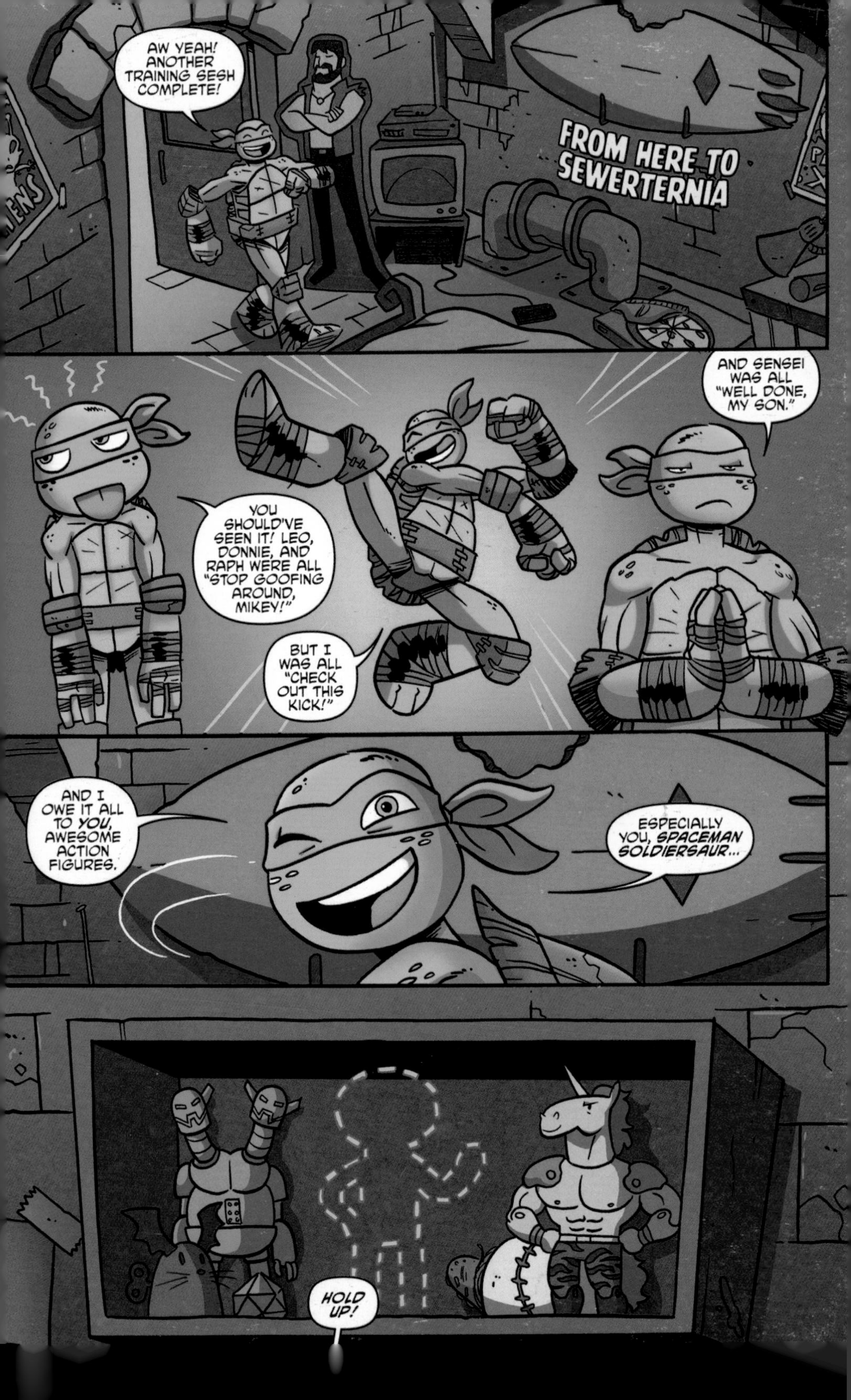
AW YEAH! ANOTHER TRAINING SESH COMPLETE!
FROM HERE TO SEWERTERNIA
YOU SHOULD'VE SEEN IT! LEO, DONNIE, AND RAPH WERE ALL "STOP GOOFING AROUND, MIKEY!"
BUT I WAS ALL "CHECK OUT THIS KICK!"
AND SENSEI WAS ALL "WELL DONE, MY SON."
AND I OWE IT ALL TO YOU, AWESOME ACTION FIGURES.
ESPECIALLY YOU, SPACEMAN SOLDIERSAUR...
HOLD UP!

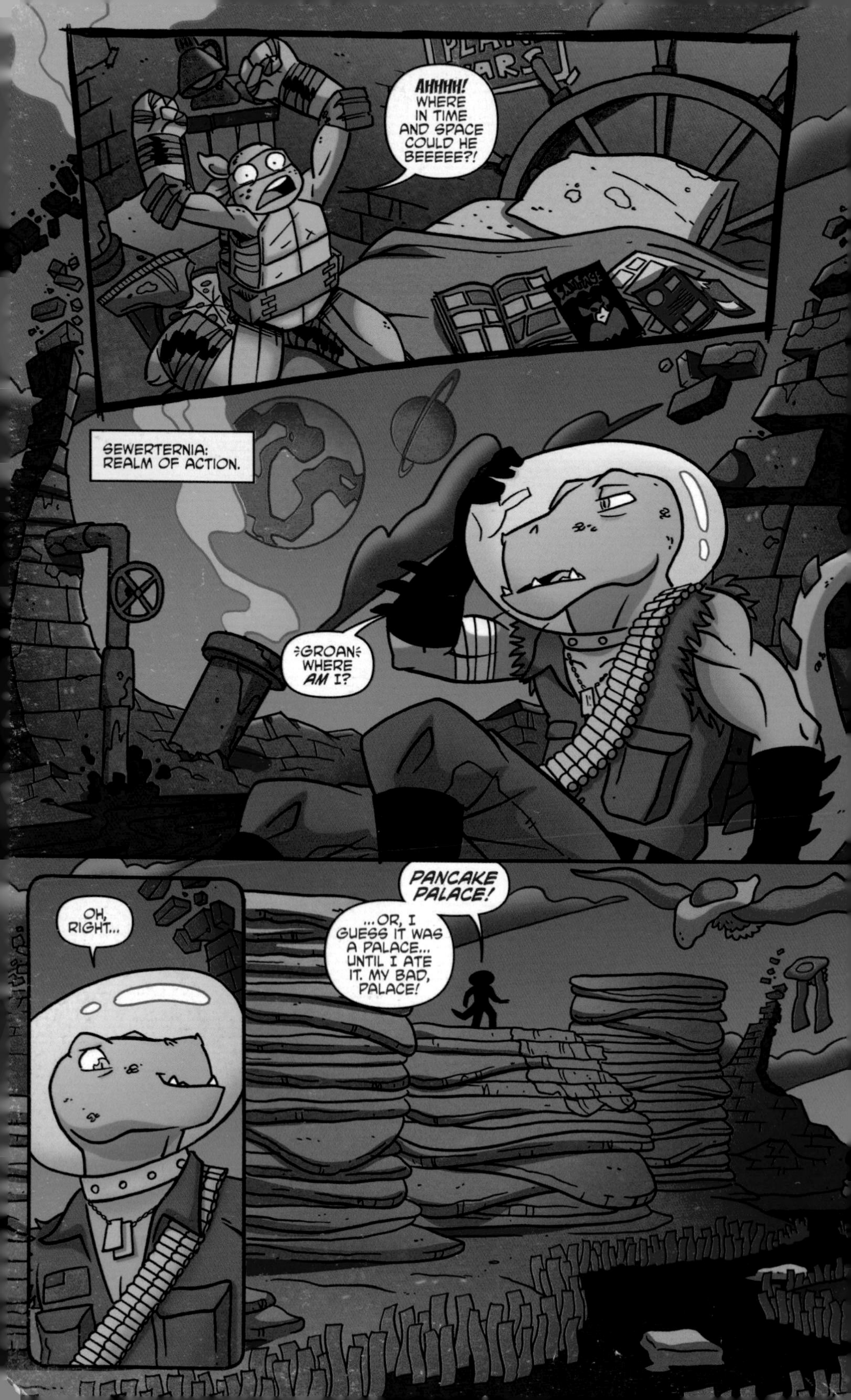
AHHHH! WHERE IN TIME AND SPACE COULD HE BEEEEE?!
SEWERTERNIA: REALM OF ACTION.
GROAN WHERE AM I?
OH, RIGHT...
PANCAKE PALACE!
...OR, I GUESS IT WAS A PALACE... UNTIL I ATE IT. MY BAD, PALACE!

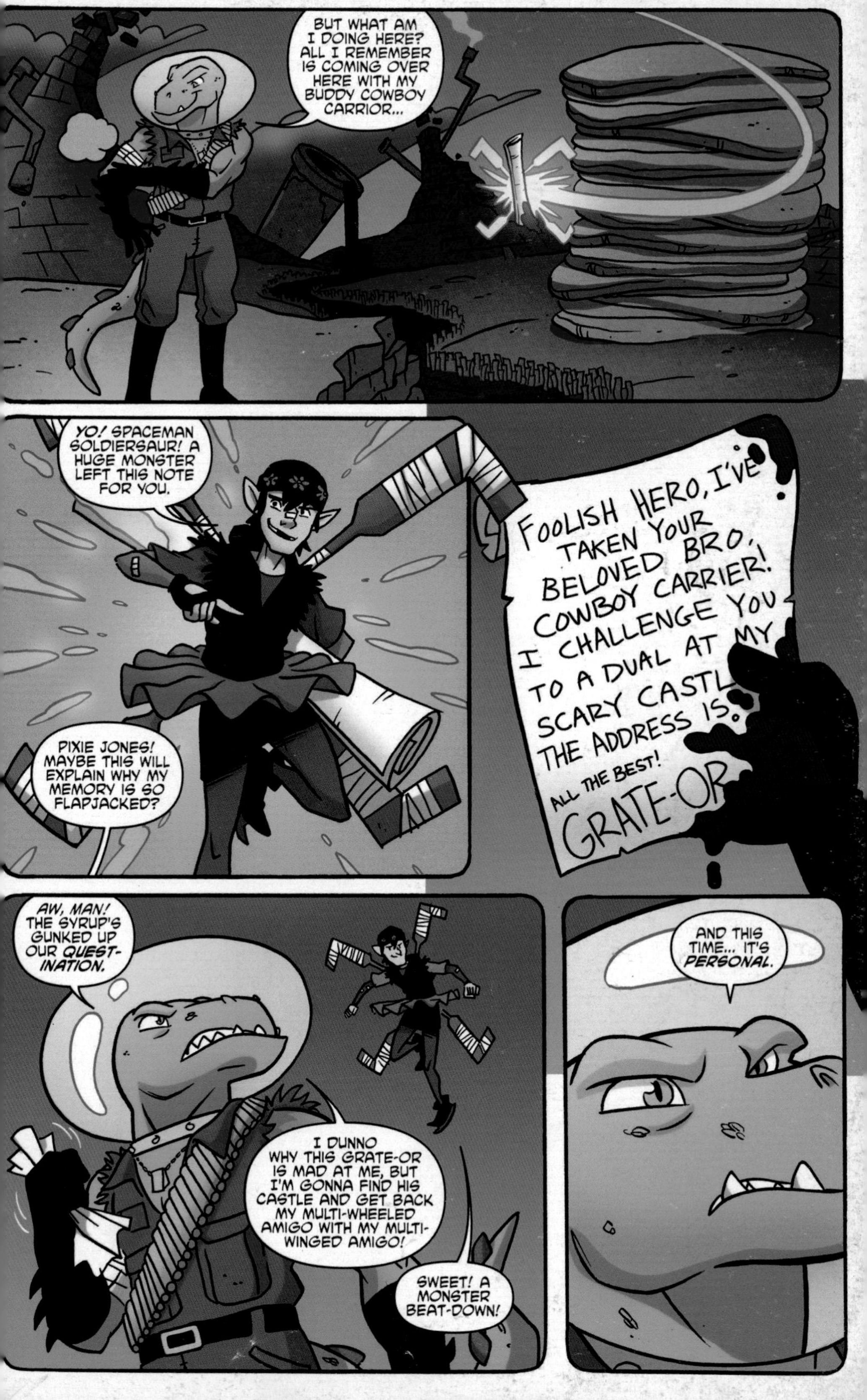
BUT WHAT AM I DOING HERE? ALL I REMEMBER IS COMING OVER HERE WITH MY BUDDY COWBOY CARRIOR...
YO! SPACEMAN SOLDIERSAUR! A HUGE MONSTER LEFT THIS NOTE FOR YOU.
PIXIE JONES! MAYBE THIS WILL EXPLAIN WHY MY MEMORY IS SO FLAPJACKED?
FOOLISH HERO, I'VE TAKEN YOUR BELOVED BRO, COWBOY CARRIER! I CHALLENGE YOU TO A DUAL AT MY SCARY CASTL THE ADDRESS IS:
ALL THE BEST! GRATE-OR
AW, MAN! THE SYRUP'S GUNKED UP OUR QUEST-INATION.
I DUNNO WHY THIS GRATE-OR IS MAD AT ME, BUT I'M GONNA FIND HIS CASTLE AND GET BACK MY MULTI-WHEELED AMIGO WITH MY MULTI-WINGED AMIGO!
SWEET! A MONSTER BEAT-DOWN!
AND THIS TIME... IT'S PERSONAL.

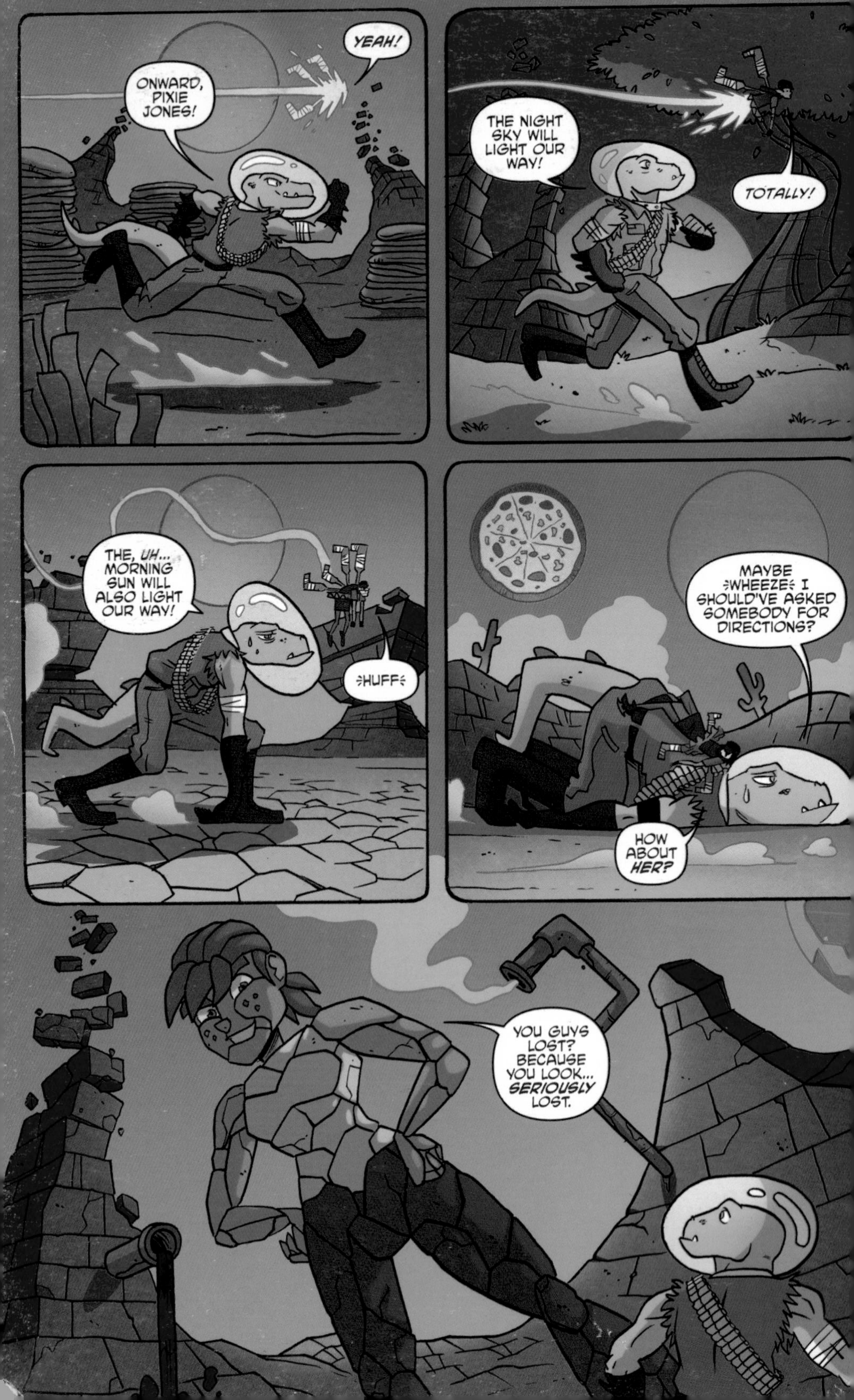
ONWARD, PIXIE JONES!
YEAH!
THE NIGHT SKY WILL LIGHT OUR WAY!
TOTALLY!
THE, *UH*... MORNING SUN WILL ALSO LIGHT OUR WAY!
⇒HUFF⇐
MAYBE ⇒WHEEZE⇐ I SHOULD'VE ASKED SOMEBODY FOR DIRECTIONS?
HOW ABOUT *HER*?
YOU GUYS LOST? BECAUSE YOU LOOK... *SERIOUSLY* LOST.

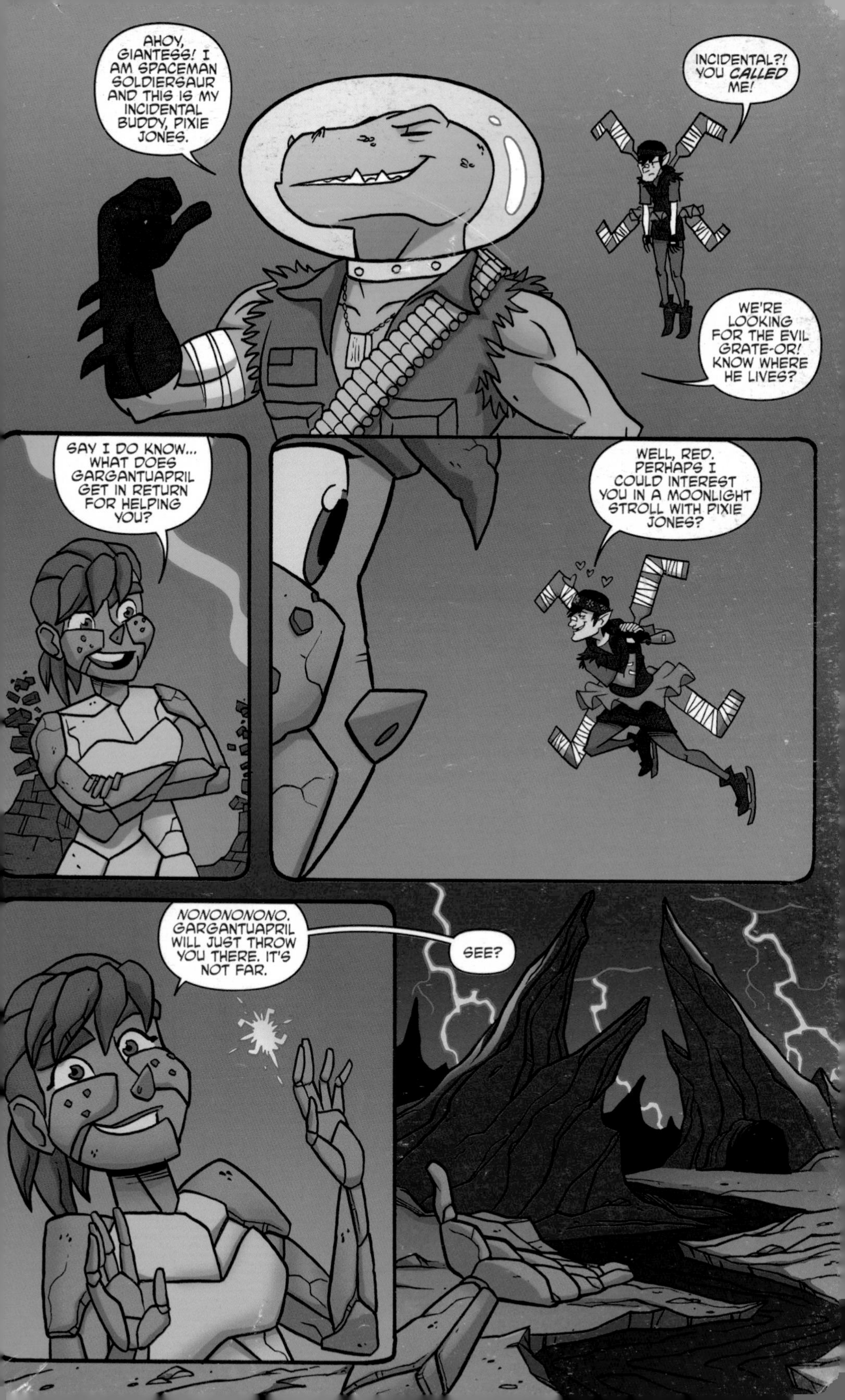
AHOY, GIANTESS! I AM SPACEMAN SOLDIERSAUR AND THIS IS MY INCIDENTAL BUDDY, PIXIE JONES.
INCIDENTAL?! YOU *CALLED* ME!
WE'RE LOOKING FOR THE EVIL GRATE-OR! KNOW WHERE HE LIVES?
SAY I DO KNOW... WHAT DOES GARGANTUAPRIL GET IN RETURN FOR HELPING YOU?
WELL, RED. PERHAPS I COULD INTEREST YOU IN A MOONLIGHT STROLL WITH PIXIE JONES?
NONONONONO. GARGANTUAPRIL WILL JUST THROW YOU THERE. IT'S NOT FAR.
SEE?

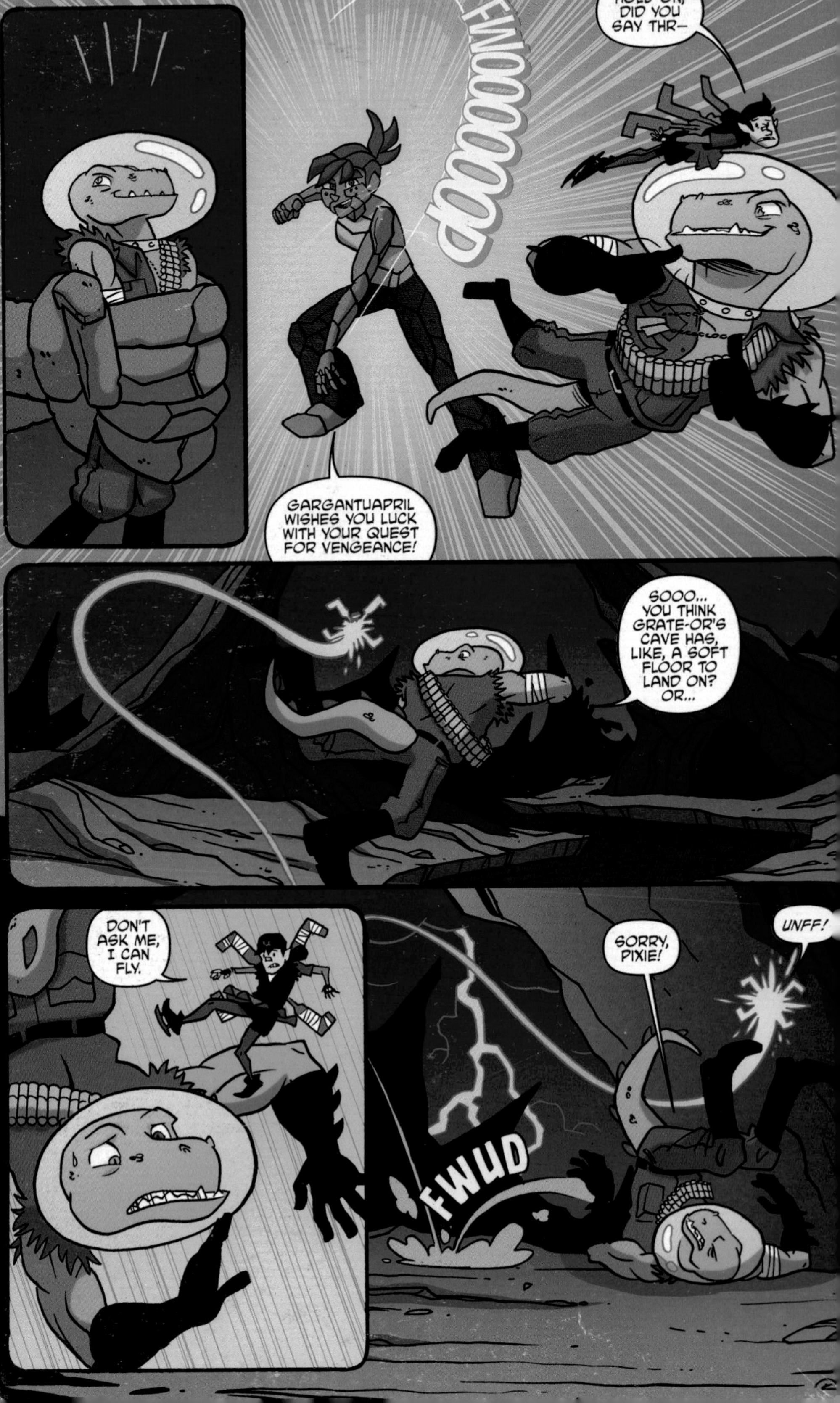
FWOOOOOOOP
HOLD ON, DID YOU SAY THR–
GARGANTUAPRIL WISHES YOU LUCK WITH YOUR QUEST FOR VENGEANCE!
SOOO... YOU THINK GRATE-OR'S CAVE HAS, LIKE, A SOFT FLOOR TO LAND ON? OR...
DON'T ASK ME, I CAN FLY.
SORRY, PIXIE!
UNFF!
FWUD

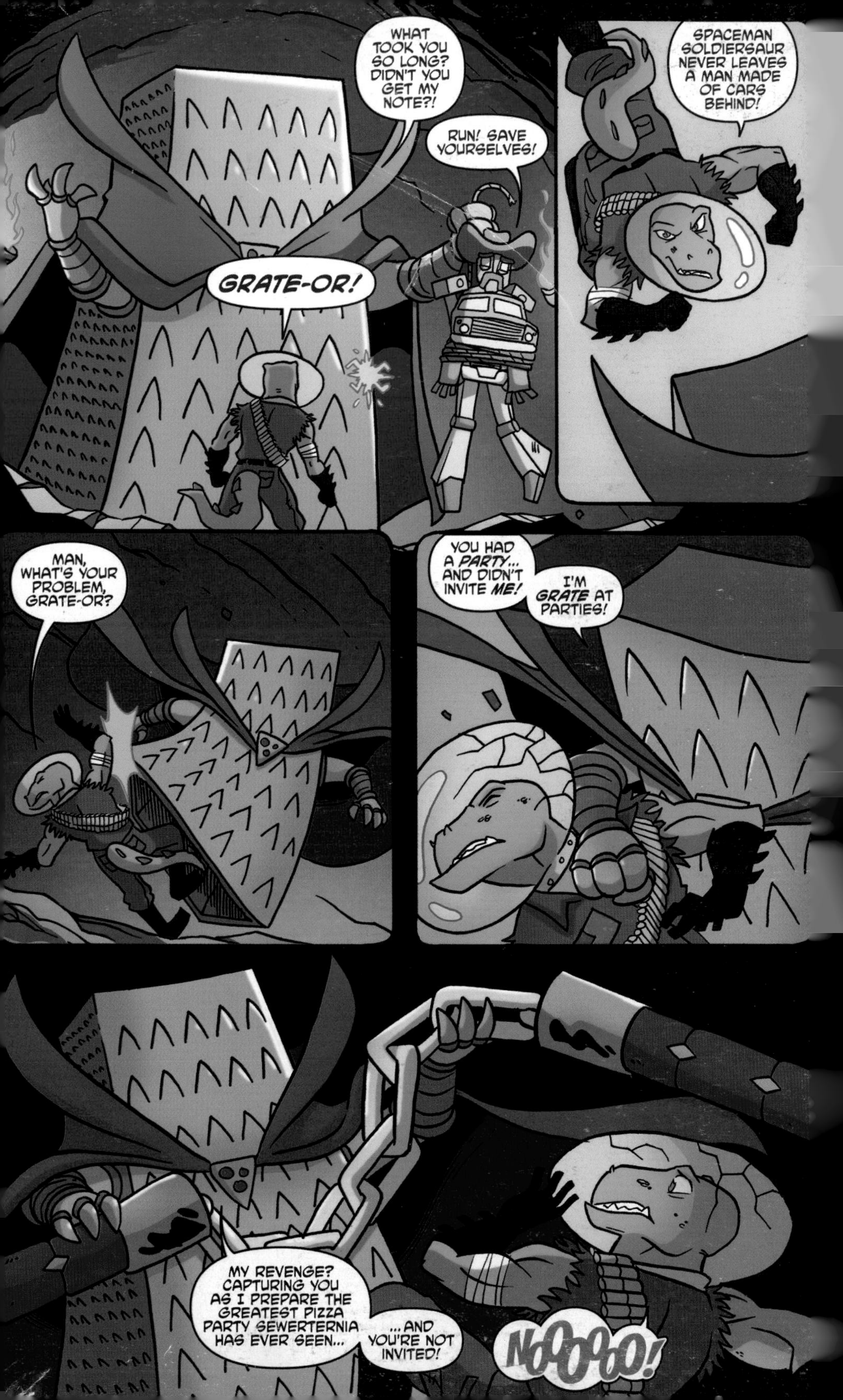
WHAT TOOK YOU SO LONG? DIDN'T YOU GET MY NOTE?!
RUN! SAVE YOURSELVES!
GRATE-OR!
SPACEMAN SOLDIERSAUR NEVER LEAVES A MAN MADE OF CARS BEHIND!
MAN, WHAT'S YOUR PROBLEM, GRATE-OR?
YOU HAD A *PARTY*... AND DIDN'T INVITE *ME!*
I'M *GRATE* AT PARTIES!
MY REVENGE? CAPTURING YOU AS I PREPARE THE GREATEST PIZZA PARTY SEWERTERNIA HAS EVER SEEN...
...AND YOU'RE NOT INVITED!
NOOOOOO!

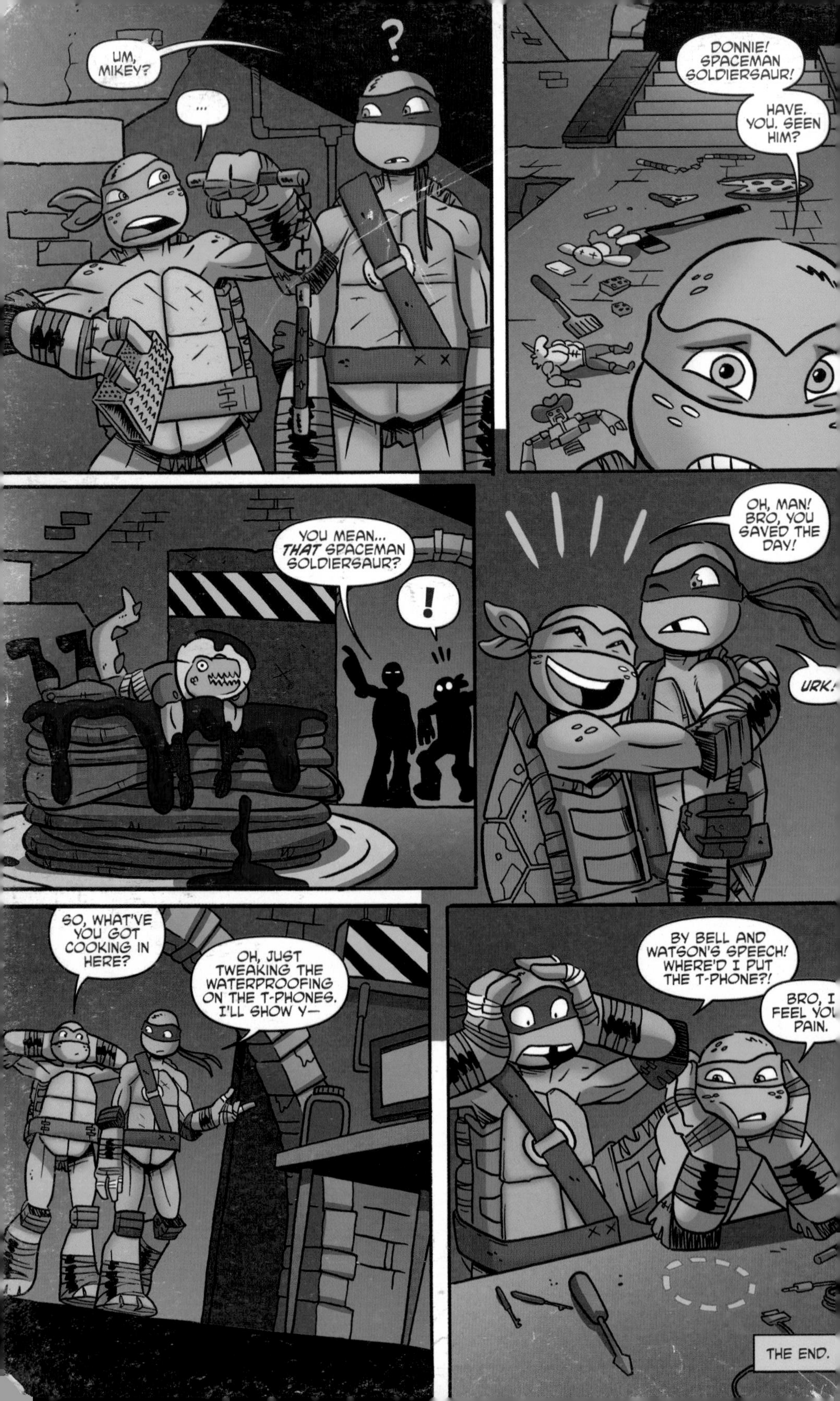
UM, MIKEY?
...
?
DONNIE! SPACEMAN SOLDIERSAUR!
HAVE. YOU. SEEN HIM?
YOU MEAN... THAT SPACEMAN SOLDIERSAUR?
!
OH, MAN! BRO, YOU SAVED THE DAY!
URK!
SO, WHAT'VE YOU GOT COOKING IN HERE?
OH, JUST TWEAKING THE WATERPROOFING ON THE T-PHONES. I'LL SHOW Y—
BY BELL AND WATSON'S SPEECH! WHERE'D I PUT THE T-PHONE?!
BRO, I FEEL YOU PAIN.
THE END.

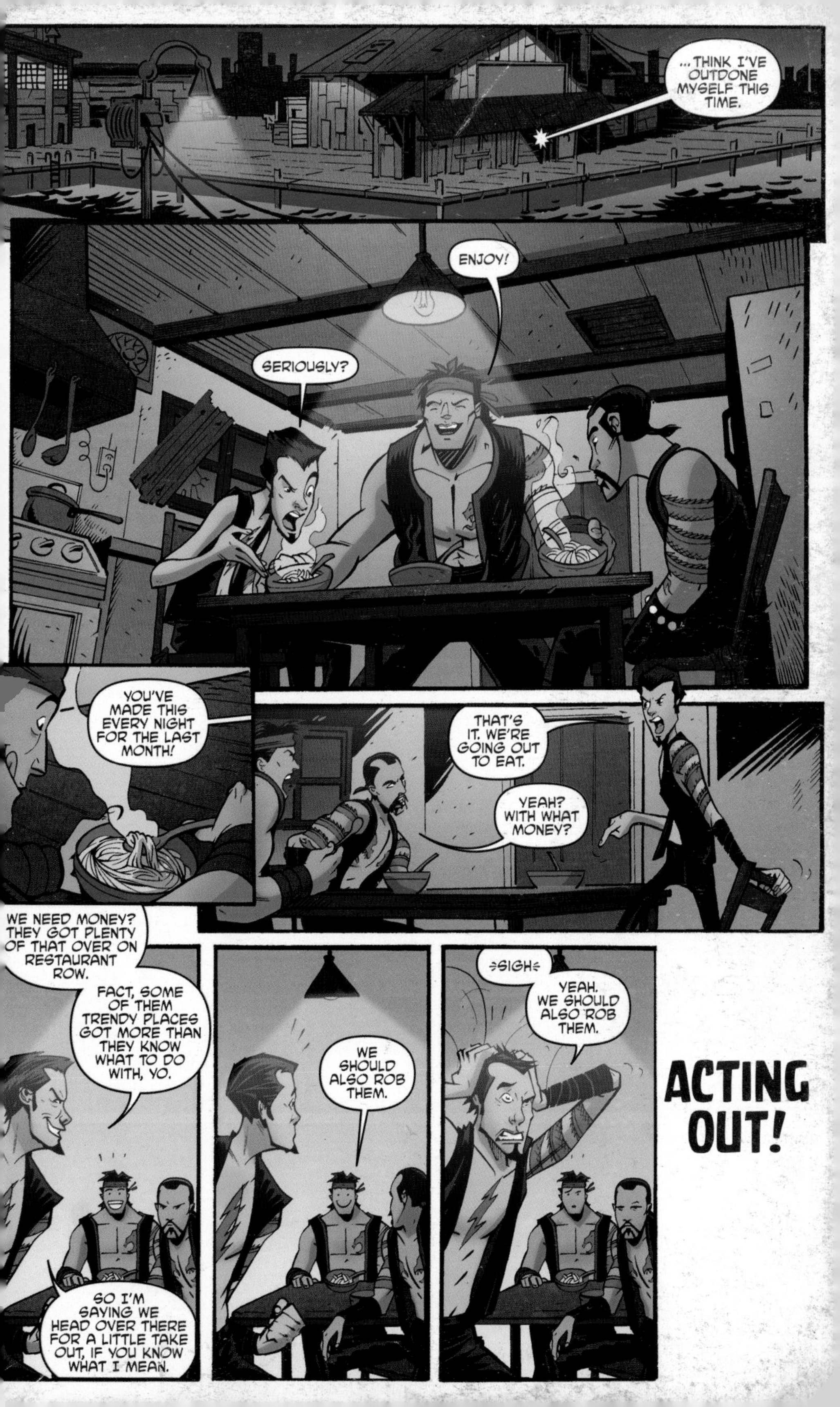
...THINK I'VE OUTDONE MYSELF THIS TIME.
ENJOY!
SERIOUSLY?
YOU'VE MADE THIS EVERY NIGHT FOR THE LAST MONTH!
THAT'S IT. WE'RE GOING OUT TO EAT.
YEAH? WITH WHAT MONEY?
WE NEED MONEY? THEY GOT PLENTY OF THAT OVER ON RESTAURANT ROW.
FACT, SOME OF THEM TRENDY PLACES GOT MORE THAN THEY KNOW WHAT TO DO WITH, YO.
SO I'M SAYING WE HEAD OVER THERE FOR A LITTLE TAKE OUT, IF YOU KNOW WHAT I MEAN.
WE SHOULD ALSO ROB THEM.
⇒SIGH⇐
YEAH. WE SHOULD ALSO ROB THEM.
ACTING OUT!

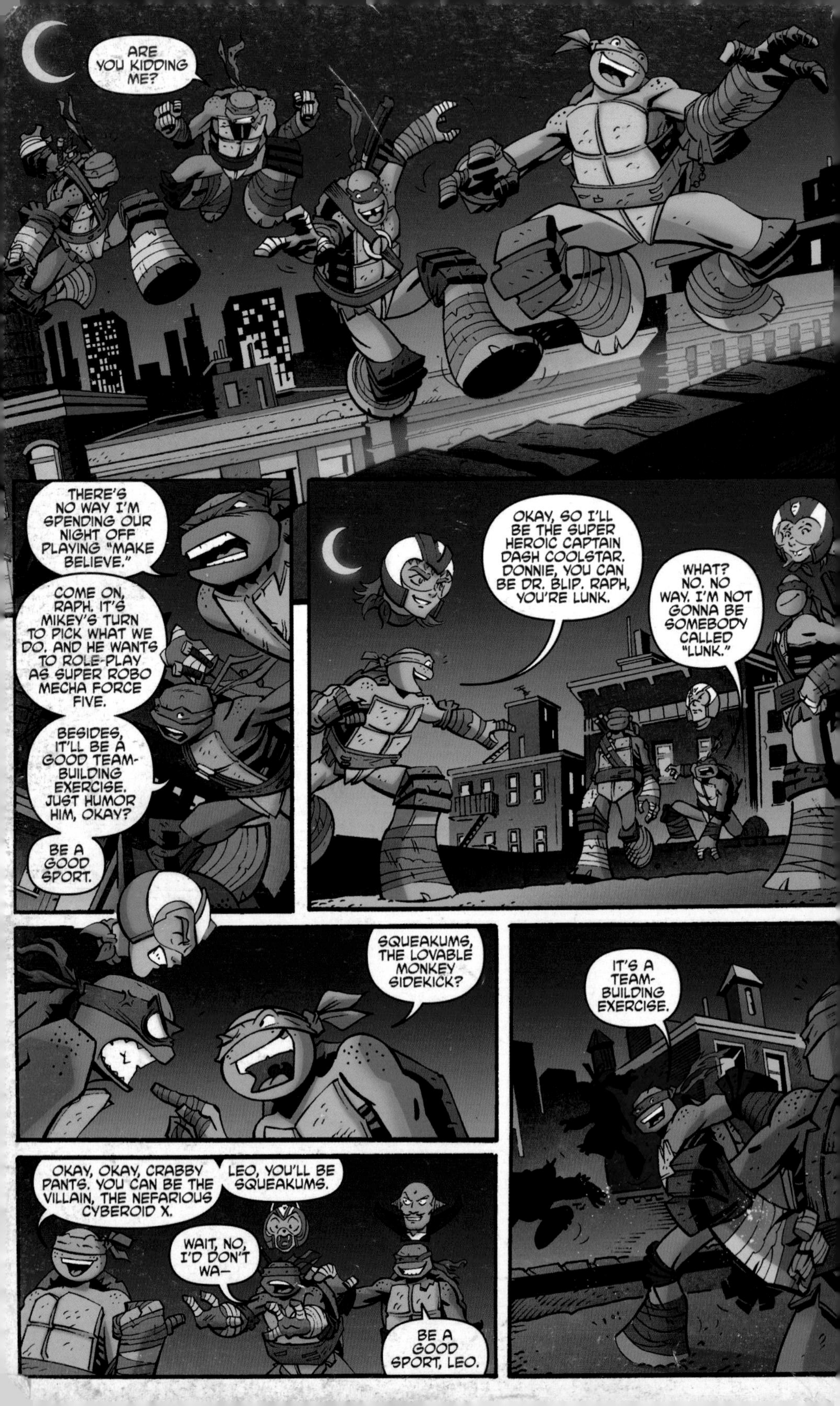
ARE YOU KIDDING ME?
THERE'S NO WAY I'M SPENDING OUR NIGHT OFF PLAYING "MAKE BELIEVE."
COME ON, RAPH. IT'S MIKEY'S TURN TO PICK WHAT WE DO. AND HE WANTS TO ROLE-PLAY AS SUPER ROBO MECHA FORCE FIVE.
BESIDES, IT'LL BE A GOOD TEAM-BUILDING EXERCISE. JUST HUMOR HIM, OKAY?
BE A GOOD SPORT.
OKAY, SO I'LL BE THE SUPER HEROIC CAPTAIN DASH COOLSTAR. DONNIE, YOU CAN BE DR. BLIP. RAPH, YOU'RE LUNK.
WHAT? NO. NO WAY. I'M NOT GONNA BE SOMEBODY CALLED "LUNK."
SQUEAKUMS, THE LOVABLE MONKEY SIDEKICK?
IT'S A TEAM-BUILDING EXERCISE.
OKAY, OKAY, CRABBY PANTS. YOU CAN BE THE VILLAIN, THE NEFARIOUS CYBEROID X.
LEO, YOU'LL BE SQUEAKUMS.
WAIT, NO, I'D DON'T WA—
BE A GOOD SPORT, LEO.

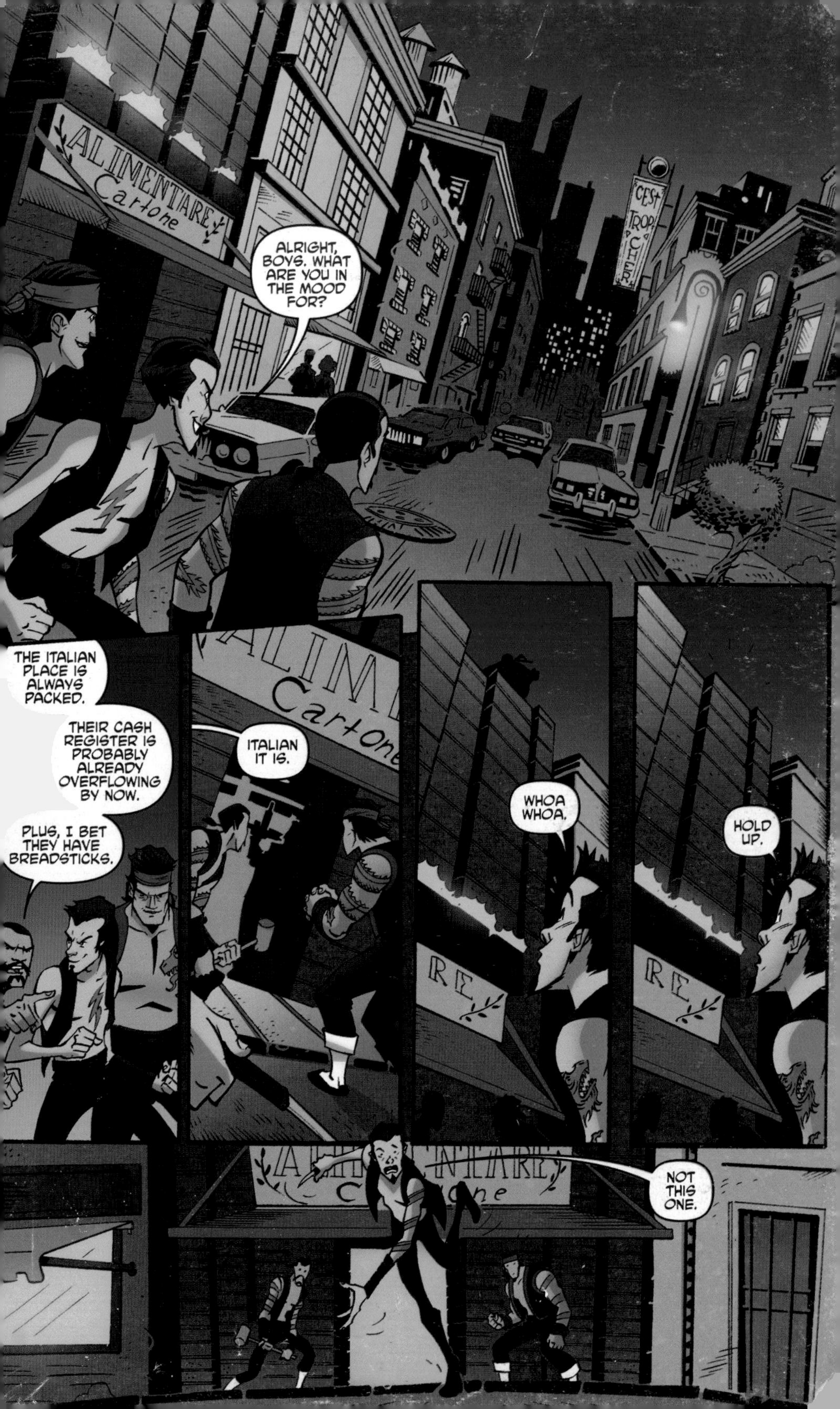
ALINENTARE
Cartone
C'EST TROP CHER
ALRIGHT, BOYS. WHAT ARE YOU IN THE MOOD FOR?
THE ITALIAN PLACE IS ALWAYS PACKED.
THEIR CASH REGISTER IS PROBABLY ALREADY OVERFLOWING BY NOW.
PLUS, I BET THEY HAVE BREADSTICKS.
ITALIAN IT IS.
WHOA WHOA.
HOLD UP.
NOT THIS ONE.

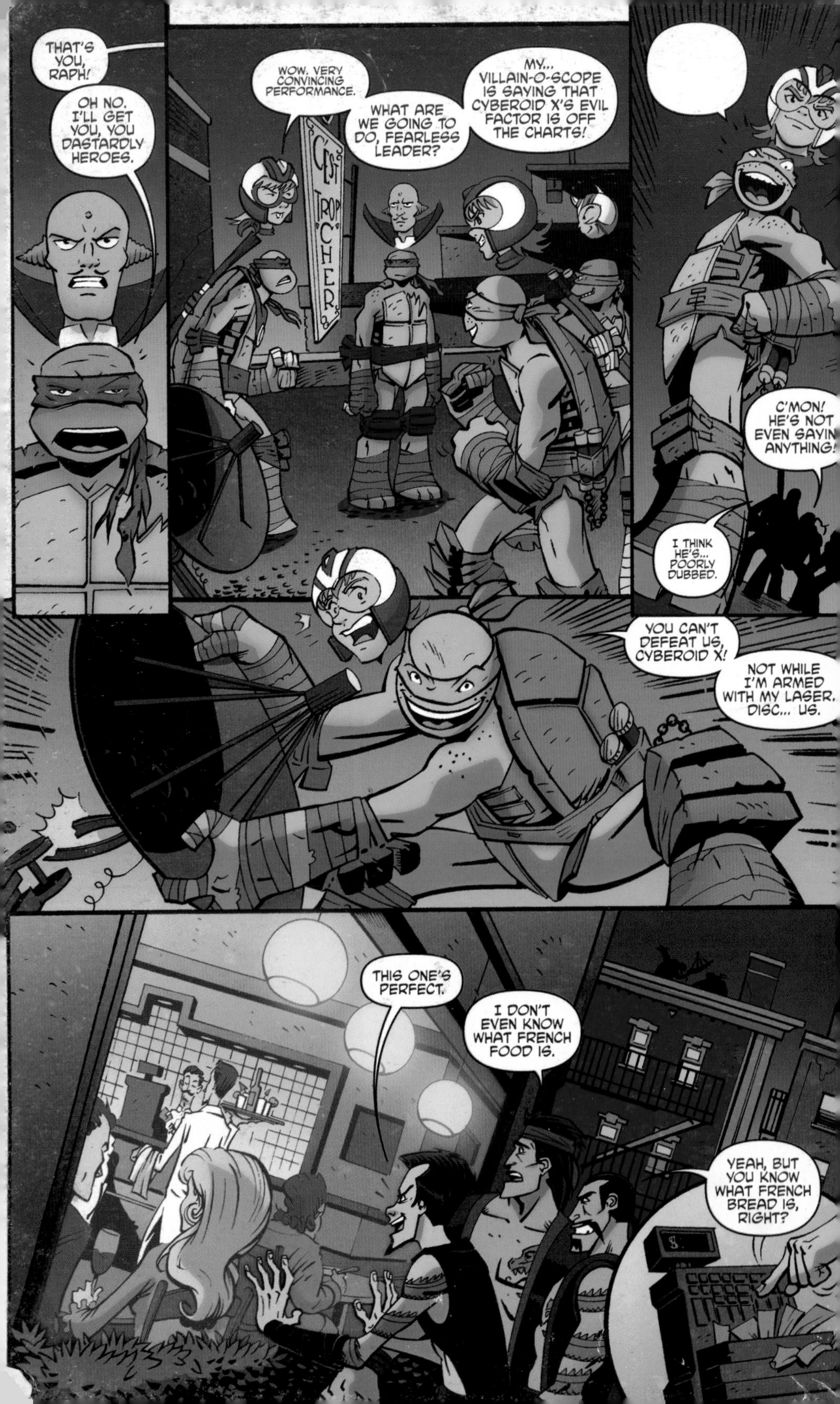
THAT'S YOU, RAPH!
OH NO. I'LL GET YOU, YOU DASTARDLY HEROES.
WOW. VERY CONVINCING PERFORMANCE.
WHAT ARE WE GOING TO DO, FEARLESS LEADER?
MY... VILLAIN-O-SCOPE IS SAYING THAT CYBEROID X'S EVIL FACTOR IS OFF THE CHARTS!
C'EST TROP CHER
C'MON! HE'S NOT EVEN SAYIN ANYTHING!
I THINK HE'S... POORLY DUBBED.
YOU CAN'T DEFEAT US, CYBEROID X!
NOT WHILE I'M ARMED WITH MY LASER DISC... US.
THIS ONE'S PERFECT.
I DON'T EVEN KNOW WHAT FRENCH FOOD IS.
YEAH, BUT YOU KNOW WHAT FRENCH BREAD IS, RIGHT?

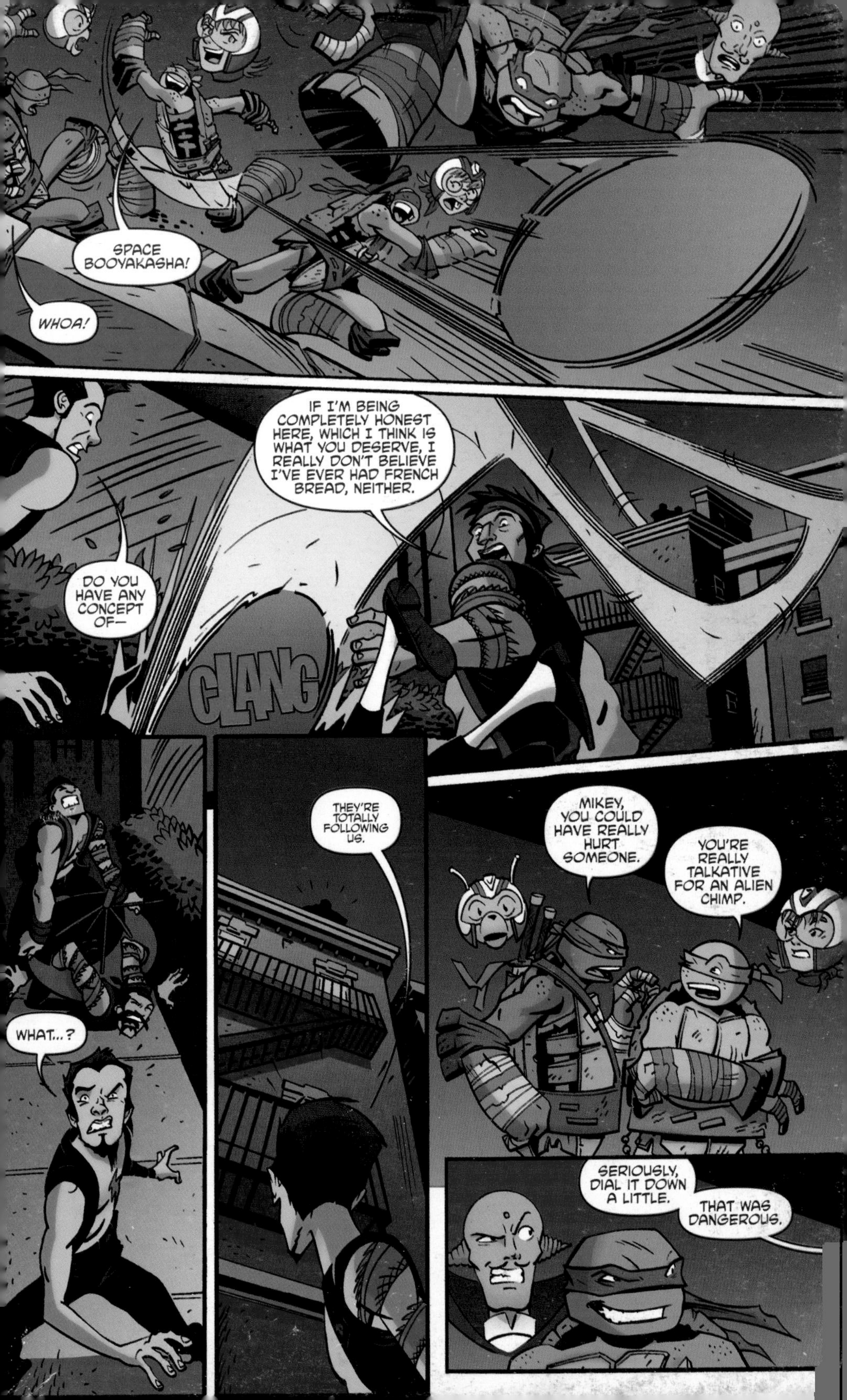
SPACE BOOYAKASHA!
WHOA!
IF I'M BEING COMPLETELY HONEST HERE, WHICH I THINK IS WHAT YOU DESERVE, I REALLY DON'T BELIEVE I'VE EVER HAD FRENCH BREAD, NEITHER.
DO YOU HAVE ANY CONCEPT OF—
CLANG
WHAT...?
THEY'RE TOTALLY FOLLOWING US.
MIKEY, YOU COULD HAVE REALLY HURT SOMEONE.
YOU'RE REALLY TALKATIVE FOR AN ALIEN CHIMP.
SERIOUSLY, DIAL IT DOWN A LITTLE.
THAT WAS DANGEROUS.

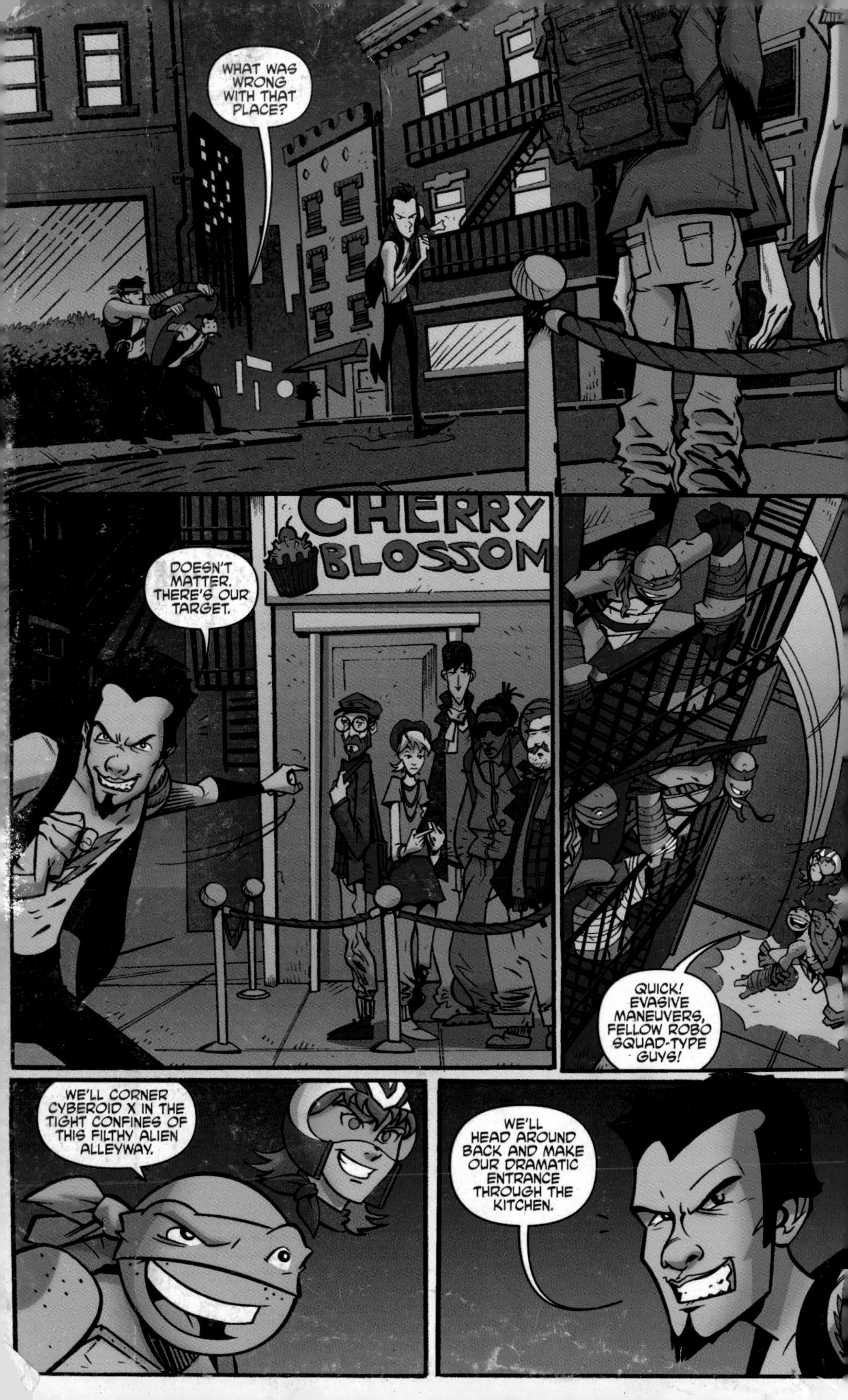
WHAT WAS WRONG WITH THAT PLACE?
CHERRY BLOSSOM
DOESN'T MATTER. THERE'S OUR TARGET.
QUICK! EVASIVE MANEUVERS, FELLOW ROBO SQUAD-TYPE GUYS!
WE'LL CORNER CYBEROID X IN THE TIGHT CONFINES OF THIS FILTHY ALIEN ALLEYWAY.
WE'LL HEAD AROUND BACK AND MAKE OUR DRAMATIC ENTRANCE THROUGH THE KITCHEN.

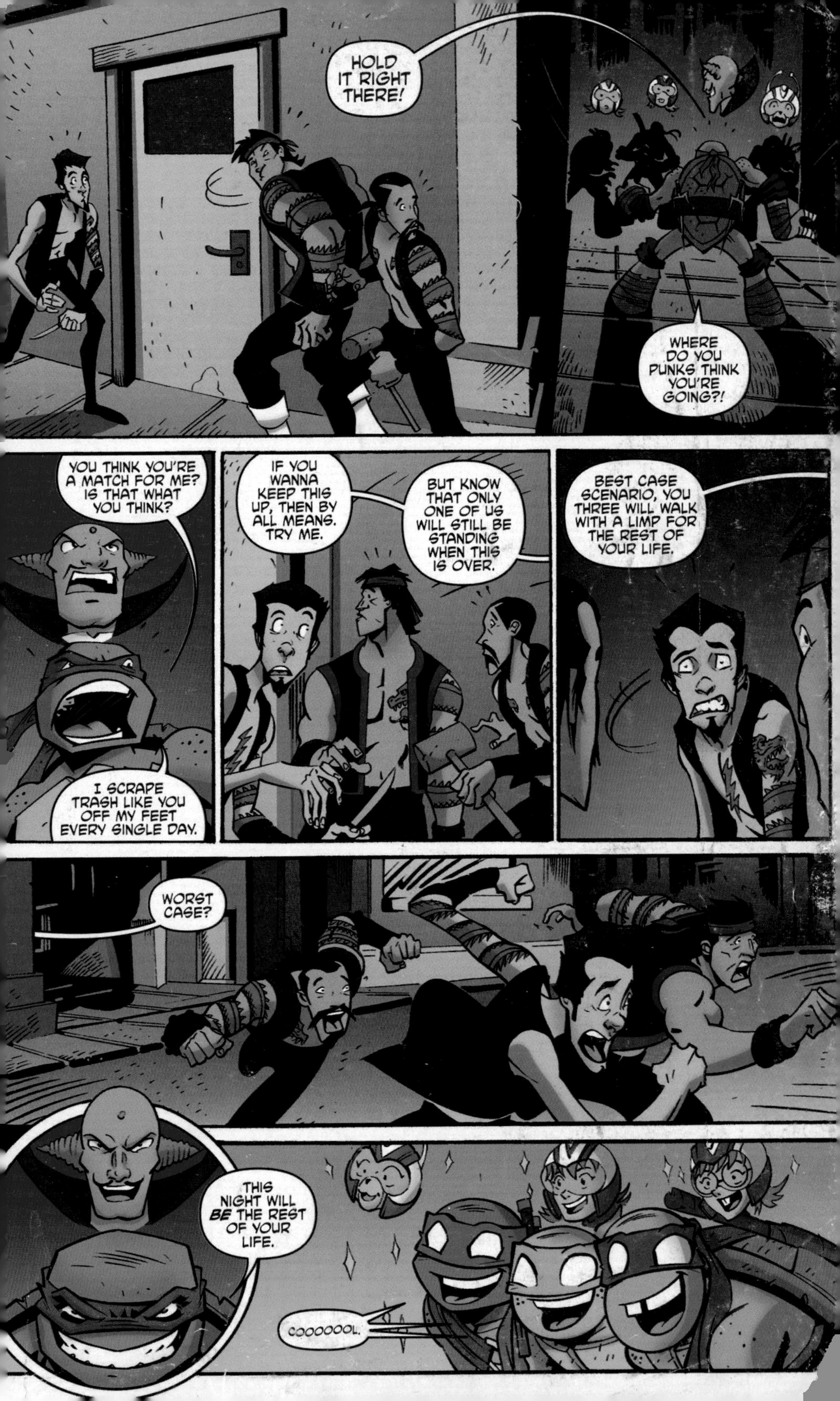
HOLD IT RIGHT THERE!
WHERE DO YOU PUNKS THINK YOU'RE GOING?!
YOU THINK YOU'RE A MATCH FOR ME? IS THAT WHAT YOU THINK?
I SCRAPE TRASH LIKE YOU OFF MY FEET EVERY SINGLE DAY.
IF YOU WANNA KEEP THIS UP, THEN BY ALL MEANS. TRY ME.
BUT KNOW THAT ONLY ONE OF US WILL STILL BE STANDING WHEN THIS IS OVER.
BEST CASE SCENARIO, YOU THREE WILL WALK WITH A LIMP FOR THE REST OF YOUR LIFE.
WORST CASE?
THIS NIGHT WILL *BE* THE REST OF YOUR LIFE.
COOOOOOL.

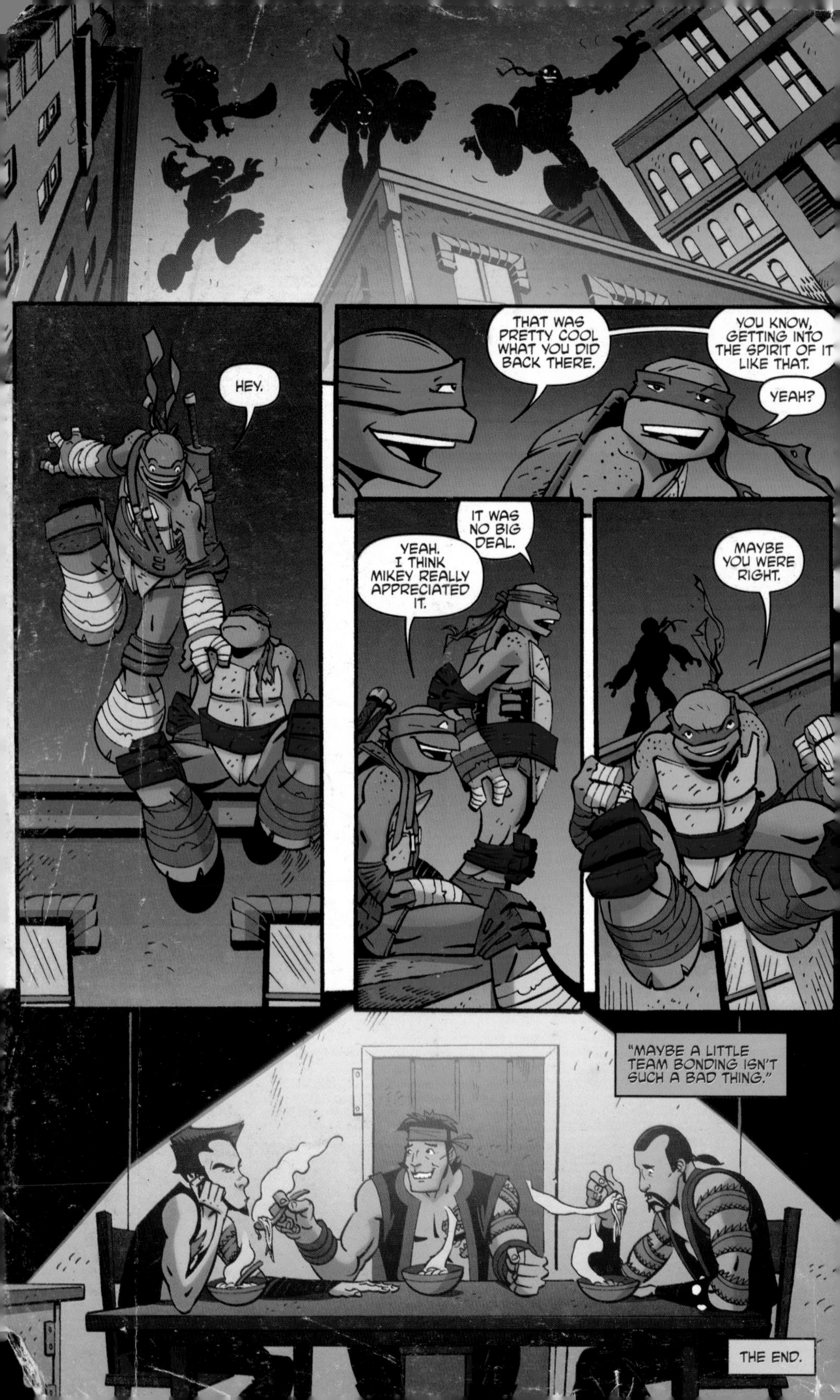
HEY.
THAT WAS PRETTY COOL WHAT YOU DID BACK THERE.
YOU KNOW, GETTING INTO THE SPIRIT OF IT LIKE THAT.
YEAH?
IT WAS NO BIG DEAL.
YEAH. I THINK MIKEY REALLY APPRECIATED IT.
MAYBE YOU WERE RIGHT.
"MAYBE A LITTLE TEAM BONDING ISN'T SUCH A BAD THING."
THE END.

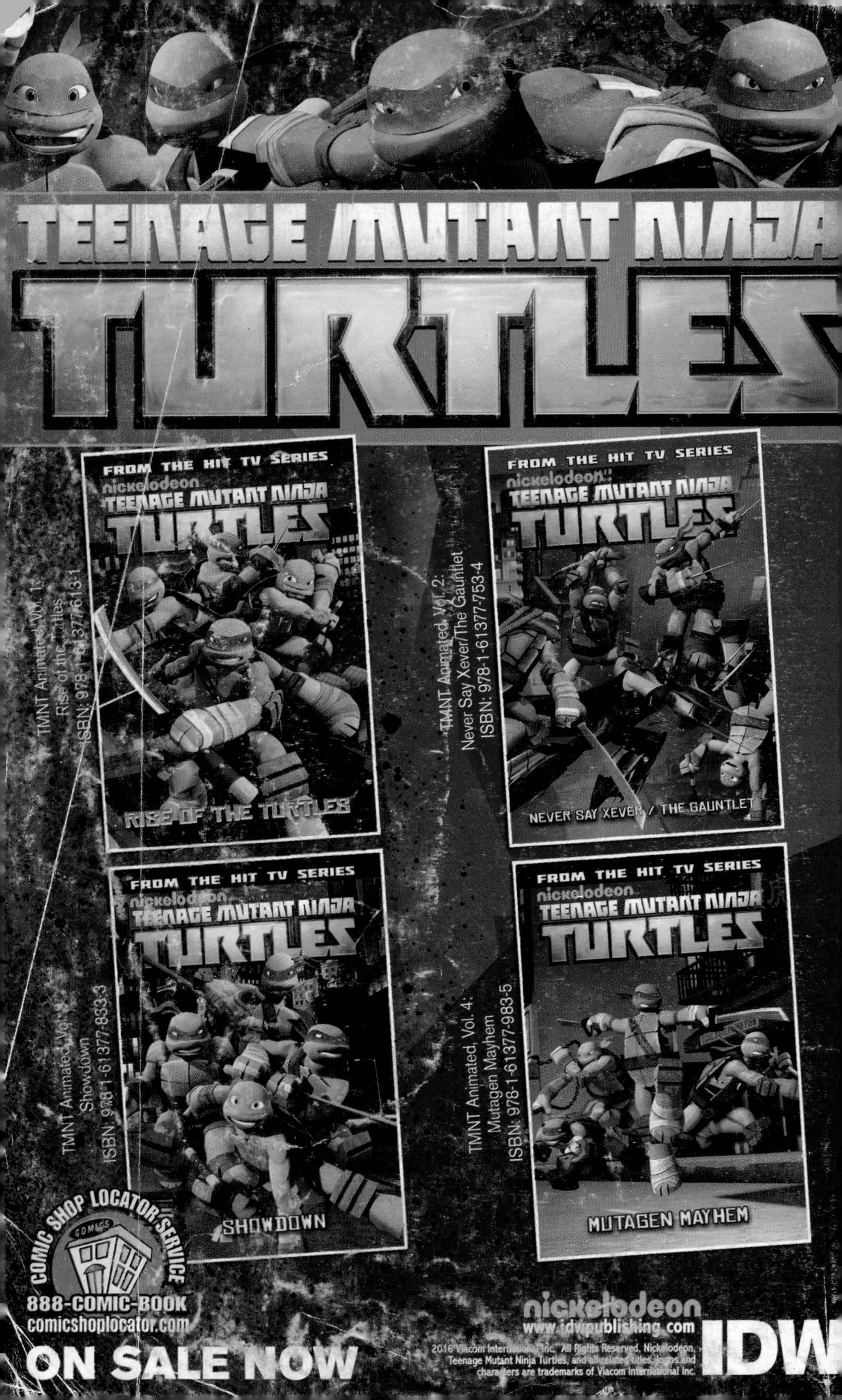

TEENAGE MUTANT NINJA
TURTLES
FROM THE HIT TV SERIES
nickelodeon
TEENAGE MUTANT NINJA
TURTLES
RISE OF THE TURTLES
TMNT Animated, Vol. 1:
Rise of the Turtles
ISBN: 978-1-61377-613-1
FROM THE HIT TV SERIES
nickelodeon
TEENAGE MUTANT NINJA
TURTLES
NEVER SAY XEVER / THE GAUNTLET
TMNT Animated, Vol. 2:
Never Say Xever/The Gauntlet
ISBN: 978-1-61377-753-4
FROM THE HIT TV SERIES
nickelodeon
TEENAGE MUTANT NINJA
TURTLES
SHOWDOWN
TMNT Animated, Vol. 3:
Showdown
ISBN: 978-1-61377-833-3
FROM THE HIT TV SERIES
nickelodeon
TEENAGE MUTANT NINJA
TURTLES
MUTAGEN MAYHEM
TMNT Animated, Vol. 4:
Mutagen Mayhem
ISBN: 978-1-61377-983-5
COMIC SHOP LOCATOR SERVICE
888-COMIC-BOOK
comicshoplocator.com
ON SALE NOW
nickelodeon
www.idwpublishing.com
IDW
2016 Viacom International Inc. All Rights Reserved. Nickelodeon, Teenage Mutant Ninja Turtles, and all related titles, logos and characters are trademarks of Viacom International Inc.

Cover by **PATRICK PARNELL**

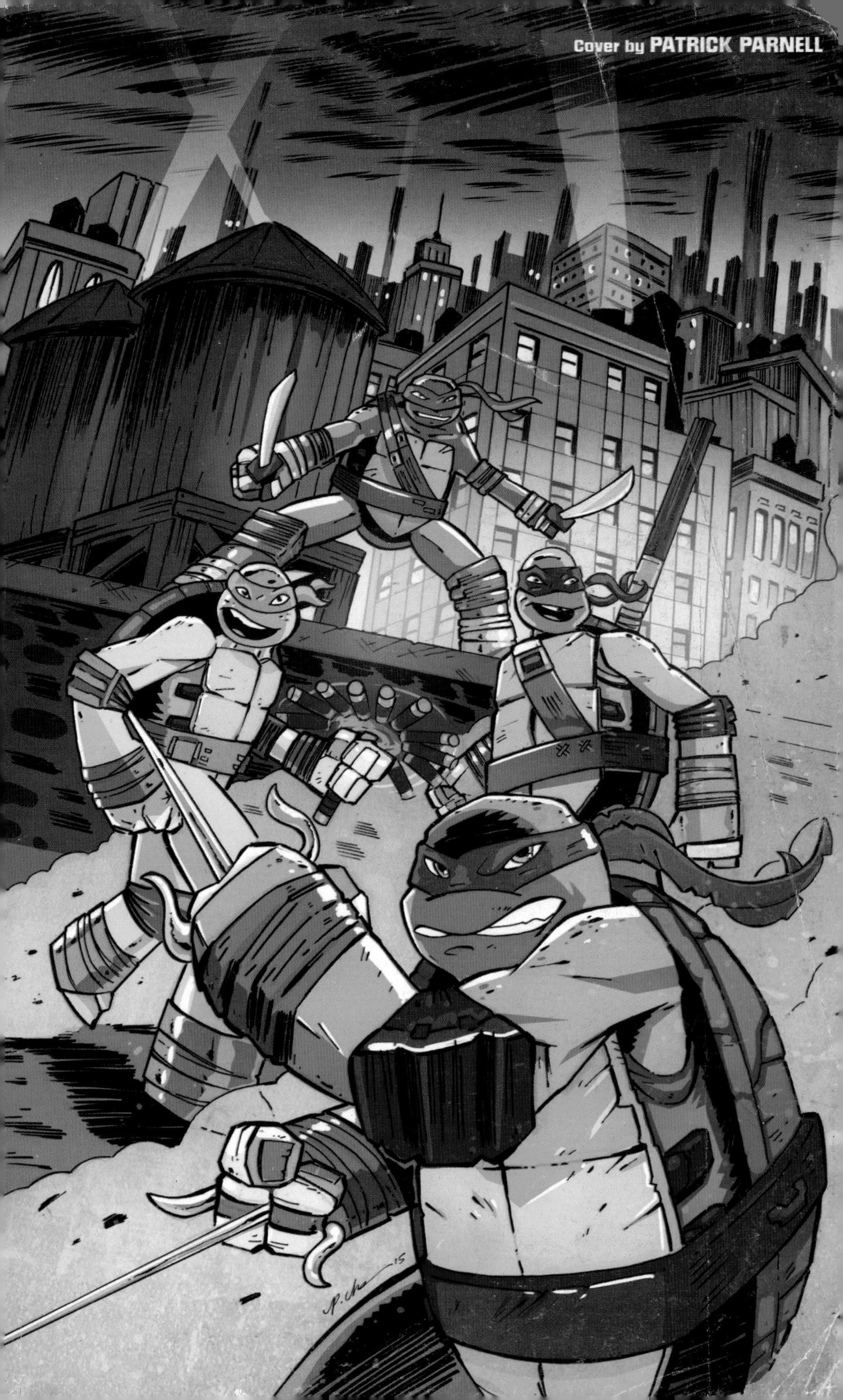